READER'S DIGEST CONDENSED BOOKS

OPPOSITE: TLINGIT INDIAN HEADDRESS (NINETEENTH CENTURY)

READER'S DIGEST
CONDENSED BOOKS

Volume 5 · 1978

THE READER'S DIGEST ASSOCIATION

Pleasantville, New York

Reader's Digest Condensed Books are published every two to three months at Pleasantville, N. Y.

The condensations in this volume have been created by The Reader's Digest Association, Inc., and are used by permission of and special arrangement with the publishers and the holders of the respective copyrights.

With the exception of actual personages identified as such, the characters and incidents in the fictional selections in this volume are entirely the products of the authors' imaginations and have no relation to any person or event in real life.

CONTENTS

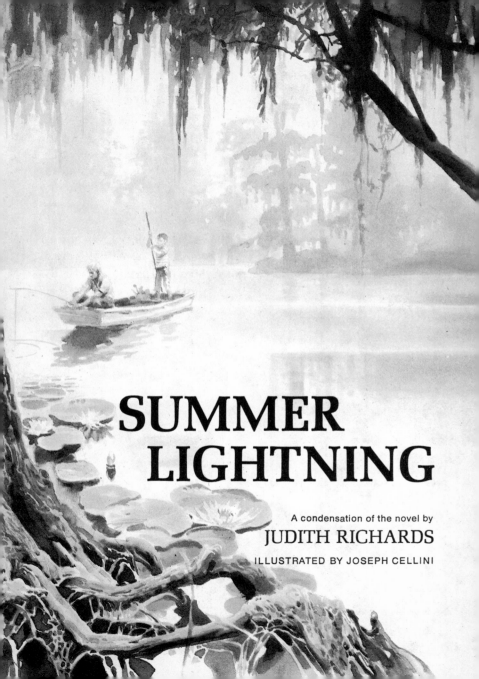

SUMMER LIGHTNING

A condensation of the novel by
JUDITH RICHARDS

ILLUSTRATED BY JOSEPH CELLINI

Terry Calder never *planned* to miss school. He simply couldn't resist—he had the spirit of a hawk and he yearned to be free as all outdoors.

Sooner or later, Terry always turned up at Mr. Mc-Cree's place at the edge of the Everglades swamps. McCree understood Terry's freedom-loving ways as no one else did. He knew that a little hawk needed to fly, to soar, to ride the air currents. It was old McCree who gave the little hawk flight—and the results were unforgettable.

This winsome tale of an irrepressible young boy is based on the childhood adventures of a real Terry, and most of the events related in the story actually happened.

A GENTLE breeze gave breath to the palms; fronds sighed, whispering, promising a good day at Lake Okeechobee. An aroma of overripe dates in the palms, and a buzz of sweat bees suckling nectar from spoiled fruit, reminded Terry that wild bananas would be a bittersweet reward if he bolted and ran.

"Eat your breakfast, Terrell."

"Yes ma'am."

Migratory workers were already in the fields. Children's voices came to his ears—going to school in Belle Glade, half a mile distant. A scent of guava mingled with the perfume of poinciana and citrus trees planted throughout Camp Osceola.

"I want you to go to school today, Terrell."

"Yes ma'am."

Through the kitchen window he saw long lines of yellow boxcars on railroad tracks above and behind the house. He heard the clink of couplings, the hiss-chug of engines as United Fruit cars were shifted, filled, iced and sent on their way north.

"There's been enough playing hooky," Mama said.

"Mickey, the boy says he's going." Daddy gazed at Terry sternly. "Didn't you, Terrell?"

"Yessir."

Daddy folded his newspaper to another page. "I don't know

9

what this country is coming to," he commented. "Now Roosevelt wants to arm merchant ships. If that happens, we're that much nearer war."

"Hurry now." Mama reached over, wiped Terry's mouth. "Wash your face and hands," she said.

"Yes ma'am."

He stood on incredibly thin legs, knees knobbed, exposed by short trousers which he detested. He hurried to the bathroom, turned on the water, wet the soap and replaced it unused. He went into the bedroom to get his books, bound with a belt like other children carried theirs.

"Terrell!" Vexation in her tone now. Aside to Daddy, "Lord, that child is slow."

"Mickey, you're always shouting at that boy."

"How do you suggest I get his attention? Whisper?"

"Terrell!" Daddy's voice. "Time for school."

"Yessir."

Mama gave him a brown paper sack: two potted-meat sandwiches with mayonnaise mixed with a sweet relish. An apple. A nickel for a drink. "Milk," Mama stated.

"Yes ma'am."

He eased the screen door closed behind him. He was aware of Mama's eyes as he crossed the backyard, climbed a cinder-strewn incline to the maze of railroad tracks and disappeared from her sight. He ducked between two stationary fruit cars, deliberately taking a path that would carry him beside the steaming locomotive.

"Can I have a ride?"

The engineer grinned. He nodded, and the fireman, who shoveled the coal to power the engine, reached down with one hand to lift Terry aboard. Terry went directly to a padded seat opposite the engineer. The engine reverberated beneath his feet and he wished he were barefoot.

"Going to school?"

It was obvious: clean, shoes, books. Terry nodded.

Far down the track a flagman waved to the engineer. The vehicle wheezed as the throttle was eased forward. The mighty engine creaked, wheels squealing as sand dropped on the rails for traction.

They didn't move far. The flagman waved again, threw a switch and waved anew. The couplings responded to the pull and they backed up, drawing a snaking curve of cars off a siding.

"You're going to be late, little buddy."

"Yessir."

The fireman lifted him over the side and down onto the cinder bed. Hot fumes blew Terry's red hair as he passed the length of the engine between tracks.

He crossed a bridge connecting Camp Osceola with the main town road of Belle Glade and cut between the packinghouses. There was no point walking on blistering hot pavement, with the wide eave and cool platform of a packinghouse so available. The building was a hive of activity, the vegetable smell of celery and foliage pungent and pleasing. Voices, machinery and water sounds formed a cadence that could hold him spellbound by the hour.

He entered the long, open shed of the three-story building. The structure was laced with ribbons of steel-rollered conveyors, each filled with crates end to end. Women wearing rubber aprons and boots packed the boxes. Terry passed a washing machine that sprayed the produce to give it a final cleansing before green shredded paper was put over it and a top was nailed on. He approached one of the aproned women.

"May I have a piece of celery?"

She tore off a stalk, gave it to him with scarcely a glance.

He passed the hot-dog stand, where a tantalizing lure of cooking sauerkraut tempted him to invest his nickel in a spoonful. Better yet, he might trade away his lunch to one of the people working here, for a dime or fifteen cents. But he didn't do it. The best deals were made closer to lunch.

Terry saw several men taking a break. He asked one of them, "Can I have a cigarette?"

"You're too young to smoke."

"Please."

"Give the kid a cigarette."

"Thank you." He put the Camel in a top pocket and crossed the packinghouse to another group. "Can I have a cigarette?"

The same protests, the same results. He did this four more times before he reached the end of the building. Six cigarettes of four different brands. These he could trade away to the boys at the high school, who paid as much as three cents for a cigarette.

He followed a circuitous route through several other packing-houses, arriving at the last one, which abutted the icehouse. Bucky Dallas was sitting on the warped steps of a shack under an eave of the building. Bucky was eleven years old and had a crossed eye. His father ran the icehouse. Bucky's parents didn't seem to care whether he went to school or not.

"Want to buy a cigarette?" Terry asked.

"I got no money."

Terry gave him a Picayune, the hardest to sell. Bucky was always good for a chunk of crystal-clear ice in the dead of summer.

"Hey, Terry, let's go swimming," Bucky suggested.

"No. I got to go to school."

Terry went across the pavement, avoiding pitch bubbles raised by the hot sun. A canal separated the school from the packing-houses. It was lined with thick growths of bamboo—a source of fishing poles, and a cool retreat for errant boys.

"School started?" His question was to three older truants.

"Long time ago."

"Teacher's already been out here looking for you, redhead. She's going to tell your mama."

The realization brought a quickening heartbeat. He crossed the rickety board linking the narrow canal banks and walked into the fenced schoolyard. From an open window he heard the pledge of allegiance; from another window, the morning prayer.

If he didn't go, Mama would be angry. If he did go, the teacher, Mrs. Wright, would send him to the principal for being late again. He entered the red brick building trembling, clutching the paper sack, then hurried across the covered walkway between the high school and elementary classrooms. From the hallway off which the first-grade room was situated he smelled chalk, heard a teacher's voice. He walked down to his room, at the other end.

"Aaaayyyy"—voices in unison—"beeee . . ."

He heard Mrs. Wright say, "Who knows what this is?"

"Ceeeee . . ."

He swallowed, put a shaking hand on the doorknob to turn it.

Across the hall, another teacher, voice booming. "All crayons must be replaced in the boxes, students."

"Effffph . . ."

Terry walked back along the hall, gaining momentum as his resolve evaporated. He hit the door at full run, bolting into the yard like an animal with a glimpse of freedom.

He reached the plank bridging the canal and in three steps cleared it, raced across hot pavement and into the packinghouse. He dashed between conveyors, skirted stacked boxes, vaulted a dolly being pushed toward a boxcar.

"Hey! Kid! Get outta here! Hey, you!"

He was settling to a slower pace. He glanced back repeatedly, as though expecting a horde of teachers led by the principal, armed with rulers and bent on dragging him to class.

"Want to buy a lunch?" Terry asked one of the workers.

"Nah. I brung my own."

Next man. "Want to buy two potted-meat sandwiches? I'll throw in a apple, too, all for a quarter."

"Dime."

"Fifteen cents."

The man fished out coins and gave Terry the money.

Twenty cents total, snug in his pocket, trouble at home tonight, but until then . . . He paused at the hot-dog stand and bought one, and a big RC, and sat amid workers taking first lunch break, savoring the onions and relish, steamed bun and mustard. He took huge swigs from the RC, maintaining suction to avoid a backwash.

He walked out to the road that led to Chosen, taking a detour through a cane field where black men with machetes were harvesting thick, juicy stalks.

"Peel me a stalk?" he inquired of a worker.

"Sure nuff."

The man's accent told Terry this was an islander from the Bahamas, come to make a few dollars American before returning to his own home.

Chewing cane as he walked, Terry wondered if he'd see McCree today. McCree called him Little Hawk and never asked discomforting questions.

Terry heard a car coming and got off the road. Miss Ramsey, the truant officer, came this way every morning, gathering the unwary to haul them back to the principal's office.

The car passed. It was not Miss Ramsey. It was the greenkeeper at the golf course, on his way to work. Terry crawled down a bank to reach canal water, ever mindful of snakes, and washed sticky cane juice from his hands. He nearly slipped. Only a quick grab for the belt around his books saved them from total loss.

He continued toward Chosen, then followed a familiar path from the road through a thicket of Australian pines to a small clearing. Here lived Eunice Washington, a stout black woman, and her sole grandchild, LuBelle.

"Hey, Eunice."

"Lord, boy, you near scared me to death! Don't come creeping up on Eunice like that."

"You seen Mr. McCree?"

"Not yet. He'll be along directly."

"Can I wait?"

"Help yourself." Eunice poked a bleached broomstick into a boiling caldron of lye soap, rainwater and "took in" clothes, which she washed and ironed for pay.

"LuBelle inside?"

"Most likely."

The house was built on stilts over hard-packed earth. There were no windows, only holes cut in the siding. The house was an odd mixture of odors. Boiling beans simmered on a wood stove, where Eunice also heated her irons, and a damp, musty aroma of dirt rose through cracks between floorboards.

LuBelle, a year younger than Terry, was sitting on a bed.

"You want some taffy?"

"No," Terry said.

"Mawmaw made it last night."

"Listen, LuBelle, you got any worms?"

"No."

"Reckon we could go dig some? I'm going to ask Mr. McCree to take me fishing."

"He ain't going. Today's his day to trade with Mawmaw."

"Ho, Eunice."

"There he is." LuBelle grinned.

"Ho, Mr. Cree"—Eunice always dropped the Mc from his name—"what you got there?"

LuBelle and Terry ran to the front porch. Mr. McCree was standing in the yard, laughing, Eunice holding him at bay with her broomstick. The old man gripped the heads of two huge catfish, one in each hand, tails flopping wildly.

14

MICKEY Calder twisted her auburn hair into a bun behind her head. She turned before a full-length mirror, examining a seam in her nylons. Her hands were perspiring. She was still irritated from her phone conversation with Gerald.

"He did it again, Gerald. Terrell skipped school."

A long silence on the line, background sounds of office activity behind Gerald's exhaled sigh. "Where is he now?"

"Gerald, how would I know? I know he isn't here!"

"All right, Mickey. All right."

"Mr. Hammond called."

"The principal?"

"Yes. And Miss Ramsey, the truant officer, came by a moment ago. This is embarrassing, Gerald. That child makes us appear to be negligent parents."

"I don't see anything we can do until he comes home tonight."

"We could go look for him."

"Where? The packinghouses? Chosen? Lake Okeechobee? He said he went to all those places last week."

"There happens to be a state law about six-year-old children attending school, Gerald, and that boy hasn't attended but three days of classes!"

"I know, Mickey. Terrell's a boy. Boys do this sort of thing."

"Gerald, really! I would appreciate a bit of maturity on your part. I'm at my wit's end and I must have help with that boy. He belongs to *both* of us, you know!"

"All right, Mickey."

"I'm going out looking."

"If you insist."

"I want that boy blistered for this tonight."

"Now, Mickey."

"I mean it! I want him worn out. He told me with a perfectly straight face he was going to school."

"We'll see, Mickey."

"Are you going to do what is necessary?" Her voice trembled.

The metallic reply on the telephone. "If you insist."

She had hung up without good-bys. Now dressed, feeling very pregnant, she cursed the wiggly line of her hose, the stray wisps

15

of hair that eluded her barrette, and the heat. She checked the calendar, a daily task. Tuesday, September twenty-third. The baby was due the first week in December.

Mickey got into the suffocatingly hot Chevrolet they had just bought, the new smell still strong. She drove down to the camp's main entrance, passed over a canal and turned toward Chosen.

Two years ago Gerald had taken the position as manager of this migratory labor camp in southern Florida. Since then they had seen their fortunes steadily recover from the utter deprivation of the Depression years in Birmingham, Alabama. A three-bedroom house was provided here, two hundred a month income, and Gerald was happy. After graduating from college, Gerald had aspired to become a writer, and he had an overwhelming need to "help" mankind. His job here satisfied the latter, anyway.

Established to give housing and medical care to migrant workers tending crops, the camp had a steady flow of laboring families arriving and departing. Before the camps, these poor people had slept in vehicles, swamps and cane fields. They had lacked health facilities, and often the result was disease of epidemic proportions.

Gerald and the Farm Security Administration were doing something good for mankind. But at what cost to Terrell? He'd been wandering far and wide at five, and now, in his first year of school, was rebelling against restrictions. Where would he be in ten years after associating with tough transient children?

"Gerald, we must curtail that child!" Mickey had demanded.

"How, Mickey?" She'd made him angry. "You suggest he play with no one? Keep him at the house? Is that it?"

"I don't know how. But he's becoming—contaminated."

"Mickey, *all* boys do what he does! Terrell will be all right. He runs hither and yon and I wouldn't have it any other way. Now if you want to make that child miserable, segregate him from his peers. Make him—and them—think he's different! All that he sees and does, good or bad, can be a growing experience. He's a fairly self-sufficient kid."

As with most of these conversations, that one had ended with sulking silence, issues unresolved, Terrell still running wild. There were evenings when the boy didn't show up until after dark.

"Where have you been, son?"

"Around the camp."

"*Where* around the camp, Terrell?"

A shrug of small shoulders, a wrinkling of his freckled nose. "I don't know. All over."

All over. Mickey had an idea of the scope of that from casual comments made by camp employees.

"That Terrell's a pistol ball! I seen him over to the sewage disposal plant walking those intake pipes like a monkey!"

"Terrell's a sight. Comes by and charms the ladies right out of sauerkraut they're canning."

"I don't want to worry you folks, but it isn't safe really . . . to play in packinghouses . . . on railroad tracks . . . in the canals. . . ."

Mickey drove the Chevrolet past the new golf course, along a dike which held the waters of Lake Okeechobee in place in time of hurricane. She paused atop the swing bridge. Below, hyacinth-choked, murky black water flowed. There were saw grass with razor-sharp cutting edges, cattails higher than a man's head, and snake-infested swamps all around. This was where Terrell had spent most of last week!

"Doing what?" Gerald had questioned gently.

"Playing."

"I know, Terrell. But playing with whom?"

"LuBelle."

"Who are her parents?"

"She lives with her grandmama, Eunice."

"What is Eunice's last name?"

"Washington."

"Where does Mrs. Washington live?"

"Chosen."

Like extracting teeth. Each question answered with an absolute minimum of words.

"Why isn't LuBelle in school?" Gerald persisted.

"She's too little."

"Younger than you?"

"Yessir. I think."

Mickey had stepped in then. "What do you do with LuBelle? Where do you go?"

A twist of Terrell's thin lips, scratching under his nose with one small finger. "Just out to play."

"Terrell, I want a better answer than that."

"Mama, we just *play*."

"Terrell, you told your mama you would not skip school and you did. Why?" Gerald asked. "Don't you like the teacher?"

"She's okay."

"Are the children unfriendly to you?"

"No sir."

"Then, what is it?"

"I don't know."

Gerald had studied the boy, the two of them soberly judging one another, the child a red-haired miniature of the father.

"You're going to school tomorrow?"

"Yessir."

So he did, Monday. Today was Tuesday. Mickey passed over the bridge, halting on the far side. She set the brake and went inside a small store scented with shellacked fishing poles and earthy aromas from boxes marked BAIT.

"Have you seen a little redheaded boy, age six?"

"Terry, you mean?"

Why did that child insist on changing his name from something as strong and masculine as Terrell to the feminine Terry?

"Yes," Mickey said, "Terry."

"Not today, ma'am. Want I should send him home, if I do?"

"Yes, please do. Thank you." She left feeling uncomfortable, huge and awkward. She drove perhaps two miles between stands of wild grasses. The hollow magnified the heat. Flitting swarms of gnats buzzed around her face. Hundreds of black, red and orange grasshoppers blanketed the dirt road, and a grisly crunch of their bodies under the wheels kept her teeth on edge. Mickey didn't look any farther. She turned around and went home.

"GERALD?"

"Yeah, hey, Burrell!" Gerald clamped the receiver between ear and shoulder. Ribbons tied to an oscillating fan wiggled in the airstream.

"Gerald, what's this I hear about Eleanor Roosevelt coming down to inspect the camps?"

The Belle Glade paper, product of its four-hundred-pound owner, Burrell Mason, was an astonishing enterprise. Its staff had produced a syndicated columnist, now in Washington, and a

Pulitzer prizewinner, who had gone on to *The New York Times*.

"That's what they say, Burrell. Rumors, mostly."

"That black camp's her pet, isn't it?"

"She has expressed a good deal of interest in it, yes."

Burrell Mason breathed into the receiver, a labored sound. "Keep me posted on it, will you, Gerald?"

"I'll try."

Through opened casement windows, the odor of freshly mowed Bermuda grass came to Gerald's nostrils, the clacking of rotating blades chewing away fast-growing lawn.

"You think there'll be war?" Dr. Phillip Norman's question brought Gerald's mind back to the man in his office.

"There already is war," Gerald stated. "The Nazis have trapped two hundred thousand Russians around Kiev."

"I don't mean that. I mean war with us?"

"I don't know, Phillip. I certainly hope not."

Dr. Norman raised himself from his chair. He accepted Gerald's signed receipts for inoculations. "I'm glad summer is over," he said. "Polio took its toll this year."

Gerald watched him go, then dialed home for the third time. Still no answer. He rubbed his eyes, massaging away the pounding. He was tired. Long hours, constant worry about a hundred things. Now this problem with his family.

He'd tried reasoning with the boy. "Punish him," Mickey had insisted. For what? For being a boy? For doing only what every child truly yearned to do—run away and play? Given a choice, would he, Gerald, sit in a seething hot classroom or go swimming at the nearest water hole?

"Mr. Calder?" The administrations officer, Marilyn.

"What, Marilyn?"

"Can you send maintenance over to section four? They have a plumbing problem in the bathhouse."

"All right. Make a note on it."

Gerald looked down at his desk; work aplenty. He began signing a seemingly endless mound of forms. He had tried to be a good father. He took Terrell up to Port Mayaca fishing, over to Pahokee swimming, out to the Seminole Indian Reservation now and then. He'd even taken him over to West Palm Beach to see *Bambi*.

"Did you enjoy the movie?"

"Yessir."

"What did you think was the best part?"

Terrell chewed his lip, thinking. "Where the daddy deer saved Bambi in the forest fire."

"Yes," Gerald had said. "That was good."

"Want to play alligator poker?" Terrell asked as they turned onto the forty-five-mile-long highway to Belle Glade.

"Sure." Count the alligators on your side. The side with the most at the end of the trip is winner.

"What did you two talk about?" Mickey later questioned.

"Oh, the movie."

"Anything else?"

"Played alligator poker."

Mickey had sighed. He rubbed her shoulders, kneading away the tension she suffered these days.

"I hope this one is a girl," Mickey said, patting her protruding stomach. "Girls don't do nose dives off the roof, or set off fire alarms just to hear bells ring."

"I spanked Terrell for that."

"Girls don't pull off grasshopper heads and stick them in keyholes." Gerald had laughed.

The telephone rang and he lifted the receiver.

"Gerald?"

"Yes, hey, Mickey. Any luck?"

"No."

"He'll be along tonight, honey. Don't worry about him."

She hung up without another word.

CHAPTER THREE

LuBelle and Terry watched Mr. McCree clean the catfish. "With your mawmaw's beans," McCree said, his voice deep, graveled, "we got us a feast ahead."

"Where's your dog?" Terry asked.

"Round about. Dog!" he hollered.

Dog was the animal's name. A mongrel with one blue eye and one green, the old man's chief companion.

"There's Dog," McCree said, pointing to a hollow under an elephant's ear plant.

"Go stir them beans, LuBelle!" her grandmother commanded.

"Yes ma'am."

"Mr. McCree, reckon we can go fishing soon?" Terry questioned.

"Not today, Little Hawk."

"You said you'd teach me how to catch fish with no bait."

"I did that, and will, too."

"You think I can do it?"

"Anybody can."

"Them beans bubbling?" Eunice called, lifting clothes that had boiled over the fire, transferring them, on the end of the broom handle, to a bucket.

"Yes ma'am," LuBelle replied.

"Eunice knows about beans," McCree said, salting the catfish.

When the clothes were done, they cooked the catfish outdoors in large frying pans over the embers, the aroma of food making their bellies churn. McCree split a section of green bamboo into slivers, and they used these to spear fish directly from the pan onto plates heaped with soft butter beans and green onions.

"Don't smack your lips," Eunice said to Terry. "If a bite's too big to shut on, make a smaller bite of it."

"Yes ma'am."

"Don't say ma'am to me, neither."

"Yes ma'am, Eunice."

McCree passed a quart jar to Eunice. It looked like kerosene. But it wasn't. Eunice helped herself to several small swallows, winced, handed it back.

"Can I have a taste?" Terry asked.

McCree gave it to him and Terry took a sip of the liquid, felt it sear to his innards.

"I don't like it," Terry said. "Tastes like coal oil smells."

"It does," McCree agreed.

"How come you drink it, then?" Terry asked.

"Punishing myself for long-ago sins," McCree said. Eunice laughed.

"What kind of sins?" LuBelle questioned.

"Minor infractions, mostly," McCree stated. "And taking the Lord's name in vain," he added.

The crickets had begun their evening serenade, the sun was settling behind the tops of Australian pines. They sat around the fire, watching the embers pulling ashen blankets over the reddish glow below. LuBelle and Terry had their young heads against McCree's chest. The old man smelled like cured tobacco, his breath a miasma of the weed he chewed.

"Some of these days a gator or cougar is going to feed on my bones," McCree stated.

"Hush such," Eunice said, but not firmly.

"As it should be. I been eating their kind nigh onto eighty-three years, more or less."

LuBelle's eyes fluttered, closed. Fluttered, closed.

Bullfrogs burping, cicadas chirping, wind whispering, bellies filled, pine smoke holding off mosquitoes, the final light of day gone, Terry sighed deeply, eyes closing.

"Where you reckon this boy's mama be?" Eunice asked softly.

"Says he ain't got none."

"You believing that! Dressed the way he do? He got a mama."

McCree gazed down at Terry sleeping. "I tell you, Eunice, about believing. What he believes *is* what is, even when I believe it ain't true."

McCree shook Terry gently. "Little Hawk, the moon's rising, the owls are coming out to play."

Terry opened his eyes as McCree caressed his shoulder. He rose and followed the old man to his battered pickup truck. "Let's go, Dog!" The pup bounded past Terry onto the front seat. Terry settled against the shuddering door of the cab, Dog's tail thumping him in the arm as McCree said so long to Eunice, and thanks.

Terry awoke at the bridge over the main entrance canal of the camp. McCree was shaking him. "Flit away home, boy."

"We going fishing sometime?"

"Whenever," McCree said. "You awake?"

"Yessir."

Terry slipped from the cab. He watched the truck go over the tracks, the sole taillight flickering. He crossed the bridge.

The lights were on in the house. He circled it and saw Mama washing dishes. Daddy was sitting at the radio console, turning dials. Terry tried to lift his bedroom screen, but Mama had double-latched it. There was nothing else to do except go in the front door.

Daddy didn't turn until he was almost to the hall. "Terrell—"

"Yessir."

"Why didn't you go to school today, son?"

"I meant to."

"Your mother has been hunting you, worrying, all day."

"I'm sorry, Daddy."

Mama, coming through the dining room, wiping her hands with a dish towel, heard their voices. She took in Terry's appearance with a glance, her lips tightly compressed.

"No talk," she said. "Wear him out. Do it, or I will!"

"Mickey, I think I should discuss this with Terrell first. I think he should be aware of why—"

"Do it!" Mickey commanded sharply.

"Terrell, you told your mother you would go to school today. You promised."

"Yessir."

"Look at you!" Mama's voice lifted. "You're filthy! Your new clothes—Gerald!"

"Son, breaking a promise is a very bad thing to do."

"Yessir. I'm sorry, Daddy."

"Gerald!"

"Mickey, go back to the kitchen. I'll handle this if you'll allow me to approach it my way."

Mama lunged at Terry, seized his arm and shoved him toward the bedroom. "This isn't fair, Gerald. It is not fair. I shouldn't have to do this myself."

"Mickey, wait a minute, now. . . ."

Mama slammed the bedroom door and tore off Terry's pants. She held him in one hand, getting a belt from the top of the dresser with her other. Terry, blue eyes wide, trembling, threw up one frail palm, crying, "Please, Mama! I'm sorry!"

The strap fell hard, wrapping a searing thong around his legs, raising blistering welts. *Whap!* "Mama!" *Whap! Whap!*

It went on and his screams choked to shattering sobs, his legs fiery red and aflame with pain.

"You will go to school tomorrow, Terrell," Mama said, her voice quivering. "You will go to school or I will wear you out every evening you don't. Do you understand that?"

"Yes ma'am."

"Go take a bath and go to bed." She guided him into the bathroom. "Use soap, too," she ordered.

Daddy stood at the end of the hall, in the living room, his face hidden by shadows, his body a silhouette, unmoving.

"Mickey, I told you I would take care of—"

"I don't want to hear it, Gerald!"

Water rushing in the tub drowned their voices. Terry closed the spigot and eased himself down, squatting in the water.

Mama appeared in the bathroom door. "Stop that and bathe."

"Yes ma'am." He forced himself to sit, wincing. Mama glared at him. He wet the washcloth, rubbed soap against it and began smearing it across his dry chest, body jerking as he muffled sobs behind closed lips. Mama's expression altered slightly.

"I don't want to ever have to hit you again," Mama said. "But I want you to go to school. From now on. Every day."

"Yes ma'am, Mama."

She knelt beside the tub, her eyes brimming. "I love you."

"I love you, Mama."

She tried to busy herself scooping water onto his back. She began to cry, bathing him gently, helping him towel dry, then holding him tightly.

CHAPTER FOUR

IN MRS. Wright's schoolroom the next morning, the blackboard reflected sunlight. A breeze fragrant with canal scents and the odor of fetid vegetation tantalized Terry. He glanced out, saw the bamboo stand, the roofs of the packinghouses.

"Do not use your wrists, students. Move your entire arm. . . ."

A wolf spider appeared on the window, hairy legs holding the iridescent body aloft, multiple eyes glistening.

"Move your whole arm and make big, round O's."

Moaning from afar, the low wail of a whistle. A train coming from the north. If Terry could see the cars— A trainman had taught him to decipher the coded chalk marks on the sides, which told where the freight was going.

"Terrell! *Terrell!* Will you sit down, please?"

"I can't see the blackboard."

"There's nothing on the blackboard."

Several students giggled, turned to stare at him.

Recess outside was carefully structured, the teachers standing in the cooling shade of the covered walk, watching boys run and throw themselves about. The girls dominated the swings, voices screeching. Terry eased toward the bamboo stand. A casual glance at the adults, quick dart, and he was across the canal.

"Hey, Terry." Bucky Dallas lounged in a well-hollowed spot, leaning against the bamboo. "How's school?"

Terry stared at the teeming schoolyard. "I hate it."

"Dump it," Bucky urged. "Let's go get some ice."

"I can't."

"You scared?"

Terry studied his companion, unbuckled his trousers and pulled down his pants, exposing bruised welts above the knees.

"Jeeze."

Terry rebuckled his trousers as a handbell announced recess was over. Without another word he retraced his steps to the yard, joined the others and marched dutifully back to class.

BURRELL Mason wore a broad-brimmed Panama hat, which he dropped on a corner of the table. He looked oddly balanced on the small soda-fountain chair. Perspiration soaked the newspaperman's collar. "Gerald, do you realize the consequences of this new camp?" he asked.

"I know it will be good for the cane growers."

"But opening up a black labor camp is going to bring darkies in here by the thousands. It's going to freeze wages for the whites who compete against them. There's going to be resentment."

"Listen, Burrell, I don't make policy for Washington. Construction is in progress and the camp will be, that's all."

"I'm against it, not because they're black. I'd be against it if they were whites. The only way to raise wages is to squeeze management where it hurts—manpower supply."

With a sudden shift in subject, Burrell grunted. "You see the Miami *Herald* yet?"

"No. What?"

"A U.S.-owned tanker under Panamanian registry was torpedoed and sunk in the South Atlantic."

"Dear God."

"Roosevelt is putting us into this war, Gerald. You know why Washington is building that new camp, don't you?"

"For more laborers."

"Well, yes. But it goes deeper than that. The whites, and blacks, are going to be sent overseas before you know it. This new camp is for Bahama laborers. To get the cane crops in, come hell or high water."

"Burrell, assume that's true. If we're at war, we'll need those Bahamians. Be reasonable."

"I'm going to fight it, Gerald. With my little newspaper, right here in Belle Glade."

"You're looking for headlines, Burrell."

The truth of that was reflected in the editor's eyes, a flicker of amusement. "That," he said, "is what it's all about, Gerald. Have they asked you to manage that black labor camp?"

"What makes you think they'd ask me?"

Burrell labored to rise. "Who else would be fool enough to take such a thankless, awful job?"

Gerald watched the thickset publisher move with astonishing agility toward the door. Who indeed? Gerald thought.

MICKEY was strolling toward the house when she heard the phone ringing. It was Marilyn. "Mrs. Calder, do you know where I might find Mr. Calder?"

"No, Marilyn, I don't. Something wrong?"

"Yes. No. I mean, Mrs. Roosevelt is coming."

Mickey's heart skipped a beat. "Today?"

"No ma'am. Next week."

"Keep it under your hat, Marilyn."

Mickey hung up. She sat on the couch and let her head fall back, both hands on her belly. Her eyes touched on a petrified wad of toilet paper which Terrell had wet and thrown up to see it stick. There had been hundreds; Mickey had somehow missed that one. "Please, the next one has to be a girl," she whispered.

PERSPIRATION trickled down Terry's sides. He was fighting a desire to close his eyes and sleep. Last night's spanking had left him aching and stiff.

"One plus one," Mrs. Wright chanted.

"Equals two"—the class response.

"Two plus one—"

Terry's mind numbed. He wondered if Mr. McCree had been looking for him out at LuBelle's. The prospect of learning to catch fish with his bare hands was so exhilarating he smiled.

"What's so funny, Terrell?"

Mrs. Wright looked hot, cheeks red, hair coming unknotted. "All right, class, let's have Terrell answer this by himself." All eyes on him now. "What is six plus one?"

"Seven."

"Eleven plus one."

"Twelve."

Her expression hardened. "Fourteen plus seven."

Imperceptibly, his fingers worked. "Twenty-one."

"Twenty-one plus thirteen."

He ran out of fingers, confused his toes. No reply.

A hand wagged insistently in the air. Curly hair, white shoes, wide freckles, Eddy Kent.

"What's the answer, Eddy?" Mrs. Wright asked.

"Thirty-three!"

A softer, forgiving tone. "Thirty-four," Mrs. Wright said. Then to Terrell, "Pay attention!"

When the bell rang, Terry went home by way of the playground at the back of the camp, where most of the boys hung out.

"Hi." He flung himself on a bench. "Know what I've been thinking about?" he said to Lonny, who was nearly eleven.

"What?"

"Running away."

The boys looked at him with varying degrees of skepticism but with mounting respect. Their interest was not in why but how.

"I'd pick a fruit car going to Kissimmee," Terry said. "There's lots of fruits and vegetables this time of year, so I could get all I wanted to eat from packinghouses and orange groves. I'd sleep nights in the hobo jungles."

"Cops'd getcha," somebody noted.

"No they wouldn't. And so what if they did? Eldridge Hopkins said the state school at Marianna had tennis and swimming."

"What if somebody tried to stomp on you?"

"I'd carry a sock with sand in the toe. It makes a blackjack." That had come from a Dick Tracy comic book.

"What about your folks? They'd get unhappy, wouldn't they?"

"They got another baby coming."

"You'd have to come home someday."

"I would. Someday. When I'm too big to whip."

He walked toward home, winding between shelters. People sat on concrete steps outside open doors. The odor of cooking heavily mixed in the air: cabbage, beans, fatback.

He wished he could, really. Run away.

CHAPTER FIVE

SATURDAY came at last.

"You may go with me to the store this afternoon, Terrell."

"I want to go play, Mama."

She almost looked relieved. "Be home before too late."

He ran out, shouting good-by, and was gone before Mickey's call could ask him where he was going. He trotted past LuBelle's and took a rutted, narrow back road to where McCree lived.

The swamp out here was a constantly moving thing. From thousands of sources came sounds which alone might go undetected. Together they formed the voice of the Glades. The hum of insect wings, the crunch of gnawing teeth; serrated blades of saw grass rasping in a breeze.

Water oozed underfoot. Terry stepped on higher ground, walking past tremendous beds of ants that were almost as high as his knees. To stir one of those was to ask for agony. He reached a small lake, a clearing of growth, and stood gazing toward a shack on the far side. He saw McCree's truck.

"Ho, McCree!" His voice bounced here, there, rippling away in echoes. The swamp was abruptly silent, creatures transfixed by the alien call. "Ho! Ho! Ho! McCreeeeee!"

The old man appeared in the darkened doorway, barely visible through wiggly waves of heat rising from the lake. "Hey! Boy!"

Terry began circling the body of water. He wove his way through mangrove trees poised like vegetable spiders on exposed roots, forming a hammock over which he climbed. Below the matted root system lay pitch-black water, swirled now and then by startled minnows. Birds beat skyward, squawking in protest as he encroached on nesting areas of cattle egrets, blue herons and roseate spoonbills.

McCree was still in the doorway, grinning. "Skeeter-bit and thorn-tore," he said. "Better suck on them scratches, boy."

Terry did this, then followed McCree inside, where it was dark, noticeably cooler and exciting.

There were no electric lights, no toilet. The table was two orange crates topped by a plank McCree had found somewhere. The seats were more crates, bottom end up and covered with burlap sacks for padding. The house was filled with enviable items: bleached skulls of beheaded snakes, shells of turtles in various states of disassembly, and burlap sacks stuffed with pinecones that seeped aromas and gave the dwelling a continuous feel of Christmas. A huge round wasp's nest hung from the rafters, and bushel baskets of various seeds were stacked everywhere.

From these things the old man earned a living. Seeds, cones and dried cattails he shipped to florist-supply houses. Skeletons, alligator skulls and snake rattles went to biological laboratories. Bobcats, raccoons and an occasional bear cub were purchased by animal dealers from Miami.

McCree held up a spiral-shaped object the size of his thumb. "If you see any of these, I have an order for a thousand."

"What is it?"

"Cocoon. The cecropia moth."

"A thousand?" The number was incomprehensible to Terry.

McCree shuffled through some papers in a pasteboard carton. "And I got me an order for three hundred bushels of Australian pinecones. Easy to fill. Good pay, too."

"Three hundred bushels?"

"Yep. Three hundred. You know what ten is."

Terry held up both hands. McCree nodded. "Ten times ten is a hundred. Thought I taught you that."

"I forgot it."

"Show me."

Ten flicks of both hands. One hundred.

"A thousand?"

Uncertainty. Then remembering. "A hundred times ten."

"I need that many cocoons. Want coffee?"

There was no coffee like McCree's. At first, Terry thought the flavor came from the boiled swamp water. But he had since learned the delicious difference was from a blue-flowered weed

30

which McCree, who called things by their "true" names, referred to as *Cichorium intybus*. "The leaves make a fine salad," the old man told him. "Roots can be boiled and eaten with butter. Or dried, ground and used as coffee. Folks think of it as a weed. Truth is, it is what it is to you. To me, it's good old chicory."

The mixture was well diluted with condensed milk, sweetened with honey stolen from a hive in a hollow stump. "Sweet enough?" McCree questioned.

"Just right! Reckon you could take me fishing today?"

"Might as well as not," McCree said. "We might have some luck this afternoon when it gets cooler, if you want to try."

A flutter of inner excitement. "I'd like to try."

"With luck, catfish will make us some good eating tonight."

McCree gathered his food stores from what he called the biggest garden in the world: the swamp. Other than salt, flour and sugar he traded for from a mill, he seldom bought anything. And when he went on treks, he relied on his ability to harvest something near at hand. Terry had observed the old man producing pancakes from cattail roots, sweetened with blackberries and covered with cane syrup. Venison, smothered in mushrooms and bamboo shoots, was often followed by sapodilla gum for dessert and to cleanse the teeth. From wild lime trees came flavoring for pan-fried fresh-caught catfish or bass.

City frills, McCree often said, "can best be done without."

The sun was a fuzzy ball of flame still half an hour above the horizon when they arrived at a selected spot in the backwaters of a canal. Here McCree tamped down grass to give them a place to sit. With a finger to his lips compelling silence, he knelt and stared down into black water.

Terry tried to see what the old man saw. Nothing. Except the reflection of McCree's unshaven face. Then, on the old man's parched lips, a fleck of foam appeared. Slowly, the bubbly spit gathered volume. Terry sat mesmerized by the silvery thread drawing longer and longer, closer and closer to the water. It dropped. Tiny ripples moved away from the disturbed surface.

One hand lifted, moved unhurried, outward. McCree reached down and picked up a tremendous catfish. He sat back, drool on his chin, looked at Terry's open astonishment and laughed.

"Nothing to it, Little Hawk. You see how I did it?"

"Yessir, Mr. McCree."

"Want to try?"

A shiver of ecstasy. "Yessir."

"Good. Be real still. The spit's got to be full of bubbles. Look straight down, and soon that old fish thinks you belong up there. When you go to reach for him, put your hand in the water like a knife, slicing down, and grab him gently. Otherwise he'll slip away. Think you can do it?"

"I'll try."

Terry leaned out, staring down. He worked spit, pushing and pulling it between his teeth, creating bubbles. The spit dropped. Unbelievably, rising in the water, unafraid and unaware, a catfish came nearer and nearer the surface. Terry's hand eased out, quivering with excitement. He kept his fingers together as McCree had shown him, eased into the water; cold flesh, alive, fingers closed. He had him!

Terry threw himself backward, the fish wild in his hand, McCree's roaring laughter in his ears.

"I did it!" Terry shouted.

"Did right good. Bigger than the one I caught," McCree said, cutting a green, pliable switch, which he ran through the gills of both fish so they could carry them.

"Did you see him slinging water and flopping?" Terry was so excited his words were a jumble, face flushed.

"Whipped water like a snapped limb." McCree smiled. "But you held him tight enough."

"I did it," Terry said, awed. "I really did it."

"Kind of surprised me, to tell the truth," McCree drawled, walking now back toward home and frying pans.

"Really?" Chest bursting with pride.

"I once taught a Seminole kid to do that. Later grew up to be a chief. But you know, it took him nigh twenty times to catch on to it. You know what *twenty* is."

Two quick flicks of the hands.

"A Indian? It took him twenty times?"

"Yessirree. And he was smart. But I never saw anybody catch on so fast as you did. First try!" McCree's hand rode easily on Terry's shoulder, both of them walking faster than was necessary.

"That was something," Terry said. "Really was."

"Sure was that. Beat the Indian chief."

Later, when McCree delivered Terry to the entrance of Camp Osceola, they were still talking about the catch, and the flavor. "Best catfish I believe I ever tasted," McCree said.

It had been, too. Sopped in the juice of a bitter lime, simmered in a saucepan of "secret" juices, eaten with a potatolike bulb dug from under a particular tree—the meal was unforgettable.

"Think you'll be out tomorrow?" McCree asked.

"I don't know."

No further questions. "Enjoyed it, Little Hawk."

"Me, too, Mr. McCree. Thanks for teaching me."

"You sure learned in a hurry, Little Hawk."

McCree pulled the door of the truck shut. The motor grumbled, and the vehicle went over railroad tracks and disappeared.

"WHERE have you been, Terrell?" Mama. Angry.

"I went out to Chosen."

Daddy looked over his newspaper. The Cities Service Band of America was on the radio.

"I am at my wit's end, Gerald. Supper comes and goes—"

"Are you hungry, Terrell?" Daddy asked.

"No sir, I ate."

"Where?" Mama demanded.

"I caught a catfish and—Daddy, it was this big!"

"Hey, that's a big catfish."

"Yessir! And—"

"Go in there and get bathed," Mama said.

"Mama, I caught the fish with—"

"You *smell* like fish. Get in there and bathe now. I made some banana pudding. Do you want some?"

"Yes ma'am!" He went to the bathroom and began running a tub. He heard Daddy laugh.

"You can't say he's a sissy, Mickey."

"Granted that."

"I like it, Mickey. Makes the boy self-sufficient. It's a good lesson for him. Drop the matter, why not."

He strained to hear a reply. Mama had gone to the kitchen.

Terry was in the tub when Daddy's head appeared in the door.

"How big?" Daddy asked, his tone intentionally skeptical.

Terry carefully held out his hands, adjusting to the truest dimension he could recall.

"That was a whopper."

Terry nodded, eyes growing vacant, remote. "Sure was," he said softly. "It was something."

CHAPTER SIX

BUCKY Dallas was sitting on the back steps when Terry finished breakfast. "Tomatoes are coming in," Bucky noted. "I got a box of salt. Want to go to the packinghouse?"

"Sure!"

Mickey, at the kitchen window, listened to the exchange.

"Mama, may I go to the packinghouse?"

"I suppose so."

She watched them walk across the yard, Bucky's arm around Terry's shoulder.

"Gerald, do you think it's all right for Terrell to run around with that Dallas boy?"

"I don't see why not. Bucky is like an older brother."

"I guess I worry too much over nothing."

"Yes," Gerald said gently, turning on the radio, seeking the football games.

Mickey sighed. She left him to his game and went to lie down.

The two boys walked unhurriedly to the Blue Goose Packing Company ramp.

"Hey!" Terry pointed. "There's Mr. McCree."

The old man was selecting hampers from a refuse pile. To ship his goods, McCree scavenged damaged crates, repairing them with brads and bailing wire from other smashed containers.

"Ho, Little Hawk. Who's your friend?"

"Bucky Dallas."

McCree extended a hand to the cross-eyed boy. "Pleased to make your acquaintance," McCree said. "What're you two up to?"

"Going to eat tomatoes, Mr. McCree. Want to go with us?" Terry glanced at Bucky. It was his box of salt.

"Where to?" McCree asked, tossing a hamper into his truck.

"In the loft," Bucky replied.

"Sounds fine to me," McCree said.

"Mr. McCree taught me how to catch catfish with my bare hands," Terry said.

"Come on!" Bucky laughed, sensing a joke.

"He did, didn't you, Mr. McCree?"

"Sure enough. Big catfish you caught, too. Bigger than mine."

Because McCree was an adult, Bucky pursued the matter no further, but he clearly didn't believe the tale.

They climbed to the third-floor storage area of the packinghouse. Here, stacked almost twenty feet high, were hundreds of crates of freshly picked tomatoes, ready to be delivered down below for packing. Bucky clambered up a service ladder and secured a precarious hold on the mountain of boxes. Safely atop these, he waved Terry and McCree up behind him. Then Bucky lifted several lids and they selected the juiciest, almost overripe tomatoes and passed around the salt.

"Delicious," McCree said, tomato seeds in his chin whiskers.

They ate until their stomachs bulged, aching.

"Want to shoot the shoot?" Bucky asked Terry.

"Sure!"

"What's this?" McCree inquired.

"Shoot the shoot," Bucky said dubiously. "It's kind of scary."

"Too scary for me?" McCree asked.

"I don't know."

"Not for Mr. McCree," Terry stated. "He's never scared."

Bucky was studying McCree. "That really true?"

"Yep."

"Want to shoot the shoot?" Bucky offered.

"Might as well as not," McCree said. "Show me how?"

They climbed down the ladder and walked through the cavernous building to a far end. Here packing crates were stored. To send them down to packing lines three floors below, the crates were placed on a spiraling chute that turned like a dizzying corkscrew from here to the main floor. There the chute straightened and became a series of rollers over which the crates passed down a fifty-yard-long incline. The remainder of the exhilarating trip was a flat track where the boxes were packed, and beyond this, the ultimate joy, was the washing machine. Triggered by the passing crates, it blew stinging jets and misty sprays from all four directions. The box was then ready to be capped and shipped.

35

Bucky completed his explanation and stood, jaw twisted, his expression unquestionable: he expected McCree to decline.

"Who goes first?" McCree asked.

Bucky shrugged. "It don't matter. But whoever goes last has to be ready to run for it, because by the time the third one gets out of the washing machine, the guard is usually on his way."

"I don't run fast as I used to," McCree said. "Might be I ought to be first, then?"

"Second would be best," Bucky advised. "That way you can see how it's done and still have time to get away from the guard."

"You run fastest," Terry told Bucky. "I'll go first. And remember, Mr. McCree, don't let your elbows or hands stick out over the sides of the crate. You might lose a finger."

Terry got into a crate, knees pulled up, elbows wedged inside, prepared for the initial spiraling, headlong fall. Bucky pushed Terry's box to the edge of the chute.

"Ready?"

"Ready!"

Bucky shoved Terry forward, the box tilted, and *zoom*—he was falling. Round and round, heat from friction causing the wood slats to smoke. Gathering momentum, Terry roared out of the corkscrew and hit the slanted ramp. Gaining speed, he shot the length of the building, over the heads of startled workers, a whine of rollers stretching out behind. Side rails narrowed, slowing the projectile. Then a conveyor belt drew Terry through the washing machine. Breathless, head spinning, he jumped out, pulled his box off to make way for McCree. He heard the old man coming.

"Aiyeeeee!"

He knew by the sounds of the rollers that McCree had reached the ramp—*zingggg! Thump!* Water sounds. In the distance, a cursing male voice, running feet. Behind McCree the squeal of another crate coming down the chute—*zoom!*

The old man was drenched, grinning, eyes wild. Terry seized his box, yanking it out of the way for Bucky.

"That was something," McCree said, not moving.

"Hurry, Mr. McCree! Here comes the guard!"

The old man stretched his legs, unknotting muscles. "Something else!" he said, stepping off the conveyor and holding Terry's shoulder for support. Terry urged greater speed, heading for a tunnel route they often used for escape. McCree barely made it as Bucky landed on the far side of the conveyor and decoyed the guard away, the man's cursing voice and shaking fist adding zest to the adventure.

McCree followed Terry, crawling between crates toward a point of light at the end of the tunnel. Terry turned and helped him up. They stood looking at one another, eyes sparkling, laughing.

"This way," Terry instructed. He went down the exit steps, ducked beneath the platform, traversed the entire width of the building and emerged near McCree's truck, where Bucky waited.

"You did it right," Terry said, grinning.

"Thank you," McCree replied. "You taught me how. The credit rightly belongs to you. I'm glad you told me to keep my hands inside. I confess, my fanny got a mite warm. That box gets hot!"

The boys laughed.

"You all want to go out to my place?" McCree asked.

Bucky shook his head. "I have to mind the ice plant."

"How about you, Little Hawk?"

"Yeah!"

They went to LuBelle's, actually, where they consumed green beans cooked with pigs' knuckles. While McCree and Eunice sat on the porch chewing Bull of the Woods, talking, Terry and Lu-Belle played a form of hopscotch they'd worked up together.

McCree delivered Terry to the camp shortly after dark.

"Did you like shooting the shoot?" Terry asked.

"Don't know when I've liked something so much," McCree said. "Tomatoes were good, too."

"Mr. McCree . . . I sure do have fun with you."

McCree's throaty chuckle came in the dark. "You keep an old man young, Little Hawk. Come see me when you can."

Mr. McCree sat in his pickup, watching Terry walk across the bridge. Terry deliberately went away from the house, not forgetting his fib that he had no home, no parents.

He didn't know why he'd told McCree that. Perhaps to avoid worry about the hours he kept. The lie had come from his lips before he was aware of its forming, and McCree had looked at him a long time, then nodded. The deception had been carefully reinforced ever since, though McCree had never brought up the subject again.

Terry recognized a car belonging to Burrell Mason. He halted on the porch, voices coming through the living-room windows.

Mr. Mason's tone was intense. "This Roosevelt-Churchill Atlantic Charter—what do you think that will accomplish, Gerald?"

"It will set up a food pool to rehabilitate Europe, Burrell."

"Ye gods and golden minnows! You believe that?"

"Then what *is* it for, Burrell?"

"It is an alliance getting ready to fight the Axis, Gerald!"

Terry walked in and the mood altered noticeably.

"Have fun today?" Mama asked.

"Yes ma'am."

"Been over at the packinghouse all day," Mama told the men. "If you want to know doing what, take a look at his clothes."

Tomato seeds had dried like burrs to the fabric of Terry's shirt. Mama was unbuttoning it.

"Mind you don't lose a toe in a fan belt over there," Mr. Mason said. Terry secretly despised him for that.

"You are careful, aren't you?" Mama asked, her face showing instant alarm.

Terry exhibited his bare feet. Daddy laughed.

"He has all his toes, Mickey," Daddy noted.

"Supper will be in a while," Mama said. "Mr. Mason is eating with us tonight."

Terry took his cue from a slight jerk of Mama's head that sent him to take a bath.

After dinner Gerald sat at the kitchen table, tapping his fingernails against the porcelain top. He had offered to help Mickey with the dishes, but she'd refused.

"You know if we have war, I'll have to go," Gerald said.

"Please, Gerald, not tonight. Burrell is so depressing. Why do we have that man out here? He insults your intelligence, and I honestly don't think he tastes a bite of what I cook."

"He consumes enough of it," Gerald noted.

Mickey stared at her husband a moment, went back to dishwashing. "Gerald, we are going to have a war, aren't we?"

"I don't know. Roosevelt says—"

"Forget Roosevelt," Mickey said. "I want to know *your* opinion. Are we going to war?" She turned to look at him again.

Gerald said nothing. He wore an expression which frightened

her. She dried her hands and walked to him, pulling his head against her stomach, holding him like a child.

"I love you, Gerald."

Terry had paused in the hallway on his way to the kitchen for a drink of water. He turned, on tiptoe, and quietly went back to bed. He wasn't quite sure what war was, but the tone of the word, the expressions it elicited, brought a quicker heartbeat and a shortness of breath. In the dark, eyes unseeing but open, he was suddenly afraid.

CHAPTER SEVEN

"TERRELL, are you going to school today?" Daddy asked.

"Yessir." He accepted the brown paper sack from Mama, kissed them both and ran out the back door. He climbed the steep cinder path and trotted toward the packinghouses.

He traded well for his sacked lunch, then ran all the way to school. Mrs. Wright met him at the door.

"You're late, Terrell."

"I'm sorry."

Mrs. Wright stepped aside, allowing him to pass. He went to his desk and sat, while she began marking math problems on the blackboard.

"Guess what I got?" A whisper behind Terry's head.

"What?"

"A jar full of tree frogs."

Terry turned, looking at Cooty Jones. The dark-skinned boy was the son of an attorney. He sniveled constantly.

"I'm going to put them in Mrs. Wright's desk."

"You are?" Terry saw the boy in a new light.

"Yep. Recess. Want to help?"

Terry grinned, nodded.

During recess, Cooty got his jar and met Terry in the rest room. The mass of pale green, sticky-footed frogs was transferred, after much grabbing and cramming, to a cigar box Terry had found.

"What's that for?" Eddy Kent asked.

"None of your beeswax," Terry said. Then to Cooty, "Don't tell him nothing."

They left Eddy Kent, curly head high, covering the sting of his rebuff with haughty sounds of superiority. On the way to their seats, Terry detoured by Mrs. Wright's desk and quickly snitched a rubber band and two thumbtacks. He attached the rubber band to the box lid with one tack, pulled open the center drawer of the teacher's desk and placed the box inside, tacking the other end of the rubber band to the underside of the desk top. This done, he carefully cut the paper which acted as a hinge for the box lid.

"When she opens the desk drawer," he reasoned aloud, "the rubber band is going to yank off the top."

"Then what?" Cooty asked.

"What's a tree frog do when light hits him?"

"Jumps."

Terry grinned. "Yep."

Several times they thought she was about to open the drawer, but her hand went to other drawers instead. The final bell rang and school was out.

"Now what?" Cooty wailed.

"I don't know," Terry confessed.

"You wasted my frogs," Cooty accused.

"Maybe she'll open it tomorrow. Yeah, she will. She has the attendance book in her desk."

Terry forgot the incident overnight. Cooty was absent the next day, so nothing made him think about it.

The students took their seats, awaiting the bell. Mrs. Wright pulled open her center desk drawer.

Terry, like everyone else, was quietly sitting with eyes forward. Suddenly Mrs. Wright threw herself backward, swatting the air, bumping the blackboard. Tiny flecks of green dotted her dress, neck, hair and arms. Then Terry remembered.

Mrs. Wright drowned the bell with a scream, and, to the amazement of her students, she clawed her hairdo to a shambles and began tearing off her clothes.

Another teacher peered through the door. "Nancy?"

Mrs. Wright was busy. She jolted as though struck from behind and began slashing at her backside. "Watch it!" she shrieked, and the other teacher mounted a nearby chair, holding her skirt above the knees.

Mrs. Wright shuddered, lifted her own dress from the floor and shook it. "I demand to know who did this," she said.

"I know!" Eddy Kent's hand, waggling. "I know, Mrs. Wright!"

She transfixed the curly-haired tattler, and Eddy Kent turned with malicious pleasure to point at Terry Calder.

TERRY felt small sitting in a chair where his toes didn't quite touch the floor.

"What are we going to do with you?" the principal asked.

"I don't know."

Terry watched the ominous man glaring down at him.

"Are you unhappy at home?"

"No sir."

"You know, if you have a problem, you can come to me any-time and I'll try to help you with it."

No reply.

"Do you dislike Mrs. Wright, is that it?"

"No sir."

"You must not like her very much! You don't come to class, or come late when you do. Then you scare her half to death."

"I'm sorry, Mr. Hammond."

"You should be. I want you to tell Mrs. Wright you're sorry. You understand? And I want you to apologize to the entire class."

"Yessir."

Mr. Hammond stood and opened the door.

The hall was a roar of activity. Terry hugged the wall opposite the lockers and started down the walk toward the elementary section. He was shaking in nervous relief, from his release from the punishment he'd geared himself to accept.

He felt all eyes turning toward him—students on the playground, teachers sitting on benches. Terry approached Mrs. Wright.

"Did Mr. Hammond spank you?" Icy cold.

"No ma'am. He told me to apologize. I'm sorry, Mrs. Wright."

She stared at him, eyes hard.

"Mr. Hammond said I ought to apologize to the class."

"Go play," Mrs. Wright commanded.

That afternoon Terry left school carrying a note from Mrs. Wright, sealed in an envelope. "I expect a reply from your mother in the morning, Terrell. Don't come to school without it."

He stopped at Bucky's on the way home. "Will you read something to me, Bucky?"

"Sure, what is it?"

Terry gave Bucky the note. Bucky tore it open.

"'Dear Mrs. Calder,'" he hesitantly recited. "'Your Terrell robbed me of ten years today. He planted a box full of frogs in my desk. I opened the drawer and they plastered themselves to me and I'm afraid I gave the children an impromptu peek at a mature female form undressing in class. The reaction here has been, for the most part, great humor at my experience or utter relief that Terrell isn't theirs! I report this for no other purpose than sympathy. Mr. Hammond put the fear of God into Terrell, and I trust that will suffice until he reaches the second grade. Best regards— Nancy Wright.'"

"Your mama will blister you for this," Bucky said.

"I know it."

"What if you didn't show her the note?"

"Mrs. Wright said don't come to school without an answer."

Bucky considered this. "What if we get somebody to write a note and you say your mama wrote it?"

Terry looked at Bucky, heart ascending. "Who'd do it?"

"Renée, at the Last Dollar Café. She writes notes for me all the time. My teacher can't tell the difference."

The jukebox was wailing groans of hillbilly music as they walked in. Men with rolled shirt sleeves sat at a counter, eating.

"Hey, Renée!" Bucky stood at the end of the counter.

"Hello, Bucky baby!" Renée carried cups of coffee stacked up her arm. "Be right back, hold on."

Water in glasses atop the counter formed tight circles of sympathetic ripples in time with the throb of music. The Wurlitzer had columns of lights going up each side, with bubbles traversing the length of the box and merging somewhere inside to reappear from the bottom. Between recordings, the human contribution to the pandemonium temporarily subsided, then lifted anew as another record was seized by a mechanical arm.

"Whatcha need, Bucky?"

Bucky told her. She read the note, looked at Terrell, and threw back her head, laughing. "You did that, kid?"

"Yes ma'am."

"Ma'am?" echoed Renée. "He's got manners, ain't he, Bucky?"

Bucky nodded.

"Okay, why not," Renée agreed. She got a piece of paper from a back room, sharpened her pencil and, with smoothly gliding strokes, wrote: "Tough luck, baby. I got a real man for a kid."

Bucky read it aloud. "I don't think that'll fool her."

"That's what I'd say was it my kid," Renée declared. But she went for another piece of paper. This time she composed more thoughtfully.

Bucky read the results: " 'Dear Mrs. Wright: I am truly sorry my boy caused all the truble. If he does such again, let me know and I will ware him out. Signed, his mother.' "

They watched Terry for judgment. He grinned.

"Think it'll work?" Bucky asked.

"Sure! Thanks, Bucky."

But it didn't. Mrs. Wright opened the note the next day and her eyes told Terry he had been betrayed, even before she asked, "Did your mother write this?"

He couldn't afford another trip to the office. Tears welled up. "No, Mrs. Wright."

"Who did, then?"

"A friend of mine."

"Where is this—friend?"

"She works at the Last Dollar Café."

Mrs. Wright's eyes closed and stayed closed a long time. When they opened, she said quietly, "Go sit down, Terrell. Let's forget the whole thing, shall we?"

"You want me to apologize to the class?"

"No, that won't be necessary. Please sit down."

The morning was excruciatingly long.

"Did it work?" Bucky inquired when Terry appeared among the bamboo stand at lunchtime.

"No. Renée must not write like Mama."

"You think Mrs. Wright will go to your mama?"

"I don't know," Terry said. "I don't care. I'm thinking about running away, anyway."

"Running away? Don't be stupid! The cops'll throw you in the hoosegow!"

Terry stared at his companion. The school bell called.

Assuming his place in line, he vowed to stay clear of cops, if he did run away.

43

TERRY finished breakfast and went out the back door. There was a leaden feeling in his stomach as he started toward school.

He plucked a dandelion, blew the snowy globe of seeds and watched them spread like miniature parachutists. He heard laughter from afar, a train spinning wheels for traction. A caterpillar wearing a prickly jacket of black and yellow bands rippled past his feet. Birds twittered on electric lines above.

He began running, no conscious decision made, his legs doing that for him. He paused to discard his shoes and socks, wiggled his toes in hot dust and began running again.

He turned out the Chosen road and met McCree just as the old man's truck had halted to enter the road. "Ho, Little Hawk!"

"Can I go with you?"

"Sure enough. Hop in."

McCree never drove fast. Most often he traveled in low gear, bumping over back roads or on the embankment beside a highway. In the rear of his vehicle were stacks of hampers, burlap sacks, and long bamboo poles with metal hooks attached to the ends.

"Going to get those pinecones, Little Hawk," McCree said. "Out Tamiami Trail be about the best place, don't you reckon?"

"Most likely."

Planted by the government along the ubiquitous canals, the trees acted as windbreaks on the flat terrain and also served to keep sleepy drivers from a watery death.

"I knew a man drove into one of those canals once," McCree said. "He fell asleep driving, him and his wife. All of a sudden he wakes up in pitch-dark, with bubbly sounds in his ears and his wife screaming like a madwoman."

Terry nodded, listening intently.

"Have I told you this before?"

"I like to hear it."

"Well sir, the water commenced pouring in the window." McCree pulled off the road and looked up at thickly needled trees. "The man told his wife to take a big gulp of air and he dragged her out. Somehow he got her to the bank of the canal. She was hurt bad, couldn't walk."

44

The next part had given Terry nightmares for weeks. He waited with macabre anticipation.

"Man went to fetch help, walked to town and woke somebody up. When they got back, his wife was dead. Rats killed her."

A shiver.

"Don't never lie down in a swamp or cane field and go to sleep, Little Hawk."

"No sir."

"Reckon we can get some cones along this stretch?"

They walked the row of trees, estimating the yield. "Looks good," McCree said. He got one of his bamboo poles and began snaring the cones. Terry climbed the tree itself, to the uppermost limbs.

"Break them off and throw them down," McCree instructed. "And mind you don't get swallowed by a giant red bug."

Terry laughed, wedging himself between two rough-barked limbs. He worked fast and expertly. Cones showered down.

"We'll have those three hundred bushels before you know it!" McCree hollered up.

"Sure will!"

"That-a-boy!"

They worked until dark. The ride back to town and then to Camp Osceola was passed with few words.

"Many thanks for your help, Little Hawk."

"I enjoyed it."

"Night," McCree said. Terry was trotting away.

Terry expected retribution the moment he stepped through the door. Instead, Mama greeted him mildly. "Supper's ready, son."

Daddy was on the telephone. "Burrell, Mrs. Roosevelt has said you can join us for inspection of the Negro labor camp. Tomorrow, about nine o'clock."

"Terrell, get washed up."

"Yes ma'am."

When Terry returned to the table, Mama was seated, waiting for Daddy to get off the telephone. She tapped Terry's hand as he reached for a biscuit, and he withdrew, also waiting.

"She's coming here first, Burrell."

"Mama, who's coming?"

"Mrs. Roosevelt. The President's wife."

"Can I meet her?"

Gerald came in as the question was posed. "Sure you can."

"What about school?" Mama asked.

"How often does a child get to meet the wife of the President, Mickey? Let's have the blessing."

ELEANOR Roosevelt was taller than Daddy. She wore a dress that fell halfway between knee and ankle. Her purse was woven white raffia. Her graying hair was piled atop her head in a rolled, bushy effect. She had buckteeth and spoke with an odd accent.

"Mrs. Roosevelt, I'd like you to meet my wife, Mickey."

"How do you do, Mrs. Calder? When is the blessed event?"

"I hope the first week in December," Mama said.

"At least by then the heat will have abated."

"And this is my son, Terrell."

Mrs. Roosevelt's hand extended, taking Terry's and holding it as though in mid-shake. The backs of her hands were laced with purple and red veins. She smelled good.

"This is our camp foreman," Daddy continued, "Randy Adams."

"Mr. Adams." Mrs. Roosevelt said everyone's name on hearing it.

"Can I go play?" Terry whispered to his mother.

"This is the newspaper's publisher and editor, Burrell Mason."

"Mama, can I go play, now?"

Mama grasped Terry's wrist and her fingernails dug into flesh.

"The lawn looks lovely," Mrs. Roosevelt commented. "How many men are required to keep it that way?"

Terry saw Daddy's instant alertness.

"We use tractors," Daddy said, "pulling seven mowers. Two men can mow it in a couple of days. You know, Mrs. Roosevelt, so few of these families have ever had a lawn on which to play."

She nodded, now smiling. "I hadn't considered that. Very nice. Shall we go?"

Mama and Terry were left standing as the others climbed into automobiles for the trip to the new camp.

"How many times do I have to tell you about interrupting people while they're talking?"

"I'm sorry, Mama."

"Change clothes. Then you may go and play."

Terry ran to the house, to get out of the stiffly starched white pants and shirt he wore. The entire day still lay ahead.

46

At the new camp, as he had at the white camp, Gerald introduced the black people, each of whom had an opportunity to shake Mrs. Roosevelt's hand.

"These people have a great deal of respect for you, Mr. Calder," Mrs. Roosevelt commented.

"And I for them, Mrs. Roosevelt," Gerald replied.

Throughout their walk over the expansive camp, Gerald had held his breath for fear Burrell would throw an embarrassing query at the First Lady. It was on their drive back to Camp Osceola that Burrell let the hammer fall: "Mrs. Roosevelt, isn't the purpose of this new camp actually to meet the manpower needs of the impending war?"

"War?" Mrs. Roosevelt asked. "It isn't impending. We've been fighting the war against poverty since men assembled in caves. Did you see the distended bellies of some of those black children?"

"Yes, Mrs. Roosevelt, but—"

"That's a dietary deficiency. Impetigo, pellagra, pyorrhea all have a common denominator, Mr. Mason—poverty. But the laborer is the greatest victim of all. Don't you agree?"

Gerald listened in absolute satisfaction as Burrell did the only thing he could do: agree.

"What is that old man doing there?" Mrs. Roosevelt leaned toward the driver's seat, speaking to Gerald.

"Gathering pinecones, apparently," Gerald said. He slowed so the President's wife could see for herself. Something high up the tree caught his eye, but traffic diverted his attention.

"My word," Mrs. Roosevelt said, "if that child fell, he would break his neck!"

"Mrs. Roosevelt, with war looming on the horizon," Burrell began anew, "wouldn't we be inundated with Bahamian laborers?"

"Mr. Mason, you should be working with the Washington newspapers, not here in Belle Glade."

"Why is that, ma'am?"

"You ask questions best directed to my husband. Not me."

"Burrell says they're going to ask you to manage the new camp, Gerald," Mickey said. Her tone was conversational, but something had Terry taut in his chair at the table, eating supper, listening. "Would you do it?"

47

"I don't know, Mickey."

"Gerald, I don't want you taking that job."

Daddy dropped his fork on uneaten food and stared at Mama. "Well?" she asked.

"Well what? I just said I *don't know* what I would do."

Mama shoved back her chair. She slammed Daddy's plate on hers, a fork skittering to the floor. Terry got down and retrieved it.

"Ten thousand things to worry about"—Daddy followed Mama into the kitchen— "and you want to talk about something that is not even happening yet. If they ask me, we'll discuss the matter."

"Go away, Gerald."

"Mickey, this is ridiculous, you—"

"Go away! Do you hear me?"

The food in Terry's stomach curled into a knot. Daddy walked past, into the living room, and turned on the radio. "Chase and Sanborn brings you . . . Edgar Bergen and Charlie McCarthy!"

Mama took Terry's plate. Over her shoulder she said, "Go to bed, Terrell. No argument. Just go to bed."

CHAPTER NINE

SEVERAL weeks later Randy Adams, camp foreman, was sitting with Daddy at the breakfast table when Terry entered. Mama motioned Terry to his seat, her face compelling silence.

"The Nazis have executed a hundred or more Frenchmen because a German officer was murdered," Randy Adams was saying. "They're killing them off like flies over there."

"I know, Randy."

The two men went onto the porch talking as Terry pushed oatmeal this way and that with a spoon.

"Do I have to eat this?"

"You certainly do."

"I hate oatmeal."

"Eat it."

Terry eased out the drawer on the kitchen table. With Mama at the sink, her attention on the talking men, he raked his oatmeal into the receptacle and shoved it closed.

Mama handed Terry his lunch sack. "What kind?" he asked.

"Mashed prunes and peanut butter."

48

"Aw, Mama! I hate prunes and—"

"Go to school!"

Terry squeezed past the men and out the front way. He left camp by the main entrance and, with little attempt to hide himself, began trotting toward Chosen and Mr. McCree. He found him filling hampers with cones.

"Mr. McCree, what's a Nazi?" Terry asked.

"I don't rightly know, Little Hawk."

"They kill people, right?"

"That's what I hear. I wouldn't know for sure."

Terry dragged over a burlap bag of cones for McCree to empty into another hamper. "What's a war?"

"Well, a war is when a whole country gets into a fight with another country."

"You think we're going to have a war?" Terry asked.

McCree halted his work, looking at the boy. "I ain't been keeping up with it much, Little Hawk. Why do you ask?"

Terry shrugged his shoulders. "I don't know."

McCree indicated Terry's lunch. "What you got there?"

"Something awful. Prunes-and-peanut-butter sandwiches."

McCree winced slightly. "Maybe I could find something better here. Why don't we give your sandwiches to my friends the birds?"

"Okay."

They walked outside. "Be real quiet now."

The old man held his arms straight out and pursed his lips, making a warbling, low note. Then he warbled again. McCree did this for several minutes, making no motion, the sandwiches held in his open palms. Suddenly, from a nearby tree, a titmouse flew down and landed on his fingers.

Enthralled, Terry watched the old man continue calling until dozens of the tiny birds were hovering around him, landing on his arms, shoulders and head. Some that arrived took a peck at the sandwiches in passing flight; others stayed to dine in leisure.

When all the food was gone, Terry, who had been standing transfixed, followed McCree back inside. "Wow. That was really something, Mr. McCree. Did you charm them to get them to come to you?"

"Your sandwiches were all the charms we needed, Little Hawk. Now let's you and me find something decent to eat."

49

"OH, THAT BOY!" Mickey cried.

"What is it?" Gerald appeared in the door.

"Terrell dumped his oatmeal in the table drawer."

Gerald laughed and Mickey's temper instantly flared. "You wouldn't think it quite so funny if you had to clean this mess!"

"I will clean it," Gerald offered as Mickey dumped the sticky contents of the drawer into the sink. "You know how much he hates oatmeal."

"That's beside the point! Honestly, I am at my wit's end."

"Don't worry. He's going through a phase."

Automobile tires on the driveway drew Mickey to the living room. She recognized the vehicle with a sinking heart. "Gerald! Miss Ramsey, the truant officer, is here."

Mickey opened the door, mustering a smile. "Good morning, Miss Ramsey."

"Good morning, Mrs. Calder." She entered to find Gerald coming from the kitchen. "Oh, good, Mr. Calder. I need to speak to both of you."

"Don't tell me," Mickey said, her face flushed.

"I'm afraid so. Terrell has been out of class again."

Miss Ramsey accepted a seat. Gerald and Mickey sat across from her on the couch, waiting, as she opened a folder.

"Terrell has been absent from class forty-three days thus far this year. The law in Florida is very explicit about truancy. In your position, Mr. Calder, I'm sure you can appreciate this. There's been so much parental abuse of children in years past, making them laborers for a few dollars."

"Child abuse?" Gerald said numbly. "Miss Ramsey, I assure you we aren't abusing Terrell."

"No, of course not. Judge Franklin said the same thing."

"Judge Franklin?" Gerald's face warmed. "What has Ike Franklin to do with this, Miss Ramsey?"

"All truancy reports which persist go to him, Mr. Calder." Miss Ramsey's trim legs touched at ankle and knee, nylons straight. Mickey felt obscenely obese.

"You see," Miss Ramsey continued, "we aren't handling Terrell very well, are we? Mrs. Calder tells me she has administered corporal punishment. We've tried reasoning. Mr. Hammond talked to Terrell about the incident with the frogs."

"Frogs?" Mickey asked hoarsely.

Miss Ramsey affected an understanding, benevolent manner. "Yes. I'd forgotten you didn't get Mrs. Wright's note."

"No," Mickey whispered, "I didn't."

"Terrell had a waitress at the Last Dollar Café attempt to forge a reply."

"What about frogs, Miss Ramsey?"

Miss Ramsey's laugh almost sounded genuinely amused. She told how Terrell had placed the creatures in Mrs. Wright's desk. She mentioned Mrs. Wright's hysterical fear, telling how the teacher had disrobed in class.

Gerald now had his hand on Mickey's wrist.

Miss Ramsey lifted her glasses from a chain hanging around her neck, put them on. "The problem is, we are fast approaching a court action that would be of no benefit to Terrell. It would prove embarrassing, at the very least. We're all caught up in the mechanizations of our structured society in this case. The laws were created to prevent child abuse, and in the eyes of the law, Terrell is in the same position as the son of a migrant worker who refuses to educate his children. Do you see what I'm saying?"

"Yes," Gerald said.

"Judge Franklin has asked me to defer the matter awhile. He suggests a meeting with the teacher, principal and both of you, with the child. I will be there, also. We should try to resolve Terrell's problem and get him started on a normal childhood."

"I see," Gerald said coldly.

"Do you know where Terrell is?" Miss Ramsey asked.

"No."

Miss Ramsey made a note. "Has he exhibited any signs of maladjustment other than skipping school?"

"No!"

"Have you noticed any indication that Terrell might need glasses or a hearing aid?"

"No."

"Have there been any problems in the home? Fighting, tensions?"

"No, Miss Ramsey."

"Would the family like the services of a professional counselor?"

"No!"

Miss Ramsey's young face hardened slightly. "Mr. Calder, I know how uncomfortable this is for you. But truant children follow a dismally predictable path. Out of school, without proper supervision, many—most—ultimately resort to criminal activities. Studies have shown us the importance of nipping these things in the bud. Now. Right now while the case is merely that of a carefree boy who wants to go swimming and fishing, rather than learn his ABC's."

Gerald stood. Neither woman moved.

Miss Ramsey continued. "If Terrell were the child of any other parents, he would be in court tomorrow. If need be, they send the truant away to state-supported schools."

"Reformatories," Mickey said flatly.

Miss Ramsey started to amend that, then nodded.

"Miss Ramsey, my wife is not feeling well. We'll discuss this and see what we can do."

"I'm afraid it has gone beyond that, Mr. Calder." Miss Ramsey rose from her chair. "You are being asked to a family-school meeting, as I said. Would tomorrow afternoon at three be acceptable?"

"Yes, fine, Miss Ramsey. Thank you." Gerald held her arm, gently but insistently pushing her toward the door.

He returned to find Mickey in bed, lying on her side, an arm over her face. "Gerald—Gerald—"

"The nerve of those bureaucratic sons of—"

"Gerald! To them, it looks like we can't control our own first grader!"

"I'll control him," Gerald snorted. "When that boy comes home this evening, I'll wear him out."

"You should have done that weeks ago."

"You're suggesting I have neglected my responsibility as a father."

"Haven't you?"

"I didn't think I had."

"The court may disagree."

"This isn't going to court, Mickey!"

"What are you going to do? Call Washington? Ask for a presidential pardon? Gerald! We are about to lose our child!"

"KNOW what I wish, Mr. McCree?"

"What do you wish, Little Hawk?" They were picking an unusually late crop of blackberries, their fingers stained purple.

"I wish you were my daddy."

"Hmm-m. That'd be something, all right."

"We could go hunting and fishing every day and I could help you get pinecones and chicory coffee."

"Mmm-hmm."

They walked toward his truck, each carrying two buckets.

"You think you'd like to have me for a little boy?"

"Put your bucket so it won't tip, Little Hawk."

"I'd get up early and make the coffee."

"I never minded getting up early."

"Yessir, but if you were to want to sleep late, I'd get up."

McCree started the engine and it roared through the rusted muffler. A covey of water birds took flight all around them.

"See," Terry said, lifting his voice, "I think they're about to kick me out back at the camp. They're getting tired of having an orphan kid around, to tell the truth."

"To tell the truth," McCree repeated.

"Anyhow," Terry said, watching for clues in the old man's eyes, "I was thinking about it."

They jostled toward McCree's shack. "I got some venison for supper, Little Hawk. You like venison?"

"Yessir."

"I'm out of limes, though. Reckon you could pick a few?"

"Yessir!"

CHAPTER TEN

GERALD sat in the living room reading the newspaper. From the radio came bursts of laughter and Molly's voice digging at Fibber McGee.

Mickey rocked gently, knitting booties. She gasped as a fetal foot jabbed her ribs. "Gerald, do you think we should call the sheriff?"

"No. Terrell will be along. He's often been later than this."

Mickey put her knitting aside and rose with great effort. Had she marked today's date off the calendar? She couldn't remember.

"What is today?"

Gerald checked the paper. "Wednesday, November nineteenth."

Two weeks more. She walked toward the bedroom and was about to enter when something across the hall caught her eye.

54

Turning on the hall light, she saw more clearly—a huddled form in Terrell's bed. She went in and pulled back the cover slightly.

A sound of even breathing. Mouth open, face filthy, Terrell was asleep. His clothes were in a heap on the floor at the foot of the bed. Mickey shuddered, relieved. She picked up the dirty clothes and put them in the bathroom hamper.

Drew Pearson's staccato delivery held Gerald, head close to the radio speaker, elbows on his knees. Mickey went to the kitchen and made a cup of weak tea.

When the news was over, she said, "Terrell is home."

"Send him in here, Mickey."

"He's asleep."

Gerald moved toward the hallway.

"Don't wake him, Gerald. There's no telling when he came. He must have sneaked in the window. Anyway, he'll need his strength for tomorrow."

"Mickey, I think I should spank that boy."

"Not tonight. Let him sleep."

"TERRELL, so far as I'm concerned, you should be worn within an inch of your life."

"Yessir, Daddy."

"You have lied to your mother. You have lied to me. You put frogs in Mrs. Wright's desk, then had someone else write a note."

"Yessir, Daddy."

"Your mother is having a hard enough time, expecting the baby, without this nonsense from you. This morning I am going to drive you to school. When school is over, we're all going to the principal's office."

"Yessir, Daddy." Terry sat, back straight, his wide eyes following every move Gerald made.

"Now, Terrell, get your teeth brushed and comb your hair."

Terry slipped off the chair and ran to the bathroom. Throughout breakfast, Mama had said nothing. Terry wet his toothbrush, replaced it, then smoothed his hair and ran back to the dining room.

"Are you ready?"

"Yessir, Daddy."

"Get in the car."

"Yessir." He ran to the automobile and got in. When Gerald

arrived, he rammed the car into reverse and backed out. Terry kept swallowing, although his tongue was tinder dry.

At the school building, his father opened Terry's door, face grim. "When school is out, Terrell, wait in Mrs. Wright's room. Your mother and I will meet you there. Do you understand that?"

"Yessir, Daddy."

Terry ran up the walk. When he didn't hear the engine start, he turned and glanced back. Daddy was watching him. He entered the building. Inside, he stopped, listening. The motor started, tires crunched on gravel.

Instantly, Terry stepped out and broke for the yard, running as fast as he could. He ran between girls doing double jump rope, shoved aside Eddy Kent and was happy to see the curly-haired tattler spill headlong in the dirt. He hit the crossing board as two older students were coming over it.

"Hey!" Terry's momentum carried him through the flailing boys and he heard cursing, water splashing.

"Catch him!" one of the boys in the canal cried.

He reached the packinghouse, his legs churning. Behind him a clatter of planks told him older feet were in hot pursuit. Terry ducked for the escape tunnel near the washing machine, crawling, shins skinned but the pain ignored. He reached the far side, heard a squish of water-filled shoes in the dark behind him.

He leaped from the platform into an open boxcar, ran through it, out the other side, and ducked into another packinghouse. He clambered atop some crates, crouched, heart pounding.

"Where'd he go?"

"Up there, I think."

Terry squeezed behind a thick I-beam and a huge box. A button snagged, pulled loose.

"There he is. Get him!" Terry counted four of them. He jumped the dizzying distance to the floor, but they had him blocked. His only escape now lay in the yawning door at the building's end.

He burst into the open like a hunted rabbit, vaulted the loading ramp and *wham!* He heard wind go from a man's lungs, arms involuntarily thrown around Terry as he sank into the man's belly.

"What the—"

"Please," Terry cried, "four boys—going to beat me up."

"Four boys?" The man's automobile, from which he'd just

emerged, was filled with black suitcases, pamphlets, the gear of a salesman.

Over the ramp came the pursuers, only to find themselves fenced between the warehouse wall, the salesman's car and the large man himself, who was pulling off a wide, thick leather belt.

"Be ashamed of yourselves," the salesman said, grabbing one sopping boy. *Whap!* The belt fell across the boy's buttocks.

"Hey, mister, wait a minute, we—"

Whap! The second boy tried to walk on air and was lifted bodily, the strap falling with a forceful delivery. The third victim was snared scrambling over the hood of the car. Glimpsing freedom, the fourth boy was off and running.

The salesman finally let the three go, crying all of them. He turned and winked at Terry. Terry grinned and winked back.

"We got 'em, partner."

"Sure did. Thanks."

Terry trotted off, grinning to himself, but slightly fearful of what another day might bring.

"TERRELL didn't go to school, Gerald."

"Mickey, I took him myself. I saw him enter."

"He's not there." Mickey's breathing sounded short through the telephone.

"Damn!" Gerald said. "What about the meeting this afternoon?"

"Miss Ramsey thought perhaps we'd kept Terrell out on purpose this morning, because of that."

"What did you tell her?"

"I didn't tell her anything. I let her believe it."

"I—I'm stunned. I don't know what to say."

Mickey sighed in Gerald's ear. "You realize what this is probably going to bring about, don't you?"

"I'm afraid so."

"My mind is numb," she said. "Do you have any suggestions?"

"I don't know. I guess I'd better call the principal and Miss Ramsey and see if I can get the meeting postponed. I'll say we sent Terrell to Tampa to see a—a psychiatrist."

"Are you kidding?"

"Why not?"

"Why not," Mickey said.

Mr. McCree was not at his shack when Terry arrived. The boy dawdled around for a while, then trudged back to LuBelle's place.

"Look what we got for Mr. Cree," LuBelle gloated. She held up a gallon jar filled with cecropia-moth cocoons.

"Where'd you find them all?" Terry asked, envious of the praise he knew the cocoons would bring from McCree.

"Mostly on citrus trees back along the dike."

"Yeah? Listen, LuBelle, will you show me where?"

The black girl looked at Eunice, who was placing neat stacks of laundry into a tremendous woven basket.

"I got to go to town," Eunice said. "If you two stays together, I'm of a mind to let you go."

Eunice twisted a bandanna until it was one rolled, thick strand. She tied the ends together, forming a ring, and placed it flat atop her head. The basket of clothes would ride on this as Eunice walked the nearly four miles to town.

Terry followed LuBelle, weaving through thickets, crawling under matted webs of vegetation, artfully skirting areas known to be infested with sandburs, mosquitoes, ticks or thorns.

"Best to pick them by the stem," LuBelle tutored, speaking of the cocoons. "You can feel them wiggling inside."

"You can?"

"Sure nuff. When we find one, I'll show you."

They walked, heads down, vigilant for the lurking threat of inert reptiles. Gnats swarmed constantly.

"See here!" LuBelle indicated a stalactite of living pupa as long as Terry's little finger. It hung, motionless, beneath the branch of a wild lime tree. LuBelle snapped it off and put it in a paper sack they'd brought. Then, remembering, she withdrew it and squeezed it slightly.

"Feel," she whispered. Terry put his fingers against the cocoon and the dormant creature pulsated.

"Wonder what's inside," Terry mused.

"Gushies. Guts and stuff. Want to break it open?"

"No. I reckon it hurts the moth."

They spent the entire day gathering cocoons. "You think Mr. Cree be happy with what we got?" LuBelle asked as they walked back toward her house.

"Ought to be."

McCree didn't show up that day. When evening came, LuBelle poked fresh kindling into the stove and maneuvered a pot of left-over beans into place.

"Eunice ought to be back by now, shouldn't she?" Terry asked.

"Sometimes early, sometimes late," LuBelle intoned.

They lit a lantern, ate beans at the bare table, watching insects bump the glass cover over the flickering wick.

"Can I spend the night here, LuBelle?"

"Sure nuff."

"Reckon Eunice will care?"

"No, I don't think so."

"Did you latch his window screens?" Gerald questioned.

"Yes." Mickey washed the last of the dishes.

"Then he has to come through the door."

"If he comes at all."

"You think he might not come home?"

Mickey gazed at her husband evenly. "Would you?"

Gerald sipped cold coffee. "Any idea where he might be?"

Mickey controlled her voice. "None whatsoever. Gerald, I think we should call the sheriff's office."

"Let's be realistic," Gerald said hoarsely. "If Terrell is with a friend, afraid to come home, the fear will pass. When it does, he'll come in here expecting to get his little fanny worn out. If we call in Sheriff Lambert, then Ike Franklin and Miss Ramsey will hear about it and we'll be in court fighting for that boy. Now, Mickey, I still stand by Terrell. He's all boy. He has to be punished, but my Lord, he's just a Tom Sawyer–Huck Finn kind of kid, that's all!"

"Remember that," Mickey said, "when you try to explain all this to Judge Franklin."

CHAPTER ELEVEN

Gerald swirled his shaving brush in a cup, working up lather. He started to apply the soap and stood looking at his reflection. His face was lined; he looked weary. His hands were shaking. Letting things get to him. Gut-knotting worry over the world, more worry about the new camp.

Gerald pulled his cheek taut, razor scraping, burning his flesh.

If there was war, he was sure to be called up. He had become obsessed with getting things in order for Mickey's sake. Now this business with Terrell. When he found that boy—

"You want me to answer the phone, Gerald?"

He swore softly. "I'll get it."

He grabbed a hand towel and took the call in the living room.

"Mr. Calder, this is Bert Arthur, Washington."

Gerald's stomach twisted. "Morning, Mr. Arthur."

"Mrs. Roosevelt has taken an interest in your work down there. More precisely, the President is aware of your work."

"I see."

"They want you to manage the new migratory labor camp."

"The black camp."

"Yes. Is that acceptable to you?"

Gerald's long pause made Bert Arthur add, "There's a twenty percent raise in pay."

"Mr. Arthur—I wonder if I could have time to think?"

"Don't tell me you don't want it! Mrs. Roosevelt came back glowing about your rapport with those people, the high respect you've earned in the community, your press relations—"

"It isn't that I don't want it," Gerald said. "I would like a day or so to discuss it with—"

"I'm afraid you don't understand, Mr. Calder. A news release has already gone out on this."

"Isn't that irregular, Mr. Arthur? Before notifying me?"

"This could be very embarrassing for the administration."

"Listen, Mr. Arthur," Gerald snapped, "all I want is a day. I'll call you tomorrow morning."

"This is very *important,* Mr. Calder. Politically. We need a man who can make a model of this camp."

"I understand. Don't worry. I'll probably take it."

"That's what I want to hear."

"Call you tomorrow." Gerald hung up.

"What's the trouble, Gerald?"

"No trouble." He walked into the bedroom. "I'm going to try to find Terrell."

"Want me to go with you?" Mickey looked tired, her complexion pallid, circles under her eyes.

"No need. I'm going to try to locate Bucky—what's his name?"

"Bucky Dallas. He lives near the icehouse."

"I'll start there." He walked out to his car to begin the search for his son.

"What's for breakfast?" Terry questioned Eunice. The black woman stood with feet planted apart, the back of one hand propped on a hip, stirring a saucepan with a wooden spoon.

"Tater pancakes," Eunice said.

"Great! I love tater pancakes."

"Boy, your mama know you was here last night?"

"I don't have a mama."

Eunice turned, pointing her spoon at Terry. "Don't come telling Eunice no lies, boy!"

Terry shrank internally, struggling to hold his ground. "I ain't got no mama! I ain't got no daddy!"

"Who looks after you, then?"

"Lots of people. Like you're doing right now."

She glared at him, black eyes sparkling, then began putting patties in a hot skillet. "You and LuBelle go wash up."

"Yes ma'am, Eunice." Terry and LuBelle went to wash in a dishpan of water on the back steps. The strong brown soap burned the scratches on their arms.

"Is Eunice mad with me?" Terry whispered.

LuBelle's eyes widened as her shoulders lifted, then dropped, expressing a lack of certainty.

Eunice was putting potato pancakes on their plates when Terry and LuBelle sat down. LuBelle reached for a fork and began eating. Terry sat looking at her.

"What's the matter?" Eunice asked.

"Aren't we going to have the blessing?"

LuBelle held a fork halfway to her open mouth, eyes cutting to Eunice. "Certainly, we going to have the blessing! Put that food down, LuBelle! Ask it, child," Eunice said to Terry.

"Heavenly Father, give us thankful hearts for this and all other blessings, we ask in Christ's name. Amen."

He lifted his head to find Eunice staring at him with an odd expression.

"Can I eat now?" LuBelle asked Mawmaw, voice low.

"Help yourself."

GERALD PULLED UP THE emergency brake and stepped out of the car. He approached a man leaning against the icehouse.

"Is Bucky Dallas here?"

"Who're you?"

"I'm Gerald Calder." Gerald extended his hand. The man contemplated the outstretched hand, then shook it. "I was hoping Bucky had seen my son, Terrell," Gerald said. "He—he didn't come home last night."

The overt distrust slowly melted. "Excuse my manners, Mr. Calder. I thought you was one of them meddling school folks. They've been sticking their noses in and around here of late."

Gerald nodded. The man went to a thick insulated door, opened it and hollered, "Bucky! Come on out. Mr. Calder is here."

The cross-eyed boy appeared, wearing a heavy apron, oversize rubber boots and gloves. A set of tongs hung from a rope tied around his waist.

"Don't be long, Bucky," the man said, walking away. "We got six thousand pounds to shred and blow this morning."

"Yessir, Pa."

"Bucky, have you seen Terrell?" Gerald asked.

"Terrell! That his name? I'll sure tease him plenty about it."

"What do you call him?"

"Terry."

"His mother and I haven't seen him since yesterday morning."

"He's something else, that kid. He said he was going to run away, but I didn't believe it."

A chill traced Gerald's shoulders, rippled down his spine.

"Would you have any idea where Terry might be, Bucky?"

"Ain't no telling. He could've hopped a freight. He knows all the trainmen, knows how to read the codes on the cars."

"You think he did that?"

"No telling. But don't worry. You could throw him in a swamp and he wouldn't go hungry. He learned that from the old man."

"What old man?"

Bucky's tone was suddenly wary. "I forget his name."

"I'd appreciate it if you could remember."

"Mac something. I met him only once, a few weeks back."

"Bucky, get on it!" his father shouted from inside the building. "Here come them fruit cars and you ain't even got the ice out!"

Gerald watched Bucky put a foot against the icehouse wall, gaining leverage to pull open the heavy refrigerator door.

"Dear God," Gerald whispered, and returned to his car.

TERRY spent the day with LuBelle, collecting more cocoons. He wanted as many as possible when he approached Mr. McCree.

"Reckon I could spend the night again, LuBelle?"

"I don't know. We can ask Mawmaw."

Terry's heart was pounding when he confronted Eunice. "Reckon maybe I could spend the night again, Eunice?"

The sizzle of fatback in a skillet and the bacon smell of it brought saliva to Terry's mouth. Eunice flipped the meat, pressed it down. "Might as well. It's dark, ain't it? But you might've asked me earlier in the day."

"I will tomorrow, Eunice."

Suddenly she bent, her face close to his. "You can't stay here forever, boy. It ain't 'cause we don't like you. We do. But there's got to be somebody out there looking for you, worrying about whether you stepped in quicksand, or got gator ate, or snakebit. When they find you and you tell them it was Eunice who had you, there ain't no guessing the trouble I'll have!"

"I'll go tomorrow, and I won't tell anybody I was here."

"Oh, child, bless your heart. Eunice don't want to drive you away. I wish to God I could help you."

"Yes ma'am."

She pulled Terry to her and stroked the back of his head. "Boy," she said brusquely, "don't say ma'am to me!"

IT WAS that twilight time between night sounds and daybreak when Terry awoke. He sat up and peered through a partly closed shutter. Etched against a dawning sky, a poinciana glistened with beads of dew strung through thousands of spiderwebs.

He slipped out of bed shivering. On bare feet, he quietly found his clothes. Eunice had washed and pressed them for him.

He moved in a cloak of ground fog, a disembodied red head in a liquid gray field, running all the way to McCree's. The old man was applying a poultice of crushed boneset leaves to Dog's neck.

"What happened to Dog?" Terry questioned, without greeting.

"Snakebit. Dog's not smart about playing with snakes."

"Need some help?"

"There's water boiling inside. Suppose you could pour it over some camphor leaves in a bowl?"

"I think so."

Terry carefully poured the bubbling liquid over the fragrant leaves. The aroma was similar to that of salves Mama rubbed on Terry's chest when he had a cold.

"What do I do with it now?" Terry called.

"Leave it awhile to cool. Later I'll put a little on Dog's neck. It holds down pain and soreness."

Outside, Terry squatted, hands clasped beneath his chin. "LuBelle and I got a lot of cecropia cocoons."

"Did you?"

"Couple hundred."

"How many is a hundred?"

Ten flicks of ten fingers. "Times two," Terry added.

"Can I stay here tonight—and tomorrow night?" Terry asked.

McCree pushed to his feet. "If it's all right with the folks you stay with."

"They won't worry," Terry said. "I told them where I'd be."

McCree nodded. "You can go with me down in the Glades, then."

THE old man loaded a flat-bottomed boat into his truck and threw in a slender pole for pushing the craft through shallow water.

The last traces of lingering fog were burning away under a rising sun when they drove through Belle Glade. The sight of the schoolyard gave Terry a secret shiver.

"I'm glad I don't have to go to school," Terry commented.

"I expect you'll like it when the time comes," McCree said. "You'll learn some interesting things. Know how many cups of seeds make a bushel?"

"It's a basketful."

"Baskets aren't all the same size, Little Hawk. Two cups make a pint. Two pints make a quart. Eight quarts make a peck. Four pecks make a bushel. So how many cups of seeds make a bushel?"

"I don't know."

"That's what you'd know by going to school."

"How many cups make a bushel?"

"A hundred twenty-eight."

"Tell it to me again."

McCree repeated the dry measures. Terry whispered them to himself. "Tell me one more time."

"Write it down."

"I can't write!"

"You learn that in school. How many in a peck?"

"I don't know."

They drove along, jolting, turning, finally leaving the paved road to push through an endless sea of grass.

"Thirty-two," Terry said.

"What, Little Hawk?"

"There're thirty-two cups in a peck."

McCree laughed, stained teeth flashing. "Thirty-two it is."

"Reckon I could drive awhile, Mr. McCree?"

"Might as well as not," McCree said. "Come on over."

Terry had done this several times, always in the open glades where there were few obstacles to hit. He climbed between the old man's bony legs, gripping the shuddering steering wheel with both hands. McCree worked the gas, gearshift and clutch when the need arose, Terry steering with a face-stretching smile.

"Go a little to your left," McCree instructed. A moment of thought, which hand, then Terry did as told.

"That-a-boy! We have to go faster now, so we don't stall and get stuck. You ready?"

"Ready!"

McCree's foot pinned the accelerator to the floor and the swish of grass intensified as the truck lunged through the glade, tires spinning when they hit wet places. Breathless, Terry turned this way and that as McCree shouted orders.

They came to a halt beside a towering stand of cabbage palmettos. Terry scampered onto the truck bed, getting the pole as McCree put his boat into water. They threw in several burlap sacks, a jug of sassafras tea, and camping supplies.

"Best rub mud on your arms and face, Little Hawk. Otherwise you'll spend your energy fighting mosquitoes."

The smelly mud, scooped from underwater, dried to a cracked glaze on face, neck and arms.

"Makes us look like alligator skins," Terry said.

"Can't say it improves our looks," McCree agreed. He stood

toward the rear of the craft, his pole jabbed down, pushing away, then retrieved in long, flowing movements that sent them gliding over mirror-smooth waters. Behind, in a widening V, the wake rippled under lily pads and rafts of watercress.

"What are we looking for, Mr. McCree?"

"Epiphytes, Little Hawk. Plants that get their nourishment from air, rain and dust. Air plants, florists call them."

The midmorning still was broken only by water dripping from McCree's pole when it was lifted, the boat riding on momentum.

"Bobcat, Mr. McCree."

"Where?" he whispered.

Terry pointed. The tawny cat was statue still in the shallow water, yellow eyes alert, tufted ears erect.

"You have sharp eyes, Little Hawk."

But it was the old man who first spied a fox bitch and her cubs and the nesting mound of a female alligator.

"Where do we look for air plants?" Terry asked.

"Trees with rough bark," McCree said. "Water oaks, mostly. We're after a particular kind called butterfly orchid."

When they found the plants, McCree poled his boat under the tree. From there he and Terry climbed up to get them.

They worked the afternoon away. The sun was a huge globe settling toward the horizon when McCree called up to Terry. "Best make camp, Little Hawk. Be night before long."

They located high ground and stomped down surrounding grasses to drive away insects. McCree sent Terry to gather firewood. The old man fashioned a lean-to with fronds of palmettos laid like overlapping shingles atop the poles. So they wouldn't be on the ground, McCree built a hammock in the structure, using bamboo and saplings trimmed of leaves.

"Seminoles call this lean-to a chickee," McCree stated.

To smother the chiggers which were surely on them, they took turns smearing black grease salve over one another. Then McCree dipped water from the lake, strained it through cloth to remove algae and boiled it for purification.

"It's going to be a one-pot meal, Little Hawk—wild potatoes, swamp cabbage, and a chunk of pork for seasoning."

"Sounds good."

With nightfall came a chilled north wind that swept the lake, bending grasses and bringing a chatter to Terry's teeth. McCree gave the boy a dank woolen blanket and put him to bed. Terry felt warmth returning as McCree put hot coals in the chickee, covering them with moss to make enough smoke to drive off mosquitoes.

"How do you feel, Little Hawk?"

Terry mumbled a satisfied reply, sighed heavily and went to sleep. His last thought was a vague concern for Mama. He wondered if she was worrying.

"WE MUST go to someone about this, Gerald," Mickey said. "He wouldn't stay gone three nights unless something had happened."

Gerald took a deep breath, exhaled slowly. "I think we should keep trying to find him ourselves. At least another day or two."

"But it's getting colder," Mickey said. She began crying.

Her husband knelt before her chair. "If Terrell gets cold, or hungry, the sooner he'll come home."

"He must not love us."

"That isn't true, Mickey. Little boys don't think."

"Gerald, I can't stand this. I'm going crazy with worry."

He held her close to him. Her sobs were silent, pulsating.

"There has to be somebody who has seen him," Gerald reasoned. "I think I'll go back to the packinghouses."

"At this hour?"

"They're running full shifts. There'll be plenty of people."

"I'll go with you."

At each of the five major packinghouses Gerald approached one person after another with a snapshot of Terrell.

"Have you seen this child recently?"

"Afraid not."

"He has red hair."

"A hundred kids hang around here, mister."

Always the same response.

"He talks about the packinghouses constantly," Mickey declared. "Somebody must have noticed him!"

"He spends a lot of time here," Gerald conceded. "But not this late at night. I'll come back for each shift tomorrow."

It was another night of sleepless tossing as Gerald or Mickey dozed, only to awake with a start as bad dreams assailed them.

The next morning Gerald finally located people at the Blue Goose Packing Company who knew Terrell well by sight. But no one had seen him for several days.

"Redheaded boy?" the guard said. "Sure, I know that boy! It's a miracle he hasn't been hurt before now. He rides packing crates from the third floor down through the washing machines. And say, who's that old man was with him the last time?"

"Old man?" Gerald's heart skipped a beat.

"That old codger ought to know better, mister. Riding the same crates. You see that chute?"

Gerald looked up a corkscrew spiral winding two floors above. "You wouldn't know the old man's name?" he asked.

"No. I see him around now and then. Drives a beat-up '34 Ford pickup. No license tag on it. That's common with transients."

"Well"—Gerald shook the guard's hand—"thanks for your help."

CHAPTER TWELVE

TERRY followed McCree toward a grove of wild tamarind, stunted water oaks and twisted Caribbean pines. From somewhere afar, the bellow of a bull gator rose, echoed, rippled away to silence.

"Watch your step, Little Hawk." McCree pointed at a seemingly firm area. "Quicksand."

They waded a shallow pool of stagnant water filled with frogs and snakes. When they gained solid footing again, Terry's bare legs were coated with a film of greenish, smelly scum.

"We're almost there," McCree said.

Terry gazed up at the rumpled blanket of low scudding clouds. Observing this, McCree said, "We could use some rain."

When they reached the trees, McCree nodded, satisfied. Hundreds of butterfly orchids dotted the limbs. The old man suggested they both climb, break off plants and drop them at random.

"We can gather them up later, Little Hawk."

With an agility that rivaled Terry's, McCree selected a particularly tall tree and climbed, stretching out along the limbs to reach the furthermost plants.

"We'll be finished before long," McCree called.

Terry was far out on a limb, trying to pull loose a plant with a tenacious root system. He heard McCree yell—

Thump. A leaden, dull sound. Terry peered through the foliage around him. "Mr. McCree?"

His voice came back, "Cree . . . ree. . . ." Echoing, gone.

Terry's heart quickened. He scooted backward along the bough and swung down. Waist-deep in grass, he circled under McCree's tree and found the old man lying face down. Heart hammering, Terry knelt at McCree's head.

The old man's eyes were half closed. His right arm was oddly twisted, blood seeping through the shirt sleeve. Terry leaned over, looking, and his stomach turned. A jagged sliver of bone had pierced the fabric just above McCree's elbow.

"Oh, Mr. McCree!"

He put a hand on the old man's sweat-soaked back. McCree wasn't breathing. He shook his friend's shoulder. Nothing.

"Mr. McCree—please—" Terry stood, looking this way and that. The Glades stretched as far as he could see. Should he go for help? How could he get out, much less back again to find this place?

From the old man came a sudden rush of air, sucking in, then exhaled. The eyes opened, winced. He turned over and cried out.

"Mr. McCree, your arm is broken."

McCree slowly sat up, taking the injured appendage with his good hand, pulling it around so he could see. He groaned, eyes turned up into his skull, and fell back unconscious.

"Gerald, this is Burrell Mason. What the hell is going on?" the newspaperman growled. "The Miami *Herald* has a story about you taking the management of the new black camp."

"Wait a minute, Burrell. I didn't actually accept it."

"Bull! I called Washington and they confirmed it!"

"They did that without my—"

"Gerald, you know I am opposed to a camp designed to house cheap imported Bahamian labor. In deference to you, I haven't taken an editorial stand. But I will now. American farm workers need to be warned what's going to happen to them."

"Burrell, be reasonable. Let's sit down and discuss this."

"Gerald, I had hoped you were working for farm labor, not against it. That camp is going to be black, isn't it?"

"Yes, black."

"For Bahamian labor."

"For *black* laborers, Burrell. We need that camp."

"You mean the growers need it! You're condemning American laborers to an indecent wage scale for years to come. For a guy who claims to be for the common man, you do odd things, Gerald."

"Burrell—"

"I'm writing that editorial today, Gerald." The line went dead.

"What on earth was that about?" Mickey asked.

"Burrell. Angry about the new camp."

"That's nothing new. What has him so mad with you?"

"Bert Arthur called me this past week. He told me Mrs. Roosevelt had recommended me to manage the black camp and—"

"You accepted." Accusingly.

"No, I said I needed time to talk it over."

"You didn't refuse it, though."

"Damn it!" Gerald exploded. "I didn't accept or refuse, Mickey. Burrell is angry because it's in the Miami paper. Washington sent out a news release to put pressure on me. I'm getting pressure from Burrell, from Washington, from you! Damn you all!"

Mickey heard the front door slam.

TERRY tried to help the old man rise. McCree cried out again, grabbing his bloodied arm. Gnats began to dart around them.

McCree was on his knees, face starkly white beneath the stains of mud and grease. "Let me get my wind," he whispered.

Together, somehow, they got McCree to his feet. The old man's hand bore down hard on Terry's shoulder, pain causing McCree to halt often.

"Go back the way we came?" Terry questioned.

"Only way to go, Little Hawk."

They sloshed through the shallow pond, McCree leaning against a tree now and then. He avoided looking at his sleeve.

Lightning streaked unexpectedly and a deafening clap of thunder followed. Instantly, driving sheets of rain began to fall.

"Notice any mistletoe about, Little Hawk?"

"No sir. Why?"

"Chew the leaves—kills pain."

In the way of the Everglades, parched soil suddenly grew boggy, shallow water stirred restlessly, invisible currents quickened and became ominous swirls of black motion.

"Got to get in the chickee," McCree whispered.

Terry felt McCree's legs wobble, buckle, then straighten. "Not much further, Mr. McCree!" he shouted over the crashing thunder.

McCree had chosen the site for the chickee with care. The thatched roof was holding well in the gusts of wind. Terry followed McCree's instructions and dug below the hammock until he found a few glowing coals left from last night. He put palmetto fronds over the embers. A short time later the chickee filled with smoke.

"Blow on it, Little Hawk."

A tiny poof! The palmetto fronds caught fire. On this, Terry put successively larger twigs. He put chicory into a pan and caught water from the thatched roof. The smell of coffee seemed to revive the old man for a moment, but then he fell back on the hammock, breathing heavily, his eyes closed.

Terry squatted by the fire, shivering despite the heat. He wished he were home, bathed, dry and in bed.

RAIN inundated the streets. Gerald peered through the windshield, using the back of his hand to clear away moisture. He turned toward home, knowing Mickey would be thinking the same haunting thoughts he was having. Was Terrell out in this?

Mickey was standing in the front door when Gerald reached the screened porch. Soaked, he took her in his arms and they held one another close for a long time.

"You need dry clothes," Mickey said, as though to a child.

"Tomorrow we'll go to the sheriff."

"No," Mickey said. "I've been thinking. We should go see Ike Franklin first. He'll call the sheriff and get more action than we will. He'll also be sympathetic to our problem, Gerald."

Numbed mentally and physically, Gerald nodded.

THE rain fell incessantly through the night. The fire fizzled and died and the roof of the chickee began to leak.

Through the dark hours, McCree moaned. The roar of water seemed so near, Terry reached down from the hammock to see if they were being flooded. Finally, before dawn, the wind died, the rain eased to a steady downpour.

Terry awoke as McCree cried aloud. He sat up, disoriented, frightened, cold and wet.

"Oh! God have mercy. Oh!" McCree spoke between teeth tightly clenched, muscles in his face corded.

"Can I help, Mr. McCree?"

"Is the fire out?"

"Yessir."

"Get—oh! Get another one—oh, *damn!*"

Terry threw off the smelly blanket and went out in the half-light of daybreak. He dug around beneath drenched plants, seeking dry tinder. He returned with what he could find.

"Shouldn't have let it die, Little Hawk."

"I'm sorry, Mr. McCree. It was my fault."

"No, Little Hawk," McCree amended softly. "Mine. You did good. I'm proud of you. Reckon you can get a fire started with that wet stuff?"

"I don't think so."

"Okay. Don't waste matches. Let's go home."

"Do you want breakfast, Gerald?" Mickey wore a flowered maternity dress she'd been saving for the drive to the hospital.

"Coffee," Gerald said, adjusting his tie. "Did you call Ike?"

"He says he can see us around ten at his office."

Gerald sipped his coffee. "You look beautiful," he said.

"I walk like a duck, I have been irritable and unresponsive. So I assume you must love me."

Gerald nodded soberly. "I do."

They drove to town in a steady drizzle, parked and walked into Judge Ike Franklin's chambers.

"Ike, we have a problem," Gerald began.

"Okay, let's talk about it." They sat down at a conference table.

"It's our son, Terrell."

Ike chuckled. "That boy is a real boy, Gerald."

"He's run away. We're worried to death, Ike," Mickey managed to say, crying. Ike reached across the table, patting her arm.

"Gerald, why don't you tell me about it?"

Gerald spoke in flat, unemotional tones. He told Ike what a carefree and pleasant child Terrell had always been. He noted the lack of suitable playmates out at the camp. Until school started, however, neither he nor Mickey had ever seriously considered Terrell a problem.

"When Miss Ramsey came to us," Gerald admitted, "we tried reasoning with Terrell. We delivered him directly to school. Still he ran off."

"Do you have any idea what's at the root of this?" Ike asked, deep voice gentle.

"No. We are a close family, I would say. Terrell is well mannered, usually obedient. He expresses himself physically, kissing and hugging both his mother and me. At first, I assumed he was just a freedom-loving child who didn't want to be confined to a classroom."

Ike stood. "That may be all there is to it."

"Yes," Gerald said, "but now he's run away."

"All right," Ike said, "the first thing to do is find him. I'll call Sheriff Lambert. We'll notify Miss Ramsey. She knows where children go to hide. I suspect we'll find him staying with a friend somewhere, safe and sound, dry as gunpowder."

"I hope so," Mickey said.

Ike extended his hand in a firm, pleasant shake. "When we get him back home, then we can go to work on changing his attitude about school. Right, Gerald?"

For the first time in several days, Gerald smiled. "Thanks, Ike."

As they stepped outside, Mickey took Gerald's arm. "Maybe that's a good sign," she said. "It just quit raining."

CHAPTER THIRTEEN

TERRY's stomach cramped. They had eaten nothing since breakfast yesterday. Thirst and hunger were sapping his strength. Now in McCree's boat, he struggled to move the craft. McCree sat forward, head hung, the fractured arm cradled in his lap.

The rain had stopped, replaced now by a sweltering humidity that intensified the heat. Not a breath of air stirred as Terry, arm muscles trembling, poled across the glasslike surface. Cattle egrets and blue herons roosting in mangroves watched them, unafraid. Alligators sunned themselves on the banks.

"Mr. McCree, I'm lost. I don't know which way to go."

"North."

"Which way is that?"

McCree straightened. His face was blanched with shock and

pain. "Listen to me," he commanded hoarsely. "East is where the sun comes up. Say it!"

"East is where the sun comes up."

"West is where the sun sets."

"West is where the sun goes down."

"Face east, then."

The sun was on the afternoon side of overhead. Terry turned slightly.

"That's east," McCree whispered. "Where's north?"

"I don't know."

McCree hissed. "Listen to me, Little Hawk! Face east . . . north is left of east."

"That way?"

McCree nodded. "Go north."

Terry pushed down on the pole, through sucking mud. *Sunrise east . . . sunset west . . . north is left of east. . . .*

They reached the truck as the sun was sinking. "Think you could get home alone from here?" McCree asked.

"No sir. I won't go without you."

"You might have to, Little Hawk."

Every move an agony, crying out or halting to suck gulps of air, McCree finally made it into the pickup. He stared at the dashboard.

"We can make it now, Mr. McCree."

"Can't drive, boy. Don't know when something ever hurt so much! Snakebit, catfish-finned, thistle-stuck—nothing like this!"

With his own heart the loudest thing he heard, Terry sat watching the old man. It was getting dark. Mosquitoes buzzed through the open windows. "Mr. McCree, we have to go now."

McCree's head was lolling. Terry touched the old man's leg. "Reckon I could drive, Mr. McCree, like we did it before."

"Won't work. Arm can't reach the gears."

"Show *me* the gears," Terry said quickly.

It seemed hours before McCree agreed and allowed the boy to stand between his legs. The old man's cries of pain, mumbled instructions and Terry's own empty stomach had tears running down Terry's cheeks.

"How do we start the motor, Mr. McCree?" A whir of mosquitoes. McCree's breathing his only response. Terry examined the dashboard, pulling one knob, then another. He found the lights.

"What do I do first, Mr. McCree?"

Aroused, the old man instructed: Turn the key, pull out choke, push starter button. The motor turned, sputtered and caught. McCree told him how to ease in the choke, adjust the throttle.

"Have to go fast, else—stuck."

"Yessir."

Somehow, lurching, headlights dipping, slashing the night sky, they began to move, shifted to second, then third, and with the wind in their faces, crossed the glade.

TERRY approached the polished counter and a nurse in crisp white clothing. "Please ma'am."

"Yes?"

"Mr. McCree is outside. He broke his arm. Please come help."

The nurse dialed a telephone, her eyes touching on Terry's face, clothing, legs. "I need an aide, please. Emergency ward."

They carried McCree inside on a stretcher. Somebody cut off the motor in the truck.

"What's your name, sonny?" the orderly asked.

"Terry."

"What's your last name?"

"McCree."

The nurse was on the telephone, talking. "Dr. Norman, this is the clinic. We have a compound fracture several days old. Man in his late seventies or early eighties. Could you come out?"

"Did you drive that truck?" the orderly asked.

"Yes," Terry said.

Terry was asleep on a bench when Dr. Phillip Norman passed in the hall. Somebody had put a pillow under the boy's head.

"Camp people?" Dr. Norman asked the nurse.

"I would think so. The child is filthy. They came in a battered pickup truck."

"Better find out who to call. The man may lose that arm."

Terry awoke, a hand on his shoulder, the nurse's face close to his. "Who can we call to come get you?"

"Is Mr. McCree dead?"

"No, he's not dead."

"I'll wait for him."

"He has to stay here awhile. Can someone take you home?"

Terry sat up, rubbing his eyes. He glanced down the hall and saw Dr. Norman. "I have to go," he said, and began running.

DR. NORMAN was getting into his automobile when he noticed McCree's pickup truck. The windows were open. He hesitated. The old man wasn't coming out for several days. He walked over to close the windows and glanced inside. A small form lay curled on the front seat, bare legs dotted with mosquitoes.

Dr. Norman returned to the hospital and called Sheriff Lambert. "He's in the parking lot in a pickup truck," the doctor related. "Come get him and keep him overnight. He'd be eaten alive by mosquitoes out here."

Terry was vaguely aware of strong arms lifting him. He sighed deeply, drugged by exhaustion. The sheriff's deputy put him on the front seat, rounded the patrol car and drove to the city jail.

THE deputy awoke Terry the next morning. He had been sleeping on a hard cotton mattress in an unlocked cell. The deputy gave him a stiff washcloth, a bar of Octagon soap and a thin towel.

"After you bathe, we'll get some vittles."

"Yessir." Terry eased into the shower.

"I'll throw these dirty duds in the washing machine," the deputy said. "When you get out, wrap the towel around yourself until the clothes are dry."

The hot water felt good. Terry put the bar of soap to his tangled hair and rubbed vigorously.

His bath complete, he downed two heaping plates of scrambled eggs and bacon prepared by an inmate cook. He drank most of his milk, although he'd have preferred coffee.

"Where're my clothes?" he asked when the cook came to collect the tray.

"In the laundry room down the hall."

"Can I get them?"

"If they're dry."

Terry dropped the towel at the dryer, slipping into his clothes. With a furtive glance back toward the cell compound as he skirted the outside of the building, he climbed a chain link fence and dropped quietly on the other side. Heading for the hospital, he avoided the main streets, darting between buildings, and cut across a side yard to enter the red brick building from the parking lot. McCree's truck was gone!

He approached the nurse on duty. "Is Mr. McCree still here?"

She telephoned someone, asking. She hung up and leaned over the counter. "He's still here, doing fine. But no children are allowed in the wards, son."

The expression on Terry's face made the nurse bend. "Would you like to see him through a window?"

"Yes ma'am."

They walked a long hall, Terry holding her hand. She pulled a stepladder to one of the two swinging doors and put her head inside. "Mr. McCree! Someone to see you at the window."

Terry saw McCree's shoulder wrapped in a rigid white cast that extended to the tips of his fingers. Terry waved, grinning. McCree waved in long swoops of the hand, smiling.

"See," the nurse said, "he's doing fine. You run home now."

"Thanks!" Terry ran ahead, going out the doors still smiling.

When he arrived at the shack, Terry found Dog hungry. Following McCree's example, he fed him, and as Dog ate, Terry removed the poultice bandanna and daubed camphor water onto the pup's inflamed neck.

He wandered around the shack, considered cooking something, then realized he had no matches. He went to LuBelle's.

Eunice was gone. LuBelle sat on the steps, drawing taut a string tied to her index fingers. On the string the whirring blur of a button "buzz saw" droned like an angry wasp.

"They been here looking for you," LuBelle said.

"Who has?"

"Some white woman. She ask Mawmaw where you went."

"What did Eunice say?"

"You went to see Cree. Mawmaw says you can't stay here again."

"Is she mad with me?"

"I reckon." The string to the button broke and curled around one of LuBelle's fingers. "That white woman says you got a mama and a daddy."

"She did?" Terry now realized it must have been Miss Ramsey. "How come you lie about your folks?" LuBelle asked.

"I don't know."

LuBelle suggested they play hopscotch. But Terry, afraid to face Eunice when she returned, said he was going home. Instead, he went to McCree's shack again.

He was sitting on McCree's stoop when he heard an automobile. He ran to a dark corner of a back room, where he could crouch behind a mound of burlap sacks. Peering out, he saw Miss Ramsey get out of her car. Like a wild animal, Terry remained motionless, every muscle tensed.

"Terrell!" Miss Ramsey was walking around the outside. "Your mother is very worried about you. Don't you think it's about time to go home?"

Did she know he was here? Or was she bluffing?

Her footsteps sounded as she entered the dark shack. Terry held his breath until his chest ached. Slowly, quietly, he exhaled, then, with tremendous control, inhaled.

Miss Ramsey bumped something. Terry saw a dim flicker. A match flame pushed at the dark, then died. A sputtering sizzle and a phosphorous smell as another match flared. He knew by the sound of her steps she was looking behind things. Terry eased down onto his knees.

"Terrell, your parents aren't angry with you. Nobody is. We only want you to come home. We can work out any problems, you know. I'll help you."

She was in the same room now. Terry heard her scrape another match, more light.

"Terrell."

He knew by her tone she had seen him. He looked up. Miss Ramsey stared at him unsmiling. She held out her hand. "Come on, Terrell. Let's go home."

They got into her automobile and Terry sat, back straight.

"Your mother and father have been very worried about you, Terrell," Miss Ramsey said as they reached the paved road and turned toward camp. "They will be so happy to have you home."

The smell of oleander came and went. Terry's mind raced with desperate thoughts: jump, run, get away!

Lights from the packinghouses came into view.

"Can you stop?" Terry asked. "I have to go to the bathroom."

"We'll be home in a second."

"I have to go now! Hurry, please!"

Miss Ramsey stopped the vehicle and Terry stepped out. A chorus of crickets and the burp of frogs rose from a familiar pond nearby.

"Watch for snakes, son," she called.

"Yes ma'am. Are you going to watch?"

"Oh, I'm sorry."

In the scant few seconds her back was turned, Terry slipped out of the red glow of the taillights and was gone.

"Are you about through?"

She knew children. She knew before she looked. She put a hand to her forehead and permitted herself a rare obscenity.

"AT LEAST you can take comfort from the fact that he is apparently hale and hearty," Miss Ramsey reported. Gerald and Mickey listened in stunned silence.

"That rascal conned me as sweetly as you please," Miss Ramsey said, managing a smile. "I wasn't three hundred yards from the entrance to the camp."

"He couldn't have gone far," Gerald said angrily.

"No," Miss Ramsey agreed. "But I suggest we wait until morning. I have a good idea where to find him now."

"Where?" Mickey demanded.

"At the old man's place. McCree. He's in the hospital with a broken arm. Eighty-three years old and fell out of a tree! He says Terrell brought him in from the Glades. I'll have another talk with him in the morning. Judge Franklin wants me to ascertain exactly where Terrell went, with whom and so forth."

"Why?" Gerald asked cautiously.

"It's standard procedure, Mr. Calder. Most runaways usually steal food, candy, that sort of thing."

"Dear Lord," Mickey groaned.

"We submit reports to the police routinely. However, I doubt that Terrell has done any of that. He spent his entire time with the black washerwoman, her granddaughter and this elderly man."

"What kind of people would take in a six-year-old child?" Mickey fumed. "Didn't they question whether he had a home?"

Miss Ramsey smiled tightly. "The kind of people who would do that are either ignorant, such as the washerwoman, or an old man who can't function as a responsible member of society."

79

When Gerald returned from seeing Miss Ramsey to her car, he took Mickey in his arms. He held her, saying nothing, tears of disappointment and humiliation in his eyes.

"We must have made a terrible mistake with Terrell, Gerald."

"Why must it be our fault, Mickey? Why can't he be what he is, without blaming us?"

Mickey sniffled. "I hate myself for feeling so angry toward him. He's just a child! But he must not love us, Gerald."

This time there was no denial.

TERRY made a bed of burlap sacks. Below, from the second floor of the packinghouse, vibrant sounds of humming machinery lulled him. He drifted off to sleep thinking about lights he'd seen burning at home, Miss Ramsey's automobile in the driveway.

He awoke before the midnight shift changed to dayworkers. He walked from person to person asking for cigarettes, and after an hour he had accumulated six. When several older boys arrived at the bamboo stand near school, he was waiting to barter.

"What kind of sandwiches do you have in your lunch?"

"Pimento cheese. One's bologna."

"I'll give you two cigarettes for your lunch."

"Make it four."

"Three."

A deal was made. Satisfied, Terry started back toward the packinghouse. Bucky Dallas spied him and ran out, grinning.

"Where'd you go?" Bucky whispered.

"New York."

"New York! How'd you get back?"

"Walked."

Skepticism crept into Bucky's eyes and Terry amended, "Part of the way. Partway I rode boxcars."

They reached the steps of the Blue Goose Packing Company. "I got to go see if I can sell this lunch," Terry said.

"Okay if I go with you?"

"Stay back is all. They don't trade so good when they see older boys around."

It took six approaches before a sale was made. The lunch went for twenty cents. This was spent on one hot dog all the way and a bottled NuGrape.

"I heard tell you were going to Marianna Boys' School," Bucky said in a low voice.

"They got to catch me first." Terry sucked mustard off a dirty finger.

"Uh-oh!" Bucky warned. It was all the alarm needed. Terry dashed one way and Bucky the other. Terry heard the packing-house guard shouting, "Catch him! Catch the redheaded one!"

Terry skirted a man with arms outstretched, raced across the building and disappeared through a maze of boxcars and shuttle engines. He slid down an embankment, legs cutting on rough shale, and raced toward a favorite place in a cane field. Only then did he permit himself to collapse, panting.

GERALD entered the newspaper office. Printing stock, liquid ink and a metallic smell of typesetting equipment were a pleasant aroma. There'd been a time when a writing career—

"Morning, Gerald!" Burrell Mason had a huge cigar clamped between his teeth, lips smiling around it.

"Burrell, may I see you privately?"

The publisher gestured grandly toward his glassed-in office and followed Gerald inside.

"Burrell, your editorial is unforgiveable. It is going to turn every white laborer into a raging racist! You surprise me. Really, this is irresponsible journalism."

"I resent that, Gerald. But how about writing a rebuttal? You may have equal space for your reply. Fair enough?"

"I can't do that and you know it. I'd have to get it approved in Washington before I could submit it. This is too delicate to be casually batted back and forth."

"Your Washington people give me a pain! I have stated my opinion. You have the wherewithal to make a meaningful reply. If you want a bureaucratic committee action, that's all right by me. Call Washington if you want and ask them what you should say!"

Gerald slammed the door on his way out.

TERRY saw Mr. McCree's truck parked inside a locked fence behind the sheriff's office. He stood, fingers hooked through the links of the fence, staring at it. How could Mr. McCree get from the hospital to home? Why had they moved it?

He walked slowly, shuffling his bare toes in dust bowls. He needed to talk to Mr. McCree.

He stopped under the marquee of the theater, looking at photographs of Tom Mix and Gene Autry. A reflection in the glass covering the posters was Terry's only warning. With an intuitive jump he was off and running.

"You little punk!" The deputy overtook Terry, grabbing the waist of his trousers and back of his shirt.

"I ought to paddle you right here and now," the deputy fumed. He locked Terry in the rear of the patrol car. The car lunged forward. They turned a corner, another corner. Terry saw the jail.

"I found him, Sheriff."

"Put him in a cell. And lock the door."

Terry was pushed into the same cell he'd slept in the night before last. The door shut with a clang, echoing through the building.

Terry heard steps, and Sheriff Lambert loomed outside the cell.

"We called your folks, boy. We called Judge Franklin and Miss Ramsey, too. Take a good look at this cell, son. Runaways and boys who play hooky end up here. You sit and think about it. Think how you'd like those iron bars and that hard bed for weeks, or months, or even years."

The sheriff walked away. A far door banged shut. Terry stood in the center of the cell, surrounded by gray walls, bars, a narrow shaft of light coming from a latticed window high overhead. Tears poured down his cheeks.

CHAPTER FOURTEEN

"What do you suppose Ike is going to say?" Mickey said flatly.

"He said he wants to talk to Terrell. I suspect he wants to see for himself what kind of child Terrell is."

Mickey completed dressing. "Terrell isn't the same child he was, Gerald. He sits and stares into space. He acts so lonely."

"He'll get over that."

"I can't draw him out. The only thing he's interested in seems to be some dog that old man owns. He said it needs food and water."

"That's certainly a sense of responsibility, Mickey. That encourages me."

IKE FRANKLIN OFFERED COFFEE to everyone. Miss Ramsey, the deputy, Sheriff Lambert, Mr. Hammond and Mrs. Wright were there. Mickey and Gerald sat stiffly. Terry sipped a soft drink.

After everyone had prepared their coffee, Judge Franklin said, "I have considered everything carefully and I think I've found the root of this little fellow's problem. Our adventurer has been under the influence of an interesting, exciting man. He has been doing what any lad of comparable age would do—he's been going where it's most fun to be. Isn't that right, Terrell?"

Not fully understanding, Terry nodded anyway.

"I want to say this, Gerald. We will be holding hearings this coming Thursday. Dr. Norman says it appears now that McCree will be all right and can be released from the hospital.

"Sheriff Lambert has issued a summons. Ostensibly it is for contributing to the delinquency of a minor, but in fact it is a legal prelude to having the man committed. We hope we can convince him to voluntarily have himself placed where somebody can look after him."

"What about Terrell?" Mickey's voice was small.

"He'll have to go to school," Judge Franklin said. He looked at Terrell. "If you don't go, son, they're going to put you in a place where the doors are locked. Do you understand that?"

"Yessir."

"Let me hear you say that you are going to school, son."

"I'm going to school."

Judge Franklin took a deep breath and his tone softened. "Terrell, I know you don't think so this minute, but someday you will be thankful all this happened. Otherwise, son, without education you would become one of the millions of people who can never become something special. We think you are a very smart little boy. We think you will make a fine member of society. Who knows, you may grow up to become President of the United States."

Judge Franklin stood. "I'll see you all in court Thursday, December fourth, at ten o'clock. I think everything is going to work out just fine." The judge smiled, putting a hand on Terrell's shoulder.

"Thank you, Ike," Mickey said. Judge Franklin hugged her gently as she blinked back tears.

Their footsteps echoed as they went down the flight of marble steps. "Anybody want a banana split?" Gerald asked.

"I shouldn't," Mickey said, "but I do."

"How about you, Terrell?"

Terry nodded. They crossed to the drugstore. It had double doors which folded back, forming an open corner of the building. Seated at a round table, Terry could gaze out at the street.

Two black children on roller skates whizzed past, metal wheels zinging. They wheeled, returned and stood watching Terry eat his ice cream. Terry took a bite, returning their gaze.

"Where are you going, Terrell?"

He carried the remainder of his ice cream to the two children and held it out. They studied him soberly, glanced at his parents, then dashed off down the street.

"That's some boy, Mickey," Gerald said gently.

Mickey stood abruptly, took the ice cream from Terry's hands.

"Come sit down," she said. "Eat, or don't eat, as you choose. But don't get up from the table again."

Terry winced as she pushed him back to his seat.

"You don't want that?" Daddy asked.

"No."

"Mind if I eat it?"

Terry pushed it toward Gerald. He sat, head hung.

"Terrell, I'm sorry," Mama said, her voice low. "I was wrong to do that. You were being very generous. I love you."

"I love you, too, Mama."

THAT evening Terry sat at the dinner table, hands in his lap, eyes down, as his parents discussed the hearing.

"What is wrong, Terrell?" Daddy said suddenly.

"Nothing."

"That can't be true, Terrell. If nothing was wrong, why would you continue to run away?"

"I don't know, Daddy."

Gerald sighed heavily. "Why do some people call you Terry?"

"I don't know."

Wham! Gerald's fist struck the table and the silverware leaped. Terry jolted, his back pinned to his chair.

"You don't like the name Terrell?" Gerald demanded.

"No sir." Trembling voice.

Daddy's tone altered. "Would you like us to call you Terry?"

Terry nodded. Gerald looked at Mickey. Nobody moved.

"Eat your supper, *Terry*," Mama said.

Terry began eating, hands shivering, the English peas falling off his fork. He chanced to glance up, fork before an open mouth, and was stunned at what he saw.

Mama and Daddy were smiling at one another.

TERRY and Bucky strolled the packinghouse platform. The guard approached them. "Your folks know where you are, Terrell?"

"Yessir."

The boy didn't run. He met the adult's eyes firmly. The guard yielded. "You boys stay out of trouble, hear me?"

"Yessir."

Bucky whispered to Terry, "Do they really know?"

"Yeah. I told Mama I was coming over here. She gave me two quarters. Want a hot dog?"

Bucky accepted. They went to the snack bar and liberally salted two hot dogs.

"Bucky, do you know what *committed* means?"

"We formed a committee once in class," Bucky dimly recalled.

"I don't think it means that. The judge said something about having Mr. McCree committed."

"That means they're going to lock him up, I bet."

"I got to go, Bucky."

"Wait a minute, Terry! Where are you going?"

"I got to see Mr. McCree."

"You said they wouldn't let you in!"

"They wouldn't. But I got to see him." Terry began to run.

THE nurse intercepted Terry as he walked down the corridor. "Whoa, young man! No children allowed in the ward."

"Please ma'am, I got to see my granddaddy."

"Who is your granddaddy?"

"Mr. McCree. I got to tell him about Grandmama."

"What about Grandmama?"

"She died."

"Died!" the nurse gasped.

"She's home in bed dead. I need to know about feeding the dog."

"Oh, God," the nurse said.

"Please ma'am, let me see him." Terry began to weep.

"Hold it. I'll see what I can do."

Terry watched her telephone someone, speak in a hushed voice. She turned to Terry, her tone sympathetic. "The doctor said Mr. McCree can come out into the hall and visit with you if he feels like it. How about that?"

"That's good."

The nurse indicated a bench where Terry could wait, and she disappeared through the swinging doors of the ward. She returned with Mr. McCree. The old man was grinning, face shaved.

"Heylo, Little Hawk! Slip over and let me sit with you."

Terry inched closer to the old man. "I told them you were my granddaddy," he whispered. "I told them I had to tell you Grandmama was home dead in the bed."

"Yes." McCree's eyes twinkled. "The nurse told me. I don't think she understood my laughing about it. I told her I never did like your grandmother too much."

Terry slipped his arm inside McCree's. "I got us in a peck of trouble, Mr. McCree."

"How much is a peck, boy?"

Terry's fingers flicked against his knee. "Thirty-two cups."

"Little slow," McCree said, "but right."

A man in white appeared and Terry looked up at a staff doctor.

"Mr. McCree, is this child your grandson?"

"You could say that," McCree said.

"He told the nurse—did you know—"

"Yes." McCree's face was suddenly sorrowful. "Terrible thing, so quick. She was all right yesterday. Isn't that what you said, Little Hawk?"

"She was fine."

"Is there anyone you'd like us to call, Mr. McCree?" the doctor asked, his voice gentle.

"No, no, I don't think so. We tend to our own, we do."

The doctor scrutinized the boy and old man. "I'm sorry, sir, but I don't believe this story. Mr. McCree, we have hospital regulations about children visiting. The boy will have to go."

"I guess that's it, Little Hawk."

"I want to talk to you, Mr. McCree."

"I'd like that, Little Hawk, but it's the man's hospital, not mine."

Terry stood, lips quivering. The doctor motioned to the nurse, who took Terry's arm and pushed him toward the exit.

"I should've known better," the nurse said sharply. "Kids who lie go to hell, did you know that?"

"Little Hawk!" McCree's voice echoed in the hall.

The nurse halted, and Terry called back, "Yessir?"

"Don't try to bury her by yourself, son!" As Terry pushed through the door, he heard McCree chuckling.

CHAPTER FIFTEEN

JUDGE Franklin sat higher than anyone else, behind a polished desk. People being questioned sat to one side of him. When they brought in Mr. McCree, he was put at a table by himself.

The attorney called Dr. Phillip Norman to the stand.

"Dr. Norman, is Jackson Cole McCree a patient of yours?"

"Yes."

"How many times have you treated him?"

"Three that I recall, most recently for a compound fracture of the right arm."

"What kind of payment did you receive from Mr. McCree for professional services rendered?"

"He was a charity patient."

"Thank you, Doctor. You may step down."

"Mr. Michael Elton, please."

A man walked toward the stand self-consciously adjusting his tie. He wore a new suit, shined shoes. It took Terry a minute to recognize him.

"Mr. Elton, what is your occupation?"

"I'm a security guard at the Blue Goose Packing Company."

"Have you ever seen this man before, Mr. Elton?" The attorney pointed a pencil at Mr. McCree.

"Yessir, I have."

"Tell us about it, please."

The guard's hands kneaded one another. As he spoke, he gazed across the heads of everybody in the courtroom.

"When I saw the old man come down that chute, I couldn't believe it. I mean, a person could get killed doing something like that. But there he went, just like the kids."

The attorney nodded and pointed at Terry. "Do you know the red-haired child, Mr. Elton?"

"His name's Terrell Calder."

"Is Terrell one of the boys you saw with Mr. McCree?"

"He was one of them. Bucky Dallas was the other."

"Thank you, Mr. Elton. You may be excused."

"Mr. McCree," Judge Franklin said, "you may question any of these people on your own behalf, if you wish."

"Thank you, Judge." McCree nodded soberly. "If I think of something, I'll ask."

"This could go badly for you. You have a right to engage counsel. Are you aware of that?"

"Long as nobody lies," McCree argued gently, "what could a high-priced lawyer do?"

Judge Franklin looked at the prosecuting attorney. "Go ahead, Mr. Garrick."

Mr. Garrick called Eunice Washington. She hesitated, eyes darting, and the judge said, "Come sit down, Eunice. We only want to ask a few questions."

Eunice avoided looking at Mr. McCree and Terry.

"Where do you live, Eunice?"

"Out close to Chosen. My grandbaby, LuBelle, lives with me."

"Eunice, do you know Terrell Calder?"

"I knows him. Terry. He comes to play with my LuBelle."

"Do you feed him when he's out there?"

"If he's hungry. What boy ain't?" Several people laughed.

"Has he ever stayed overnight at your house?"

Eunice tensed visibly. She mumbled something.

"You are not in any trouble," Mr. Garrick said softly. "We are trying to establish where the boy spent a week of his time."

"Yessir. He stayed two nights."

"What about his people? They would worry, Eunice."

"He said he didn't have no people."

"Did you believe that?"

"No."

"Then why did you let Terry stay with you?"

Eunice shook her head. "If he figured he needed someplace to stay, I didn't want to send him out to sleep in the swamps."

"Why did Terry finally leave your house?"

"I told him to go home to his people."

"All right. Now, how long have you known Mr. McCree?"

"Oh, Lawd. Twenty, thirty years, maybe."

"What is your relationship with him?"

Eunice cut her eyes warily. "What do that mean?"

"I mean, does he buy from you, or sell things to you?"

"Yessir. He comes on trading day. Brings fish and things."

"What do you give him for the fish and things he brings?"

"Mostly, I cooks. When he gets a yen for hot food, he'll stop by to take a meal with us."

"I see. No further questions, Your Honor."

Judge Franklin said to Mr. McCree, "Would you like to ask this woman any questions?"

"No. She said it right."

Judge Franklin turned to Eunice. "You may go, Eunice."

"Yessir, Judge. Can I say something?"

"If you wish."

"That man is a good man, Judge. He looks after us. Comes to fetch firewood, brings us to town when LuBelle got the mumps, mended my roof after the hurricanes. Mr. Cree's a good man."

"Thank you, Eunice."

"Terry's a good boy, too. Him and that old man is two of a kind."

"Thank you, Eunice. You may step down."

Eunice walked out the side door of the courtroom.

"Sheriff Edward Lambert," the attorney called. The large law officer walked heavily to the stand. He sat, legs spread.

"Sheriff, you are holding a 1934 Ford pickup truck?"

"I am."

"Who is the registered owner of that vehicle?"

"It isn't registered. Mr. McCree claims ownership."

"Why are you holding it?"

"Operating without a license. The taillights are faulty, brakes are bad, the muffler is no good."

"Sheriff, do you know the child Terrell Calder?"

"He's one of Miss Ramsey's truants."

"You were given orders recently to pick him up?"

"For running away, yessir."

The judge looked at McCree. The old man shook his head no.

"Thank you. Step down, Sheriff."

"I think we should take a break for lunch," Judge Franklin announced. "Everyone under subpoena is to return here promptly at one o'clock." He struck his desk with a gavel.

"Can Mr. McCree eat with us?" Terry asked his mother.

"Absolutely not," she said.

"Daddy? He can't find things to eat in town like he can out in the swamps."

"I'm afraid not, Terry." They walked across the street to a drugstore and sat at a table which allowed Terry to see the courthouse door. Mr. McCree came down the broad white steps slowly. He stood uncertainly on the sidewalk, then moved down the street, pausing to look through shopwindows or up at signs overhead. Finally he went into a supermarket.

Terry began to cry.

"Stop that this minute, young man," Daddy said evenly.

After a while, Mr. McCree emerged from the store, a small sack in hand. He shuffled back to the courthouse and found a bench in the shade of an oleander bush. Terry watched as he opened a can of what looked like sausages, a package of crackers.

After their lunch, Terry broke away from his father's hand as they crossed the street, and ran across the courthouse lawn.

"Terrell!"

He reached McCree as the old man was putting the empty can and cracker wrappings into the paper sack. "Mr. McCree?"

"Yes, Little Hawk?"

"I'm sorry, Mr. McCree."

"No need to be."

"I caused you all this trouble." Terry's lips twisted. McCree enveloped Terry with his good arm and patted him gently.

"I think your pappy wants you, Terrell."

The use of his name shocked Terry. "I'm sorry, Mr. McCree."

Gerald took Terry's arm as McCree's hand slipped away. Daddy's grip was very strong, Terry's arm throbbing from the pressure as they walked fast toward the courtroom.

MR. HAMMOND told of meetings with Mrs. Wright and Terry's parents, of the day he had the boy in his office for putting frogs in Mrs. Wright's desk. Everybody laughed except Terry, his parents, Mr. McCree and Mrs. Wright.

Terry heard himself described as intelligent, perceptive, well mannered but a paradox. He didn't understand the word paradox but soon decided that it meant he wasn't truly intelligent, perceptive and well mannered.

Miss Ramsey told how many days Terry had missed school. She said she had chased him from cane fields to packinghouses to Lake Okeechobee. She said he was her most persistent truant.

"Now, Miss Ramsey," Mr. Garrick questioned, "tell us what you've discovered in the past few weeks about Terrell Calder."

"He's been drawn to the man McCree," Miss Ramsey said. "The old man is colorful. His house is a shack in the swamps with no electricity, no sanitary facilities. If there was a bed, I didn't see it. Junk of all kinds litters every inch of space."

"In your opinion, Miss Ramsey, as a trained social worker, did Mr. McCree exert a favorable influence on this child?"

"No sir, he did not."

"In what way, Miss Ramsey?"

"They ate what they could find, scavenging for seeds and roots, and slept in the open during the time they were out, under a makeshift thatched shack of palmetto fronds. Under the spell of the old man, Terrell invented fanciful tales, resorted to lying. McCree told Eunice Washington he did not question Terrell's stories, accepting them as truth.

"In an interview with me in the hospital, McCree admitted Terrell drove the truck out of the swamps. He said the child had been allowed to steer the truck on other occasions. When they are together, McCree almost always takes advantage of the child, using him as a laborer to gather the seeds, cones and berries which he sells. They had been climbing trees in search of air plants the day Mr. McCree fell and broke his arm. If McCree had died out there, it is a virtual certainty that the child would have perished, also."

"Miss Ramsey, in your professional opinion what has been the problem with Terrell Calder?"

"The problem is, as I see it, that Terrell has been mesmerized by Mr. McCree. He was a lonely child and the old man was lonely. Each served a need to the other."

"And what can be done about this?"

"First, the child should be separated from McCree."

"No!" Terry screamed.

"Terrell!" Mama snatched him back down onto the seat.

"No!" Terry yelled.

"Terrell!" Judge Franklin was hitting his desk with the wooden gavel. "Terrell, be quiet!"

Miss Ramsey continued. "In my opinion, Mr. McCree is incapable of looking after his own welfare, much less that of a child. The boy has attached himself to McCree and under his influence has developed poor value judgment. He resents the restrictions of society, yearning to live a life of uninhibited freedom."

"Thank you, Miss Ramsey."

Mr. Garrick whispered to Judge Franklin and the judge leaned across the bench. "Mr. and Mrs. Calder, we would like to have Terrell on the stand."

JUDGE Franklin spoke softly. "Terrell, do you know what it means to swear to tell the truth?"

"Yessir."

"What does it mean?"

"If I lie, I go to jail."

A man held out a Bible and Terry did as he'd seen the adults do—placed one hand on the book, raised the other.

"Do you swear to tell the truth, the whole truth, and nothing but the truth, so help you God?"

"Yessir."

Mr. Garrick smiled at Terrell. "Some people in this court call you Terry. Which should I call you? Terrell or Terry?"

"Terry."

"Terry, how did you meet Mr. McCree?"

"Out at LuBelle's."

"How long have you known Mr. McCree?"

"About—two years."

"Do you like him?"

"Yessir."

"Why do you like him?"

"He takes me with him when he goes hunting things."

"Things like what?"

"Australian pinecones, cocoons, air plants—"

"So you work for him?"

Uncertain, Terry mumbled, "Yes." Pause. "Sir."

93

"Do you get paid for your work?"

"No. But he's nice to me and he teaches me things!"

"Oh, such as what?"

"How to charm birds, and catch fish with no bait."

The attorney laughed. "How do you catch fish with no bait?"

"You sit real still, staring at the water. You have to mix bubbles in your spit and let it fall. When you see the fish come up, you put your hand in the water and just pick him up."

"Just pick up the fish. You've seen Mr. McCree do this?"

"I did it, too."

"You did!"

Terry's eyes narrowed suspiciously. "Yes."

"Terry, let's talk about the day you and Mr. McCree went to the packinghouse. What were you doing there?"

"We went to eat tomatoes."

"Did you pay for these tomatoes?"

"No sir."

"You just helped yourselves?"

"Sure, everybody does it."

"Well, not quite. If everybody did, the packinghouses wouldn't have very many tomatoes to sell, would they?"

Terry considered this. "I guess not."

"Then you decided to ride in a packing crate down a spiraling chute. Is that true?"

"Yessir."

"Mr. McCree rode one, too?"

"Yessir."

Mr. Garrick nodded. He turned a page of a yellow pad of paper with notes scribbled on it. "How many times have you driven Mr. McCree's truck?"

"I don't know."

"Many times?"

"I guess."

"How did you manage to drive?"

"I stood between Mr. McCree's legs, steering."

"That must have been exciting. Did you go fast after Mr. McCree's accident?"

"Yessir! We would've gotten stuck if we went slow."

"When Mr. McCree fell out of the tree, tell us what happened."

94

"The bone was sticking out of his arm, so I knew it was broken. I helped him get back to the chickee."

"What's a chickee, Terry?"

"That's what the Seminoles call it. It's a lean-to with palmetto for a roof."

"Was it cold and rainy that night?"

"Yessir."

"Did you have anything to eat?"

"Nothing."

"Terry, the hospital staff says you told them Mr. McCree was your grandfather and that you had to see him because your grandmother was home dead in the bed."

Terry answered the attorney over laughter from the people listening. "Yessir."

"Terry"—Mr. Garrick leaned nearer—"you really love that old man, don't you?"

Terry glanced at his parents. Mama's eyes were frightened. Daddy sat holding her hand.

"Yes."

"You'd do almost anything for him. You worked for no pay, you ate little or nothing without complaint, isn't that so?"

"Yes."

"In fact, you saved his life, didn't you?"

"I don't know."

"Terry, did Mr. McCree ever tell you to go home?"

"No sir." Terry swallowed hard. "But he drove me to the camp at night."

"Oh, he did? So he knew where you lived, then?"

"Not really. I always got out at the bridge."

"All right, Terry. Unless Mr. McCree has some questions, you may go back and sit with your mama and daddy."

Mr. McCree shook his head without looking up.

Mr. Garrick said, "I now call Mr. Jackson Cole McCree."

Mr. McCree's chair scraped the floor as he rose. He walked slowly to the seat Terry had just vacated, and sat down.

"State your name, please."

"Jackson Cole McCree."

"What is your occupation, Mr. McCree?"

"I sell seeds and things."

"Seeds and what things?"

"Wildlife, raccoons, possums, snakes, moths, whatever folks want to order that I can catch."

"Do you make a living at this?"

"I get by."

"Mr. McCree, how much did you pay in taxes last year?"

"I don't recall paying any."

"You have, in fact, never paid taxes, have you?"

"No, I reckon not."

"Do you qualify for Social Security?"

"Don't rightly know. I never asked."

"Mr. McCree, did you know there is a law requiring that all motorized vehicles have a license tag?"

"Yessir."

"Why haven't you bought one?"

"I used to bring my horse to town," Mr. McCree said. "They told me I'd have to stop that. So, for a while, I'd leave my horse at the edge of town and walk the rest of the way. When the horse died, I bought that truck of mine. I never come to town in it, either. Always leave it at the edge and walk in."

"Do you know there's a law about such things as faulty lights, brakes and muffler?"

"Nobody ever told me that."

"Ignorance of a law is no excuse, Mr. McCree."

"They keep telling me that the last day or so."

"Did you know there are laws prohibiting the use of child labor, with or without pay?"

"Me and the boy never rightly thought of it as work."

"You sold what he gathered, didn't you?"

"I did."

"You have been charged with contributing to the delinquency of a minor. Do you know what that means?"

"I think I do. It ain't true."

"It isn't? Wouldn't you say you have encouraged this boy to stay away from school, run away from home, and lie?"

"I didn't think so, no."

"Did you encourage the child to steal?"

"No. Never stole in my life, sir."

"Who paid for the tomatoes you ate?"

"Well, sir, about the tomatoes—"

"Mr. McCree, do you have a hunting or fishing license?"

"No."

"Do you have a business license?"

"No."

"Do you own property?"

An imperceptible shake of the head.

"Do you have a family, Mr. McCree?"

"No."

"How old a man are you, Mr. McCree?"

"Eighty-four come February."

The attorney walked around the room, studying his notes. "Mr. McCree, tell me what you think of Terry."

"He's a fine boy."

"He deserves an education, don't you think?"

"Be a shame if he didn't get educated."

"Yes, it would. You're fond of that boy, aren't you?"

"Mighty fond."

"He saved your life, didn't he?"

"I'd of died if he hadn't got me back."

"If you had died, he would have also. Is that fair to assume?"

"It's what kept me going."

"Your Honor," Mr. Garrick said, "I think we've pretty well established what the court needs to know."

"Yes, Mr. Garrick. Mr. McCree, is there anything you'd like to say on your own behalf?"

"Yessir." Mr. McCree turned toward the judge. "I'd like to ask my little friend some questions, now."

"The boy?"

"Yessir. If you don't mind."

Judge Franklin looked at his watch. "How long will it take?"

"I don't rightly know. I don't want to hurry none."

"Very well," Judge Franklin said, his tone slightly irritated. "This court stands adjourned until tomorrow morning at ten." He stood, banged the gavel and walked out, frowning.

"Mr. McCree." Terry leaned over the rail separating them.

"Yes, Little Hawk?"

"I want to talk to you, Mr. McCree."

"Tomorrow, Little Hawk. We'll talk tomorrow."

CHAPTER SIXTEEN

TERRY sat in the chair beside Judge Franklin's high mahogany bench. An overhead fan whirled, blowing warm air down from the ceiling.

"You remember what you promised yesterday, Terrell?" Judge Franklin asked.

"To tell the truth."

"That's right." Then to Mr. McCree, "You may begin."

Mr. McCree gazed at Terry solemnly.

"How's your arm, Mr. McCree?"

"Itches something awful."

"I knew a boy with a broken leg. He said his itched, too."

"Mr. McCree," Judge Franklin stated, "let us begin."

The prosecuting attorney slumped in his chair.

"Yesterday," McCree said to Terry, "you and me looked kind of bad. To hear them tell it, we broke about every law there is."

"That's what my daddy said."

"Know something, Little Hawk? I don't feel that way about it. Do you?"

"No sir, I don't."

"Your Honor, please," Mr. Garrick said.

"I agree. Mr. McCree, let's try to get to the point."

"Now, Your Honor," McCree said, smiling, "I didn't rush anybody yesterday. I sat by and listened to how I made this boy into a criminal. I didn't open my mouth one time. I'd appreciate the same from this gentleman. He's got a mighty bad opinion of me and I'd like to change his mind, if I can."

"That's what we're here for. But let's get on with it."

"Good. Little Hawk, I don't ever recollect you telling me how old you were. Did you ever tell me that?"

"No sir."

"How about school? You ever mention going to school?"

"I said I didn't want to go. You said, when the time came, I'd like it. You said I'd learn lots of things."

"Hm-m. More than you'd learn with me, for sure."

"I learned a lot with you."

"Oh? You don't say. What?"

"About how to find something to eat in the swamps."

"That's important, all right, if you're in a swamp. Now, about those tomatoes we swiped. What kind of tomatoes were those? Were they green ones, or blue ones?"

Terry laughed. "Red ones, ripe and juicy."

"Don't they usually throw out real ripe tomatoes?"

"Yessir, they rot in the hamper if they're too ripe."

"Reckon anybody minded us eating those real ripe tomatoes?"

"No sir."

"All right. Now, it's true we did shoot the shoot."

"Yessir."

"That was something, wasn't it?"

"It sure was!" Terry wiggled in his seat.

"We didn't get hurt, did we? Tear up anything?"

"No sir."

"Listen, Little Hawk, about this business of working you for no pay. I didn't mean to cheat you."

"I didn't want any money."

"I know that. But you did help me, didn't you?"

"Yessir. We got three hundred bushels of pinecones!"

"I bet you don't even know what a bushel is."

"Yes, I do. Two cups make a pint, two pints make a quart, eight quarts make a peck, four pecks make a bushel."

"You said that mighty fast. Could have memorized that. Let's see—how many cups are in a bushel?"

"A hundred twenty-eight."

"Not bad, Little Hawk. You say we got three hundred of these bushels? How many is that?"

Ten flicks of ten fingers. "Times three," Terry said.

McCree nodded. "What else did we gather?"

"Cecropia cocoons."

"What's that?"

"You know what that is!"

"I do. These folks might not."

"It's a kind of moth."

"Little Hawk, let's talk about the day I fell out of the tree. Let's say I couldn't of got up. What would you have done?"

"You said go north."

"Which way is north?"

99

"The sun comes up in the east and sets in the west. North is left of east."

"Which is your left, Little Hawk?"

Terry lifted his left hand.

"What if you'd got stuck out there at night by yourself?"

"I'd build a chickee."

"You think you could do that?"

"Yessir." Terry told how he'd get only green fronds because dead ones broke easily. He explained the overlapping to keep out rain, and how stems had to be interlocked to hold against wind.

"What about mosquitoes?"

"Cover coals with moss to drive off mosquitoes."

"How about water?"

"Strain it, and boil it hard so it won't make you sick."

"Food?"

"Swamp cabbage, *Daucus carota*—"

"What's that?"

"Wild carrot. Mama calls it Queen Anne's lace."

"Anything else?"

"Berries, nuts, most everything can be eaten if you know what to look for and how to cook it."

Mr. McCree nodded, looking at the floor. He propped his bad arm on the judge's bench.

"How's Dog?"

"He's doing okay. I threw away the poultice of boneset leaves and put camphor water on his bite."

Judge Franklin cleared his throat. "What is this?"

"My dog, Dog," McCree said. "Got bit by a rattlesnake and I haven't been back to tend to him. Little Hawk did it for me. Now, Little Hawk, if I ask you a straight question, will you give me a straight answer?"

Terry's eyes dropped. "Yessir."

"Do you love your ma and pa?"

"I sure do."

"You don't want to hurt them, do you?"

"No sir."

"You might not have meant to, but you did. I saw it in your ma's face when Eunice told how you said you didn't have any folks."

"I'm sorry, Mr. McCree."

"I am, too, Little Hawk. But let's see if we can figure why you said such a thing. You have any friends, Little Hawk?"

"Aren't you my friend?" Terry had tears in his eyes.

"I am that. I mean, any other friends."

Terry thought a long time. "Bucky, I guess."

"You don't sound too sure. I judge a friend by whether the other person will do the same for me that I'd do for him. Would Bucky do for you?"

"No."

"Who would?"

"You."

"Anybody else?"

"Mama. Daddy."

"Anybody else, Little Hawk?"

"No." Terry hung his head.

"Nothing to be ashamed of," McCree said. "Most folks don't have even one friend. But you have other friends."

"Who?"

"Eunice and LuBelle."

"Oh. Yessir."

McCree took his arm off the judge's bench and walked away, looking stooped. He halted before Mr. Garrick and looked at the attorney a long moment.

"When you was a boy, Mr. Garrick, did you ever want to take off all your clothes and go swimming?"

"I suggest you confine your questions to the child, Mr. McCree," Mr. Garrick said, not harshly.

To Judge Franklin, McCree said, "When I first came to the Everglades nigh onto sixty-five years ago, birds rose up on the wing, so many the sky turned dark for an hour. They don't have flocks like that anymore. Gators big as tree trunks were common as grass. The day's coming when they'll all be gone."

McCree turned to Mama and Daddy. "Everybody's been worrying about why this boy wants to stay out of school. That's no mystery to me. He's a—little hawk. He needs to fly, soar, ride the air currents, before they clip his wings forever."

McCree looked at Terry, a shimmer of water in his eyes.

"Ya'll asked me was I fond of him?"

The old man paused, brushed under his eyes quickly. "Truth is, he came to me like he was God-sent. This skinny little boy with a spirit yearning to be free as all outdoors. Me and him had something special, we did. From riding through the swamps, doctoring Dog's snakebite and even shooting the shoot! That was a lot of fun, wasn't it, Little Hawk?"

"Yessir, it was." Terry began crying softly.

"Now, you might lock up old McCree's body. But I pine for this boy the way I'd pine for a bobcat kitten in a cage, who'll never know the smell of swamp water and the taste of wild food.

"If I'm supposed to be ashamed of giving this little hawk flight, I just can't find myself feeling it."

McCree came to Terry and put a quaking hand on the boy's shoulder, shaking it gently. "We had us something special, boy. Something few men and boys ever know. Someday, I'm betting, it won't be learning to spell and add you'll think about, because you'll have them memory-locked. I'm betting you remember old man McCree."

McCree went back to his table and sat down. Mama and Daddy were staring at Terry, eyes moist. Judge Franklin sat a long time in a room silent except for the circling fan overhead.

"Monday morning, ten o'clock, December eighth," Judge Franklin said brusquely. "I'll deliver a decision then."

SUNDAY, December 7, 1941, Terry was eating cookies while Daddy listened to the football game on radio. Suddenly Daddy cried out, a sound so visceral that Terry would never forget it.

Daddy's face was starkly pale as he grabbed Mama, holding her. "The Japanese attacked Pearl Harbor, Mickey."

Terry saw her eyes go wide, frightened.

"That means war. Now. Today. Dear God."

That evening Burrell Mason called and said he was retracting his editorial about the new camp. Terry watched Daddy talk into the phone in urgent tones, something about the President speaking tonight.

"They want me to join the International Red Cross," Daddy told Mama, hanging up from yet another long-distance call.

"What about the camp, Gerald?"

"War changes priorities, Mickey. They'll send someone else to manage the camps. I'll have to go to Fort Pierce for a day or two."

"The baby, Gerald."

"I know."

On Monday the world looked the same, but all talk was of war. When Terry and Mama arrived in court, they and McCree were the only ones there.

Judge Franklin came in, looking older since Friday, and sat heavily, gazing down at a folder before him.

"Mr. McCree," Judge Franklin said, his voice strangely choked, "last Friday was a thousand years ago."

"Yessir."

"Somehow, today," Judge Franklin said, looking at Terry, "I think there are few people in the world who would begrudge the freedom of a little hawk."

McCree nodded.

The gavel hit the bench. "Dismissed," Judge Franklin said.

"What does that mean, Mama?"

"It means they're going to forget everything," Mama said, standing. She winced suddenly, holding her stomach, mouth open.

"You all right, Mrs. Calder?" McCree asked.

"I think—I'm—"

McCree helped Mama sit again. "I'll have the judge call somebody, Mrs. Calder," he said.

IN THE hospital corridor, Daddy stood with Burrell Mason, doctors and nurses, listening to a radio. Mama was in another room trying to have a baby. Terry sat close to McCree.

Daddy and Burrell walked by Terry and the old man. "No need recriminating," Mr. Mason was saying. "We need that camp now."

Terry put a hand on McCree's knee. "Mr. McCree, my daddy says we're moving away from Belle Glade."

"That a fact?"

"He's going to fight the war."

McCree nodded.

"Reckon I could come live with you in the swamp?"

"Reckon not, Little Hawk. Your mama ain't going to have a man around the house with your pa gone to fight. And with the new baby, she's going to need you mighty bad."

Terry blinked his eyes quickly.

"Summer's over, Little Hawk."

103

"This is December, Mr. McCree. This is winter."

McCree grunted. "The Seminoles used to say, so long as it's hot, it's summer. When it's cold, it's winter. Well, Little Hawk, you had a Seminole summer. Now it's past. Time for new things and new places. You got to grow up some. Go to school. Understand?"

"Mr. Calder!"

"Yes?"

"It's a girl!"

Terry saw a strange mixture of expressions cross Daddy's face. "How's my wife? How's Mickey?"

"Fine!"

"Did you tell her it was a girl?" Daddy asked.

"Yes, we did. She said, 'Thank goodness.'"

Daddy turned and grabbed Terry, hugging him too tightly. "We have a little sister in the house now. You'll have to help your mama look after her."

"Yessir. Mr. McCree told me."

Daddy had tears in his eyes, looking at Terry. He kissed the boy ever so gently. "I don't know if I told you, Little Hawk. But I sure do love you."

Terry hugged Daddy. "I love *you*."

"Here comes the baby!"

"Look at that!"

The red-faced, fretting child looked like a prune! Somebody said, "Looks just like Mickey."

Terry turned to sit down, fuming. That baby looked like nobody. Ugly! Red! "Beautiful!" everybody was saying.

Terry looked for McCree where they'd been sitting.

The old man was gone.

Forever.

There Really Is a Terry

Judith Richards

"*Summer Lightning* is true and not true," says Judith Richards. There really is a Terry. As a child he was wild and free-spirited and "all boy." That much is true. The name Calder is fiction.

"His real name is Terry Cline," says the author, who has known him and his parents for the past ten years. "Today he's a successful writer. He and his whole family are all great storytellers." *Summer Lightning* seemed to evolve naturally from conversations with them. "The book is based on a lifetime, the family's lifetime. The challenge was to try to write the story from a child's perspective, yet show the other side as well."

The real Terry, Judith Richards says, "was even wilder than the Terry in the book." He had run away from home three or four times by the time he was six. Before he turned seven he had traveled from Florida to Montana all by himself. "He knew what the chalk markings on the boxcars meant, and he knew where all the hobo hangouts were."

Terry himself remembers it all with a half smile. "I gave up on school after one day," he says, "because when I got home the first afternoon, I picked up a book and found that I *still* couldn't read. My running away wasn't because I didn't like home or love my parents. I just had a yen to travel, to see things, to meet people."

It was Terry who helped Judith Richards in her writing career. Nowadays, she and Terry edit each other's manuscripts. "It feels natural to work this way," she says, "and it certainly takes the loneliness out of writing." Their partnership seems likely to endure. Shortly after *Summer Lightning* was published, Terry and Judy announced plans to get married.

TARA KANE

A CONDENSATION OF THE NOVEL BY

GEORGE MARKSTEIN

ILLUSTRATED BY GUY DEEL

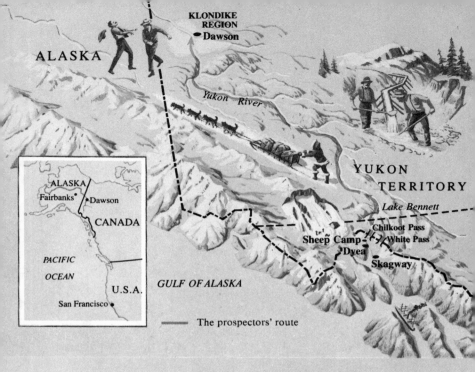

ALASKA

KLONDIKE REGION
●Dawson

Yukon River

YUKON TERRITORY

Lake Bennett

Chilkoot Pass
Sheep Camp
White Pass
Dyea
Skagway

ALASKA
Fairbanks●
●Dawson
CANADA
PACIFIC OCEAN
U.S.A.
San Francisco ●

GULF OF ALASKA

—— The prospectors' route

A young woman journeys to
the Klondike to find something
more valuable than gold.

It was the year Queen Victoria celebrated her diamond jubilee and William McKinley took the oath as the twenty-fifth President of the United States. Air conditioning was patented, the electron was discovered, and the cause of malaria isolated.

In Europe, Spain's prime minister was assassinated by an anarchist, Freud was delving into the mysteries of sex, Stalin was seventeen, and a schoolboy called Adolf Hitler learned the three R's.

It was the year of the Klondike Gold Rush.

It was 1897.

CHAPTER ONE

SHE made a strikingly attractive mourner. Black enhanced Tara Kane; it silhouetted her slim figure and complemented her deep auburn hair. Under the dark veil tears ran down her pale cheeks. Her generous mouth, which like her large oval green eyes reflected her moods, was turned down at the corners. Hers was a private grief she could share with no one and all the sadder for its solitude.

The funeral of her nine-month-old daughter, Gabrielle, had taken place ten days earlier in San Francisco's Laurel Hill Cemetery. The gravedigger, who was scooping out fresh earth nearby, remembered her clearly. It had been an austere burial with only two people present, the woman in black and the minister. No family. No husband. Afterward she had walked off alone, and the gravedigger had wondered who the sad, elegant woman might be.

Now she was back, staring at Gabrielle's grave. Bending down, she placed a small bunch of flowers on the ground that covered the tiny coffin. For a moment she knelt, silent, her eyes blurred with tears. Then, gathering her cloak around her, she stood up and walked off among the bending willows.

Tara looked back only once. At the cemetery gate she stopped, her eyes searching among the rows of graves for where, in the distance, Gabie lay. But the plot was already hidden from sight. She sighed. Tomorrow she would be gone, and there would be no one to visit the forlorn little grave. She turned, raised her head high, and walked out of the cemetery, her face set with determination. What she was about to do was the most desperate decision of her life, but there was no other course.

TARA had hired a hack to take her and her cabin trunk to the ship, but once through the dock gates, movement was impossible. Across a sea of heads she could see the *North Fork*, smoking from its three stacks. Even from this distance she looked what she was, a rusty and battered tramp steamer, more suited for the breaker's yard than a voyage to Alaska.

"Can't go no further," announced the cabby with finality as he dumped her trunk on the sidewalk.

"How am I going to manage?" Tara asked him despairingly.

"That's your problem," he replied as he jumped back into his hack. It was hopeless for her to try to move the trunk herself. None of the hundreds of jostling people took the slightest notice of her. KLONDIKE OR BUST someone had chalked on a warehouse wall, and that seemed to be the goal of all of them. She came near to panicking. She could visualize herself still trapped in this madhouse when the *North Fork* cast off in three hours' time. The ship sounded its steam whistle imperiously. Somebody pushed Tara and she almost fell down.

"Whoa!" said a man she was flung against. "Take it easy." He was large, muscular, and looked like a sailor.

"Please," Tara gasped, "can you get my trunk to the ship? I'll pay you five dollars." She knew she was throwing her money away, but she was so near now that nothing was going to stop her.

"Let's try it," he said, picking up the trunk with a grunt and hoisting it on his shoulder.

Slowly the man began to force his way through the dense mob. Tara followed and tried not to see the angry, harassed faces that flashed in front of her. People dug her in the ribs, stepped on her feet, jostled her. Grimly she kept a firm hold on the valise and purse she was carrying, and forged on.

Suddenly from behind her came shouts of protest and howls of rage. She heard the cracking of a whip, and then a wagon began to force its way through, the driver furiously lashing people who blocked him. In the wagon Tara saw dozens of dogs chained together, barking and snarling as they were driven to the ship.

The *North Fork* loomed over the pierhead, already crowds of people lining the railings. At the gangway, the man put her trunk down. "That's it," he said. "The rest is up to you."

"I'm so grateful to you," she said, pressing five dollars into his hand. "Thank you so much."

"Going to the Yukon?" he asked, smiling wryly. "Good luck! Hope you survive." Then he was engulfed by the crowd.

Close up, the soot-encrusted *North Fork* appeared even more squalid. "I'm a passenger," Tara shouted to a villainous-looking seaman who was blocking the gangway. "I need help with my trunk."

"Nobody more comes aboard," the man growled. "We're full."

"You have room for me," Tara cried. "I'm joining my husband." She held up the precious ticket for which she had queued for hours in a mile-long line of Alaska-bound prospectors trying to get passage north before the winter freeze-up.

"You're too late." The man grinned unpleasantly. "But maybe I can fix you up. For a little extra."

All Tara wanted was to get on that deck, and it was only a few yards away. If it needed a bribe, so be it. She took twenty dollars out of her purse and gave it to him.

"Okay, I'll get you on board." He turned and shouted to a sailor. "Hey, Rusky, get this trunk."

Tara followed the sailor up the long gangway, each step leading her into a frightening unknown. Yet she felt strangely elated. Despite all odds she'd got a ticket, was on the boat, and soon she would be on her way.

On deck every inch of space seemed to be occupied. Neighing horses reared and kicked in wooden pens that had been erected as temporary stables. Rows of dog cages were roped to the deck, the animals inside snarling and snapping. Overhead swayed crates and other cargo being hoisted aboard. The sight of the crowd still pushing toward the gangway was frightening.

"I want to go to my cabin," Tara said to the sailor.

"The captain will fix you up." He nodded at a man with a walrus mustache standing near a lifeboat. Unconcerned about the chaos on his ship, the captain leaned against the railing and puffed at his pipe.

"Captain?" said Tara, walking up to him.

"Yes, ma'am, Captain Swain," he said, taking the pipe out of his mouth. "What's the trouble?" The familiar way he eyed her made Tara's hackles rise.

"I want to know where my cabin is. I have a reservation."

"All by yourself?" There was something insulting about his manner. "There'll be a surcharge. One hundred dollars."

"Don't be ridiculous," she exclaimed. "I've paid my passage."

"Ladies on their own are a problem. Not easy to fit females into this vessel. We're not built for it. You can see for yourself."

"I've already had to bribe one of your men—"

"My men don't take bribes," Swain cut in. "If you don't like this ship, get off it. I'll have your luggage removed."

Tara was outraged. "If you put me ashore, I'll call the police!" she cried so fiercely that even he seemed shaken. "I'll have you arrested, the whole lot of you! You won't sail without me, I promise you, Captain Swain."

He sucked at his pipe, then asked, "What's your name?"

"Mrs. Kane."

"Well, Mrs. Kane, there's no need to fly off the handle. I guess we can squeeze you in. The only question is, ma'am, do you have the hundred bucks?"

By now she knew she had no choice. She wouldn't be able to get another ship for weeks, not in the middle of the Gold Rush, with men fighting for a passage to the Klondike. "All right," Tara agreed through gritted teeth as she counted out the money.

"Welcome aboard, Mrs. Kane." He smiled, stuffing the dollars into his pocket. "I'll have you shown to your quarters."

"I want my own cabin," Tara warned. "First class," she added. "I've paid enough."

"First class it is," the captain said. He ordered a seaman over. "Take this lady and her trunk to cabin four."

Tara turned and followed the man below. The stench in the bowels of the ship was nauseating. Here on the lower deck, as everywhere else, soiled sawdust and wood shavings were strewn on the floor to soak up all manner of refuse. Tara felt faint.

"Here you are, cabin four," the seaman said, stopping before a door and kicking it open.

Tara stepped into what she had imagined would be her own cozy cabin. Instead it was what had apparently been a storeroom converted into a dormitory for four people. The woodwork was not painted, and the only illumination came from two oil lamps swinging from the low ceiling. It was shabby, rough, and cramped.

"This can't be right," Tara cried as the seaman dragged in her trunk. "I'm traveling first-class."

A broad grin spread across the sailor's face. "We ain't got first class on this tub. Unless this is it. You're lucky, ma'am. You got a bunk, and there's only four in here, being all ladies. The men are stacked ten to a cabin half this size. We got three hundred passengers and sleeping berths for only half that. So maybe you got first class." He closed the door, leaving an alarmed Tara looking around her new home.

The other occupants had already moved in. Flamboyant and garish clothes were strewn about, and Tara smelled the odor of cheap perfume. One bunk in the corner did not seem to have been claimed. A thin straw palliasse served as a mattress. There was no pillow, and the single blanket was so dirty that the thought of it covering her made Tara squirm.

From outside there was laughter, and then the door flew open. The two women who entered the cabin stopped still when they saw Tara. "What have we here?" asked the taller of the two. She was blond, in her twenties, her face smothered with thick makeup.

Her companion was fat, and her eye shadow and red lipstick did nothing to enhance her sweaty face. The top of her dress was undone, and she carried a half-empty bottle of gin.

"I'll be sharing with you," Tara said, swallowing hard.

"Well!" said the blonde. "What do you think of that, Flo?"

"You'd better find somewhere else, honey." Flo hiccupped. "We're full up. There's no room."

Tara was at the end of her tether. "Believe me, I don't want to be here either, but I'm staying," she said, sitting on her bunk.

"What's your name?" Flo asked.

"Tara Kane."

Flo had spotted her wedding ring. "Married, are you?"

"I'm sailing to join my husband."

Flo sat down on the bunk beside Tara. "Well, Tara, you got to understand," she explained. "There's seven of us using this cabin."

"Seven!" Tara echoed, horrified.

"Only me, Maggie, and Belle sleep here, but us and our friends will be using it. Connie, Lola, Pearl, and Frenchy. We need this shack for business. We got to earn our passage, honey."

Tara knew that if she gave up these few feet of space she was lost. "I can see your problem," she said quietly. "But this is where I stay."

Flo studied Tara. "Okay," she said. "But don't say I didn't warn you, *Mrs.* Kane. The girls may not take it kindly."

"All right, Flo. Thank you for making it so clear. I will try to cause you and your friends as little trouble as possible."

Flo looked at her, amazed. Her experience on the Barbary Coast had not led her to expect politeness. She stood up. "Let's go, Maggie," she said to the blonde.

"The stuck-up little prude," Maggie hissed.

To Tara's surprise, Flo turned on her friend. "Just leave it," she said. "She knows the score."

After they had gone, Tara sat staring at the wall, utterly miserable. The prospect of long weeks on this ghastly ship had been bad enough, but how was she going to cope with seven prostitutes in a floating brothel? She sighed and thought, One day at a time, somehow I'll learn to live with everything.

She went up on deck to get some fresh air, but the confusion and noise were as great as ever. The ship's whistles shrieked, and underneath her feet the engines began to thump. The mooring ropes were released, and then, suddenly, amid a great cheer, the *North Fork* slowly began to move. Gradually it edged away from the dockside, from San Francisco, out toward the Golden Gate, toward the ocean, toward Alaska.

Tara stayed at the rail for a long time watching the docks and harbor front recede. Her elation had gone. Not even the thought that she had started the long journey to find Daniel could ease her melancholy. She opened her purse to look for the little compass he had given her.

"Think of me, look at the needle," he had said. "It will always point to where I am."

As Tara held it in her hand, the tiny needle quivered, but as always, its direction was northward. To the Klondike. To Daniel. To the future.

LIFE aboard the *North Fork* grew grimmer with every passing day. The weather was rough, and the overloaded ship had difficulty riding a storm. Every wave caused her to roll unmercifully.

The ship's facilities were nonexistent. Toilets were buckets, and washing had to be done in dirty tubs of seawater. Only when Tara stood on deck and the salt water swept over the rails, dousing all of them, was there a moment of tangy, freezing freshness.

By the second week she gave up sleeping in the cabin at night because she was too often awakened by giggles from the other berths. She resorted to sleeping in her bunk during the day and walking around the deck at night, even though that was also nerve-racking. Time after time Tara was scared by the men who stood in the shadows. Rough hands would reach out for her and she would run for a better lit part of the ship.

Her experiences with Captain Swain and his crew made Tara abandon her plan to place her money in the care of the ship's purser. She secreted her roll of bills in a little pouch, which she pinned to the inside of her bodice.

Flo noticed the pouch one day when Tara was changing her dress. "What do you keep in there, the family jewels?" she asked.

"Nothing," shrugged Tara. "Just a couple of trinkets." She could feel herself blushing. She wasn't a good liar. Flo exchanged a look with Maggie but said nothing more.

Mealtimes on the *North Fork* were disgusting. The saloon also served as the dining room. The first time Tara went to eat, the sight of the overcrowded saloon festooned with carcasses hung from hooks in the ceiling made her rush out, and for several days she could not return. Then hunger became too much. She nerved herself to face the ordeal and managed to find a seat. A plate of congealed stew was slung at her, but despite her hunger she could not bring herself to eat.

Sitting next to her was a bespectacled man in a crumpled city suit. He pushed his own plate away, then gave her a sympathetic smile. "Awful, isn't it?" He had a distinct foreign accent.

Tara nodded. He appeared to be in his late thirties, and had a trim mustache and small sideburns. Tara liked him immediately, especially the laugh lines around his clear, blue eyes.

"I wish I could force it down," she said, shuddering.

"I don't think we need go hungry," the man said. "Follow me."

On deck, Tara took a deep breath. "I know," commiserated the man. "I feel like that myself. Now close your eyes."

She studied him for a second, then shut her eyes.

"Open them!" he commanded. He was grinning when she looked at him. In his hand were two shiny green apples. "One for you, one for me."

She bit into the hard apple and it tasted delicious. "You're very kind," Tara said. "Thank you very much, Mr. . . ."

"Ernst Hart," he announced, giving a little bow. He finished his apple and tossed the core over the side. "You have not told me *your* name."

"Mrs. Kane."

"Oh. You are traveling with your husband?"

She shook her head. "No. I am joining him."

"In the Klondike?" He seemed surprised. "By yourself?"

"Mr. Hart, this is 1897, not the Middle Ages. Women can look after themselves quite well, you know."

He smiled. "You must understand. I am from Germany, and there a woman's place is in the kitchen and the nursery. Not on a ship like this. Why did you not go with your husband? It would have been simpler."

"I . . . I had to look after our baby," she explained falteringly. "She died. She had meningitis. It was so sudden, after he'd left. He doesn't even know."

"I'm sorry," Hart murmured gently. "Your husband . . . he has found gold?"

"I haven't heard but, knowing Daniel, I'm sure he's doing well."

"Good." Hart seemed pleased by her confidence. "I hope he becomes a millionaire." He paused. "Tell me. What made him go?"

"What makes any of them go?" asked Tara a little wistfully. He followed her glance. All kinds crowded the decks: clerks in city clothes, roughnecks from the slums, fresh-faced students, hard-bitten adventurers; each one counting the days until he would step ashore at Dyea, at the foot of Chilkoot Pass, and begin the trail.

"Gold fever," explained Tara.

Hart frowned. "He just left you and the baby?"

"It wasn't like that," Tara said. "He provided for us, and he did what he thought was right. I wouldn't have dreamed of standing in his way. If it hadn't been for the baby, I would have gone with him." Her lips trembled for a moment, remembering when Daniel had first told her he was going to get their pot of gold. She had been heartbroken at the thought of separation from him for at least a year. But he had pointed out that to achieve anything in life one had to make sacrifices. And what rewards that year would bring! They could buy a house on Nob Hill, Gabie could have a private nurse, they could take trips to Europe. . . .

She pulled herself together. "What about you, Mr. Hart? Are you off to make a fortune too?"

"No, Mrs. Kane. I'm not interested in gold. I go looking for people."

He saw her puzzled expression.

"I am a photographer. I wish to record this madness for posterity. What Mathew Brady did for your Civil War, I want to do for this Gold Rush, so that people will always be able to see what it was like." He stopped, a little embarrassed. "It must seem foolish. Here is everybody out to become a millionaire, and all I want to do is take photographs."

"Not at all," Tara replied. "I think it sounds fascinating."

He glanced at her sharply. Then he nodded. "Yes. I think perhaps you do understand." He pulled out his watch. "Excuse me. I must see that everything is in order." He had arranged, he explained, to store his equipment in the purser's office.

They saw a lot of each other after that. They walked together on the deck, and if they found the space, they sat together and talked. He had secreted a little hoard of food, and he often produced delicious tidbits for her—a bar of chocolate or even a piece of cheese.

Hart loved studying people. When Flo and Maggie flounced by,

Hart looked at them, intrigued. *"That's* what I want to photograph," he said. "When I get up to the Klondike I want to photograph the street girls, the saloons, the gamblers."

Tara smiled at him. "First, Ernst, we have to get there."

"What are you going to do when we do arrive?" he asked.

"Get to Skagway as quickly as possible. My husband is prospecting somewhere around there."

Hart's eyes opened wide. "But my dear lady, there is no gold at Skagway. To find gold you have to go to the creeks, hundreds of miles to the north."

For a moment Tara was stunned. "I always thought . . ." she began, then stopped. "Well, Skagway's where he made for, and I shall find him."

"I can see you love him very much," Hart said. "To come all this way, to put up with this terrible journey . . ." He stared down at the ocean. "One day I will find a woman like you. Until then, I suppose, I have my camera."

ONE morning a few days later, Tara and Hart stood watching the sea. He seemed to be preoccupied.

"What's the matter, Ernst?" Tara asked.

He glanced around nervously. "I don't want to frighten you."

Tara stiffened. "What is it?" she asked apprehensively.

He hesitated, then said, "Everybody on the ship is in great danger. We may all be blown sky-high at any moment."

"What do you mean?"

"Last night I couldn't find a place to sleep. Two roughnecks had taken my bunk. There was no room on deck, but I managed to squeeze into one of the cargo holds. It was pitch-dark, so I struck a match. I saw stacks of wooden cases. I took a closer look and they are all marked 'Danger—High Explosive.' Tara, we are sitting on hundreds of pounds of dynamite."

Tara stared at him. "What can we do?" she whispered.

"Nothing. We are trapped."

They both looked out at the ocean, where the occasional pieces of drift ice heralded the distant northern shores, still days away. The *North Fork* rolled uneasily in the swell.

That afternoon, desperate for sleep, Tara made her way down to the smelly little cabin. Flo and Maggie were there with one of their friends, Frenchy, a dark-haired girl with narrow catlike eyes, who wore huge brass earrings.

They were all chattering, but when Tara entered, they lapsed into silence. "You haven't met our lodger, have you?" Flo asked Frenchy. "Our Mrs. Kane."

"No. But I heard about you," Frenchy replied, giving Tara an unfriendly glance.

Tara squeezed through to her bunk, thinking how nice it would be if she could have a bath and curl up on a soft mattress between clean sheets for twelve uninterrupted hours of sleep. But existence on the *North Fork* and a growing awareness of how primitive her new life would be were gradually teaching Tara to look on as luxuries what she had formerly considered essentials.

She was just about to lie down when Frenchy started shouting, "Maggie, where did you get that?" Frenchy tugged at a thin gold chain around Maggie's neck, and the chain broke.

"Why, you lousy rat," Maggie screeched, and slapped the dark-haired girl across the face. They flew at each other, spitting and screaming. Frenchy grabbed the blonde's hair, and Maggie scrabbled for her face with long, clawing fingers. They staggered to and fro in the tiny cabin, squealing and cursing.

"For heaven's sake, stop it," Tara cried. "Flo, stop them."

Flo gave Tara a contemptuous smile. "If you're so bothered, why don't *you* stop it, Mrs. Kane?"

"All right, I will." Tara jumped off her bunk and grabbed the two struggling women, trying to separate them. Suddenly she found herself in a tangle of arms, legs, and bodies. Somebody hit her hard. Tara, in blind pain, struck out, and then realized that Flo had also joined in the fight and now she was struggling against all three women. Somebody kicked her, and somebody else knelt on her and was clawing at her bosom.

Then, as if by a signal, the fighting stopped. The women got to their feet. "Okay, girls, that's enough," panted Flo.

Tara slowly stood up. Her lip was bleeding, and her whole body ached. As she crawled onto her bunk, the three women started drinking from a bottle and giggling. Now and then one of them glanced at Tara, and then they all burst into ugly laughter.

"Let's go, Flo," Frenchy said.

"Yeah," Maggie agreed. "Leave madam to cry herself to sleep."

When they had gone, Tara lay there, her body throbbing. She smoothed out her rumpled dress. Then, as if she had had a sudden electric shock, she sat upright. Her pouch was gone. Her money had vanished. She could see the rip in her bodice where the pouch had been torn away. They had planned it all.

Tara went at once to the bridge. "Yes, Mrs. Kane?" asked Captain Swain. He was sweeping the horizon through binoculars.

"I have been robbed. All my money's been stolen," Tara told him, incensed.

"That is an extremely serious allegation," he said, lowering his binoculars. "Who is supposed to have done this?"

"The women in my cabin."

"Have you any proof?" Swain asked.

"They've got my money," Tara insisted doggedly.

"You do get confused about such things, don't you, Mrs. Kane? I remember you wildly accused one of my men of extortion when you came aboard."

"Captain Swain, I remember very well what happened when I came on board," Tara said.

He cleared his throat. "Mr. Jensen," he shouted, "take over. I have some business to attend to. Come along, Mrs. Kane."

She followed him below to cabin four. Her roommates had returned. Flo was in her bunk, and Maggie was arranging her hair. "Do come in, Captain," Maggie said. "We are honored."

Swain sat down on the one chair. "Your fellow passenger here is alleging that you ladies stole her money," he announced.

"Mrs. Kane, how could you?" Flo gasped, looking shocked.

Tara stood her ground firmly. "They are thieves."

"Mrs. Kane, kindly observe the basics of polite behavior," Swain huffed. "These ladies are passengers on my ship."

"I want my one hundred and sixty-five dollars," Tara demanded. "It was torn from my bodice. I kept it in a pouch pinned there."

Swain was impressed. He gave the prostitutes a closer look. "That's a lot of money. You say they attacked you and took it?"

"Not exactly attacked me. They staged a fight, and in the confusion—" Tara faltered. It wasn't easy to explain.

"She is telling a pack of lies," Flo interrupted. "The truth is that this woman drinks. When she is under the influence she becomes violent. It has made life very difficult for us, sharing this cabin. She attacked my friend Maggie. She has the strength of three men, and we eventually had to use force. Now she is trying to get back at us."

Swain gave Tara a cold look. "Well? What do you say to that?"

Tara shrugged. "What's the point, Captain? You don't want to believe me."

"We are quite prepared to have our things searched, Captain," offered Flo.

"I don't think that will be necessary. I am quite satisfied. Mrs. Kane," Swain growled, "I'm evicting you from this cabin."

"I paid my passage," Tara cried. "It's my right—"

"You've got no rights, lady. I make the decisions. These ladies are entitled to comfort and privacy, not wild accusations."

"Where am I supposed to sleep?" Tara cried.

He grinned savagely. "That's your problem now. I imagine you'll find a corner to bed down."

Tara turned and left the cabin. Hart found her on deck, huddled against a horse pen, trying to find shelter from the bitter northerly wind. *"Gott im Himmel,* what has happened to you?" he asked when he saw her swollen lip.

"Oh, Ernst." Tara burst into tears. "My money's been stolen. Everything I have." And then she told him the whole story.

Hart stood up. "You wait here." He was back after a few minutes with a small tin. He gently brushed her lip with some ointment, and then said, "Give me your hand."

Hesitatingly she held out her hand, and he pressed something into it. She opened it, and found he had given her thirty dollars.

"It's not much, but I haven't got a lot left."

"I can't take it," Tara protested.

Hart drew himself up stiffly. "The matter is closed," he said. "It is my pleasure and my privilege as a gentleman."

Even in her misery Tara had to smile at his stilted manner. "All right, thank you. It's very good of you. As soon as I meet up with Daniel, I will pay you back."

They had been at sea nearly three weeks, and although it was only the middle of September, the weather grew harsher and the cold more intense as they sailed north. Tara had become one of the homeless, constantly on the hunt after dark for some free space to bed down in. When she had found a place, sleep remained uneasy throughout the night. Once Tara woke up to find a man's leering face a few inches from hers. She shot up and ran off, and for the rest of the bitter, freezing night she walked around the deck, too frightened to settle down anywhere else.

She felt filthy and uncomfortable and was ashamed of her appearance—her hair unwashed, her face drawn and tired, her eyes bloodshot from lack of sleep.

"We must sleep together," Hart said.

She didn't know what to say.

"No, no," he protested, reddening. "I do not mean like that. Do you think me to be so dishonorable as to take advantage of you? It's that you will not be molested if you are with a man."

But that night there was no sign of Hart. She finally found him in a corner of the saloon. He was slumped over a table, an empty bottle rolling to and fro in front of him. "Ernst," she whispered, shaking his shoulder.

He opened one bleary eye and stared up at her, uncomprehending. "Come and sit down, Tara," he invited woozily.

"No," she said. "I'll see you in the morning."

He lurched to his feet. "Nonsense. I will go with you." He insisted on coming on deck with her, she having to support him as they looked for somewhere to sleep.

Eventually, in a passageway, Tara managed to find space between two snoring men. She helped Hart lie down, then sat beside him. He leaned against her, and in a moment he was deep asleep.

Tara sat open-eyed, staring into space. "I love you so very much," Daniel had said. "Fate cannot keep us apart for long."

"And I love you," Tara whispered into the darkness. Everything would be all right once this terrible voyage was over.

CHAPTER TWO

WHEN at last, after four weeks, the Alaskan land appeared, it looked inhospitable. Tara shivered as she surveyed the mountain-locked inlet of the Lynn Canal, just off the supply center of Dyea, where the ship had anchored for the night. She had expected some kind of port, but there were no piers, no harbor front, only the beach, and some tents and rough wooden shacks in the distance.

Disembarkation was barred until morning. "If you stay up here, you'll catch your death," Hart said, when he found a half-frozen Tara standing by the rail in the twilight, looking at the shore.

They went below and found the saloon packed with people. Bottles of whiskey passed from hand to hand. Toasts were drunk to the future, to each other, to wealth and success, and to gold. Somebody produced a mouth organ, others started clapping in tempo with the tune.

Flo and Maggie were in their element. Flo's lipstick was smeared, and she was shrieking with laughter. Maggie was locked in an embrace with a thickset individual, and Frenchy danced by herself, holding up her skirt for all the world to see her knickers.

Suddenly there was a scuffle. Two men were at each other, and one of them knocked against an oil lamp swinging from a hook in the low ceiling. It all happened so quickly that many people were not even aware of it.

Frenchy screamed, and Tara, horrified, saw her skirt on fire, and then the rest of her flared up like a torch. The oil lamp, lying smashed on the floor, sent a stream of burning oil cascading across the sawdust.

Tara looked around for a blanket, a rug, anything to wrap around the pyre that had been the dark-haired Frenchy. But already people were screaming and falling over each other as they tried to escape the flames that began to spread.

Hart grabbed Tara and dragged her up the companionway to the deck. There was a wild stampede of people behind them, clawing and fighting to escape from the blazing saloon.

Tara vaguely heard a bell clanging, and then smoke began to swirl across the deck. "You have to get off the ship," Hart yelled at her. "You must swim ashore."

"I can't," she cried. "I can't. . . ."

"Don't you understand?" Hart shouted at her. "The *dynamite!*"

He pulled her to the rail. All she could see was the darkness of the sea. "No, Ernst," Tara screamed.

Around them the ship had turned into bedlam, horses desperately kicking out, dogs howling, smoke pouring across the deck, and the ugly crackling sound of flames growing louder.

"Go on, jump," Hart shouted. "It's your only chance."

She stared at him wide-eyed, her legs paralyzed. Roughly Hart lifted her over the *North Fork's* rail. Disbelieving, she found herself in midair, plunging down into the black abyss. When she struck the icy water it was as if her breath had been cut off. She was numb with cold and panic. She started thrashing about in blind fear, then began to swim away from the ship. She heard a thundering, roaring sound, followed by a huge flash which lit up the whole sea. She blacked out.

Tara never knew who it was that had saved her. She never saw the boats that had set off from the beach to pick up survivors, but for long afterward she was haunted by the memory of the water around her lit by the blazing ship, and the terrifying screams.

The stinging pain of her face being slapped roused her. Hart, white-faced, soaking, was kneeling by her side, shaking her. It was daylight, and she was lying in a freezing pool of water on a beach. "On your feet," he ordered, putting his arm around her and pulling her upright. "Walk. Keep moving."

Gradually sensation returned. She started hobbling along, supported by Hart. "The ship?" she asked.

"There is no ship. It blew up." He was staggering, dragging his big camera case and other gear with him. "A boat came alongside just before the explosion. I threw everything in."

She was still dazed. "How many were saved?"

He pointed to the few dozen survivors crouched around fires on the beach.

Slowly they trekked toward the little huddle of habitations that was Dyea. For weeks it had been the name that represented to Tara the gateway to the Klondike and the first step to Daniel. She had thought it would be a bustling, lively community. What she saw were clusters of tents a quarter of a mile inland, and then groups of rickety-looking wooden shacks. The place was littered with rubbish, broken-down carts, and abandoned cabins. It was dreary and unwelcoming.

The people who had survived the *North Fork* straggled in the same direction as Tara and Hart, the lucky ones weighed down by belongings they had managed to salvage. All Tara had left was the purse she had pinned to her dress, with the little compass, thirty dollars of borrowed money, her mother's silver locket on a chain, and the icy, wet clothes she stood in.

Dyea had one main thoroughfare, a glorified muddy track, proclaimed on a rough wooden sign to be TRAIL STREET. It was flanked by shacks that led to a frozen river. Beyond that was a narrow canyon that rose toward a pass.

"There's the Chilkoot Pass," Hart said. "The route I'll take."

There was one solidly constructed building on the street. GENERAL STORE read a notice over the entrance. Hart led the way up the wooden steps, Tara wearily trailing behind him.

Inside the store there were great piles of food and clothing. Stacked against the walls were sleighs and rolled-up camping equipment. But above all, there was an enormous stove in the center of the floor, with the chimney pipe going straight to the roof. They went over to the stove, holding out their hands.

A fat man in rubber boots and a checked shirt waddled over. "The lady needs some clothes," Hart said to him.

"Help yourself," he invited, indicating the store. "Got most things here. Better get some mukluks too."

"Mukluks?"

"Boots. Five dollars," he said.

"That's a lot of money," Hart said.

"Don't need to have 'em. Lose your toes instead. Up to you."

Tara selected some clothes from the stacked piles. "Where do I change?" she asked.

"Right there, lady," the fat man said. "Behind those sacks."

Tara felt herself go red. She grabbed the clothes and went to the corner where cases and sacks came up to her shoulders. As quickly as she could she got out of her wet, torn dress. Wearing rough woolen long johns and no corset felt strange. She emerged finally, her whole appearance changed. Except for her auburn hair, which hung damply around her shoulders, she looked boyish in a checked shirt, sweater, a parka trimmed with wolverine, and heavy flannel-lined trousers. She wore a pair of mukluks, heavy, watertight, and very comfortable, like overgrown moccasins.

"Fits you perfect," the fat man said. "Don't it?"

"How much?" Tara asked coldly.

"Well now, guess twenty-eight dollars will cover it."

As Tara counted out the dollar bills the fat man asked Hart, "Is she your woman?"

"Yes," Hart said.

She was annoyed until she realized why he had said it. In this land a woman had to be owned—or she was free game.

"Man ought to pay for his woman," the storekeeper said. "Otherwise somebody might jump his claim."

"Mind your own business," Tara said fiercely.

"We need a hotel for tonight," Hart interjected.

"Try the Klondike, down the street," the fat man said. "Beds twenty-five cents a night. Sort of rough, but it's warm and dry. No lice either."

The Klondike Lodging House was a two-story timber building, across the street from the Ritz Bar. Its proprietor, Joe Gibbons, evidently did not believe in home comforts. The floors had no covering, the stairs were rickety, the tables stained, the plates tin, the cutlery bent and broken. The place had never been painted.

Some kind of meeting was going on. Gibbons, a man who boasted proudly that he had not had a bath for twenty-one years, presided from a table in the center of the room near the big stove, which was surrounded by spittoons. Spread on the table in front of him were boots, pots and pans, a sleeping bag, some field glasses. Rough-looking men were lolling about on chairs, drinking.

Gibbons hammered on the table with the butt of a pistol. "Okay," he yelled, "what am I bid for these boots? We got to bury Tommy good and decent."

"Any blood on them?" called out a voice.

"You ought to know better." Gibbons grinned. "He wasn't shot in the feet. Fifty cents, anybody?" Tara wondered what had happened to the dead man, how he came to be shot.

Gibbons held up the dead man's sleeping bag. "Kept him dry and snug," he announced. "Clean too. No bugs."

To Tara's amazement, Hart raised his hand. "One dollar, please."

"Okay. Going for a dollar once, twice. Sold."

"What did you buy that for?" Tara asked.

"You need a sleeping bag," Hart replied matter-of-factly.

Gradually Gibbons auctioned off the late Tommy's belongings. When everything had been sold, Gibbons counted the money. "Well, fellows," he announced jovially, "I don't calculate there's sufficient to bury Tommy, but we got enough to adjourn and drink his health. On the house."

"They even cheat a dead man," Tara remarked bitterly.

"It doesn't matter to him," Hart said. "He's past caring, whoever he was."

Hart went over and asked Gibbons for two rooms for the night.

"Rooms? Place is full up. But if you can find space, you can bed down on the floor. For two dollars each."

"At the store they said twenty-five cents for a bed," Hart protested. "What do you mean, two dollars to sleep on the floor?"

"Take it or leave it," Gibbons grunted.

That night, lying on the hard wooden floorboards in the dead Tommy's sleeping bag, surrounded by strange, snoring men, Tara made a promise to herself. She was going to survive. Tomorrow, for the first time in this new world, she would be completely on her own. She would be sorry to say good-by to Hart, and also a little afraid. Until she met up with Daniel in Skagway, there would be no one to help, no one to protect her. The prospect made her feel apprehensive, but the challenge excited her too.

CHAPTER THREE

TARA could hear hymn singing. A drum was beating in time and someone was shaking a tambourine. A handful of voices croaked about Our Lord in ages past.

When she emerged from the lodging house, the group was standing in front of the Ritz Bar. The singing had stopped, and a tall, gaunt man with deep-set staring eyes was declaiming as he thumped a Bible in his hand. The big drum was strapped to a sad-looking Indian, and beside the tall man stood a buxom woman, her lips a thin, disapproving line. She was the one with the tambourine. Next to her stood another Indian carrying a banner reading BISHOP BEAUCHAMP's KLONDIKE CRUSADE.

Their audience consisted of two grinning prospectors chewing tobacco, a trapper swaying slightly in an alcoholic haze, and another Indian. A few feet away was Hart, camera on tripod, cloth over his head and shoulders, photographing the group.

"The moment of salvation has come for you sinners," cried the tall man. "I have come to guide you to salvation, to bring the word of the Lord to these unfortunate heathen, and to return to them this fine land which is being corrupted by the men of Babylon and their painted harlots."

Bishop Beauchamp looked around challengingly. The prospectors went on chewing their tobacco undeterred. "You miserable pagans," the bishop cried. "You have joined Satan in pursuit of the evil yellow metal, but all the gold in the world will not buy your way out of the hellfire that is to come."

"Amen," the woman intoned.

"Today the crusade will depart for Skagway on the first stage of its great work," the bishop announced. "Come travel with us and help us to raise the banner of the Lord in that den of iniquity."

Tara swallowed and took a step forward. "I'll go to Skagway with you," she called out.

"A sinner repenteth," the bishop cried. "Lord, I thank thee."

Tara bristled, but she knew her great chance was here. These people would take her to Skagway.

"What's your name?" the grim woman demanded.

"Tara Kane."

"Welcome," the bishop said, smiling. "Perhaps you had to come here to see the light."

"What are you doing in Dyea?" asked the woman. She did not seem utterly convinced that Tara had seen any light.

"I'm joining my husband," Tara said. "But a woman traveling on her own needs respectable company."

The bishop's hard, fanatical eyes stared straight into hers. "We trust that you *are* truly seeking to do the Lord's work. And remember, those who take His name in vain shall burn eternally in hell's fire."

"Pack your things on one of the sleds. We leave at twelve," said the woman, who Tara gathered must be the bishop's wife.

Later, in the lodging house, Tara said good-by to Hart. He embraced her. "Look after yourself, Tara," he said. "You're a very special woman." He pressed her to him.

"Good luck on your way north, Ernst." She kissed him and left him looking after her for a long while.

Three sleds were drawn up on Trail Street, each with a team of dogs. One of the sleds was loaded with wooden crates lassoed securely together. "We have a precious cargo," the bishop explained. "Holy Scriptures. Paid for by our benefactor in Skagway. He also built our mission hall there."

"He must be a very generous man," Tara remarked.

The bishop nodded. "Mr. Jefferson Smith is a gentleman. There are some left, even in this wilderness. Now, you will ride with

Mrs. Beauchamp," he continued. "Matthew will drive your team."

Tara eased herself in beside the large woman. Matthew, the Indian who had beaten the drum, stood behind them controlling the four pairs of growling huskies. The other Indian took the rear sled loaded with the crates and the luggage.

The bishop drove the front sled. "Mush!" he yelled, and Tara held on as the little cavalcade shot off, the huskies yelping excitedly, a whip cracking, and the wind blowing in their faces.

It was a great moment for Tara, and she felt exhilarated. Hart had said the dogsleds could cover thirty miles a day, which meant they would be in Skagway in three or four hours—after all these months of waiting.

Mrs. Beauchamp interrupted her thoughts. "Does your family approve of your traveling in this wild territory?" she questioned.

"Both my parents are dead," Tara said.

"I'm sorry," Mrs. Beauchamp apologized. Then she pressed on. "Where is your husband? He's not a gold prospector, I trust."

Tara hesitated. "He's a Mountie. Up north," she lied.

Mrs. Beauchamp shot her a peculiar look. "But they're not allowed to marry."

"He's an officer," Tara said haughtily.

"Tell me, can you teach Sunday school?"

"Why of course I can," Tara said.

"Good. Mrs. Constantine and I—"

"Mrs. Constantine?"

"I'd have thought you'd have known. *Inspector* Constantine's wife. He commands the Mounted Police detachment in Dawson. She and I have a great problem finding helpers. We are looking for somebody to assist us—"

"Mrs. Beauchamp," Tara said hastily, "I don't want to make a decision right now."

Mrs. Beauchamp lapsed into a frosty silence.

The convoy of sleds made good time over the hard, frozen snow, and in the bright sunshine even the cold seemed less harsh. For the first time Tara saw the real beauty of Alaska, snowcapped mountains and cascading waterfalls.

Suddenly they were in Skagway, heralded by huts and tents and timber buildings. It was a makeshift, rough sprawl inhabited by thousands of people. The main street was named Broadway.

Tara could see the landing stage, with a couple of steamers at anchor. All around her the snow had been churned into mud by carts and wagons. There were innumerable tree stumps, standing mutely beside the huts that had been built out of their timber.

Many of the signs were bizarre: EGGS FRIED IN BEER—$1.50, read one. A log building had an old pair of trousers slung on a line in the front, with MEALS daubed on the seat in white paint.

The convoy came to a halt in front of a little wooden hut which had SKAGWAY MISSION painted on it. The hut was completely over-shadowed by a two-story building next to it, a garish sign identifying it as THE PALACE OF FORBIDDEN DELIGHTS.

At the door of the mission stood a burly man in a black hat with a broad brim, and a thin string tie. As the sleds came to a halt, he walked forward, smiling, and greeted Beauchamp.

"The Reverend Charles Bowers," explained the bishop, introducing Tara. There was something suspicious about the man's glittering eyes, his smile. He was the last person she would have taken to be a clergyman. And the last person she would have trusted. She was quite sure "Reverend" was assumed.

"May I unload the precious cargo?" asked Bowers diffidently.

"Of course." The bishop rubbed his hands. "Tell me, how is our benefactor?"

"Mr. Smith is well," Bowers said. He snapped his fingers, and the two Indians started to unload the third sled, piled high with crates marked FRAGILE—BIBLES.

Bowers courteously led the bishop and his wife into the small mission hall. He looked back at Tara.

"Won't you join us?" he invited.

"In a moment," Tara said. To her surprise, the men didn't carry the cargo into the mission hall but marched straight into a back door of The Palace of Forbidden Delights. Tara grabbed her sleeping bag, stuffed with her belongings, and followed them.

The saloon inside was like a barn, with a long bar running the length of the room. A bull-like bartender was counting out a wad of dollars for the two Indians, who had stacked the crates in front of the bar. Two other men began breaking them open. Each crate contained at least two dozen bottles of whiskey—and no Bibles. But this aroused no curiosity. Evidently it was a normal delivery.

A few men were lounging about the saloon, drinking or playing

131

cards. "Won't you join me in a drink of mountain tea?" a soft voice asked.

Tara turned and saw Bowers standing beside her, grinning. He was much better suited to this setting than to his role as a cleric. He signaled to the bartender. "Two of the best."

Tara didn't trust him, but she liked something about this rogue. He didn't pretend with her. "No, thank you. But can you tell me why they said our cargo was Bibles?" she asked.

"Bless you, child," he said. "Don't you know hooch is illegal in this territory? We look to the good bishop to bring it in. He brings us all kinds of good things, unknowingly. Like you."

"My husband's here," Tara said, reading his thoughts. "I've come to join him. Do you know a man named Daniel Kane?"

"Never heard of him," Bowers said.

"I'm sure he's here," Tara insisted. She turned to leave.

"Where are you off to?" Bowers asked.

"The U.S. marshal," she replied.

When she entered his office, Marshal Colson had his feet on the desk and was filing his fingernails. "Are you the marshal?" Tara asked doubtfully.

"Yeah," he grunted.

Tara cleared her throat. "I'm looking for my husband," she announced. "He arrived here early in August. On the steamship *Humboldt* from San Francisco. How can I find him?"

The marshal scratched his stomach. "I don't know. He'll have moved on, lady, most likely. Nobody stays in Skagway long."

"His name is Daniel Kane," Tara said. "He's about five feet eleven. Brown hair. Hazel eyes. Quite good-looking. . . ."

"He's prospecting for gold?"

She nodded.

"No gold around these parts, lady." He laughed. "The diggings are way north. Up the Yukon. Better make for Dawson."

"Dawson—how far's that?"

"Seven hundred miles north. Up the White Pass." Colson nodded at a map of the Yukon area, vast and unpopulated.

Tara stood undecided. It was all going wrong. Daniel had never mentioned going to Dawson; he had always talked of Skagway. She had only the vaguest idea of the geography of this territory. She thought they found gold all over.

"Since you're on your own, you'll be looking for a bed for the night, I figure," said Colson, looking her up and down.

"I'll find one somewhere," Tara said, wishing she was as confident as she sounded. She turned and walked out into the street.

The Indians called the town Skagus, which meant home of the north wind, and Skagway lived up to its name. In the weak afternoon sunshine it had seemed a city in the making, brash but colorful. Now, in the gloom, it was suddenly unfriendly, the wind whistling around corners, the narrow paths full of shadows and lurking dangers.

Tara started wandering aimlessly in no specific direction, a nagging, unwanted thought beginning to grow. Suppose something had happened to Daniel? A fight? A robbery? Eventually she stopped outside a window with SKAGWAY INTELLIGENCER—THE KLONDIKE'S BIGGEST LITTLE PAPER spelled out on the glass.

She went in and asked an old man behind a counter for the editor.

"I'm the editor," he said, peering over the top of his glasses.

"If anything happens in Skagway, you hear about it, don't you?" The old man nodded.

"Have you heard of a man called Daniel Kane? I'm his wife. I've just arrived in town."

The old man looked at her sympathetically. "Well, Mrs. Kane, I don't think he's shot anybody or anybody's shot him. We haven't had a good shooting for a couple of months. And nobody's drowned lately. I don't think you need to worry about him having had a misadventure."

Tara's heart felt lighter. At least Daniel had survived Skagway.

She left the newspaper office. Now her immediate problem was securing a roof over her head, food, and warmth. There was the mission hall, but she could not swallow more doses of the Beauchamps' brand of salvation.

Ahead of her was a sign: LOANS—CASH FOR ANY ITEM.

She tried to think of something on which she could raise a few dollars. She had only the little silver locket containing her mother's miniature. She hated the idea of pawning it. Yet she couldn't walk around Skagway all night.

She crossed the street and pushed through the swing doors. Waiting their turn in front of a counter with a grille, like a bank teller's window, were half a dozen haggard, shabby men, standing silently in line. This is the other side of the Gold Rush, she thought. The man behind the counter, a gun belt strapped around him, was called Sam; they all seemed to know him.

The man ahead of Tara waited, his hands empty. When it was his turn at the grille, he took off his spectacles and handed them to Sam, who gave him a dollar. The eyeglasses were added to a collection on a rack marked ALL ONE PRICE.

"What's this?" asked Sam as Tara handed the locket across the counter. "This ain't worth a bent dime to me."

"It's sterling silver," Tara pointed out.

Sam ignored her. "You got any gold?"

She shook her head. Her face was drawn, pale with fatigue.

He seemed to feel sorry for her. "I'll tell you what," he said, pulling his ear. "I'll lend you five dollars on this."

"All right," Tara agreed reluctantly.

"No deal." It was a soft voice, with a southern drawl, but it had authority. She swung around.

Standing by the door was an immaculately dressed man. He was tall, in his middle thirties, and across his black vest was looped a heavy gold watch chain hung with charms. Above a well-trimmed mustache he had chiseled features. His eyes were gray, shrewd, alert.

"Give it back to the lady," he ordered.

"Yes, boss," Sam said hastily. He thrust the locket at her.

"No," insisted Tara. "I want my money."

"My regrets, ma'am," the stranger said, shrugging.

"You keep out of it," she cried. "It's none of your business."

He smiled. "On the contrary, this is my business. I own it."

"Who are you?" she asked, staring at him with hostility.

"The name is Smith, Jefferson Randolph Smith."

"Mr. Smith, I need that money."

"May I?" he said. He took the locket out of her hand and looked at the painted miniature. "Very attractive. Is she your kin?"

"My mother."

"I should have guessed." He turned the locket over, looked at the words inscribed on it: *To Tara*. He glanced up at her. "So tell me, Tara, what brings a looker like you to this hole?"

The way he appraised her was unnerving. "I'm here to find my husband, Daniel Kane," she replied. "Have you come across him?"

"Should I have?"

Tara felt increasingly uncomfortable. His eyes did not leave her face. "Can I have my money?" she demanded.

He shook his head. "Unfortunately this locket is worthless to me." He handed it back. He took out a cheroot, bit the end, and lit it. "We're interested in gold," he continued, exhaling a cloud of Havana smoke. "I'll tell you what I'll do. Jefferson Smith never lets a lady go broke. I'll make you an offer."

"For what?" she asked curtly.

"*That's* gold," he said, and pointed at her wedding ring. "I'll give you fifty dollars for it. Now that's a mighty generous offer. That's the going rate for three ounces of gold."

Her green eyes narrowed. "No."

"Can you afford not to?" Smith asked.

It was true that she couldn't. If she didn't get some money, what would she do? Freeze to death? Starve? Fifty dollars could take her a long way toward Dawson.

"Take it or leave it," Smith said carelessly.

Tara hesitated, then she slowly twisted the ring off her finger. It had never been off her hand since Daniel put it there three years ago when they had exchanged rings. She passed over to Smith the very symbol of her marriage vow.

"Pay the lady," Smith ordered Sam. Then, to her fury, he slipped the ring on the little finger of his left hand.

Sam counted out the money, and as Tara took it she said to Smith tersely, "It's only a loan. I'll get the ring back."

"It'll always be a pleasure to do business with you, Mrs. Kane," Smith replied, inclining his head.

Out in the dark, cold night air, snow was falling lazily. Tara shivered. Next to a little store that sold cigars stood the wooden façade of the Mondame Hotel. It looked quiet, respectable.

The dingy hallway contained a bell marked VISITORS. Tara's summons was answered by a polite Chinese couple. A single room would cost ten dollars for the night. For the comfort of a mattress, a pillow, and privacy, she thought it was cheap at the price.

After she had wolfed down a hearty meal served in her room, there was a knock on the door. The couple carried in a tub and a copper kettle of steaming water. The stove in the corner heated the room well, and Tara felt like Cleopatra as her body sank into the tub. When she emerged, she knew she could face anything.

She put out the lamp and lay curled up in the bed. It was bliss to be alone without fear of intrusion. It was only when she touched her bare finger and thought of her ring and the man who now had it that the warmth and comfort felt less secure. She closed her eyes, but Jefferson Smith could not be shut out. He kept bowing mockingly, with a debonair, challenging smile.

When Tara came downstairs in the morning, the hefty figure of the Reverend Bowers rose from a wicker chair to greet her. "Good morning, Mrs. Kane. I trust you slept well."

"Yes, thank you," Tara said warily.

"Praise be," he said piously. "We were very anxious about your welfare. May I ask what your plans are?"

"Yes. I'm leaving for Dawson," said Tara brusquely.

"That is not a journey for a Christian woman on her own."

He could see that his clerical act was making no impression on Tara and dropped it suddenly. "You're not being very smart, are you?" he said. "If you stick around, I could fix you up with a good job. All it needs is a word to the boss. Mr. Smith can do anything for a girl. He's taken quite a fancy to you."

Tara looked Bowers straight in the eye. "You can tell your boss I'm not interested in anything he has to offer."

"Don't be dumb," Bowers said. "You're on your own. You need protection. He'll look after you."

Tara drew herself up. "I can imagine. And you can also give *this* message to your Mr. Smith. Tell him I'll get my wedding ring back." She stalked out of the hotel.

In the street something important was happening. A shouting mob of men swept by, half pushing, half dragging a pale, terrified-looking man whose hands were tied behind his back. He made no sound, and his eyes were glassy. Leading the mob was Marshal Colson, carrying a shotgun.

The crowd formed a circle around a tall birch tree. Tara looked at the screaming, distorted faces and saw nothing but crazed hate and eager anticipation. She knew this was a lynching.

The marshal raised his hand to silence the throng. "This here execution is being carried out according to law, sentence of death having been passed by the citizens of this community."

A roar went up from two hundred voices.

A horse was led into the center of the circle and the white-faced man was hoisted on it.

"Cal Mason," the marshal called out, turning to the man sitting rigid on the horse. "You're going to be hanged for the murder of Serena Bradley. Is there anything you want to say?"

Marshal Colson didn't wait for an answer. He raised a coiled rope high above his head. It had already been knotted into a noose. He swung it over a bough of the tree. Tara felt sick. She turned and walked away from the crowd. Then she stopped.

Marching up the street toward her were six men, walking abreast, their faces set. Tara could see the high-necked collars of scarlet tunics under their fur-trimmed jackets, and a broad yellow stripe down the length of their blue breeches. Their bearing was upright, military. The leader's pistol holster was already unbuttoned, and the other five also carried rifles.

The crowd around the tree was too preoccupied to notice them. Colson put the noose around the neck of the wretched man on the horse. "Let's get on with it," Colson yelled, raising his hand.

From behind the mob there was a shot. The Mountie sergeant had fired into the air. "Stop," he shouted.

The mob parted as Colson walked through to face the Mounties. "Keep out of this, Sarge," he rasped. "You've got no jurisdiction. This is United States territory."

"Release that man," said the sergeant.

"This is a legal execution," Colson bawled.

"It's a lynching," said the sergeant tersely. "Unlawful anywhere." The Mounties advanced, but the crowd closed ranks. Colson smiled complacently. The men at his back gave him confidence.

"Run 'em out of town," somebody yelled. A piece of frozen snow was hurled, and hit one of the Mounties in the face. It was followed by a rock. Tara saw the crowd surge forward.

"No damn Canadian Mountie tells us what to do," Colson yelled. "I'm the U.S. marshal, and what I say goes. You got no rights in Skagway." The Mounties ignored him. Slowly, deliberately, they advanced with their guns at the ready. Colson swung around, facing the mob. "Are you going to let these red bellies get away with it?"

"Marshal!" called out a commanding voice. Across the street a man had appeared on a white horse. Tara recognized Jefferson Smith. He cantered over until he was between the Mounties and the mob.

"Gentlemen," Smith declaimed. "Remember that we are all law-abiding citizens." He edged his horse through the crowd. He stopped next to Mason. Leaning over, he lifted the noose from the man's neck.

Then Smith walked his horse to the center of the throng and held up his hand. He was like a general commanding a rabble. His authority was unchallenged. He *does* own the place, Tara thought.

"My friends, we are all proud of the way we run this town, and we must certainly cooperate with the officers here," said Smith.

"This ain't their territory," a man yelled. "Tell them to get back to Dawson."

"On the contrary, if these officers feel they have jurisdiction, it is not for us to argue."

"You're selling out, Soapy," shouted somebody from the back. "You're letting the Canucks take over."

A man pushed forward and went up to Smith. "Throwing your weight around, ain't you," he accused. "Trying to run the town your way. It's you they should arrest."

Smith looked down at him with contempt.

"I'm doing it by the book, Reid. Nice and legal," he retorted. "If you know what's good for you, you'll agree with me."

"You murdering devil, Cal," cried a wild-eyed man in the crowd. He tried to push his way nearer to the prisoner. "You're not going to get away like this."

"He isn't going to get away with anything, Matt," he said. "Take it easy."

"I want him strung up," yelled the man. "Serena was my woman."

"Serena will get the best funeral money can buy, I promise you," Smith said. "But there'll be no lynching."

"You're yellow, Soapy," Matt yelled. "Six red bellies from the Yukon with popguns, and you turn yellow."

There was stunned silence. Quietly a dozen tough-looking individuals formed a protective ring around Smith. Two carried clubs and the rest had guns.

"Cal Mason killed my woman, and I'll get him, even if your whole gang is there," Matt cried.

"You'd better get out of town, Thatcher," growled a hoodlum who appeared suddenly behind Matt and twisted his arm until he bent double with pain.

Smith trotted back to the prisoner, who was still sitting upright, hands tied. He took the bridle of the horse and led it through the crowd. He stopped in front of the Mounties, who eyed him warily. "Here's your man, Sergeant," Smith said. "He's your responsibility now. Do your duty. Get him out of town if you don't want a riot."

"We're hitting the trail to Dawson today," the sergeant said. He gave a command, and one of his men untied the prisoner and then helped him down from his horse. Without a second look at Smith or the sullen crowd, they handcuffed Mason and marched him off.

"My compliments to Inspector Constantine," Smith called after them. Then, turning his horse around, he faced the assembly. "Gentlemen," he shouted. "Drinks at my place. On the house."

Smith's gang gave a ragged cheer, and the rest joined in. They started drifting down the street in the direction of the saloon. Smith urged his horse forward, and it began to trot lazily after them. Just as Tara was turning to go, Smith spotted her. He cantered to her side and took off his hat politely. "That invitation includes you, Mrs. Kane. I'd be flattered if you'd join us."

Without a word Tara turned on her heel. Smith rode off. He was smiling.

Back at the Mondame Hotel, Tara got some ink and paper. She had little time, but this mustn't be botched. She began writing a letter:

My dear Tara,

The Constantine household is in quite a tizz at the thought that you will be arriving here soon. I am dying to hear all the latest news from home. You have a long journey ahead of you, and since this is no easy venture for a gentlewoman on her own, your dear brother-in-law insists that as soon as you arrive in Skagway you approach the local post of the Northwest Mounted Police, and ask them if they have a detachment proceeding to Dawson in whose company you might travel. They are *splendid* men, and we know they will take good care of you. We eagerly await your arrival.

Your loving sister,
Sarah

Tara backdated the letter to June 30, 1897. She thought that under the circumstances she had done an admirable job. She knew that the commander of the Mounties at Dawson was an Inspector Constantine. She knew he was married. But she had no way of knowing whether Mrs. Constantine's name was Sarah, or if she had a sister. There was only one way to find out.

Outside the Mounties' post, four sleds were drawn up with their dog teams. Tara walked in, introduced herself, and told a startled Sergeant Campbell how grateful she was for their help in getting her up to Dawson. She handed him the letter.

The sergeant stood by the stove reading it, a worried look on his face. "Nobody told me about this," he said.

"That's just like Sarah." Tara laughed. "She probably forgot. She must have taken it for granted you'd know."

"We got no orders, and without orders . . ."

"Sergeant, you can't just leave me here," Tara gasped.

"We have a prisoner," Campbell pointed out. "We're not equipped to carry ladies. Not across the White Pass."

"I can look after myself," Tara said hastily. "I won't be any burden, I promise. And, Sergeant, think how angry my brother-in-law would be if you left me behind."

"I guess we could fit you on one of the sleds," Campbell conceded. "Where is your luggage, Mrs. Kane?"

"I've only a sleeping bag," she said. "Everything was lost on the *North Fork*."

Campbell paused. "I depend on you to sort it out with Inspector Constantine if he gets mad at me for bending regulations."

"I'm sure he'll be more than grateful to you, Sergeant," Tara said. So far her plan to get to Dawson had worked.

CHAPTER FOUR

ARA admired the expertise with which Sergeant Campbell handled his team. He had a whip with a long, braided sealskin lash that cracked like rifle fire, but he relied far more on his voice. It ordered, threatened, encouraged, but was always obeyed.

For hours after leaving Skagway they traveled across flat, frozen timberland, following a kind of primitive road, the route of thousands of travelers north. The snow fell steadily as the convoy began to ascend the White Pass, and the temperature dropped to twenty below zero. Tara felt pain in her nose; inside her nostrils the tiny hairs froze into sharp little barbs which, as she breathed in the biting air, drew blood.

They were now hundreds of feet up, traveling along a corkscrew trail which was dominated by ugly slate cliffs. Below the sheer fall, rocks were strewn with skeletons and the wreckage of wagons that had tried to edge their way along the track and failed. Tara clutched at the sled, pushing away fear.

The daylight was fading as they made camp behind some six-foot-high boulders. The dogs were unhitched, cooking gear unpacked, a tent pitched. Two Mounties gathered wood and began cutting it up. The dogs were fed first; that was a golden rule.

Inside the tent, the stove was lit, and everyone gathered around it. One of the men stuck a big lump of frozen snow on a branch. As the snow melted from the heat of the stove, the water was caught in a pan. The Mounties had supplies of beans, corned beef, and potatoes, which they boiled in the water. And there was hot coffee. The meal was delicious, and Tara ate with vigor, although the prisoner ate his food listlessly. They had taken off his handcuffs. He was as silent as ever, staring into the glow of the stove.

Campbell started rolling himself a cigarette. "If the weather holds, we'll make the post at Summit Hill in a day or so. If we stay lucky, I reckon we'll reach Lake Bennett in four or five days."

Tara was thankful for one thing. So far Campbell hadn't once asked her about her "sister" or the Constantine family. Sometimes, though, she thought she saw the lantern-jawed sergeant looking at her thoughtfully. She wondered if he was growing suspicious of her. Outside, the wind shook the canvas, and Tara thought she could hear a wolf howling. Now and then the dogs whined.

"Most important thing you can have here is a reliable dog team," the sergeant explained. "If you're out on your feet, you can't drag your dog team anywhere. But, by heavens, they can get you to safety. The dogs are your life. You can't look after them too well. And if you're starving, you can always eat 'em."

"*Eat* the dogs?" Tara made a grimace. "I'd rather starve."

"Hope you never run out of food," Campbell said quietly. He stretched himself. "I guess we'd all better have some shut-eye." He hesitated and looked at Tara. "Normally, Mrs. Kane, we all bed down in the tent. But seeing as you are a lady . . . I mean, if you prefer . . ."

"Sergeant Campbell." Tara smiled. "Why don't we do just that? I've got my sleeping bag, and I'd feel much safer."

"That's dandy, then. You'll have that corner all to yourself, and I'll be right here." He was obviously relieved. He handcuffed the prisoner again, then turned down the oil lamp, but the red glow from the stove continued to illuminate the tent.

They broke camp early the following morning. It was a bright, hoary day, crystal clear and as sharp as a diamond. As the convoy progressed, Tara for the first time saw the price the White Pass demanded of those who braved it. They passed exhausted prospectors, moving at a snail's pace, short on supplies, whipping their tired, half-starved dog teams.

"Crazy fools," one of the Mounties said. "Greenhorns got no business in this godforsaken country."

They traveled on in silence. Suddenly there was a shot. Then another one. "Keep down," Campbell yelled. The prisoner, Cal Mason, sagged, face up, halfway out of his sled, and in the middle of his forehead was a neat little hole.

"Over there," the sergeant shouted to two Mounties, pointing at a clump of fir trees. "I'll cover you."

Tara scrambled out of the sled and flung herself on the ground, feeling her heart pounding against the frozen earth. Three more shots whizzed past the two Mounties who were racing toward the trees. Campbell fired back from behind the sled. Two further shots rang out from the wood.

"You're surrounded, you don't stand a chance," Campbell yelled. "Come out with your hands up."

They waited tensely. Then a man emerged, holding his hands high above his head. He was dark-haired, dressed like a trapper, and seemed vaguely familiar.

As she scrambled to her feet Tara was shaking. She had seen a man murdered in front of her eyes.

"Is he dead?" the man asked, looking at Mason's slumped body.

"Dead as he'll ever be. What's going on, Matt?"

"I swore I'd get him," Matt Thatcher said with satisfaction. "I trailed you from Skagway. He killed my woman," he added simply.

"I heard she was anybody's woman," the sergeant growled. He

had unlocked the dead man's handcuffs, and now he clicked them on Thatcher's wrists.

Before they moved off, they buried Mason. One of the Mounties nailed a rough cross together. CAL MASON they carved on it, DIED SEPT. 22, 1897. Then they stuck it on top of the grave.

Mason's death had a marked effect on the sergeant. When they next made camp, he remained aloof from the others. "He's got his hands full," one Mountie whispered to Tara. "You don't lose a prisoner, not in the Mounties."

They did not need to tell Tara when they were passing through Dead Horse Gulch. The snow in it was packed hard, the trail trampled by thousands who had relentlessly pursued the route north. The wailing of the sharp wind sounded to her like the screams of dying animals and the shrieks of desperate men who had met their end in this macabre graveyard.

It was thirty degrees colder than on the coast. She longed for warmth, not only a physical temperature, but something warm for the eye. Her surroundings were dazzlingly white, hard, cold: in the shadows, gray white; in the cold sun, blue white; on the peaks in the distance, silver white.

The final thousand feet to the top of Summit Hill was the worst ordeal Tara had yet had to face. To lighten the dogs' burden she and Thatcher had to make the climb on foot. She groped her way along, slipping and sliding, panic-stricken.

"You can have a rest when we get to the police post," the sergeant said, trying to encourage her. "It's right ahead."

Four hours later it seemed no nearer. To Tara the post at Summit Hill began to assume the image of a distant paradise. For the Mounties it was the official frontier, the border between United States territory and British Columbia. She looked forward to it with growing excitement. But all she saw as they trudged on was the same inhospitable landscape. She thought of Daniel struggling up this trail, gritting his teeth, each step heavier than the last.

Finally she saw the sergeant's team halt. Tara's heart jumped. She could see a cluster of huts and two poles, one flying the Stars and Stripes and the other the Union Jack. This was the border. Then the Yukon; not the end of the trail, but the beginning.

Once inside the post, Tara was the center of attention. The Mountie in charge, a sergeant called Grayburn, fussed over her like a mother hen. She was immediately given a berth in an empty bunkhouse. A tub of steaming water was brought to her, and she was invited to join the men for dinner in the mess.

She expected it to be a rough-and-ready affair. But the Mounties turned out in their scarlet tunics, buttons flashing, cavalry boots polished like mirrors, and they observed strict protocol. Every man remained on his feet until Tara sat down.

The food was coarse but good. There was caribou steak, pancakes, beans, and fried potatoes, served all together. In this climate Tara was constantly hungry, and she consumed enormous helpings of food she would never have touched a few months ago.

Then came the moment that she had been dreading. "You lost your husband, Mrs. Kane?" Grayburn asked sympathetically. She was aware that Campbell, on her other side, was listening intently.

For a moment Tara did not know what to say. "Lost?"

"I notice that you don't wear your wedding ring," he said.

Tara tried to collect her thoughts. If she had to answer questions about her husband, her story about being Constantine's sister-in-law would collapse. "Oh, that." She dismissed it lightly. "I wear it on a chain around my neck, where it's closest to me." She changed the subject. "Tell me, Sergeant Campbell, that man Smith in Skagway, does he rule the place?"

"Soapy?" Campbell smiled grimly. "He's town boss all right."

"Biggest bunko man in the territory," Grayburn snorted. He noticed her confused expression. "Con man, Mrs. Kane. Trickster."

"But why the name Soapy?"

"Someplace in Colorado he sold shaving soap for five dollars a piece to anyone who believed his story that there was a twenty-dollar bill under the wrapper. Made a small fortune. . . ."

"Guess he knows how to fool 'em," Campbell said. "He even laid a telegraph wire that only ran for six miles and got people to pay five bucks to send ten words anywhere in America."

"And when they found out?" Tara asked.

Campbell shrugged. "Mrs. Kane, folks have two rules about Soapy Smith. One, they don't argue with him. Two, they keep their eyes in the back of their heads when he's around."

So the elegant man who lorded it over Skagway with his smooth manner and soft drawl was just a cheap crook. Every time Tara felt her bare finger her anger rose. And yet . . .

For some reason she was curiously intrigued by him.

They rested for twenty-four hours at Summit Hill, and Tara discovered that the border post was the end of the line of many a man's gold rush. As would-be prospectors came along the trail to cross into British Columbia, and thence to the Yukon, the Mounties checked each man's supplies. If he didn't have 1150 pounds of food, one year's supply, he was turned back. Tara wondered if Daniel had passed this test.

Next morning they set off once more. Soon after the huts of the frontier post receded, a blizzard struck. The Mounties, driving their teams, became strange, mute, frost-encrusted forms. The dogs' fur turned white, the sleds were thick with icy snow. The howling sleet and wind made the convoy look like phantoms. To protect them from frostbite their faces had to be completely covered. Tara realized that without the goggles Sergeant Grayburn had given her at Summit Hill she would have gone blind. As it was, they kept frosting up, and she was unable to see most of the time.

They were only able to cover a few yards an hour. At intervals the wind was so violent, and the flurries of snow so thick, that they all seemed motionless, straining against an invisible wall. Despite the fury of the wind, Tara found herself nodding off once or twice. It was her first brush with the lure of the white death—the curious desire to fall asleep in the middle of the wilderness. Her driver saw Tara's head nod and shook her shoulder roughly. People in blizzards who went to sleep rarely woke up again.

After a few hours the weather changed gradually. Tara was able to uncover her face and breathe properly once more. The dogs perked up and started moving faster. Now there was total and frightening silence enveloping them, and Tara wondered if she had become deaf. A group of caribou appeared in the distance. Up in the sky some geese passed in a ragged V, but they made no sound. After the raucous wind of the blizzard it was eerie. Three hours later they made camp. No one talked. They were too exhausted.

Before the Gold Rush, Lake Bennett, gateway to the Yukon River, had been one of the loveliest places in the territory, as if nature were trying to prove that the Yukon was not merely a cruel, savage, icy wilderness.

Now the lake was encircled by thousands of tents, large and

small. There were dog tents, army tents, tent barbershops, and canvas saloons. The snow-covered lakeside echoed with the whine of saws, the blows of axes, the shouts of men warning of falling timber.

Presently, Lake Bennett was one giant boatyard. Everyone here was building boats to go up the river when the ice thawed; boats that would have to be sailed, rowed, dragged through some of the most treacherous waters known to men.

After the loneliness of the White Pass, Tara found the sight of this swarming canvas township cheering. Campbell thought otherwise. He looked around at tree stumps. "They're tearing the guts out of the place, and they don't put anything back. Those trees took centuries to grow."

The Mounties pitched tents by the shore. Tara looked across the frozen lake at the river that reached beyond like a white highway. Along that river was their route to Dawson.

"But it's frozen," Tara exclaimed, dismayed. "How can we?"

"We travel on the ice," Campbell said. "It's easier in a boat, but we haven't got time to wait for the thaw."

After resting for two days, they followed the frozen river to the Whitehorse Rapids. Tara gazed down on a curtain of raging torrent where the water never froze. It cascaded and thundered, white crests rising four feet high, a swift current of water spiked with sharp rock teeth lurking treacherously to rip the bottom off any craft. The walls rose sheer on either side of the foaming crest. "We're going the long way round," Campbell announced. "I'm not shooting that with a woman."

It took two and a half days to manhandle the sleds along six miles of cliff overlooking the rapids. They had to be dragged, pushed, and at one point even carried through tiny rock passages, up and down slippery trails, sometimes a few inches from a plunge to death. The dog teams, unhitched, had to be led step by step.

Tara's body ached, muscles she never knew she had hurt, and the sheer strain of dragging herself along the trail was so exhausting that all she wanted was to sink to her knees.

They stopped briefly at a mound of rocks. On it a primitive cross had four words only: HE NEVER MADE IT.

Who was the man who never made it? Tara wondered. Daniel must have come along this route. At the foot of the cliffs on the other side she could see more graves—tiny crosses—all of them men for whom this was the end of the Gold Rush.

A Mountie named Hennessy came to join her. "Guess I owe you an apology, ma'am," he said.

Tara looked at him. "What on earth for?"

"Well," he said, scratching his head. "I told Sergeant Campbell this might be too tough for you. You proved me wrong. You can handle yourself okay."

He could not have pleased her more. She knew that they had all been watching her, and she had passed the test.

That night they camped near Lake Laberge. Tara was warming herself over the fire, and Campbell handed her a mug of coffee. "How much longer to Dawson?" she asked him.

"Couple of weeks maybe," the sergeant said noncommittally.

She sipped the coffee. "Sergeant, what's Inspector Constantine like?" It was out before she realized what she had said.

"Your brother-in-law? Why, don't you know?"

"Not . . . not really. I don't know him very well."

"Hmm," Campbell said, and threw another piece of wood into the flames. "I guess he'll have a lot of questions to ask you."

Of course he knew the truth. He was saying as much. Giving Tara a curt nod, he left her to her thoughts and misgivings.

Some days later they met up with another Mountie patrol. Campbell conferred with the man in charge. Tara caught an occasional word, "sister," "letter," "expecting her." The officer walked toward her, and she knew that it meant trouble and more lies.

He saluted her. "I hear you're on your way to Dawson to meet with your brother-in-law." His American accent was unexpected. Most of the Mounties she had met so far had been British. "It's amazing," he went on. "I never would have believed you're Alice's sister if I hadn't been told."

Alice! And she had signed the letter Sarah. "Anyway, I'm sorry you're in for a disappointment," he said. "Your sister's at Fort Constantine. Didn't she tell you?"

Tara had never heard of the place. "Isn't that near Dawson?"

"Not exactly. It's across the river from Fortymile. One of the empire's most northerly outposts."

"Oh." She wasn't sure what to say.

"Guess Inspector Constantine will have lots to talk about with you." He smiled broadly. "I leave you in Sergeant Campbell's good hands, meantime." Tara's heart was pounding as the officer walked back to his teams.

Campbell started up the convoy. "Guess Zac Wood knows your sister right well," he said genially. "He's a great guy and a real troubleshooter. Nothing escapes him."

Tara had the uneasy feeling that Campbell was only too right.

CHAPTER FIVE

Only two years before, Dawson had been a wilderness, at the junction of the Yukon and Klondike rivers, a pasture for moose, unclaimed by men. Now thousands of prospectors were making fortunes, going bankrupt, gambling, and drinking twenty-four hours a day. Deep in the heart of Yukon region, Dawson had turned itself into an American frontier town on Canadian soil. Nine out of ten men there were Americans, drawn by the gold, and the Stars and Stripes flew defiantly in the main street. Here a man who didn't have gold was worth less than a sled dog. Much less.

The handful of Mounties headquartered in a log cabin acted as a reminder that somewhere beyond this wild isolated town there was a Canadian government. Presiding was a sardonic-looking man with a hook nose and a Vandyke beard. He was Charles Constantine, the commander of the Mounties' Yukon detachment.

A Union Jack hung outside the police cabin. As Campbell's patrol drew up in front of the ramshackle headquarters, Tara steeled herself for her confrontation with the inspector.

"Let's go, Mrs. Kane," Campbell said. Inside the cabin, he indicated a wooden chair. "Wait here," he ordered. Then he went through a door marked Commanding Officer. When he emerged a few minutes later, he said flatly, "This way, Mrs. Kane."

She walked with him out of the headquarters building, around to the back, to a wooden hut. "In here," he said.

She found herself facing four cells. Thatcher sat on a bunk in one of them, his head in his hands. He looked up through the bars, puzzled, when he saw Tara.

Campbell held one of the cell doors open.

Tara stared at him. "In . . . in there?" she faltered.

"I'm acting under orders," Campbell said awkwardly.

She stepped into a bare cell with a bunk and one stool. She shivered and turned to Campbell, but he had slammed the door and was locking it. She sank onto the stool in disbelief. She was in jail. Surely they couldn't do this without even talking to her.

Then she heard the door of the lockup open. An officer appeared and unlocked her cell. His pointed beard was neatly trimmed, and he wore polished riding boots. He didn't have to tell her he was Constantine. He studied her coldly. Tara braced herself. "Am I under arrest?" she asked.

He held out his hand. "The letter from my wife, please."

Nervously she pulled out the scrap of paper. He took it and glanced over the writing, then tore it up.

From his tunic Constantine took a folded piece of paper and handed it to her. "The bill, madam," he said frigidly.

"What bill?" Tara asked dully.

"You owe the government for transportation and food and shelter. Two hundred dollars will pay for the facilities you have obtained by false pretenses and forgery."

"I haven't got the money," said Tara in a low voice.

"Of course not. That is why you are in here. Obtaining goods and services by deception is a serious criminal offense."

"I'm terribly sorry," Tara said contritely. "I was stuck in Skagway. So I told a story, hoping—"

"A *lie*, madam."

"I don't make a habit of it. Please believe me."

He walked over to the bunk and sat on it. "All right," he said. "What the devil made you embark on your charade anyway?"

She told him, then waited anxiously for his reaction. It came like a cold shower. "Frankly, Mrs. Kane," he said, "you have little chance of finding your husband. Much of the Yukon is uncharted. He could be anywhere. You are friendless and alone. You should return home."

Tara lowered her head. "I'll find him," she insisted. "I must stay here and go on with the search. My mind is made up."

"Then so is mine," he said. "I'd give a man who cheated the government thirty days' hard labor. Since you won't remove yourself from Dawson, thirty days' hard labor it shall be."

She watched, still disbelieving, as he got up and walked from the cell, slammed the door, and locked it.

An hour later Sergeant Campbell returned. "Come along, Mrs. Kane," he said. He took her arm and led her outside. He towered above her as they marched through the town, she carrying her sleeping bag, trying to keep up with his long strides.

"Where are we going?" Tara panted.

"Mrs. Miles's place," he said curtly. He avoided her eyes, and she knew her punishment had already begun. He steered her across the main street to a wooden, two-story house. There was a No Vacancies sign on the front door. "In you go," Campbell ordered, and followed her inside.

The hallway had a smell which, at first, Tara couldn't place. Then she realized what it was. The house smelled clean. An Indian rug covered the floor. This was the first home she had been in since San Francisco.

"Mrs. Miles," Campbell called out. A severe-faced woman emerged from the kitchen in the rear, and Tara's heart sank. She was in her late fifties, with every steel-gray hair in place. Her starched apron creaked as she walked. She was the personification of a prison matron.

"Hello, Linda," Campbell said. "Can I have a word with you?" A door closed behind them, but not before Tara heard Campbell saying, "Inspector Constantine sent this letter . . ."

A few minutes later Mrs. Miles came out with the inspector's letter in her hand, followed by Campbell. "Mrs. Kane," she said briskly. "Mr. Constantine has asked me to work you like a skivvy for thirty days. Now I need a domestic, but she has to be decent and respectable."

Tara's eyes smoldered defiantly. "I'll do the work. However, I would like to make it clear, Mrs. Miles, that I am not a trained domestic."

"By the time I'm finished, you will be," Mrs. Miles assured Tara grimly. She turned to Campbell. "But if she's no good, Mr. Constantine gets her back. Be sure you tell him that."

"We appreciate that," Campbell said, beating a hasty retreat.

"Now you and I have to get a few things straight," said Mrs. Miles, leading Tara through to the kitchen. "This is a respectable rooming house. You don't socialize with the lodgers. You don't go out in the evening without my permission. You are allowed no visitors. You don't whistle, nor do you sing. You will get up

151

at six every morning and make up the fires, scrub the floors, clean the rooms, black the grates, and keep the place generally tidy. I do the cooking. At all times I shall expect you to be willing and cheerful."

"Of course," Tara concurred, her lips twitching.

"In return, you will have your lodging and full board."

"Oh, that is kind," Tara said. But her feeble attempt at irony was lost on Mrs. Miles.

"Well, come along, then. I'll show you your quarters."

Although it wasn't a cell, it was the smallest room Tara had ever seen. But she liked it. At long last she would have privacy. The small window actually had a tiny chintz curtain. Like the rest of the house, the room was clean and neat.

"I think I'll be very comfortable," Tara said, and she meant it.

"If you need anything, tell me. But I don't want any mess in here," Mrs. Miles added gruffly, as if she was ashamed of sounding too nice. "Get settled in, and then we'll have a cup of tea."

Tara dragged her sleeping bag upstairs, then sat on the bed and tried to collect her thoughts. This was not how she had planned it. She had come thousands of miles, and now she was a domestic servant. She took out the little compass. The needle kept pointing to—where, she wondered. In San Francisco it had pointed this way. High up on the pass it had kept pointing. Always farther—to the beyond.

Tara went to the window and looked out at the street below. This was where she had to begin her search, among the saloons, the stores. Here, somewhere, she would find news of Daniel. "That's right, isn't it?" she whispered to the compass, balancing it in her hand. "I'll find him, won't I?"

"Tara!" came a shout up the stairs.

In the kitchen, she found Mrs. Miles surrounded by steaming pots and pans, preparing the evening meal. "They're hungry men, and there's got to be plenty for them."

There were five boarders, Tara discovered as she sipped a big mug of tea, none of them gold prospectors.

Mrs. Miles eyed Tara's trousers disapprovingly. "You'll have to wear a dress, understand? I can't have you looking like that."

"I lost my clothes," Tara said.

"I'll have to find you a dress. Come along." She marched Tara up the stairs. From a cupboard she produced some underwear, black lisle stockings, and a gray dress with a high collar.

"There," she said, "these ought to fit you. They belonged to the last girl." Tara wondered about the last girl. Had Mrs. Miles acquired her also from the ranks of errant ladies who had fallen afoul of the law? "Wear this apron tonight to serve the supper," Mrs. Miles continued. "You'll eat in the kitchen, then clean up."

Tara got her first glimpse of the boarders when she carried the huge soup tureen into the dining room. Mrs. Miles was presiding at the head of the table, the five lodgers arranged on either side of her. There were the Bartlett brothers, who operated a successful freight-haulage business; Harry Robbins, the town's dentist; Eugene Brock, a storekeeper; and Joe Lamore, a sawmill owner, who had turned timber into his own kind of gold mine.

Dinner was an unending succession of carrying in hot plates and taking out dirty dishes. At one point Tara caught part of a conversation. "This place could become another Skagway if we let him get away with it," the dentist was saying.

"That's the truth," Brock agreed. "I tell you, Soapy Smith is taking over Dawson. Already he owns four saloons."

"So what's the law doing about it?" asked one of the Bartletts. "This is Canadian territory. We don't need to allow Yankee hoodlums in here."

"But ninety percent of the people in Dawson are American citizens," Lamore pointed out. "What can a handful of Mounties do?"

"They should have hanged Soapy Smith years ago," commented Robbins, but Tara missed the rest of it because she had to bring in the apple pie. In the kitchen, the words echoed in Tara's ears. Soapy Smith! His influence also here in Dawson?

TARA was up first thing in the morning doing chores. She began by scrubbing the hallway on her hands and knees.

"Where is Mr. Kane?" Mrs. Miles suddenly asked. "Or should I ask, is there a Mr. Kane?" She fixed her eyes on Tara's left hand. "After all, a married woman wears a wedding ring."

Tara held her temper in check. "Since you're so curious, there is a Mr. Kane, and I don't wear a wedding ring because I had to pawn it." Mrs. Miles's eyes opened wide. "I had no choice," Tara went on. "I was starving, destitute, and alone in Skagway."

Mrs. Miles softened a bit. "What were you doing in Skagway?"

Tara told her story yet again. Mrs. Miles shook her head. "How on earth do you expect to find him here? Do you know what it takes for a female to survive on her own in these parts? You're too soft. You're not up to it."

"Don't worry, Mrs. Miles, I'll make out. You managed all right, didn't you?"

Mrs. Miles grunted. "I was left with a broken wagon and a few supplies when my husband died in '95." She told Tara how she had got hold of a stove, baked bread, and sold it for fifty cents a loaf until she had earned three hundred dollars. Then she opened an eating place and served good, cheap meals. When she had enough capital, she opened her lodging house.

"This is where I've made my stake, and it's all mine," she said fiercely. "I'm not beholden to anybody, and I know how to look after myself. Which is more than you can do."

"I've got this far," Tara said. She was gaining respect for Mrs. Miles. Dour and formidable she might be, but Tara found herself admiring the starched lady.

"You have, but on other people's backs." Mrs. Miles said it without rancor, more like a mother putting a daughter straight. "You haven't stood on your own feet. Anyway, all this talk won't get the housework done," she growled, turning to go.

"Mrs. Miles," Tara said. "I need some time off."

"Time off!" Mrs. Miles boomed. "You haven't even started working properly and you want time off?"

"I've got to start looking for Daniel."

"You mean wander round Dawson, talking to strangers, going into saloons, all on your own?" Mrs. Miles was appalled.

"Yes. Stand on my own feet."

Mrs. Miles studied her hands, then looked at Tara sternly. "Very well. You can have an hour now and then. And you may call me Linda," she added, quickly disappearing into the kitchen, as if embarrassed by her momentary lapse.

After their conversation Mrs. Miles seemed to think more kindly of her. She put a woven Indian blanket on Tara's bed, and even smiled at her occasionally. When Tara fell into bed, dog-tired after sixteen hours' work, she knew she was proving herself capable, a quality Mrs. Miles respected.

THE MONTE CARLO Saloon was packed. Tara stood blinking, trying to adjust herself to the smoke-laden atmosphere and the deafening noise. Every man's path crossed the Monte Carlo, and here somebody could well have heard of Daniel. She mustered up her courage to begin inquiries at the bar.

"Let's have a whirl," a lumberjack said. He grabbed her and, without waiting for her reply, swung her around the dance floor, pressing her close. Suddenly Tara felt as if she had been struck by a giant; only the lumberjack's firm grip kept her on her feet. She looked around to see what had hit her. A gigantic woman was bear-hugging a man whose head reached only to her massive bosom. She must have weighed at least three hundred pounds. She wore a huge, sequined dress, which covered her body like a tarpaulin. The most disconcerting thing of all was her eye. She had only one, and it glared at Tara, bloodshot and furious. Where the other eye should have been was an empty socket.

"Watch your big feet," the woman snarled at Tara.

The lumberjack pulled Tara away. "Phew," he said. "The last girl that bumped into the Grizzly Bear lost her scalp. I'd rather tangle with an elephant."

"She looks pretty fierce," Tara said, mesmerized.

"Fierce? How do you think she lost her blinker?"

Tara shook her head.

"Buffalo Liz gouged it out with her nails over at Sam Bonnifield's place. The Grizzly broke three of her ribs."

The music stopped, and he dragged her toward the bar. "I'll get us some bubbly." He thumped the counter. "Hey, Pierre, pint of fizz."

The bartender produced a bottle and two glasses. "Thirty bucks."

The lumberjack brought out a thick wad of money. "Nothing's too good for any little lady I go with. And you've made two bucks, honey, haven't you?"

"Two bucks?"

"Hasn't Soapy told you? You get two bucks commission on every bottle of fizz the customers buy."

"Soapy Smith? What's he got to do with it?" Tara asked.

"He owns the joint. Aren't you one of his girls?"

Tara put the glass down. "I'm sorry. You've made a mistake."

The lumberjack gave Tara an evil look and shuffled off muttering.

155

She turned to the bartender. "I'm looking for a man called Daniel Kane. Do you know if he's come in here?"

"Kane? Wait a moment." Pierre went to the back of the bar, opened the cash register, and took out a small pile of notes.

Tara's heart jumped as he came back to her, holding one of the pieces of paper. "Yeah," said Pierre. "I remember the guy. He owes us forty-five bucks."

She looked excitedly at the paper. "What's that?" she asked.

"His marker. He was going to get the cash and gave us an IOU."

"Let me see," she said, reaching for the note. It was Dan's handwriting all right. At least she knew now that he had come to Dawson. "When was this?" Tara asked.

"Four, five weeks ago. What's he to you anyway?"

"He's my husband," Tara replied quietly.

"Oh, is he? Well then, in that case, lady, you'd better pay his debt," he said coldly. "The boss don't like cheaters."

"My husband doesn't cheat," Tara protested indignantly.

"Mort," Pierre yelled. A stocky man dressed in black came over. "Got a marker here for forty-five bucks. The guy ran out on us. Now his wife's showed up. She doesn't want to pay."

Mort nodded. "We got pretty strict house rules, lady, and the boss don't make exceptions. You'd better pay up."

"Tell Mr. Smith he can say that to my face," Tara retorted.

He looked at her dubiously. "You a friend of his?"

"Yes," Tara said. "I know him quite well."

"Well, in that case . . ." said Mort. "We'd better leave it for the moment. The boss will be arriving in a couple of days."

"Good night," Tara said. She turned and pushed her way out into the cold air of Front Street.

"And how is Mrs. Kane doing?" asked a voice at her elbow. Sergeant Campbell stopped her as she came out.

"I'm being very law-abiding, Sergeant," said Tara.

"Not sergeant anymore," he said, pointing at his sleeve. The three chevrons had gone. "You're talking to a constable now."

"What happened?" she asked, dismayed.

"Got busted." He sighed. "The inspector took the stripes away."

"Because of me?" It must be her fault. "Oh, I *am* sorry."

"No, not entirely." He gave her a little smile. "It's been a lousy deal all around. Thatcher strung himself up in his cell. Constantine was up all night writing the report. He's worried about jurisdiction. Maybe I should have left the other guy in Skagway."

"But you couldn't let him be lynched," Tara said.

"When you bend regulations, you either come out smelling like a rose, or you pay. I paid." He shrugged. "Have you found your husband yet?"

"I know he's been in Dawson. Now I'm looking around the town to see if anyone knows where he is."

"You just stay out of trouble, Tara," he said. "Find your husband, then get out."

"That's all I'm trying to do, Sergeant Campbell. . . ."

"Name's Andrew," he said. "Just watch yourself."

During the next few weeks, in her search for a clue to Daniel's whereabouts, Tara learned that in Dawson people lost their identities. "Daniel Kane?" they asked. "What's his name?"

At first she was at a loss for words. Then she began to understand. Phantom Archibald. Waterfront Brown. Limejuice Jim. These were the names men were known by, and that's what their friends put on their tombstones when they were buried.

"I'd like to help you, honey," a dance-hall caller told her. "But who'd call himself Daniel Kane? Doesn't he have a moniker? Frisco Dan? Faro Kane?"

Tara shook her head. She had to admit that Daniel's description could fit any one of a thousand men. And she didn't even know what he looked like now. Was his hair long, or had he kept it short? Had he grown a beard? But relentlessly she pursued her quest.

One day Mrs. Miles handed Tara a letter. She ripped the envelope open as Mrs. Miles stood watching. It was a short note:

Dear Mrs. Kane,

I may be in possession of some information which could be of interest to you. I look forward to the pleasure of your company tonight at supper. I will call for you at six o'clock.

Yours most sincerely,
Jefferson R. Smith

Tara's head was in a whirl. She passed the note to Mrs. Miles, whose face clouded over as she read it. "Well, that's out of the question," she decreed. "You can't go out with him."

"If he's got information about Daniel . . ."

"The man's a blackguard, and probably lying," exploded Mrs. Miles. "Good heavens, Tara, you couldn't think of accepting."

"I must, Linda. I'd have supper with the devil if he'd lead me to my husband. It is possible that he knows something. So I must go. Will you give me the time off? I've served my thirty days."

"Please yourself," Mrs. Miles said. "You're over twenty-one. But don't say you weren't warned."

The grandfather clock downstairs was striking six when Mrs. Miles banged on Tara's door. "He's come for you," she called out gruffly. "But he's outside. He's not coming into my house."

Tara pinched her cheeks to heighten her color and smoothed her dress. Mrs. Miles, busy in the kitchen, did not look up when she appeared. If she had, she would have seen a Tara who looked almost elegant, her luxuriant dark auburn hair swept up and carefully arranged. Here was a young woman who didn't need jewelry or furs to make her beautiful. Her natural loveliness was more than sufficient.

As Tara emerged from the house, Smith came toward her and raised his broad-brimmed hat. "What a pleasure to see you again," he drawled. "May I?" He offered her his arm. She looked at his hand. There on the little finger was her wedding ring.

"I must be back soon," Tara said coldly, ignoring his proffered arm. "I hope we're not going far."

"Hardly. And I promise to bring you back safe and sound."

They began walking down the street toward the center of Dawson. "Where are we going, Mr. Smith?" she asked.

"Oh, a little place I have," he murmured. It was called the Regina Café. Tara had noticed the four-story building under construction, without realizing what it would become.

When she stepped inside, she was amazed. There was wall-to-wall deep red Brussels carpeting. Hanging from the ornate ceiling were glass chandeliers. The wood-paneled walls were decorated with gold leaf. No sawdust, and no spittoons.

"It will be Dawson's finest hotel," Smith said, looking around proudly. "Fifteen rooms, all steam-heated, all lit by electric. I'll get the power from a ship on the river. It's going to have class."

This was a new angle on Smith's operations. She associated him with rackets and cheap saloons.

Smith was well aware that she was impressed, as he had intended. He led her along a corridor and opened a door. Inside she saw a table laid for two. On it were candles in a tall holder, already lit. At her place was a small silver vase with wild flowers in it. Bone china plates were on a snow-white tablecloth. All this luxury seemed strangely out of place in Dawson.

Smith tugged at a bell rope. For a hotel still under construction the amenities were already functioning smoothly. There was a soft tap at the door, and a little Chinese entered. He handed Tara a printed menu. "I hope you're hungry," Smith said.

She couldn't believe such fare existed in these parts. There was *consommé à la jardinière,* Rock Point oysters, broiled caribou chops *aux champignons,* pears and peaches, and chocolate cake. And to drink, apart from the wine cooling in the bucket on a side table, there was a thirty-nine-year-old port, and Napoleon brandy.

Smith played the perfect host. He filled their glasses and then silently raised his, looking across at her. She was beginning to find his smooth attentiveness disconcerting.

When she took her first taste of the food, Smith watched her reaction closely. "What do you think?" he inquired. "The chef's on trial tonight. I've imported him from the Palace Hotel in Frisco. Now we're going to find out if he lives up to his reputation."

"Delicious," Tara said, and meant it. The mere fact that Smith could produce such luxuries so far from civilization earned her grudging respect for his ingenuity.

"You said you had some information which could interest me," she said, breaking a long and oddly intimate silence.

"There's plenty of time to talk about that," he protested.

"No," Tara said firmly. "This is not a social occasion, Mr. Smith. That's why I'm here."

He took a sip of wine. "I guess you've heard the most terrible stories about this scoundrel Soapy Smith. What a rogue he is. How he runs all the rackets. Correct?"

"Why should I listen to stories about you, Mr. Smith? I've seen you in action. I know how you operate."

Now he was smiling broadly. "Sure. I'm a businessman."

Tara pushed her plate away. "Businessman? Selling people ten-cent bars of soap for five dollars? Rigging up fake telegraph lines? You call that business?"

159

"You really don't understand, do you? I'm a kind of educator. I teach people how easy it is for a sucker to be parted from his dough. I figure that's a public service. Now, doesn't that appeal to you?"

Tara glared at him. "No. It so happens I'm honest, Mr. Smith."

He leaned back and looked at her cynically. "My, that's quite a statement, coming from you. I reckon you haven't much cause to preach me sermons. But any dame who succeeds in taking the Mounties for a ride certainly merits closer acquaintance."

Tara's green eyes blazed. "How dare you . . ."

He grinned at her. "Don't look so worried. I admire you. You're a good-looking woman all right, but you got real talent as well. I got a feeling you and I sort of fit."

"Mr. Smith," Tara said, an edge to her voice. "I don't."

"One day you will, I promise you," he said softly.

"You flatter yourself," she snapped. "Now what have you heard that could interest me?"

"Ah, about your husband. There's a rumor that a man called Daniel Kane from Frisco is prospecting around Fortymile. I'll take you there if you like."

Tara studied him suspiciously and was about to speak when the door burst open. Framed in the doorway was a stunning-looking woman. She wore a silver-fox jacket over a figure-hugging black gown, her hair piled on top of a good-looking, hard face with generous lips. Perhaps the most startling thing about her was the belt encircling her slim waist. It was made entirely of gold nuggets. There was a fortune there, and Tara gaped at it.

"Miss Cad Wilson," Smith said lazily, "Mrs. Tara Kane."

"I heard she was your new filly," Cad said insultingly.

"You know better than to believe everything you hear, Cad," retorted Smith, his tone mocking. "And now that you've met Mrs. Kane, I'm sure you have other matters to attend to."

Cad's glance swept the table. "My, my. Champagne, wine, candles. You *are* trying hard, Soapy."

"I don't like you calling me that, Cad," Smith said. They stared at each other angrily, the atmosphere between them full of unspoken threats.

Cad turned to Tara. "You don't belong in Dawson, honey. If I were you, I'd get out, and that's good advice."

"Cad, it's time you were getting back to work," Smith said.

She leaned forward, picked up his wineglass, and poured what was left onto the white tablecloth. "Sweet dreams." She smiled, her eyes sharp knives ripping through Tara. At the door she blew a kiss to Smith and swept out.

Smith replenished his glass. "Well," he said, ignoring the interruption, "what do you say? Are you coming to Fortymile?"

"Why should I trust you?" Tara demanded. "I'd like to know exactly what you've heard about my husband."

"It's kind of thirdhand, but it sounds like Daniel Kane. From Frisco. Rumor has it he's a pretty sharp poker player too."

It could be Daniel. "And how did you . . ."

"I sort of kept a few ears open," Smith said airily.

"Why?" she asked sharply.

"Because he owes me money and . . ." He paused. "And because I am interested in you. So I put the word out. I'll be leaving in the morning."

Tara stood up. "If I decide to join you, I'll be ready by then." She picked up her purse and walked over to face him. "By the way, I'd like my wedding ring back, please."

"Ah," he sighed. He looked down at the gold band on his finger. "Despite what you might have heard, I'm a man of principle, and one of my strongest is never to mix business with pleasure. I'd hate to spoil a delightful evening by discussing sordid money matters. You're talking about a deal we made. Remember, Tara, you're at liberty to reclaim it at any time, but right now I guess the price is a little too steep for you."

"I could pay you by installments, say two dollars and fifty cents a week."

Smith's eyes twinkled. "One hundred and fifteen dollars paid off at—"

"You only advanced me fifty," exclaimed Tara.

Smith felt in his pocket and pulled out a piece of paper. "The balance is made up by this," he said, unfolding Daniel's IOU. "Plus a surcharge for late payment."

"Of all the low, rotten—"

"Now, now, Tara, business is business."

"One day," Tara said through gritted teeth, "you *will* give it back, and it might be sooner than you think."

"That, Tara, is the day I'm waiting for. Until then, since the sight of it aggravates you so much, I'll keep it in a safe place." He removed the ring from his finger and put it in his vest pocket.

Smith insisted on walking her home. Tara noticed three men following them. "They're deputies," Smith said, wearing his arrogant smile.

"Your gang, you mean?"

He shrugged. "Somebody has to keep law and order. Businessmen like me have investments, and they have to protect them."

As they approached Mrs. Miles's house, Smith said, "Tara, be careful. About Cad. Don't take any chances if she's around."

"Your lady friend?" said Tara coldly. "I really don't think we've much in common. I wouldn't worry about it."

"I know Cad," Smith said. "She can be dangerous."

They were outside Mrs. Miles's house. "Good night, then, Mr. Smith. I'll think about Fortymile," Tara said, pulling out her key.

He shook his head. "You know something, Tara? You're the first woman I've ever spent an evening with who at the end of it still called me Mr. Smith."

"You forget," Tara reminded him, "that ours is strictly a business acquaintance." She turned her back on him and disappeared inside the front door.

That night she lay in the darkness, looking at the ceiling. She knew she would risk anything, even traveling alone in Soapy Smith's dubious company, if Daniel were at the end of the trail. In the morning she packed her few belongings, then sat down and wrote a note to Linda, explaining where she was going. She tiptoed downstairs and left it on the kitchen table, where Mrs. Miles was bound to find it.

CHAPTER SIX

THEY spoke little on the sled journey north. When they camped, Smith prepared the food, made sure she was comfortable, but virtually ignored her. He was polite, correct, and just a little superior. All of which made him intensely annoying to Tara.

"That's Alaska over there," Smith said, pointing into the distance with his whip. "The United States–Canadian border. And *that's* where we'll look for your husband."

Unlike Dawson, Fortymile did not even pretend to be civilized. It was a bleak and windswept settlement that had established itself at the junction of two frozen rivers, the Yukon and the Fortymile. In the middle of the Fortymile River was a small rocky island. To Tara's surprise, Smith guided the team of huskies across the frozen river onto the shale beach of the island. A group of men ran over to them as Smith helped Tara out of the sled. Eagerly she scanned their faces. They were bearded, and wore a strange variety of furs, skins, and Indian anoraks.

"Greetings, General, welcome to Paradise," a white-haired man cried out, sweeping off his cap and bowing low.

"My friends," Smith called out. "This lady has come from Dawson. She is looking for her husband. Daniel Kane."

"Daniel Kane, did you say?" asked a man behind Tara. She swung around. He was a tall man in a scout's hat and buckskin jacket. "Sure, I know him. Allow me to introduce myself. Colonel Lee, ma'am, at your service. Late of the Sixth U.S. Cavalry."

"You know my husband?" Tara stammered.

"Indeed, ma'am." The colonel walked her out of earshot. "He saved my life."

Tara looked at him, startled. "No! When was this?"

"Well," the colonel said, pulling his goatee. "We were cut off. Only me and Dan left. And, by jiminy, you know what he did? Killed six of the savages, got through to the fort, and brought the relief column. Custer was a fool, but with men like me and Dan, he would have survived."

"What are you talking about?" she stuttered. "That's not my husband. That's not Daniel Kane."

"Sure it is," the colonel insisted. "Hey, wait a moment. Lord, you're right. Come to think of it, he got killed in '89. In New Mexico." He looked sad.

Tara didn't know whether to cry with rage or pity, she felt so let down. Smith, who had been walking among the men, slapping them on the back, laughing at their stories, appeared at her side and looked at her inquiringly. "Any luck?"

"Luck?" Tara said bitterly. "Is *he* all the information you had for me? He's crazy. He's still with General Custer."

Smith shook his head sorrowfully. "That's what happens sometimes in the Klondike. It gets too much for some people."

"I don't think there is any point in going on with this charade," said Tara grimly. "Shall we go?" They walked to the sled, and by the time they drew up outside the one ramshackle building in Fortymile which passed for a hotel, Tara's anger was at boiling point. "You didn't really think I'd find out anything about my husband, did you?" She faced him accusingly.

"We're staying here tonight," Smith said, ignoring her question.

Her eyes swept the front of the seedy, uninviting hotel. "Looks delightful," she said scathingly. "I suppose you own this too. Another of your rackets?"

Smith burst out laughing. "Oh, Tara, you should just see yourself when you get indignant."

"I'm glad you find it so amusing, Mr. Smith, hoodwinking me into coming to this godforsaken place on a wild-goose chase." Smith saw her lift her hand to slap his face, but he adeptly grabbed her wrist. He caught her other hand and, holding her arms above her head, he started to dance her around the sled, humming a lively polka. A group of bystanders laughed.

"Stop it," she cried helplessly. The crowd gave a cheer.

"Why, Tara, I had no idea you danced so well." Then, abruptly, he stopped dancing and kissed her hard on the lips. The men whistled and applauded. Smith turned and bowed.

"Come on," he said, seizing her hand. He half pulled, half dragged her into the shabby building, up the rickety staircase to the landing. He kicked open the door at the top, dragged her across the room, and threw her down on the bed.

"Now, you stay there until I get back," he said mildly.

She got off the bed and stood, panting. "How dare you?"

"Dare?" He looked at her, amused. "I dare anything, Tara, believe me." Smith looked at his watch. "High time I did my collection. Part of my public duties here includes running the post office. Every month I have to collect the takings. Tomorrow we return to Dawson. While I'm gone, do not leave this room. Understand?" He went out, gently closing the door.

Tara, shoulders heaving, cried with the disappointment and injustice of it all. She hated herself for being such a gullible fool. Smith had played a cruel hoax on her; to cap it all, he had publicly humiliated her.

Gradually her tears subsided. She sat up and became aware for the first time of the room she was in. Her lips tightened. Smith's things were neatly arranged on the chest of drawers; a shaving mug and brush, a stick of soap, a razor. This must be his usual pied-à-terre on his visits to Fortymile.

There was a closet too. Inside hung male clothing, obviously Smith's. And there was a woman's robe on a hanger. Tara's lip curled. How convenient. Fury engulfed her. "All right, Mr. Soapy Smith," she said, walking around the room. "You want to play games, we'll play games."

The window overlooked Fortymile's main street. Tara tried to open it. It was frozen shut. She smashed the glass. She took the shaving mug and the beaver-bristle brush and threw them out. Then she took a fur jacket from the closet and flung it out, followed by Smith's trousers and shirts. Under the window a little group had now gathered, fascinated by the barrage landing around them.

Tara spotted a leather gladstone bag on the far side of the bed. She rushed over and opened it. There were papers inside, a box of Havana cheroots, and a silver hip flask. Tara bombarded the street with them, item by item. Finally the gladstone bag, with *JRS* embossed on the calf hide, went out the window.

The crowd below had grown to thirty or forty people, and they were loving it all. "Hey, lady," somebody yelled up at Tara, "are you going to throw Soapy out too?"

She waved, but she wasn't finished yet. She looked under the bed. Yes, there it was, the chamber pot. Triumphantly she carried it to the window, then grandly flung it to the crowd below.

The sight of Soapy Smith's chamber pot sailing into Fortymile's main street was heralded with a burst of whistles and applause. Tara grinned. That was the most satisfying of all. They were laughing at Soapy Smith. The king of the Klondike would never be respected quite as much again.

Suddenly she spotted Smith striding purposefully through a barrage of cheers and catcalls toward the hotel. Tara rushed to the door and locked it. She heard him thundering up the stairs.

"Let me in, Tara," he yelled, rattling the door handle.

She smiled complacently. For the first time since she'd met this arrogant joker she had got the better of him.

Then, with a splintering of wood, the door gave way. "What the hell—" began Smith, looking wildly around the room.

"Excuse me," Tara said serenely, and tried to push past him.

He grabbed her arm. "You're not going anywhere."

"Mr. Smith, there are a lot of people outside. If you don't let me pass, I shall scream."

His eyes were blazing. "Just how do you expect to get back to Dawson?"

"I'll manage," Tara replied, pushing past him.

She came out into the street to find the crowd still standing around. They parted, almost reverently, to let her through. A man called out, "Hey, lady, just a moment." She turned. He was a young man in a stiff collar and a neat necktie. "I'm a reporter on the *Nugget*. What was that all about at the hotel?"

"I don't want to talk about it. Excuse me," she said.

"If only that German photographer had been there," said the reporter sorrowfully. "I can still see that chamber pot—"

"What photographer?" Tara asked.

"Herr Hart. He's crazy about shooting things as they happen."

"Is he here? In Fortymile?" she demanded in excitement.

"Sure. He's set up just behind the general store. Taking portraits of everyone in town."

She rushed off. Hart, here in Fortymile. She couldn't believe her luck. A familiar face at last. She found his tent. YOUR PICTURE TAKEN FOR FIVE DOLLARS read the notice hanging from it.

Just then Hart's head popped out of the flap of the tent. When he saw her his eyes opened wide. "Tara," he gasped. He rushed out, kissed her on both cheeks, and drew her inside.

"Ernst," Tara said. "How have you been?"

He raised his hands. "Fantastic. You would never believe it. I have hundreds of photos. What an exhibition I will make." Then he stopped. "Have you found Daniel yet?"

She shook her head and told him what had happened since they had parted company in Dyea. When she described the scene at the hotel, he laughed.

After she had finished, Hart said firmly, "I shall take you back to Dawson on my sled."

"Can you manage it? Have you got the room?" She looked anxiously around the tent, littered with boxes and chemicals.

"I've always got room for you, Tara," Hart said. "I have completed my work here anyway, so there is no problem."

WHEN THEY ARRIVED in Dawson, Tara and Hart parted company again. He looked crestfallen at losing her so soon, but Tara promised to come and see him when he had set up shop.

"Oh. It's you," was Mrs. Miles's greeting when Tara walked into the lodging house. "It was a wild-goose chase, wasn't it, and now you've got nowhere to stay?"

Tara nodded.

Mrs. Miles sniffed. "Well, I'll take you back as a servant girl. I'll pay you five dollars a week, and you get your keep and lodging. That's all. You have disappointed me."

"Linda," protested Tara. "If you'll only listen to what really happened."

Mrs. Miles shot her a quick glance. "You do agree, don't you, that trust is the most important—"

"Please don't lecture me," Tara cried. "I got my just reward in Fortymile."

Mrs. Miles's manner softened. "Very well." She nodded. "Just do your work, and we won't talk about it again."

The following day Tara was alone in the house when she heard someone knocking at the front door. To her astonishment, there stood Cad Wilson, wrapped in a magnificent fur cape with a hood.

"Good morning, Mrs. Kane. Aren't you going to invite me in?"

She stepped into the hall, and Tara closed the door. "Yes?"

"I've come here because I've found out something about your husband, so I thought I'd pass it on."

"All right," Tara said warily. "Come in." She opened the door to the parlor and Cad went in.

"Thank you," murmured Cad. "I have something I want to show you." She opened her handbag and gave Tara a wrapped object.

Tara looked at her mystified, and then unwrapped the piece of cloth. It was a man's silver watch. She stared at it in disbelief. It was her father's watch, which she had given to Daniel. There were the words she had had engraved inside it: *To my darling husband Daniel, with eternal love from his devoted wife Tara Kane, 1897.* "Where did you get this?" Tara whispered.

"Your husband sold it," Cad said. "He needed money for supplies. I understand he's teamed up with a man called Jake Gore. They've got a digging."

"Where?" gasped Tara.

"Oh, a hundred miles from here, in Hell's Kitchen, up in Tagish country."

"What is it? A town?"

"A hole. The end of the line."

"How did you come by the watch?" asked Tara.

"Jake's brother bought it from your husband, then he had bad luck at faro at the Monte Carlo. So he paid his debt with it. I saw the name and asked him how he came by it."

"There's one thing I don't understand," said Tara, turning the watch over in her hands. "Why are you trying to help me?"

"Listen, Mrs. Kane. I don't want you around Jeff. Is that clear enough? He's my property. We belong to one another."

Tara stared at her. "Believe me, Miss Wilson, you're welcome to him. If I never see him again, I'll be happy."

Cad drew on her sealskin gloves. "You know where your man is now. Find him and get out of the territory."

After Cad left, Tara rushed to her room. She pressed the watch to her cheek. At last a tangible clue to Daniel's whereabouts. Hell's Kitchen, she mused. Only a hundred miles from Dawson. It could not be all that bad, not if Daniel was there.

Her requirements were simple, she decided. She needed a sled, a dog team, supplies, and a map. She thought of the lodgers. She was sure she could get a sled and team from the Bartlett brothers; weren't they in the haulage business? Then Mr. Brock might advance her sufficient supplies for the journey. As for a map, who better to approach than Hart?

Tara hurried to the temporary studio Hart had set up in the center of town. Even after she had shown him the watch and explained what Cad had told her, he seemed unconvinced. He described the terrain she would have to cover. It was no place for a woman on her own. So, in the interests of a photographic record of the Klondike, he would accompany her.

"Well, if you really want to come . . ." said Tara.

"Of course. You don't think I would let you go alone. I will close shop and prepare my equipment for the journey. There will be room enough on my sled for you too."

"It's all right. I've hired my own team." Tara smiled at him. "With the watch and my compass, and you to guide me, I know we will find Daniel."

CHAPTER SEVEN

EARLY the following morning Tara trudged with the Bartlett brothers to their depot, where she picked up a sled and team. From there she went to Brock's store and collected supplies. Then she drove the sled to Hart's studio.

"Well, Mrs. Tara Kane," Hart said, going over to his sled and picking up the reins, "let's get going and find your husband."

The hundreds of miles she had traveled in other people's sleds, watching them handle their dog teams, had not been wasted. For the first few miles she was frightened, but then she realized the dogs were traveling the way she wanted, obeying her.

They were circling Lousetown, on the trail north, when she noticed a horseman following them. He was galloping furiously, and Tara tightened her lips when she recognized Jefferson Smith.

To Tara's annoyance, Hart slowed his team. Smith pulled up alongside them and looked down at her. "There's a rumor you're going north, Mrs. Kane. It's no place for a woman."

She stared straight through him.

Hart cleared his throat. "You need have no worries about Mrs. Kane. She will be well protected."

"Listen, mister," Smith said menacingly, moving his horse nearer to Hart. "You look after her well. Because I'm telling you fair and square, if anything happens to her"—he reached out and grabbed Hart by his coat collar—"I'm going to hold you responsible."

Tara had never seen Smith like this. For the first time she realized that he actually cared what happened to her.

Smith released Hart and turned his horse to Tara. "Since you won't change your mind, you'd better have this." It was a stubby pistol, a tiny .22 derringer, beautifully made, with an engraved mother-of-pearl handle. "If anyone gets too close for comfort, use it." He swung his horse around and galloped off.

Tara looked at the pistol. It fitted her hand perfectly. Inscribed along the squat barrel was *A Sure Thing from JRS*.

"What are we waiting for, Ernst?" Tara said, putting the pistol in her bag. It was as if she had communicated her sense of urgency to the dogs. They streaked through the snow, moving ahead of Hart's sled. She felt as she'd never felt before, free, completely in control of her destiny, no longer beholden to somebody else. At last the vast territory didn't threaten her. Now she was part of it.

When they camped, Tara set up a stove inside the tent, while Hart collected firewood. She melted snow as she had seen the Mounties do, and made sure that her dogs were fed. She was like a woman of the Klondike.

Once, she saw Hart watching her. "Why are you staring at me?"

"Because you've changed," he said. "You're not the shivering, timid, frightened orphan I met on the ship."

"What am I now, then?"

"You're a woman who can look after herself," he said, a little grudgingly. "You'll survive, no matter what."

During the night Tara stirred uneasily. She opened her eyes and then sat up, stifling a scream. A man with long hair and earrings stood over her, a hideous grin on his face and a pistol in his hand.

"Howdy," he said genially. He stuck his pistol in his belt and hauled her to her feet.

Stupefied with fear, Tara watched wide-eyed as his ugly face came nearer. She turned her head in a feverish effort to escape his repulsive embrace.

The man grinned malevolently and dragged her from the tent. "Look what I found, boys," he announced triumphantly.

Two other men stood by the sleds. They both had rifles. Hart was lying motionless on the ground.

"Ernst!" she cried, rushing toward him. She knelt by him and took his head in her hands.

His eyes flickered. "Tara," he gasped. "Are you all right?"

The three men were standing around laughing. The other two were as forbidding as their companion with the earrings. One had a black eye patch and was dressed like a trapper. The other had a red beard and a brutish face.

"What do you want from us?" she demanded.

"You'd never guess," said the one with earrings.

"I'm sorry, Tara," Hart apologized. "They crept up on me, and then somebody hit me."

"He's okay," said the man with the eye patch. "Hank never hits 'em too hard."

Hank was the one with the earrings. He grabbed Tara's chin and turned her head toward him. "She and me fancy each other," he said. "Ain't that right, sweetheart?"

"Keep away from me," she spat, kicking out at him.

"Where are you making for?" asked the man with the eye patch, who seemed to be in charge.

"We're going north," Tara said.

"Got any gold?"

Tara shook her head.

"She's lying, Duke," Hank said.

"So what's on the sled?" Duke asked. "Supplies?"

"Equipment," replied Tara. "Mr. Hart is a photographer."

They stared at her, disbelieving. Then Hank went over to Hart's sled and pulled back the tarpaulin covering the cases and boxes. Duke picked up a box of plates and looked at it curiously. "What kind of pictures do you take?"

"I take portraits of important people," Hart said.

"We should get our pictures made. You willing to picture me and the boys?"

"You'll have your own portfolio. I'll do you in a group and then individually," Hart said eagerly, struggling to his feet.

Tara wondered if this display of enthusiasm was genuine, or merely an attempt to get them out of a tight spot.

"We got a little hideaway," Duke said. "We'll take you. The rest of the boys there will want to be took too."

"What about her? Who gets her?" demanded the red-bearded one, without even looking in Tara's direction.

Hank swung around. "I do."

"Like hell you do—"

"Keep your hair on," intervened the man with the eye patch. "There's plenty for all of us."

Tara was petrified. She wondered wildly how they could escape.

"Where is this place?" Hart demanded.

"Mister, you ask too many questions," Duke said coldly. "Get hitched up. Move."

Little was said once they were on the trail. Duke had a sled, with a pack of dogs as villainous as the trio. Hank and the red-bearded man, whose name was Shorty, trekked along on snowshoes beside Tara and Hart, who were driving their own sleds.

The landscape provided no clue to where they were going. It was more barren, more deserted than any terrain Tara had seen so far. In the distance were great mountains, their summits obscured by frozen mist. Eventually they halted, and Hank approached Tara. A great uneasiness swept through her.

"Relax, sweetheart. I ain't going to harm you." He tied a scarf securely over her eyes.

"I can't drive the team like this," Tara objected.

"Hank'll take over," Duke said. "You can ride like a lady."

She had no idea how long they traveled nor in what direction. Then a shot rang out.

"It's okay," Hank said. "Nothing to worry about." Three more shots followed, fired from just behind. Hank pulled the sled to a halt. "You can look now," he said, pulling off the scarf.

She blinked, her eyes unaccustomed to the sudden brightness. The sleds had pulled up in a clearing, surrounded on all sides by high cliffs. There were a few tents and two rough wooden shacks.

Duke was talking to a tall man wearing the scarlet jacket of a Mountie. When Tara looked more closely she saw that most of the brass buttons were missing and there was a hole, edged by a stain, where the Mountie's heart had once been. Behind him stood three other men.

"How much do you want for her?" the man dressed as a Mountie asked Duke.

Duke shook his head. "She's not for sale. She belongs to us, Blue. Me and the boys found her, so she's ours."

Tara stared straight ahead, trying to conceal the raw fear she felt in the pit of her stomach. "Where is this?" she asked.

"Paradise." Blue smiled. "Least that's my name for it. Some call it Hell's Kitchen. You've fallen among thieves."

"Hell's Kitchen," she repeated slowly. She glanced at Hart, who was as shaken as she was to discover they'd reached their intended destination. "I am Daniel Kane's wife. From San Francisco."

"So?" asked Blue. It meant nothing to him.

"Where's Jake Gore, his partner?"

"You know Jake, eh?" said Blue. "Fancy that." He turned to one of the men behind him. "A friend of yours, Jake?"

Jake was a sallow-faced man with long black hair tied at the nape of his neck. He had a shoulder holster under his left armpit, but instead of a gun it held a knife sheath. He wore a gold ring on every finger. Tara stared at him incredulously. Was this Daniel's partner?

173

Jake turned to Blue. "I think she and me got some private business," he said.

"You ain't doing any claim jumping while I'm around," Hank threatened, his hand going toward his gun.

"We got business," said Jake very softly. He turned as if to walk away; then, with the speed of a rattlesnake, he whirled around and threw something. Hank sank to his knees, Jake's knife protruding from his chest. He slumped forward and lay still.

Slowly Jake walked up to Hank's lifeless body, turned it over with his foot, and drew out the knife.

"One moment, please!" shouted Hart, carefully sidestepping Hank's body. "I would like to take a picture."

"What for?" Jake growled.

"To photograph you. Here on the spot. As it happened."

Hart's cold-bloodedness shook Tara. He unloaded his sled, set up his camera, posed Jake Gore by Hank's body, disappeared under his blanket, and exposed the first plate. When he had finished, the men applauded and cheered. Hart told them he was available for anyone wishing to have his portrait taken.

Jake Gore went up to Tara, who was standing by, pale and numb from what she had seen. "Come on, let's talk," he said, leading her to a tent. Inside there was only a bearskin rug. "So, you're his wife?"

She nodded.

"Who told you I was here?"

"Cad Wilson," Tara said, reaching in her bag and bringing out the watch.

He looked at it, then at her. "Yeah, that's his."

"Where is he?" she asked.

"Camped a few miles from here. At the claim."

"Can we leave now?"

He shook his head. "Weather don't look good. First thing in the morning, Mrs. Kane."

Once outside, Tara hugged herself with excitement. She had to find Hart. From the direction of a cave in the rock she could hear men shouting, so she went toward it.

The interior of the cave was illuminated by a roaring log fire and oil lamps hanging from the walls. The place was packed; obviously this was Hell's Kitchen's nighttime haunt. Hart, oblivious to everything, was adjusting his camera on its tripod.

Tara edged her way through the crowd to him. "Ernst," she said urgently. "I'm meeting Daniel in the morning."

"I don't think I have any pictures," Hart grumbled. "This light is too dim."

"Ernst," Tara exploded. "I have found Daniel. He's camped a few miles away. He's got a claim."

"That's wonderful," he said, but he didn't sound enthusiastic. "I'm so happy for you. I know you think I am a cold-blooded fish, yes? Here you are, all excited, and I am only interested in taking pictures. But you see, this is my mission out here."

She kissed him on the cheek. "Jake Gore and I start at dawn."

Hart regarded her gravely. "He is a very bad man."

"He knows where Daniel is. He's taking me to him. That's all that matters."

"Wait until I can come with you."

"Oh, Ernst, you don't think I can *wait*, do you?"

"No, perhaps not." He sighed. "You are always impetuous, Tara. Your trouble is you won't change your mind."

CHAPTER EIGHT

IT was not only the sounds of revelry and drunkenness that kept Tara awake most of that night. It was the thought that by this time tomorrow she and Daniel would be together again. It filled her with a strange combination of excitement and apprehension. Excitement at seeing him, being in his arms, kissing him; apprehension at what he might have become.

Toward dawn she packed away her few things, put the derringer Smith had given her in her pocket, and hitched up her team. Jake was waiting beside his sled. "Follow me," was all he said. There was no blindfold this time.

They traveled through a narrow ravine, then down a bumpy trail. Finally they emerged onto open ground. She wanted to ask how long it would take, but Jake's sled kept too far ahead. All the time she hoped for some sign of their destination, but white emptiness stretched for miles on every side.

Four hours later Tara saw in the distance what looked like a frozen lake, with some haggard pine trees around it. Pitched by the edge was a tent. Her excitement grew and she lashed away

175

at the dogs, urging them to go faster in the biting wind. "Is that it?" she yelled as she drew level with Jake's sled.

Jake nodded.

Tara felt a sense of triumph. She had found Daniel.

As she drew nearer she could see snow heaped against one side of the tent, where winds and blizzards had drifted it. She brought her sled to a halt a few yards from the tent and rushed forward, tumbling and sliding through the snow in her eagerness.

"Daniel! I'm here!" she called out, her eyes shining as she pulled aside the tent flap. The tent was empty.

For a moment she stood stunned. She could see enough to know that this was certainly somebody's quarters. Some clothes were lying about, and there were cooking utensils, mining tools.

She looked around, puzzled; then slowly Tara turned and walked toward Jake. His sled stood beside hers. "Where is he?" demanded Tara. "Where's Daniel?"

"This way," Jake said.

She followed him to the back of the tent.

"There he is," Jake announced, stepping aside. A few feet in front of her was a little mound. Stuck on the top of it were two pieces of wood, tied together into a cross.

Tara stared in disbelief, the blood draining from her face. "No," she whispered, "no."

"That's him," Jake said. "Say howdy."

Her whole body felt numb. This could not be. Daniel buried here in the frozen ground, alone, abandoned? No, never.

"That's how I got his watch, see," Jake said. "He never was a willing giver."

She looked at him, her face a mask of horror.

"I guess you're a widow woman now. But don't worry." He smiled. "You ain't going to be lonesome." He reached out and grabbed her.

"No!" she shrieked, clawing at his face. He swung a fist, and she could feel herself falling. Then everything went black.

When she came around a few seconds later, she was on the ground, his full weight on top of her. He was tearing at her clothes, ripping them. "I'm going to have you," he snarled. "Then I'm going to kill you, just like I told Cad."

He didn't notice her pulling the gun from her pocket. She

rammed the stocky muzzle against his head and without hesitation squeezed the trigger. Jake went rigid, his eyes opening wide. Then his body went limp.

"Oh, God!" she screamed. With all her strength she pushed Jake off her body. He lay on his back, his sightless eyes staring up at the graying sky.

Tara couldn't believe that Jake was dead. She stared at him, sobbing like a child. She was alone, with a dozen dogs, a dead man, and a grave for company. She did not know where she was; she had no idea in what direction they had traveled. The tent billowed soundlessly in a cold wind whispering across the snow.

There was the grave. It could not be Daniel's, a voice in her head insisted. Like a sleepwalker, she slowly got to her feet. She had to know who was in that lonely mound.

She grabbed a pickaxe from the tent and ran to the grave. With the strength of a lunatic she started hacking away at the rock-hard soil. It began to crack. Now she could see the outline of a body. She fell to her knees, and with her bare hands started clawing at the earth. She had to see his face. She was almost hysterical, mouthing prayers as she brushed away the last veil of soil.

She was looking on the hard-set face of a middle-aged man. His eyes were frozen shut, as if he were sleeping—sleeping with a hole through his heart. He had been murdered. But he was not Daniel.

"Aaah!" she screamed, jumping to her feet, her eyes wild. "He's not dead!" she cried to the vast emptiness around her, not noticing how the wind began to blow. "Jake Gore lied!" She stood in the raging wind, snow now swirling around her, and she laughed.

Gradually her elation receded, and she became aware of the swirling snow and the frenzied yapping of the dogs. Her teeth began to chatter. She recalled what the Mounties had told her: once you start freezing, you're finished. She quickly gathered some wood, lit the stove in the deserted tent, and prepared coffee to warm herself. As she drank the scalding liquid she looked around the tent.

There were some canned foods, a pair of snowshoes, and some clothes. She took off her torn jacket and shirt and put on a large parka. Then she saw a tin deedbox in the corner of the tent.

Tara opened the lid. There were five dollars, a rabbit's paw, a necklace with an Indian pendant. None of it meant anything to her. There were also several stained letters. She threw them aside impatiently. Then she spotted handwriting she recognized. "Mrs. Tara Kane, 110 Fulton Street, San Francisco, Cal., USA" read Daniel's script. Her mind reeling, she tore open the envelope.

My own most dearest Tara,
    I do not know if you will ever receive this. Yet I must write to you, because I miss you more than words can describe. Things have not gone well so far and the only thing that keeps me going is the thought of you and our daughter. I love you, Tara, as no man has ever loved a woman.
    This is a dismal hole and I am not at all sure I am on the right trail. Supplies are low and I have developed an irksome cough. The worst thing is the isolation. I have not seen a human face for days. I never dreamed it would be like this. But take no notice. We shall all be rich. One way or another. Isn't it insane how usless gold is, though? You cannot eat it. Out here it doesn't even keep you warm. Why do we worship it? One thing, though, I know now. I will come back to you, Tara. In this world, or another. We will never be parted, you and I.

Her eyes were brimming with tears as she finished reading the letter. "Oh, Dan," she sobbed. "Dan."

Through her tears she tried to reason it out; the letter looked months old, but how had it got here? How had Jake Gore got hold of Daniel's watch? And how did Cad Wilson fit in?

Tara vaguely recalled something Jake had said before she killed him. Then it came back to her; his words about killing her as he'd told Cad he would. Could it be that Cad was so insanely jealous of her that she had hired Jake Gore to lure her out here to kill her?

She could hear the dogs snarling. They hadn't been fed for hours. There was some dried moose meat packed among her things, but she was frightened. A terrible gale had started up, and the sound of the wind, the howling of the dogs, and the two dead bodies filled her with foreboding. But she had to feed the dogs. Without them she would never get back to civilization.

She pocketed Daniel's letter and battled her way out to the sled and unwrapped the meat. She picked up her whip and went over to Jake's mangy malamutes. As she approached, they growled at her, so she cracked the whip.

"Down!" she cried as one beast snapped at her ankles. Quickly she unwrapped the meat, and then unharnessed the team. She had forgotten the golden rule: each dog had to be fed individually and unharnessed one at a time to eat.

As she returned to her own sled, where the tethered dogs were getting restless, Jake's team, free from their traces, streaked across the snow like a pack of wolves. "Come back!" Tara yelled, but they took no notice. Then she saw what had caused the stampede. The dogs were tearing, biting, ripping Jake's body.

Tara's own team responded by yapping and snapping with excitement, straining at their harnesses in their eagerness to join in. Tara's stomach turned over, but fear of what this maddened horde might do next overwhelmed her disgust.

She knew she had little time. If the malamutes turned on her, she was finished. She ran over to Jake's sled and, with shaking hands, untied his rifle from the handlebars. She pushed back the safety catch and, aiming as best she could through the snow the wind hurled against her, pulled the trigger.

She kept firing until the rifle clicked, its magazine empty. She had killed two of the dogs and wounded another. Then, like a grisly epilogue, two of the survivors launched themselves at the crippled dog and sank their teeth into his body. The third watched for a moment and then flung himself into the melee.

"Oh my God," Tara sobbed as the frenzied animals fought each other. Here was a primitive lust to kill, fed on the oldest urge of all, survival. It didn't last long. The dogs lay strewn around the snow, dead or dying. Jake's pack had destroyed itself.

She dashed to her sled and, without a backward glance, cracked her whip and urged her team ahead. They pulled the sled willingly. They were hungry, and a ravenous dog made a willing worker.

The swirling snow made visibility bad, and she didn't know in which direction she was going. Although she had no map she decided she was north. She had to get back to Dawson, which she reasoned must lie to the south. She riffled through her bag and took out the compass, but it was a pitiful aid to navigation.

She continued traveling through the night. Like a phantom team, the dogs pulled through the darkness, and she relied on them to keep traveling along the right track. In her delirious condition she thought at times she was lying safely in bed and all this was a dream. Then she would realize where she was. Once Tara screamed so terrifyingly that the dogs turned their heads and stared at her, their eyes puzzled.

"Somebody please help me! Save me!" she yelled dementedly to the empty landscape. "I don't want to die."

Then she saw it. She watched, awestruck, as an indescribable yellow light sprang from the whiteness of the snow to the heavens above. An unearthly golden glow spread across the sky, streamers of brilliant, dazzling colors dancing along the horizon, bathing the sky in a divine fireworks display.

The lights, vivid reds and yellows and blues, imbued the whole firmament and spread before Tara's hypnotized eyes. After the blackness, the grays, the whites, the monotones, this darting stream of color was like the promise of another land. Tara had never seen, but she had heard of, the aurora borealis—the northern lights. Standing there, a lone human figure witnessing the sky on fire, she was enraptured by its beauty and hidden meaning. It was the omen that made all the difference.

"Thank God," Tara sobbed. "Oh, thank God."

Those glorious rays, reflecting the brightness of all the hopes of the Yukon, more dazzling than all the gold in the Klondike, gave her faith as nothing else could have.

It was a sign from heaven. There was hope.

She turned her back on the phenomenon and faced the direction the miracle had now confirmed was south. Although she was consumed by fatigue, she gritted her teeth and thrust the sled forward, determined to make it to Dawson.

CHAPTER NINE

THE woman who staggered, robotlike, into Dawson three days later had no memory of her long, delirious trek. She stumbled down the main street, driven by the inner compulsion that had kept her traveling through the snowy wastes.

Suddenly she stopped. She was holding on to a hitching post, staring blankly at the wooden façade of the Monte Carlo Saloon.

Dizzily she realized that before her was the place where Cad Wilson worked. She was the only one who could tell Tara the truth.

She slowly mounted the wooden steps, pushing open the swing

doors of the saloon. With unseeing eyes she walked toward a man behind the bar. "Where is Cad Wilson?" she croaked.

The man raised his eyebrows. Tara's clothes were stained, her hands caked with dried blood, her face weather-beaten, her lips covered with scabs. "Miss Wilson's upstairs."

Clutching the banister, Tara climbed the stairs. She made her way down the corridor, looking for Cad in each room, leaving angry prostitutes in her wake. Finally she reached the last door.

Inside was a large and ornately decorated boudoir. Tara floated across a sea of thick carpet toward a chaise longue on which Cad Wilson reclined, dressed in a multicolored kimono.

Cad stood up. From miles away Tara heard her gasp, "You!"

"He didn't kill me," Tara said.

"I don't know what you're talking about," Cad retorted.

"What happened to my husband?" Tara asked in a low voice.

"Don't tell me you didn't find him, Mrs. Kane." Cad laughed.

Tara slapped her across the face. Cad fell back onto the sofa, staring up at Tara.

"You knew Daniel wasn't there. You used his watch to get me out of your way," screamed Tara. "You hired Jake Gore to kill me, didn't you? Only it didn't quite work out the way you planned it, because Jake Gore is dead."

Cad looked at her fearfully. "You're crazy!"

"I killed him! Now tell me where my husband is." Tara grabbed Cad by the shoulders and shook her like a rag doll.

Cad escaped her grip and ran to the door. "You're not well, Mrs. Kane. Get out before I have you thrown out."

Tara turned and looked at Cad standing beside the open door. Beyond her a gaggle of prostitutes crowded into the corridor. Tara started through them, her head ringing. At the top of the stairs she fainted, falling down the entire flight and collapsing in a heap on the saloon floor.

She never heard the uproar. Smith had entered the saloon in time to see Tara crash down the stairs. He dashed to where she lay and carefully turned her over.

"What happened?" he demanded, still kneeling beside Tara.

Cad rushed forward. "Oh, Jeff, the poor woman came to my room raving, and when I told her she was sick, she went quite wild, ran out of my room, and you saw the rest."

"Mort!" shouted Smith, getting up. "Get some blankets. I'm taking Mrs. Kane home."

The sight of Jefferson Smith walking down Front Street carrying the seemingly lifeless body of a woman wreathed in blankets was unusual even in Dawson. But he ignored the gaping passersby, mounted the steps, and knocked on Mrs. Miles's front door.

She gasped when she saw Tara, limp in his arms.

"Mrs. Kane has collapsed," Smith said quietly. "She needs your help desperately."

"This way," she said.

They mounted the stairs in silence, Mrs. Miles leading the way to Tara's room. She hovered, while Smith gently laid Tara on the bed. "Now leave my house. I don't want to see you here again."

"Of course," he agreed amiably. In the hallway, he paused. "Before I go, ma'am, I want to assure you that anything you may require will be at your disposal. I will arrange for the doctor to stop by. If I can be of—"

She slammed the bedroom door on him before he had time to finish.

After the doctor had examined the unconscious Tara, his face was grave. The fall down the stairs had been the last straw. She was suffering from exposure. She had bronchitis, which could be turning into pneumonia, and she was half starved.

Day and night Mrs. Miles nursed Tara like her own daughter. She attended her every need, sitting hour after hour by her bedside, watching her toss and turn, delirious with fever.

It was several weeks before the doctor announced that Tara could go downstairs for the first time. Mrs. Miles lit a huge fire in the parlor. There Tara spent the next few days, her mind becoming clearer and her body stronger. Slowly her eyes grew brighter, the scabs cleared from her lips, her skin began to glow once more.

Her gradual improvement was partially due to her decision that the nightmare events at the grave belonged to another world. Tara wanted to tell Linda Miles what had happened, but she could not face the thought of having to admit that she had murdered. The terrible memories began to recede, but each time she dozed, weird and frenzied images haunted her dreams. Often, when alone, she reread Daniel's desperate letter, wondering where he had written it, who he had given it to, where he had gone after sealing it.

One day there was a peremptory knock on the front door. Mrs. Miles was out shopping, having left firm instructions that Tara should stay in the fireside armchair.

The knocking sounded again, hammering urgently. Tara's legs still felt shaky as she opened the front door.

"Hello, Tara," said Sergeant Campbell. He was in uniform, and Tara noticed that he had been given his three stripes back.

"Andrew." Tara held out her hand. "How have you been?"

Campbell cleared his throat. He seemed ill at ease. "This is official business, Tara. I've come to ask you some questions."

"What about?"

"An allegation has been made." He paused. "I am following up a report that a man was murdered up north, near Hell's Kitchen, in Tagish territory. Is there anything *you* want to tell me?"

"About what?" she mumbled, clenching her hands.

Campbell hesitated. "Tara, did you kill a man?"

"Kill a man," she repeated dully. The nightmare turned into reality again. "Yes," she croaked. "I killed a man."

"Jake Gore?" prompted Campbell.

She was trembling. "I didn't want to . . . He tried to . . ."

"Was it self-defense?" asked Campbell.

No one heard Mrs. Miles come in. "What's going on?" she demanded, standing in the doorway of the parlor.

"I'm investigating a killing," said Campbell. "There's a man in town by the name of Arne Gore, who says that Tara killed his brother Jake."

"I don't believe you," exploded Mrs. Miles.

"Gore's threatened to whip up feeling against her and get the whole of Dawson on his side if we don't do our duty as law officers." He turned to Tara. "Did Jake try to assault you? Was he going to kill you?"

"Yes," she screamed, the tears pouring down her face. "Yes!"

"Oh, my dear," said Mrs. Miles, putting her arm around Tara's shoulders. "Why didn't you tell me? Oh, you poor thing."

"Tara, you'll have to make a formal statement," said Campbell. He turned to Mrs. Miles. "Please try to understand that I can't afford trouble. Inspector Constantine is away and I've got to do it by the book. Otherwise, the Citizens' Committee or the Miners' Court might take the law into their own hands." Campbell went to the door. "Bring her over to the post as soon as she's fit, and I'll take a deposition."

After he had left, Mrs. Miles led Tara upstairs and helped her into bed. She sat beside her and took her hands. "Why don't you tell me about it?" she said very softly.

Tara looked at her, and then, her voice choked with emotion, her green eyes pools of sadness, told Mrs. Miles the whole story.

CAMPBELL had not been exaggerating when he said that Gore was stirring up bad feeling in Dawson. The next night men carrying flaming torches gathered in front of Mrs. Miles's house, shaking their fists and yelling. Tara could not make out what it was they shouted.

Mrs. Miles came into her room. "Get away from that window," she ordered. "Don't let them see you."

For the first time Tara could hear the words the mob was yelling. "Tara Kane, we've come for you. Tara Kane!"

"What do they want from me?" she whispered.

The mob was being waved on by a tall, lean man, his long hair tied back. His blazing brand illuminated sharp features, an ugly, snarling mouth. What she could see in the flickering light reminded Tara of the man she could never forget. Jake Gore.

"We're coming in to get you," the man yelled.

Mrs. Miles rushed from the room, Tara following her. The lodgers had gathered in the hallway. They were all armed.

Fists hammered on the front door. "Open up," came a voice. "We want the Kane woman. Orders of the court."

"It's the Miners' Court," the lodger Lamore said.

Tara froze. This was the reckoning. As Campbell had predicted, the Miners' Court had decided to settle the matter themselves.

"She's sick," Mrs. Miles told them through the door. "Leave this business to the Mounties."

The only reply she got was a furious pounding; then a window smashed upstairs. One of the Bartletts ran past Tara.

"The first man that tries to come in, we'll blow his head off," he yelled from the first-floor window.

"What are we going to do?" asked Lamore. "They won't give up. They'll burn the house down."

"Linda! Open the door!" Tara said, hardly recognizing her own voice. "There's no other way. They've a right to hear the truth, and I want to tell it to them."

Reluctantly, Mrs. Miles unlocked the door. As it opened, Tara saw a three-man deputation standing on the steps.

"There she is," yelled the tall man, holding his torch high and pointing at her. "There is the woman who killed my brother."

One of the three men took her arm. "Where are you taking me?" Tara asked, looking around for a familiar face, but the lodgers and Mrs. Miles were lost from sight. She was alone.

"Courtroom," grunted the leader, escorting her down the steps.

Tara found herself marching with the three vigilantes. The whole town appeared to have turned out for this grim procession. In the glow of torches she caught glimpses of hard, set faces. Leading the way, his blazing brand held aloft, ran Jake Gore's brother.

Halfway down Front Street, the Reverend Charles Bowers suddenly appeared at Tara's elbow. Under his black coat a gun belt was visible. It was the first time Tara had seen him since Skagway.

"Keep your powder dry," he whispered urgently. "Plead not guilty, whatever they say, see?" He merged back into the throng behind them.

The procession halted at the Eldorado Saloon.

"Here she is," Arne Gore yelled from the steps. "Why don't we get a rope now and save a lot of time?"

The vigilante leader had his finger on the trigger of his rifle. "Stand aside, Gore," he commanded. "This is all going to be done according to miners' law."

Gore wavered for a moment, then grudgingly stood aside, and the throng rushed forward, propelling Tara through the doors.

Inside, the saloon had been transformed into a crude courtroom. A table had been dragged in front of the bar; opposite it, on the dance floor, was another table; to its right, a lone chair. At the back, rows of chairs lined the walls. Now people stampeded wildly, pushing each other out of the way to get a good seat.

The vigilantes ordered Tara to the vacant chair.

She looked around. Cad Wilson, dressed in a magnificent silk dress, was in the front row, sitting between the fat Grizzly Bear and Diamond Tooth Gertie, one of Dawson's toughest saloon queens, whose vixenish grin bared an enormous diamond fixed between her two front teeth.

Tara clenched her hands, willing herself to keep calm. She couldn't believe that this was happening to her, that she was actually on trial for her life in this parody of a court of law.

A white-haired man appeared at the table in front of the bar and held up his hands. "Quiet," he yelled. "Silence in court."

The buzz of conversation ebbed. Through the swing doors a man was pushed in a wheelchair. Gold-rimmed glasses perched on his nose; his skin was gray and pasty, his thin lips tinged with blue.

Slowly he maneuvered the wheelchair between the bar and the table, then faced the crowd. His piercing eyes fixed unblinkingly on Tara while the white-haired man declaimed, "This court's now in session. The Honorable Judge Elmer Rickless presiding."

"Court's ready," the judge said, rapping for order with a hammer. "Where's the jury?"

Twelve men immediately stood up and trooped behind the bar. They sat down on high stools, facing the saloon. They looked almost identical—tough, villainous, shifty.

The judge nodded at the white-haired man, who appeared to act as court usher. "Okay," he said. "Let's start. Who's prosecuting, and what's the charge?"

Arne Gore was on his feet. "I am, Your Honor, and the charge against that woman is murder." He pointed at Tara. "She killed my brother."

"Okay." The judge nodded. "What's your name?" he wheezed, staring at Tara.

"Kane. Mrs. Tara Kane."

"Are you pleading guilty or not guilty?"

"Not guilty," replied Tara quietly.

"You got a defense counsel?"

"I'll defend myself."

"Okay. It's your neck. So, Mr. Prosecutor. Tell us how she killed your brother."

"Your Honor," Gore said. "She hired Jake up in Tagish country as a guide. Then out on the trail she shot him for his money. She's a hustler down on her luck. Jake had sixty dollars and three ounces of gold dust."

"Did you witness the murder?" the judge asked.

"No, Your Honor."

"Then how do you know she did it?" he queried.

187

Arne Gore grinned. "Miss Cad Wilson will testify to that."

The judge opened a book he had brought into court with him. He began thumbing the pages, then looked up. "Without a body you don't have a murder. So who's seen the body?"

"I have," said Gore. "I went looking for my brother, and I found what was left of him. She'd set the dogs on him." There was a rustle in the saloon, and Tara could feel the hostility.

"Okay," said Judge Rickless. "Let's hear from your witness."

Gore looked over to the spectators. "I call Miss Cad Wilson."

"Hold it!" yelled the judge, turning to the usher. "Where's the witness stand? A courtroom's gotta have a witness stand."

The usher dragged a wooden crate from behind the bar and put it in the middle of the floor. "How's that?" He beamed.

"Better," growled the judge. "Makes it decent and formal. Okay, Miss Wilson. You take the stand."

"Thank you, Judge." As she stepped on the crate she looked elegant, glamorous, and completely at ease.

"You swear to tell the truth, the whole truth, and nothing but the truth so help you God?" intoned the usher.

"On a stack of Bibles, Judge," Cad demurely agreed.

"Just tell 'em what you know," urged Gore.

Cad took a deep breath. "She's a fortune hunter. She heard that Jake had struck it rich, and she asked me how to locate him. Later on I heard that she and a friend set off for Jake's camp. When she returned to Dawson, she told me she'd killed Jake Gore. Then she threatened me, saying that I'd be the next person she'd kill."

"Hmm," said the judge. He looked across at Tara. "You want to ask her something?"

Tara stared at Cad, horrified. "She's a liar. There's no point in my asking her anything."

"Gentlemen, I appeal to you!" Cad cried angrily. "Ain't a lady entitled to some protection from that murderess?"

The judge banged for order with his hammer. "I can't have witnesses yelling like that. You are excused, Miss Wilson."

Cad returned to her seat.

"Mrs. Kane, take the stand," ordered the judge. Tara sat paralyzed with fear. As she looked around, not one single face in this mob seemed remotely sympathetic. There was no sign of a scarlet tunic; even Bowers had forsaken her. It was up to her to win over this kangaroo court, and her only defense was that she was the one person who knew the whole truth.

Tara stood and slowly climbed onto the crate vacated by Cad Wilson. In a low voice she repeated the promise to tell the truth.

"So what happened?" asked Judge Rickless.

"I killed Jake Gore, but I had to kill him because otherwise he would have killed me."

"Are you saying it was self-defense?"

Tara nodded. Cad Wilson emitted a high, sneering laugh.

"Okay," said the judge. "If a woman says she killed a man in self-defense, that makes it justifiable homicide," he told the jury. "But she's got to prove it. Explain to the court, Mrs. Kane."

Tara swallowed and, white-faced, her voice shaking, told the whole grisly story. At the end, tears were streaming down her cheeks. She looked up, and for the first time noticed Jefferson Smith standing to the side of the crowded room. He was watching her closely, and there was nothing mocking in his expression.

Tara concluded in a trembling voice. "I didn't even know he had any gold. The dogs tore his body to pieces. Do you think I'll ever forgive myself for taking a human life? Do you think I'll ever be able to wipe from my memory what I've been through? But Jake Gore had taken many lives and he would have taken mine."

Tara pointed at Cad Wilson. "That woman hired Jake Gore to kill me. His only mistake was that he tried to assault me first."

"She's lying," screamed Cad.

"Order, order," hammered the judge. His bleary eyes blinked at Gore. "Prosecution wants to cross-examine the accused?"

Arne Gore smiled coldly. "Hell no, Judge," he said. "She don't even deny she killed Jake. I say she's a murderess. I went to the Mounties, and you can see what they did about it. They couldn't care less if a Yank gets killed. I want justice for my brother's death. It's your duty as true Americans to see that I get it. I say we should hang Tara Kane—"

"Okay, Gore. You've made your point," the judge intervened. He paused as footsteps echoed around the silent saloon. Jefferson Smith had come forward and stood near the front row of chairs, his arms folded.

Judge Rickless cleared his throat. "Now, there's two sides to every story. The accused here says Jake attacked her and she shot him.

Does her credit. What kind of woman is it who lets a man do that? Arne Gore says it was robbery and murder, and she says it was self-defense. Now it's up to you jurors to say who's telling the truth. Go away now and consider your verdict. Court's recessed."

The men behind the bar didn't bother to move. One of them, in a tartan shirt, stood up. Tara got the impression that they had not even consulted each other.

"Okay, Judge," he said. "We're decided."

"So what's the verdict?" asked Judge Rickless.

"Not guilty."

There was pandemonium in the saloon. Many people applauded, others booed. Tara stepped down from the crate, thanking God that she had survived.

Cad Wilson approached her. "You'd better get out of town," she warned. "Fast—"

"You're late for work, Cad," interrupted a cool voice. Smith had appeared by her side. "Get going."

She glared at Tara, her mouth curling with contempt, then sauntered off.

"Drinks on the house," shouted Smith. He walked over to the bar, where the jurors were standing in a group. "Gentlemen," he declared. "You've served the town well." They laughed as Smith poured champagne and raised his glass with them. Suddenly the Eldorado was its old self again, the piano tinkling away, the faro wheels clicking, people laughing and shouting.

Tara was exhausted and yearned for the peace of her own room. She started edging through the celebrating crowd when, unexpectedly, she came face to face with Arne Gore. A hush descended over the festivities, and Tara shrank back from the venom in his eyes.

"You!" spat Gore. "You're dead."

"That's enough, friend," intervened Smith. He reached out and grabbed Gore by the collar, pulling his face close to his. In various corners of the saloon, armed men who were Smith's shadows wherever he went began to move forward. "You get out of here and keep walking. Don't come back." He hurled Gore against a nearby table.

Gore tottered, his eyes shifting uneasily. Then he turned and slunk toward the doors of the saloon.

"Mr. Gore," Smith called out. "You forgot something." His eyes had become chips of ice. "You forgot to apologize to the lady."

Slowly Gore turned. A nerve twitched in his face as Smith eyed him lethally. "I'm sorry," Gore said through gritted teeth. Without another word he walked out.

"I haven't had the chance to congratulate you, Tara," drawled Smith. "You had every man in the room on your side."

"I only told the truth," she said quietly.

"I know. And it won you the day. Now I'll escort you home." He took her arm and propelled her through the crowded saloon.

They walked in silence until they reached Mrs. Miles's house. On the steps he faced her. "Tara, can't we at least be friendly?"

"I don't think we've enough in common even for that."

She closed the door, but Smith did not move for a long time. He stood staring after her. Then slowly he made his way into the dark town. There was a smile on his face.

CHAPTER TEN

THE next morning Tara entered Inspector Constantine's office. If she had expected sympathy for her ordeal, he quickly disillusioned her.

"I was hoping you'd have quit looking for your husband," he said. "You might not be so lucky next time."

"So you would have let me hang?" Tara asked.

"You weren't in any danger," he said frostily. "It was a carnival, and you took the starring role."

"What on earth are you talking about?"

"Nothing was going to happen to you. It was all staged."

"Staged? By whom?" asked Tara incredulously.

"The man who rigged the jury. Your protector, Soapy Smith."

"I don't believe you," gasped Tara.

"Please yourself." Constantine shrugged. "They got well paid, so I understand."

"No," breathed Tara. "That isn't so. That wasn't why."

"Oh no?" He smiled coldly. "They were on the rampage. They wanted blood. So why the change of heart to let you off so easily, then? You're lucky you got that sort of friend."

Tara winced. "I . . . I didn't know," she said quietly.

"Mrs. Kane, I want you out of Dawson. Out of the Yukon. Since you've been here you've been nothing but trouble, and I don't need it or want it. And remember, your benefactor may not always be around."

"Damn him!" Tara said fervently, and stormed out. She marched to the Monte Carlo, where the bartender told her Smith was in his office in the Regina Café. She strode through the town and into the Regina. The two men behind the desk were hardly hotel managers. Both wore guns. "I'm looking for Mr. Smith," Tara said.

"Sure, Mrs. Kane," said one. "I'll take you up." She followed the man up a staircase. He stuck his head in a door and said, "Mrs. Kane, boss."

Tara marched into the room. Smith rose from behind his desk, flashing her a welcoming smile. "Tara, my dear," he said, delighted to see her. "Please sit down."

He pushed an ornate chair forward for her. The office was certainly not the sort Tara expected a racketeer to have. On one wall was a framed map of Alaska and a portrait of President McKinley. In a corner, on a flagstaff, was the Stars and Stripes.

Tara sat stiffly, but before she could say anything, Smith waved a hand. "How do you like my office?"

"I didn't come to see your office," she said coldly. "I've come to tell you I think you're contemptible. You think you can bribe and corrupt, buy anything and anyone with money. Even your kangaroo courts."

He reached into a bottom drawer and brought out a bottle of brandy and two cut crystal glasses. He poured, and pushed one drink across to Tara.

"Tara," he said gently. "I didn't fix that trial. Cad Wilson did. She bribed the jury to find you guilty. So I bribed those twelve men not to let themselves be bribed. That pretty neck of yours deserves a better fate. As for Cad, she's leaving Dawson."

He took a drink and set the glass down. "Truth is you handled it beautifully. I'm proud of you. You didn't need anybody's help."

Tara glared at him, hating him and yet believing him.

"You've got guts, Tara. A mighty proud lady. Only one trouble. You don't know how to look after yourself."

"You've no need to worry about me, Mr. Smith."

"But I do," he said gently, sipping his brandy. "If I'm not around you, you get into big trouble. Figure out if you can afford it."

"Afford what?"

"To be without me," he said simply.

"You mean the widow needs a protector," Tara suggested.

He didn't rise to that. "I have plans, Tara. Big plans."

"More saloons, bigger and better rackets?"

Smith grinned. "I'm not interested in penny-anteing, Tara. I'm talking about politics. The railroad that's being built from Skagway to the Yukon. The future of Alaska. Sure, it sounds crazy, but a man can do anything he sets his mind to, provided he's got the right woman beside him."

"I hope you find her one day," Tara said.

"I'm returning to Skagway. I'm going to put that little place on the map in a big way. It needs me. Governor of Alaska."

"Alaska a state?" she asked, amused.

"I'm going to add that star to the flag," promised Smith. He raised his glass. "Here's to great days," he proposed.

She hesitated. There was a plea in his eyes. She picked up her glass. "To great days," she toasted.

"So," went on Smith, as if it had all been decided. "I want you to come to Skagway with me. How about it?"

She looked him straight in the eyes. "All right. I'll come to Skagway if you'll help me to find Daniel."

He threw back his head and laughed. "I talk about opening up the world, and you just talk about him. I'll do anything for you, Tara, but that's one job you got to do on your own." He started playing with some dice on his desk. The clicking infuriated her.

"Well," he said. "Are you coming to Skagway with me?"

"No," replied Tara.

"I play long odds," he said.

"There are no odds, Mr. Smith."

He grinned. "I'm a born gambler, Tara. And I never lose."

So it was that just when Dawson could boast two banks, two newspapers, and five churches, as well as the biggest saloon district outside the Barbary Coast, Jefferson Randolph Smith decided to sell out.

Tara heard people say that Smith couldn't have chosen a better time to depart, and that the prospect of a civilized Dawson made him realize that his rich pickings were over. The railroad was becoming a reality. Slowly, mile by mile, it was going to forge northward, and its arrival would mean a different Dawson, a place where Smith would find his buccaneering more restricted, fast communication curtailing his scope.

The political friction between the United States and Canada was increasingly discussed in Dawson. Although it was a Canadian city, four-fifths of its population owed no allegiance to Queen Victoria. When the gold royalty was upped to twenty percent of any mine's output exceeding five hundred dollars a week, the Yanks rebelled. But any move on their part to make the Yukon American would have to start at Skagway, where the Stars and Stripes already flew. There the United States faced an unclear frontier line between Alaska and British Columbia. If anyone wanted to wipe out that line, he had to begin where Soapy Smith was now heading.

Meanwhile Tara continued her search for Daniel.

THE arrival of spring and the thawing of the Yukon River heralded the opening of the 1898 lucky strikers' season. Claim markings shot up all over the sprawling creek land, along every tiny stream and rivulet that emptied into the basin of the Klondike, Indian, and McQuesten rivers. Tara borrowed a horse and rode out to the creek land to look for Daniel herself.

But the sheer effort of scouring eight hundred square miles of gold claims was daunting. In whatever direction Tara looked, tents dotted the landscape, fires burned to thaw out the ground, and men hacked fiendishly at the frozen earth and streams so that they could pan the gravel.

Some of the friendlier sourdoughs talked of the gold lore: how gold water had its own flavor, how you had to stay on the right side of the Yukon, no good going upriver and looking for gold where the moose roamed. Trees had to lean the right way; trees at a wrong angle meant no gold.

"There's going to be trouble soon," one old man told her. "Gold's running out." Tara stared at him, bewildered. "What with newcomers, there ain't going to be enough to go round."

"But there's talk of millions to be found," Tara said. "A man in Dawson sold his claim for seven hundred and fifty thousand dollars and said he'd already had a million out of it."

The old man shrugged.

For days Tara rode through the claims, asking if anyone had seen or heard of Daniel Kane. But most men she spoke to either eyed her suspiciously or shook their heads.

It's hopeless, she thought, pausing at the foot of Cheechako Hill, by a tree on which had been hammered a primitively carved notice:

TO WHOM IT MAY CONCERN!
I do, this day, locate and claim, by
right of discovery, five hundred feet,
running upstream from this notice.
Located this 17th day of August 1896.
G.W. Carmack

So this is where it all began. On this spot, less than two years ago, Carmack and his partners had found the nugget that started the Gold Rush.

Tara went back to Dawson, despondent. She returned the horse and began trudging back to Mrs. Miles's house. An impressive sign on a building near the barbershop caught her eye. PHOTOGRAPHS! it proclaimed. ALASKA VIEWS, PORTRAITS. ERNST HART.

Her heart began to pound. So much had happened since she had last seen her friend. She rang the bell and went inside. Hart emerged from behind a curtain. "My dearest Tara." He held her close. "I only just returned to Dawson and heard what terrible things you have been through. I blame myself; I should never have let you go off alone with that man Jake."

"Dear Ernst," she said softly. "It's over. None of it matters now. The important thing is that Daniel is still alive."

"Of that you're sure?" he asked.

"Of course, Ernst," she replied, with a brave attempt at a smile. "I don't quite know where to go from here, but you know my motto: 'One day at a time.' I'll find him."

"Of course you will," he agreed, patting her hand. "By the way, I've finished processing the photographs of my trip around the territory. Please, will you look at them?"

As Hart spread each print in front of her, it was as if Tara were looking at the whole of the Gold Rush unfolding in one long panorama. He had effectively recorded the vast and sweeping views, as well as the small and personal. There were photographs of a weary gold prospector who had fallen asleep as he panned, a man gnawing at a frozen slab of bread, a good-time girl brazenly lifting her skirt to show her legs. Hart, Tara realized, was a sensitive artist, using his photographic plates like a canvas.

"I've never seen pictures like these. They're superb, truly marvelous. What are you going to do with them?" she asked.

"Take them back to the States, show them in exhibition. A pictorial history of the Gold Rush."

Hart had stacks more photographs. She saw his views of prospectors, of Mounties, of Indian guides, of snow-covered shacks, of lonely graves, of . . . Tara stopped. She stared at a photograph in her hand. "Where did you take this?" she asked very quietly.

"Oh, that one. At Sheep Camp, below the Chilkoot Pass. Why?"

"That man," she said, her hand shaking.

"What about him?" He looked at the picture again. The man was in front of a tent, perched on a crate, his right leg stiffly extended. He was holding a crude crutch. A dog team was beside him.

"That's Daniel," she exclaimed. "I'm sure it's Daniel. When did you take this?"

"A few weeks ago. I did not ask his name. I photographed him because I thought he looked like a man marooned. He'd broken his ankle. He couldn't continue up the Chilkoot until the bone had mended. I felt sorry for him. The Gold Rush was passing him by."

"Ernst, he must be there now." Her eyes were shining with excitement. This was Daniel, no doubt about it. His eyes, his mouth. Despite the straggly beard, she could tell it was her husband. "I have to get to Sheep Camp as quickly as possible." She took Ernst's hand. "You've found him," she said, her eyes filling with tears of happiness. "You've found him, alive."

Tara told Mrs. Miles her plans the following morning. "You won't be coming back, then," Mrs. Miles said sadly.

"No," Tara said. "It's good-by to Dawson. There's nothing more for me here. Daniel's at Sheep Camp, and the thought of being with him again is all that's kept me going all these months. And your kindness, Linda. Without you I don't know what would have happened to me."

"You would have survived," said Mrs. Miles. "I didn't think that when I first saw you, but now I don't worry. You know, over the past few months I've seen you gradually turn into one of us. You belong now. I've watched you deal with the hardships of this place, and yet you've remained very much a woman."

"Thank you," Tara said as Mrs. Miles fussed over the coffeepot, embarrassed by what she had said.

Later that day Mrs. Miles went into Tara's bedroom and found her poring over a map Hart had given her. "How do you plan on getting to Sheep Camp?" Mrs. Miles asked.

"I'll hire a dog team and make my way down to the lakes and through the Chilkoot Pass. Sheep Camp is a few miles on the other side, beyond the border."

"But you should wait till the river is completely thawed," cautioned Mrs. Miles. "There'll be dozens of prospectors leaving Dawson then."

"*Wait!*" exclaimed Tara. "*You* wouldn't, would you?"

"No, I suppose not." Mrs. Miles shrugged; she knew it was no good. Once Tara had made up her mind, it was pointless to argue. "All right. I'll go talk to Mr. Brock right now about getting your supplies at cost."

Mrs. Miles accompanied Tara to Brock's store early the next morning. There the sled and team Tara had hired from the Bartletts waited, piled high with equipment and provisions. Tara tucked her sleeping bag, filled with her belongings, under the tarpaulin, and then turned to Mrs. Miles.

"Linda, you've got me enough stuff to last a lifetime. How can I begin to thank you?"

"Don't begin," Mrs. Miles said, tears in her eyes. They embraced. "Godspeed, travel safely."

She pressed Tara's hand reassuringly. Tara walked to her sled and picked up the whip. She turned and waved to Mrs. Miles, at the same time shouting, "Mush!" The dogs moved off.

CHAPTER ELEVEN

SHEEP Camp—so named because, it was said, hunters had once camped there, seeking mountain sheep—lay in a deep basin scooped out of the surrounding mountains, the last staging point beyond Dyea, and four miles south of the treacherous Chilkoot.

The White Pass was terrible, but the Chilkoot had a cold, fearful majesty all its own. An endless line of men climbed its slippery slope, draping the steep incline to the summit of the mountain like a human garland. They were going north, to the destiny they were all dreaming of, the goldfields of Dawson, Eldorado, Bonanza, and beyond. Tara's route was in the opposite direction, south over the pass, and down Long Hill to the outpost they called Stone House.

A thick blanket of heavy snow blinded Tara as she slipped and slithered down a gradient of thirty-five degrees. It became almost impossible to guide the dog team, and she had to leave the animals to make their own way. At times she fell on her hands and knees, but, finally, exhausted and freezing cold, she reached the settlement at the foot of the hill. Although she was only a few miles from Sheep Camp, her body and the threatening sky told her that she couldn't go on. She found a protected spot, tucked away the sled, made sure the dogs were safely fastened, then rigged up the tent and crawled inside.

When the blizzard came, it charged with the ferocity of a tornado. The wind howled; gusts tore at the guy ropes and pummeled the canvas. Then, after what seemed like hours, the howling eased. In the sudden quiet she thought she heard one or two distant rumblings that sounded like faraway artillery fire, some ghostly bombardment in the Chilkoot.

When she emerged from the tent the next morning, it was curiously calm. The sky was clear, and there was a hint of sunshine. Hastily she bolted down some breakfast, fed the dogs, dug out the sled, and loaded up her tent and supplies.

The going was slow, the snow so deep that the dogs and the sled sank into it. After an hour, in which she only covered a few hundred yards, she heard the same dull rumbling as the night before. This time it seemed louder, threateningly sinister.

Finally, in the distance, she could make out the sprawling sea of tents and shacks that was Sheep Camp. Hart had told her the place was a madhouse of nearly fifteen hundred people. On the far side of the basin, on the slopes leading down to it, were other dwellings. That was where Hart had photographed Daniel.

Once more the ominous rumbling echoed in the muffled stillness.

Three hours later she entered Sheep Camp, driving her dogs along the slushy camp road leading to the slope a mile away, where she would find him.

"Thank God," she whispered, eyes riveted on the mountainside.

Then it happened. She could feel the tremors under her as the rumbling thunder crescendoed in a tremendous roar, a fearful crashing sound. Before Tara's disbelieving eyes, the top of the mountain she was heading toward slid twenty-five hundred feet down and enveloped everything in its path—huts, tents, the specks of life on the slope. Tara screamed as she saw the people sucked under the expanding white tide. The avalanche roared on, blanketing the slope encampment under thirty feet of snow and ice—crushing, suffocating those entombed under its weight. It was April 3, 1898, date of one of Alaska's worst disasters, when more than sixty persons died in the avalanche on the Chilkoot trail.

In the eerie silence that followed, Tara stood numb with horror. From all over Sheep Camp people came running out of shacks, saloons, and tents. They stood gaping at the awful spectacle of the avalanche's destruction. Then they rushed toward the slope.

Daniel, Daniel, was the only thought that pounded through Tara's head. I've got to get to him. I must get him out before it's too late. She joined the crowd stampeding forward wildly, carrying spades and pickaxes. At the slope, people were already digging frantically. They were standing on tons of snow, sinking into it, with who knew how many people buried beneath it, some dead, some slowly suffocating.

Tara grabbed a gold pan and began hacking at the frozen layers. They could hear a man's voice coming from the depths. They all stopped and listened, then attacked the snow with renewed vigor. When, finally, they lifted him out, they were too late.

More corpses were gradually dug out and laid in lines, like dead soldiers on parade. Tara studied each face. None was Daniel's. She lost count of the number of eyelids she closed, the frozen faces she covered with blankets. She tried group after group of rescuers, who were now digging by the light of hurricane lamps. "Has anyone come across Daniel Kane?" she demanded. They were too busy to answer. Tara sank to her knees. "Oh, please," she cried. "Somebody help me find my husband!"

Then a hand shook her. "You!" barked a gruff voice. "We need you." A black-bearded man yanked her to her feet. "There's a woman we just dug out over there about to give birth. Get her to Sheep Camp before it's too late."

"I'm not leaving until I find my husband!" Tara shouted. "Get somebody else. Why doesn't her husband look after her?"

"He's down there," the man said, pointing at the snow, "just the same as yours is." Unexpectedly he put his arm around her. "I know what you're going through, lass. We'll try to find your husband. You can help her. Come on."

Tara followed him. The woman, about seventeen or eighteen, had been covered with a fur pelt, but Tara could clearly see the outline of her swollen belly. She was pale, with blue-tinged skin stretched over prominent cheekbones. She gave a cry of pain and clutched Tara's hand. "My baby," she whimpered, "my baby."

Compassion flooded through Tara. Amid so much death, this woman was going to give life.

Tara wearily called to three bystanders to strap the woman onto a sled. She held the woman's hand as the three men gingerly negotiated the slippery descent to Sheep Camp. There they took the woman to a tent and lifted her onto a pallet.

Tara turned to the men. "I need plenty of hot water. Get me a stove, pans, extra blankets, a sharp knife. And I'll want a crate or a drawer, something to put the baby in. And if someone could bring my sled—it has supplies that would be useful now."

Then she knelt down by the woman. "Everything will be all right," she said, trying to sound reassuring.

The woman opened her eyes. "My husband," she whispered.

"They're looking for him. I'm Tara," she said gently. "What's your name?"

"Suzanna Lacey. The baby isn't due for another two weeks. We thought we could make it to Dawson. Then the avalanche." Suzanna groaned, her pain more intense. "I'm going to die."

"That's nonsense. You won't die. You're going to have a beautiful baby, and I'm going to help you."

"But if I do," she whispered, "until they find John, promise me you'll take care of the child."

"I promise."

"Thank you," sighed Suzanna. "I'm not worried anymore."

The men returned with the items Tara had requested, but they hadn't found her sled yet. She began melting snow on the stove, all the while trying to remember her little practical knowledge of childbirth.

Suzanna's labor pains had started again, and Tara soothed and comforted her as she tossed and turned. Waiting for a new life to make its appearance, Tara remembered that first glorious moment when they had put Gabie in her arms. The way Daniel had smiled at both of them—the happiest moment in her life.

"Stay with me," sobbed Suzanna.

"Don't worry, I'm not going to leave you," Tara said quietly.

The pains were coming faster now. Suzanna gave an agonized cry. "Try to help by pushing, Suzanna," Tara said. "It's coming; push harder." Very quickly the child was delivered. "It's a boy," Tara announced, bundling the baby in a blanket.

"Look," she said, placing the infant in his mother's arms. "Hold your son. Isn't he perfect?"

Suzanna smiled weakly as she cradled the child, but she was too exhausted to speak. Suddenly she began to hemorrhage. Her eyes opened wide with horror. Tara tried to stanch the flow, but it was hopeless. She made the woman as comfortable as possible, willing herself to believe that the inevitable would not happen.

"Tara," came a whisper from Suzanna. "Love him for me."

Tara nodded, too full of emotion to speak. She bent closer to hear what Suzanna was trying to say. It sounded like "John." "Always," she whispered. "Always keep him, no one else."

"Please don't die," pleaded Tara, clutching Suzanna's hand. But Suzanna's head fell to one side. As Tara stared down at her she stopped breathing. Frantically, Tara felt for the pulse, but it had ceased. She sank to her knees, exhausted. Death seemed to be everywhere around her.

A terrible fatigue swept through her, making it impossible to keep her eyes open. She collapsed on the floor.

She was brought back to consciousness by someone roughly shaking her shoulder. The black-bearded man and another man peered down at her. "What happened?" the bearded man asked.

"I did everything I could," Tara whimpered, "but she's dead."

"What about the baby?"

"A boy. Have you found the father?"

"That's what we came to tell you," the other man said. "We found him, close to where we dug her out. He's dead. Crushed by the snow."

She looked at him, her unspoken question evident.

"No," he said. "There's no news of your husband." Then he told her that her sled had apparently been stolen.

Tara got up and went over to the baby. "Don't worry, John," she said. "You'll be safe. I promised your mother."

Perhaps this was what fate had intended all along. She had been robbed of her own child; she had failed to find Daniel. Everything seemed to have been taken from her.

Until now. She picked up the baby and rocked it to and fro. "We've got one another," she told him. "We need one another."

THE rescue operation continued. Silently people from Sheep Camp watched and waited, although every hour that passed lessened the chances of anyone being brought out alive. There was still no news of Daniel. In the tent Tara cradled the baby. He was asleep, but soon he would need milk and she had none to give him. She was determined that little John was going to survive. Not just because of a promise she had given a dying woman, but because she had been given a second chance, someone to love.

For the first three days she boiled snow, added sugar, let it cool, then soaked a piece of linen in the liquid. John sucked hungrily at the syrupy cloth. But milk was essential. With the baby bundled up in blankets inside her parka, Tara ventured out to find some. The catastrophe overshadowed the entire camp. People stood in groups, talking in subdued tones. Some of them were gathered around a log cabin, staring at a newly painted sign nailed to the door. It read CORONER. She had not realized that officials from Skagway were already in Sheep Camp.

Tara entered the cabin. Inside was a trestle table, on which lay a thick ledger, an inkwell, and a stack of papers. Behind the table sat Soapy Smith.

"Tara!" he gasped. Then he glanced down and saw John Lacey's head protruding from her coat. "Who the hell is that?"

"That's no concern of yours," she replied. "I'll come back when the coroner is here."

"But he is, Tara." He stood and bowed. "I'm sort of acting coroner from Skagway for the Chilkoot division of the territory."

"Self-appointed, I suppose?"

"Of course. Somebody had to take on the onerous task of safeguarding the victims' valuables until we locate the next of kin, although most of the stuff could have belonged to anyone. But, Tara, I want to hear about you. What happened? And who is that?" Smith asked again. He peered at the top of the baby's head. "Sit down and tell me all about it."

Tara sank into a chair. "His name is John Lacey. His father was killed in the avalanche. His mother was dug out, and I delivered him, but she died." She stopped, then stared Smith straight in the eye. "He needs milk, and he needs it quickly. He won't survive if he doesn't get some soon."

Smith contemplated her. "Fortunately, in my official capacity, I'm not only the coroner but also registrar of births and deaths." He opened a ledger. "Father's name John Lacey, right? Mother's name . . ." He looked at Tara questioningly.

"Suzanna."

Smith wrote in the ledger, and then on a form.

"Do you have to do that now?"

"It won't take a minute," he said smoothly. "This makes him legal." He handed Tara the form.

She stared at the printed birth certificate. The name of the child was listed as John Jefferson Randolph Lacey.

"What are these names—Jefferson Randolph?" asked Tara.

"Well, after all, I am his godfather," Smith said. Tara stared at him, amazed that he was serious. "It's quite customary for a child to have a godfather, you know. And it's a proud southern name. My father was an officer in the Confederate Army."

"A godfather looks after his godchild's spiritual and moral welfare. I wouldn't have thought you were much up to that kind of responsibility."

Smith grinned. "Maybe that'll be your department. But I've got a few talents he'll find useful, believe me."

Tara wished that she could tell him that neither she nor the baby needed his help. But it wouldn't be true. She felt relieved that some of the responsibility for John's survival was being shared with someone else, even if it was Soapy Smith.

Back in the tent, she wondered if she was deluding herself. Despite misgivings, she was placing a certain amount of faith in Smith's ability to help. Her soothing voice and comforting arms could no longer placate the hungry baby.

The flap of the tent was pulled aside, and Smith stood there, holding a piece of rope. On the other end of the line was a goat. "Here's the milk."

"How do I get it?" Tara asked, eyeing the animal nervously.

"You milk the goat," Smith replied. "How else?" He tied the animal to a peg outside the tent.

"Here," Tara said, handing John to Smith. "Hold him firm."

Smith took the baby somewhat gingerly and sat down, keeping a very straight face, while Tara gathered up a crate and saucepan and went outside. As best she could she emulated the pastoral paintings she had seen of rosy-faced milkmaids. Placing the pan under the goat, she put her hands on the udders and pulled. When she returned with the milk, she felt triumphant.

Smith handed her the baby and picked up his hat. "I'll be back, my dear," he said.

Tara began to feed the baby. "Thank you, Jeff, for the goat."

He stopped at the tent doorway. It was the first time she had ever thanked him for anything, and the first time she had used his name. But if he felt a triumph, he showed no sign. Instead he went over to her, knelt down beside her, and said very gently, "Tara, somebody has to look after you."

"I'll be all right."

"You can't bring up an infant in this shantytown." He paused. "I want to get you both to Skagway. To make sure you've got a decent roof over your heads, to make sure you get what you need. I beg you."

"Why, Jeff? You don't need us. You've got money, power. Why do you want to do this?"

"I think you know, Tara." The rest remained unsaid.

"Are you going on with the search for Daniel?" he asked after a while. "Because I don't think there's any point. The bodies out there are twenty feet down. Many won't be found until the thaw."

She put the baby down and looked at him, her eyes filling with tears. "And I don't even know if he's among those still buried on that slope, or if he'd left here before it happened."

He put his arms around her. "In any case, Tara, you and the baby can't stay here any longer. You must come with me."

Tara did not resist the comforting warmth of his body. He held her tight, and she felt him stroke her hair; then his lips brushed against her cheeks. He was more comforting, more kind, more reassuring than she would have thought possible. She and John would have to go with Jefferson Smith. Fate had decided for her.

And she found that now she allowed herself to wonder about a possibility, the shadow of which she had always before shut away. Suppose Daniel were dead? Had she been sentenced to a monotonously gray future without her husband's love?

CHAPTER TWELVE

WHEN Tara had arrived in Skagway in 1897, Smith had been the unchallenged town boss. But during the first three months of 1898, industry and commerce began to make their mark, encouraged by the town's designation as the starting point for the forthcoming rail link with Whitehorse, in the Yukon.

With the completion of the first stage of the track, future prospectors would be able to reach the summit of the White Pass by train. So thousands of sourdoughs thronged the trail from Dyea to Skagway, to prepare for their journey to Dawson via this easier route. The sidewalks teemed with prospectors, trappers, and traders, and, for the first time in the Yukon, a new class—businessmen, with city clothes peeping out of their parkas, who were reaping healthy profits from the spending power of lucky strikers.

Since Tara had been away, the amenities of Skagway had improved to keep up with its growth. The town's residents were now provided with better entertainment, better hotels, and even better opportunities to lose money, but Skagway was as lawless as ever. However, as the respectable element prospered, they became increasingly critical of the likes of Soapy Smith and his men.

It had taken Smith and Tara three days to reach Skagway from Sheep Camp. As they neared the end of their journey, Smith was in high spirits. But if he had expected a welcoming committee, he was in for a shock. During his absence some of the townsfolk had decided it was time to clean up Skagway. They had printed a notice:

WARNING

All con men and other objectionable characters are notified to leave Skagway immediately. Failure to comply with this warning will be met by prompt action.

Smith stood in front of the first poster he came across, seething. Then he ripped down the notice and threw it in the mud. "That's the trouble with newcomers," he said, "always getting too big for their breeches."

There was the sound of hoofs from behind them, and Tara turned to see a man galloping toward them. "Hi, boss," the Reverend Charles Bowers called out. "And good day to you, Mrs. Kane," he said, eyeing her and the baby with a look of surprise. "The boys will be glad to know you're back in town."

"Where's Colson?" Smith asked without ceremony.

Tara remembered the U.S. marshal who had led the lynch party and who was jokingly referred to as Skagway's law.

Bowers leaned forward. "He's dead. He got shot at Fay's place."

"What happened?" Smith asked.

"Well, boss, a guy called McGrath walked into the saloon. Put down a bill for a drink, and Fay wouldn't give him change."

"So?" Smith shrugged. "What's wrong with that? Local custom, ain't it?"

"Yeah, but McGrath started a ruckus, and Colson rushed in. Fay kind of lost his head and Colson got his."

"Ah, well," Smith sighed. "Guess we'd better get ourselves a new marshal. And get rid of those damn posters. I want them down."

"Sure, boss." Bowers galloped off.

"You see what happens when I turn my back?" remarked Smith.

"The baby and I need a place to stay," Tara said coldly, ignoring this latest evidence of Smith's racketeering.

"Sure," he agreed. "Got to get the important things done first."

Half an hour later Smith had installed Tara in a log cabin. It was neatly furnished: bright Indian rugs covering the rough floorboards, curtains at the windows, a roomy wooden bed, and a range. To Tara it was a palace.

"Whose is this?" she asked, looking around.

"Yours," Smith said. "My men will bring you wood, food, and supplies, and I'll get a basket for John." Smith paused. "This is okay for you, Tara, isn't it?"

"It's the nicest place I've been." She smiled. "Thank you."

"I've got things to do," he said, pulling on his gloves. "You'll be safe here, Tara. I promise." Then he was gone.

A couple of hours later, Smith's men arrived with food, cooking utensils, kerosene lamps, linen—every household item she could possibly want. As she was putting it all away she heard someone hammering outside the cabin. A poster had been nailed to the cabin wall:

PUBLIC WARNING

The men who have been usurping civic authority are hereby notified that any overt act committed by them will promptly be met by the law-abiding citizens of Skagway. The Law and Order Society, consisting of over three hundred citizens, will see that justice is dealt out.

Jefferson R. Smith, The Law and Order Society.

Soapy Smith had declared war. It hadn't taken him long to warn Skagway that he commanded an army of followers, and that he ruled the town again. Tara ripped down the handbill, tore it in pieces, and threw them to the wind.

Even the luxury of lying on a feather-filled mattress, between crisp sheets, didn't help Tara sleep that night. She knew she had to tell Smith that her acceptance of his kindness did not indicate approval of his lawlessness.

The next day Smith turned up at the cabin with a basket. "This should be safe and snug for Johnny boy."

Tara pushed in a pillow for a mattress and gently placed the baby in it. "It's exactly right," she said.

"Got another surprise for you," Smith said, disappearing outside and immediately returning with an Indian woman. She was young, her thick black hair in two long plaits. She smiled at Tara.

"Here's your milk supply," Smith said. "Her papoose died. Meet Lydia. She'll help take care of John."

"Do you speak English?" asked a startled Tara.

"Not a word," intervened Smith, "but she's perfect with the baby talk. Now, you introduce her to John."

Lydia cooed with delight as she and Tara bent over the basket. Then Lydia picked the baby up, and he gurgled happily.

"There, you see, they get on perfect." Smith beamed. "And there'll be somebody here, so I can take you out."

"I don't remember saying I was going out," Tara said stiffly. "I think it's time you and I had a serious talk."

"My pleasure," said Smith, "but now there's business I've got to attend to. I'll be seeing you soon."

Tara was left staring at the closed cabin door. Then she saw an envelope on the table. She ripped it open. Inside were fifty one-dollar bills and a note with just one word: "Housekeeping."

Tara held the money, at first undecided about what to do. There were things she needed to buy for the baby: material to make him clothes, proper diapers instead of the torn towels he had worn since his birth, and ointments.

"All right." Tara put the money in her pocket. "I'll take it because John needs things, but, my goodness, Jeff Smith, don't think fifty dollars can buy me."

That afternoon Tara went out shopping, accompanied by Lydia, with John on the Indian girl's back, wrapped up like a papoose. The excitement she felt at gazing in shopwindows lifted Tara's spirits. So many varieties of stores had opened since she had been away. There were milliners, dress shops, and even a Viennese pastry shop.

Soapy Smith's posters were much in evidence. The people who gathered around appeared hostile as they discussed them. She shuddered as she heard one man complain to another, "Damn blackguard. Must think he owns the place."

"He'll get his comeuppance soon," prophesied the other.

After purchasing all the items John needed, they returned to the cabin. Within a few minutes there was a knock on the door and three men staggered in carrying a bathtub loaded with boxes, and a folding rosewood screen upholstered in damask. "Compliments of Mr. Smith," puffed one of them, handing Tara a small envelope. Without further ado they all left.

She opened the envelope and read the card inside. "This isn't meant as an insult. Just pamper yourself."

She undid the boxes and gasped as she took out an extravaganza of feminine luxury. There were jars of bath salts, bars of soap, several bottles of perfume, and enormous white Turkish towels. "I don't know if you're hinting, Jeff Smith"—Tara smiled, pressing a soft towel to her face—"but this bath will be a treat."

And it was. Tara washed and scrubbed her sore and tired body, feeling the grime of the past weeks float off her. Afterward she tingled from head to foot with pleasure as she dropped into the soft bed. Her last thought before falling asleep was that tomorrow, when she put on her freshly laundered clothes, she would look like a different woman, one ready to confront Jefferson Smith.

The following morning Smith called for her. "I'm taking you out, so we can have that serious conversation you wanted."

With evident pride he walked her through the center of Skagway, stopping at a restaurant with a white, immaculate façade. This was Jefferson Smith's Oyster Parlor, his seat of power in the town. He held open the door, and Tara entered a barroom, complete with flags of American states, a big mirror over the polished mahogany counter, and, to Tara's astonishment, electric lights.

Next door to the bar was the restaurant, with fretwork screens and artificial palm trees. Unbelievably, there were waiters in boiled shirts and white bow ties, their appearance somewhat spoiled by one or two of them having blackjacks stuck in their belts.

Smith and Tara were greeted by Mort, who ran the Monte Carlo for Smith, and by a sinister, soft-spoken man in a blue suit. "Yeah Mow," Smith said to him, "this is Mrs. Kane. Anything the lady wants, she has. Understand?"

"Sure, Mr. Smith," said Yeah Mow diffidently.

"What did you say his name was?" Tara asked, following Smith to the back, where there was a lady's parlor.

"Yeah Mow. It's Chinese," Smith told her, leading the way upstairs. "Means wildcat. He bodyguarded some Tong lords in Frisco—the only American who used an axe better than the Chinese." Smith opened the door to his office. It was even more palatial than the one in Dawson.

Tara looked at the map of the North American continent, the framed copy of the Declaration of Independence, and the bust of Julius Caesar on a shelf.

Smith ushered her to a huge leather armchair in front of his desk. "Well, my dear, what is it you want to talk about?"

"Jeff," Tara said falteringly. "I want you to know I'm very grateful for the help you've given me with John, for your thoughtful gifts, and for your friendship, but I don't want you to think that because I might appear reliant on you at the moment that I approve of the sort of man you are or the things you do."

"And tell me, my dear, what sort of man is it that you think I am?" he asked softly.

"I think you're a crook. You take advantage of innocent people."

"And what are all the others doing?" he demanded, his eyes steely. "Everyone here has come to use someone. The sourdoughs are tearing the territory apart so that they can make themselves rich on its gold. The city slickers are here to cash in on the sourdoughs. And I'm here to entertain all those poor suckers. But they needn't be entertained by me or by any other crook, as you so charmingly put it, unless they want to."

"And you think that makes you decent?" Tara challenged.

Smith laughed derisively. "You know what the trouble is with you? You want it all ways, and however I play it, I can't win. If I'd left you in Sheep Camp to fend for yourself, I'd have been a scoundrel. If I provide you with a roof over your head, which I can easily afford, it's so I can woo you into a lawless way of life."

She looked at him. "Why did you help me, then?"

"Because I wanted to," he said quietly.

"I don't believe you, Jeff, because I don't believe you've ever done anything without an ulterior motive."

"What a pity that such a kindhearted woman has so little faith," he mused. "I bow to your superior knowledge, Mrs. Kane. But before you go I'm going to put you straight about me. If you think owning faro games is my ambition in life, you're as wrong as if you think you came to these parts to find that missing husband of yours."

"So what am I here for?"

"You ran away to find yourself, to learn something you would never have found out back in San Francisco. That you can stand on your own feet and own the world."

Tara was taken aback. "I have no interest in owning the world. That's your desire, not mine."

"We'll see," said Smith. From a drawer he brought out a heavy piece of rock into which was set a brass plate. It was engraved *Jefferson Randolph Smith, Governor of Alaska.*

"Another sure thing?" she asked acidly.

"Exactly," he said. "Alaska, the Yukon, the Klondike. All under one flag. The richest slice of real estate in the world. And I aim that the whole territory will belong to the United States."

"And to you?"

"Sure. A few acres will. Commission, so to speak."

"And just how do you intend to go about this mighty mission?"

"I've already begun," he said softly. "I know the most important thing already. I know that as much as you hate to admit it, you believe in me, Tara, and that's fine for starters. And I'm going to offer you a job, a chance to earn clean money. Be my right-hand woman, my assistant. Help me achieve a decent future for this godforsaken territory."

His eyes were bright as he spoke. Tara was lost for words.

"If you're the woman I think you are, Tara, you'll accept my challenge. That way perhaps you'll stop being ashamed of having a friend in Jefferson Smith. That way we can help one another, because the one thing I haven't got you can give me."

"What's that?"

"Class," he replied. He laughed a little wryly. "You can make me respectable."

He got up, went to the door, and opened it. "Don't give me your answer straightaway. Consider my proposition carefully, but let me know soon."

In a daze she moved out the door.

Walking down Broadway, Tara felt strangely stimulated by Smith's words. Was it because he had offered her an opportunity to prove herself, to be financially independent? She brooded over what Smith had said about her coming to the Yukon to find her identity. He seemed to have taken it for granted that she had given up her search for Daniel, but that wasn't true.

If Daniel had survived Sheep Camp, there was only one way for him to get back to San Francisco—by sea. He would have to pick up a boat in Juneau, Dyea, or Skagway, the main ports serving the Gold Rush. Gradually a plan began to form in Tara's mind, and the key to it was the Skagway *Intelligencer*.

She hurried to the newspaper office. Behind the counter, men were pounding furiously at typewriters, presses were clattering.

Tara shouted over the din, "I want to place an advertisement."

Eventually one of the men glanced up and came over to her. "What do you want to say?"

" 'Daniel Kane' in big letters across the top, and underneath, 'a reward will be paid to anyone knowing his whereabouts. Contact his wife care of box number,' et cetera. Does the paper sell in Dyea too?"

"It sells all over," the man replied. "I've seen them read the Skagway *Intelligencer* as far afield as Dawson, so don't expect an instant reaction. It could take months."

"That's all right. I'll still be here. Please keep running it until I tell you to stop."

That afternoon Tara wrote a letter to Jefferson Smith:

Dear Mr. Smith,

With reference to your offer of employment, I am writing to advise you that I would be happy to accept the post of assistant to yourself, provided the following terms are agreeable:

I understand that my exclusive employer will be yourself, Jefferson Smith, and that I won't have to deal with any business appertaining to Soapy Smith. I would require a remuneration of one hundred dollars per month with free board and lodging for myself and John. I can commence working for you when it suits you.

Yours faithfully,
Tara Kane

Tara sealed the envelope and went back to the Oyster Parlor. She handed it to the bartender, saying, "Please give this to Mr. Smith." She went back to the cabin and nervously awaited his reply.

"TARA, you're incorrigible!" were Smith's first words when he walked into the cabin. He was holding her letter.

"What's the problem?" she asked anxiously.

"Money. I intend to pay my assistant a minimum of two hundred dollars a month."

Tara's eyes opened wide. "Two hundred dollars?"

"You'll have to be my hostess when necessary, and be available to work whenever I say. And I want your company whenever I please. Naturally, I'm willing to pay for the additional socializing required. You need a job. I need somebody I can trust, to be around me, to keep my books, and to do my letters."

"Well," said Tara slowly. "I can do your accounts. I'm a reasonable bookkeeper, I suppose."

"Sure, and you'll make a fine hostess at a business function." He smiled. "Mrs. Kane, you're on the payroll now." He pulled out a bundle of notes. "Get yourself a dress and a decent coat," he said, pressing the money into Tara's hand. "You start at nine o'clock tomorrow morning. At the Oyster Parlor."

Without a backward glance he left.

CHAPTER THIRTEEN

S MITH barely noticed Tara's arrival at the Oyster Parlor the next morning. Like a theatrical producer of a gala performance, he was busily instructing Yeah Mow on the wine that was to be served at a dinner party that evening.

Tara watched for a while, then mounted the stairs to Smith's office. A small writing table had been placed opposite his desk. It was covered with writing materials. On top of them was a box, and on that lay a newspaper with an item circled in blue crayon. Her advertisement in the *Intelligencer* had caught Smith's eye.

"You'll never give up, will you?" Smith remarked, going over to his desk. Tara glanced up. She hadn't heard him come in.

"No. Not while I believe there's a chance."

"If you want my opinion, you're wasting your time and money."

"I don't recall requesting your advice." Smith didn't answer. "What's in the box?" she inquired.

"A dress. I want you to wear it tonight."

"I'm quite capable of buying one myself, thank you," she said.

"Don't let's argue. Wear it," he instructed. "You'll look stunning, and I aim to cash in on it."

Tara glared at him.

"Here's the menu," he went on, handing her a sheet of paper. "I want you to do four copies of it, then do the place cards. I'll be out for the rest of the day. You sort out any problems here, then go home and change, but be back by six thirty sharp. I don't want any hitches tonight. I'm negotiating an important business deal, and this dinner may well clinch it."

While she wrote out the place cards, Tara wondered why "Sir Thomas Tancrede" and "Mr. Michael J. Heney" warranted such extravagant consideration. Then it struck her that Smith had given her a splendid opportunity. What fun it would be to show up that arrogant scoundrel in front of two people he was falling over himself to impress. He would learn that Tara Kane was not a woman to dazzle the suckers while he conducted his shady deals.

Once home, Tara undid the dress box and took out a sensational black taffeta evening gown, with a plunging neckline. Quite out of the question. She laughed to herself and returned the exotic creation to its box.

She took painstaking care with her hair, sweeping it up but leaving wisps to frame her face, and dabbed perfume behind her ears. Then she put on the old trousers and shirt she had worn on the trail. When she finally entered the Oyster Parlor, she was well aware she was twenty minutes late. She went directly to the private dining room. Without knocking, she opened the door and stepped into the candlelit chamber. Smith, who was wearing evening dress, looked around, but not a flicker on his face betrayed his surprise at her appearance.

"Ah, Tara," he said smoothly, his diamond cuff links twinkling in the subdued lighting. "You're just in time."

He turned to the two well-dressed gentlemen standing in front of the fireplace. "Gentlemen, may I present Mrs. Tara Kane." She smiled brilliantly.

"This is Sir Thomas Tancrede," he went on, indicating a bean pole of a man with a sardonic smile.

"Enchanted, my dear," said Sir Thomas in a clipped English accent. "What a surprise."

"And this is Mr. Michael J. Heney." Smith glanced at him. "Known as Big Mike to his friends." The granite-faced man did not smile but nodded curtly. "These gentlemen are on the board of the railroad," explained Smith.

Now she knew why he had gone to so much trouble over the dinner. This was the get-together at which he intended to make his bid for a share of the White Pass and Yukon Railroad.

"My goodness, Jeff, you should have told me," Tara said, not the slightest bit sorry for having messed up his well-laid plans. "If I'd realized this was going to be such an important occasion, I would have dressed more formally."

Smith did not blink an eyelid. "Mrs. Kane is a real pioneer lady," he said, turning to his guests. "She is more at home with a rifle and a dog team than with the frills of the salon. As you forge your railroad into the interior, you'll meet more of her kind in the set- tlements. Don't let their sex fool you. They're as tough as nails."

"I wouldn't say tough, Jeff." Tara laughed. "It's just we're more

215

used to dealing with the practicalities of life than to being treated as pretty ornaments."

Smith's eyes raked her, then he reached for the bellpull. "Shall we eat?" He smiled coldly at Tara. "We're a little late, but you probably had to feed the dogs first."

"Jeff, how you exaggerate!" She turned to Sir Thomas. "Why, you'll have your guests believing everything you say."

They sat down at the large oval dining table, resplendent with crystal glasses and silver cutlery. Throughout the four courses Tara acted the perfect dinner companion, keeping up a spirited conversation, and all the time stopping Smith from getting down to the business at hand. But he went along with her, attentive, amusing, a gentleman very much at ease, all the while watching her like a hawk.

When they reached the brandy stage and the cigars came out, Tara started to leave. "No, Tara," Smith said firmly. "I'd like you to stay."

There was political talk. Of the war with Spain and how long it would last. In the United States "Remember the *Maine*" had become a national slogan, and Teddy Roosevelt was raising a band of volunteers to fight in Cuba. They discussed the probable scale of the war.

Then Sir Thomas cleared his throat. "Why don't we get down to business? People say you're interested in our railroad, Smith. Is that right?"

"Damn right," said Smith. "I know a good investment when I see one."

"What exactly is your proposition?" Heney asked.

Carefully, Smith knocked the ash off his cheroot. "We all have a dream, gentlemen, to make this territory a great land, a land which can make more money for all of us than anyone has imagined. The key to that land is the railroad. Open up the territory, and you shrink it to a manageable size. Cut the distances, and you've conquered it."

"I say"—Sir Thomas winked at Tara—"he can dress up things."

"Well?" cut in Heney, unimpressed.

"The point is, Mr. Heney, I'd like us all to be partners." Smith beamed at them. His watch chain and diamond cuff links danced in the candlelight.

"Sorry," said Heney gruffly. "No deal."

Smith remained unruffled. "But you haven't heard me out."

Sir Thomas sighed. "Mr. Smith, we're an Anglo-Canadian consortium. We don't want American involvement."

"We're businessmen, all of us," Smith said. "Since when hasn't some extra capital been useful? You got big costs coming."

"Maybe," grunted Heney. "But we don't want you in, Smith. We don't want your kind of money."

"So you don't think my dough's good enough," said Smith very quietly. "You only like nice clean capital." He laughed mirthlessly. "Tell me, Sir Thomas, did your folks never ship any slaves? Never conquer any colonies?"

"We don't need lectures from a brothel owner," spat Heney.

Smith's eyes blazed. "Gentlemen, maybe you forgot a couple of things. You need a lot of supplies, a lot of men to build that one hundred and eleven miles of railroad. You haven't got any of it."

"Right now, Smith," Heney said triumphantly, "ships are on their way to Skagway with everything we need. Labor, supplies, horses."

Smith nodded. "Of course. And within twenty-four hours of their arrival you'll start laying the track," he said smugly.

Heney's eyes narrowed. "What are you getting at?"

"I have a certain, let's say, influence on the waterfront. The men listen to me. I daresay, gentlemen, that if I didn't get a look into your railroad, they might not unload your ships."

Heney pushed back his chair unceremoniously and stood up. "Now, you listen, Smith," he snarled. "Our railroad has the blessing of the authorities. You try to stop us unloading, you start your bullyboy tricks, and we'll have a battalion of United States infantry in Skagway so quick you won't know what hit you."

He glanced at Sir Thomas. "I think it's time we went."

The Englishman stood up and bowed to Tara. "I do apologize, dear lady," he said. "Business can get so tedious."

"Business, Sir Thomas," she replied, smiling politely, "is never tedious. It interests me enormously."

"We'll see ourselves out," Sir Thomas said, nodding at Smith.

For a while Tara and Smith sat in silence. It was perhaps the first time she had known Jefferson Smith not to have the last word. She felt rather sorry for him. "Well?" she asked at last.

"I'll get my way. It might just take a little longer than I'd thought." He sipped his brandy. "What do you think, Tara?"

She looked at him in surprise. "Do you care?" she asked.

"Yes I do," he said. "Very much."

She looked into his eyes, and she knew it was time for her to be his friend.

"What are you thinking about, Tara?"

"I was wondering if I could help you."

"Well," he said accusingly, "what about this evening? Why didn't you help me then? Look at yourself. Some hostess. What stopped you wearing the gown?"

"Jeff, I will not be an ornament. I didn't wear it because you only wanted me to be a pretty doll. That's not me. I'm not Cad Wilson. I'm not a plaything. It didn't make any difference anyway. They'd made up their minds before they got here. You know that."

Smith lit another cheroot, exhaled the smoke, and paused. "All right," he said at last. "If that's the way it's got to be." He gave his twisted grin. "Kind of expensive lesson. That gown cost me two hundred and fifty bucks." He became serious. "You and me got a lot in common. So let's share it. You want me to tell you things, I'll tell you things."

He told her of his schemes to secure control of the railroad.

Tara became increasingly uneasy, for she began to realize that if Smith did not achieve his means peacefully, he would do it by force. If he couldn't use a dock strike to win a say in the railroad, he would bring in his hired guns. Skagway would be ripped apart by bloodshed.

"You'd be surprised what can go wrong when you lay tracks, Tara. Accidents. Landslides. Explosions." He smiled. "Believe me, let them experience a few armed men and a load of dynamite—then they might find it cheaper my way."

"Jeff, if you try to stop them—they'll kill you."

"Maybe I've got a little more experience at that kind of game."

"No," Tara said. "That's not the way, Jeff. Violence never solves anything. Where would it end?"

"It's the only way. What alternative have I got?"

"To give in."

Smith laughed derisively. "You crazy?"

"Jeff, if you're serious about achieving your political ambitions, about really becoming governor, you must prove to the townsfolk now that you're after the best for Skagway, the best for Alaska, not just the best for Soapy Smith. If you allow the railroad to go ahead without a fight, you'll gain their confidence. You'll be looked on as somebody worthy of respect, worth voting for. Bring in gunmen, tear the town apart, and you'll be despised. And when you get killed, as most certainly you will, they'll all cheer." Tara went over to Smith and knelt beside his chair.

Smith sighed wearily. "Okay, I'll do it your way. They can build their railroad. But I'll get what I want . . . eventually."

She was surprised at how readily he'd agreed. Then that crooked, disarming grin of his appeared. He put his hands on her shoulders and gazed into her eyes. "Tara, maybe your way is the right way. And if that's your price—"

"I don't have a price," Tara whispered. "I don't ask anything. Only I don't want to see you with a bullet in your back."

He kissed her, a sudden, warm embrace, holding her tight for a fleeting moment. Then he smiled.

"I've got to be careful, Tara. If I don't watch it, you'll be educating me."

OVERSHADOWING the talk in the bars, the barbershops, the stores, was the war with Spain. It was far removed from Alaska, did not touch the life of the gold miners, but as the news filtered through, patriotic fervor grew. In the Oyster Parlor miniature Stars and Stripes sprouted everywhere. Uncle Sam posters appeared. A picture of Teddy Roosevelt hung prominently over the bar.

"I got to get into this war," Smith told Tara.

"Are you volunteering?"

"Maybe," he said thoughtfully.

When she arrived at his office a few mornings later, she stopped dead in her tracks. The door had been forced, and inside it was chaos. Drawers had been pulled out of his desk, a metal deedbox had been jimmied open, letters were strewn all over.

Tara started to tidy up the mess, trying to sort out what had been taken. But nothing seemed to be missing. The cashbox had been opened, but the money had not been touched.

Smith appeared in the doorway. "What the hell—" he began, looking around. "Are you all right?"

"Somebody broke in," Tara said. "But I don't think anything's been stolen. Do you know what they were after?"

He glanced at her with an expression of studied innocence. "How would I know?"

"They went through everything. I think they even read the ledgers, but they left them."

"They wouldn't find anything there," he said, looking pleased.

He was playing it so casually that she began to get a feeling that maybe there were documents he kept hidden. Maybe that's what the intruders had been after.

"Listen," he said, "me and the boys are going to have a little council of war. No need for you to be here."

That meant Bowers, Yeah Mow, Mort—the inner circle. "Jeff, is there anything wrong?" Tara asked.

"Now, what could be wrong?" he countered.

But from then on an armed man hovered outside the office day and night. New locks were fitted to the door, and for the first time there was a safe in the office.

"Merely precautions," Smith explained. "You'd be surprised how many rogues are in town."

"Jeff, what are you afraid of?"

"Nothing, nothing. I just don't like people poking their nose into our affairs."

"*Your* affairs," she reminded him firmly.

Little could surprise Tara about Smith, or so she thought. Then, a few days later, a hand-painted sign appeared on his door: OFFICE OF THE COMMANDING OFFICER.

He made a grand entrance in the uniform of a U.S. Army officer and snapped to attention when he saw Tara. "Captain Jefferson Smith, ma'am, commanding officer, Company A."

"Company what?" she asked. "Jeff, what are you playing at?"

"Company A, First Regiment, National Guard of Alaska."

"I don't believe it!"

"We're at war, woman," he replied loftily. "I'm raising a volunteer outfit, Skagway's own National Guard company."

"You mean you're raising your own private army," she said.

"Damn it, Tara, you can be the most aggravating female," he shouted. He took a sheet of paper from his desk and thrust it at her. "Private army, indeed," he growled.

The paper had an officially printed letterhead embossed with the legend OFFICE OF THE SECRETARY OF WAR, WASHINGTON, D.C. It read:

Dear Captain Smith,

The President joins me in commending your patriotic spirit in forming your militia unit. You and your volunteer forces and the enthusiasm with which you have rallied to the colors in this hour of your country's need are a tribute to the people of Alaska.

Your offer to put your unit at the disposal of the United States Army and to lead your men in an invasion of Spanish Cuba is greatly appreciated, but I can assure you that the forces we have available are adequate and there is no need for the War Department to require your services overseas.

Russell A. Alger, Secretary of War

"Well?" He stood beaming at her. "You still think I'm planning to start some cockeyed private war?"

She had to admit that it wasn't what she had expected.

Smith became totally committed to Company A. Recruitment posters went up in town overnight. He dictated to Tara a flamboyant order of the day, urging all "red-blooded Americans to follow the summons to arms in our country's hour of need." Near the Oyster Parlor a recruitment marquee was raised.

Along with many others, Tara went to the recruitment rally at Jackson's music hall. Smith was on the platform, dressed in his uniform. He pointed at a crowd of unshaven characters lounging in the front rows and told them, "You are fine and brave men, and I'm sure you will follow me anywhere and at any time."

Everybody cheered. Then Mort and some other men went around the audience with collection boxes. When Mort came to Tara, she asked, "What are you collecting for?"

"It's the welfare fund. For the company's orphans and widows."

"Yours must be the only unit in the world that collects for its widows and orphans before it's even got recruits."

"Absolutely," he agreed. "But you got to think ahead." He handed her a little wad of paper. "Here," he said. "Like you to sell some of those. Dollar a ticket. It's a lucky draw."

"A benefit for the widows?" she inquired.

Smith nodded. "We want to sell fifteen hundred."

"What's the prize?"

"Seventy-five bucks," he said. "Not bad for a dollar, eh?"

"Who keeps the other one thousand four hundred and twenty-five dollars?"

"Who do you think? The company paymaster." Smith shrugged. "I have to train my men. Hell, I'm the CO of the outfit. I have to get military supplies. Uniforms, rifles, sidearms. I'm having them shipped in. You don't want my soldier boys to have wooden swords, do you?" He laughed as if that were a good joke.

Smith transformed Skagway. Huge banners declaring FREEDOM FOR CUBA and DOWN WITH TYRANNY spanned the streets. All over town, people were wearing buttons reading REMEMBER THE *Maine*, COMPLIMENTS OF SKAGWAY MILITARY COMPANY, JEFF R. SMITH, CAPTAIN. However, the town did not see much outward evidence of Smith's army. He discouraged too many questions.

"Why be so mysterious?" Tara asked.

He smiled at her. "Skagway's going to see plenty of its militia when the time comes, I promise you."

All that was swept from her mind when, next day, Mort came into the office at the Oyster Parlor. "That German fellow is here."

"The photographer? Herr Hart?"

Mort nodded, unenthusiastic. "I'll tell him to go away."

But Tara was already rushing down the stairs, and there he was, his blue eyes lighting up behind their glasses when he saw her. He opened his arms to her and held her tightly.

"Oh, you don't know how good it is to see you, Ernst," she said.

Hart looked at her solemnly. "Tara, we must talk—but not here."

He seemed nervous, ill at ease. Tara led him upstairs to the office, and they sat opposite each other. "What's the matter, Ernst?" she asked, frowning. "Tell me, how did you track me down?"

"I heard you were with Smith."

She had a lot to explain, she knew that. "Ernst, I didn't find Daniel—" she began, but he cut her short.

"I know," he said softly, almost sadly. "Tara, Daniel is dead."

It seemed an infinity before the words assumed meaning. "No. He can't be." Tara's voice faltered. "How do you know?"

He reached for her hand. "He was murdered in Circle. Somebody knifed him. He was found in a back alley."

"Oh my God." Tears were running down her face.

"Inspector Constantine identified him from this." Hart pulled out a handkerchief. In it was a gold wedding ring.

She took it, her fingers trembling. She could see the inscription inside the band: *Tara to Daniel.* It was his ring, the twin of the one she had worn.

"No," Tara moaned, her voice full of despair. She buried her face in her hands and was racked by sobs.

"I'm sorry," Hart whispered. "I think it must have happened very quickly, Tara. He had no pain, I'm sure."

She looked up, her face ashen. "Did you see him . . . ?"

He nodded. "Yes, I did see the body. He had been stabbed in the side. Just below the birthmark."

"You said birthmark—"

"Yes," he said. "The funny-shaped one, under his left arm."

"That's not Daniel," whispered Tara. "He had no birthmark." She leaned back and closed her eyes. "Thank God."

"But the Mounties are sure he must be Daniel."

"I tell you they're wrong," she snapped, almost savagely.

"Please, Tara, you must not delude yourself. The ring is proof—"

"What does a wedding ring prove?" Tara cried. "I haven't got mine, have I? Maybe he sold it. Maybe it was stolen."

They sat in silence, and then Hart said, "I am sorry to have given you such a shock. If you're sure it is the wrong man, I wish we knew how he came to have the ring."

"We'll find out," Tara said confidently, "when I am reunited with Daniel. I'm running an ad for him in the paper. Someone is bound to answer."

It was like a bad dream they wanted to forget; they didn't talk about it anymore. Instead Hart eyed her admiringly. "Well, I must say you're looking very chic, Mrs. Kane. You might not have found Daniel, but it would appear you've struck gold."

She told him what had happened at Sheep Camp, but she did not mention the baby or Jefferson Smith. Somehow she was reluctant to admit to Hart the role Smith had been playing in her life.

"Ernst, I have a little cabin now. Come over on Sunday at noon. Have some home cooking."

He rose and blew her a kiss. "I'll count the hours."

The next day, when Smith turned up at the Oyster Parlor, he

glowered at Tara. "What's that Sir Galahad with the tripod hanging around for?" he rasped.

"Ernst is passing through Skagway, so he looked me up."

"Yes, I heard. I don't want him in my place, you got that?"

"Anything else?" she asked coldly.

Their eyes locked, and he got up and left the room without a word. But he came back after an hour. She ignored him, her pen scratching in the ledger she was balancing.

"Tara," he said at last. "Sorry I bit your head off."

He walked around the office like a man making up his mind about something. Then he faced her. "Let's take a day off and go somewhere. You and me and the kid. We'll have a picnic, out in the country. All day Sunday."

Inwardly she groaned. "Sunday?"

"What's wrong with Sunday?"

"Ernst is coming to have a meal. He won't be here long and—"

"Oh, I see. Herr Hart. A little tryst with Sir Galahad."

She stood up, flushed. "What's it to you, anyway?" she cried. "I don't have to ask your permission, do I?"

"You're wasting your time with a gump like that," Smith said. "You can do better, honey."

"He's a *friend*," she yelled at him. "You don't even know what that means . . . and don't call me honey."

"Okay," he said mildly. "We'll have our picnic some other time. You enjoy yourself with Hart."

"I will," said Tara, and walked out the door.

WHEN Ernst arrived on Sunday, he handed Tara a bottle of wine. Then he noticed the Indian girl, holding little John in her arms. "I didn't know you were sharing this place," he remarked.

"Lydia works for me, and the baby is mine," Tara said uneasily.

He stared at the baby, then at Tara. "Yours?" he gasped.

"By adoption, so to speak."

"Why didn't you tell me?" Hart's tone was reproachful.

"Ernst, there is a great deal I haven't told you."

"Well," he said, "you'd better start."

He listened intently while she told him about the avalanche and about the baby's birth. When she finished, she looked at him questioningly. "You are not angry with me?"

"Why should I be? No, I admire you. Taking in that child, keeping him alive, looking after him. Now I understand."

"Understand what?"

He looked away as he replied. "Why you are with Smith."

"Ernst, I am not with Smith. I work for him. I needed a job, and he gave me one. I earn my wages."

"Tara," he said gravely. "You must get away from him. He is a bad man. There are rumors he is planning something dangerous. I hear stories."

"I'm not interested in gossip," she retorted.

"No, you must listen," Hart said urgently. "He is raising an army, shipping in weapons, ammunition. He plans a *Putsch*, a revolt. When he has enough men and guns, he will take over the town, the railroad, seize the Chilkoot, the White Pass."

"That's crazy!" she cried.

"I beg you, Tara, you must leave here. Before it's too late."

"Ernst, I don't believe any of—"

"I will protect you from him," he burst out. "I will look after you and the baby. You need not have anything to do with the man ever again."

Tara said nothing. He was speaking rapidly. He grabbed her hand. "I will arrange everything. One day, God willing, we will marry, and we will be so happy, my dearest, together always."

Tara looked at him, unbelieving. Hart raised her hand to his lips and kissed it. "And the little baby, of course, he will be my son too. Thank God, *Liebchen*, I can save you from Smith."

"No." Tara pulled her hand away. "I don't want to live with you. I am married, and if I wasn't, I wouldn't marry you."

She softened when she saw his wounded expression. "Oh, I don't mean to sound unkind, Ernst. But this . . . this is absurd."

"So," he said, and there was bitterness in his voice, "you prefer that hoodlum to me. You like Smith better."

She stared at him, amazed. "Jeff has been a friend to me, don't you understand that? I know what he is. I know what people say. But to me he has been generous, kind. I'm grateful to him. I like him—" Tara stopped. It was the first time she had ever admitted it, even to herself.

"He is a *Schuft*, a scoundrel."

"You're jealous," she said gently.

To Tara's horror, Hart fell on his knees in front of her and clung to her dress. "I love you," he whimpered. "You're the only woman I have ever met who's meant anything to me. Please, please say yes."

"Ernst," she said. "For heaven's sake, pull yourself together. I like you, but I don't love you. Please get up, I beg of you."

At that moment the cabin door opened. Tara saw Jefferson Smith standing on the threshold, a bunch of flowers and a bottle of champagne in his arms. "My, my, what a touching scene."

"What do you want?" Tara demanded.

Smith's voice brought Hart to his senses. He got up, brushing dust from his trousers in an effort to cover his embarrassment.

"Have I arrived at an inopportune moment, my dear?" Smith asked solicitously. He sniffed the aroma from the stove. "Smells good. Yes, I think I'd like some lunch. How kind of you."

"Jeff, I don't recall inviting you," she began, but he handed the flowers and champagne to her.

"I'm sure you meant to," he said blandly. "Shall I open the bubbly? A drink to our hostess, Mr. Hart?"

"Tara." Hart cut Smith dead. "I'm not staying for lunch."

"Oh, for Pete's sake, there's plenty of food for everybody. Please stay, Ernst." She hastily laid an extra place at the table.

"How's my godson?" Smith asked.

"Godson? I thought Tara had adopted him," Hart said coldly.

"We both did." Smith smiled. "Sort of a joint stake."

The two men did not speak to one another while Tara served the soup. Smith then turned to Hart. "I hope I wasn't interrupting anything by bursting in on you folks," he said casually.

Hart looked at him viciously. "I have asked her to marry me," he said.

Smith poured the champagne. "Have you?" he snapped. "You want to marry her, protect her? You couldn't look after a lame cat. She goes on the trail with you, and gets back alone, half out of her mind, two-thirds dead, and wanted on a murder charge. I'll never forgive you for that."

"I . . . I couldn't stop her," Hart said in a low voice. "She went off on her own. What could I do?"

"If I'd been in your boots, nothing in the world could have stopped me staying with her. No, you were too busy taking your pretty pictures. You're not worth a woman like that." Smith pushed back his chair and turned to Tara. "I'm sorry about all this. I had no idea he was going to ask you to—" He stopped, staring at the wedding ring on the middle finger of her left hand.

She followed his look and nodded. "Yes, Jeff. It's Daniel's. Ernst brought it to me from Circle. They found it on a dead man, but the man wasn't Daniel."

"What happened to him, then?"

"I don't know. But one thing's for sure, Jeff," she said gently. "I'm not marrying anybody. I'm married already."

He gave a wry little smile. "I hope I'll see you tomorrow." He left the cabin without saying a word to Hart.

"I'm going now," Hart said, putting on his coat.

"Yes," said Tara quietly. "I think that's best."

"I don't think we should see one another again." His voice faltered. "Take care, dear Tara. I will always love you, and I only hope and pray you have made the right choice."

"There is no choice, Ernst. There's only one man I love."

Hart nodded. "Yes. Mr. Smith."

Tara was immediately on the defensive. "Of course not!"

Hart shrugged. "You know, my dear, I think you are hoodwinking yourself. I believe you have fallen in love with that man."

"You're wrong," she snapped, but although her voice was firm she could not meet his gaze.

Hart inclined his head. "Good-by," he said. "I am sailing back to San Francisco. I have over a thousand pictures of the Gold Rush, and my work is finished. Any other reason I have had for staying is over. It is all finished."

"Good-by, Ernst. Thank you for everything," she whispered as she watched him walk away.

CHAPTER FOURTEEN

Tara's mood was buoyant as she rode along the trail to Dyea. Since there was still no response to her ad, she intended to check the town's lodging houses, try to find someone who might know something about Daniel.

She had traveled this route with Bishop Beauchamp, unwittingly smuggling Soapy Smith's liquor by way of the spurious Reverend

Bowers. Then, the countryside had been white and freezing. Now, with the coming of summer, it was warm and ablaze with flowers. Goldenrod, daisies, and poppies jostled with a myriad of ferns. The sun would not set until after ten o'clock; even then, there would only be twilight.

Dyea had changed. Soldiers in dark blue uniforms were everywhere. Tara left her horse in the stables next to the blacksmith shop, checked into a hotel, then set out to make inquiries about Daniel. Ever since Hart had left, she had been torn with doubt. Was she, as he had said, hoodwinking herself? Was she falling in love with Jeff Smith? She had to prove to herself that Daniel was still alive and that she loved him, more than anyone.

She had a meal in an eating house, and just as she was paying her bill, the door opened. A U.S. Army officer with the silver bar of a lieutenant and the insignia of the infantry stood looking around. As soon as he saw Tara he went toward her and saluted.

"Colonel Bradshaw's compliments, ma'am. The colonel wonders if you could spare him a few minutes."

"What is it about?" Tara asked.

"I'm sure the colonel will tell you himself, ma'am." She had the feeling that it was not so much an invitation as an order.

At army headquarters, Tara was ushered into the colonel's office. "Mrs. Kane, sir," announced the lieutenant, and Tara found herself facing two men. The colonel, a gray-haired man with sharp eyes, rose from behind his desk. The other man, who had also risen, was a civilian, in a city suit, with gold-rimmed glasses.

"I appreciate your coming here, Mrs. Kane," said the colonel without warmth. "I'm Colonel Bradshaw, and this gentleman is Mr. Wilkins, from the War Department in Washington."

He sat down again and cleared his throat. "Mrs. Kane, there is a reason for our presence in Dyea. The government has moved in the army, in case of certain eventualities—"

"Let's put it this way, ma'am," interrupted Wilkins. "You are an . . . an associate of Mr. Smith. In Skagway."

"I know Mr. Smith," she said curtly.

"Are you here on Mr. Smith's business, ma'am?" asked the colonel crisply.

"Of course not." Her tone was hard. "If you must know, I'm here on a private matter. I'm trying to locate my husband."

"We're only interested in Mr. Smith, in his activities, and the people around him," Wilkins said flatly.

"Mr. Smith's activities are of very little concern to me," declared Tara. Certain things were coming back to her that Hart had said about Smith's militia and arms shipments.

"Well, Mrs. Kane, whatever you're doing here, you can give Mr. Smith a message." The colonel's voice was icy. "Tell him the government has moved a battalion of infantry into Dyea. Their orders are to keep the peace and to uphold law and order."

He opened the door for Tara. "Good day, ma'am."

She went to her hotel room to find a man waiting for her. "Forgive the intrusion, Mrs. Kane." He handed her a card. "I'm Edward Cahill, newspaper correspondent from Seattle."

"Please go," Tara said, indicating the door.

"I think you'd better listen," he said authoritatively.

She hesitated, then sat down.

"You've got yourself in bad company, Mrs. Kane. I am a reporter, but I also work for the U.S. government. That's why I'm interested in Jefferson Smith. Just as the military gentlemen are," he added with a smile. "We've sort of checked on things and we believe that maybe you don't really know what's going on."

She sat silent. She knew he was going to ask her to betray Smith, and she knew what her answer had to be.

"You must help us, Mrs. Kane," he went on. "We suspect Smith is planning to take over Skagway by force of arms. We think he wants to seize the railroad, the passes, maybe Juneau, Dyea. Take over Alaska, maybe invade British Columbia, seize the Yukon. Pretend he's claiming it for the United States. It's a disputed border anyway, and you can guess what that would do. Maybe war between us and the Canadians."

"That's rubbish. All he wants to see is Alaska as part of the Union," intervened Tara.

"He wants to control the gold that's coming out of the Klondike," said Cahill brutally. "He wants to squeeze the prospectors by controlling the whole place, the ports, transportation. He'll take his cut out of every ounce of gold that's found."

"How could he?" Tara asked.

"What do you think he's raising his phony National Guard for? It's nothing but a private gang; tough, hard mercenaries, dressed up in army uniforms to fool everybody. He's shipping in arms, Mrs. Kane, maybe Maxim guns, even light field guns. We suspect he's got an arsenal somewhere in Skagway. A warehouse, perhaps. We're trying to find out. We've got an agent working in Skagway."

"This agent of yours, did he break into Smith's office at the Oyster Parlor?" she asked.

He said nothing.

"Mr. Cahill," Tara said slowly. "I don't have any part in all this. I'm terrified of what you say he's doing. But you must also know this. He's been a good friend to me, and I can't repay it by . . ."

Cahill looked at her gravely. "All right," he said. "I believe you. Only, this is insurrection. Don't put your neck in a noose."

He went to the door. "Be careful, Mrs. Kane. Skagway is going to be a mighty dangerous place."

TARA could almost smell the tension when she returned to Skagway. Men were standing around in clusters, grim-faced, and the usually crowded streets were strangely quiet. The atmosphere of unease was even more evident outside the Oyster Parlor. A cordon of Smith's men were cradling shotguns and scrutinizing strangers.

Inside, Mort gave her a nod. He had his six-gun buckled on. "Welcome back, Mrs. Kane," he grunted.

She looked at the bouncers sitting near the door, one of them with a Winchester across his knees. "What's happened?"

"Well"—Mort contemplated Tara—"there's been a shooting."

It was not all that unusual. Guns were part of the scene all over—Dawson, Fortymile, Skagway. Even a periodic shoot-out was not unknown. But this was different. Whatever had happened, people were angry and resentful. Something was simmering.

"Who was it?" Tara inquired.

"Some greenhorn. Better ask the boss."

Slowly, Tara got the story out of Smith. "Yeah Mow got trigger-happy," he said. "Fellow called Glen Ashbury. Been hanging around the place." He shrugged. "It'll pass over. Folks are pretty worked up at the moment, but they'll soon forget."

The shooting had taken place in broad daylight. In front of dozens of passersby Yeah Mow had shot down an unarmed man.

"Do you know anything about Ashbury?" she asked nervously.

"Why should *I* care?" But she could see he was worried.

He snapped his fingers suddenly. "Maybe I'll fix a trial. We'll get Yeah Mow acquitted, and then everybody will calm down."

He waited for her reaction, but all she said was, "I've seen enough of your trials, Jeff."

Killing Ashbury was a big mistake. Tara saw a slogan white-washed on a wall: HANG SOAPY. People kept away from the Oyster Parlor. Three days later Smith told Tara that there had been an inquest. "Verdict's self-defense," he announced. "Yeah Mow got cleared. Six witnesses testified they saw Ashbury draw a gun first."

"But he wasn't armed, you said so yourself."

"I wasn't there, honey. These guys saw it."

There was a celebration that night in the Oyster Parlor, with Yeah Mow as guest of honor. The six witnesses drank with him—men whose faces were not unknown in the establishment.

The town did not forget the Ashbury shooting. At a time when Skagway promised to be the most important landing stage for the goldfields, thanks to the rail link with Lake Bennett, Smith's re-gime was threatening everything. The traders, the railroad, the backbone of the community, knew that if news of Soapy Smith's hold over Skagway reached Seattle and San Francisco, it could put an end to the town's prosperity.

All the more reason, Jefferson Smith thought, for his making the forthcoming Fourth of July the most dazzling event in the history of the Klondike. "It's going to be the biggest, fanciest Independence Day Alaska has ever seen," he announced to Tara. There would be a huge carnival, military bands, and a parade. *"That's* when we unveil the militia, and I'll invite every important citizen— the railroad people, the bankers, even the governor."

Tara was writing out the invitations at the desk when she came across some papers she hadn't noticed before—bills of lading and cargo manifests that Smith had forgotten to lock away in his drawer. She picked one up and found he was importing "kitchen equipment" to the amount of five thousand dollars and "gardening gear" to the tune of four thousand dollars. What use did he have for gardening gear and that much kitchen equipment? She knew what she was looking at. Consignments of arms. Evidence the government had sought in the office break-in.

Tara had been keeping her ears open too. Several times she had heard mention of "the warehouse." When she asked Smith about it, he had said something about the place where he stored his liquor. There was only one way to find out if Cahill had been right about the existence of an arsenal.

The warehouse stood by itself at the side of a disused lumber mill. Tara dismounted from her horse and concealed herself behind a tree. Suddenly she froze. A man with a rifle came around the corner of the warehouse, looking about him like a sentry on patrol. She saw a mule train approaching, accompanied by two armed horsemen. Each mule was weighed down by two heavy crates. They came to a halt before the warehouse.

Tara watched as the sentry unlocked the door of the warehouse and the men carried the heavy crates inside. Then she stepped out from behind the tree and crept over to the big shed. The door was ajar, and she could hear voices. She peered through the gap and caught her breath as she saw row after row of rifles, boxes of ammunition, Maxim guns on tripods, and six machine guns.

"You shouldn't be here, Mrs. Kane," Yeah Mow said. She spun around. She hadn't heard him come up behind her. "Does the boss know you're here?" He was pointing a pistol at her.

"Of course," she lied.

"Okay," he said. "You and me are going to say hello to him."

They rode back to town in silence. Yeah Mow spoke only once. "You're a pretty lucky lady. Usually when people go snooping around that place we shoot first and ask questions afterward."

"Like the way you killed Glen Ashbury?" Tara asked.

"Guys don't break into the boss's office and get away with it." Then she knew they had killed the U.S. government agent.

Yeah Mow shoved Tara into a storeroom of the Oyster Parlor. "Get Mr. Smith right away," blustered Tara. "He's going to be mighty sore at you."

Yeah Mow smiled coldly. "You'll see him all right." He shut the door, and she heard the key turning in the padlock. As time passed, she felt more and more apprehensive.

Finally she heard the key turning again, and Smith came in. He walked slowly over to a crate and sat down on it. "What were you doing there?" His tone was quiet.

"Finding out the truth for myself."

"Why did you have to sneak off to the arsenal? Why didn't you

233

tell me you wanted a look? And you found just exactly what I've been telling you. I've been shipping in arms for my little outfit."

"Some little outfit. There's enough arms to equip a small army. To kill thousands. You didn't start this whole business to fight in the Spanish War. You're planning rebellion."

Smith stared at her. He said nothing. He sat rigid.

"I'm waiting," she said. "Deny it. Please."

"Why should I?" asked Smith. "It's the truth."

"No. You can't be that cold-blooded." Her voice was controlled, her hands clenched. "Don't tell me you don't care about what will happen. The people you'll kill. The bloodshed." She leaned forward. "Jeff, the government knows what you're up to. They've got troops ready to move in. I've seen them. Ashbury was investigating you. He was a government agent."

"Come on now, that's mighty emotive talk. Nobody's moving in troops. All they need is a little persuasion—like a good front-row view of Skagway's finest—and they'll get that on the Fourth." He laughed. "It'll all be finished before they know it. There ain't going to be no shooting, unless somebody else starts it."

"They will, Jeff. That's why those troops are in Dyea. You know what they'll do the moment you take over. Thank God I won't be there."

"What's that?"

"I'm pulling out, Jeff," she said very quietly. "I'll be in San Francisco when they hang you. I've had enough."

For the first time he looked worried. "You can't," he said. "I won't let you. Never." He took her in his arms and stroked her hair. Before she knew how it happened he was kissing her on the lips, first gently, then more passionately, and Tara did not resist. She closed her eyes and luxuriated in his embrace, her body yielding to him, her arms folding around him.

Then, slowly, he released her. They stood looking at one another, the atmosphere between them charged. He was imbued with a magnetism she had never felt in him. It left her breathless.

"You're so important to me, Tara," he said softly.

"If that's true, Jeff," she said, gazing into his unwavering eyes, "give up your crazy scheme. Promise me you'll never use your men against this town, the territory, anyone."

He looked into the distance, then turned back to her. "All right, stay until the Fourth. More than anything I want you there. You'll be the hostess, the first lady. If you do that . . . maybe I can do it all your way." He took her hand and kissed it. "Well?" he said. "Is it a deal?"

She nodded. "Yes," she said slowly. "I think it is."

CHAPTER FIFTEEN

ONG before the big parade was due to begin, red-white-and-blue bunting waved from rooftops and flagpoles, and Skagway's streets were filled with people in their Sunday best. Prospectors shot off pistols and rifles, and steamships in the harbor sounded their whistles.

Tara could hear the sounds of revelry as she dabbed perfume behind her ears. She was dressed in a new frock, her auburn hair swept up, her green eyes bright with excitement and happiness.

She dressed John in a little suit Lydia had made for him and wrapped him in a big embroidered shawl. "My John." Tara smiled proudly, balancing the curly-haired baby on her knee. "I need you as much as you need me. Together we can face the world and cope with anything. As soon as I can I'm taking you home, and there you'll have a proper life. I want to be a good mother."

When Smith came for them he was wearing his army uniform, complete with sword. For a moment he stood and admired Tara openly. "I'm a very lucky man. I've not only got the honor of escorting a beautiful woman, I've also got the company of an extremely stylish young man." He stroked the baby's cheek.

"If you're both ready, the carriage awaits," he announced formally, leading her to the door. Outside stood an open four-wheeled carriage drawn by two magnificent horses and complete with driver.

Smith helped her into the carriage, and they set off through the streets of Skagway, Tara holding the baby and Smith bolt upright beside her, waving his hand, performing to perfection his role of military commander, civic leader, and would-be statesman. Thousands of onlookers stared in amazement. Such handsome, fashionable people simply did not exist in that region.

They stopped in front of a dais dominated by a giant Stars and Stripes. A loud roar rang out, and Smith stood acknowledging the town's welcome. Then a brass band began playing "Dixie."

"My signature tune." Smith grinned crookedly as he helped Tara out of the carriage. He led her to one of the three chairs that had been placed on the platform, another one of which was occupied by a bearded man in a frock coat. He rose as they approached.

"Governor," Smith said, "may I present Mrs. Kane."

The governor bowed, and Tara held out her hand to the man Smith wanted to kick out of the territory.

"As you know, my dear," purred Smith, "Governor Brady is doing us the honor of taking the salute."

"I must say, Captain Smith, you're doing the town proud," rumbled Brady. "Looks like there's going to be a fine show."

"You haven't seen anything yet, Governor." Smith seated Tara on the chair next to Brady and winked at her. He then sprinted down the steps of the dais, disappearing out of sight.

The little brass band played Sousa marches, and soon Tara could hear the sound of hundreds of pairs of marching feet in the distance. The parade was approaching from the upper end of Broadway, and Tara craned her neck and saw a man carrying Old Glory. He was followed by Jefferson Smith, mounted on a white charger, his sword drawn, a heroic figure riding in front of his army.

Drummers beat a blood-stirring tattoo, and the First Regiment, National Guard of Alaska, tramped down the street, marching in very creditable military style considering its ranks included Smith's bouncers, bartenders, and croupiers, who had been pressed into service alongside genuine volunteers. None of the arms from the arsenal was on display.

Brady was on his feet, his hand on his heart, taking the salute. "Magnificent. A wonderful body of men. A credit to Alaska."

If only you knew, Tara thought. Smith had promised Skagway the greatest show it had ever seen, and he kept his word. Three Scots pipers headed a series of wagons converted into floats, depicting Skagway's gold mining, the railroad, shipping, banking. Then came a second brass band, followed by a wagon loaded with dance hostesses blowing kisses. Across the wagon was a big poster: JEFF SMITH FOR GOVERNOR. STATEHOOD FOR ALASKA.

Brady swallowed at that but managed a sickly smile as cheers went up from the crowd. Then, while the tail end of the parade was still passing, Smith appeared beside Tara on the dais. He sat down and whispered to her, "Well, how did that look?"

"The best parade a kid could wish to see," Tara whispered back. "But I don't think the governor was amused by that sign."

The procession had finally passed, but the crowd still stood, packed. Smith moved to the front of the platform and raised his hand for silence.

"Fellow citizens of Skagway," he began. "This great nation is at war, and we Skagway folk are going to play our part in licking the tyrants of Havana. We're doing our duty, but we believe also that we deserve a square deal. The people of Alaska call on the Republicans in Congress to keep their faith with us and give us our own elected congressmen."

The crowd stamped their feet, and guns were fired into the air.

"Now, we don't want anything but our just dues," cried Smith. "What's Washington done for us? Made some lousy laws, taxed us, but what else? For years we've been the orphan. Hell, until the railroad we only had one wagon road running for two miles. That's going to change. This great territory, Alaska, is going to be right up there." He pointed to the Stars and Stripes fluttering in the breeze. "It's going to be one of those states.

"We need men in Washington who will speak for us," Smith continued. "Men of vision. Men who believe in Alaska and its future. Let's send those men to Washington. The future belongs to us."

He sat down, and the crowd threw their hats into the air and cheered. Tara felt certain that he had meant every word he'd said.

"Great speech, Captain Smith," Brady broke in uneasily. "The party needs men like you."

"You think so, Governor?" Smith drawled. "Maybe we ought to talk about it sometime."

The noise and excitement became too much for young John. He began to cry, and Tara decided it was time to take him home. She excused herself to Brady, who looked unhappy and dour. He stood alone, whereas Smith was surrounded by well-wishers. Then Tara saw a scowling stranger go over to the governor and say something. A complacent smile spread across Brady's face, and he walked off with the man, his arm around his shoulder.

Tara forced her way through to Smith's side. "Jeff," she said, "I'm going back to get changed for the ball."

"I'll send Bowers with the carriage for you." She started to move off, but Smith caught her hand. "And thank you, Tara. You don't know how much you've helped me."

SMITH's Independence Day Ball was the nearest thing to a society event Skagway had ever seen. The Princess Hotel was ablaze with light, and when the carriage drew up outside, Tara could hear orchestral strains drifting out of large French windows.

Bowers held her hand as they mounted the steps to the entrance hall. Tara was well aware of the glances people gave her, and she smiled brilliantly as she swept into the hallway. Let them stare, she said to herself. I'm going to enjoy every minute of this.

Bowers led the way to the enormous ballroom, where hundreds of candles reflected in the crystal pendants of a dozen chandeliers. Already guests were milling around drinking champagne. Tara was so enchanted she only became aware of Smith's presence as he gently removed her shawl and ran his eyes admiringly over her black taffeta gown. "My dear Tara," he said, kissing her hand. "You look stunning." He beckoned to a hovering waiter bearing a silver salver with glasses of champagne.

Smith raised his glass. "To the loveliest woman in the world and the belle of my ball," he toasted, and they both drank.

"Come," he went on, handing their glasses to Bowers. "It's time for us to start the dancing." He held out his arm and led her onto the floor. The other guests parted to let them through. The orchestra broke into a lively Strauss waltz, and Tara allowed herself to be swept around the floor, feeling exuberant, euphoric, marvelous. Gradually other couples joined in, so that the floor became a mass of whirling color.

"How does it feel," he asked as he turned her this way and that, "to be the center of attention, to have every man in the room desire you and every woman envy you?"

"That's nonsense, Jeff," Tara said. But she was pleased.

When the waltz stopped, he led her to the buffet heaped with food—platters of poached salmon in aspic, cold poultry and meat, dishes of sliced cucumber, trays of cheeses, and an exotic collection of desserts. They walked to a table, their plates piled high.

As Smith was about to sit down a man approached. Tara recognized him immediately. He was middle-aged, his face weather-beaten, his eyes crafty. She had seen him that very afternoon, when he had buttonholed the governor after the parade.

"Must have cost you a pretty penny or two," the man remarked coldly, nodding at the dance floor, "but it won't buy us."

"I don't recall inviting you, Reid," observed Smith coolly. He turned to Tara. "My dear, my apologies. This gentleman is Frank Reid. He likes to think of himself as the city engineer—Mr. Public-Spirited Citizen."

Reid nodded at Tara curtly.

"Don't see your vigilante friends around," Smith drawled.

"They wouldn't come near one of your functions." Reid bent closer. "I just wanted to warn you, Smith. You're finished. You're not going to shoot people down again, I promise you. The decent people of this town have had enough."

"I think I have too. Right now you're boring me." Smith's eyes were like hard, cold diamonds. "If you want to talk business, you know where to find me."

"All right, Smith. I've said my piece so you know what to expect. My respects, ma'am." He nodded at Tara and walked off.

Tara sighed in relief. "What an awful man."

"The dregs," Smith said. "I found that out a long while ago. We used to be partners."

Tara was amazed. "What happened?" she asked.

Smith shrugged. "Let's just say he and I no longer get on."

For some time they ate in silence, Smith deep in thought. Reid's appearance had brought Tara down to earth. Had all the magic been a dream? she wondered. The veneer of Skagway's attempt to emulate fashionable society was beginning to wear thin. Everyone was getting louder and brasher. Elegant dancing was being replaced by thumping feet.

"Come," Smith said, getting up. "There's something I want to show you." Together they walked out, past the potted plants and intoxicated guests, and mounted the red-carpeted staircase. Smith took Tara's hand as he led her down the corridor. He opened a door and Tara found herself in a plush sitting room, lit only by candles. There was a large sofa upholstered in red velvet, and the walls were covered with fabric.

"Now, sit down, take your shoes off and relax," he ordered, going over to a bar. She sat, her posture the epitome of propriety.

"Try this for size," he invited, returning with two balloon brandy glasses.

There was an explosion of light outside the window, followed by the sound of people cheering. "It's the fireworks," Smith said.

"Come on, we must watch them," insisted Tara, going over to the French windows.

Down in the street Smith's militia were handing out sparklers, while overhead, Roman candles, rockets, catherine wheels zoomed, and rained a web of shooting color in the twilight.

"Oh, they're beautiful," sighed Tara as she watched a thousand stars exploding in the sky. "They remind me of the northern lights. Did I ever tell you how they saved me? Like a sign from heaven to guide me back to Dawson." They watched the fireworks display for some time, until the noise of people yelling and laughing made them close the window.

Smith pulled the heavy drapes and Tara returned to the sofa and kicked off her shoes. She looked very attractive, the sheer blackness of the gown setting off the whiteness of her shoulders and the dark fieriness of her hair. She sipped the brandy.

"What was it that you wanted me to see, Jeff?" she asked.

"It's a little gift I've got for you." He came over and sat on the sofa. "It's something that's yours by right, Tara." He took her hand and dropped her wedding ring into her palm.

She gazed at the inscription: *Daniel to Tara.*

"Put it on," Smith said, "next to that one."

She looked at him, her expression a mixture of confusion and happiness. Then, slowly, she slipped the ring onto the fourth finger of her left hand. "Thank you, Jeff, so very much." Her eyes were misty. He had given her only what was hers, but it was the greatest gesture he could have made. She was flooded with affection for him.

"Maybe you should ask why?" Smith suggested quietly. "I'd say a fellow who loves a woman is crazy to give her another man's wedding ring."

She glanced up at him sharply and was about to speak, but he put a finger gently on her lips.

"No, let me say it. I want to put my cards on the table, the whole darn pack; no joker. I started figuring why I was holding on to that little band of gold. To kid myself it didn't exist? To con myself that there wasn't anybody else? One thing a good gambler mustn't do, he mustn't kid himself. I was acting like somebody scared of a ghost." He touched the ring. "*That* ghost. Because your husband is a ghost, Tara. Daniel's dead."

"Don't ever say that," whispered Tara, choking back tears.

"He's dead," Smith repeated insistently. "You can't live with a ghost. You can't sleep with a dream. He's dead, and you've got to come to terms with that fact." He drew her to him, and she laid her head on his shoulder. "Tara," he said, stroking her hair. "I want you to marry me. I love you. I know you love me too."

"Even if Daniel is dead," she sobbed, "I wouldn't marry you. I don't love you, Jeff. I'm sorry, but you made me say it."

"I think you're lying, Tara. If you didn't love me, you couldn't have looked so happy, so beautiful, so in love this evening."

"Jeff, I don't . . ." But she couldn't meet his eyes. "Not yet, anyway," she added, lowering her head.

"Because you won't let yourself, Tara. You want to run away from me because you're scared of the truth. Daniel's just a convenient excuse. Not facing the reality of his death means you're safe, because he's there to fall back on, even though he's only a memory. You know that you and I fit. We belong. Let's join forces and build a future. For one another—for John."

"Jeff, I'm taking John back to San Francisco. You know I've made up my mind. Nothing will ever change that decision."

"I'm not trying to alter that decision, Tara," Smith reasoned. "I want to come back to Frisco with you and John. We'll get married here first, and then we'll go back, the three of us, together."

"But what about Skagway? Alaska? Statehood?"

"They don't matter, Tara. Only we do."

"You'd give up everything?" she asked incredulously.

"That's how much I love you. Without you there is no future. If you say no, I'll stay here and run this territory. I'll own it. But if you agree to marry me, it'll be different. I'd feel a complete man because I respect you, I listen to you. With you I think right, I act right, I do right."

He pulled her closer. "It is crazy. The way a man usually shows a woman that he wants her is to kiss her, not sit talking. . . . And then he has her. That's what I've done with every woman I've ever wanted. Except you." He studied her. "You look so beautiful,

Tara." And she did. Her face was tear-stained, her hair awry, but her eyes betrayed her passion for Smith, and there was nothing she could do to hide it.

Then he kissed her and she clung to him. They lingered together, not speaking, for there was nothing to say for a long while. Slowly he removed the pins from her hair. One by one each auburn curl cascaded to her shoulders. She gazed into his clear gray eyes, and they told her that he was going to make love to her, and she knew she wanted him to. She put her arms around him and leaned back against the sofa.

Smith loved her, and he proved it. For both of them, making love was the fulfillment of something they had wanted. They sought one another's mouths, their lips pressing together, his hands on her body, hers stroking his.

After the passion had faded, they lay in one another's arms. "Tara," he whispered, "I love you so very much."

She looked up at him and smiled. "I think I love you too, Jeff," she replied softly.

Later they walked back to the cabin in silence, Smith holding Tara close to him all the way. Outside the door, he stopped. "Tara," said Smith, taking her hands, "don't tell me what you've decided now. Take a few days to think over my proposal."

He bent and kissed her lightly on the lips. "And always remember, my dear, no matter what your answer is, I'll understand. There'll be no recriminations, no arguments. I just pray, oh how I pray that you'll say yes."

Then he walked off, Tara watching him go, a part of her wanting to run after him. But she remained where she was and, true to character, Smith never once looked back.

CHAPTER SIXTEEN

TARA knew that she loved Smith. She also knew what she owed to him. He had mocked and humiliated her in the past, but without him she would never have survived. And she had learned the most important thing from him. If the Mounties had taught her the practicalities of survival, from Smith she had picked up self-confidence. He had given her a belief in herself and her own capabilities.

Yet she could not marry him. What would happen if one day Daniel did return? If she were married to Smith, that would make her a bigamist. That was unthinkable. She and John would have to leave for home very soon. It was the only course.

As she made her way along Broadway she rehearsed how she would tell Smith. She was just about to open the door of the Oyster Parlor when Mort, Bowers, and the deadly Yeah Mow rushed out, nearly sending her flying. They were all wearing guns.

"Sorry," apologized Bowers, steadying Tara. "We got trouble at the docks. A vigilante meeting. Reid called out the boss." He ran off with the others.

A terrible fear swept through Tara as she started half walking, half running toward the waterfront. Ahead of her she saw a rapidly growing crowd gathering by a warehouse. She pushed through the throng. Some of Smith's gang stood blocking the sidewalk, their hands hovering near their guns. Beyond them were two men.

Tara squeezed her way to the front and stopped dead in her tracks, heart racing. All around, everyone was silent. Jefferson Smith and Frank Reid stood poised. Smith was holding a Winchester rifle like an elongated handgun, the barrel pointing at Reid, his finger lightly resting on the trigger. Reid stood a few feet away. He wore a gun belt and the butt of his pistol was outside the flap of his jacket. His fingers twitched near the gun butt.

"Jeff! Don't!" Tara cried out. Smith's hooded eyes remained fixed on Reid.

Reid took a step toward Smith. "It's the end of the road, Soapy," he shouted. "We've had enough of you and your men. I know what you've got planned for this town. You and your rat pack got twelve hours to get out of the territory. And take your cardsharps and fancy women with you."

Smith laughed. Reid spat at Smith's feet.

"You got a lot of nerve all of a sudden, Frank," goaded Smith. "Found your guts at last?"

The rifle was absolutely steady. Reid and Smith were only a foot or two apart, their eyes locked. Then, quite deliberately, Reid grabbed the barrel of Smith's rifle with his left hand, and tried to force it down. In his right hand he held his six-gun.

"You fool, don't make me kill you," warned Smith, ignoring the gun inches from his chest.

Horror-stricken, Tara saw Reid's finger tighten on his trigger. Then the hammer clicked, the chamber spun, but there was no shot. The bullet was a dud.

"Sorry about that," Smith drawled, his eyes not blinking. He jerked up the barrel of his rifle and fired in one movement. Reid rocked, his face a grimace of agony. He still held the six-gun, and he pulled the trigger once more, before he collapsed. Glass tinkled as the bullet shattered a windowpane behind Smith.

Smith stood looking down at Reid. His face was expressionless. He was about to turn when a voice called out, "Smith!"

From the crowd, his back to Tara, stepped a man.

"What do you want, mister?" Smith cried, facing him.

"You . . ." the man said in a low voice. He wore a gun belt, and his right hand hovered over the holster.

Smith nodded. "That figures."

Out of the corner of her eye Tara saw Mort move forward, but Smith waved him back. "Anybody interferes, and they're dead," called out Smith. "This is between me and him."

The gunman went for his .45 just as Smith raised his Winchester again.

But the gunman fired first.

Smith staggered but managed to pull his trigger. The gunman reared like a stricken creature, then fell to the ground.

Smith dropped the Winchester and slowly sank to his knees. The gunman's bullet had gone through his chest.

Tara screamed and ran forward. She had no eyes for Tancrede, the railroad boss, standing to one side, like a privileged spectator who had been specially invited, or for anyone else. All she wanted was to be near Smith. She dashed to where he lay, a few feet from Reid. Nobody bothered about the dead gunman.

"Jeff! Jeff!" she sobbed as she knelt beside him. Smith groaned, his eyes shut.

Tara felt herself roughly pushed aside and Bowers and Mort bent over Smith. Then they picked him up and carried him through the murmuring crowd. As they walked, his head lolled and his arms hung limply. Above the blackness of his vest a red stain was growing.

Tara caught up with them and seized Smith's freezing hand. "You've got to live," she prayed as they headed down State Street.

She never let go of his hand during that terrible journey through the strangely still streets to the Oyster Parlor. All the way they were escorted by Yeah Mow and others from Smith's militia, who surrounded the grim procession, their guns drawn, eyes raking the gaping bystanders, daring them to come forward.

Somebody had already summoned a doctor, and by the time they arrived, he was standing by the bar with his little black bag. Gently, Mort and Bowers carried Smith upstairs and put him on the couch in his office.

The doctor bent over him. "He's alive," he announced, "but he hasn't got long."

"Can't you get the bullet out?" Bowers asked.

"No point," replied the doctor. "He's shot to hell."

He left, and somebody covered Smith with a blanket. Then they all stood around, uncertain, gazing down at Smith as if they expected him to take charge again and issue orders.

Tara gradually became aware of a droning noise, like a swarm of angry bees closing in. There was the sound of crashing glass downstairs. Almost immediately the door flew open and the bartender burst in. "We got to get out," he yelled. "There's a mob down there. The whole town's going wild. They've heard the boss is dead. They're grabbing guns and looking for us."

Yeah Mow checked the magazine of his gun.

"Come on," said Mort. "Let's go."

They all ran out, leaving Tara and Bowers alone with Smith. Tara knelt down beside Smith, searching his drawn, white face for some flicker of life.

"Here," Bowers said, pouring her a brandy. "You need this."

Tara shook her head; then Smith spoke. "Hell, Tara, never turn down a good brandy." His eyes were glazed but open, looking at her. His voice was hardly audible, but he managed to smile.

They could hear the crowd in the street. It was an ugly sound, just like it had been in Dawson when the lynching party arrived outside Mrs. Miles's house.

"Charley," Smith muttered to Bowers. "Just leave us."

Bowers hesitated. "I'll be around," he said, and went out.

Smith smiled at Tara. "You know what I want to know. You don't have to tell me if you don't want to. But it would be nice if you could." His face contorted as pain shot through him.

"I love you, Jeff," choked Tara, forcing back her tears. It was the truth.

"You'll marry me?" he whispered.

"Of course."

He sighed. There was a look of great relief on his face. "Well, Mrs. Smith, aren't you going to kiss the bridegroom?"

He was so weak he could not hold her, but his mouth sought hers urgently. She closed her eyes and pressed her lips to his.

"I never wanted anything more in the world than you," he murmured. "Tara, hold my hand."

Then she knew he was losing feeling. She had been grasping his hand tightly, and yet he hadn't even known.

"Tara, you're so very beautiful," he whispered. "I love you. I want to . . ." He tried once more. "See you . . . only you . . ."

His face was still turned toward her, his eyes were on her, but they could no longer see.

Jefferson Smith was dead.

She bent down and held him to her for a long while. Then she kissed his cold, lifeless lips. "Good-by, my dear, true friend," she said softly. Gently she closed his unseeing eyes.

The door opened quietly, and Bowers walked in. For a moment he stood silent, looking down at Smith's body. "Guess he was right," he said at last. "He always said they'd never hang him."

He coughed. "We'll have to get out of here. Those worthy citizens will string us all up if they get the chance. You too."

"Me?" she asked, dazed.

"You were his woman." He looked at Smith's body. "He made me promise that if anything ever happened to him, I'd make sure that you were okay. Now that's the last thing I can do for him."

Tara said nothing; she felt numb. Bowers insisted on escorting her home, taking her out through a secret exit. Downstairs all the windows of the Oyster Parlor had been smashed. In the middle of Broadway the very people who had so willingly joined in Smith's Independence Day celebrations were now burning his effigy.

Bowers guided Tara through back streets and alleys to the cabin.

Gangs of Reid's followers were brandishing a special edition of the Skagway *Intelligencer*, announcing that the king was dead. Reid was dying. The dead gunman's identity was a mystery.

That night bloodthirsty, rampaging bands of citizens gathered for the kill. Smith's men fled for their lives, hiding in the woods and hills around Skagway, followed by murderous posses. Toward midnight the Oyster Parlor was set on fire. In the cabin, Tara watched the glow in the sky, silhouetting the town's skyline.

The virtuous, law-abiding people had taken over Skagway. The vigilantes, who prided themselves that they were cleaning up the town and had at last driven out its evil spirit, meted out cruel violence as they roamed the streets. Skagway had never been more lawless.

Dazed and heartbroken, Tara sat alone in the dark cabin, next to John. Lydia had run off when she saw the smoke rising over the town. Tara stared into space, her mind a blank, her face pale and drawn. Then she heard the sound of horses outside, and the creak of a wagon, followed by a hurried knocking on the door.

She opened it cautiously and saw Bowers standing there. "You and the kid got to get away," he said. "They're going to burn you out." He picked up John from his basket, put him in her arms, and pushed her out the door. "Quick," he ordered, and helped her into the wagon. Then he climbed on and took the reins.

Tara shivered, clutching the baby to her. She noticed a coffin in the back of the wagon. She knew without asking that lying in that wooden box was Jefferson Smith.

The wagon creaked and bumped along a path away from town toward the forest. They had been rumbling along for some twenty minutes when Bowers reined in the horses and pointed into the darkness. They were overlooking the sprawl of Skagway, and she could see her cabin. Suddenly a glow appeared, and the cabin flared up.

Without a word Bowers picked up the reins, and the wagon moved onward again, into wooded territory. Finally he pulled up and she was taken into a cold cave, where he lit a fire.

"Nothing's left," said Bowers at last. "They've looted everything, the scavengers. Law-and-order men! Well, they got their law and order now."

"What about the others? Yeah Mow?" she asked quietly.

"He's dead." Bowers shrugged. "They strung him up before he could get out of town. Mort's hightailing it to Dyea."

"What happens now?" Tara asked.

"Well, I got him outside." He didn't have to explain more, and he knew it. "We'll take him to the graveyard at dawn and bury him. Couple of the boys will be there." He looked at her sharply. "We owe it to the boss."

"Yes," she said simply.

"After that we'll get you and the kid away."

Toward dawn they set off from the cave, Tara huddled in the back of the wagon, the baby in her arms, staring at the wooden casket. And as they bumped along, she was sobbing silently. If Bowers was aware of her sorrow, he never said so.

Skagway's graveyard was at the start of the trail northward. The drizzle that had begun when they left the cave had ceased by the time Bowers helped Tara off the wagon. He nodded to two men who were leaning on shovels. They walked around to the back of the wagon and began dragging off the coffin.

Bowers guided Tara to the gaping hole that already yawned in the muddy ground. The two men carried the casket to the grave and lowered it into the ground. Then they started unceremoniously shoveling in the earth.

"It's been good knowing you, boss," Bowers murmured. Then he threw in Smith's dice and a deck of cards. "Keep a game going for me. The boys send their best, but you know how it is. Too many necktie parties going on, so they asked me to say it for 'em."

He stopped and glanced at Tara. She was staring into the grave, the tears drying on her face. She was not crying just for the man who had loved her; she was crying for the child she had lost, for the man she had not found, for all of them.

"Can you say a prayer for him?" Tara whispered. "Please."

Bowers shook his head. "Don't want to offend you, but the boss would die laughing. Me saying a prayer for him? No. You just think one."

So this is the end of the man who had been king, she thought, watching the plain coffin finally disappearing under the muddy earth. This furtive, hasty little excuse of a funeral. How he would have resented it. No honor guard. No muffled drums. No saloon girls dressed in black. Jeff Smith—who would have arranged to have himself planted in magnificent style.

She held the baby close as she looked for the last time on Smith's resting place. Then she turned and climbed back in the wagon. Bowers got in and picked up the reins. Slowly they moved off; and, at least, in true Smith style, Tara never once looked back.

"I've got you a ticket for a berth on the *Columbia*," Bowers told her as they moved along. "She sails for Frisco tomorrow on the tide. The sooner you and the boy are out of this, the better."

Tara said nothing. Of course this was the only way. She gazed at the distant mountains, the rolling forests, and at that moment they looked beautiful. The memory of the hardships, the misery, the cruelty of the territory, melted away because this country had given her so much more. She had John. She had regained her self-respect. She had found love again. And perhaps, one day, Daniel would come back and they would be together again.

Bowers took them to a shack among some fir trees. "You'll be okay here until the ship leaves," he assured her. "I'll get you aboard the boat, never worry."

She knew he was risking his life to stay behind and protect her. He could have gotten out of town with Mort. There would be little justice in Skagway for Smith's right-hand man.

After he had gone, the tears came again. A couple of times the timbers of the log shack creaked. Tara raised her tear-stained face to the door as if she expected to see Smith standing there, smiling at her nonchalantly, puffing his ever-present cheroot, slowly walking over, taking her in his arms. But it was only the wind.

When Bowers came for her in the morning, his appearance was citified; to the eyes of the townsfolk he was a dude to his toe caps. He brought a big shawl to cover Tara's head.

"If anyone stops us, you're my lady wife," he said. "Mr. and Mrs. Jenkinson, and their little boy. I work for the White Pass Railroad Company."

The journey through Skagway passed without incident. The town had calmed down after its orgy of violence. Bowers pulled up at the quay. The *Columbia* already had steam up.

"You'd better get on," said Bowers gruffly, handing her the ticket.

"Charley . . . " began Tara, but the words died on her lips.

"This is for you too. From Jeff." He pulled out a sealed envelope and gave it to her. Then he turned and rapidly walked away, like a man not trusting himself to say anything more.

Holding John tightly in her arms and clutching the ticket and the envelope, Tara slowly walked up the gangway. The *Columbia* was a smart, well-appointed ship. Tara found, to her surprise, that Bowers had booked her a first-class passage. She was shown to a tidy cabin.

She went back on deck, John in her arms. A young boy was selling the Skagway *Intelligencer* and Tara bought a copy, her final souvenir of the Klondike. As each ship line was taken in, another link with Alaska was broken and her heart seemed to ache a little more. The engines grew louder, and around her, passengers waved to the well-wishers on the dockside. Bowers had disappeared.

"Good-by, Alaska," Tara whispered. As the ship eased away from its mooring, her sense of loss was like a physical pain. She stayed on the deck for a long time, watching the majestic panorama of the Lynn Canal as the *Columbia* steamed through. The great icy kingdom had been a challenging world she would never forget. She had survived it, and it would always be part of her.

When finally the *Columbia* passed the last tip of British Columbia, Tara knew the past had gone.

Then she remembered the envelope Bowers had handed her. She went below to her cabin and sat down, with John on her lap. Slowly she opened it. There was a note:

My dearest Tara,
You won't get this unless I've finally thrown in my cards. I hope that will never be, because there's so much I want to do with you. So you'll never read this, if I'm lucky. I love you.

Jeff

There was something else in the envelope. She held in her hand a banker's draft addressed to the Bank of California, San Francisco. A certified draft payable to Mrs. Tara Kane for the sum of one hundred thousand dollars in gold, signed, with a flourish, Jefferson Randolph Smith.

For a long time Tara stared at the check. Then she put John's tiny hands on it. "It's yours, my love. With love from your godfather."

AFTER she had put John down, Tara sat on her bunk and opened the newspaper. The front page was dominated by a photograph of Reid, lying dead, surrounded by several worthy-looking Skagway citizens. Under it was an article headed:

SMITH'S KILLER NAMED
GUNMAN WAS ON RAILROAD PAYROLL

The man who shot down Jefferson Smith was a newly hired railroad employee. According to company officials he was a down-on-his-luck gold miner whose prospecting fortunes had failed. He had been hired only twenty-four hours before to ride shotgun on high-value consignments. But Sir Thomas Tancrede, railroad boss, told the *Intelligencer* that the man at the time of the shoot-out "was not on company business. While we are not unhappy that the community is rid of Mr. Soapy Smith and his ilk, we did not hire a gunman to kill him." Asked why the killer should have taken on Mr. Smith, Sir Thomas Tancrede said he had no idea "but there must be a lot of people who had their own reasons for wanting to see Smith dead." The gunman, after firing the fatal shot, died immediately from Smith's bullet. He never spoke, but the railroad has named him as Daniel Kane, 27, of San Francisco.

"It can't be true," Tara pleaded. She could not believe that she had seen Daniel kill Smith without knowing. That she had been less than ten feet away from him and not recognized him. That she had gone off with Smith and left her own husband dying in the street alone, abandoned. And that while Daniel lay dying, she had agreed to become another man's wife.

Stunned and desolate, Tara wrapped herself in her cloak and went up on deck. She stared across the black sea. Before her stretched a rippling astral carpet, the silvery moon undulating in a liquid abyss. It was beautiful, hypnotic, calling.

And it reminded Tara of another natural phenomenon—the aurora borealis. That had been a sign from heaven in the frozen wilderness. This was also a promise.

"Dear God," she sobbed, looking up at the sky. "You have taken so much from me, but You've given me the greatest gift of all. I have John, a future to live for. Who knows what lies ahead, but with Your help I'll get through." Always one day at a time.

"Tara is quite simply my ideal woman...."

George Markstein was out of breath when he arrived at the restaurant, scarcely five minutes late, for our lunch.

George Markstein

"I'm so sorry to have kept you waiting," he apologized. "The little flat where I do my writing has been burgled. But they've only taken a few papers from a book I'm writing about Göring's death and the rise of neo-Nazism."

"You don't mean to say . . ." I began.

"In this world of ours, all sorts of extraordinary things are possible," George pointed out. "I make my living writing about them. When I first became a journalist, it was my luck to work on many exciting stories, concerned at that time with the more shadowy areas of the cold war. I have always been lucky."

Ever in search of excitement, he was one of the pioneers of British independent television. He devised two top-rated series, "The Prisoner" and "Special Branch." For the cinema he scripted the box-office hit *The Odessa File*.

As for *Tara Kane*, he said, "The idea came to me when I discovered in a secondhand bookshop a collection of vivid photographs of the Klondike Gold Rush taken by a German called Eric Hegg. Here was an amazing world, peopled with prospectors and prostitutes, charlatans and con men, even a bishop with a changed name."

George began to do serious research and unearthed a gold prospector's manual loaded with information. More and more historical characters clamored to join the cast—Inspector Constantine, the Reverend Bowers, Governor Brady, Soapy Smith, Cad Wilson. What was needed to pull the whole story together was a heroine. . . .

"Tara," George told me, "is quite simply my ideal woman. She is positive, full of ingenuity, and couldn't care less what people think of her."

As we were leaving the restaurant I asked him if he had ever met his ideal woman. "Yes," he told me, in his typical half-amused, half-enigmatic fashion. "I mentioned earlier I have always been very lucky in life. You can tell your readers that I have met my Tara." —N.D.B.

FLIGHT INTO

A condensation of the novel by

ARTHUR HAILEY AND JOHN CASTLE

ILLUSTRATED BY JIM SHARPE

DANGER

Suddenly, four miles above the earth, an ordinary flight becomes a journey into terror. The lives of everybody on board the airliner are placed in the hands of three courageous, frightened people:

DR. BRUNO BAIRD: *"I know nothing about flying. All I know is this. There are people on this plane who will die within a few hours. . . ."*

STEWARDESS JANET BENSON: *"I know they use that to talk to the ground, but I don't know which switches you have to set."*

SALESMAN GEORGE SPENCER: *I am a passenger on this airplane. Correction: I was a passenger. I am now the pilot."*

Co-authored by Arthur Hailey (*Hotel, Airport, The Moneychangers*), *Flight into Danger* is his earliest, least-known novel, yet surely one of the most gripping he has ever written.

Steady rain slanting through the harsh glare of its headlights, the taxi swung into the approach to Winnipeg airport and, braking hard, came to a spring-shuddering stop outside the reception building. Its passenger leaped out, tossed a couple of dollar bills to the driver, seized an overnight bag, and hurried inside.

He turned down the collar of his damp topcoat, glanced at the wall clock, then half ran to the departure desk of Cross-Canada Airlines, deserted now except for a passenger agent checking through a manifest. As the man reached him, the agent picked up a small microphone on the desk and with measured precision began to speak.

"Flight 98. Flight 98. Direct fleetliner service to Vancouver, with connections for Victoria, Seattle, and Honolulu, will be leaving immediately. All passengers for Flight 98 are asked to proceed to gate four, please."

A group of people rose from the lounge seats and made their way thankfully across the hall. The man in the topcoat opened his mouth to speak but was elbowed aside by an elderly woman.

"Young man," she demanded of the passenger agent, "is Flight 63 from Montreal in yet?"

"No, madam," he replied smoothly. "It's running approximately thirty-seven minutes late."

"Oh, dear. I've arranged for my niece to be—"

"Look," said the man in the topcoat urgently, "have you got a seat on Flight 98 for Vancouver?"

The passenger agent shook his head. "Sorry, sir. Not one. With the big football game on in Vancouver tomorrow, things are chockfull. I doubt if you'll be able to get out of here before tomorrow afternoon."

The man swore softly and dropped his bag to the floor. "Of all the lousy deals. I've got to be in Vancouver by tomorrow noon."

"Don't be so rude," snapped the anxious old woman. "I was talking. Now, young man, my niece is bringing—"

"Just a moment, madam," cut in the passenger agent. He leaned across the desk and tapped the man's sleeve with his pencil. "Look, I'm not supposed to tell you this—"

"Well, really!" exploded the old lady.

"But there's a charter flight in from Toronto on its way to the coast for this game. They were a few seats light when they came in. Perhaps you could grab one."

"That's great," exclaimed the man in the topcoat, picking up his bag again. "Where do I ask?"

The agent pointed across the hall. "Right over there. The Maple Leaf Air Charter. But mind, I didn't say a thing."

"This is scandalous!" stormed the old lady. "My niece—"

"Thanks a lot," said the man. He walked briskly over to the charter company's desk.

The agent there looked up, pencil poised, all attention, as the man arrived. "Sir?"

"Have you by any chance a seat on a flight to Vancouver?"

"Vancouver. I'll see." The pencil checked rapidly down a list. "Yes, just one. Flight's leaving straightaway, though."

"That's fine. Can I have that seat, please?"

The agent reached for a ticket. "Name, sir?"

"George Spencer." It was entered, with the flight details.

"That's sixty-five dollars for the one-way trip, sir. Thank you; glad to be of service. Any bags, sir?"

"Only one. I'll keep it with me."

"Here you are, sir. The ticket is your boarding pass. Go to gate three and ask for Flight 714."

Spencer nodded, turned to give a thumbs-up to the Cross-Canada desk, where the agent grinned in acknowledgment over the old lady's shoulder, and hurried to the departure gate. Outside, he was directed across the floodlit apron to a waiting aircraft whose four propellers were shining silver disks in the light of the overhead arc lamps. Already men were preparing to disengage the passenger ramp. Bounding across puddles, Spencer reached them, handed over the detachable half of his ticket, and ran lightly up the steps. He ducked into the aircraft and stood there fighting to regain his breath. He was joined by a stewardess who smiled and made fast the door. As she did, he felt the motors start.

"Out of condition, I guess," he said apologetically.

"Good evening, sir. Pleased to have you aboard. There's a seat forward."

Spencer walked to the vacant seat and with some difficulty bundled his coat into an empty spot on the luggage rack, remarking to the neighboring passenger, "They never seem to make these things big enough." He disposed of his bag under the seat and sank gratefully down onto the soft cushions.

"Good evening," came the stewardess' voice over the public address system. "The Maple Leaf Air Charter Company welcomes its new passengers to Flight 714. We hope you will enjoy your flight. Please fasten your seat belts and observe the 'No Smoking' sign. We shall be taking off in a few moments."

As Spencer fumbled with his belt catch, the man next to him grunted, "That's a pretty sobering sentence," and pointed to a small notice on the back of the seat in front reading YOUR LIFE PRESERVER IS UNDER THE SEAT.

Spencer laughed. "I'd certainly have been sunk if I hadn't caught this bus," he said.

"Oh? Pretty keen fan, eh?"

"Er—no," Spencer said. "I hadn't given the game a thought. I hate to admit it, but I'm rushing off to Vancouver to keep a business appointment."

His companion lowered his voice conspiratorially. "I shouldn't say that too loudly. This plane is crammed with fans who are going to Vancouver to root for their boys. They're quite likely to do you harm if you use such a light tone about it."

Spencer chuckled again and leaned out from his seat to look around the crowded cabin. There was evidence in plenty of a noisy but good-natured party of football fans traveling with the one objective of triumphing with their team. To Spencer's immediate right sat a man and his wife, their noses buried in sports magazines. Behind them, four supporters were pouring rye into paper cups and arguing the respective merits of various players; a snatch of their conversation came over to him. "*Haggerty?* Don't give me that. He's not in the same league as the Thunderbolt. Now *there's* a man. . . ." Behind the slightly alcoholic foursome were other team supporters, mostly big, red-faced men, wearing team regalia.

Spencer turned to the man beside him. Trained to observe detail, he noted the quiet suit, of good cut but well crumpled, the lined face and graying hair, the indefinable impression of confidence and authority. Behind him, the blue lights of the perimeter track had begun to slide past as the aircraft rolled forward.

Spencer said conversationally, "I'm on a sales trip, and a mighty important one."

His companion showed polite interest. "What do you sell?"

"Trucks. The local salesmen don't like me too well because they say I'm the sharpshooter from the head office with special prices; I come in and clinch a deal they've spent weeks nursing. I get called when a sale involves maybe thirty to a hundred trucks. Selling has its little problems, all right. Still, it's a reasonable living."

Spencer stretched his legs in front of him. "Man, I'm tired. It's been one of those days. First this Winnipeg guy decides he likes a competitor's trucks better than ours. Then, when I've sold him after all and figure I can close the order over supper tonight and be back with my wife and kids tomorow night, I get a wire telling me to be in Vancouver by lunchtime tomorrow because a big contract is going off the rails there—and fast." Spencer sighed, then said in mock earnestness, "Hey, if you want forty or fifty trucks today, I can give you a good discount."

The man beside him laughed. "Sorry, no. They're a bit outside my usual line of work. I'm a doctor. I couldn't afford to buy one truck, let alone forty. Football is the only extravagance I can allow myself. Hence my trip tonight."

Leaning back in his seat, Spencer said, "Glad to have you around, Doctor. If I can't sleep, you can prescribe me a sedative."

As he spoke, the engines thundered to full power, the whole aircraft vibrating as it strained against the wheel brakes. The doctor put his mouth to Spencer's ear and bellowed, "A sedative would be no good in this racket. I never could understand why they have to make all this noise before takeoff."

Spencer nodded; then, when the roar had subsided sufficiently for him to make himself heard without much trouble, he said, "The run-up for the engines is always done before the plane starts its takeoff. Each engine has two magnetos, in case one packs in during flight, and in the run-up each of the mags is tested separately. When the pilot has satisfied himself that they are running OK, he takes off. Airlines have to be fussy, thank goodness."

"You sound as though you know a lot about it."

"Oh, I flew fighters in World War II, but I'm rusty now."

The engine roar took on a deeper note, and a powerful thrust in the backs of their seats told them the aircraft was gathering speed on the runway; almost immediately a slight lurch indicated that they were airborne, and the engines settled back to a steady hum. Still climbing, the aircraft banked steeply.

"You may unfasten your seat belts," announced a voice over the public address system. "Smoke if you wish."

"Never sorry when that bit's over." The doctor released his belt. "By the way, I'm Bruno Baird."

"Glad to know you, Doc. I'm George Spencer of the Fulbright Motor Company."

The two men lapsed into silence. Spencer's thoughts were somber. He had decided there would have to be a showdown when he got back. Although he had explained the position on the telephone to the local Winnipeg salesman before leaving for the airport, that order would take some holding on to now. It would have to be a big show in Vancouver to justify this snafu. It might be a good idea to use this as a lever for a pay raise when he got back. Or better yet, promotion. If he were a manager in the sales division, Mary and he, Bobsie and little Kit, could move up to Parkway Heights. Or pay off the bills—the new boiler, installments on the car, and the hospital charges for Mary's last pregnancy.

Dr. Baird found himself thinking about the small-town practice he had abandoned for a couple of days. I wonder how Lewis Evans will cope, he thought. Doris would keep him on the right track. Doctors' wives were wonderful like that. Had to be. That was a thing young Lewis would have to learn: to find the right woman.

The couple in the seats across the aisle were still engrossed in their sports magazines. The four fans in the seats behind were starting their third round of rye. Three were of the usual type: beefy, argumentative, out to enjoy themselves, with all the customary restraints cast aside for two memorable days. But the fourth was a short, lean-featured man of lugubrious expression who spoke with a Lancashire accent and rejoiced in the nickname of 'Otpot. "'Ere's t'Lions t'morrer," he called, raising his paper cup. His friends acknowledged the toast solemnly.

One of them, his coat lapel displaying a badge which appeared to depict a mangy alley cat in rampant mood but presumably represented the king of beasts himself, remarked, "Never thought we'd make it. Not after having to wait in Toronto with all that fog around. Still, we're only a few hours late and we can always sleep on the plane."

"Not before we eat, though, I hope," said one of the others. "When do they bring round the grub?"

"Should be along soon, I reckon. Everything's been put behind with that delay."

"Never mind. 'Ave a drink while you wait," suggested 'Otpot.

The rest of the fifty-six passengers were reading or talking, all glad to be on the last leg of their journey.

The twinkling blue and yellow lights of the last suburbs of Winnipeg could be seen from the port windows before they were swallowed in cloud. In the galley, Stewardess Janet Benson prepared for a dinner that should have been served over two hours ago. The mirror above the glassware cabinet reflected the swing of her blond hair from beneath her airline cap and the movements of her trim body as she busied herself efficiently. Taking napkins and cutlery from the built-in cupboards, Janet hummed contentedly to herself. Waitressing was the least attractive part of a stewardess' duties, and she knew she was in for an exhausting hour catering to a planeload of hungry people, but she was filled with the exhilaration she always felt at the beginning of a flight. At twenty-one, Janet was just tasting life and finding it good.

Forward on the flight deck, the only sound was the steady drone of the engines. Both pilots sat still except for an occasional leg or arm movement, their faces faintly illuminated in the glow of light from the myriad dials on the instrument panels. From their headsets came the crackle of conversation between another aircraft and the ground. Around their necks hung small boom microphones.

Captain "Dun" Dunning stretched himself in his seat and blew through the luxuriant growth of his mustache in a mannerism that his crew knew well. He looked older than his thirty-one years. "How are the cylinder-head temperatures on Number 3 engine, Pete?" he asked, his eyes flickering to the first officer.

Pete stirred and glanced at the panel. "OK now, Skip. I had it checked at Winnipeg."

"Good." Dun peered ahead. A thin moon shone bleakly down on the banks of cloud. Shredded wisps of cotton wool lazily approached, to suddenly whisk by; or occasionally the ship would plunge into a tumble of gray-white cloud. "With a bit of luck it'll be a clear run-through," he commented. "The weather report was reasonable for a change. Doesn't often happen on this joyride."

"You said it," agreed the first officer. "Come winter, it'll be a very different story."

The aircraft began to bump and roll a little as she hit a succession of thermal currents, and for a few minutes the captain concentrated on correcting her trim. Then he remarked, "Are you planning to take in this football game in Vancouver?"

Pete hesitated before answering. "I don't know yet," he said. "I'll see how it works out."

The captain looked sharply at him. "If you've got your eyes on Janet, you can take them off again. She's too young to come under the corrupting influence of a Casanova like you."

Few people looked less deserving of this description than the fresh-faced, thoughtful-eyed first officer, still in his twenties. "Go easy, Skipper," he protested, coloring. "I never corrupted anyone in my life."

"Well, don't aim to start with Janet." The captain grinned. "Half the airline personnel of Canada have tried to. Don't make life hard for yourself."

Twelve feet away from them, on the other side of a sliding door, the subject of their conversation was collecting orders for the evening meal, offering a choice between lamb chops or grilled salmon.

George Spencer and Dr. Baird both chose the lamb, but many others ordered fish.

Back in the galley, Janet spent the next half hour preparing and serving meals. When everyone who felt like eating had been served with a main course, she picked up the telephone in the galley and pressed the intercom buzzer.

"Flight deck," came Pete's voice.

"I'm finally serving dinner," said Janet. "What'll it be—lamb chops or grilled salmon?"

"Hold it." She could hear him putting the question to Dunning. "Janet, the skipper says he'll have the lamb—no, he's changed his mind. Is the fish good?"

"Looks OK to me," said Janet. "Had no complaints."

"Skipper will take salmon, then. Better make it two. Big helpings, mind. We're growing boys."

"All right—double portions, as usual. Two fish coming up."

She quickly arranged two trays and took them forward, balancing them with practiced ease. Pete opened the sliding door for her and relieved her of one tray. The captain had completed his switchover to automatic pilot and was now halfway through his routine radio check with control at Winnipeg.

"Height 16,000," he continued, speaking into the tiny microphone held before his mouth on a slender plastic arm. "Course 285 true. Air speed 210 knots. Ground speed 174 knots. ETA Vancouver 0505 Pacific time. Over."

He switched from transmit to receive, and there was a clearly audible crackle from his headset as the acknowledgment came on the air. "Flight 714. This is Winnipeg Control. Roger. Out."

Dun reached for his log sheet, made an entry, then slid his seat back so that he was well clear of the controls but within easy reach if it were necessary for him to take them over again quickly. Pete was starting to eat, a tray resting on his knees.

"Shan't be long, Skip," he said.

"There's no hurry," replied Dun. "I can wait. Enjoy it. How is the fish, anyway?"

"Not bad," mumbled the first officer, his mouth full. "If there were about four times as much, it might be a square meal."

The captain chuckled. "You'd better watch that waistline, Pete." He turned to the stewardess, who was waiting behind the seat. "How are the football fans, Janet?"

She shrugged. "Very quiet now. Four of them have been knocking back rye pretty steadily, but there's been no need to speak to them about it. It'll help to keep them quiet. It looks like it will be a peaceful, easy night—fingers crossed."

Pete raised a quizzical eyebrow. "Unh-unh, young woman. That's the kind of night to watch. I'll bet someone's getting ready to be sick right now."

"Not yet," said Janet lightly. "But you warn me when *you're* going to fly the ship and I'll get the bags ready."

"I'm glad you found out about him," said the captain.

"How's the weather?" asked Janet.

"Let's see. General fog east of the mountains, extending nearly as far as Manitoba. There's nothing to bother us up there, though. It should be a smooth ride all the way to the coast."

"Good. Well, keep Junior here off the controls while I serve coffee, won't you?"

She slipped away before Pete could retort, made her way through the passenger deck taking orders for coffee, and then brought a tray to the pilots. Dun had eaten his dinner, and he now drained his coffee with satisfaction. Pete had taken the controls and was intent on the instrument dials as the captain got to his feet.

"Keep her steaming, Pete. I'll just tuck the customers up for the night."

Pete nodded without turning around. "Right, Skipper."

The captain followed Janet out into the passenger section and stopped first at the seats occupied by Spencer and Baird. "Good evening. Everything all right?"

Baird looked up. "Very nice meal. We were ready for it."

"Yes, I'm sorry it was so late."

The doctor waved aside his apology. "You can hardly be blamed if Toronto decides to have a bit of fog." He settled himself back in his seat. "I'm going to get my head down for a doze."

"That goes for me as well." Spencer yawned.

"I hope you have a comfortable night," said Dun. "The stewardess will bring you some blankets." He passed on down the aisle, saying a few words to each of the passengers.

"Well, it's me for dreamland," said Spencer. "One thing, Doctor—at least you won't be getting any calls tonight."

"How long is it to Vancouver?" murmured Baird drowsily.

"A good five hours, anyway," grunted Spencer. "Better make the most of it. Good night, Doc."

Now blanketed off by thick cloud into a cold, remote world of her own, the aircraft droned steadily on her course. Sixteen thousand feet beneath her lay the silent prairies of Saskatchewan.

When Dun reached the whiskey-drinking quartet, he politely forbade further consumption of liquor that night. "You know," he told them with a reproving grin, "this sort of thing isn't permitted. Don't let me see any more bottles or you'll get out and walk."

"Any objection to playing cards?" inquired one of the party.

"None at all, if you don't disturb the other passengers."

"Pity you, Captain," said the man from Lancashire. "What's it like—taking a massive job like this through t'night?"

"Routine," said Dun. "Just plain, dull routine."

"Comes to that, every flight is just routine, I s'pose?"

"Well, yes. I guess that's so."

"Until summat happens—eh?"

There was an outburst of chuckles in which Dunning joined before moving on. Only the Lancastrian, through the haze of his evening's drinking, looked thoughtful at his own words.

CHAPTER TWO

THE captain had almost completed his rounds when his eyes fixed on the stewardess, farther along the aisle. She was bending over a woman, her hand on the passenger's forehead. As he approached, the woman, who slumped rather than sat in her seat, suddenly grimaced. The captain touched the stewardess on the arm.

"Anything wrong, Miss Benson?"

Janet straightened. "The lady is feeling a little under the weather, Captain," she said. "I'll get her some aspirin."

Dun took her place and leaned over the woman and the man beside her. "Sorry to hear that," he said sympathetically. "What seems to be the trouble?"

The woman stared up at him. "I—I don't know," she said in a small voice. "It seemed to hit me all of a sudden. I feel sick and dizzy and—and there's an awful pain . . . down here." She indicated her stomach. "I'm sorry to be a nuisance—I—"

"Now, honey," murmured her husband. "Just lie quietly." He glanced at the captain. "A touch of airsickness, I guess?"

"I expect so, sir," answered Dun. He looked down thoughtfully

266

at the woman, taking in the perspiration beginning to bead on her pallid forehead, the whiteness of her knuckles as she gripped the armrest of the seat. "I'm sorry you don't feel well," he said gently. "Try to relax as much as you can. If it's any comfort, I can tell you that it should be a calm trip." He moved aside for Janet.

"Now here we are," said the stewardess, handing down the aspirin. She eased the woman's head forward, to help her take a few sips of water from a glass. "And let's make you a little more comfortable." She tucked a blanket around the woman. "How's that?" The woman nodded gratefully. "I'll be back in a few minutes to see how you're feeling. If you need me quickly, just press the call button by the window."

"Thank you, miss," said the husband. "We'll be OK in a little while." He looked at his wife with a smile, as if to reassure himself. "Try to rest, dear. It'll pass over."

"I hope so," said Dun. "I know how unpleasant these things can be. I hope you feel better soon, madam."

He continued down the aisle and waited for Janet in the galley. "Who are they?" he asked when she returned.

"Mr. and Mrs. Childer. She was all right fifteen minutes ago."

"Let me know if she gets any worse and I'll radio ahead. I don't like the look of her. Could be airsickness or just a bilious attack, I suppose—but it seems to have hit her pretty hard." The captain looked worried. "Have we a doctor on board?"

"No one who's listed as a doctor," replied Janet, "but I could ask around."

Dun shook his head. "Don't disturb them. Most of them are getting down to sleep. Tell me how she is in half an hour or so. The trouble is," he added as he turned to go, "we've got over four hours' flying before we reach the coast."

Making his way to the flight deck, he stopped for a moment to smile down at the sick woman. She attempted to smile, but a sudden stab of pain closed her eyes and made her arch back against the seat. For a few seconds Dun stood studying her. Then he continued forward, closed the door of the flight deck behind him, and slid into his seat.

Pete was flying manually. Scattered banks of cloud seemed to rush at the forward windows, envelop them momentarily, and then disappear. "Cumulonimbus building up," he commented.

"Rough stuff," Dun said. "I'll take it. We'd better try to climb on top. Ask for twenty thousand, will you?"

"Right." Pete pressed a button on his microphone to transmit. "This is 714 to Regina," he called.

"Go ahead, 714," crackled a voice.

"We're running into some weather. We'd like clearance for twenty thousand feet."

"Stand by, 714. I'll ask Air Traffic Control."

The captain peered into the cloudy turbulence ahead. "Better switch on the seat-belt sign, Pete."

"OK." Pete reached for the switch on the overhead panel. There was a brief shudder as the plane freed herself from a wall of cloud, only to plunge almost instantly into another.

"Flight 714," came the voice on the radio. "ATC gives clearance for twenty thousand. Over."

"Seven fourteen," acknowledged Pete. "Thanks and out."

"Let's go," said the captain. The note of the engines took on a deeper intensity as the deck began to tilt and the altimeter needle registered a climb of 500 feet a minute. The windshield wiper swished rhythmically.

"Shan't be sorry when we're clear of this muck," remarked the first officer.

Dun didn't answer, his eyes on the dial in front of him. Neither of the pilots heard the stewardess enter.

"Captain," she said urgently. "That woman's worse, and I have another passenger sick now—one of the men."

Dun stretched up an arm and switched on the landing lights. Ahead of them the sharp beams cut into driving rain and snow. He turned off the lights and began to adjust engine and deicer switches. "I can't come right now, Janet. You'd better see if you can find a doctor. And make sure all the seat belts are fastened. This may get pretty rough. I'll come as soon as I can."

"Yes, Captain."

Emerging from the flight deck, Janet called out in a voice just loud enough to carry to the rows of passengers, "Fasten your seat belts, please. It may be getting a little bumpy." She leaned over the first two passengers to her right. They blinked up at her, half asleep. "Excuse me," she said casually, "but do either of you gentlemen happen to be a doctor?"

The man nearest her shook his head. "Sorry, no," he grunted. "Is there something wrong?"

"No, nothing serious."

An exclamation of pain snapped her to attention. She hurried along the aisle to where the sick Mrs. Childer lay half cradled in her husband's arms, moaning, with eyes closed, and partially doubled over. Janet knelt and wiped the glistening sweat from the woman's brow. Childer's face was creased with anxiety.

"What can we do, miss?" he asked her. "What d'you think it is?"

"Keep her warm," said Janet. "I'm going to see if there's a doctor on board. I'll be back straightaway."

Janet got to her feet, looked down briefly at the suffering woman, and moved on to the next seats, repeating her question in a low voice.

"Is someone ill?" she was asked.

"Just feeling unwell. It sometimes happens, flying."

A hand clutched at her arm. It was one of the whiskey quartet, his face yellow and shining. "Sorry, miss, to trouble you again. I'm feeling like hell. D'you think I could have a glass of water?"

"Yes, of course. I'll get it right away."

"It's my insides," said the sick man. "Feels like they're coming apart." His hands clenched his stomach.

Janet shook Spencer gently by the shoulder. He opened one eye, then both. "I'm very sorry to wake you up, sir," she said, "but is anyone here a doctor?"

Spencer gathered himself. "A doctor? Yes, this gentleman beside me is a doctor."

"Oh, thank goodness," breathed the stewardess. "Would you wake him, please?"

"Sure." Spencer looked up at her as he nudged the recumbent form next to him. "Come on, Doc, wake up."

The doctor shook his head and grunted.

"Are you a doctor, sir?" asked Janet anxiously.

He snapped awake. "Yes, I'm Dr. Baird. What's wrong?"

"We have two passengers who are quite sick. Would you take a look at them, please?"

"Yes, certainly."

Spencer stood up to let the doctor out.

"I think you'd better see the woman first, Doctor," said Janet, leading the way and calling out quietly, "Fasten your seat belts, please," as she passed along.

Shivers of pain racked Mrs. Childer's nearly prostrate body. She breathed heavily, with long, shuddering gasps. Her hair was wet with sweat.

Baird knelt and took her wrist.

"This gentleman is a doctor," said Janet.

"Am I glad to see you, Doctor," Childer said fervently.

The woman opened her eyes. "Doctor. . . ."

"Just relax," said Baird, looking at his watch. He released her wrist, felt in his jacket, and took out a pocket flashlight. "Open your eyes wide," he ordered gently, and examined each eye in the bright pencil of light. "Any pain?" The woman nodded. "Where? Here? Or here?" As he palpated her abdomen, she stiffened suddenly, choking back a cry. He felt her forehead, then stood up. "Has this lady complained of anything in addition to the pain?"

"My wife's been very sick, throwing up everything." Childer looked helplessly at Janet. "It's all come on so suddenly."

Baird nodded reflectively. He moved away, taking Janet's arm and speaking very quietly so as not to be overheard by the nearby passengers. "Have you given her anything?"

"Only aspirin and water," replied Janet. "That reminds me. I promised a glass of water to the man who's sick—"

"Wait," said Baird. His sleepiness had vanished. "Where did you learn your nursing?"

Janet colored at his tone. "Why, at the airline training school."

"Well, it's no use giving aspirin to anyone who is actually vomiting—you'll make 'em worse. Water only."

"I—I'm sorry, Doctor," Janet stammered.

"I think you'd better go to the captain," he said. "Tell him we should land at once. This woman has to be taken to a hospital. Ask to have an ambulance waiting."

"Very well, Doctor. While I'm gone, will you take a look at the other sick passenger? He's complaining of the same pains."

Baird looked at her sharply. "Where is he?"

Janet led him forward to where the sick man sat, bent over, retching. Baird crouched down. "I'm a doctor. Will you put your head back, please?" As he made a quick examination, he asked, "What have you had to eat in the last twenty-four hours?"

"Just the usual things," muttered the man, all the strength appearing to have been drained from him. "Breakfast," he said weakly, "bacon and eggs . . . salad for lunch . . . a sandwich at the airport . . . then dinner here." A trickle of saliva ran disregarded down his chin. "It's this pain, Doctor. And my eyes. Can't seem to focus. I keep seeing double."

His companion appeared to find it amusing. "That rye has got a real kick, yes sir!" he exclaimed.

"Be quiet," said Baird. He rose, to find Janet and the captain standing beside him. "Keep him warm—get more blankets round him," he told Janet. The captain motioned him down to the galley. As soon as they were alone, Baird demanded, "How quickly can we land, Captain?"

"That's the trouble," said Dun briefly. "We can't."

Baird stared at him. "Why?"

"It's the weather. I've just checked by radio. There's low cloud and fog right over the prairies this side of the mountains. Calgary's shut in completely. We'll have to go through to the coast."

"What about turning back?" Baird asked.

Dun shook his head, his face taut. "That's out, too. Winnipeg closed down with fog shortly after we left. Anyway, it'll be quicker now to go on."

Baird grimaced. "How soon do you expect to land?"

"About five a.m., Pacific time." Dun saw the doctor glance at his wristwatch, and added, "Three and a half hours from now."

"Then I'll have to do what I can for these people until we arrive at Vancouver. I'll need my bag. Do you think it can be reached? I checked it at Toronto."

"We can try," said the captain. "Let me have your tags."

Baird dug into his hip pocket for his wallet. He took out two baggage tickets and handed them to Dun. "There are two bags, Captain," he said. "It's the smaller one I want."

He had barely finished speaking before a violent lurch of the aircraft sent the two men sprawling to the far wall. There was a loud, persistent buzzing. The captain was on his feet first and sprang to the intercom telephone. "Captain here," he rapped out. "What's wrong, Pete?"

The voice of the first officer was struggling and painful. "I'm sick . . . come quickly."

"You'd better come with me," said Dun to the doctor, and they hurried out of the galley. "Sorry about the bump," Dun remarked affably to the upturned faces as he and the doctor walked along the aisle. "Just a little turbulence."

As they burst into the flight deck, it was only too apparent that the first officer was very sick; he was slumped in his seat, clutching the control column, his face streaming perspiration.

"Get him out of there," directed the captain urgently. Baird and Janet, who had followed the men in, lifted Pete out while Dun slipped into his own seat and took the control column in his hands. "There's a seat at the back of the flight deck, for when we carry a radio operator," he told them. "Put him in it."

Pete vomited as they helped him to the vacant seat. Baird loosened his collar and tie and tried to make him as comfortable as the conditions would allow.

"Doctor," called Dun. "What's happening?"

"I'm not sure," said Baird grimly. "But there's a common denominator to these attacks. Has to be. The most likely thing is food. What did he have for dinner?"

"The first officer had fish." Janet's face began to register alarm.

"Do you remember what the two passengers had?"

"No—I don't think so—"

"Go back quickly and find out, will you, please?"

The stewardess hurried out. Baird knelt beside the first officer. "Try to relax," he said quietly. "Here." He reached up and pulled down a blanket from a rack. "You'll feel better if you stay warm."

Pete opened his eyes a little and ran his tongue over dry lips. "Are you a doctor?" he asked. Baird nodded. Pete said with a sheepish attempt to smile, "I'm sorry about this. I thought I was going to pass out."

"Don't talk," said Baird. "Try to rest."

Janet returned. "Doctor." She spoke rapidly, hardly able to get the words out quickly enough. "Both passengers had salmon. There are three others complaining of pains now."

"I'll come, but I'll need that bag of mine."

Dun called over his shoulder, "Janet, take these tags and dig out the smaller of the doctor's two bags, will you?" Janet took the tags, and Dun continued, "I'm going to radio Vancouver and report what's happening. Is there anything you want me to add?"

"Yes," said Baird. "Say we have three serious cases of suspected food poisoning and that there seem to be others developing. We suspect that the poisoning could have been caused by fish served on board. Better ask them to ban all food from that same source."

"I remember now," exclaimed Dun. "That food didn't come from our usual caterers. We had to get it from some other outfit because we were so late getting into Winnipeg."

"Doctor, *please*," Janet implored him. "I do wish you'd come and see Mrs. Childer. She seems to have collapsed altogether."

Baird stepped to the door. The lines in his face had deepened, but his eyes were steady as rock.

"See that the passengers are not alarmed," he instructed Janet. "We shall be depending on you a great deal. Now if you'll be good enough to find my bag and bring it to me, I'll attend to Mrs. Childer." He pushed back the door, then stopped her as something occurred to him. "By the way, what did *you* eat for dinner?"

"I had meat."

"Thank heavens for that." Janet smiled and started to leave again, but he gripped her suddenly by the arm. "I suppose the captain had meat, too?" He shot the question at her.

She looked up at him, as if trying both to remember and to grasp the implications of what he had asked. Then, suddenly, shock and realization flooded into her. She almost fell against him, her eyes dilated with an overpowering fear.

Bruno Baird regarded the stewardess thoughtfully. Behind the calm reassurance of his blue-gray eyes his mind rapidly assessed the situation. He released the girl's arm.

"Well, we won't jump to conclusions," he said, almost to himself. Then, more briskly, "You find my bag—just as quickly as you can. I'll have another word with the captain."

Baird turned and moved forward. They were now in level flight, above the turbulence. Over the pilot's shoulder he could see the cold white brilliance of the moon converting the carpet of cloud below them into a seemingly limitless landscape of snow, with here and there what looked like a pinnacle of ice thrusting through the surrounding billows. The effect was dreamlike.

"Captain," he said, leaning over the empty copilot's seat. Dun looked around, his face drawn and colorless in the moon's glow.

"Yes, Doctor. What is it?"

"I presume you ate after the other officer did?"

"Yes, that's so." Dun's eyes narrowed. "About half an hour later. Maybe a little more." The point of the doctor's question suddenly hit him, and he sat upright with a jerk. "Holy smoke, that's right. I had fish, too. But I feel OK."

"Good." Relief showed in Baird's voice. "As soon as I've got my bag I'll give you an emetic. You can't have digested it all yet. Anyway, not everyone who ate fish will be affected."

"I'd better not be," muttered Dun, staring now into the moonlight ahead.

"Is there any way of locking the controls of this airplane?"

"Why yes," said Dun. "There's the automatic pilot. But that wouldn't get us down—"

"I suggest you switch it on, just in case. If you feel ill, yell for me immediately. I can't do much, but if you get any symptoms, they'll come on fast."

The knuckles of Dun's hands gleamed white as he gripped the control column. "OK," he said quietly. "What about Miss Benson, the stewardess?"

"She's all right. She had meat."

"Well, that's something—look, for heaven's sake hurry with that emetic. I can't take any chances, flying this ship."

"Miss Benson is hurrying to get my bag. Are you absolutely certain that we've no other course but to go on to Vancouver?"

"Certain," answered Dun instantly. "I've checked and doublechecked. Thick cloud and ground fog until the other side of the mountains. Calgary, Edmonton—all closed."

The doctor stepped back to leave, but halted when Dun said, "Oh, Doctor . . . glad you're aboard."

Baird left without another word. Dun took a deep breath, experiencing not for the first time in his flying career acute apprehension and awareness of his responsibility for the safety of a huge aircraft and nearly sixty lives. He felt an icy premonition of disaster. In the space of half an hour a normal, routine flight had changed into a nightmare.

He pushed these thoughts from him in self-disgust, flicked the switches on the automatic pilot panel, waiting until the appropriate indicator light gleamed to show that the next stage of the switching over could be started. Ailerons first, needing a slight adjustment to bring them fully under electrical control; then rudder and elevators were nursed until all the four lights set into the top of the panel had ceased winking and settled down to a steady glow. Satisfied, he took his hands off the wheel and let the aircraft fly itself while he carried out a thorough cockpit check.

To an inexperienced eye, the flight deck would have presented a weird sight. Just as though two invisible men sat in the pilots' seats, the twin control columns moved slightly forward, backward, then forward again. Compensating for the air currents as they gently buffeted the aircraft, the rudder bar moved also.

His check completed, Dun reached for the microphone that hung on its hook beside his head, quickly clipped it to his neck, and adjusted the padded earphones. Well, he thought, here goes.

"Hello, Vancouver Control. This is Maple Leaf Charter Flight 714. I have an emergency message. I have an emergency message."

His earphones crackled instantly: "Maple Leaf Charter Flight 714. Come in, please."

"Vancouver Control. This is Flight 714. We have three serious cases of suspected food poisoning on board, including the first officer, and possibly others. When we land we shall want ambulances and medical help standing by. We think the poisoning may have been caused by the fish served at dinner. You'd better put a ban on all food coming from the same source. We understand that owing to our late arrival at Winnipeg the food was not supplied by the regular contractor. Please check. Is this understood?"

He listened to the acknowledgment, his eyes gazing bleakly at the frozen sea of cloud below and ahead. Vancouver Control sounded as crisp and impersonal as ever, but he could guess at the burst of activity his words would have triggered. Almost wearily, he ended the transmission and leaned back. He felt strangely heavy and tired, as if lead had begun to flow into his limbs. The instrument dials seemed to recede until they were far away. He was conscious of a cold film of sweat on his forehead and he shivered in a sudden uncontrollable spasm. Then, angered at the perfidy of his body, he flung himself with all his strength and concentration into rechecking their flight path, their estimated time of arrival, the expected crosswinds over the mountains, the runway plan of Vancouver.

Back in the body of the aircraft, Dr. Baird tucked fresh blankets around the limp form of Mrs. Childer. The woman lay back helplessly, her eyes closed, moaning quietly. The top of her dress was stained and damp. As Baird watched her she was seized with a fresh paroxysm. Her eyes did not open.

Baird spoke to her husband. "Keep her mopped up and as dry as you can. And warm. She must be warm."

Childer reached up and grabbed the doctor by the wrist. "She's pretty bad, isn't she?" His voice was shrill.

Baird looked again at the woman. Her breathing was rapid and shallow. "Yes," he said, "she is."

"Well, can't you give her something?"

Baird shook his head. "She needs drugs we haven't got."

"But surely even some water—"

"No. She'd gag on it. Your wife is nearly unconscious, Childer. That's nature's own anesthetic." Baird added hastily as the other man half rose in alarm, "Don't worry. She'll be all right. Your job is to watch her and keep her warm."

Baird moved to the next row of seats. A middle-aged man, collar undone and hands clasping his stomach, sat slumped partly out of his seat, his face glistening with sweat. He looked up at the doctor, drawing back his lips in a rictus of pain.

"It's murder," the man mumbled. "I've never felt like this before."

Baird took a pencil from his jacket pocket and held it in front of the man.

"Listen to me," he said. "I want you to take this pencil."

The man tried to grasp the pencil, but it slipped through his fingers. Baird's eyes narrowed. He lifted the man into a more comfortable position and tucked a blanket in tightly around him. The stewardess hurried toward him holding a leather bag.

"Good girl," said Baird. "That's the one I want. Not that I can do much. . . . Where's your public address system?"

"I'll show you," said Janet. She led the way aft to the galley and pointed to a wall telephone. "How is Mrs. Childer, Doctor?" she asked.

Baird pursed his lips. "She's seriously ill," he said. "And there are others who'll be as bad before long."

"Do you still think it's food poisoning?" Janet's cheeks were very pale.

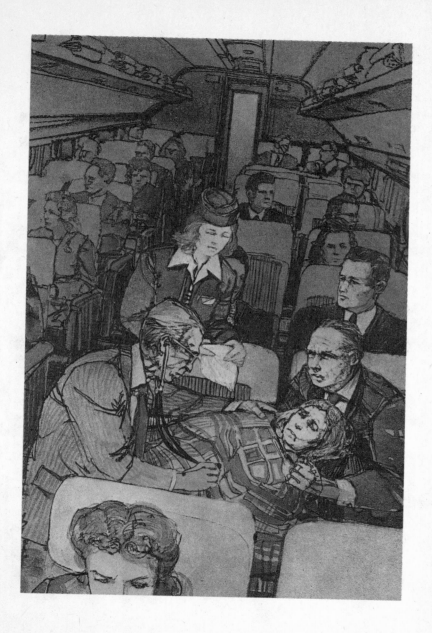

"Tolerably certain. Staphylococcal, I'd say, though some of the symptoms out there could indicate even worse."

"Are you going to give round an emetic?"

"Yes, except of course to those who are already vomiting. That's all I can do." Lifting the telephone, Baird paused. "As soon as you can," he told her, "I suggest you organize some help to clean up a bit. Squirt disinfectant around if you've any. Oh, and as you speak to the sick passengers you'd better tell them not to lock the door of the toilet—in case any pass out in there."

He pressed the button of the public address system. "Ladies and gentlemen, may I have your attention, please?" He heard the murmur of voices die away, leaving only the steady drone of the engines. "First of all," he went on, "my name is Baird and I'm a doctor. You are wondering what this malady is that has stricken our fellow passengers, and I think it's time everyone knew.

"Well, as far as I can tell, we have several cases of food poisoning on board and I believe the cause of it to be the fish some of us had for dinner." An excited hubbub broke out. "Now, listen, please. There is no cause for alarm. The passengers who have suffered these attacks are being cared for, and the captain has radioed ahead for medical help to be standing by when we land. If you ate the fish for dinner, it doesn't necessarily follow that you are going to be affected. However, we *are* going to take some precautions, and the stewardess and I are coming round to you all. If you ate fish, we'll tell you how you can help yourselves."

Baird took his finger off the button, replaced the telephone, and turned to Janet. "All we can do now is to give immediate first aid," he said. "To begin with, everyone who had fish must drink several glasses of water—that will help to dilute the poison. After that we'll give an emetic. If there aren't enough pills in my bag, we'll have to use salt. I'll start at the back here with the pills, and you begin bringing drinking water to those people already affected, will you? Take some to the first officer, too."

Stepping out of the galley, Baird practically cannoned into the lean, lugubrious Lancashire man called 'Otpot. "Anything I can do, Doctor?" he asked.

Baird allowed himself a smile. "Thanks. First, what did you have for dinner?"

"Meat, thank heaven," breathed 'Otpot fervently.

"Right. Then will you help the stewardess hand water round to the passengers who are sick? I want them to drink at least three glasses—more, if possible."

'Otpot entered the galley, returning Janet's rather tired little smile. In normal circumstances that smile of hers could be guaranteed to quicken the pulse of any man, but 'Otpot could see the hint of fear that lay behind it. He winked at her.

"Don't you worry, miss. Everything's going to be all right."

Janet looked at him gratefully. "I'm sure it is, thanks. Here's the water tap and there are the cups, Mr. —"

"The boys call me 'Otpot."

"'Otpot?" Janet burst out laughing.

"There, that's better. Come on, lass, let's get started. A fine airline this is. Gives you your dinner, then asks for it back again."

IT TAKES a very great deal to upset the equilibrium of a modern airport, but the control room at Vancouver when Dun's emergency call came through presented a scene of suppressed excitement. In front of the radio panel an operator wearing headphones transcribed Dun's incoming message onto a typewriter, pausing only to punch an alarm bell on his desk. He carried on imperturbably as a second man appeared behind him, craning over his shoulder to read the words. The newcomer, summoned by the bell, was Airport Controller Grimsell, a man who had spent a lifetime in the air and knew travel over Canada as well as he knew his own garden. He got halfway through the message, then stepped sharply back, cracking an order over his shoulder to the telephone operator.

"Get me Air Traffic Control quickly. Then clear the teletype circuit to Winnipeg. Priority message." Grimsell picked up a phone, waited a few seconds, then said, "Vancouver controller here." His voice was deceptively unhurried. "Maple Leaf Charter Flight 714 from Winnipeg to Vancouver reports emergency. Serious food poisoning among the passengers. The first officer is down with it, too. Better clear all levels below them for priority approach and landing. Can do? Good. ETA is 0505. Right. We'll keep you posted."

The controller glanced at the wall clock; it read 0215. He put down the phone and barked at the teletype operator, "Got Winnipeg yet? Good. Send this message: Controller Winnipeg. Urgent. Maple Leaf Charter Flight 714 reports serious food poisoning

279

among passengers and crew believed due to fish dinner served on flight. Imperative check source and suspend all other food service originating same place. Understand source was not, repeat not, regular airline caterer." He swung around to the switchboard. "Get me the local manager of Maple Leaf Charter, Harry Burdick. After that I want the city police—senior officer on duty." He leaned over the radio operator's shoulder again and finished reading the now completed message. "Tell the captain of Flight 714 that all altitudes below him are being cleared and that he'll be advised of landing instructions later."

On the floor below, an operator of the Government of Canada Western Air Traffic Control swiveled in his chair to call across the room, "What's flying in Green One between here and Calgary?"

"Westbound, there's an Air Force North Star at eighteen thousand. Just reported over Penticton. Maple Leaf 714—"

"Maple Leaf 714's in trouble. They want all altitudes below them cleared."

"The North Star's well ahead and there's nothing close behind. There's an eastbound Constellation ready for takeoff."

"Clear it, but hold any other eastbound traffic for the time being. Bring the North Star straight in when it arrives."

Upstairs, Grimsell had scooped up the telephone again. "Hello, Burdick? Grimsell here. Look, we've got an emergency on one of your flights—714 ex Toronto and Winnipeg. The first officer and several passengers are down with food poisoning. I told Winnipeg to trace the source of the food. You'd better come over as soon as you can." He jabbed down the telephone cradle with his thumb and nodded to the switchboard operator. "The police—got them yet? Good, put them on. Hello, this is the controller, Vancouver airport. . . . Look, Inspector, we have an emergency on an incoming flight. Several passengers and one of the crew have been taken seriously ill with food poisoning. We need ambulances and doctors out here. The flight is due in about five o'clock local time. Will you alert the hospitals, get the ambulances, set up a traffic control? Right. We'll be on again as soon as we've got more information."

Within five minutes portly little Harry Burdick had puffed into the room. He stood with his jacket over his arm, gasping for breath after his hurry and swabbing the moonscape of his face with a blue-spotted handkerchief. "Where's the message?" he grunted. He ran his eye quickly over the sheet of paper the radio operator handed him. "It would be quicker to go into Calgary."

"No good, I'm afraid," Grimsell said. "There's fog right down to the grass everywhere east of the Rockies as far as Manitoba. They'll have to come through."

A clerk called across from his phone, "Passenger agent wants to know when we'll be resuming eastbound traffic. Should he keep the passengers downtown?"

Grimsell called back, "Yes. We don't want a mob out here."

"Have you got medical help lined up?" asked Burdick.

"The city police are working on it."

Burdick turned to the switchboard operator. "Get me Dr. Davidson, will you?" Then he shook a worried head. "Say, suppose the captain takes sick, Controller? Who's going to . . ." He left the sentence unfinished.

"I'm praying, that's all," said Grimsell.

CHAPTER THREE

NEARLY four miles above the earth, the aircraft held her course. In every direction, as far as the eye could see, stretched the undulating carpet of cloud.

Inside the aircraft, fear was taking root, like a monstrous weed, in the minds of most of the passengers. The hubbub of dismay and conjecture following the doctor's words had soon died away, to be replaced by whispers and uneasy snatches of conversation.

Baird had given Janet two pills. "Take them to the captain," he told her in a low voice. "Tell him to drink as much water as he can to dilute the poison. Then he's to take the pills. They'll make him sick—that's what they're for."

When Janet entered the flight deck, Dun was completing a radio transmission. He signed off and gave her a strained grin. "Hello, Jan," he said. "How are things back there?"

"So far, so good," said Janet. She held out the pills. "Doctor says you're to drink as much water as you can, then take these. They'll make you feel a bit green."

"What a prospect." He reached down into the deep seat pocket at his side and took out a water bottle. "Well, down the hatch." After a long draft, he swallowed the pills.

Janet looked anxiously down at him as he sat before the panel of flickering gauges and dials. She touched his shoulder. "How do you feel?" She was watching his pallor, the beads of perspiration on his forehead. She prayed to herself that it was just the strain he was undergoing.

"Me?" His tone was unnaturally hearty. "I'm fine." He looked over at the first officer, now prone on the floor, his head on a pillow. "Poor Pete," he murmured. "I hope he'll be all right."

"That's up to you, isn't it, Captain?" said Janet urgently. "The faster you can push this thing into Vancouver, the quicker we'll get him and the others into a hospital." She stepped over to Pete and knelt to adjust a blanket around him.

Dun was troubled as he regarded her. "You think a lot of him, Jan, don't you?" he said.

"I—I suppose so," she replied. "I've begun to like him during the past few months since he joined the crew and this . . . this horrible business has made me—" She checked herself and jumped up. "I've got a lot to do to help the doctor."

She smiled at him and opened the door to the passenger deck. Baird was halfway along the starboard side, talking to a middle-aged couple who stared at him nervously.

"Did you have fish or meat?" Baird asked.

The man's bulbous eyes seemed about to depart from their sockets. "Fish," he exclaimed. "We both ate fish." Indignation welled up in him. "I think it's disgraceful that such a thing can happen. There ought to be an inquiry."

"I can assure you there will be." Baird handed them each a pill, which they accepted as gingerly as if it were a high explosive. "Now, you'll be brought a jug of water. Drink three glasses each—four, if you can. Then take the pill. It'll make you sick, but that's what it's for. There are paper bags in the seat pockets."

He left the couple staring hypnotically at their pills and in a few minutes, after progressing along the rows, had reached his own empty seat with Spencer sitting alongside it.

"Meat," said Spencer promptly, before Baird could ask him.

"Good," said the doctor. "That's one less to worry about."

"You're having a heavy time of it, Doc, aren't you?" Spencer commented. "Can you do with any help?"

"I can do with all the help in the world," growled Baird. "But there's not much you can do, unless you'd like to give Miss Benson and 'Otpot a hand with the water."

"Sure I will." Spencer lowered his voice. "Some of them back there sound in a bad way."

"They *are* in a bad way. The devil of it is I've got nothing I can give them that's of any real use. You travel to a football game—you don't think to pack your bag for food poisoning. I don't know why I threw in a bottle of emetic pills, but it's a good thing I did. In these cases, the serious thing is dehydration, the loss of body fluids. And I have nothing with me to help to preserve them."

Spencer rubbed his chin. "Well," he said, "thank God for lamb chops. I just don't feel ready for dehydration yet."

Baird frowned. "Perhaps you see some humor in this situation," he said sourly. "I don't. All I can see is my complete helplessness while people steadily get worse."

"Don't ride me, Doc," Spencer protested. "I meant nothing. I'm only glad we didn't get sick like the other poor devils."

"Yes, yes, maybe you're right." Baird passed a hand over his eyes. "I'm getting too old for this sort of thing."

Spencer got to his feet. "Now, hold on there, Doc," he said. "You're doing a fine job. The luckiest thing that ever happened to these people is having you on board."

"All right," Baird retorted, "but you can spare me the salesman's pep talk."

The younger man flushed slightly. "Fair enough. Well, tell me what I can do. I've been warming my seat while you've been hard at it."

"Until Miss Benson needs you, maybe you'd better stay in your seat. There's enough traffic in the aisle already."

"I'm here if you want me." Spencer resumed his seat. "But tell me—just how serious is all this?"

"It is *very* serious," Baird said curtly, and moved along to the group of football fans who had earlier imbibed whiskey with such liberality. The quartet was now reduced to three, and one of these sat shivering, a blanket drawn across his chest. His color was gray.

"Keep this man warm," said Baird to the other two. "Has he had anything to drink?"

"That's a laugh," replied a man behind him, shuffling a pack of cards. "He must have downed a couple of pints of rye."

283

"It has helped to dilute the poison, I don't doubt," Baird said. "Have any of you men got some brandy?"

One of the men leaned forward to get at his hip pocket. "I might have some left in the flask."

"Give him a few sips," instructed Baird. "Do it gently. Your friend is very ill."

"Poor old Andy." The man with the flask unscrewed the cap. A thought struck him. "He'll be all right, won't he?"

"I hope so. Make sure he doesn't throw off that blanket."

As Baird stepped away, the man with the cards flicked them irritably in his hand and demanded of his companion, "How d'you like this for a two-day vacation?"

Farther along the aisle, Baird found Janet anxiously bending over Mrs. Childer. He raised one of the woman's eyelids. She was unconscious.

"How is she?" implored her husband.

"She's better off now than when she was conscious and in pain." Baird hoped he sounded convincing. "When the body can't take any more, nature pulls down the shutter."

"She will be OK, won't she? I mean . . ."

"Of course she will," said Baird gently. "There'll be an ambulance waiting when we land. Then it's only a question of treatment and time before she's well again."

Childer heaved a deep breath. "It certainly is good to hear you say that."

Yes, thought Baird, but supposing I'd had the guts to tell the truth?

"You still think it was the fish, do you, Doctor?"

"I think so. Food poisoning can be caused either by the food just spoiling—the medical name is staphylococcal poisoning—or it's possible that some toxic substance has accidentally got into it during its preparation. I can't be sure which this is, but from its effects I'd suspect a toxic substance. We won't know until we're able to make proper tests in a laboratory. With the careful way in which airlines prepare food—the chances against this happening are a million to one. I can tell you, though, that our dinner tonight didn't come from the usual caterers."

Childer nodded. Funny how people seem to find comfort in a medical man's words, Baird reflected. Maybe we haven't come so far from witchcraft; there's always the doctor with his box of magic, to pull something out of the hat. Most of his life had been spent in coaxing, cajoling, bullying—reassuring frightened people that he knew best, and hoping each time that his skill had not deserted him. Well, this could be the moment of truth, the inescapable challenge which he had known would face him one day.

He was aware of Janet standing beside him. He questioned her with his eyes, sensing her to be on the edge of hysteria.

"Two more passengers have been taken ill. At the back there."

"Right. I'll get to them straightaway. Will you have another look at the first officer? He might like a little water."

He had barely reached the new cases and begun his examination before Janet was back again.

"Doctor, I'm terribly worried. I think you ought to—"

The buzz of the galley intercom cut across her words like a knife. Baird was first to move. The buzz continued without a break.

"Don't bother with that thing," he rapped out. "Quick!"

Moving with an agility quite foreign to him, he raced along the aisle and burst into the flight deck. There he paused momentarily, and in that instant something inside him, mocking in its tone but menacing, too, said, *You were right—this is it.*

The captain was rigid in his seat, sweat masking his face and streaking the collar of his uniform. One hand clutched at his stomach. The other was pressed on the intercom button on the wall beside him. In two bounds the doctor reached him and leaned over the back of the seat, supporting him under the armpits. Dun was swearing between his clenched teeth, quietly and viciously.

"Take it easy," said Baird. "We'll get you away from there."

"I did . . . what you said . . ." Dun gasped, squeezing the words out in painful jerks. "It was too late. . . . Give me something, Doc. Got to hold out . . . get us down. . . . She's on autopilot but . . . got to get down. . . . Must tell control . . . must tell . . ." With a desperate effort he tried to speak. Then his eyes rolled up and he collapsed.

"Quick, Miss Benson," called Baird. "Help me get him out."

Panting and struggling, they pulled Dun's heavy body out of the pilot's seat and eased him onto the floor alongside the first officer. Baird took out his stethoscope and made an examination. In a matter of seconds Janet had produced coats and a blanket; as soon as the doctor had finished, she made a pillow for the captain and covered him. She was trembling as she stood up.

"Can you bring him round long enough to land the plane?"

Baird thrust his stethoscope back in his pocket. In the dim light from the battery of dials his features seemed suddenly much older, and unbearably weary.

"You are part of this crew, Miss Benson, so I'll be blunt." His voice was so hard that she flinched. "Unless I can get all these people to a hospital quickly—very quickly—I can't even be sure of saving their lives. They need stimulants, intravenous injections for shock. The captain, too. He's held out too long."

Barely audible, Janet whispered, "Doctor—what'll we do?"

"Let me ask you a question. How many fish dinners did you serve?"

"About fifteen. Most of the fifty-six passengers had meat."

"I see." Baird regarded her steadily. "Miss Benson, did you ever hear of long odds?"

Janet tried to understand what he was saying. "Yes, I suppose so. I don't know what it means."

"It means this," said Baird. "Our one chance of survival depends on there being a passenger aboard this airplane who is not only qualified to land it but who also didn't have fish for dinner."

As THE doctor's words penetrated her mind, Janet met his eyes steadily, well aware of his unspoken injunction to prepare herself for death. Until now a part of her had refused to accept what was happening. While she had busied herself tending the passengers, something had insisted that this was a nightmare. At any moment she would wake up to find half the bedclothes on the floor and the clock buzzing to herald another morning. But now that sense of unreality was swept away. She knew this was really happening, to her, Janet Benson.

"I understand, Doctor," she said levelly.

"Do you know of anyone on board with any experience of flying?"

Janet cast her mind over the passenger list. "There's no one from the airline," she said. "I don't know . . . about anyone else. I suppose I'd better start asking."

"Yes, you'd better," said Baird slowly. "But try not to alarm them, or we may start a panic. Some of them already know the first officer is sick. Just say the captain wondered if there's someone with flying experience who could help with the radio."

"Very well, Doctor," said Janet quietly.

"Miss Benson—what's your first name?" he asked.

"Janet."

"Janet—I think I made some remark earlier on about your training. It was unjustified and unforgivable—the comment of a stupid old man who could have done with more training himself."

Color returned to her cheeks as she smiled. "I'd forgotten it." She moved toward the door, anxious to begin her questioning.

"Wait," Baird said. His face was puckered in an effort of concentration, as if something at the back of his mind were eluding him. "I've got it. I *knew* someone had spoken to me about airplanes. That young fellow in the seat next to mine. George Spencer. I forget exactly, but he seemed to know something about flying. And he had the meat. Get him up here, will you? Then carry on asking the others, too, in case there's someone else."

Baird paced the narrow cabin nervously while she was gone, then knelt to feel the pulse of the captain lying flat and unconscious beside the first officer. At the first sound of the door opening behind him, he jumped to his feet, blocking the entrance. Spencer stood there, looking at him in bewilderment.

"Hello, Doc," the young man greeted him. "What's this about the radio?"

"Are you a pilot?" Baird shot out, not moving.

"A long time ago. In the war. I wouldn't know about radio procedures now, but if the captain thinks I can—"

"Come in," said Baird.

He stepped aside, closing the door quickly behind the young man. Spencer's head snapped up at the sight of the pilots' empty seats and the controls moving by themselves. Then he wheeled around to the two men stretched on the floor under their blankets.

"No!" he gasped. "Not both of them?"

"Yes, both of them. Listen," said Baird urgently. "Can you fly this aircraft—and land it?"

"No!" Spencer put out a hand to steady himself. "Not a chance!"

"But you just said you flew in the war," Baird insisted.

"That was thirteen years ago. I haven't touched a plane since. And I was on fighters—tiny Spitfires about an eighth of the size of this ship and with only one engine. This has four. The flying characteristics are completely different."

Spencer's fingers, shaking slightly, probed his jacket for cigarettes, found a pack, and pulled one out.

Baird watched him as he lit up. "You could have a go at it," he pressed.

Spencer shook his head angrily. "I tell you, the idea's crazy," he snapped. "I wouldn't be able to take on a Spitfire now, let alone all this." He jabbed his cigarette toward the banks of instruments.

Baird said, "Let's hope there's someone else who can fly this thing—neither of these men can." He looked down at the pilots.

The door opened and Janet came into the flight deck. "There's no one else," she said. Her voice was flat.

"That's it, then," said the doctor. He waited for Spencer to speak, but the younger man was staring forward at the row upon row of dials and switches. "Mr. Spencer," said Baird, measuring his words, "I know nothing about flying. All I know is this. There are people on this plane who will die within a few hours if they don't get to a hospital. Among those left who are physically able to fly the plane, you are the only one with any kind of qualification to do so." He paused. "What do you suggest?"

Spencer looked from the girl to the doctor. He asked tensely, "You're quite sure there's no chance of either of the pilots recovering in time?"

"None at all, I'm afraid."

The salesman ground his cigarette under his heel. "It looks as if I don't have much choice, doesn't it?" he said.

"That's right. Unless you'd rather we carried on until we were out of gas—probably halfway across the Pacific."

"Don't kid yourself that this is a better way." Spencer stepped forward to the controls and looked ahead at the white sea of cloud below them, glistening in the moonlight. "Well," he said, "I guess I'm drafted." He took off his jacket, slipped into the left-hand pilot's seat, and glanced over his shoulder at the two behind him. "If you know any good prayers, start brushing up on them."

Baird moved up to him and slapped his arm lightly. "Good man," he said with feeling.

"What are you going to tell the people back there?" asked Spencer, running his eye over the gauges in front of him and racking his memory to recall some of the lessons he had learned in a past that now seemed very far away.

"For the moment—nothing," answered the doctor.

"Very wise," said Spencer dryly. He studied the bewildering array of instrument dials. "Let's have a look at this mess. The flying instruments must be in front of each pilot. That means the center panel will probably be engines only. Ah—here we are: altitude 20,000. Level flight. Course 290. We're on automatic pilot—we can be thankful for that. Air speed 210 knots. Throttles, pitch, trim, mixture, landing-gear controls. Flaps? There should be an indicator somewhere. Yes, here it is. Well, they're the essentials, anyway—I hope. We'll need a checklist for landing, but we can get that on the radio. Where are we now, and where are we going?"

"From what the captain said, we're over the Rockies," replied Baird. "Because of fog, we're going through to Vancouver."

"We'll have to find out more." Spencer looked about him in the soft glow. "Where *is* the radio control, anyway?"

Janet pointed to a switch box above his head. "I know they use that to talk to the ground," she told him, "but I don't know which switches you have to set."

"Ah yes, let's see." He peered at the box. "Those are the frequency selectors—we'd better leave them where they are. What's this? Transmit." He clicked a switch, lighting up a small red bulb. "That's it. Now we're ready for business."

Janet handed him a headset with the boom microphone attached. "You press the button on the mike when you speak," she said.

Adjusting the earphones, Spencer spoke to the doctor. "You know, whatever happens, I'm going to need a second pair of hands up here. You've got your patients to look after, so I think the best choice is Miss Canada here. What do you say?"

Baird nodded. "I agree. Is that all right, Janet?"

"I suppose so—but I know nothing of all this." Janet waved helplessly at the control panels.

"Good," said Spencer breezily, "that makes two of us. Sit down and make yourself comfortable—better strap yourself in."

Janet struggled into the first officer's seat, taking care not to touch the control column as it swayed back and forth. There was an anxious knocking on the flight-deck door.

"That's for me," said Baird. "I must get back. Good luck."

289

Alone with the stewardess, Spencer summoned up a grin. "The name's Janet, isn't it? Mine's George." His tone became serious. "Janet, this will be tough."

"I know it."

"Well, let's see if I can send out a distress call. What's our flight number?"

"Seven fourteen."

"Right. Here goes, then." He pressed the button on his microphone. "Mayday, Mayday, Mayday," he began in an even voice. It was one signal he could never forget. He had called it one murky October afternoon above the French coast, with the tail of his Spitfire all but shot off, and two Hurricanes had mercifully appeared to usher him across the Channel like solicitous old aunts.

"Mayday, Mayday, Mayday," he continued. "This is Flight 714, Maple Leaf Air Charter, in distress. Come in, anyone. Over."

He caught his breath as a voice responded immediately.

"Hello, 714. This is Vancouver. We have been waiting to hear from you. Vancouver to all aircraft: this frequency now closed to all other traffic. Go ahead, 714."

"Thank you, Vancouver. Seven fourteen. We are in distress. Both pilots and several passengers . . . how many passengers, Janet?"

"It was seven a few minutes ago. May be more now, though."

"Correction. At least seven passengers are suffering from food poisoning. Both pilots are unconscious and in critical condition. We have a doctor with us who says that neither of them can be revived to fly the aircraft. If they and the passengers don't get to a hospital quickly, some may die. Got that, Vancouver?"

The voice crackled back, "Go ahead, 714. I'm reading you."

Spencer took a deep breath. "Now we come to the interesting bit. My name is Spencer, George Spencer. I am a passenger on this airplane. Correction: I *was* a passenger. I am now the pilot. For your information, I have about a thousand hours total flying time, all of it on single-engined fighters. Also I haven't flown an airplane for nearly thirteen years. So you'd better get someone on this radio who can give me some instructions about flying this thing. I am on automatic pilot. Our altitude is 20,000, course 290 magnetic, air speed 210 knots. Your move, Vancouver. Over."

"Vancouver to 714. Stand by."

Spencer wiped the gathering sweat from his forehead and

grinned across to Janet. "Want to bet that's caused a bit of a stir in the dovecotes down there?"

She shook her head, listening intently to her earphones. In a few seconds the air was alive again, the voice as measured and impersonal as before.

"Vancouver to Flight 714. Please check with doctor on board for any possibility of either pilot recovering. Over."

Spencer pressed his transmit button. "Vancouver, this is Flight 714. Your message understood, but doctor says there is no possibility whatever of pilots recovering to make landing. Over."

There was a slight pause. Then: "Vancouver Control to 714. Your message understood. Will you stand by, please."

"Roger, Vancouver," acknowledged Spencer, and he switched off. His hands played nervously with the control column in front of him, following its movements, trying to gauge its responsiveness as he attempted to call up the flying skill that had once earned for him quite a reputation in the squadron: three times home on a wing and a prayer. He smiled to himself as he recalled the wartime phrase. But in the next moment, as he looked blankly at the monstrous assembly of wavering needles and the unfamiliar banks of levers and switches, he felt himself in the grip of an icy despair. One wrong move might shatter in a second the even tenor of their flight; if it did, who was to say that he could bring the aircraft under control again? He began to curse the head office which had whipped him away from Winnipeg to go troubleshooting across to Vancouver at a moment's notice. The prospect of a promotion to sales manager now seemed absurdly unimportant. It would be damnable to end like this, not to see Mary again, not to say to her all the things that were still unspoken. As for Bobsie and Kit, he should have done more for those poor kids, the world's best.

He lit a cigarette. "I don't suppose this is allowed," he said to Janet, "but maybe the airline can stretch a point."

CHAPTER FOUR

WITH an accelerating thunder of engines the last eastbound aircraft to take off from Vancouver that night had gathered speed along the wetly gleaming runway and climbed into the darkness. Its navigation lights, as it made the required circuit of the airport, had been shrouded in mist. Other aircraft, in process of being towed back from their dispersal points to bays alongside the departure buildings, were beaded with moisture. It was a cold night. Ground staff, moving about their tasks in the yellow arc lights, slapped their gloved hands around themselves to keep warm. None of them spoke more than was necessary. One last slowly taxiing aircraft came to a stop and cut its engines at a wave from the indicator torches of a groundman. In the sudden silence the swish of its propellers seemed an intrusion. Normally busy Vancouver airport prepared itself with quiet competence for emergency.

Within the brightly lit control room the atmosphere was tense. Replacing his telephone, Controller Grimsell studied a wall map, then turned to Burdick. Perched on the edge of a table, the plump manager of Maple Leaf airline had just finished consulting the clipboard of information he held in his hand.

"Right, Harry," said the controller. "As of now, I'm holding all departures for the east. We've got nearly an hour in which to clear the present outgoing traffic in other directions, leaving plenty of time in hand. After that, everything scheduled outwards must wait until . . . until afterwards, anyway." He addressed an assistant who sat holding a telephone. "Have you raised the fire chief yet?"

"Ringing his home now."

"Tell him he'd better get here—it looks like a big show. And ask the duty fire officer to notify the city fire department. They may want to move equipment into the area."

"I've done that. Vancouver Control here," said the assistant into his telephone. "Hold the line, please." He cupped his hand over the mouthpiece. "Shall I alert the Air Force?"

"Yes. Have them keep the zone clear of their aircraft." Grimsell turned to Burdick. "Have you any pilots here at the airport?"

Burdick shook his head. "Not one. We'll have to get help."

The controller thought rapidly. "Try Cross-Canada. They have most of their men based here. Explain the position. We'll need a man fully experienced with this type of aircraft who is capable of giving instruction over the air."

"Do you think there's a chance?"

"I don't know, but we'll try. Can you suggest anything else?"

"No," said Burdick. "But I sure don't envy anyone that job."

The switchboard operator called, "The city police again."

"Put them on," said the controller.

"I'll see the Cross-Canada people," said Burdick.

The controller lifted the telephone as Burdick hurried out of the room. "Controller speaking. Ah, Inspector, I'm glad it's you. That's fine. Now listen, Inspector. We're in bad trouble, much worse than we thought. First, we may have to ask one of your cars to collect a pilot in town and bring him here just as fast as possible. No, I'll let you know the address later. Second, in addition to the urgency of getting the passengers to the hospital, there's now a very serious possibility that the plane will crash-land. I can't explain now, but when the ship comes in she won't be under proper control." He listened for a moment to the man at the other end. "Yes, we've issued a general alarm. The fire department will have everything they've got standing by. The point is, I think the houses near the airport may be in some danger." He listened again. "Well, I'm glad you've suggested it. I know it's a hell of a thing to wake people in the middle of the night, but we're taking enough chances as it is. I can't guarantee at all that this plane will get down on the field. We're lucky that there are only those houses out towards Sea Island bridge to worry about. We'll route her well clear of the city. . . . No, can't say yet. We'll probably try to bring her in from the east end of the main runway." Another pause, longer this time. "Thank you, Inspector. I'll keep in touch." The controller clicked the telephone back, his face etched with worry.

"The fire chief is on his way," reported his assistant. "I'm on to the Air Force now. They ask if they can give any assistance."

"We'll let them know, but I don't think so. Thank them." He returned to his study of the wall map as Burdick came back into the room, breathing noisily.

"Jim Bryant at Cross-Canada says their best man is Captain Paul Treleaven. He's ringing him now. He's at home and in bed, I suppose. They'll get a police escort; I've told them we need him in the worst way. Do you know Treleaven?"

"I've met him," said the controller. "He's a good type. We're lucky he's available."

The switchboard operator broke in. "I've got Seattle and Calgary waiting, sir. They want to know if we got the message from 714 clearly."

"Tell them yes," answered the controller. "We'll work the aircraft direct, but we'd appreciate them keeping a listening watch in case we meet with reception trouble."

"Right, sir."

The controller crossed to the radio panel and picked up the stand microphone. He nodded to the dispatcher, who threw a switch to transmit. "Vancouver Control to Flight 714," he called.

Spencer's voice, when he replied, spluttered from an amplifier high in a corner of the room. Since his Mayday call all his conversation had been channeled through the loudspeaker. "This is 714. Go ahead, Vancouver. I thought you were lost."

"Vancouver to 714. This is the controller speaking. We are organizing help. We shall call you again very soon. Meanwhile do nothing to interfere with the present set of the controls. Do you understand? Over."

Despite the distortion, the asperity in Spencer's voice came through like a knife. "Seven fourteen to Vancouver. I told you I've never touched a job like this before. I certainly don't aim to start playing fool tricks with the automatic pilot. Over."

The controller opened his mouth as if to say something, then changed his mind. He signed off and said to his assistant, "Tell reception to get Treleaven up here fast when he arrives."

"Right, sir. The duty fire officer is clearing all runway vehicles, and the city fire department is bringing all the equipment they've got into the precincts."

Burdick said suddenly, "Hey, with the city departments on to this, we'll have the press at any time. Front page everywhere. I can just imagine it. Planeload of people, many of them sick. No pilot. Maybe evacuation of those houses towards the bridge. And—"

The controller cut in, "Let public relations handle it. Get Cliff Howard here, at the double." Burdick nodded to the switchboard operator, who ran his finger down an emergency list and then began to dial. "Cliff will know how to play it, Harry. Tell him to keep the papers off our backs. We've got work to do."

Burdick picked up a telephone impatiently. "Have you been able to reach Dr. Davidson?" he demanded of the operator.

"He's out on a night call. I've left a message."

"If he doesn't check in in ten minutes, get the hospital. That doctor on 714 may be in need of advice."

On the outskirts of the town, a telephone was ringing incessantly.

A smooth white arm emerged from bedclothes and groped slowly in the darkness for the switch of a bedside lamp. The lamp clicked on. With her eyes screwed up against the brightness of the light, Dulcie Treleaven, an attractive redhead, reached drowsily for the telephone. She mumbled, "Yes?"

"Mrs. Treleaven?" demanded a crisp voice.

"Yes," she said. "Who is it?"

"Mrs. Treleaven, may I speak to your husband?"

"He's not here."

"Where can I find him, please? It's imperative that we contact him without delay. This is Cross-Canada."

"He's at his mother's place. His father is ill." She gave the telephone number.

"Thank you. We'll ring him there."

She replaced the receiver and swung her legs out of bed. As the wife of a senior pilot she was accustomed to unexpected calls for her husband, but part of her still resented them. Was Paul the only pilot they ever thought of when they were in a fix? Well, if he was having to take over a plane in a hurry, he would call home first for his uniform and gear. There would be time to make up a flask of coffee and some sandwiches. She drew on a robe and stumbled sleepily down the stairs toward the kitchen.

Two miles away, Paul Treleaven slept deeply on the davenport in his mother's parlor. That vigorous old lady had insisted on taking a spell by the side of her sick husband, ordering her son to rest. The news from the family doctor the previous evening had been encouraging: the old man had passed the dangerous corner of his pneumonia and now it was a matter of careful nursing. Treleaven had been thankful for a chance to sleep. Only thirty-six hours previously he had completed a flight from Tokyo, and since then, with the crisis of his father's illness, there had been scant opportunity for more than an uneasy doze.

He was aroused by his arm being shaken, and looked up to find his mother bending over him. "The airport is on the telephone," she said. "I told them you were sleeping, but they insisted."

"OK. I'll come." Pulling himself off the davenport, he padded in stockinged feet to the telephone in the hall. He was already half dressed, having removed only his jacket, tie, and shoes for comfort. "Treleaven," he said.

"Paul, this is Jim Bryant." The words were clipped, urgent. "We're in real trouble here. There's a Maple Leaf Charter—an Empress C6—on its way from Winnipeg, with a number of passengers and both pilots seriously ill with food poisoning."

"What! *Both* pilots?"

"That's right. It's a top emergency. Some fellow is at the controls who hasn't flown for years. Fortunately the ship is on autopilot. Maple Leaf hasn't got a man here, and we want you to come in and talk her down. Think you can do it?"

"It's a tall order." Treleaven looked at his wristwatch. "What's the ETA?"

"Zero five zero five," Bryant said.

"But that's under two hours. We've got to move! Look, I'm on the south side of town—"

"What's your address?" Treleaven gave it. "We'll have a police car pick you up in a few minutes. And good luck, Paul."

"You're not kidding."

He strode back to the parlor and pulled on his shoes without stopping to tie the laces. His mother held out his jacket for him.

"What is it, Paul?" she asked apprehensively.

"Bad trouble at the airport, Mother. They need my help." He looked around for his pipe and tobacco and put them in his pocket. He stopped in his tracks. "How did they know I was here?"

"Perhaps they rang Dulcie first."

"Yes, that must be it. Would you give her a ring, Mother, and let her know everything is all right?"

"I will. But what is the trouble about, Paul?"

"A pilot is sick on an aircraft due here soon. They want me to talk it down, if I can."

His mother looked puzzled. "What do you mean—talk it down? If the pilot's sick, who's going to fly it?"

"I am, Mother—from the ground."

"I don't understand."

Maybe I don't either, Treleaven thought to himself five minutes later, seated in the back of a police car as the driver pulled away from the sidewalk and slammed into top gear. The speedometer crept steadily to seventy-five as the siren sliced into the night.

"Looks like a big night over at the field," remarked the police sergeant beside the driver. "Every available car has been sent over to the airport in case the houses near the bridge have to be cleared. I'd say they're expecting a hell of a bang."

"You know what?" interjected the young driver. "I bet there's a busted-up Stratojet coming in with a nuclear bombload."

"Your trouble is you read too many comics," said the sergeant with heavy scorn.

They crossed the estuary to Sea Island, where police crews were already talking to bewildered homeowners in doorways, and sped along the last stretch of Airport Road.

At the reception building, Treleaven was out of the car, through the doors, and had crossed the concourse before the wail of the siren had died behind him. He could move remarkably fast for a man of his size. His loose-limbed agility, combined with a solid physique and fair hair, had long made him an object of interest to women. His hard, lean features, angular and crooked, looked as if they had been inexpertly carved from a chunk of wood. He had a reputation as a disciplinarian, and more than one crew member had had cause to fear the cold light in those pale blue eyes.

As he entered the control room, Grimsell stepped quickly over to greet him. "I'm certainly glad to see you, Captain," he said, and he gave him the story quickly. "Burdick has just got his president out of bed in Montreal. The old man sounds far from happy."

"What else can we do?" Burdick was pleading anxiously and deferentially on the phone. "Captain Treleaven, Cross-Canada's chief pilot, just walked in the door. We'll get on the radio with a checklist and try to talk him down. . . . Of course it's a terrible risk, sir, but can you think of something better?"

Treleaven took from the dispatcher the clipboard of messages from 714, read them carefully, and consulted the latest weather reports. Then he laid the papers down, raised his eyebrows somberly at the controller, and produced his pipe, which he proceeded to fill.

Burdick was still speaking. "I've thought of that, sir. Howard will handle the press at this end—they aren't on to it yet."

"What do you think?" Grimsell asked Treleaven.

The pilot shrugged without answering and picked up the clipboard again, drawing steadily on his pipe.

". . . ETA is 0505 Pacific time," Burdick was saying with increasing exasperation. "I've a lot to do, sir . . . I'll call you as

297

soon as I know anything more. . . . Yes, yes . . . G'by." Putting
down the telephone, he blew out his cheeks with relief, then turned
to Treleaven. "Thank you very much for coming, Captain."

Treleaven held up the clipboard. "This is the whole story?"

"That's everything we know. You'll have to talk this guy right
down onto the ground. Can you do it?"

"I can't perform a miracle," said Treleaven evenly. "The chances
of a man who has only flown fighter airplanes landing a four-engine
passenger ship are slim, to say the least!"

"I know that!" Burdick exploded. "But do you have any other
ideas?"

"No," Treleaven said slowly. "I guess not. I just wanted to be
sure you knew what we were getting into."

"The biggest air disaster in years, that's what we're getting into!"
shouted Burdick angrily.

"Keep your temper," said Treleaven coldly. "We'll get nowhere
fast by shouting." He glanced at the wall map. "This is going to
be tough and a very long shot," he said. "I want that fully understood."

"You are right to emphasize the risk, Captain. We fully accept
that," said the controller.

"Very well, then, let's get started." Treleaven walked over to the
radio operator. "Can you work 714 direct?"

"Yes, Captain. Reception's good."

"Call them."

The operator switched to transmit. "Flight 714. This is Vancouver. Do you read? Over."

"Yes, Vancouver," came Spencer's voice through the amplifier.
"We hear you clearly. Go ahead, please."

The operator handed the stand microphone to Treleaven. "OK,
Captain. It's all yours."

Holding the stand microphone in his hand, its cable trailing to
the floor, Treleaven turned his back on the other men in the room.
Legs braced apart, he stared unseeingly at the wall map, his cold
eyes distant in concentration. His voice, when he spoke, was steady
and unhurried, easy with a confidence he did not feel. As he began,
the other men visibly relaxed, as if his natural authority had temporarily relieved them of a crushing responsibility.

"Hello, Flight 714," he said. "This is Vancouver. My name is

Paul Treleaven and I'm a Cross-Canada Airlines captain. My job is to help you fly this airplane in. We shouldn't have too much trouble. I see that I'm talking to George Spencer. I'd like to hear a little more about your flying experience, George."

CHAPTER FIVE

SPENCER tensed, shooting an involuntary glance at the girl in the seat beside him. Her eyes were fixed on his face. He looked away again, listening carefully. Treleaven was saying, "The message here says you've flown single-engine fighters. Have you had any experience at all with multiengine planes, George?"

Spencer's mouth was so dry that he could hardly speak. He cleared his throat. "Hello, Vancouver. Seven fourteen here. Glad to have you along, Captain. But let's not kid each other. I think we both know the situation. My flying up to now has been entirely on single-engine aircraft, Spitfires and Mustangs—I'd say about a thousand hours in all. But that was thirteen years ago. I've touched nothing since. Over."

"Don't worry about that, George. It's like riding a bicycle—you never forget it. Stand by, will you?"

In the Vancouver control room, Treleaven pressed the cutout button on the arm of the microphone in his hand and looked at a slip of paper Grimsell held out for him to read.

"Try to get him on this course," said the controller. "The Air Force has just sent in a radar check." He paused. "Sounds pretty tense, doesn't he?"

"Yes—who wouldn't be, in his shoes?" Treleaven grimaced reflectively. "We've got to give him confidence. Whatever happens, he mustn't lose his nerve." He released the cutout. "OK, 714. This is Treleaven, George. In a minute you can disengage the autopilot and get the feel of the controls. When you've had a bit of practice with them, you are going to change your course a little. When you start handling the airplane, the controls will seem very heavy and sluggish compared with a fighter. Don't let that worry you. It's quite normal. Watch your airspeed all the time you are flying and don't let it fall below 120 knots while your wheels and flaps are up or you'll stall. Now, one other thing. Do you have someone up there who can work the radio and leave you free for flying?"

"Yes, Vancouver. I have the stewardess here with me and she'll take over the radio now. It's all yours, Janet."

"Hello, Vancouver. This is the stewardess, Janet Benson. Over."

"Why, it's you, Janet," said Treleaven. "I'd know that voice anywhere. You're going to talk to me for George. Now, Janet, I want you to keep your eyes on that airspeed indicator. Remember that an airplane stays in the air because of its forward speed. If you let the speed drop too low, it stalls—and falls out of the air. Any time the ASI shows a reading near 120, you tell George instantly. Is that clear, Janet?"

"Yes, Captain. I understand."

"Back to you, George. Very slowly, I want you to unlock the autopilot—it's clearly marked on the control column—and take the airplane yourself, holding her straight and level. Watch the artificial horizon and keep the airspeed steady. Climb-and-descent indicator should stay at zero. All right. Start now."

Spencer put his right forefinger over the autopilot release button on the control column. His face was rigid. Feet on the rudder bar and both arms ready, braced, he steeled himself.

"Tell him I'm switching over now," he told Janet. She repeated the message. His hand wavered for a moment on the button. Then, decisively, he pressed it hard. The aircraft swung a little to port, but he corrected the tendency gently and she responded well enough to his feet on the rudder bar.

"Tell him OK," he gasped, his nerves taut as cables.

"Hello, Vancouver. We're flying straight and level." Janet's voice sounded miraculously calm.

"Well done, George. As soon as you've got the feel of her, try some very gentle turns, not more than two or three degrees. Can you see the turn indicator? It's almost directly in front of your eyes and slightly to the right. Over." Treleaven's eyes were closed with the effort of visualizing the cockpit layout. He opened them and spoke to the dispatch messenger. "Listen, we ought to start planning the approach and landing while there's plenty of time. Get the chief radar operator up here, will you?"

Very gingerly Spencer extended his left leg and eased the control column over. This time it seemed an age before the aircraft responded to his touch and he saw the horizon indicator tilt. Gratified, he tried the other way; but now the movement was alarming.

He looked down at the ASI and was shocked to see that it had dropped to 180 knots. Quickly he eased the control column forward. Then he breathed again as the speed rose slowly to 210. He would have to treat the controls with the utmost respect until he really understood the time lag; that was evident. Again he tried a shallow turn and pushed at the resisting weight of the rudder to hold it steady. Gradually he felt the ship answer. Then he straightened up, so as to keep approximately on the course they had been steering before.

Janet had lifted her eyes momentarily from the instrument panel to ask in a small voice, "How is it?"

Spencer tried to grin, without much success. "Tell him I'm on manual and doing gentle turns, coming back on course each time."

Janet gave the message.

"I should have asked you this before," came Treleaven's voice. "What kind of weather are you in up there?"

"It's clear where we are right now," answered Janet. "Except below us, of course."

"Better keep me informed. Now, George, we have to press on. You may hit cloud layer at any time, with a little turbulence. If you do, I want you to be ready for it. How does she handle?"

Spencer looked across to Janet. "Tell him—sluggish as a wet sponge," he said between clenched teeth.

"Hello, Vancouver. As sluggish as a wet sponge," repeated Janet.

The group at Vancouver Control exchanged smiles. "That's a natural feeling, George," said Treleaven, serious again, "because you were used to smaller airplanes."

The dispatch messenger cut in. "I've the radar chief here."

"I'll talk to him as soon as I get a break," said Treleaven.

"Right."

"Hello, George," called Treleaven. "You must avoid any violent movements of the controls, such as you used to make in your fighter airplanes. If you do move the controls violently, you will overcorrect and be in trouble. Is that understood? Over."

"Yes, Vancouver, we understand. Over."

"Now, George, I want you to try the effect of fore-and-aft control on your airspeed. To start with, adjust your throttle setting so as to reduce speed to 160, and cruise straight and level. But keep the airspeed over 120. The elevator trim is just to your right on the control pedestal, and the aileron trim is below the throttles, down near the floor. Got it? Over."

Spencer checked with one hand, holding the plane steady with the other and with braced legs.

Time ticked away as the speed slowly dropped. At 160, George adjusted the trim tabs and held up his thumb to Janet.

"OK, Vancouver. We've got 160 knots on the indicator."

Treleaven waited until he had struggled out of his jacket before speaking. "Right, George. Try a little up and down movement. Use the control column as carefully as if it were full of eggs, and watch your speed. Keep it at 160. Get the feel of the thing. Over." He put the microphone down. "Where's the radar chief?"

"Here."

"At what range will this aircraft show on your scope?"

"Sixty miles, thereabouts, Captain."

"That's no good for a while, then. Well," said Treleaven, partly to himself, partly to Burdick, "you can't have everything at once. Next call, we'll check his heading."

"Yeah," said Burdick.

"If he's stayed on the same heading," continued Treleaven, looking at the wall map, "he can't be that much off course, and we can straighten him up when he gets in our radar range. That Air Force radar check is a help."

"Can't he come in on the beam?" asked Burdick.

"Right now he's got enough to worry about. If I try to get him on the beam, he'll have to mess around with the radio, changing frequencies and a lot of other stuff. I'd sooner take a chance, Harry, and let him go a few miles off course."

"That makes sense," Burdick conceded.

The pilot turned to the radar chief. "I'll do the talking. He's getting used to me now. As soon as he shows up on your scope, feed me the information and I'll relay it. Can you fix up a closed circuit between me and the radar room?"

"We can take care of that," said the dispatcher.

"How about the final approach?" asked the radar chief.

"We'll handle that the same way," said Treleaven. "Directly we've got him on the scope and he's steady on course, we'll move to the tower. You report up there, and we'll decide on the runway and plan the approach."

"Yes, sir."

The controller was replacing a telephone in its cradle. "Dr. Davidson is downstairs," he told Treleaven. "From the information we've got, he agrees with the diagnosis of food poisoning. Could be botulism. Shall we get the doctor and put him on the air?"

"No, Mr. Grimsell. It's more important right now to fly this airplane. We'll let them call for medical advice if they want it. I don't want Spencer's mind distracted from the job. But have Davidson stand by." Treleaven spoke into the microphone. "Hello, George Spencer. Don't forget that lag in the controls. Just take it steadily. Do you understand that?"

There was a pause. Then, "He understands, Vancouver. Over."

To Spencer it seemed as if Treleaven had read his thoughts. He had moved the column slowly forward and then back again, but there had been no response from the aircraft. Now he tried again, easing the stick away from him. Imperceptibly at first, the nose of the aircraft began to dip. Then, so suddenly that he was momentarily paralyzed with shock, it plunged downward. Janet bit hard on her lip to avoid screaming. The ASI needle began to swing around . . . 180 . . . 190 . . . 200 . . . 220. Putting all his weight on the column, Spencer fought to bring the aircraft back. In front of him the instruments on the panel seemed alive. The climb-and-descent indicator quivered against the bottom of the glass. On the altimeter the 100-foot hand whirred backward; the 1000-foot hand less quickly but still terrifyingly fast; while the 10,000-foot needle had already stopped, jammed at its nadir.

"Come on!" he shouted as the nose at last responded. He watched the altimeter needles begin with agonizing slowness to wind up again, registering gradually increasing height. "Made it!" he said in relief to Janet, forgetting that he was overcorrecting.

"Watch it—watch the speed!" she exclaimed.

His eyes flicked back to the dial, now rapidly falling again. One sixty . . . 150 . . . 140. Then he had it. With a sigh the aircraft settled down on an even keel once more and he brought it into straight and level flight.

The door to the flight deck opened behind them, and Dr. Baird's voice called, "What's wrong?"

Spencer did not move his eyes from the panel. "Sorry. I'm trying to get the feel of her."

"How are you doing?"

"Fine, just fine, Doc," said Spencer, licking his lips. The door closed again, and Treleaven's voice came on the air.

"Hello, George. Everything OK? Over."

"All under control, Vancouver," replied Janet.

"Good. What's your present heading, George?"

Spencer peered down. "Tell him the magnetic compass is still showing about 290." Janet did so.

"Very well, George. Try to stay on that heading. You may be a little out, but I'll tell you when to correct. Right now I want you to feel how the ship handles at lower speeds when the flaps and wheels are down. But don't do anything until I give you the instructions. Is that clear? Over."

Janet got Spencer's nod and asked Treleaven to proceed.

"Hello, 714. First of all, throttle back slightly and get your airspeed steady at 160 knots. Adjust your trim to maintain level flight. Then tell me when you're ready. Over."

Spencer straightened himself and called, "Watch that airspeed, Janet. You'll have to call it off to me when we land, so you may as well start practicing now."

He eased the throttles back. "What's the speed, Janet?"

"One ninety, 180, 175, 165, 155, 150 . . . That's too low!"

"I know. Watch it!"

His hand nursed the throttle levers, almost caressing them into the exact positioning to achieve the speed he wanted.

"One fifty, 150, 155, 160 . . . It's steady on 160," Janet said.

Spencer puffed out his cheeks. "Phew! Tell him, Jan."

"Hello, Vancouver. Our speed is steady on 160. Over."

"OK, 714." Treleaven sounded impatient, as if he had expected them to be ready before this. "Now I want you to put on just 15 degrees of flap. The flap lever is at the base of the control pedestal and marked plainly; 15 degrees will mean moving the lever down to the second notch. The flap-indicator dial is in the center of the main panel. Have you got both of those? Over."

Spencer located the lever. "Confirm that," he told Janet, "but *you'd* better work the flaps. Right?"

She acknowledged to Vancouver and sat waiting, her hand on the lever.

"Hello, 714. When I tell you, push it all the way down and watch that dial. When the needle reaches 15 degrees, pull the lever up and leave it at the second notch. All clear?"

"We're ready, Vancouver," said Janet.

"Right. Go ahead, then."

She started to depress the lever, then jerked her head up in alarm. "The airspeed! It's down to 125."

Spencer's eyes flicked over to the airspeed indicator. Desperately he pushed the control column forward. The lurch of the aircraft brought their stomachs to their mouths. Janet almost crouched in front of the panel, intoning the figures.

"One thirty-five, 140, 150, 160, 170, 175 . . . Can't you get it back to 160?"

"I'm trying, I'm trying." Again he leveled off and jockeyed the controls until the ASI had been coaxed back to the required reading. He passed his sleeve over his forehead. "It is 160, isn't it?"

"Yes, that's better."

"That was close." He sat back in his seat. "Look, let's relax for a minute, after that." He managed to smile. "You can see the kind of pilot that I am. I should have known that would happen."

"No, it was my job to watch the airspeed." She took a deep breath to steady her pounding heart. "I think you're doing wonderfully," she said. Her voice shook slightly.

It was not lost on Spencer. He said with exaggerated heartiness, "You can't say I didn't warn you. Come on, let's get going."

"Hello, George," Treleaven's voice crackled in the earphones. "Are your flaps down yet?"

"We're just about to put them down, Captain," said Janet.

"Hold it. I omitted to tell you that when the flaps are down you will lose speed. Bring it back to 140. Over."

"Well, I'll be—" Spencer exclaimed. "That's mighty nice of him. He cut it pretty fine."

"It's probably hectic down there," said Janet, who had a very good idea of the scene taking place at the airport. "Thank you, Captain," she said, transmitting. "We're starting again. Over." At a nod from Spencer she pushed the lever down as far as it would go, while Spencer watched the indicator carefully.

"Right. Now back to second notch."

With infinite caution he cajoled the ASI needle until it rested steadily at 140.

"Tell him, Janet."

"Hello, Vancouver. Our flaps are down 15 degrees and the airspeed is 140."

"Right, 714. Are you still maintaining level flight?"

Spencer nodded. "Tell him yes—well, more or less, anyway."

"Hello, Vancouver. More or less."

"OK, 714. Now the next thing is to put the wheels down. Then you'll get the feel of the airplane as it will be when you're landing. When you are ready—and make sure you *are* ready—put down the landing gear and let the speed come back to 120. You will probably have to advance your throttle setting to maintain that airspeed, and also adjust the trim. Is that understood? Over."

"Ask him," said Spencer, "what about propeller controls and mixture?"

At Janet's question Treleaven said in an aside to Burdick, "Well, this guy's thinking, anyway. For the time being," he said into the microphone, "leave them alone. Later on I'll give you a full cockpit check for landing. Over."

"Tell him, understood," said Spencer. "We're putting down the wheels now." He looked apprehensively at the selector lever by his leg. It seemed a much better idea to keep both his hands on the column. "Look, Janet, I think you'd better work the landing-gear lever and call off the airspeed as the wheels come down."

Janet complied. The arrest in their forward flight was so pronounced that it was like applying a brake, jerking them in their seats.

"One thirty, 125, 120, 115 . . . It's too low."

"Keep calling!"

"One fifteen, 120, 120 . . . Steady on 120."

"I'll get this thing yet," Spencer panted.

Treleaven's voice came up, with a hint of anxiety. "All OK, George? Your wheels should be down by now."

"Wheels down, Vancouver," Janet reported.

"Look for three green lights to show you that they're locked. Also there's a pressure gauge on the extreme left of the center panel, and the needle should be in the green range. Check."

"Yes, Vancouver. All correct."

"And say she still handles like a wet sponge," Spencer murmured, "only more so."

"Hello, Vancouver. The pilot says she still handles like a sponge, only more so."

"Don't worry about that. Now put on full flaps and then you'll have the proper feel of the aircraft on landing. Now follow me closely. Put full flap on, bring your airspeed back to 110 knots, and trim to hold you steady. Adjust the throttle to maintain the altitude. Over."

"Did you say 110, Captain?" Janet queried nervously.

"Yes, 110 is correct, Janet. Are you quite clear, George?"

"Tell him yes. We are putting on full flap now."

Once more her hand pushed hard on the flap lever and the airspeed started to fall.

"One twenty, 115, 115, 110, 110 . . ."

Spencer's voice was tight with the effort of will he was making. "All right, Janet. Let him know. By God, she's a ton weight."

"Hello, Vancouver. Flaps are full on and the airspeed is 110."

"Nice going, George. We'll make an airline pilot of you yet. Now we'll get you back to where you were and then run through the procedure again, with certain variations regarding props, mixture, boosters, and so on. OK? Over."

"Again?" Spencer groaned. "I don't know if I can take it. All right, Janet."

"OK, Vancouver. We're ready."

"Right, 714. Using the reverse procedure, adjust your flaps to read 15 degrees and speed 120 knots. You will have to throttle back slightly to keep that speed. Go ahead."

Reaching down, Janet grasped the flap lever and gave it a tug. It failed to move. She bent closer and tried again.

"What is it?" asked Spencer.

"Sort of stiff. I can't seem to move it this time."

"Shouldn't be. Give it a good steady pull."

"It must be me. I just can't make it budge."

"Here. Let me." He took his hand off the column and pulled the lever back effortlessly. "There. You've got to have the touch."

"Look out!" she screamed. "The airspeed!"

It was 90, moving down to 75.

Bracing himself against the sudden acute angle of the flight deck, Spencer knew they were in a bad stall, an incipient spin. Keep your head, he ordered himself savagely—*think*. If she spins, we're finished. Which way is the stall? It's to the left. Try to remember what they taught you at flying school. Stick forward and hard opposite rudder. *Stick forward.* We're gaining speed. Opposite rudder. Now! Watch the instruments. They can't be right—I can feel us turning! No—trust them. Be ready to straighten. That's it. Come on. Come on, lady, *come on.*

"The mountains!" exclaimed Janet. "I can see the ground!"

Ease back. Not too fast. Hold the airspeed steady. We're coming out . . . we're coming out! It worked! We're coming out!

"One zero five, 110, 115 . . ." Janet read off in a strangled tone.

"Get the wheels up!"

"The mountains! We must—"

"Get the wheels up, I said!"

The door to the flight deck crashed open. There were sounds of crying and an angry voice. "There's something wrong! I'm going to find out what it is!"

"Get back to your seat." This was Baird's voice.

"Let me through!"

The silhouette of a man filled the doorway, peering into the flight deck. He lurched forward and stared in petrified disbelief at the back of Spencer's head and then at the prostrate figures of the two men on the floor. His mouth worked soundlessly. Then he impelled himself back to the open doorway. His voice was a shriek. "He's not the pilot! We'll all be killed! We're going to crash!"

CHAPTER SIX

WREATHED in woolly halos, the neon lights at the entrance to the reception building at Vancouver airport glistened back from the wet driveway. At the turnoff from the main highway into the airport approach, a police car stood angled partly across the road, its roof light blinking a constant warning. Those cars which had been allowed through along Airport Road were promptly waved by a patrolman to parking spaces well clear of the entrance to reception. Fire rigs and ambulances halted there for a few seconds to receive directions to their assembly points. A gleaming red salvage truck roared away, and in a small pool of silence the sound of a car radio carried clearly. "Here is a late bulletin from Vancouver airport. The authorities stress that although the Maple Leaf airline

flight is being brought in by an inexperienced pilot, there is no cause for alarm in the city. Residents in the airport area are being warned and emergency help is streaming out to Sea Island. Stay with this station for further announcements."

A mud-streaked Chevrolet swung into the parking lot and stopped abruptly. On its windshield was a sticker: PRESS. A big thickset man, with graying hair, wearing a trench coat, got out, walked rapidly over to reception, and hurried inside. He made his way to the Maple Leaf airline desk. Two men stood there in discussion with a passenger agent, and at the touch of the big man one of them turned, smiling in greeting.

"What's the score, Terry?" asked the big man.

"I've given the office what I've got, Mr. Jessup," said the other man, who was much younger. "This is Ralph Jessup—Canadian International News," he added to the passenger agent.

"I think Mr. Howard is about to make a statement in the pressroom," said the agent.

"Let's go," said Jessup. He took the younger man by the arm. "Is the office sending up a camera team?" he asked.

"Yes, but there'll be pretty full coverage by everyone."

"H'm. Remind the office to cover the evacuation of houses near the bridge. The same man can stay on the boundary of the field. He may get one or two shots of the crash—and get away quicker than the others. Who is this guy who is flying the plane?"

"A George Spencer of Toronto. That's all we know."

"Well, the office will get our Toronto people on to that end. Now grab a pay booth in reception here and don't budge out of it. Keep the line open to the office."

"Yes, Mr. Jessup, but—"

"I know, I know," said Jessup sadly, "but that's the way it is. If there's a foul-up on the phones in the pressroom, we'll need that extra line."

His coat flapping behind him, Jessup strode across to the pressroom. Newsmen were already gathered, three talking together, another rattling at one of the typewriters on the large center table, and others using two of the telephone booths that lined both sides of the room. On the floor were leather cases of camera equipment.

"Hi, Jess," greeted one of the men. "Have you seen Howard?"

"On his way, I'm told. It's easy to see who's doing the work here," he said, indicating the two newsmen in the telephone cubicles.

Abrahams of the *Post-Telegram* cut in. "We'd better start shouting for some action."

They turned as a youngish man entered, holding some slips of paper. This was Cliff Howard, high-spirited and energetic, whose crewcut hair, rimless spectacles, and quietly patterned English ties were a familiar and popular sight at the airport. Most of these newsmen were personal friends of his.

"Thanks for staying put," he told them, and the two men at the phones terminated their calls and joined the others.

"Let's have it, Cliff," said one of them.

Howard glanced down at the papers in his hand. There was a film of perspiration on his forehead as he said that one of the fifty-six passengers was at the controls of the plane because the pilot and copilot were ill. "Captain Paul Treleaven, Cross-Canada's chief pilot, is talking him down—but the authorities thought it advisable to take precautionary measures in clearing the area and bringing in extra help in case of accident."

"Come on, Cliff, what are you giving us?" protested Abrahams. "How does it happen *both* the pilots are ill?"

Howard shrugged uncomfortably. "We don't yet know for sure. It may be some kind of stomach attack—"

Jessup interrupted. "Everything you've just said, our offices knew before we got here. What's the truth about the rumor of food poisoning? And who is the guy who's piloting the ship?"

Howard made a dramatic gesture of flipping notes to the floor. "Look, boys," he said expansively, "I'll lay it on the line for you. But if I stick my neck out, I know you'll play along with me. That's fair, isn't it? We don't want to get the thing out of perspective. What's happening tonight is a big emergency—I won't pretend it isn't—but everything that's humanly possible is being done to minimize the risk. The story, so far as my information goes, is that there has been an outbreak of sickness on the plane, which may very possibly be food poisoning. The Empress was late on arrival at Winnipeg, and the normal caterers were not available. Food obtained from another firm included fish, and some of that fish, gentlemen, may, and I repeat *may,* have been contaminated."

"The guy at the wheel! Who is he?" asked a reporter.

"Luckily there was a passenger on board who had piloted before, and he took over the controls with the most remarkable smoothness. Name of George Spencer. He flew extensively in the war in smaller aircraft—"

"What kind of smaller aircraft?" Jessup demanded.

"Spitfires, Mustangs, quite a wide range of—"

"Hold it. This man was a fighter pilot during the war? And you mean that an ex-wartime pilot who was used to single-engine fighters has now, after all these years, to handle a multiengine airliner?" Jessup said almost disbelievingly. There was a scramble as two of the newsmen broke away to the telephone booths.

"How long have we got before the crash?" Abrahams pressed.

Howard jerked around to him. "Don't assume that," he retorted. "She's due in round about an hour, maybe less."

"Suppose she overshoots into the water?" someone asked.

"That's not likely, but the police have alerted every available launch to stand by."

"Cliff," said Jessup, "how long will the gas last in this plane?"

"I can't say, but there's bound to be a safety margin," answered Howard, loosening his tie. He sounded far from convinced.

Jessup looked at him for a second or two with narrowed eyes. Then it struck him. "Wait a minute," he shot out. "If there's food poisoning on board, it can't be only the pilots who've come down with it?"

"A number of passengers are ill, but there's a doctor on board who is giving what treatment he can. We have further medical advice available on the radio if required."

Jessup pursued relentlessly. "The time factor in food poisoning is everything. If those people don't get down pretty damn soon, they could even die!"

"That's about it," Howard agreed, tight-lipped.

"But—but this story is of worldwide interest! What's the position up there now?"

"Well, about ten, fifteen minutes ago—"

"That's no good!" Jessup roared. "Get the position *now*, Cliff. Who's duty controller tonight? Ring him—or I will, if you like."

"No, not for a while, Jess, please. I tell you they're—"

Jessup gripped the public relations man by the shoulder. "This will be the biggest air story for years, and you know it. In an hour's time this place will be stiff with reporters, TV, the lot. You've got to help us now, unless you want us busting out all over the airport. Get us the exact present position and you can take a breather while we get our stories through."

"OK, OK. Ease off, will you?" Howard picked up an internal telephone from the table. "This is Howard. Control room, please. Hello, is Burdick there? Put him on, it's urgent. Hello, Harry? Cliff. The press are crowding up, Harry. They want the full situation as of now. They've got deadlines to meet."

"Of course!" snorted Burdick sarcastically in the control room. "Certainly! We'll arrange for the flight to crash before their deadlines. Anything for the newspapers!"

"Take it easy, Harry," urged Howard. "These guys are doing their job."

Burdick lowered the telephone and said to the controller, "Mr. Grimsell, things are boiling up a bit for Cliff Howard. Do you think Stan could take a few minutes out to talk to the press?"

"I think so," answered the controller. He looked over to his assistant. "We'd better keep those boys under control."

"And no point in holding back," Burdick advised. "Tell 'em the whole thing—up to and excluding this," and he nodded to the silent radio panel.

"I get it. Leave it to me." The assistant left the room.

"The assistant controller is coming down, Cliff," said Burdick, and he rang off. He heaved his bulk over to the radio panel, mopping his face with a crumpled handkerchief. "Are you getting anything?" he asked in a flat voice.

Treleaven shook his head. His face was gray with fatigue. "No," he said dully. "They've gone."

The controller rapped to the switchboard operator, "Teletype Calgary and Seattle, priority. See if they're still receiving 714."

"Come in, 714. Vancouver Control to 714. Come in, 714," called the radio operator steadily into the microphone.

Treleaven leaned against the radio desk. "Well," he said wearily, "this could be the end of the line."

"Calling 714, 714. Do you hear me? Come in, please."

"I can't take much more," said Burdick.

"Hold it!" exclaimed the radio operator.

"Did you get something?" asked the controller eagerly.

"I don't know. . . . I thought for a minute . . ." Bending close to the panel, the operator made adjustments to his fine-tuning controls. "Hello, 714, 714, this is Vancouver." He called over his shoulder, "I can hear *something* . . . it may be them. If it is, they're off frequency."

"Tell them to change frequency," said Treleaven.

"Flight 714," called the operator. "This is Vancouver. This is Vancouver. Change your frequency to 128.3. . . ."

Burdick plumped back onto a corner of the center table. "This can't happen—it can't," he protested, staring at the radio panel. "If we've lost them now, they'll die—every last one of them."

Like a man in a nightmare, his face streaked with sweat, Spencer fought to regain control of the aircraft, one hand on the throttle lever and the other gripped tightly on the wheel. Within him, oddly at variance with the strong sense of unreality, he felt scorching anger and self-disgust. Somewhere along the line, and quickly, he had not only lost altitude but practically all his airspeed, too. His brain refused to go back over the events of the last two minutes. Something had distracted him, that was all he could remember.

He felt an almost uncontrollable desire to scream. To scramble out and away from the controls and abandon everything. Run back into the warm, friendly-lit body of the aircraft, crying out, *I couldn't do it. I told you I couldn't do it, and you wouldn't listen to me. No man should be asked to do it. . . .*

"We're gaining height," came Janet's voice, incredibly level now. He remembered her with a shock, and in that moment the screaming inside his head became the wild shrieks of a woman passenger in the compartment behind.

He heard a man shouting, "He's not the pilot, I tell you! They're stretched out there, both of them. We're done for!"

"Shut up and sit down!" rapped Baird clearly.

"You can't order me about—"

"All right, Doctor," came the adenoidal tones of 'Otpot, the man from Lancashire, "just leave him to me. Now, you . . ."

Spencer shut his eyes for an instant in an effort to clear the dancing of the illuminated dials. Behind him he could hear the woman passenger, sobbing loudly now. He shot a glance at Janet. In the light from the instrument panel, her pale face looked almost translucent. He felt very ashamed.

"Trying to get the bus up as fast as I can," he said. "Daren't do more than a gentle climb or we'll lose way again."

Baird's voice called from the doorway, above the rising thunder of the engines, "What *is* going on in there?"

Spencer answered, "Sorry, Doc. I just couldn't hold her."

"It was my fault," said Janet.

"No, no," protested Spencer. "If it hadn't been for her, we'd have crashed. I just can't handle this thing."

"Rubbish," said Baird curtly. Then his voice was raised loudly to address the passengers. "Now listen to me, all of you. Panic is the most infectious disease of the lot, and the most lethal, too." The door slammed shut, cutting him off.

Janet said calmly, "I ought to be reporting to Captain Treleaven."

"Yes," agreed Spencer. "Tell him what's happened and that I'm regaining height."

Janet pressed her microphone button to transmit and called Vancouver. For the first time there was no immediate acknowledgment. She called again. There was nothing.

Spencer felt the familiar stab of fear. He forced himself to control it. "What's wrong?" he asked. "Are you sure you're on the air?"

"Yes—I think so."

"Blow into your mike. If it's alive, you'll hear yourself."

She did so. "Yes, I heard all right. Hello, Vancouver. This is 714. Can you hear me? Over."

Silence.

"Let me," said Spencer. He took his right hand from the throttle and depressed his microphone button. "Hello, Vancouver. Hello, Vancouver. This is Spencer, 714. Emergency. Come in, please."

The silence seemed as solid and as tangible as a wall.

"I'm getting a reading on the transmitting dial," said Spencer. "I'm sure we're sending OK." He tried again, with no result. "Calling all stations. Mayday, Mayday, Mayday. This is Flight 714, in serious trouble. Come in anybody. Over." The ether seemed completely dead. "That settles it. We must be off frequency."

"How could that have happened?"

"*Anything* could have happened, the way we were just now. You'll have to go round the dial, Janet."

"Isn't that risky—to change our frequency?"

"It's my guess it's already changed. All I know is that without the

315

radio I might as well put her nose down right now and get it over. I don't know where we are, and even if I did, I certainly couldn't land in one piece."

Janet slid out of her seat and reached up to the radio panel. She clicked the channel selector around slowly. There was a succession of crackles and splutters. "I've been all the way round," she said.

"Keep at it," Spencer told her. "You've got to get something. If we have to, we'll call on each channel in turn." There was a sudden, faraway voice. "Wait, what's that?" Janet clicked back hurriedly. "Give it more volume!"

". . . to 128.3," said the voice with startling nearness. "Vancouver to Flight 714. Change to frequency 128.3. Reply, please. Over."

"Keep it there," said Spencer to the girl. "Is that the setting? Thank our lucky stars for that. Better acknowledge it, quick."

Janet climbed back into her seat and called rapidly, "Hello, Vancouver, 714 answering. Receiving you loud and clear. Over."

A relieved voice came back. "This is Vancouver, 714. We lost you! What happened? Over."

"Vancouver, are we glad to hear you!" said Janet. "We had some trouble. The airplane stalled and the radio went off. But it's all right now—except for the passengers, they're not taking it too well. We're climbing again. Over."

"Hello, Janet." This time it was Treleaven speaking, in the same measured manner as before but clearly with immense thankfulness. "I'm glad you had the good sense to realize you were off frequency. George, you *must* watch your airspeed all the time. But there's one thing: if you've stalled and recovered, you obviously haven't lost your touch as a pilot."

"Did you get that?" Spencer asked Janet incredulously. They exchanged nervous smiles.

Treleaven was continuing. "You've probably had a bit of a scare, so we'll take it easy for a minute or two. While you're getting some height under you, I want you to give me readings from the instrument panel. We'll start with the fuel-tank gauges."

While Spencer recited the information the captain wanted, the door to the passenger deck opened and Baird looked in again, about to call to the two figures forward. He took in their concentration on the instrument panel and checked himself. Instead, he entered quietly, closed the door behind him, and dropped on one knee beside the forms of the pilot and first officer, using his ophthalmoscope as a flashlight to examine their faces. Dun had rolled partly out of his blankets and was lying with his knees drawn up, moaning softly. Pete appeared to be unconscious.

The doctor readjusted the covers, wrapping them in tightly. He remained crouched in thought for a few seconds. Then he rose, bracing himself against the tilt of the steadily climbing airplane. Janet was relaying figures into her microphone. Without a word the doctor let himself out, carefully sliding the door closed.

The passenger deck resembled a vast casualty ambulance. At intervals along the crowded cabin sick passengers lay swaddled in blankets. One or two were quite motionless, scarcely breathing. Others were twisting in pain while friends or relatives watched them fearfully or replaced damp cloths on their foreheads.

Bending over the man he had recently thrust back into his seat, 'Otpot was saying, "I don't blame you, see? 'Appen it's better sometimes to let off steam. But it don't do to go shouting off in front of the others who're feeling poorly, especially the ladies."

Temporarily subdued, the passenger, who was twice the size of 'Otpot, stared stonily at his own reflection in the cabin window by his seat. 'Otpot came along to the doctor, who patted his arm.

"You're quite a wizard," said Baird, in thanks.

"I'm more scared than he is," 'Otpot assured him fervently, "and that's a fact. Doctor . . . what d'you make of things now?"

"I don't know," Baird replied. His face was gaunt. "They had a little trouble up front. It's hardly surprising. Spencer is under a terrible strain. He's carrying more responsibility than any of us."

'Otpot put to him as quietly as he could, "What d'you really think, Doc? 'Ave we got a chance?"

Baird shook the question off in tired irritation. "Why ask me? There's always a *chance*, I suppose. But keeping an airplane in the air and getting it down without smashing it are two mighty different propositions. Either way, it isn't going to make much odds to some of the folk here before long."

He squatted down to look at Mrs. Childer, noting her pinched face, dry skin, and quick, shallow breathing.

Her husband demanded hoarsely, "Doctor, is there *nothing* we can do for her?"

Baird looked at the closed, sunken eyes of the woman. He said slowly, "Mr. Childer, you've a right to know the truth. We're making all the speed we possibly can, but at best it will be touch and go for your wife." Childer's mouth moved wordlessly, and Baird went on. "I've done what I could for her and I'll continue to do it, but it's pathetically little."

Childer found his voice. "I won't have you say that. Whatever happens, I'm grateful to you, Doctor."

"Of course he is," interposed 'Otpot heartily. "No one could've done more than you, Doc. An absolute marvel, that's what."

Baird smiled faintly, his hand on the woman's forehead. "Kind words don't alter the case," he said. "You're a man of courage, Mr. Childer, and you have my respect." The moment of truth, he thought bitterly; inside another hour we shall all very probably be dead. No romantic heroics—just the plain truth.

"I'm telling you," Childer was saying with emotion, "if we get out of this, I'll have everyone know what we owe to you."

Baird collected his thoughts. "What's that?" he grunted. "I'd give plenty to have two or three saline drips aboard." He rose. "Carry on as before, Mr. Childer. Make sure she's really warm. Keep her lips moistened. Your wife has lost a very critical amount of body fluids."

In the control room at Vancouver, Harry Burdick was replacing some of his own body fluid with a container of coffee. In addition to the microphone held in his hand, Treleaven now had on a telephone headset, and into the latter he was asking, "Radar. Are you getting anything at all?"

From another part of the building, the chief radar operator answered in a conversational tone, "Not a thing yet."

"I can't understand it," Treleaven said to the controller. "They ought to be in range now."

Burdick volunteered, "Don't forget he lost speed in that last practice."

"Yes, that's so," Treleaven agreed. Into his headset he said, "Radar, let me know the instant that you get something." To the controller, "I daren't bring him down through cloud without knowing where he actually is. Ask the Air Force for another check, will you, Mr. Grimsell?" He nodded to the radio operator. "Put me on the air. Hello, 714. Now listen carefully, George. We are going to go through that drill again, but before we start I want to explain a few things you may have forgotten or that only apply to big airplanes. Are you with me? Over."

Janet replied, "Go ahead, Vancouver. Over."

"Right, 714. Now before you can land, certain checks and adjustments must be carried out in addition to the landing drill you just practiced. I'll tell you when and how to do them later. Now I just want to run over them to prepare you. First, the hydraulic booster pump must be switched on. Then the brake pressure must be showing about 900 to 1000 pounds a square inch. Next, after the wheels are down, you'll turn on the fuel booster pumps and check that the gas feed is sufficient. Lastly, the mixture has to be made good and rich and the propellers set. We'll take it step by step as you come in so that Janet can set the switches. Now I'm going to tell you where each of them is. Here we go. . . ."

Janet and Spencer identified each control as directed.

"Hello, Vancouver. We're OK on that."

"Right, 714. Check again that you are in level flight. Over."

"Hello, Vancouver. Yes, flying level now and above cloud."

"Right, 714. George, let's have 15 degrees of flap again, speed 140, and we'll go through the wheel-lowering routine. Watch that airspeed like a hawk. If you're ready, let's go. . . ."

Grimly, Spencer began the procedure, following Treleaven's instruction with complete concentration while Janet anxiously counted off the airspeed and operated the flap and landing-gear levers. Once again they felt the sharp jolt as their speed was arrested. The first streaks of dawn were glimmering to eastward.

In the control room, Treleaven gulped some cold coffee. He looked haggard, with a blue stubble around his chin.

"How do you read the situation now?" Burdick said.

"As well as can be expected," said the captain, "but time's running short. He should have at least a dozen runs through this flap and wheels drill. With luck we'll get about three in before he's overhead—that is, if he's on course."

"You'll give him practice approaches?" put in the controller.

"I must. Without them I wouldn't give a red cent for his chances, not with the experience he's got. I'll see how he shapes up. Otherwise . . ." Treleaven hesitated.

"Otherwise what?" Burdick prompted.

Treleaven rounded on them. "We'd better face facts," he said. "That man up there is frightened out of his wits, and with good reason. If his nerve doesn't hold, they may stand more chance by ditching offshore in the ocean."

"But—the impact!" Burdick exclaimed. "And the sick people! And the aircraft would be a total loss."

"It would be a calculated risk," said Treleaven icily. "If our friend looks like he will pile up all over the field, your airplane will be a write-off anyway."

"Hell, yes, I guess so," said Burdick uncomfortably.

"And with the added danger," continued Treleaven, "that if he crashes here, fire is almost certain and we'll be lucky to save anyone. Whereas if he puts down on the ocean, he'll surely break up the airplane, but we stand a chance of saving *some* of the passengers. With practically no wind the water is pretty calm. We'd belly-land him by radar as near as we could to rescue craft."

"Get the Navy," the controller ordered his assistant. "Air Force, too. Air-sea rescue are already standing by. Have them put out off-shore and await radio instructions."

"I don't want to do it," said Treleaven, turning back to the wall map. "It would amount to abandoning the very sick passengers. But it may be necessary." He spoke into his headset. "Radar, are you getting anything?"

"Still nothing," came the even reply. "Hold it, though. This may be something coming up. . . . Yes, Captain. I have him now. He's ten miles south of track. Have him turn right to a heading of 265."

"Nice work," said Treleaven.

He nodded to be put on the air as the switchboard operator called across, "Air Force report visual contact, sir. ETA thirty-eight minutes."

"Right." He raised the microphone. "Hello, 714. Have you carried out the reverse procedure for flaps and landing gear?"

"Yes, Vancouver. Over," came the girl's voice.

"Any trouble this time? Flying straight and level?"

"Everything's all right, Vancouver. The pilot says—so far." They heard her give a nervous little laugh.

"That's fine, 714. We have you on radar now. You're off course ten miles to the south. I want you to bank carefully to the right and then place the aircraft on a heading of 265. Is that clear? Over."

"Understood, Vancouver."

Treleaven glanced out of the window. The darkness outside had lightened very slightly. "At least they'll be able to see a little," he said, "though not until the last minutes."

"I'm going to put everybody on standby," said the controller. He called to his assistant, "Warn the tower, Stan. Tell them to alert the fire people." Then, to the switchboard operator, "Give me the city police."

Treleaven had slumped into a chair, his head bowed, a hand over his eyes, not hearing the confused murmur of voices about him. But at the first splutter as the amplifier came alive he was on his feet, reaching for the microphone.

"Hello, Vancouver," called Janet. "We are now on a heading of 265 as instructed. Over."

"Right, 714. You're doing splendidly," said Treleaven cheerfully. "Let's have it all again, shall we? This will be the last time before you reach the airport, George, so make it good."

Beside him the controller was speaking with quiet urgency into his telephone. "Yes, they'll be with us in about half an hour. Let's get the show on the road."

CHAPTER SEVEN

SPENCER tried to ease his aching legs. His whole body felt pummeled and bruised. In the effort of concentration he had expended enormous quantities of nervous energy; the moment he relaxed, he was left utterly drained of strength. He was conscious of his hands trembling and made no attempt to check them. All the time an interior voice, now every bit as real to him and as independent as the one in his earphones, kept telling him, *Whatever you do, don't let go. Remember, it was like this in the war. You thought you'd reached the end, with not another ounce left in you. But every time there was something left in the bag—one last reserve you never knew you had.*

He looked at Janet, willing himself to speak. "How did we make out that time?" he asked, knowing he was near collapse.

"We did pretty well," she said brightly. "I thought Captain Treleaven sounded pleased, didn't you?"

321

"Hardly heard him," he said, turning his head from side to side to relieve the muscles in his neck. "How many times have we done the flap and wheel routine now—three? If he asks us to do it once more, I'll . . ." *Steady on*, his inner voice admonished him. *Don't let her see what a state you're in.*

"Have you noticed, the sun's coming up behind us," said Janet. She leaned over to wipe his face and forehead with a handkerchief.

"Why sure," he lied, lifting his eyes. Even ahead, to the west, the carpet of cloud was tinged with pink and gold, and there, too, the vast canopy of sky had perceptibly lightened. To the south, on the port beam, he could see two mountaintops, isolated like islands in a tumbling ocean of cotton wool. "We won't be long now." He paused. "Janet."

"Yes?"

"Before we go down, have a last—I mean, another look at the pilot and copilot. We'll probably bump a bit, and we don't want them thrown about."

Janet flashed a grateful smile at him and slipped off her headset. As she rose from her seat, the door to the flight deck opened and Baird looked in.

"Oh—you're off the radio," he observed.

"I was just going to have a look at the captain and copilot, to make sure they're secure," she said.

"No need to," he told her. "I did it a few minutes ago, when you were busy."

"Doctor," called Spencer, "how are things with you back there?"

"That's why I looked in," said Baird tersely. "We're running out of time fast. I'd like to have a diagnostic check with a doctor down there, but I guess it's more important to hold the air open for flying the machine. How long is it likely to be now?"

"Well under the half hour, I'd say. How does that sound?"

"I don't know," Baird said doubtfully. "There are two patients in a state of complete prostration, and there are several others who'll soon be just as bad, unless I'm very wrong."

The earphones came to life. "Hello, 714. This is Vancouver."

Spencer waved Janet back into her seat and she hurriedly donned her headset.

"Well, I'll get back," said Baird. "Good luck, anyway."

"Wait a minute," Spencer told him.

"This is 714," Janet was acknowledging into her microphone. "We'll be with you in a moment. Hold, please."

"Doctor," said Spencer quickly. "I don't have to fool you. This may be rough. Just about anything is liable to happen." The doctor said nothing. "They may get a bit jumpy back there. See that they're kept in their seats, huh?"

Baird replied in a gruff tone, "Do the best you can and leave me to take care of the rest." He thumped the younger man lightly on the shoulder and made his way aft.

"OK," said Spencer to the girl.

"Go ahead, Vancouver," she called.

"Hello, 714," responded the clear, confident voice of Treleaven. "Now that you've had a breather since that last run-through, George, we'd better press on again. You should be receiving me well now. Will you check, please? Over."

"Tell him I've been having a few minutes with my feet up," said Spencer. "And tell him he's coming in about strength niner." Strength niner, he thought. You really have dug that one up out of your past.

". . . a short rest," Janet was saying, "and we hear you strength niner."

"That's the way, George. Our flying practice has slowed you down a bit, though that's all to the good as it will be getting light when you come in. You are now in the holding position and ready to start losing height. First, I want to speak to Janet. Janet, when we make this landing we want you to follow the emergency crash procedures for protection of passengers. Over."

"I understand, Captain. Over."

"One more thing, Janet. Just before the landing we will ask the pilot to sound the emergency bell. And George—the switch for that bell is right over the copilot's seat and it's painted red."

"Can you see it?" asked Spencer without looking up.

"Yes," said Janet, "it's here."

"Janet," continued Treleaven, "that bell will be your warning for final precautions, because I want you to be back then with the passengers."

"Tell him no," Spencer cut in. "I must have you up front."

"Hello, Vancouver," said Janet. "I understand your instructions, but the pilot needs me to help him. Over."

There was a long pause. Then, "All right, 714," Treleaven answered. "I appreciate the position. But it's your duty, Janet, to see that all crash precautions are taken before we can think about landing. Is there anyone you can delegate this to?"

"What about the doctor?" suggested Spencer.

She hesitated, then pressed the button to transmit. "Hello, Vancouver. Dr. Baird will have to keep a watch on the sick passengers as we land. I think he's the best person to carry out the emergency drill. There's another man who can help him. Over."

"Hello, Janet. Very well. Leave the radio now, go aft, and explain the procedure very carefully to the doctor. There must be no possibility of error." Janet laid aside her headset and climbed out of her seat. "Now, George," Treleaven went on, "watch that you keep to your present course; I'll give you any corrections as necessary. In a minute I'll give you a cockpit check of the really essential things. Some of them you'll remember from your old flying days. Be certain you know where they are. We'll have as many dummy runs as you like, but when you do finally come in the procedure must be carried out properly and completely. We'll start on the first check as soon as Janet gets back on the air."

In the control room at Vancouver, Treleaven looked up at the electric wall clock and back at the controller. "How much gas have they got?" he demanded.

Grimsell picked up the clipboard from the table. "In flying time, enough for about ninety minutes," he said.

"You figure there's plenty of time for circuits and approaches, don't you?" Burdick asked.

"There's got to be," said Treleaven. "This is a first-flight solo. But keep a strict check on it, will you, Mr. Grimsell? We must have plenty in hand for a long run-in over the ocean if I decide as a last measure to ditch."

"Mr. Burdick," hailed the switchboard operator, "your president is on the line."

Burdick swore. "Tell him I can't speak to him now. Tell him 714 is in holding position and his prayers are as good as ours."

The assistant to the controller, his hand cupped over an internal telephone, called to his chief, "It's Howard. He says the press are—"

"I'll take it." The controller seized the telephone. "Listen, Cliff. We're accepting no more nonoperational calls. Things are far too critical now. . . . Yes, I know. They'll see for themselves." He replaced the receiver with a bang.

Paul Treleaven stood by the radio panel, his fingers drumming absently, his eyes fixed on the clock.

OUTSIDE the airport, in the first light of dawn, the emergency measures were in full swing. At a local hospital, a nurse hung up the telephone and spoke to a doctor working at an adjacent table. They hurried out and a few minutes later the overhead door to the vehicle bay of the hospital slid up, letting out two ambulances.

At the sound of a bell in a city firehouse, one of the crews held on reserve slapped down their cards, snatched up their equipment, and raced for the door.

Near Sea Island bridge, police were shepherding families from a group of houses into two buses. Most of the people had thrown street clothes hastily over their night attire. A small girl, staring intently at the sky, tripped over her pajamas. She was picked up by a policeman and deposited in a bus. He waved to the driver to get started.

"HELLO, Vancouver," called Janet, a little breathlessly. "I've given the necessary instructions. Over."

"Good girl," said Treleaven with relief. "Now, George," he went on quickly, "the clock is running a little against us. First, reset your altimeter to 30.1. Then throttle back slightly, but hold your airspeed steady until you're losing height at five hundred feet per minute. You'll have a long descent through cloud."

Spencer spread his fingers around the throttles and gently moved them back. The climb-and-descent indicator fell slowly and a little unevenly to 600, then rose again to remain fairly steady at 500.

"Here comes the cloud," he said, as the gleams of daylight were abruptly blotted out. "Ask him how high the cloud base is below."

Janet repeated the question.

"Ceiling is around two thousand feet," said Treleaven, "and you should break out of cloud about fifteen miles from the airport. Now, George, this is a little tricky. Keep a constant check on that descent indicator, but at the same time, if you can, I want you to pinpoint the controls in a first run-through of landing procedure. Think you can manage that?"

Spencer did not trouble to answer. His eyes fixed on the instrument panel, he just set his lips and nodded.

"Yes, Vancouver," said Janet. "We'll try."

"OK, then. If anything gets out of hand, tell me immediately." Treleaven frowned in concentration as he looked at the blank spot on the wall, visualizing the cockpit of the aircraft. "George, this is what you will do as you come in. First, switch the hydraulic booster pump *on*. Remember, just fix these things in your mind— don't do anything now. The gauge is on the extreme left of the panel, under and to the left of the gyro control. Got it? Over."

He heard Janet's voice reply, "The pilot knows that one, Vancouver, and has located the switch."

"Right, 714. Surprising how it comes back, isn't it, George?" Treleaven pulled out a handkerchief and wiped the back of his neck. "Next, you'll have to turn off the deicer control. That's bound to be on and will show on the gauge on the right of the panel, just in front of Janet. The flow control is next to it. That one's easy, but the control must be off before you land. Watching the descent indicator, George? Next item is brake pressure. There are two gauges, one for the inboard brake and the other for the outboard. They're immediately to the right of the hydraulic boost which you've just found. Over."

After a pause, Janet confirmed. "Found them, Vancouver. They're showing 950 and—er—1010 pounds—is it per square inch?—each."

"Then they're OK, but they must be checked again before landing. Now, the gills. They must be one-third closed. The switch is right by Janet's left knee, and you'll see it's marked in thirds. Are you with me? Over."

"Yes, I see it, Vancouver. Over."

"You can work that one, Janet. Next to it, on the same bank of switches, are the port and starboard intercooler switches. They're clearly marked. They will have to be opened fully. Make sure of that, Janet, won't you? The next and most important thing is the landing gear. You've been all through the drill, but go over it thoroughly in your mind first, starting with the flap movement and ending with the wheels fully down and locked. Full flap should be put on when the plane is very near touchdown and you're sure you're going to come in. I shall direct you on that. Is this understood by both of you? Over."

"Tell him yes, thanks," said Spencer, his eyes on the panel.

"OK, 714. When you're on the approach, and after the wheels are down, the fuel booster pumps must be turned on. Otherwise your supply of gas might be cut off at the worst moment. The switch for these is at five o'clock from the autopilot, just behind the mixture controls."

Janet was scanning the panel in a daze. "*Where?*" she almost whispered to Spencer. He peered at the board and located the little switch.

"There." His finger pointed at it.

"All right, Vancouver," she said weakly.

"Now the mixture is to be changed to auto rich. I know George has been itching for that, so I won't say any more—he'll handle that all right. Then you have to set the propellers until the green lights under the switches come on. They're just about touching George's right knee, I should think. Got them?"

"Pilot says yes, Vancouver."

"Lastly, the superchargers. After the wheels are down, these must be set in the takeoff position—that is, up, on your aircraft. They are, of course, the four levers to the left of the throttles. Well, now. Any questions about all that? Over."

Spencer looked at Janet despairingly. "We'll never remember."

"Hello, Vancouver," said Janet. "We don't think we'll be able to remember it."

"You don't have to, 714. I'll remember it for you. There are some other points, too, which we'll deal with when we come to them. I want to go over these operations with you thoroughly, George, so that when I give the word you'll carry out the action without too much loss of concentration."

"Ask him about time," said Spencer. "How much have we got?"

Janet put the question to Vancouver.

"As I said, George, you've got all the time in the world—but we just don't want to waste any. You'll be over the airport in about twelve minutes. Don't let that bother you. There'll be as much time as you like for further practice." A pause. "Radar reports a course adjustment necessary, George. Change your heading five degrees to 260, please. Over."

Treleaven switched off his microphone and spoke to the controller. "They're well on the glide path now," he said. "As soon as we've got visual contact, I'll level them off and take them around for circuits and drills. We'll see how they shape up after that."

"Everything's set here," said the controller. He called to his assistant, "Put the entire field on alert."

"Hello, Vancouver," came Janet's voice over the amplifier. "We have now changed course to 260. Over."

"OK, 714. Let's have a check on your height, please. Over."

"Vancouver," answered Janet after a few seconds, "our height is twenty-five hundred feet."

"That's fine, George," Treleaven said. "You'll be coming out of cloud any minute. As soon as you do, look for the airport beacon. Over."

On his headset Treleaven heard the radar operator report, "Fifteen miles from the field."

"Bad news," Burdick told him. "The weather's thickening."

"Can't help that now," rapped Treleaven. "Get the tower," he told the controller. "Tell them to light up—put on everything they've got. And we'll be going up there in a minute. I'll want their radio on the same frequency as this."

"Right!" said the controller, lifting a telephone.

"Hello, 714," Treleaven called. "You are now fifteen miles from the airport. Are you still in cloud, George? Over."

A long pause. Suddenly the radio crackled into life, catching Janet in midsentence. She was saying excitedly, ". . . it's lifting very slightly. I thought I saw something. . . . Yes, there it is! Do you see it, Mr. Spencer? It's right ahead. We can see the beacon, Vancouver!"

"They've broken through!" Treleaven shouted it. "All right, George," he called into the microphone, "level off at two thousand feet and wait for instructions. I'm moving to the control tower now, so you won't hear from me for a few minutes. We'll decide on the runway to use at the last minute, so you can land into wind. Before that you'll need to make some dummy runs, to practice your landing approaches. Over."

They heard Spencer's voice say, "I'll take this, Janet." There was a broken snatch of conversation in the plane, then Spencer came on the air again, biting off his words.

"No dice, Vancouver. The situation up here doesn't allow. We're coming straight in."

"He can't!" Burdick shouted.

"Don't be a fool, George," said Treleaven urgently. "You've *got* to have some practice runs."

"I'm holding my line of descent," Spencer intoned deliberately, his voice shaking slightly. "There are people up here dying. Dying! Can you get that into your heads? I'll stand as much chance on the first run-in as I will on the tenth."

"Let me talk to him," appealed the controller.

"No," said Treleaven, "there's no time for argument." His face was white. A vein in his temple pulsed. "We've got to act fast. By all the rules he's in command of that airplane. I'm going to accept his decision."

"You can't do that," Burdick protested. "Don't you realize—"

"All right, George," Treleaven called, "if that's the way you want it. Stand by and level off. We're going to the tower now. Good luck to us all. Listening out." He ripped off his headset and shouted to the others, "Let's go." The three men leaped out of the room and raced along the corridor, Burdick bringing up the rear. Ignoring the elevator, they bounded up the stairs and burst into the tower control room. An operator stood at the shining sweep of window, studying the lightening sky through night binoculars. "There he is!" he announced. Treleaven snatched up a second pair of glasses, took a quick look, then put them down.

"All right," he said, panting. "Let's decide on the runway."

"Zero-eight," said the operator. "It's the longest and it's pretty well into the wind."

"Radar!" called the captain.

"Here, sir."

Treleaven crossed to a side table on which appeared, under glass, a plan of the airport. He used a thick chinagraph pencil to mark the proposed course of the aircraft.

"Here's what we do. We'll turn him so he begins to make a wide left-hand circuit, and at the same time bring him down to a thousand feet. I'll start the prelanding check here, then we'll take him over the sea and make a slow turnaround on to final. That clear?"

"Yes, Captain," said the operator.

Treleaven took a headset that was handed to him and put it on. "Is this hooked up to the radar room?" he asked.

"Yes, sir. Right here."

The controller was reciting into a telephone-type microphone, "Tower to all emergency vehicles. Runway is zero-eight. Zero-eight. Airport tenders take positions numbers one and two. Civilian equipment number three. All ambulances to positions numbers four and five. No vehicle will leave its position until the aircraft has passed it. Start now."

Leaning down on the top of a control console, the captain flicked the switch of a desk microphone. At his elbow the spools of a tape recorder began to revolve.

"Hello, George Spencer," he called in a steady, even tone. "This is Paul Treleaven in Vancouver tower. Do you read me? Over."

Janet's voice filled the control room. "Yes, Captain. You are loud and clear. Over."

From the headset the calm voice of the radar operator reported, "Ten miles. Turn to a heading of 253."

"All right, George. You are now ten miles from the airport. Turn to a heading of 253. Throttle back and begin to lose height to a thousand feet. Janet, put the preliminary landing procedure in motion for the passengers. Neither of you acknowledge any further transmissions unless you wish to ask a question."

Removing his hands one at a time from the control column, Spencer flexed his fingers. He managed a grin at the girl beside him. "OK, Janet, do your stuff," he told her.

She unhooked a microphone from the cabin wall and pressed the button, speaking into it. "Attention please, everyone. Attention please." Her voice cracked. She gripped the microphone hard and cleared her throat. "Will you please resume your seats and fasten your safety belts. No smoking, please. We shall be landing in a few minutes. Thank you."

"Well done," Spencer complimented her. "Just like any old landing, eh?"

She tried to smile back, biting her lower lip. "Well, not quite."

"You've got plenty of what it takes," said Spencer soberly. "I'd like you to know I couldn't have held on this far without—" He broke off, his eyes on the instruments. "Janet," he said, "we haven't much more time. But I want to make sure you understand why I must try to get her down—somehow—on the first shot."

"I do understand," she said quietly. She had clipped her safety belt, and her hands were clenched together tightly in her lap.

"Well, I want to say thanks," he went on, stumblingly. "You know, if anyone does, just how lousy I am at this. But taking turns around the field won't help. And some of the folks in the back are getting worse every minute. Better for them to . . . to take their chance quickly."

"I told you," she said. "You don't have to explain."

He shot her a look of alarm, feeling somehow exposed to her. She was watching the airspeed indicator; he could not see her face. He glanced away, back along the broad stretch of wing behind them. It was describing with infinite slowness the tiny segment of an arc, balancing on its tip the misty blue-gray outline of a hillside twinkling with road lamps. Sliding under the body of the aircraft, on the other quarter, were the distantly blazing lights of the airport. They seemed pathetically small and far away, like a child's carelessly discarded string of red and amber beads.

He could feel his heart thumping as his body made its own emergency preparations, as if aware that what remained of its life might now be measured in minutes, even seconds.

He heard himself say, "Here we go, then. This is it, Janet. I'm starting to lose height—*now*."

CHAPTER EIGHT

HARRY Burdick lowered his binoculars and handed them back to the tower controller.

From the observation balcony which girdled the tower, the two men took a last look over the field, at the gasoline tankers pulled well back from the apron and, clearly visible in the half-light, the groups of figures watching from the boarding bays. The throb of truck engines from the far end of the field seemed to add to the oppressive, almost unbearable air of expectancy that enveloped the whole airport.

Searching his mind for any possible fault, Burdick reviewed Treleaven's plan. The aircraft would arrive overhead at something just below two thousand feet and then carry on out over the Strait of Georgia, descending gradually on this long, downwind leg while the last cockpit check was executed. Then one wide about-turn on to the final approach would give Spencer maximum time to regulate his descent and settle down carefully for the run-in.

A good plan, one which would take advantage, too, of the slowly increasing light of dawn. What would it mean to those of the passengers who were well enough to care? They would watch Sea Island and the airport pass beneath them, followed by the wide sweep of the bay, then the island getting shakily nearer again as their emergency pilot made his last adjustments to the controls. Burdick sensed, as if he were up there, the suffocating tension, the dreadful choking knowledge that they might well be staring death in the face. He shivered. In his sweat-soaked shirt, without a jacket, he felt the chill of the early morning air like a knife.

"We are on a heading of 253." The girl's voice carried to them from the radio amplifier. "We are now losing height rapidly."

His eyes shadowed with anxiety, Burdick glanced meaningfully into the face of the young man at his side. Without a word they turned and reentered the great glass surround of the control tower. Treleaven and Grimsell were crouched before the desk microphone, their features bathed in the glow from the runway light indicators set into the control console in front of them.

"Wind still OK?" asked the captain.

Grimsell nodded. "Slightly across runway zero-eight, but that's still our best bet."

"Radar," said Treleaven into his headset, "keep me fed the whole time, whether or not you can hear that I'm on the air. This won't be a normal talk-down. Scrap procedure the instant 714 runs into trouble. Cut in and yell."

Burdick tapped him on the shoulder. "Captain," he urged, "what about getting him to hold until the light's better and he's had—"

"The decision's been made," said Treleaven curtly. "The guy's nervy enough. If we argue with him now, he's finished." He continued in a quieter tone, "I understand your feelings, Harry. But understand his, too. He's on a razor-edge."

"What if he comes in badly?" said Grimsell. "What's your plan?"

"He probably will, let's face it," Treleaven retorted grimly. "If it's hopeless, I'll try to bring him round again, unless it's obvious he doesn't stand a chance. Then I'll try to insist that he put down in the ocean." He listened for a moment to the calm recital of radar readings in his earphones, then pressed the switch of the microphone. "George. Let your airspeed come back to 160 knots and hold it steady there."

The amplifier came alive as 714 took the air. There was an agonizing pause before Janet's voice intoned, "We are still losing height. Over."

Like a huge and ponderous bird, the Empress moved slowly over the Fraser River. To the right the bridge from the mainland to Sea Island was just discernible.

"Good," said Treleaven. "Now set your mixture controls to take-off—that is, up to the top position, George." He fixed his eyes on his wristwatch, counting the sweep of the second hand. "Take your time. When you're ready to adjust your carburetor controls, they're just forward of the throttles."

In the aircraft, Spencer peered apprehensively from one control to the next, his face a rigid mask. He heard Treleaven's voice resume its inexorable monologue. "The next thing, George, is to set the air filter to ram and the superchargers to low. Take your time, now." Spencer looked about him wildly. "The air-filter control is the single lever below the mixture controls. Move it into the up position."

"Can you see it, Janet?" asked Spencer anxiously.

"Yes. Yes, I have it." She added quickly, "Look—you can see the long main runway!"

"*Plenty* long, I hope," Spencer gritted, not lifting his head.

"The supercharger controls," continued Treleaven, "are four levers to the right of the mixture controls. Move them to the up position also."

"Got them?" said Spencer.

"Yes."

"Good girl." He was conscious of the horizon line dipping and rising in front of him, but dared not release his eyes from the panel. The roar of the engines took on a fluctuating tone.

"Now let's have that 15 degrees of flap," Treleaven instructed. "Down to the second notch. The indicator dial is in the center of the main panel. When you have 15 degrees on, bring your airspeed back slowly to 140 knots and adjust your trim for level flight. As soon as you've done that, switch the hydraulic booster pump on—extreme left, by the gyro control."

Through Treleaven's headset the radar operator interposed, "Turn on to 225. I'm getting a height reading, Captain. He's all over the place. Nine hundred, up to 1300."

"Change course to 225," said Treleaven. "And watch your height. It's too irregular. Try to keep steady at 1000 feet."

"He's dropping off fast," said the operator. Eleven hundred . . . 1000 . . . 900 . . . 800 . . . 700. . . ."

"Watch your height!" Treleaven warned. "Use more throttle! Keep the nose up!"

"Six fifty . . . 600 . . . 550. . . ."

"Get back that height!" barked Treleaven. "Get it back! You need a thousand feet."

"Five fifty . . . 450 . . ." called off the operator, calm but sweating. "This isn't good, Captain. Four hundred . . . 400 . . . 450 . . . He's going up. Five hundred. . . ."

For a moment Treleaven cracked. He swung around to Burdick. "He can't fly it!" he shouted. "Of course he can't fly it!"

"Keep talking to him!" Burdick spat out, seizing Treleaven's arm. "Keep talking! Tell him what to do."

Treleaven grabbed the microphone. "Spencer," he said urgently, "you can't come straight in! Listen to me. You've *got* to do some circuits and practice that approach. You've enough fuel for two hours' flying. Stay up, man! Stay up!"

But Spencer's voice came through. "I'm coming in. Do you hear me? *I'm coming in.* There are people up here who'll die in less than an hour, never mind two. I may bend the airplane a bit—that's a chance we have to take. Now get on with the landing check. Wheels down, Janet."

"All right, George," said Treleaven heavily. He had recovered his composure, but a muscle in his jaw twitched convulsively. He spoke with his former crispness. "If your landing gear is down, check for the three green lights, remember? Keep your heading steady on 225. Increase your throttle setting slightly to hold your airspeed now the wheels are down. Adjust your trim and keep all the height you can. Check that the brake pressure is showing around 1000 pounds. Then set the gills to one third closed. D'you remember, Janet? The switch is by your left knee and it's marked in thirds. Answer me only if I'm going too fast. . . ."

As Treleaven went on, his voice filling the hushed control tower, Burdick moved to the plate-glass window, searching the sky low on the horizon. The dawn light was murky, retarded by the thick cloud banks. He heard Treleaven instruct a gentle 180-degree turn

334

to the left, to bring the aircraft back for its approach, impressing on Spencer to take it slowly while the last checks were carried out. The captain's precise monotone formed a somber background to Burdick's frantically worried thoughts.

"Now advance your propeller settings," Treleaven was saying, "so that the tachometers give a reading of 2250 rpm on each engine. Don't acknowledge."

Spencer repeated the rpm figure to himself as he made the adjustment. "Janet," he said, "let me hear the airspeed."

"It's 130 . . ." she began tonelessly, "125 . . . 120 . . . 125. . . ."

In the control tower, Treleaven listened to the steady voice from the radar room. "Height is still uneven. Nine hundred feet."

"George," said Treleaven, "let your airspeed come back to 120 knots and adjust your trim. Repeat, airspeed 120." He looked down at his watch. "Take it nice and easy, now."

"Still losing height," reported the radar operator. "Eight hundred feet . . . 750 . . . 700. . . ."

"You're losing height!" rapped out Treleaven. "Open up—open up! You must keep at around a thousand feet."

Janet continued her reading of the airspeed: "One ten . . . 110 . . . 105 . . . 110 . . . 110 . . . 120 . . . 120 . . . steady at 120. . . ."

"Come up . . . come up!" Spencer growled between his teeth, hauling on the control column. "It doesn't respond! It doesn't respond at all."

"One twenty-five . . . 130 . . . 130 . . . steady on 130. . . ."

"Height coming up to 900 feet," intoned the radar operator. "Nine fifty . . . on 1000 now. Maintain 1000."

Treleaven called to the tower controller, "He's turning on to final. Put out your runway lights, except zero-eight." He spoke into the microphone. "Straighten out on a heading between 074 and 080. Watch your airspeed and your height. Keep at a thousand feet until I tell you."

In one series after another the strings of lights half sunken into the grass beside the runways flicked off, leaving just one line on either side of the main landing strip.

"Come out of your turn, George, when you're ready," said Treleaven, "and line up with the runway you'll see directly ahead of you. It's raining, so you'll want your windshield wipers. The switch is down at the right on the copilot's side."

335

"Find it, Janet," said Spencer.

"Hold your height at a thousand feet, George. We've taken you a long way out, so you have lots of time. Have Janet look for the landing-light switch. It's in the panel overhead, a little left of center."

"Can you find the switch?" asked Spencer.

"Just a minute . . . yes, I've got it."

Spencer stole a quick look ahead. "My God," he breathed. The lights of the runway, brilliant pinpoints in the blue-gray overcast of dawn, seemed at this distance to be incredibly narrow, like a short section of railway track.

"Correct your course," said Treleaven. "Line yourself up straight and true. Hold that height, George. Now listen carefully. Aim to touch down about a third of the way along the runway. There's a slight crosswind from the left, so be ready with gentle right rudder." Spencer brought the nose slowly around. "If you land too fast, use the emergency brakes. You can work them by pulling the red handle immediately in front of you. And if that doesn't stop you, cut the four ignition switches which are over your head."

"Janet, if I want those switches off, it'll be in a hurry," said Spencer. "So if I shout, don't lose any time about it." His throat was parched; it felt full of grit.

"All right," Janet replied in a whisper. She clasped her hands together to stop them shaking.

"It won't be long now. What about the emergency bell?"

"I hadn't forgotten. I'll ring it just before touchdown."

"Watch that airspeed. Call it off."

"One twenty . . . 115 . . . 120. . . ."

"Begin descent, four hundred feet a minute," said the radar operator. "Check landing gear and flaps. Hold present heading."

"All right, George," said Treleaven, "put down full flap. Bring your airspeed back to 115, adjust your trim, and start losing height at 400 feet a minute. I'll repeat that. Full flap, airspeed 115, let down at 400 feet a minute. Hold your present heading." He turned to Grimsell. "This is it. In sixty seconds we'll know."

They listened to the approaching whine of engines. Treleaven took a pair of binoculars the controller handed him.

"Janet, give me full flap!" said Spencer. She thrust the lever down all the way. "Height and airspeed—call them off!"

"A thousand feet . . . speed 130 . . . 800 feet, speed 120 . . . 700 feet, speed 105. We're going down too quickly!"

"Get back that height!" Treleaven shouted. "Get back! You're losing height too fast."

"I know, I know!" Spencer shouted back. He pushed the throttles forward. "Keep watching, Janet."

"Six fifty feet, speed 100 . . . 400 feet, speed 100. . . ."

Eyes smarting with sweat in his almost feverish concentration, Spencer juggled to correlate speed with an even path of descent, conscious with a deep, sickening terror of the relentless approach of the runway, nearer with every second. The aircraft swayed from side to side, engines alternately revving and falling.

Burdick yelled, "Look at him! He's got no control!"

Keeping his glasses leveled at the oncoming aircraft, Treleaven snapped into the microphone, "Open up! Open up! You're losing height too fast! Watch the airspeed, for God's sake. Your nose is too high—open up quickly or she'll stall! *Open up!*"

"He's heard you," said Grimsell. "He's recovering."

"Me, too, I hope," said Burdick.

The radar operator announced, "Still a hundred feet below glide path. Fifty feet below glide path."

"Get up—up," urged Treleaven. "If you haven't rung the alarm bell yet, do it now. Seats upright, passengers' heads down."

As the shrill warning rang out in the aircraft, Baird roared at the top of his voice, "Everybody down! Hold as tight as you can!"

Moving clumsily in his haste, Childer tried to gather his motionless wife to him, then leaned across her as far as he could. From somewhere midship came the sob-racked sound of a prayer and, farther back, an exclamation from one of the rye-drinking quartet, "God help us—this is it!"

"Shut up!" rapped 'Otpot. "Save your breath!"

In the tower, Grimsell spoke into a microphone. "All fire-fighting and salvage equipment stand fast until the aircraft has passed them. She may swing." His voice echoed back metallically from the buildings.

"He's at two hundred feet," reported radar. "Still below glide path. One fifty feet. Still below glide path. He's too low, Captain. A hundred feet."

Treleaven jumped to his feet, holding the microphone in one

hand and the binoculars in the other. "Maintain that height until you get closer in to the runway. Be ready to ease off gently. . . . Let down again. . . . That looks about right."

"Damn the rain," said Spencer. "I can hardly see." Ahead he had only a blurred impression of the beginning of the runway.

"Watch the airspeed," cautioned Treleaven. "Your nose is creeping up. Straighten up just before you touch down and be ready to meet the drift with right rudder. . . . All right. Get ready to round out. . . ."

The gray runway, two hundred feet across, slid under them.

"Now!" Treleaven exclaimed. "You're coming in too fast. Lift the nose up! Throttles right back! Hold her off. Not too much! Be ready for that crosswind. Ease her down, now. Ease her down!"

Landing gear within a few feet of the runway surface, Spencer moved the control column gently back and forth, trying to feel his way down onto the ground, his throat constricted with panic because he now realized how much higher this cockpit was than that of any other plane he had flown, making judgment almost impossible for him.

For what seemed an age, the wheels skimmed the runway, making no contact. Then with a jolt they touched down. There was a shriek of rubber and a puff of smoke. The shock bounced the aircraft right into the air again. Then the big tires were once more fighting to find a purchase on the concrete.

A third bump followed, then another, and yet another. Cursing, Spencer hauled the control column back, all the nightmare fears of the past few hours now a paralyzing reality. The gray stream below him jumped up, receded, jumped up again. Then, miraculously, it remained still. They were down. He eased on the toe brakes, then held them hard, using all the strength in his legs. There was a high-pitched squeal but no drop in speed. From the corner of his eye he could see that they were already more than two thirds down the runway. He could never stop the aircraft in time.

"You're landing too fast," roared Treleaven. "Use the emergency brakes! Pull the red handle!"

Spencer tugged desperately on the handle. He hauled the control column back into his stomach, jammed his feet on the brakes. He felt the tearing strain in his arms as the aircraft tried to slue. The wheels locked, skidded, then ran free again.

"Cut the switches!" he shouted. With a sweep of her hand Janet snapped them off. The din of the engines died away, leaving in the cabin the hum of gyros and radio equipment, and outside the screaming of tires.

Spencer stared ahead in fascinated horror. With no sound of engines, the aircraft was still traveling fast, the ground leaping past them in a blur. He could see a big checkerboard marking the turn at the end of the runway. In the fraction of a second his eyes registered the picture of a fire truck, its driver falling to the ground in his scramble to get away.

Treleaven's voice burst into his ears with the force of a blow. "Ground-loop it to the left! Hard left rudder!"

Making an instantaneous decision, Spencer put his foot on the rudder pedal and threw all his weight behind it, pressing it forward savagely.

Veering suddenly from the runway, the aircraft began to swing in an arc. Flung over to the right side of his seat, Spencer struggled to keep the wings clear of the ground. There was a rending volume of noise, a dazzling flash, as the landing gear ripped away and the aircraft smashed to the ground on its belly. The impact lifted Spencer clean from his seat. He felt a sharp pain as his safety belt bit deeply into his flesh.

"Get your head down!" he yelled. "We're piling up!"

Gripping their seats against the maniacal violence of the bouncing and rocking, they tried to curl themselves up. Still under momentum, the aircraft continued to slither crabwise, plowing grass in vicious furrows. With a screech of metal it crossed another runway, uprooting the runway lights, showering fountains of earth into the air.

Spencer prayed for the end. Like a prisoner in some crazy, helpless juggernaut, blood appearing in the corner of his mouth from a blow as yet unfelt, he waited for the inevitable tip-over, the splintering crash that would disintegrate into a thousand fiery pinpoints of light before they were swallowed into darkness.

Then, quite suddenly, they were moving no longer. For the space of seconds there was no sound at all. He braced himself against the awkward sideways tilt of the deck and looked over at Janet. Her head was buried in her hands. She was crying silently.

In the passenger compartment, there were the murmurs and rustlings of people incredulously finding themselves still alive. Someone laughed hysterically, and this seemed to let loose half a dozen voices speaking at once.

He heard Baird call out, "Is anyone hurt?"

The noises melted into confusion. Spencer closed his eyes. "Better open up the emergency doors," came the adenoidal tones of 'Otpot, "and then everyone stay where he is."

From the door to the flight deck, jammed open in the crash, he heard the doctor exclaim, "Wonderful job, Spencer! Are you both all right?"

"I ground-looped!" he muttered in disgust. "We turned right around the way we came. What a performance—to ground-loop!"

"Rubbish—you did magnificently," Baird retorted. "As far as I can tell, there are only bruises and a bit of shock back here. Let's have a look at the captain and first officer—they must have been thrown about some."

Spencer turned to him. It was painful to move his neck. "Doctor, are we in time?"

"Yes, just about. It's up to the hospital now."

Spencer tried to raise himself in his seat, but at that moment he became aware of the sound of crackling. He felt an upsurge of alarm. Then he realized that the noise was issuing from his headset, which had slipped to the deck. He reached down and picked it up, holding one phone to his ear.

"George Spencer!" Treleaven was calling. "Are you there?"

Outside, there was a rising crescendo of sirens from crash tenders and fire trucks and ambulances.

"Yes," he said, "I'm here."

Treleaven was jubilant. Behind his voice there were sounds of excited conversation and laughter. "George. That was probably the lousiest landing in the history of this airport. So don't ever ask us for a job as a pilot. But there are some of us here who'd like to shake your hand, and later we'll buy you a drink. Now hold everything, George. We're coming over."

Janet had raised her head and was smiling tremulously.

Spencer couldn't think of a thing to say to her. No witticism, no adequate word of thanks. He knew only that he was intolerably tired and sick to the stomach. He reached over for her hand and grinned back.

Flight into Danger— *"and nothing was ever quite the same again...."*

Even now, twenty-three years later, I remember that night—in vivid detail, and with a sense of excitement which will never leave me.

It was April 3, 1956, in Toronto, Canada. *Flight into Danger,* my first major piece of fiction writing, was to be performed live on television. In our home my wife, Sheila, and I had dinner, then hurriedly cleared away the dishes so we could watch.

Arthur Hailey

I was thirty-six, a successful sales and advertising executive, though not too happy in my work. What I really wanted was to be a professional writer. However, some six months earlier I had decided to face reality: it wasn't going to happen. I had had a few things published, but a great deal more rejected. Obviously, I told myself, I lacked the needed talent. Ergo, my long-established dream would remain a dream, and nothing more.

That April evening not only canceled out my acceptance of "reality"; it changed my life in countless ways, so that nothing was ever quite the same again.

The whole thing had begun the previous December. I had been on a week-long business trip to the Canadian west coast and was flying home on a Friday. During the eight-hour flight, most of it after dark, I read myself to tiredness, then tried to sleep but couldn't. The reason was simple: the airplane was a Trans-Canada Air Lines North Star, a four-engined propeller job—probably, from a passenger's standpoint, the noisiest aircraft ever.

So, instead of sleeping, I daydreamed.

The daydream opened with a question: Could I, a wartime RAF pilot trained to fly small, fast fighter airplanes, who hadn't entered a cockpit in eight years, handle and land the lumbering great bus in which I was now a passenger? Well ... *maybe;* in certain circumstances. *What circumstances?* Okay ... *let's think.*

I did think, for several hours more, during which the notion of *Flight into Danger* took shape.

My wife met me at Toronto airport and I told her, "Honey, I've a good idea for a play. It might work on TV."

"Well, write it!" she urged me.

For the next ten days, during evenings and weekends at home, I labored over a typewriter. Looking back, I find it extraordinary how fast it all came together. Since then I have not written *anything* with the same assurance or speed. Afterward, expecting one more rejection, I put the completed play in an envelope and mailed it to the Canadian Broadcasting Corporation.

Eureka! In January came notice that CBC would buy the play, and less than three months later—the night on which my life changed—it was aired on the Canadian TV network.

The reaction was like a fairy tale. Our phone rang for hours with congratulations from people we knew and others we didn't. During the days and weeks which followed I wrote two more plays for television and received offers of contracts to write still more. *Flight* was performed worldwide; after its U.S. performance on NBC, it was bought as a film and I went to Hollywood to write the screenplay. At my wife's urging I abandoned my sales and advertising career. I *was* a professional writer after all.

Then a young British publisher, Ernest Hecht, who had watched *Flight* on BBC television, suggested I adapt the story as a novel, which he would publish. I said no. For one thing, I now had all the writing I could handle for television and film. For another, I was not sure I could write a novel, so why be greedy and attempt too much?

Ernest persisted, however. Would I accept a collaborator who would convert my play into a book? My response this time: Why not?

John Castle (a pseudonym for two British writers) did a competent job of rewriting the play as a book. But when I read it I thought, Why didn't I do this myself? My story was there, unchanged; so was all my dialogue. Consequently, when the U.S. publishing house Doubleday asked if I would write *another* of my plays as a book, I agreed at once. That became *The Final Diagnosis,* which is still very much around, and I enjoyed doing it so much that I've written nothing but books since.

A postscript: Ernest Hecht, who really started me writing books, has since become my regular British publisher and a close friend. My novels, I'm happy to say, now appear in thirty languages. And, oh yes, I've just finished a new one, *Overload*.

—ARTHUR HAILEY

The moving story
of Raquela Prywes,
whose life mirrors her country's
tumultuous history,
its triumphs and tragedies

RAQUELA
A Woman of Israel

A CONDENSATION OF THE BOOK BY
RUTH GRUBER

AUTHOR'S FOREWORD

A few years ago I flew to Israel on a quest: to find a woman—not Golda Meir, not a powerful, world-renowned figure—but one whose life would define what it means to be a woman of Israel.

I wanted a woman who had been on the front lines in Israel's four wars; a woman who had known in her own life the joy and agony of growing up in the Biblical land.

I found her. She's Raquela Prywes, a ninth-generation Jerusalemite. A nurse and midwife, who worked with dedication in hospitals during the wars. And she was so beautiful that, as one doctor told me, "every man in Jerusalem wanted to marry her."

Five minutes after I met her, in the King David Hotel in Jerusalem, I knew my search was over.

This, then, is Raquela's story. —RUTH GRUBER

"A truly beautiful and inspiring work about a remarkable woman. Ruth Gruber knows the Israeli scene better than almost anyone I can think of and brings it to life magnificently in this gripping story."

—GERALD GREEN, author of *Holocaust*

PART ONE

Jerusalem, August 1929

The handsome black-robed woman walked regally, carrying on her head a basket laden with eggs and freshly picked figs. Five-year-old Raquela Levy flung open the garden gate. Mama was already waiting on the little flagstone patio.

"*Salaam aleikum*, Aisha," Mama greeted her friend in Arabic.

"*Salaam aleikum*, Mrs. Levy." Aisha eased the basket from her head as though it were filled with precious jewels.

Mama brought out a shiny copper tray with demitasse cups filled with Turkish coffee while Raquela stood in the center of the patio, an eager participant.

"Aisha," Mama said, "I need the freshest eggs you have. My husband has the flu and all he wants to eat is soft-boiled eggs."

Aisha drained her little cup. "Today I brought you eggs so fresh, this minute the chickens laid them."

"Then give me twenty-five. And I'll take a kilo of figs."

From her basket Aisha lifted a small scale, measured the figs, and threw in an extra handful. "My present." She smiled and bent to hug Raquela. "And you, little beauty, you will break many hearts in your time."

Raquela closed her eyes, letting Aisha wrap her in a cloak of musk and incense. She loved both these women, who could hardly have been less alike. Mama was tiny with high-boned Slavic cheeks, a delicate nose, and long chestnut hair. Aisha was exotic,

347

mysterious, her body robed in a voluminous Bedouin gown, her hair shrouded in a muslin shawl.

The morning transaction was over. Aisha gathered up her basket and scales and disappeared down the street.

Early that afternoon Raquela was helping Mama pick flowers in the garden when Zayda, Mama's father, bolted in.

Raquela had never seen him so excited. At home, in his cottage in the Mea Shearim section of New Jerusalem, he was always laughing with Bubba, Mama's mother, so happy even his beard seemed to bob with joy. Now his eyes were full of fear. "Trouble in Jerusalem," he panted. "The Arabs are rioting in the Old City."

The panic in his voice sent Raquela hiding in Mama's skirt.

"I was praying at the Wailing Wall. I heard screams. So I ran down the street to see. There were maybe two thousand Arabs marching, shouting, 'Death to the Jews. There is no God but Allah.'" Zayda was frantic. "Get your family together, Tova. Run."

Mama patted Raquela on the back reassuringly. "We have time. We're three miles away from the Old City."

"Three miles! You think up here, in Bet Hakerem, with your gardens and your playgrounds, you'll be safe? They can get here in an hour. Run, I tell you."

"What's all the commotion?" Papa stood in the doorway. His voice was raspy and he was shivering, even though it was August.

"Nissim, with your fever you should be in bed," Mama scolded.

"Sick or not, Nissim"—Zayda shook his finger—"you must get the family to safety. Mobs of Arabs are leaving the Old City, carrying guns and sticks. Some are already in Mea Shearim. Houses are burning. Who knows how many have been killed?"

"Is no one stopping them?" Papa demanded. "The British? The Haganah?"

The Jews of Palestine had formed small groups to defend themselves, called the Haganah—the Hebrew word for self-defense.

"I saw some Haganah men with guns," Zayda said. "Wherever they appeared, the Arabs ran away. And I saw some British policemen on horseback chasing the Arabs. But they were only a handful. The Arabs are thousands. Nissim, take the family and hide. Now I have to leave." Zayda flew out the garden gate.

"We must go straight to the seminary." Papa looked past the gate, down the street. "Ah, thank God, here come our boys."

Twelve-year-old Jacob and nine-year-old Yair entered the garden. Jacob was a runner for the Haganah. "You've heard?" he asked his father.

Papa nodded.

Jacob caught his breath. "I have five blocks to cover; I have to tell the people to go to the seminary. I'll meet you up there."

PAPA held Raquela's hand. Mama and Yair hurried out of the house with the two baskets kept ready for just this emergency— one filled with clothing, the other with food. They ran down their street and raced to the David Yellin Seminar, a teachers' seminary and school.

The seminary was set on a hill. Not yet completed, it cut the sky, a huge bird of honey-colored stone with three arches in front and two long wings folded back. Someday there would be broad entrance stairs. Now there was a concrete incline, and inside, wooden planks formed a runway from floor to floor.

Looking up at the parapets, Raquela saw two seventeen-year-old boys she knew, holding rifles, scanning the road for Arabs. Grasping Papa's hand tightly, she ran up the incline.

The neighbors had long ago decided that if trouble came, the fortresslike building would be their sanctuary. Each family's space had been staked out. The Levys' space was in the synagogue, where other families were already camping.

Mama spread blankets on the tiles and bedded Papa down. The sun was sinking behind the hills. It was dusk, the beginning of Shabbat, the Jewish Sabbath, which lasts from sundown on Friday until sundown on Saturday. Mama lighted two candles, set on a white cloth, and recited the Sabbath prayer.

More candles were lighted in the little campsites, and the magic of Shabbat cast its spell. Raquela forgot the terror outside.

Suddenly shots rang out. Bullets rocked the building. Raquela dived under Papa's blanket, frozen with fear.

After a while, one of the young sentries entered the synagogue. "We've driven them off," he announced.

Raquela heard prayers of thanks going up around the room.

"We saw them from the roof," the sentry explained. "A whole gang of Arabs coming across the wadi from Deir Yassin." Deir Yassin, an all-Arab village, was a hotbed of fanatics. "When they

349

saw us shooting from the roof, they beat it back to their village. We're safe now. You can all go to sleep."

The next day, Saturday, flames lighted the sky. "Motza is burning!" The words raced through the seminary. Everyone knew someone in Motza, a picturesque resort village in the hills of Judaea.

Menachem Orshansky, a burly man who represented the Haganah in Bet Hakerem, called the people together in the auditorium to hear news from a messenger from Haganah headquarters.

Raquela's grandparents, Bubba and Zayda Levinrad

"Jerusalem is secure!" the messenger said. "We were lucky. The British police really tried to quell the riot, along with the Haganah. And we had a group of Oxford students—Christians touring the Holy Land. When they saw what was happening, they asked the police for guns. Those students helped save Jerusalem."

"Thank God," Papa said to Mama in a hushed voice.

"Now I will tell you about Motza." The messenger began talking rapidly. "Yesterday morning, when the people of Motza heard about the riots in Jerusalem, a few of them said, 'Let's go to Jerusalem and ask the Haganah for protection.' But they didn't go, because the sheikh of Colonia, the Arab village near Motza, came and swore that if any Arabs from Jerusalem attacked them, he would return with his own Arabs and defend them. Were they not his good friends? The people of Motza were reassured."

The messenger's voice was the only sound in the auditorium. "The Arabs did not come from Jerusalem. They came from Colonia. Yes, the sheikh himself was leading them. They knew all the houses. They broke down the doors. Murdering, looting, burning."

Raquela burrowed into Mama's body.

"They broke into one of the rest homes, butchered the owner, his children, and a guest—an eighty-five-year-old rabbi."

"Where were the British?" Papa called out.

"Where were the British?" Orshansky mocked. "Where are the

British here in Bet Hakerem? True, they were in Jerusalem. But they're still trying to be 'neutral.' They allow the Arabs to carry as many rifles as they want. We're arrested if they catch us with even a rusty old pistol."

Cold sweat gathered on Papa's forehead.

The messenger went on. "When word came to Haganah headquarters that Motza was burning, a group of us jumped into a car and drove up the mountain to the village. The moment the Arabs saw our guns, they fled. They attack only defenseless Jews."

All that night the families sat in the seminary, talking. Were the Arabs rioting in other parts of Palestine?

This was the second serious riot. The first had erupted when a handful of Arab terrorists protested the Balfour Declaration.

The Balfour Declaration! On November 2, 1917, as World War I raged on, British prime minister Lloyd George, a deeply religious man, grateful to the Jews for their part in the war and sympathetic to the Zionist dream of a Jewish homeland, authorized his foreign secretary, Arthur Balfour, to proclaim to the world,

Raquela's parents, Tova and Nissim Levy

"His Majesty's Government view with favour the establishment in Palestine of a national home for the Jewish people."

There had been celebration throughout the Jewish world. The Zionist dream of returning to the Promised Land was to be fulfilled.

After the war, the Allies, meeting in San Remo, Italy, confirmed the pledge given in the Balfour Declaration. In the Middle East, British and French rulers replaced the Turks of the Ottoman Empire, and in 1922 Great Britain was given the "Mandate" by the League of Nations to administer Palestine and establish the "national home for the Jewish people."

A small fringe of the Arab community went on a rampage, denouncing the Mandate. "There will be no Jewish homeland in

Palestine!" they shouted. But they had little influence on the masses of Arabs.

Under Turkish rule they had received almost no medical care. Under the British it was inadequate. Medical care came from their neighbors, the Jews. Moreover, the Arabs who worked for Jews in the towns and farms were paid the same wages as Jewish workers, often three times more than they received from Arab employers. These Arabs had refused to join the anti-Jewish mobs. And for a few years there was relative peace in the land.

Why, now, in 1929, this second riot?

SLEEPING fitfully under a blanket, Raquela heard Papa saying, "Why should they attack us in Bet Hakerem? We didn't steal this land. We bought it from the Greek patriarch of St. Simeon Church in Jerusalem. It was wasteland."

Papa had often told Raquela how Bet Hakerem had looked when he first saw it, seven years ago, in 1922—a barren mountain with not a single person living there, inhabited only by jackals and cratered with huge boulders bleached white in the sun.

The men in the blacked-out synagogue, now talking in whispers, were the very pioneers who had left their work in downtown Jerusalem each afternoon and lugged pickaxes three miles to these hills to break up the boulders and build their homes. Their dream was to make this outpost of Jerusalem like the Holy City of King David's day, when each man could sit beneath his fig tree in his own vineyard. Indeed, they named their colony Bet Hakerem— House of the Vineyard.

The house Papa built on his half an acre was typical: a simple stucco cottage with a pink tile roof, a porch in front, a small patio on the side, and a garden in which he planted the calla lilies he loved and a tree for each of his three children.

The little colony of Bet Hakerem was surrounded by Arab villages, most of them friendly. The hostile ones, like Deir Yassin, were a few small groups within the Arab community.

Now, sitting on the floor of the synagogue, the people pieced together the events of the last few days. A week ago some two hundred Jewish boys and girls had come from Tel Aviv and gathered at the Wailing Wall in Jerusalem's Old City, raising the blue and white flag of Zion. It was to protest harassment by Arab agitators who for months had marched their camels in front of the wall and played cymbals and beat drums to drown out the prayers of the worshippers.

The young people had come from Tel Aviv to demand that the British protect the Jews' right to pray before the holy wall as they had prayed for two thousand years.

The Arabs had used the demonstration as their excuse to spread rumors throughout the country. "The Jews have held a warlike demonstration against us," their newspapers said. They carried the headlines COME TO JERUSALEM! and DO WHAT MUST BE DONE!

On Friday morning, August 16, a mob of Arab Moslems had begun marching and shouting. The people at the wall heard them and fled through the streets of the Old City. The *shammash* remained at his post to guard the prayer books. The mob attacked him, then burned the holy books.

The next day a young Jewish boy, retrieving his soccer ball in an Arab garden, was stabbed. Thousands of Jews joined his funeral cortege.

SUNDAY afternoon Orshansky called the people back to the auditorium. Raquela heard him lash out: "There is not one Jew left in Hebron!"

"Impossible!" someone shouted. Jews had lived in Hebron since the days of Abraham. It was one of the four sacred Jewish cities: Jerusalem, Hebron, Safad, and Tiberias.

Orshansky was bitter. "You know the pharmacist, Ben Zion Gershon. The man who healed hundreds of Arabs. Sixty-five years old. A gang of Arabs broke into his home. They cut off his nose and hands. They pierced his eyes. They killed his children."

Raquela saw Mama's face. It was white with horror.

"I'll tell you about one more victim. Many of us know Rabbi Slonim. They broke into the house of his son, Eliezer Dan Slonim. The Arabs killed him and his family. Then the mob moved to his father's house, screaming, 'Kill the rabbi!' But suddenly the rabbi's Arab landlord rode his horse in front of the crowd, shouting, 'Over my dead body will you enter this house.' The rabbi was saved, with his wife and his daughter. But he is a broken man.

"Sixty-six Jews were murdered in Hebron," Orshansky said. "Fifty-eight wounded." He paused. "You're wondering about the

British. When the Arabs attacked, their war cry was The government is with us." He looked around the room. The people were silent. "Finally the British officer in Hebron called for police from Jerusalem. Twenty-four men came and they were enough to drive the Arabs off. Now the police have rounded up not the Arabs but the Jews, more than six hundred, taken them to Jerusalem, and locked them in the police station. For protection, they say. They have told them they will never again be allowed to live in Hebron."

Orshansky's face contorted with anger. "These riots have shown that we can rely only on the Haganah. Wherever the Haganah intervened, even with only two or three men, the mobs fled. There was no Haganah in Hebron. Look what happened!"

For two weeks the people lived inside the seminary. Finally the riots were over and the families went home.

Peace returned to Jerusalem. But the element of fear had entered Raquela's life and she was scarred.

September 1929

Saturday belonged to Papa's mother, Senora Vavá. She lived just outside the walls of the Old City, in Yemin Moshe. Her house was halfway up a hill of yellow stone stairs, amid a cluster of gardens, olive trees, and sun-dappled houses.

She greeted Papa and Mama and the two boys, and bent to kiss her favorite grandchild, Raquela.

"*Shalom*, Senora Vavá," Raquela said. This Sephardic greeting meant, literally, Mrs. Grandmother, a fitting tribute of courtesy for the tall, elegant matriarch. Senora Vavá was, as always, a portrait in brown. Her long, full dress was a rustle of brown silk, with tiny mother-of-pearl buttons from her high collar to her waist. A richly brocaded stole of brown damask draped her shoulders, and a brown silk kerchief covered her long blond hair.

Her house smelled of Shabbat. The tile floors sparkled. The bright Oriental carpets caught the sunlight. The oak table was festive with a white lace cloth and brass candlesticks. Raquela drank in the rich Middle Eastern odors of *barakhas,* little cakes stuffed with meat or vegetables, and a special Shabbat stew.

They seated themselves around the table. "Senora Vavá," Raquela asked hesitantly, "were there Arab riots when you were a little girl?"

354

"No, Raquela, we lived peacefully together inside the Old City. Even though there were different quarters—Jewish, Armenian, Christian, and Moslem—we played together. We were in and out of one another's houses all day long."

She went on. "But outside the Old City there was danger. Gangs of Bedouins used to rob and even kill travelers coming up to Jerusalem to pray at the Wailing Wall."

"Senora Vavá," Yair spoke up. "Abdullah—he's an Arab shepherd boy I meet sometimes—he says the Arabs killed all these people because it was their country and they were here before us."

Senora Vavá looked serious. "You tell your friend your great-great-great-great-great-great-great-grandfather came here in 1650."

"From Spain," twelve-year-old Jacob added.

"Yes, indirectly," she said. "We were in Spain until 1492. Then our family went to Italy, and from Italy they came to Jerusalem."

"But Abdullah says they were here before us," Yair persisted.

She was angry now. "What does your friend mean, they were here before us? Abraham was here more than four thousand years ago. Thousands of years before Mohammed, who died in 632 A.D." Senora Vavá's eyes were flashing. "Never forget that you children are ninth-generation Jerusalemites. You are as much part of this land as the rocks and boulders you play on.

"Your links go back even in your names." She looked at Jacob, her firstborn grandson. "You, Jacob Mordechai, were named for a long line of spiritual men—rabbis. Only your father broke the line. He became a teacher." She smiled. "It's not bad having a famous son who's head of the important Elementary School for Boys."

Raquela felt a surge of pride. She knew Papa was special. Now Senora Vavá, who carried so much in her head, confirmed it.

The afternoon sun fell in bars upon the carpet. Soon the Sabbath would be over. Senora Vavá bade good-by to the family and embraced her five-year-old granddaughter. "When you come, I see my childhood all over again in you. It is good you bear my name—Raquela."

Jerusalem, 1936

After the Arab riots of 1929, tensions continued to build in Palestine. Hitler came to power in 1933. By 1936 seventy thousand German Jews had found refuge from the Nazis in Palestine.

355

The Arab mufti of Jerusalem, Haj Amin el-Husseini, went on a rampage to halt the Jewish immigration. Husseini was a notorious terrorist. In the early 1920s the British had appointed him mufti of Jerusalem, the highest Moslem post in Palestine, reasoning that power and money would make him turn respectable, and amenable to British rule. At first it seemed the British had chosen well. The red-bearded mufti abandoned his terrorist tactics until he was elected president of the Supreme Moslem Council. This post gave him control over the mosques, the courts, the schools, and all Moslem religious funds in Palestine.

Raquela with her brothers, Yair and Jacob

Now, in 1936, he discarded his cloak of respectability. He used his money and power to win over illiterate Arabs, and sought to terrorize not only the Jews but also the British, hoping to drive them all out of Palestine.

The mufti sent his cohorts to roam the highways and rob trucks for money to buy more guns. They murdered and rioted.

The Haganah, outlawed by the British, grew stronger. Many farm settlements became fortresses, like the seminary. And the seminary itself became the Haganah's secret training ground for western Jerusalem. Here, too, young men and women of eighteen, idealistic and courageous, were sworn in.

Raquela's brother Jacob, not yet nineteen, formally joined the secret group.

MAMA and Raquela entered the bus to go shopping downtown. Raquela could hardly sit still, anticipating her bas mitzvah, November 2, 1936. It was her twelfth birthday—her coming of age in the Jewish community. They were to spend the day buying a white party dress, white pumps, and an assortment of cakes at the Patt Bakery.

They were driving through Romema, an Arab section of New Jerusalem. On the sidewalk, Arab men with long black gowns sat on stools in front of their shops, smoking hubble-bubbles.

In a few more minutes the bus would be in the Jewish section. Suddenly two Arabs, wearing red and white checkered headdresses, leaped out of nowhere and aimed their rifles into the windows. Mama pushed Raquela to the floor. A bullet crashed through the window and over their heads. A woman screamed, "They've hit me." The bus swerved.

A third Arab hurled a hand grenade. The grenade ricocheted and killed him.

The driver raced on to the Hadassah Hospital. The wounded were carried in. Shaken, Raquela and Mama got out of the bus and crossed over to the Street of the Prophets, to the Patt Bakery. Raquela's knees were buckling.

Inside the busy bakery, Mrs. Patt greeted them. "*Shalom,* Mrs. Levy. *Shalom,* Raquela." She was statuesque, with fair skin and startlingly blue eyes.

"*Shalom,* Mrs. Patt," Mama said. "Did you hear all the excitement? The Arabs shot at our bus. Even threw a bomb at us."

The customers surrounded Mama, all talking at once. Mrs. Patt came around the counter. "Both of you go inside and have tea. Your nerves must be shot."

The garden tearoom was a mass of white uniforms. Young doctors and nurses from the Hadassah Hospital sat at little tables.

Raquela, sitting with Mama, looked furtively at the open yard behind the bakeshop. Two men in civilian clothes sat nearby. Raquela could see a bulge near their back pockets. In the center of the yard was the cistern used to catch rainwater. But Raquela knew that this cistern had been emptied of its water, and that every evening thirty young Haganah men climbed down the cistern's stepladder to an underground cavern that stretched beneath the yard and the bakery. Silently they marched, they drilled, they learned to shoot. For the Patt apartment, which was right over the shop, was headquarters for the Haganah high command, and Jacob Patt, Mr. Patt's brother, was Jerusalem commander.

When they finished their tea, Raquela and Mama returned to

the shop to make their selection for the bas mitzvah. Raquela chose cheesecake, a honey cake, cookies, apricot pie, and her favorite, Mrs. Patt's apple strudel.

A bell rang. Mrs. Patt whispered, "It's the British. The bell is to warn us. The Haganah boys on the terrace must have seen them."

Raquela saw the men with bulging pockets dash in from the garden. Mrs. Patt grabbed their pistols, pushed open the back door, and tossed the guns into a pile of soft dough that a baker was kneading. In seconds, the guns disappeared.

Back behind the counter, she casually began writing up Mama's order. The glass door opened. Raquela's heart began thumping so loudly she was sure the British policemen could hear it.

Afraid to lift her eyes, she saw two policemen—their khaki shoes, their khaki socks, their khaki shorts. She raised her eyes a little. Attached to their belts were black holsters.

"What can I do for you?" Mrs. Patt asked the policemen.

"We're sorry to trouble you, but we have a search warrant."

"Search," Mrs. Patt said expansively. "But may I ask what for?"

"Mrs. Patt, you know very well what we are searching for." The policemen entered the garden tearoom. All the customers were frisked. Then they opened the back door to the kitchen and approached the bakers. Raquela sent a silent message through the air: Dear God, don't let them look in the dough.

The policemen strode past the bakers' table to the icebox. They looked in, found nothing. They returned to the bakeshop.

"Will you gentlemen have a few cookies?" Mrs. Patt asked.

"You're very kind. Don't mind if we do."

She stuffed two large bags with cake and cookies.

"Thank you, ma'am." The policemen smiled and walked out.

Mrs. Patt turned to Mama. "Now back to Raquela's bas mitzvah!"

PART TWO

January 1943

Raquela jumped out of bed to find snow swirling around her open window. Snow rarely fell in Jerusalem.

She saw nothing moving on the road. She watched the uncertain daybreak. Was the city paralyzed already? And she was due at

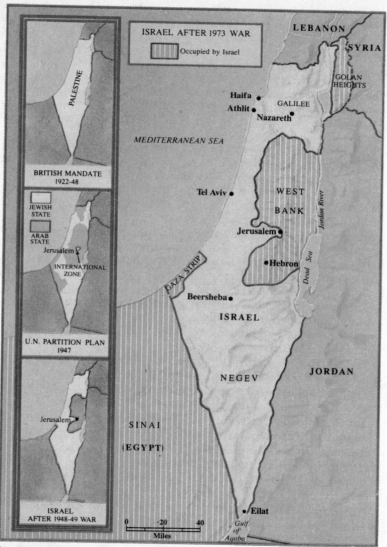

ISRAEL AFTER 1973 WAR
Occupied by Israel

LEBANON
SYRIA
GOLAN HEIGHTS
Haifa
Athlit
GALILEE
Nazareth
MEDITERRANEAN SEA
Tel Aviv
WEST BANK
Jerusalem
Jordan River
Hebron
GAZA STRIP
Dead Sea
Beersheba
ISRAEL
NEGEV
JORDAN
SINAI
(EGYPT)
Eilat
Gulf of Aqaba
0   20   40
Miles

PALESTINE
BRITISH MANDATE
1922-48

JEWISH STATE
ARAB STATE
Jerusalem
INTERNATIONAL ZONE
U.N. PARTITION PLAN
1947

Jerusalem
ISRAEL
AFTER 1948-49 WAR

Israel as Raquela knew it: four stages

eight for her first day at the Hadassah—Henrietta Szold School of Nursing.

Swiftly she pulled on a woolen skirt and a sweater. She glanced in the mirror as she brushed her long hair, now chestnut brown with hints of gold.

Raquela was eighteen. In the six years since her bas mitzvah she had grown tall, like Papa and Senora Vavá. She held the hairbrush motionless for a moment, mourning the beloved grandmother, who had died just before World War II engulfed the Middle East.

How would Senora Vavá have reacted to my becoming a nurse? she wondered. She remembered her grandmother's benediction on the day of her bas mitzvah. *May you be as Rachel, your namesake in the Bible. May you be, like her, a mother in Israel.* Be a mother in Israel. . . . Was nursing wounded soldiers back to life—was that not being a mother in Israel?

Raquela finished packing and joined Papa and Mama at the dining table. Papa was quiet, a faraway look in his eyes. Mama kept talking. "And remember, Raquela, if you don't like the school, you can always come home."

"I'll be all right. Don't worry." Raquela downed her coffee.

"Just don't be ashamed. If you're not happy, just tell them—"

Raquela jumped up. "I'd better be going." She got her suitcase. Papa came and embraced her. "May God go with you."

She kissed Mama.

"Put a scarf on your head, Raquela," Mama said. "Don't catch a cold your first day."

Raquela smiled as she pushed the door open. Mama and Papa watched her crunch through the snow to the bus stop.

Bus 8 stopped directly in front of her. Raquela lugged the suitcase up the steep steps, slid it under a seat, and sat by a window.

Downtown, she changed buses. Cold and uneasy, she peered out as the bus lumbered up the slippery road to Sheikh Jarrah, now the most dangerous district in all Jerusalem.

Here were the stone palaces of the wealthiest Arab families, many of them leaders in the Arab riots. Here was the villa of the mufti, reviled and feared even by other Arabs. The mufti was not at home; he was in Berlin, creating a Nazi-Arab axis.

Raquela tried to think of her mother's Arab friend Aisha, but her mind refused to relinquish the memory of the bus attack before her bas mitzvah, in 1936. For three years those attacks had continued. Then, in 1939, the riots ended abruptly. The mufti had achieved his goal, a spectacular capitulation from the British.

Ninteen thirty-nine: the year Hitler sealed the borders of Germany, trapping Jews; the year Great Britain issued its "white paper" proclaiming that for the next five years the number of Jews permitted to enter Palestine would be cut drastically. Then, in 1944, no Jews at all would be allowed to enter. Jews could no longer buy any land in Palestine. Nor could they settle the land they already owned.

The Arab terrorists could afford to wait until 1944. For the white paper meant the end of the British promise to establish a Jewish homeland.

Now the Jews were caught in a terrible dilemma.

When the war broke out in 1939, England had been magnificent, saving Western civilization, holding off Hitler's hordes. Then Denmark fell, and Norway. Holland, Belgium, Luxembourg, and France were overrun. The list seemed endless. Mussolini joined forces with Hitler. The gallant British had to be helped by every able-bodied Jewish man and woman in Palestine.

Yet in Palestine itself, the hated white paper had become the law of the land. To save Jews who could still escape from Europe, the Haganah organized shiploads of immigrants and beached them, at night, on the coasts of Palestine.

But the white paper had declared these Jewish immigrants illegal.

The British diverted sorely needed troops to halt the "illegals." It was an enigma. England was fighting on two fronts—the war against Hitler, in Europe, and the war Churchill later called the "sordid" war against the Jews, in Palestine.

David Ben-Gurion, the chairman of the Zionist Executive, spoke for the Jews: "We shall fight the war as if there were no white paper and we shall fight the white paper as if there were no war."

Jacob and Yair Levy, with tens of thousands of other Jews in Palestine, rushed to join the British forces to fight the Nazis. Desperate for manpower, the British agreed to let the Jews join—men in the regular forces and the RAF, women in the ATS (Auxiliary Territorial Service)—provided that for each Jewish volunteer there would be an Arab volunteer. One hundred and thirty thousand Jewish men and women of military age volunteered. But few Arabs came forward.

THE bus stopped to unload Arabs in Sheikh Jarrah. Raquela looked down at her hands. Sunburned, callused. She only recently had returned from working eight months on a farm. Like high school graduates all over Palestine too young to join the army, she had volunteered for "national service." The farmers were desperate for help. She chose to go to Tel Adashim, a cooperative village in the Valley of Jezreel.

Raquela and the other girls woke every morning at six, and for three days of the week did farming. Then they spent three days being secretly trained by the Haganah in defense.

Now she stared out of the snow-flecked bus window with relief. They had left Sheikh Jarrah, and looming ahead was the highest mountain in Jerusalem, Mount Scopus. Then she saw her destination. Set back from the highway in a pine grove, white, starkly beautiful: the Hadassah Hospital, a garden, the nursing school.

Somewhere she had read that Erich Mendelsohn, the hospital's German-Jewish architect, had written that he wanted to create something to fit into the eternal hills of Jerusalem "in the light of the monumental austerity and serenity of the Bible." The building of glistening white tiles was indeed monumental and serene.

The bus stopped opposite the nursing school, a three-story building, which was linked to the hospital by a pergola. Raquela entered and was greeted by a buxom, motherly woman with black hair and lively dark eyes.

"*Shalom.* My goodness, your hand is freezing. Come in. What is your name?"

Raquela introduced herself.

"And my name is Hannah Simonson—Mrs. Simonson, the house-mother. You're the first girl in our special wartime class to arrive. Take your wet coat off. We have to get you warmed up."

Raquela hung her coat on a rack and set her suitcase beside it. Her teeth were chattering. Was it nerves?

She followed the housemother into a luxurious living room.

"Do sit here and warm up, Miss Levy," Mrs. Simonson said.

Raquela perched on the edge of a chair while the housemother went back to the foyer and called, "Judith, can you please come down?" She returned and said, "I've fetched your mother."

"My mother?" Raquela was bewildered.

Mrs. Simonson smiled. "Every freshman gets her own 'mother.' She's a second- or third-year student who shows you around and helps you adjust to the nursing school. Now, while we're waiting, let me begin with some of the things you ought to know. The first six months are a trial period. You'll be on probation."

Six months' probation! I've got to make it, Raquela thought.

"You may receive men visitors in this living room. They must leave early in the evening. All lights in the dormitory must be out at ten and the windows drawn with black muslin curtains for the blackout. Ah, here is your mother."

A slender young woman stood at the door. "I'm Judith Steiner." She extended her hand. "I'll show you to your room."

Raquela gathered her coat and suitcase and followed her, thinking, She's not more than two years older than I. But she seems old—really old. Why?

They walked down a warm and friendly corridor lighted by a bank of windows and graced with ivy, green ferns, and miniature palm trees.

They climbed a stairwell to the third floor and entered a bedroom. Two sofa beds flanked one wall. Along another wall were two wardrobes, two desks, and two chairs. There was an attached balcony.

"Your roommate is Debby Kahana," Judith said. "She's a term ahead of you. She's a nice girl, but she seems to be having a hard time. She's still on probation."

The ominous word again—probation.

Raquela lifted her suitcase to a chair.

"Do you mind if I stay a few minutes while you unpack?" Judith asked.

"Not at all. Won't you sit?"

Judith pulled up a chair. "Watching you take your things out brings back memories of Czechoslovakia. Of my mother packing me up to go to Palestine in 1939. With ten hats."

Raquela turned from the closet. "Ten hats! What were you supposed to do in Palestine with ten hats?"

"Hitler didn't allow us to take out any money. Only clothes. So

363

my mother gave me the best clothes we had in the house, along with the ten hats and twelve pairs of shoes."

Raquela shook her head.

"We couldn't take out any jewelry, either. The Nazis at the border yanked a gold ring off my finger."

"What a terrible experience." Raquela shuddered. "Have you heard from your mother since the war began?"

Judith's blue eyes clouded over. "Not one word. Four years, and not one word about my entire family."

Is that why she looks so much older than I do? Raquela thought.

Judith stood up. "I'd better go now."

Soon after she left, a young woman entered. "I'm Debby," she said. "I guess you're my new roommate." She was short, with red hair cropped like a boy's, and freckles.

"How do you do? I'm Raquela."

Debby gave her a limp handshake, then flopped on her bed. "I'm exhausted. They work you to death here. Lord only knows why I ever thought I could be a nurse."

"What made you decide to become one?" Raquela asked.

"I did it to please my boy friend. He joined the British Army. I felt I had to become a nurse to show him I was patriotic, too." She pointed to a framed photograph dominating the shelf over her bed. "That's him. His name is Carmi Eisenberg. We're planning to get married when the war's over."

Raquela glanced up at the photograph of a young man with a brilliant smile, light hair, and strong yet sensitive features. Raquela thought him the handsomest man she had ever seen.

THAT afternoon the new student nurses were called down to the lounge for tea. They were all in uniform: white probationers' caps, and blue cotton dresses with white aprons.

A hush fell on the room as an attractive woman of medium height sailed in. "That's Mrs. Cantor, the director," Judith whispered to Raquela.

Shulamit Cantor was a commanding vision in white, from her nurse's cap, nesting in a bower of magnificent white hair, her starched white uniform, down to her white stockings and shoes.

"Welcome to the Hadassah–Henrietta Szold School of Nursing," she said. "You've chosen a difficult profession, but we'll help you overcome the difficulties. You'll start with theory and practice. During the next three years you will rotate in all the wards, learning every branch of medicine. We keep tight discipline, and we expect you to give your best."

Raquela listened with a mixture of fear and respect. Mrs. Cantor sounded tough, stern, yet beneath her starched exterior Raquela sensed something feminine, delicate. The director continued. "I believe there is not a nobler profession in the world than the one you have chosen. If you will devote yourselves, with your hearts and minds and bodies, you'll have no problems in our school. And now, young ladies, help yourselves to tea and cake."

THE next morning Raquela woke at five forty-five and stepped out onto the little balcony. The snow had disappeared. Pastel lines of orange and pink were penciled in the sky, lighting up the hills of Moab in the distance, then the Dead Sea, and, closest to her, the Judaean desert. At times like this she sensed the whole history of the land. She was part of it, part of all the generations who had built it.

She dressed in her uniform, breakfasted with Judith in the hospital cafeteria, then went to the nursing school for class.

A senior nurse was in charge. "Today," she said to the twenty newcomers, "I'm going to teach you how to make beds with tight corners, proper folds."

For the next few hours Raquela maneuvered among the hospital sheets, pulling them until they were so taut she could have bounced on them and not left a wrinkle.

Finally lunch. Rest. Classes at five. More beds.

At nine o'clock that night Raquela fell into her own bed. She was asleep within seconds. At midnight she woke with a start. Mrs. Simonson, the housemother, flashed a light in her face.

Raquela shot out of bed. "What is it? A bomb attack?"

Mrs. Simonson held her fingers to her lips. "It's just the nightly check. Go back to sleep."

A FEW days later Raquela was called into Mrs. Cantor's office. "Miss Levy." The director smiled. "I hope you would like to go to a dance for the soldiers tonight. The Women's Committee for Soldiers asked me to send fifteen of my prettiest nurses."

Raquela was delighted.

That evening she and the others stood shyly at the entrance of the soldiers' club. A committeewoman spotted them. "We're so glad you're here. Come. We need help pouring tea."

They walked across the ballroom floor. Men and women in British uniforms milled around, holding drinks, talking.

Long tables stacked with food lined the walls. Raquela began pouring tea. Words floated to her. Tobruk . . . North Africa . . . Italy. Palestine had become not only British headquarters but also the favorite rest and recreation area for soldiers from elsewhere on leave.

A middle-aged major asked Raquela to dance.

A woman next to her spoke up quickly. "Go right ahead, dear. I'll pour."

They were fox-trotting when a tall, blond second lieutenant tapped the major on the shoulder. "May I cut in, sir?"

"Of course." The major handed Raquela over reluctantly.

She stared. She had seen this face every night. On Debby's shelf.

The fox-trot had changed to a Strauss waltz. The lieutenant was holding her close, whirling her around, smiling.

"You're Carmi Eisenberg," Raquela said. He stopped dancing. "You're Debby's boy friend. She's my roommate."

His cheeks flushed. "I *was* her boy friend. We're finished."

He put his arm around her and they began to dance again. "You haven't told me your name," he said.

"Raquela Levy."

"Raquela! I've never heard that name before."

"It's the Spanish for Rachel, Raquel, with a Russian ending."

"Let's go down to the garden," he said impulsively. "It's too hard to talk with all this noise."

They walked down a short flight of stairs. The garden, filled with palms and fragrant flowers, lay in wartime darkness.

"How did you recognize me?" Carmi asked.

"Debby has your picture right next to her bed."

"She's refused to face reality. We broke up weeks ago. We just weren't meant for each other. You do believe me, don't you?"

"I hope you don't lie." She wanted very much to believe him.

Carmi cupped her face in his hands. "You know, if I were wounded— If I woke up and saw a white uniform and your beautiful face, I would never want to get well. I'd want you to take care of me forever."

Through the open door they could hear the musicians strike up a tango. Carmi assumed the stance of a flamenco dancer. He brought Raquela toward him, gracefully flung her away, then drew her back and kissed her.

She shut her eyes. She had never felt so intoxicated.

But what if he were lying about Debby? What if he were one of those soldiers who believed everything was fair in love and war? Live today, for tomorrow you may be . . .

"Raquela," Carmi whispered. "It's the most beautiful name in the world." He drew her close. "Raquela . . . Raquela . . ."

THE next afternoon Raquela was called to the phone.

"Hello, Raquela." Her heart catapulted.

Carmi was talking urgently. "I've just got orders. My unit is leaving tomorrow. I have to see you before I leave."

"Of course. But I have classes until seven o'clock."

"I'll be there then. Good-by . . . Raquela."

Carmi Eisenberg as a lieutenant in the Jewish Brigade of the British Army

She struggled through her classes. She kept seeing Carmi's face, hearing him whisper in the dark, flower-scented garden, *If I were wounded and saw your face . . .*

Promptly at seven, Carmi appeared in the lounge. Raquela raced down the stairs to meet him. He took her hands in his. "Can we go someplace where we can be alone?"

"We can walk right here on Mount Scopus," she said. "I'll go up and get a sweater."

In their room, Debby lay on her bed, watching Raquela take a white sweater from the closet. "Got a date?" she asked.

Raquela turned and glanced at Carmi's photo. "Debby, are you still seeing Carmi Eisenberg?"

Debby looked stunned. She opened a textbook. "Sure," she said. But her voice sounded unsure. "Look, you've got a date. And I'd

367

better study this or I'll be kicked out. Then what'll Carmi say?"

Raquela was confused. Who was telling the truth?

She returned to the lounge. Carmi took her arm and led her out of the school. They walked along the narrow dirt ridge that led to the campus of Hebrew University, some two hundred yards from the nursing school. Mount Scopus seemed to divide two worlds. On the southwest lay the Old City and New Jerusalem, rising on the hills; on the east, the Judaean desert, then Transjordan, Iraq. For six thousand miles eastward this was the only university and Hadassah the only medical center.

Three Arab boys approached them on donkeys. They waved and smiled. They were probably on their way to Issawiya, a village that lay on the slope of a hill just below the hospital. The Arabs of Issawiya were in and out of the hospital constantly, as workers and as patients. As the boys descended the ridge, their donkeys' bells seemed to toll peace on the Biblical mountain while Carmi was to march off to war.

Raquela and Carmi entered a terraced garden and made their way toward a circular bench with an unobstructed view of the Old City below them.

The wind hurried through the Jerusalem pines. Carmi took Raquela in his arms and kissed her. She shivered, exhilarated and uncertain. The luminous panorama of the Old City looked magical. The golden Dome of the Rock stood like a jewel amid the spires and battle walls that framed the ancient city in which David had reigned and Solomon had built his Temple. Beyond the Old City, up on the gentle hills, rose New Jerusalem.

"Carmi"—Raquela broke the spell—"I must know the truth. Debby says you still see each other."

"It's not true. We haven't even spoken for weeks."

"She told me you plan to get married when the war ends."

Carmi put his hands on her shoulders. "Now, listen to me, Raquela. Debby and I had it out. She's too jealous. She was always complaining that I didn't love her enough. Every time I sneezed, she thought it was an excuse not to see her."

"I guess her pride is hurt," Raquela said slowly. "Maybe that's why she still keeps your photo on her shelf. It's very fashionable to have a boy friend who's in the army."

He smiled. "Now you have one, too." He embraced her again.

"I'll be thinking of you every minute I'm away," he whispered. "And I'll write you every day. Wait for me, Raquela."

She trembled in his arms. "I'll wait, Carmi."

AT LUNCH the next day, Judith pulled up a chair beside Raquela. "Debby's telling everyone you stole her boy friend."

"What?" Raquela stopped eating. "I'm going to talk to her right now." She ran out of the dining room.

Upstairs, Debby was tossing clothes into her bag. "I never want to see you again," she shouted at Raquela.

"Debby, please don't leave. Is it because of Carmi?"

"I hate you. I hate you both!" Debby shoved her aside and stormed out of the room.

Raquela stepped out to the balcony. Tears welled in her eyes.

Judith's voice brought her back into the room. "I just heard the news, Raquela. Debby's probationary period ended today. She failed all her exams. She's been expelled."

CARMI was somewhere in Egypt with the British Eighth Army. His first letter took weeks to arrive:

Dear Raquela:

We traveled 24 hours by train to get to this base. Dust and sand are everywhere—in the water, in the food, in our lungs. It's very hard to get used to camp life now that I've met you. On the whole train ride, I thought about you every minute. My soul is tied to yours. I love you, Raquela, and I will love you until I die.

In May Carmi came back to Jerusalem for a week's home leave.

Raquela met him in the lounge at seven. They drove off in a cab to a café in Zion Square, too happy to talk.

Dance music was playing. Carmi gave the waiter their order and reached across the table for Raquela's hand. "Raquela, I walk through the camp and think only of you." He lifted her hand and kissed it. "I love you, Raquela."

She drew his hand toward her and placed her cheek against his warm palm. She heard herself say it aloud for the first time. "I love you, too, Carmi."

They danced waltzes, they sipped drinks.

"You know, Carmi," Raquela said, "in a way we're still strangers. I don't know very much about you."

He smiled. "I can give it all to you in a few words. My father's a judge in Jerusalem. I went to agricultural high school. After the war I want to be a farmer and marry you."

Raquela tried to visualize Carmi, resplendent now in uniform, as a farmer in blue kibbutz shorts, bending over his crops.

Suddenly she glanced at her watch. "Oh, it's nearly ten o'clock. Mrs. Simonson will have my head."

"Won't she understand this is a special night for us?"

"She doesn't accept any excuses. I must go."

In the taxi, Carmi asked, "Don't any of the girls cheat?"

"Of course. Sometimes they fix their blankets to look as though they're in their beds."

"Do you cheat sometimes, too, Raquela?"

She shook her head. "I've never stayed out late."

"Never?"

Raquela detected an edge of suspicion. "I'm an obedient, law-abiding person, Carmi. I believe if you want something, you have to accept the rules. Right now, I want to be a nurse more than anything in my life. And I don't want to do a single thing that will cause them to expel me."

THE wartime class was assembled in the lounge when Mrs. Cantor breezed in, her face wreathed in smiles. "I am happy to tell you," she said to the young women, "that you have all passed your six-month probation period."

The twenty women pulled off their probationers' caps. Carefully they draped starched white cowls over their hair. This would be their headdress for the next two and a half years.

Raquela worked tirelessly in the wards, her life punctuated by Carmi's home leaves—one week every three months.

By now thousands of Jewish men and women from Palestine were serving under the British flag in France, England, Greece, Crete, Ethiopia, Libya, Cyprus, and Iraq. They had distinguished themselves in battle. Yet they yearned to serve in their own unit, to fight Hitler under their own flag.

Finally, on September 20, 1944, the British War Office made an announcement which electrified the Jews of Palestine:

H. M. Government have decided to accede to the request of the Jewish Agency for Palestine that a Jewish Brigade group should be formed to take part in active operations.

Carmi wrote to Raquela, "I volunteered the first day. Now at last we will fight Hitler as a unit."

He arrived in Jerusalem soon after his letter. He had two weeks' leave before being shipped to Italy. Raquela saw him every evening. They walked, they sat in cafés, they danced, they went to the movies. Time sped by.

They decided to spend his last evening in Jerusalem in the garden on Mount Scopus, overlooking the Old City. As they sat together on the stone bench, he pressed her to him. "I want to marry you, Raquela, but I don't dare ask you to become engaged until this is all over. If anything happens to me . . ."

View of Jerusalem and the Old City, looking toward Mount Scopus

She dug her head into his shoulder. She could feel the Jewish Brigade patch he wore so proudly on his arm.

"You won't believe how I feel," he continued. "On the one hand, I can't wait to set foot on the soil of Europe— to get a chance to destroy Hitler before he destroys the world. On the other hand, I want desperately to come back to you."

"You must come back," she whispered.

A rustle in the garden startled them. A young intern approached. "Hello, Raquela."

Carmi dropped his arms abruptly.

"Hello, Shmuel," she said. "I'd like you to meet Carmi."

Shmuel extended his hand. Carmi shook it reluctantly.

"Beautiful evening, isn't it?" Shmuel said, and walked away.

"Who's he?" Carmi demanded.

"Just a young doctor in the hospital."

"Is he in love with you?"

Raquela stared at Carmi. "I hardly know him."

"I didn't like the way he looked at you."

Raquela moved away on the bench. "Carmi, you didn't like it when Debby was jealous of you. Now don't *you* be jealous."

"I can't help it, Raquela. In camp I went crazy thinking somebody was kissing you."

"You can put your mind to rest. Nobody's kissing me but you." She was in love with this man, and his jealousy troubled her.

It was after midnight when they walked along the ridge of Mount Scopus toward the nursing school. At the door, Carmi held her fiercely in his arms. "I adore you, Raquela."

A few days later a letter arrived:

Dearest Raquela,

It is just thirty-six hours since we said good-by. On the train back from Jerusalem I relived every moment we spent together. I will love you forever. Am I correct that you feel the same?

November 1944

The tile floors were sponged, the rooms aired. Henrietta Szold was coming to the nursing school directly from the hospital. The legendary American woman who had founded Hadassah in America and helped to build this hospital and the nursing school on Mount Scopus was to convalesce here after a near fatal bout with pneumonia.

The whole staff waited at the garden door. A frail woman with white hair approached slowly, assisted by a doctor.

"Welcome, Miss Szold," Mrs. Cantor said. "We've set up two rooms for you on the second floor, with a view of the city."

"You're very kind." Her voice was low, musical. "I hope I haven't inconvenienced anyone."

"It is an honor to have you with us," Mrs. Cantor assured her.

For the next three months the staff and students focused largely on making their famous, gentle patient comfortable.

Gradually Raquela learned some of Miss Szold's story. She had been born in Baltimore, Maryland, in 1860. Her father, a rabbi from Hungary, treated her as the son he never had. He became her teacher, instilled in her his scholarship, his sense of the truth and beauty of Judaism.

When he died she moved to New York City with her mother.

She applied for admission to the Jewish Theological Seminary and was accepted on condition that she would not become a rabbi.

At the seminary she met Dr. Louis Ginzberg, a great scholar from Germany. For Henrietta it was love at first sight. She was in her early forties.

As she had worked with her father, so now she worked with this man—translating his material, editing it, polishing it. The first volumes of his *Legends of the Jews* acknowledged her role as translator and editor. For her the relationship meant fulfillment, commitment, happiness.

Then, one summer, Dr. Ginzberg returned to Germany. When he came back to New York he announced to Henrietta that he was engaged to a young German woman.

Henrietta's pragmatic seventy-seven-year-old mother, seeing her daughter brokenhearted, proposed they go to Palestine. It was 1909. The two women were shocked by the filth and poverty and disease in the Holy Land.

Henrietta's mother made a suggestion. "Here is work for you. You have a study group at home. Let your ladies do something for these people instead of talking, talking."

They returned to America, where Henrietta organized her women. On February 24, 1912, they met in Temple Emanu-El in New York and created Hadassah; its name was the Hebrew for Queen Esther, who had saved the Jews. They took their motto, "The healing of the daughter of my people," from Jeremiah 8:22. Hadassah was to become the world's largest organization of Jewish women.

In 1920, at the age of sixty, Henrietta brought a team of American doctors and nurses to Palestine. They established hospitals, clinics, and laboratories. And a school of nursing that was, Miss Szold insisted, to be of the highest standards, as in America.

The Jewish leaders of Palestine recognized Miss Szold's impact and in 1927 chose her to be a member of the Zionist Executive. Three years later she was elected a member of the Jewish National Council for Palestine and was put in charge of social welfare, which she revolutionized as she had revolutionized medicine.

Then, in 1933, when Hitler came to power, she saw long before most that he was bent on exterminating the Jews.

At the age of seventy-five she went to Germany. "If we cannot save all the Jews," she cried, "let us at least save the children."

Youth Aliyah, created by Recha Freier in Berlin to rescue children from Hitler's Germany, became Henrietta Szold's obsession and love. In Germany, she brought her talents to the Children's Migration, which, despite the war and despite Britain's white paper, would eventually bring thousands of children to Palestine. They were never called orphans, though most of their parents had died in concentration camps.

Rain or shine, Miss Szold drove from her home in Jerusalem to Haifa to meet every ship and to shake the hand of every parentless child she had rescued. Around the world, people began calling her "the mother of ten thousand children."

And now here she was, the first lady of Palestine, convalescing in the nursing school she had created and loved. After being there for some weeks, on the morning of Tuesday, February 13, 1945, Miss Szold fell into a coma. That afternoon she died as she had lived— quietly, with consummate dignity.

Thousands of mourners came to Mount Scopus to pay their last respects. Miss Szold's body was taken to the sacred burial place on the Mount of Olives, where for thousands of years pious Jews had buried their dead.

Henrietta Szold,
founder of Hadassah

March 1945

Raquela was in the labor room, mopping the forehead of her sister-in-law, Meira, Jacob's wife.

"How much longer, do you think?" Meira asked weakly.

Raquela tried to comfort her. "It can't be too much longer." But she was worried. Contractions had started, then stopped. Meira was weak with fatigue. Her pretty face was chalk white, her dark hair stringy and wet.

Seeking to divert her, Raquela said, "Would you like to hear Carmi's last letter? It's about Italy and the Jewish Brigade."

"Please. I'll try my best to listen."

Raquela pulled the letter out of her pocket. She began:

"Wherever we go in Italy—in the areas our Allied forces have just begun liberating—the people come out on the road and stare at our trucks with the Star of David. They wave, they shout greetings, they throw kisses at us, toss flowers—"

A doctor entered the room. Raquela jumped to her feet. "And how are you this morning, Meira?" "Feeling better now that I see you, Dr. Brzezinski," Meira said.

Aerial view of Mount Scopus, Hadassah Hospital in the foreground, Hebrew University in the background, 1943

"This is my sister-in-law, Raquela, Jacob's sister."

The doctor smiled at Raquela. "I remember you from my class. I had no idea you two were related."

Raquela was flustered. Dr. Aron Brzezinski, deputy chief of gynecology and obstetrics, had noticed her. His face was more kindly than handsome. He was in his middle thirties, slightly paunched and an inch shorter than she, yet he moved in an aura of warmth and compassion.

He examined Meira. "Not yet. I don't want to induce labor unless we have to."

Meira shut her eyes. In minutes she was asleep.

Dr. Brzezinski turned to Raquela. "Would you like to have coffee with me? There's still plenty of time."

375

In the cafeteria, Raquela noticed doctors and nurses watching her as she stood self-consciously in line for coffee, then made her way to a table with Dr. Brzezinski. What were they thinking?

"Well, young lady," he began, "how do you like nursing?"

"I love it. I can't wait until next February to graduate and really dig in."

"That's good. I like to see enthusiasm in our young nurses."

They sipped their coffee slowly. Dr. Brzezinski leaned across the table and picked up her hand. "Yours could be the hands of a surgeon. Or a musician. Do you play some instrument?"

"I played the violin. At one time I considered becoming a professional violinist. I chose nursing, I guess because of the war."

"I'm glad you made this choice, Raquela. May I call you Raquela?"

She felt flattered and uneasy. Her hand dropped to her lap. Carmi's letter burned through her pocket. . . . *I love the most beautiful and fantastic girl in the world.*

"WHERE did you disappear to?" Meira asked.

"Dr. Brzezinski invited me for coffee."

Meira raised her eyebrows. "Really? That's nice. I think all the nurses around here are in love with him."

Raquela busied herself straightening the sheets.

Meira went on. "He has time for everybody. He treats you as if there's nobody else in the world. He always has advice for everybody. And he can shift from one language to another. You should hear him—Yiddish, Polish, Russian, French, German, English. Oh, and Hebrew, of course."

Raquela felt a cold sweat of guilt beneath her uniform.

"Raquela!" Meira shrieked. "I think the baby's coming."

Raquela ran to the nurses' station. "Get Dr. Brzezinski."

Within minutes he arrived and examined Meira, talking in a low voice. "You're ready," he said.

Raquela and an orderly wheeled Meira into the delivery room. They put her on the table and waited for Dr. Brzezinski.

When he appeared, in a green operating-room uniform, Raquela stood to the side. She watched as Dr. Brzezinski's capable hands drew life from Meira's body.

A cry pierced the delivery room. Meira had a son.

EACH DAY RAQUELA listened to the radio reports and clipped articles from the newspapers. Allied forces were racing across Europe. Liberating parts of Germany, Austria, and Poland, they came upon the concentration camps whose names no one had heard before: Dachau, Bergen-Belsen, Treblinka, Auschwitz.

Raquela read that tough British and American generals wept when they entered the death camps. Battle-hardened soldiers fainted when they saw the charred bodies inside huge ovens, when they saw bodies piled on top of one another, tossed together by the retreating Nazis. They gave rations to cadaverous-looking survivors, some of whom died from the food their emaciated bodies could no longer accept. Doctors gave morphine to alleviate the suffering of the half-dead concentration-camp victims.

Raquela felt anger. Disbelief.

One evening she heard Moshe Sharett on the radio. Head of the political department of the Jewish Agency, Sharett had landed in Italy in April to visit the Jewish troops. Now he was reporting what he had seen: "Thousands of our young men and women have gone to Italy, not as exiles, but as liberators. Not as victims, but proud of their strength . . . in fulfillment of a mission to fight with the sons of other nations against the foe of their people and all mankind."

Raquela felt a surge of pride. Sharett was talking of Carmi and others like him.

"They appear as the messengers of the beginning of their people's rebirth."

People's rebirth. The words had never had so much meaning. After the war. After the obscene deaths. Now the rebirth.

CARMI wrote constantly. He had been gone more than a year and a half, and Raquela found him receding in her consciousness.

"You write less and less," he complained in his last letter. "Has anything happened? Are you sick?"

How little we know each other, she thought. Only his letters and those brief visits on home leave. Can one really know another human being this way?

The traditional Friday afternoon peace settled on Jerusalem. Offices and shops closed early for the Sabbath. Men hurried home bearing flowers for their wives. The Shabbat crier, in a long black coat, walked through the city, blowing the shofar—the ram's horn.

Raquela, working the late Friday shift, felt the Shabbat peace envelop the hospital. She was at the nurses' station when Dr. Brzezinski approached. "Do you have time for coffee?"

It was eleven p.m. "I'll be off duty in one hour," she said.

"I'll come back."

The corridor was eerily quiet when he returned, carrying a bouquet of flowers. "I picked them for you from the garden."

Moslem quarter of the Old City

"Thank you," Raquela murmured.

"I'm sorry we can't have coffee," he said. "I've just been called on an emergency. Are you free tomorrow morning? We could go for a walk."

"I'm free," she said.

Dr. Brzezinski was waiting in the lounge the next morning as she entered. They set off, descending Mount Scopus, cutting across Sheikh Jarrah down to the crenellated walls surrounding the Old City. The hills were carpeted with spring flowers.

They entered the Old City through the huge vaulted Damascus Gate. The narrow streets were crowded. Jewish men in long black silk coats were hurrying toward the Wailing Wall to pray. Synagogues rang with the sounds of men and women at prayer. The Jewish shops and kiosks were shuttered, but in other quarters the Moslems, whose Sabbath was Friday, and the Christians, who closed on Sunday, called to them, "Come inside . . . beautiful jewelry. . . . You want rug . . . copper tray . . . ?"

"Let's go into this shop," Dr. Brzezinski said. From a tray he chose a necklace of blue beads made of Hebron glass. He draped the necklace around Raquela's throat.

"But—but, Dr. Brzezinski. I—"

"No arguments, Raquela. I like what blue beads do for you."

She glanced at herself in the mirror on the counter. She saw red spots on her cheeks.

"I know a small restaurant right outside the Damascus Gate

that has the best fresh fish in Jerusalem," he said. "Let's go there and have some lunch."

They entered the little restaurant and a young Arab showed them to a table. They ordered St. Peter's fish, brought down from the Sea of Galilee.

Raquela wanted to ask Dr. Brzezinski about himself. She knew only that he lived in the bachelors' quarters in the hospital and that he had come from Europe.

"A piaster for your thoughts, Raquela."

"I was just about to ask you about yourself, Dr. Brzezinski."

"What would you like to know?"

"Where are you from?"

"I was born in Poland. In Lodz. I wanted to be a doctor. But a Jew couldn't study medicine in Poland. So my father sent me to Paris in 1928. I spent seven years in medicine at the Sorbonne. I came here in 1935."

This man, gracefully dissecting the fish on his plate, was different from anyone she had known before, Raquela thought. He had European charm and manners—like a courtly gentleman. She compared him with Carmi. Carmi was far more handsome, but immature and self-absorbed.

Dr. Brzezinski continued. "You've never known what it is to live in a country like Poland, where you're hated for one crime, that of being a Jew." He seemed to turn inward. "You are a sabra," he said thoughtfully, "born in the Holy Land. You sabras are a new kind of Jew in the world." He leaned across the table. "Maybe that's why you intrigue me so, Raquela."

"Your background intrigues me, too. I'd like to know more."

He patted her hand. "You will. In time."

Lunch was over.

They walked back in the afternoon sun to Mount Scopus. The wind sang through Raquela's hair. She felt lighthearted and happy. "May I ask your advice, Dr. Brzezinski?"

"With pleasure."

She smiled. "They're starting a special course in midwifery. And even though I'm still a student nurse, I was chosen to be in the class. What do you think?"

"You are a lover of life, Raquela. And those who love life have a duty to bring new lives into the world. Not only do I think you

379

should become a midwife, but I will be happy to assist you in your first delivery."

"I really don't know what to say. Thank you. Thank you, Dr. Brzezinski."

"Please call me Arik."

She stopped walking. "You really want me to—to call you Arik?"

"Yes, Raquela."

May 8, 1945

Soon Raquela was ready to perform her first delivery. She had worked, studied, assisted the nurse-midwife-teacher until she knew every stage of the delivery.

"Let me know," Arik had told her, "when you take your patient to the delivery room. I'll do the supervising myself."

It was seven in the morning, and Raquela, apprehensive, was waiting behind the desk at the nurses' station for the first pregnant woman to arrive. Before long, two women approached the desk. "Are we in the right place?" the older of the women asked Raquela. "My daughter—she's going to have a baby."

"Yes, this is the maternity wing," Raquela said. "Do sit down. I'll need some information from you." On a chart she recorded the young woman's statistics. Name, Batya Ovadiah. Age, twenty-one. (Exactly my age, Raquela thought.) Second pregnancy. Husband's name, Shimon. Away at war.

Raquela took the chart. "Now come with me." She turned to the older woman. "You can either wait here or come back later."

"I'd better go home. We left Batya's little girl with a neighbor." She kissed her daughter and left.

In the examining room, Raquela handed her patient a hospital gown. Then she weighed her. Took her temperature. Pulse. Blood pressure. Urine. She listened through her stethoscope to the baby's heartbeat. It was strong and steady.

A pain convulsed Batya's body. She stifled a scream.

"You're ready," Raquela said. She helped Batya off the bed and into the labor room. "Try to relax between the pains." They were coming closer. Ten minutes apart. Seven. Four. Three. Two.

Finally it was time to call Arik. He met them in the delivery room. The best obstetrician in the hospital, Raquela thought, taking precious time for me. I must not make a single mistake.

She braced herself. "Batya, listen carefully. I will tell you what to do." With each new contraction Raquela commanded, "Push down." Batya pushed. "Good. Now relax again." The next pain came instantly. "Push, Batya! Push! Push!"

Raquela forgot Dr. Brzezinski was watching. For suddenly she saw it—the tiny skull covered with a mat of black hair.

Raquela moved swiftly, instinctively, remembering what she had been taught. Soon, wet and red and trailing its umbilical cord, the baby completed its journey, entering the strange new world. Crying out.

"Batya," Raquela called out, "you have a beautiful girl."

Quickly Raquela placed the baby on a sterile diaper and with a tube sucked the amniotic fluid out of the baby's mouth. Next she cut the umbilical cord.

"Is she normal?" Batya asked anxiously.

"Normal? A genius. She has ten fingers and ten toes."

Raquela heard Dr. Brzezinski laugh. She washed the baby and put a drop of silver nitrate in each eye. Then she wrapped her in a cloth and laid her on Batya's abdomen.

Batya's eyes were shut, but there was ecstasy on her face, and her hands moved eloquently as she caressed her baby.

But there was still work to be done. The placenta—the afterbirth that had transferred oxygen and nourishment from Batya to her baby—was still inside her uterus.

Raquela placed the baby in a bassinet. Then she massaged Batya's abdomen. At last, after twenty minutes, the placenta began moving. Raquela drew it out.

Now Raquela shouted joyfully, "Mazel tov!" Congratulations.

Raquela lifted the baby into Batya's arms. The baby's eyes opened, as though she wanted to see the face of this stranger in whose body she had swum and slept and survived. For Raquela this was the moment of magic.

Batya, lost in rapture, stroked her baby's cheeks. Finally she whispered, "She is beautiful. Dear God, let Shimon come home from the war and see his little daughter."

"You were so good," Arik told Batya, "that you can come back next year."

Later, as Arik and Raquela walked out together, he said, "I'm proud of you. It was a perfect delivery."

THAT EVENING THE student nurses and teachers stood in the lounge listening to Winston Churchill on the BBC: ". . . the evildoers, who are now prostrate before us . . ." The war in the West was over.

From the House of Commons they heard the opening of "God Save the King." Proudly they joined in the singing. When the broadcast ended, they sang their own anthem, "Hatikvah"—a song of hope.

Raquela saw tears rolling down her friend Judith Steiner's cheeks. She put her arms around her. "Maybe you'll hear something about your family in Czechoslovakia now."

"It's six years since I saw them. And not one word." Then slowly, as if she were dredging the words out of a well of pain, Judith said, "If I could only get one letter—one little note from my mother telling me she's alive."

Raquela wanted to comfort her. But she could find no phrases.

She looked around the lounge. For each woman the victory had a special meaning. She knew which ones were waiting for their husbands, boy friends, fathers, brothers to come home. For her the end of the war meant Carmi. Now, in the mixture of joy and anxiety that filled the room, his face seemed clearer, closer to her than it had for months. She saw the jaunty cap. The moviestar smile. Soon he would be home, soon he would hold her in his arms.

But Carmi did not come home. The men of the Jewish Brigade were detained by the British in Europe. It was clear that Whitehall feared the demobilized soldiers might use their military skill to help Jewish survivors enter Palestine.

For Raquela and the other lonely women the waiting during the postwar days seemed interminable.

July 26, 1945

Again, elation in Jerusalem. The Labour Party in Britain was swept into office in the July elections. For years the Labour Party had denounced the white paper, deploring the pro-Arab stance of the Conservatives. Even Churchill, who called himself a proud Zionist, had continued the old policy all during the war. Now Churchill and the Conservatives were out. The British people, exhausted from the deprivations and tragedies of the war, weary of the long separations from their families, wanted a change, a clean sweep, new faces, and more democratic goals.

The news seemed to herald the long-awaited end of the white paper. But within days, Ernest Bevin, the Labour Party's new foreign minister, reneged. Election promises were only promises. The white paper was still the law of the land in Palestine.

"Why?" Raquela asked Arik. He was her mentor in politics, as in medicine.

It was early evening. They were sitting on a wide window ledge overlooking the Arab village of Issawiya, which lay just below.

"Why?" he repeated. "Because oil talks louder than promises."

"Where do we go from here, Arik? To whom do we turn?" Her glance followed his down the mountain.

"The United States," he said. "They're the new world power. They will decide our fate."

October 1945

In the dining room, Raquela looked up. "Carmi!" she shouted.

"Who's he?" Arik asked, looking at the tall young officer in the doorway.

"My friend. He's back from Italy." She rose from the table and ran toward Carmi.

He enveloped her in his arms. "I can't believe it," he whispered. "You're real. I'm not dreaming this."

"Carmi! You didn't write me you were coming home."

"There was no time. A ship was leaving Italy and they let some of us from the brigade go aboard."

She took his hand. "I want you to meet one of the gynecologists I'm working with. You remember I wrote you about Dr. Brzezinski?" She led him around the dining-room tables. Arik stood up.

"Dr. Brzezinski, may I present Lieutenant Eisenberg?"

The two men shook hands. "Pleased to meet you, Lieutenant. Will you join us?"

"Am I interrupting something—a medical meeting, or a—" Carmi's eyes moved from Arik to Raquela.

"Not at all." Arik was expansive. "We're just having lunch together. It's an honor to have you with us."

"Carmi, you sit right down here next to Arik. I'll get you a tray of food."

She walked to the cafeteria line, "Carmi is back" singing in her ears. The two men who meant most to her in the world were now sitting together. Carmi, boy friend, war hero. And Arik, her wise, philosophical teacher.

The line moved slowly. She filled Carmi's tray and carried it through the dining room.

At the table, she stopped short. The two men were silent. Carmi looked sullen and glum, Arik baffled.

She sat down. "Carmi, tell Arik some of the things you did with the Jewish Brigade."

He glared at her. "I'm not in the mood!"

Arik said, "It's all right. I understand."

Carmi shoveled the food angrily into his mouth. Finally he exploded. "Do you two eat lunch together every day? How long has this been going on?"

"Carmi!" Raquela snapped. "You have no right to ask that."

Arik moved his chair away from the table.

"Please don't go, Arik," Raquela said.

"I'm sure you want to be alone together. Good-by, Lieutenant." Carmi nodded.

Raquela tried to eat but couldn't. Her mind was churning. Carmi doesn't trust me, she thought. Maybe he's incapable of trusting any woman. How can I live with that kind of jealousy? "Let's go," she said.

Silently they walked to the garden and descended to the circular bench, where they sat close together, as they had before, but in stony silence.

Finally Carmi asked truculently, "Who is this friend of yours?"

Raquela burst out, "He's one of the most respected doctors in the country. And my teacher."

"The way he looks at you, I'd say he's a lot more than your teacher."

"Stop it, Carmi! I've been loyal to you. Dr. Brzezinski is a good friend."

Raquela stared at him. He was somehow frightening. She bit her lip, feeling guilt. He's been away so long, she thought, fighting Nazis, liberating the death camps. I must give him time.

She gave him time. After work they walked, they sat in cafés, they went to the movies. Raquela was determined not to give

Carmi a single reason for jealousy. Yet she felt restless, vulnerable, confused.

One day they decided to go to the beach near Tel Aviv. The October day was flawless, the air clean and cool. Carmi spoke with quiet conviction as they walked along the promenade. "My dream, after all those years in Egypt, in Italy, in Europe, is for the two of us to spend our lives in a farm village." He put his arm around her waist.

Raquela walked in silence. Could she spend her life on a farm? What about her work? The thought of nursing brought Arik to mind. Guilt rose again. Why should she think of Arik while she was with Carmi? She looked at Carmi's bronzed profile as they walked. There was so much to admire in him—his good looks, his sensitivity, his readiness to lay down his life for the land he loved. But his jealousy filled her with apprehension. "Let's walk in the sand," she said.

They descended the few steps to the beach, took off their shoes, and sat down. The Mediterranean was green-blue and inviting. Impulsively Raquela jumped up and ran to the water's edge. She tucked up her skirt around her thighs and waded into the water, letting the sea lap about her legs.

Two soldiers approached her. *"Shalom, motek"*—Hi, sweetheart.

Raquela smiled, and the next moments were a blur of water splashing, of Carmi shouting at the soldiers, grabbing her arm, pulling her out of the sea. His mouth twitched angrily.

"Why were you flirting with those soldiers?" he demanded.

"Carmi, I was not flirting," Raquela insisted. She was confused. The energy suddenly drained from her. "We'd better go back to Jerusalem."

Soon they were on the bus, climbing the hills once more. They hardly spoke. At Mount Scopus, Carmi pleaded, "Don't go in yet. Let's walk to the garden."

They sat on the stone bench, the city below them washed in the afternoon haze. Raquela said, "Carmi. Let's end it now, before we hurt each other too deeply. I can't live with your jealousy."

"Forgive me, Raquela. It's only because I love you so much." His lips trembled. "But I'll change. I promise."

She shook her head sadly.

"Give me another chance. Please, Raquela."

She was frightened by her own strength. "Carmi, for both our sakes, let's say good-by. Now."

He drew himself up, turned, and walked away.

Raquela watched him disappear. She ran back to the nursing school and up to her room. She flung herself on her bed and wept.

FOR Judith Steiner that October of 1945 was a desperate time. She searched the lists of survivors for news of her family. She put ads in the newspapers in Palestine and in the camps for displaced persons in Germany, Austria, and Italy, where hundreds of thousands of refugees were being sheltered. Finally she received an answer from a school friend:

Dear Judith,

I saw your ad on the wall newspaper in a DP camp near Frankfurt where I and other Jews are waiting. After the liberation—I had been working in a Nazi slave-labor camp—I went back to our home. I looked for my family. But they were all dead. Then I looked for the families of my friends. Judith, dear, it grieves me to tell you that your family, too, were exterminated.

Judith's tears blotted the note. Six years of nightmares had become reality. She forced herself to go on reading:

The only one for whom I could find no witnesses and no records is your little brother Joseph.

Joseph! He had just had his bar mitzvah when she left, in 1939. Could Joseph be alive, wandering somewhere across Europe?

Judith was numb, torn between grief and a glimmer of hope.

In the next weeks Raquela watched her go about her work, serious, never missing a day teaching or comforting other students and nurses who were now learning of their families' fates.

Raquela, longing to comfort her, invited her home on weekends, hoping Mama and Papa might give her the warmth, the sense of family that she had lost.

One weekend Jacob and Meira and their baby were visiting. Jacob, who knew the most about the tragedy in Europe, understood best how to comfort Judith.

"The word is hope. Let me tell you what's happening there," he said. "A mass migration—such as the world has never seen. The Jews who went to their old homes and couldn't live there anymore are now migrating by the thousands to displaced persons camps. And now, from the camps, they're making their way instinctively to Palestine."

"Someone has to help them," Papa said. "Who's helping?"

"We are, Papa. The Haganah. We have two arms helping—on land and sea. The Bricha and the Mosad." He explained that the Bricha—the word means flight—was a clandestine body of emissaries from Palestine who were guiding the mass movement across the frontiers of Europe. The Mosad—the Committee for Illegal Immigration—headed by top Haganah leaders, was in charge of buying boats, outfitting them, and getting the DPs onto the ships.

Jacob turned to Judith. "Nearly every able-bodied person in the DP camps wants to get on one of our boats. Maybe one of them will be Joseph."

Judith whispered, "Dear God, make it happen."

Now the ships were coming, landing in the dead of night. Haganah men and women waded into the water, helped the refugees jump off the ships, then rushed them into kibbutzim and towns along the coast. They hid them until they could get them ID cards, give them a history and a past, and teach them the answers to give police if they were stopped.

When the British caught wind of the operation, they sent vessels into the Mediterranean to halt the mass movement, and they patrolled the coast of Palestine with planes and ships.

Some of the boats escaped the dragnet, but many were caught. The British put the people on trucks and transported them to a place called Athlit.

An ancient and beautiful port, Athlit lay just below Haifa. In the Middle Ages the Crusaders had built a castle overlooking the harbor. The castle ruins were still standing. Here, during the Arab riots of the late thirties, the British erected one of their chain of police stations, Tegart Fortresses, named for Sir James Tegart, the architect who had planned them. Now the British were adding a new chapter in Athlit's history: a detention camp for the survivors of concentration camps.

By the fall of 1945 the camp was already overflowing with more than two hundred captured refugees, herded into tents and barracks and caged behind barbed wire. In the wake of the tragedy in Europe, now there was a detention camp on the soil of the Holy Land itself.

The tougher the British became, the stronger the resistance grew.

The Haganah joined forces with two other national liberation movements—the Irgun, under the leadership of Menachem Begin, and the Lehi, or the Stern group. Together they formed the Jewish Resistance Movement. In a united front, resistance fighters began sabotaging bridges, railways, military installations, and the British patrol boats that were scouring the coast for illegal ships.

In Europe, more and more Jews were streaming into the DP camps and more and more boats were being outfitted to carry the survivors through the British blockade to Palestine.

President Truman, shocked by the conditions in the DP camps and the continued suffering, asked England's foreign minister, Ernest Bevin, to allow one hundred thousand DPs to enter Palestine. Truman felt that Bevin dared not refuse. The Labour Party needed American aid to bolster the crumbling British Empire. On November 13, 1945, Bevin announced the creation of the Anglo-American Committee of Inquiry on Palestine. It was the eighteenth commission on Palestine since the Mandate. Meanwhile, the white paper would remain the law of the land.

PART THREE

February 7, 1946

Raquela hung her student uniform away. She trembled a little as she slipped her new white uniform over her head and pinned on the new cap that marked her as a graduate nurse. It was a simple white cap with a red Star of David in the center. She fluffed some powder on her nose and hurried through the pergola into the hospital.

The vast entrance hall was transformed. Hundreds of people had crowded into the lobby, talking in low, excited voices. Raquela took her place with her class. Behind the nurses, in rows of wooden chairs, sat their relatives and friends. Raquela turned her head and saw Mama and Papa sitting proudly. Dr. Brzezinski sat near the back. Their eyes met and held.

After the speeches, Mrs. Cantor called each girl forward to present her with a large round silver pin, with HADASSAH superimposed over the Star of David. Circling the edge of the pin in tiny Hebrew letters were the words, THE HEALING OF THE DAUGHTER OF MY PEOPLE and the name, HADASSAH—HENRIETTA SZOLD SCHOOL OF NURSING, JERUSALEM.

"Raquela Levy." She heard Mrs. Cantor call her name again. "Will you please come forward?"

She walked to the speaker's table. Mrs. Cantor was beaming. "You have been selected as the outstanding student in your class. I am proud to present you with the Elsa Sterling Award. It's an award from America given in memory of a young woman who was president of Junior Hadassah."

Mrs. Cantor handed her two medical volumes. "I hope, Miss Levy, that you will find these books useful for the rest of your life. There's also a gift of money, but I'm sure you would like to donate it to Miss Szold's favorite project—Youth Aliyah."

A ripple of laughter broke out in the hall.

Raquela smiled. "I'm pleased to give it in memory of that wonderful woman." The hall burst into applause. Returning to her seat, she caught a glimpse of Papa's face wreathed in smiles. Arik Brzezinski's hands, high in the air, were applauding her. She sat down, her heart beating wildly.

The ceremony was over. The people spilled out into the garden, set with tables of food and drinks. Mama and Papa embraced Raquela.

Arik approached. "Mazel tov, Raquela. I was sure you'd be chosen best student."

She blushed, trying to hide her pleasure.

"I'd like to help you celebrate," Arik said. "Are you free for dinner?"

"I am, but first I want you to meet my parents."

She introduced him to Papa and Mama. Shaking Papa's hand, he said, "I know your school, Mr. Levy, and your reputation as one of the great teachers of the Bible."

Papa smiled modestly. "I am afraid Raquela exaggerates."

Raquela slipped her arm through Papa's. He was all strength

and tenderness. And now, looking at Arik, she sensed those same qualities in him.

"Excuse me," she said to Mama and Papa. "I've got to go up and change."

Mama nodded. "We're leaving now. Good-by, Dr. Brzezinski."

He bowed slightly and kissed her hand.

HESSE'S Restaurant was up a flight of stairs in downtown Jerusalem. A waiter led Raquela and Arik to a table in the far corner.

They ordered shish kebab and a bottle of red wine.

Arik raised his glass. "To you, my dear. To a brilliant future."

Raquela's eyes shone. She clinked her glass against his. "And to you, Arik. To my teacher."

They sipped the wine slowly, watching each other's faces.

It seemed to Raquela that Arik was looking at her differently now that she was a graduate. Was graduation a kind of climax? An end, and a beginning?

Arik had taken a volume of Sholom Aleichem's stories from his coat pocket and was thumbing through the pages. "Listen to this," he said, reading. " 'You've got to stay alive even if it kills you.' That's Sholom Aleichem's philosophy. And it works for me, too. It tickles my patients."

She laughed, watching his face radiate love for the Yiddish writer.

" 'You may as well laugh,' Sholom Aleichem says. 'Even if you don't see the joke, laugh on credit. You may see the joke later, and if not, you're that much to the good.' "

She chuckled. She wanted to tell Arik how she felt. He would always be her teacher, in medicine, literature, politics, life. She wanted to be open with him, to know him better. But now he was entering her life in a new way. And she could not talk.

Was it possible to fall in love with a man nearly fifteen years older than she? She looked again at his face. It seemed the kindest face in the world.

AFTER graduation Raquela moved back with Mama and Papa. But whenever shootings and explosions made it too dangerous to get home, she and other nurses and doctors stayed on Mount Scopus.

The Holy Land had become a police state. There were now one hundred thousand British soldiers there. Jerusalem's streets were blocked off by great rusted coils of barbed wire. Hotels and office buildings were guarded by concrete pillboxes dubbed dragon's teeth. Tanks and armored cars patrolled the streets. Newspapers were censored. Civil liberties were dead.

Curfew was imposed from seven at night to five in the morning. Anyone caught in the streets without permission could be arrested. Raquela had special permission to be out during curfew, as did all the doctors and nurses. But when she had night duty, Hadassah's station wagon called for her at home.

Raquela and Arik spent all their free time together. Often, while he worked at his desk, she sat reading on his divan. Then, his work finished, they would walk in the garden, holding hands as they strolled among the Jerusalem pines and the spreading eucalyptus trees.

She felt happy and safe. Yet she had doubts about him. He was attentive, affectionate. He brought her gifts. When a flu epidemic felled her for a week in the infirmary, he brought her a rose every morning. But not once had he said he loved her. Until he said it, she would not be sure.

March 1946

One night they sat in Arik's room glued to the radio. Dr. Chaim Weizmann, president of both the Jewish Agency for Palestine and the World Zionist Organization, was testifying in Jerusalem before the Anglo-American Committee of Inquiry on Palestine.

Raquela had seen photos of this old, weary, nearly blind man. It was hard to believe those photos now as she listened to his voice. Strong. Passionate.

"We warned you," he said. "We . . . told you that the first flames that licked at the synagogues of Berlin would set fire, in time, to all the world." He paused. "I ask you to follow the course of least injustice in determining the fate of Palestine."

Arik whispered, "The least injustice."

"European Jewry cannot be expected to resettle on soil drenched with Jewish blood. Their only hope for survival lies in the creation of a Jewish state in Palestine. The leaky boats in which our refugees come to Palestine are the *Mayflowers* of a whole generation."

The next witness was David Ben-Gurion, chairman of the Executive of the Jewish Agency, the stocky leader with a halo of white hair. The committee was asking him to define a "Jewish state." His powerful voice blared through the radio. "By 'Jewish state' we mean Jewish independence. We mean Jewish safety and security. Complete independence, as for any other free people."

Ben-Gurion's words carried new hope. This Anglo-American Committee was different from all the others. It had six Americans sitting with the six Englishmen. The Americans understood the meaning of a "free people." The Americans would make a difference.

After the hearings the committee flew to Lausanne, Switzerland, to write their report. They sincerely believed Bevin's promise that if their report was unanimous, he would carry it out. After a month of debates and compromises, the twelve men voted unanimously to accede to President Truman's request: one hundred thousand DPs would be allowed to enter Palestine.

Joy spread through the DP camps and Palestine. But almost overnight the joy turned to bitterness. British Prime Minister Clement Attlee announced that the Haganah and all private armies must be disarmed before any large-scale immigration could begin.

The report of the eighteenth commission was scuttled.

The Jewish Resistance Movement organized mass demonstrations and fought the British Army and police. They blew up all the bridges on the borders of Palestine.

Two weeks later the British decided to break the back of the Jewish Resistance Movement and, they hoped, to crush the Jewish will to establish a state.

At four fifteen a.m. on "Black Saturday," June 29, Raquela, sleeping in her bedroom at Bet Hakerem, was awakened. Tanks and armored cars rumbled through the streets. In a countrywide military action, soldiers burst into homes, searched attics and cellars looking for ammunition, and arrested twenty-six hundred men and women.

The leaders of the country, men like Moshe Sharett, were imprisoned in the police fortress at Latrun.

Golda Meir, who had already distinguished herself in the Palestine labor movement, was chosen as acting head of the political department of the Jewish Agency, to replace Sharett.

David Ben-Gurion was in Paris, and he escaped.

Menachem Begin, leader of the Irgun, eluded the search.

Dr. Weizmann, who was not arrested, held a press conference.

That night Raquela sat with Mama and Papa in the living room, listening to Dr. Weizmann on the radio. "First the situation is allowed to deteriorate almost beyond hope," he said. "Then it is the victims of that deterioration that are punished. Is it not a most grotesque state of affairs that the mufti should be sitting in a palace in Egypt, enjoying freedom, while Moshe Sharett, who raised an army for Britain of more than twenty-five thousand men, is behind barbed wire at Latrun?"

A voice on the radio announced, "We interrupt this broadcast to bring you a news flash. A pogrom today in Kielce, Poland, has taken the lives of many Jews. Exact details are not yet known." The broadcast was over.

Papa switched off the radio and began to pace restlessly. "These are the Jews who went back to their homes in Poland. These are the people who believed the propaganda that the world had changed, that there is no more anti-Semitism."

The Kielce pogrom started a new mass migration to the DP camps. More ships were outfitted to carry the DPs to Palestine. The white paper war continued, and as the struggle intensified, fear and terror spread throughout the Holy Land.

July 1946

Menachem Begin was the object of an intense manhunt by the British, his clean-shaven, bespectacled face on every "wanted" billboard. Begin was posing as Reb Israel Sassover, a bearded scholar, living in a small house in Tel Aviv. He spent much of his time in a synagogue, studying.

While his former house was under constant surveillance by the British police, Begin and the Irgun planned a daring attack on the headquarters of the British government at the King David Hotel in Jerusalem.

At first the Haganah command would not approve the plan. They feared that an attack on the headquarters would inflame the British to even more repressive measures.

But after Black Saturday, June 29, the Haganah command approved Begin's plan.

393

Just before noon on July 22, Irgun men dressed as Arabs carried large milk cans into the basement of the southern wing of the hotel. Inside the cans were explosives.

The next steps were carefully planned to prevent casualties. To clear the streets, a small firecracker was exploded opposite the hotel. Then a young woman made three calls. First she phoned the hotel, warning that explosives were to go off in a short time. Next she called the Palestine *Post,* warning about the bombs. Her final call was to the French consulate, next to the hotel, telling them to open their windows to prevent shattering. They followed her instruction.

Twenty-five minutes passed. Reporters from the Palestine *Post* had already reached the King David Hotel. Yet, to the horror of the underground fighters, there was no evacuation.

Later the Haganah radio reported that Sir John Shaw, the chief secretary of the British administration, had refused to accept the telephone warning, saying, "I don't take orders from Jews."

Twelve thirty-seven p.m. The whole city seemed to shake. The entire southern wing of the hotel exploded in the air. Ninety-one people were killed and forty-five injured. The French consulate was undamaged.

The British arrested three hundred and seventy-six people and sent twenty thousand troops to find Begin and the other leaders. Begin's cover held.

The British were desperate. No more Jews must enter Palestine. The patrols on the Mediterranean found the illegal ships that continued to sail, and imprisoned their passengers in Athlit. In August 1946, when Athlit could hold no more, the British opened new camps on the island of Cyprus.

Now there were two places of detention for the refugees captured on the high seas: Cyprus and Athlit.

March 1947

Raquela was finishing in the delivery room when a nurse told her that Dr. Yassky wanted to see her.

Raquela had been working as a registered nurse-midwife for a whole year now—ever since graduation—and had not once been called to his office.

Now, as she hurried down the corridor, her mind was churning.

What could he want? To most of his staff Dr. Yassky was a remote figure. He was the boss, the director general of the Hadassah Medical Organization.

Arik had told her stories of how Dr. Yassky and his wife, Fanny, had fled the Russian Revolution and come to Palestine in 1919. How appalled he had been to find that the large majority of Arab children, and nearly half the Jewish children, had eyes scarred with trachoma.

He had become a school doctor in Haifa, treating trachoma with a copper-sulphate stick. He cured the children. Henrietta Szold asked him to take the fight against blindness to the whole country. He became *the* itinerant ophthalmologist, traveling with a little cart and horse or on a donkey.

Raquela relaxed, picturing Dr. Yassky, six feet tall, his legs dangling, sitting on the back of a donkey. But as she knocked on his door her body grew tense again.

"Come in," he said. He was sitting behind his desk, smoking a cigarette in a silver and black holder. He looked austere, aristocratic. "Sit down, Miss Levy," he commanded. "I am sure you know about Athlit." She nodded. "It has nearly three thousand refugees. They've asked us to send a midwife."

Raquela blurted, "A midwife in a detention camp!"

"Even in a detention camp, men and women find ways to be together." He wafted smoke in the air. "You're the youngest midwife in our hospital." His austere face broke into a smile. "But even in this office I hear when a nurse is gifted, when she is completely dedicated to her patients." He got up, walked around the desk, and put his hand on her shoulder. "Can you imagine what it would mean to these survivors, still homeless nearly two years after the Holocaust, to have a young woman from Jerusalem helping them bring children into the world? It won't be an easy job. We would like you to stay three or four weeks." He looked at her face. "Will you accept it?"

"When would you like me to go?"

"The moment you're ready."

SHE knocked at Arik's door.

He was at his desk, reading. He looked up. "You've accepted," he said.

She stopped short. "Then you knew?"

"Dr. Yassky asked my opinion. He knew all about you; his only hesitation was that you are so young."

She walked to the divan. He followed her and put his arm around her.

"It's good you're going," he said. "Not only for the refugees but for us."

"Why?"

He took her face in his hands. "I've been monopolizing you, Raquela. It's not right. I'm too old for you."

"Fourteen years isn't such a big gap. Your beloved Sholom Aleichem would see that I'm twenty-two going on thirty. And you're thirty-six going on—let's say—thirty-three. So you're only three years older than I am."

He kissed her cheek. "Let's not discuss it," he said. "Your mission is important. You're going to be the first Hadassah nurse these refugees will have seen." He paused. "A ninth-generation Jerusalemite—you're the fulfillment of their dreams."

They walked hand in hand to the hospital entrance to wait for the station wagon that would take her through the silent, curfewed streets to Bet Hakerem.

April 1947

The bus driver called out, "Athlit," and stopped. Raquela hurried down the steps with her suitcase.

Two doctors stood in front of an ambulance. They introduced themselves—Dr. Mossberg, Jewish Agency doctor in charge of health services in the camp; Dr. Altman, eye, ear, nose, and throat man. Each day, they explained, a different specialist came to the camp from Haifa. Raquela and the doctors climbed into the ambulance for the mile drive down the access road.

The camp loomed before her. Watchtowers, manned by British soldiers, pierced the sky. Rows and rows of barbed wire stretched around an arid landscape.

At a barbed-wire gate the doctors and Raquela produced their ID cards. The gates were unlatched. Raquela followed the doctors, then stopped abruptly.

Hundreds of people were milling together on a dirt road, dressed in tattered rags. Dirty brown wooden barracks stood in martial rows, interspersed here and there with army tents. Everything looked dusty and threatening.

Near the entrance, Raquela saw the delousing station, where British soldiers sprayed people with DDT powder.

"The women are in the barracks at the left," Dr. Mossberg told her, "the men at the right. And over here is the hospital."

Each compound was surrounded by barbed wire. Camps within camps, Raquela thought dismally. She felt as if a giant lock were being turned. She was trapped.

"This first hut," Dr. Mossberg said as he led her into a white barracks, "is the clinic. Here you'll find dozens of patients waiting for you at all hours."

Some thirty people sat on camp chairs, their legs covered with open sores. Flies and mosquitoes buzzed around them.

A nurse burst into the room. "I didn't believe I'd ever get a replacement," she said. "Let's not waste time. I'm due back at the British Government Hospital in Haifa. You'll be the only midwife here. Is there anything you want me to tell you?"

"I'd like to see the delivery room and the equipment."

"What equipment?"

Raquela was flustered. "Well, I mean, you must have clamps and sputum tubes. What about sterilized sheets and towels?"

"Where do you think you are? Mount Scopus? Who has anything sterilized here?"

The doctors left as the nurse led Raquela to the delivery room. Inside was a leather delivery table. "Here's a sheet. The only time a woman sees one is in this room or in the hospital."

Nausea overcame Raquela. She leaned against the delivery table. The midwife looked worried. "Don't you feel well?"

"I'll be all right. Just show me where I'm to sleep."

They walked out to a second white barracks. "This is the hospital," her guide explained. They moved on to a third barracks. This one was partitioned into a dining room, kitchen, storage room for food, and three small bedrooms for the hospital staff.

"This is your room," the midwife said. "You won't have much time to be in it."

Raquela set down her bag.

"You're sure you're all right?" the midwife asked.

"Positively. Thank you."

"You're pretty young to be sent to this hell on earth." She picked up her carpetbag and walked out.

Raquela washed her hands and face. Then she hurried to the hospital and went from bed to bed, talking to the patients, learning what she could of their illnesses.

Lunch was at one o'clock. She entered the barracks dining room. A young woman in a spotless white shirt and pleated black skirt put out her hand. "*Shalom*," she said. "I'm Ruth Berman. I'm the Jewish Agency liaison officer between the British and the refugees. Welcome to Gan Eden."

Raquela smiled. "The Garden of Eden with barbed wire."

"After a while you won't notice the barbed wire. It's the other things that will bother you."

After lunch of bully beef, pea soup, white bread, and coffee, Raquela left to make rounds.

Down the length of the camp was a long dirt road called the Walkover. Here hundreds of people milled together, talking, shouting. Raquela walked among them. Some stared at her curiously. Others brushed past her, turned in on themselves. They seemed like people from another planet.

Raquela felt hot anger. These people had survived the death camps. They had come to the Holy Land. Yet it was denied them.

At seven, exhausted, Raquela returned to her room. Her legs were blotched with mosquito bites. She was smearing them with calamine lotion when suddenly a woman walked in.

"My time has come," she said.

Raquela led her into the delivery room and examined her. "You still have time," she said. But how could she send a woman in labor back to the overcrowded barracks? "You can stay here," Raquela said softly. She helped her off the table and tried to make her comfortable in a chair.

The woman's name was Pnina Kaczmarek; her husband was Gershon. She told Raquela she was born in Czechoslovakia. When she was fourteen the Nazis had deported her and her family to Auschwitz. Children of fourteen were almost always sent directly to the gas chambers. Pnina pretended to be sixteen. She was sent to the barracks.

Gershon, also fourteen, had made the journey to Auschwitz from Poland. He, too, had lied that he was older.

They were liberated in April 1945, nearly dead of hunger and typhus. They had gone back to their homes, found no one, and returned to Germany, where they met in a DP camp. They married and vowed they would get to Palestine. The route had led to Athlit.

"How old are you now?" Raquela asked.

Pnina looked forty, but she had to be much younger. "Nineteen," she said, trembling. "What if the war years did something to me? What if I have an abnormal baby?"

Raquela heard the panic mounting. "Don't be afraid. You've come through Auschwitz, the war. You'll come through this." She wiped Pnina's forehead with a damp cloth. "Just think. Your baby will be a sabra."

"I hope I have a daughter. I'll name her Etya, for my mother. She died in Auschwitz."

The contractions were coming at shorter intervals now. Raquela helped Pnina back on the table and soon delivered the baby.

"You have a daughter," she said.

Pnina's face relaxed. She studied her baby, stroked her forehead. Suddenly Pnina was young and radiant. "She's the image of my mother," she said.

THE worst disease of the refugees was boredom. All day they herded up and down the Walkover, endlessly waiting. Occasionally they glanced up at the hill outside the camp. They hated the hill. It separated them from the Mediterranean, blocking the cool sea breezes. Beyond the hill lay freedom.

A few internees escaped by burrowing under the barbed wire. But most were caught and arrested by the ever vigilant sentries.

Each month a few hundred were allowed to leave legally. Under the white paper, fifteen hundred certificates were allotted every month until the day, envisioned by the paper, when no more Jews would be allowed to enter Palestine. The war had sidetracked the original date—1944—when all immigration was to have ceased. The certificates were given to the Jewish Agency to administer: seven hundred and fifty for the Jews in Europe, and seven hundred and fifty for the refugees in Athlit and Cyprus. The rule in the camps was "First in, first out."

At four in the morning, a week after her arrival, Raquela walked out into the night air. She saw a figure moving about with a flashlight. It was Ruth Berman.

"What are you doing out at this hour?" Ruth asked.

"I can't sleep. What are *you* doing up?"

"Making my nightly head count," Ruth said. "It's lucky the British trust *me* to do it. How would you like to have British soldiers check the women's barracks every night?"

Ruth put a key in each barracks door, entered quietly, and made her check. When the head count was finished, they started back toward the hospital. A soldier in a watchtower beamed his light on them.

"They greet me this way every night," Ruth said. "They're victims, too. You can't blame all the British people for their government's policy. A lot of British soldiers are decent, compassionate. The policy is monstrous, not the boys. Never forget, these soldiers are not Nazis. They're interning our people, not killing them."

Raquela glanced up. The sentries were waving to them. She felt a pang of homesickness.

"If you're not ready to go to sleep," Ruth said, "why don't we have a cold drink in my tent?"

The tent had a table, a few chairs, a narrow cot. Ruth lighted a kerosene lamp and poured *gazoz*—fruit-flavored soda—into two glasses. They sat for a while in silence. Then Ruth said, "Camps like this dehumanize people. That's what the Nazis tried to do— dehumanize our people." She refilled their glasses. "When the war ended I was coldly hysterical. Every time I saw a Jewish survivor, I felt guilty that I was alive. We should have done more to save our people. We should have marched on Whitehall. We should have screamed, Save our people!"

She stopped and stared into the light. "When the Jewish Agency asked me to come here, I felt maybe I could do something for the survivors. Then I saw the results of Nazi dehumanization. People with no belief in the future. Dirty, apathetic, quarrelsome. I tried to bribe some of the women to wash their hair. They don't care what they look like."

She went on. "One day I asked some of them, 'Why do you behave this way?'

"'Madame Ruth,' they said, 'what do you want from us? Maybe

once we're out of here we'll change. We'll do the things you'd like us to do. But for now, leave us alone.'"

Two weeks passed. There were no telephones in Athlit. Raquela wondered how Dr. Yassky would get word to her to go home.

Four weeks passed. Six. Seven weeks. She knew she could go to Haifa, telephone Dr. Yassky, and ask him to send a replacement. She never telephoned.

On a boiling-hot afternoon she lay on her cot for a nap. Rats scampered overhead on the tin roof. Often they kept her awake at night. They terrified her. Now she shut her eyes.

Suddenly she screamed. A rat had found its way into her room and leaped, landing in her long hair. She shook her head free of it and raced in panic out of the barracks. I've got to get away from here! she thought frantically. I can't take any more.

She was running down the Walkover toward the entrance gate. Men and women crowded around, some touching her arm.

"My baby is sick. . . ."

"The sore you bandaged is healing. . . ."

"How can I thank you . . . ?"

"You look so pale. Take care of yourself. We need you. . . ."

She stopped running. She felt currents of love eddying toward her from the ragged people. What was a rat, compared with their agony and need? She turned around and reentered the hospital compound.

Late in the afternoon she put on a bathing suit beneath her uniform and took a shortcut across the hill to the sea and the sand. She stepped out of her uniform and ran into the water.

June 1947

A car drove up to the barbed-wire gate. A tall man made his way to the hospital.

"*Shalom*, Miss Levy."

"*Shalom*, Dr. Yassky."

They looked at each other in silence. Finally Dr. Yassky spoke. "I've seen the camp. Take a holiday, Miss Levy. I'll send a replacement for you at once. Go home and rest for a few weeks. Then, if you decide not to come back, I'll understand completely. Your job is always waiting for you at the hospital."

Raquela nodded.

Two days later her replacement arrived. She said good-by to her patients, boarded the intercity bus to Jerusalem, and slept most of the way.

At home, she kissed Mama and Papa, then retired to her room. She slept around the clock. For three days she called no one.

At last she phoned Arik. He hurried from Mount Scopus to Bet Hakerem, held her in his arms, then stood away to look at her.

"You look good," he said. "How about going downtown? There's a Philharmonic concert tonight. Let's have dinner early and celebrate your homecoming."

Soon they were on the bus, riding in the old Jewish quarter of Jerusalem. Raquela looked at the little stone houses and open kiosks, at the men in long black coats and curled earlocks, the women dressed in traditional long-sleeved Hasidic garb despite the summer heat.

"You're so quiet, Raquela," Arik said. "Still tired?"

"A little. Though I should be slept out."

They were now in the bustling modern quarter of New Jerusalem. Women in summer dresses, men in shorts and cool open shirts, walked briskly.

"Look at those people." Raquela shook her head in disbelief. "Sitting in cafés as if nothing has happened. Talking, laughing. Don't they know about Athlit?"

"This is reality, too, Raquela. I'm worried about you."

"I don't think I can sit through dinner and a concert," she said.

"What would you like to do?"

"Let's go up to Mount Scopus."

Raquela felt her spirits lift as they strolled arm in arm on the mountain she loved. The flower-scented air, the serenity, Arik's nearness were like balm. At last the words came, released in a torrent. She began to tell him about the rats, the lack of privacy, the despair, her feelings of guilt when she sought refuge in the sea.

He took her hand. "You had a right to push the camp away for a few hours. Doctors and nurses live with tragedy every day. If we don't escape occasionally, we can't function. We can break under the pressure."

Tears formed in her eyes. "But Arik, *I* could run away from the camp. The refugees couldn't."

RAQUELA STROLLED THROUGH New Jerusalem, looking at shop-windows. She entered a dress shop and rummaged through the racks. She'd been gone only two and a half months and already the styles had changed. The skirts were longer and the shoulders of suits were padded.

The salesgirl held up a voluminous taffeta dress. "It's the 'new look.' Christian Dior designed it. Why don't you try it on? With your height and figure, you'd look—supercolossal."

Raquela smiled. In the fitting room, she tried on the dress. It was brown, Senora Vavá's favorite color. That was good. She looked at herself in the mirror. It had another advantage. It made her look older than the cotton skirts and blouses she usually wore. Would Arik notice?

"I love it," she told the salesgirl. "I'll take it."

RAQUELA spent the next days at home. Jacob and Yair came with their wives, and Arik came in the evenings. But Raquela's mind kept wandering back to Athlit. She would have to make a decision. Return—or stay.

All conversation stopped when Papa turned on the radio in the living room for the nightly broadcast of the UNSCOP hearings.

UNSCOP, the United Nations Special Committee on Palestine, was composed of delegates from eleven small, neutral countries.

Earlier in the year Bevin had finally given up and announced to Parliament that he was turning the Palestine problem over to the United Nations. With the exception of the revolt of the American colonies and of Ireland, Palestine was the greatest political failure in the history of the British Empire.

The United Nations had held a special session on Palestine. The fifty-five member nations voted to send another committee to investigate and make recommendations. But this one was to be different. For the first time Britain was not part of the group investigating her own role in the Holy Land.

Raquela sat beside Arik on the sofa. She heard the radio announcer describe the eleven members of UNSCOP. Eleven strangers trying to decide the fate of Palestine, she thought. The fate of the Jews, the Arabs, and the British. Eleven Solomons pondering what to do with the "baby." Give it to one of the mothers? Give it to the foster-mother—Britain? Or cut it in half?

"What the Jews need," Ben-Gurion told the committee, "is immigration and statehood. What the Arabs need is economic development and social progress."

Immigration and statehood. That's what my people in Athlit want. She heard Ben-Gurion say, "We feel we are entitled to Palestine as a whole, but we will be ready to consider the question of the Jewish state in an adequate area of Palestine."

So they might cut the baby in half after all, Raquela thought.

A few nights later Arik came to the house for dinner. Afterward he and Raquela were to go to the Philharmonic. She wore her new brown dress.

Arik noticed it instantly. "Turn around, Raquela. Gorgeous."

Delighted, she asked, "And don't you think it makes me look older?"

He laughed. "Positively ancient."

The family ate in the little foyer. After the meal they took their coffee cups into the living room. Papa switched on the radio. Dr. Weizmann was addressing the committee: "Why Palestine . . . a country which has been neglected and derelict for centuries?"

He then talked of Moses and of the Biblical promise. That's why they had come. Four thousand years ago. This was the Land of the Promise.

He went on. "For us, the question is of survival, and it brooks no delay. All that you have seen here constitutes national progress. All of it we did with our own hands. Here in Palestine there were marshes and we have drained them; there were no houses and we have built them. All that has been done here, from the modest cottage of the settler to the University on Mount Scopus, is the work of Jewish planning, Jewish genius and of Jewish hands . . ."

Arik stood up. "I wish we could stay, but it's late."

They hurried into town. Inside the concert hall, Arik whispered, "You look so beautiful. Everybody's looking at you."

Raquela beamed with pleasure.

After the concert they walked along Jaffa Road and entered a coffee shop. Raquela knew she must resolve her conflict over Athlit. "Arik," she said, "we have carefully avoided discussing something very much on my mind."

"I waited for you to bring it up," he said.

"What do you think about my going back?"

"I think you've given so much of yourself that you shouldn't feel any guilt if you decide to stay in Jerusalem."

"It's not guilt that would make me go. It's all that's happened since I came home. UNSCOP. Listening to Ben-Gurion and Weizmann. It makes me see Athlit in a different perspective."

He nodded and waited for her to go on.

"Even in the misery of Athlit, prisoners are asserting their right to a home for their babies. They need me to help bring those babies into the world. How can I let them down?"

"I'll miss you, Raquela," he said.

THE days seemed shorter now in Athlit; the weeks meshed. One morning Dr. Carr, the camp gynecologist, came to the hospital with a message for Raquela. "I've just come from Haifa. A friend of yours—Judith Steiner—will be here this afternoon."

"Judith!" Raquela exclaimed. "But I thought no visitors were allowed in Athlit."

"She's not a visitor. She discovered her brother is here."

So Joseph had survived. Thank God.

"We're telling the guards," Dr. Carr explained, "that she's coming as a nurse to replace you for a little while."

When Judith arrived, Raquela threw her arms around her. She noticed Judith was wearing sunglasses. Was it to hide her tears?

"Sit down for a few minutes, Judith."

Judith steadied herself in the chair. "I don't know if I'll even recognize him. I haven't seen him for seven years. He was thirteen—" Her voice broke.

Raquela drew up a chair beside her. Slowly Judith tried to regain composure. "Everyone in Jerusalem sends you love. Dr. Brzezinski wants to know when you're coming back."

"I've no idea. So long as they need me . . ."

Judith stood up. "I'm feeling better now, Raquela."

"Do you want me to look for your brother with you?"

Judith shook her head. "I must find him myself. Just tell me where to look."

They went out to the Walkover. "The men's barracks are on this side. They've been kept together pretty much according to their countries of origin. Just ask where the Czechs are."

Judith started down the Walkover. Raquela saw her stop several men. "Can you tell me where Joseph Steiner is?" Judith asked. Farther along, she stopped a young man. "I'm looking for Joseph Steiner."

"I am Joseph Steiner."

The sister and brother embraced and wept.

July 18, 1947

Raquela heard a commotion on the Walkover. She stepped outside the clinic. "What's happening?" she asked a man.

"Somebody just brought us news from the Haganah radio," he said. "The biggest refugee ship in history is on its way to Haifa. They say forty-five hundred people are aboard."

"Forty-five hundred!" She looked at the man in disbelief.

"That's right. The name of this ship is *Exodus. Exodus 1947.*"

She had to know more. She ran to Ruth Berman's old tent. Ruth's tour of duty had ended, and now new Jewish Agency liaison people sat there, listening to a shortwave radio.

"You're just in time," a young man told her. "Kol Israel is picking up a broadcast that's coming from the *Exodus.*"

The radio came alive. An American voice spoke urgently. "This is the refugee ship *Exodus 1947*. Before dawn today we were attacked by five British destroyers and one cruiser at a distance of seventeen miles from the shores of Palestine, in international waters. The assailants opened fire, threw gas bombs, and rammed our ship. . . . On our deck there are one dead, five dying, and one hundred twenty wounded. The resistance continued for more than three hours. Owing to the severe losses and the condition of the ship, which is in danger of sinking, we were compelled to sail in the direction of Haifa, in order to save the forty-five hundred refugees on board from drowning."

In the afternoon word came that the forty-five hundred were dragged off the ship in Haifa and transferred to three prison ships. The British announced they were sending them to Cyprus.

Days passed. The ships did not arrive in Cyprus.

The air in Athlit was charged with desperation. Where were the British taking the *Exodus* people?

Finally the refugees were taken back to Port de Bouc, in the south of France, the port from which they had sailed for Palestine. But the refugees refused to leave the prison ships. "We will disembark only in Palestine," they said, defying the British.

For three weeks they refused to leave the ships. Bevin tried to pressure the French into forcing them off. The French refused.

Raquela read the newpaper report of an American journalist the French had smuggled aboard one of the ships, disguised as a nurse. She described the ships as "floating Auschwitzes."

"There were a thousand orphans on the *Exodus*," the journalist wrote. "Now on these prison ships, it is the children who keep morale high. There are schools in the iron cages; the children are learning the Hebrew language and literature and the Bible story of the Exodus.

"On one of the prison ships, the *Empire Rival*, the . . . officer has ordered all books in Hebrew and Yiddish burned. Among the books is the Bible. These are the people of the Book and the Land, and on these prison ships both have been taken from them."

Would she, Raquela wondered, have had the strength to go on as did the people of the *Exodus*?

On August 22 Raquela rushed out to the Walkover. The refugees were screaming curses at the guards. "Haven't you heard?" a man shouted at her. "The British are taking the people of the *Exodus* to Hamburg. To Germany." His voice and face changed. "They will fight back. They will get on more ships. They will come home. Now you will see the birth of a Jewish state."

On August 31 the members of UNSCOP finally finished their report. They recommended to the General Assembly of the United Nations that the British Mandate be terminated and Palestine divided into a Jewish state and an Arab state.

All that fall the debate raged at the U.N., which was meeting at Lake Success, New York. Arab leaders denounced the recommendations. Jewish leaders declared that partition meant "a very heavy sacrifice." They had been promised all of Palestine, yet reluctantly they would accept partition.

In Athlit, Raquela and the refugees waited. Would there be a Jewish state and an Arab state where Jews and Arabs could live side by side, helping one another, in peace?

While the debate continued, Britain still held the Mandate, still sent illegals to the refugee camps of Athlit and, even worse, to Cyprus. Athlit, at least, was on the soil of the Holy Land. Cyprus was more than two hundred miles away.

November 1947

Early in November, Raquela's replacement arrived. When word spread that Raquela was leaving Athlit, men and women streamed into the hospital bearing gifts. A woman brought a small mirror; a man came with a carved wooden bird. Raquela blinked back tears at the people's giving her their most precious possessions.

Back in Jerusalem, Raquela picked up the telephone. "Arik!" she shouted. "Arik, I'm home!"

RAQUELA returned to the routine she loved—delivering babies in the clean white delivery room on Mount Scopus.

Two weeks after she arrived home, Dr. Yassky called her into his office. "Miss Levy, you must know how proud we at Hadassah are of the job you did in Athlit. Now we have an even tougher assignment for you. Cyprus."

The word ripped through her like a blade.

"There aren't many young women I would ask to serve there. The facilities for delivering babies are better than in Athlit. But the place itself might be a lot tougher. This time I promise you—it will be for only six weeks."

"I will let you know, Dr. Yassky," she said.

She left his office and walked to Arik's room. She knocked. There was no answer. She entered and stretched out on the divan.

He came in after dark. "Raquela! What a pleasure."

"Arik, I need your advice."

He walked toward her and waited for her to speak.

"Dr. Yassky has asked me to go to Cyprus."

"Cyprus." He said the word slowly.

"What do you think?"

"Are you ready for another descent into hell?"

"Arik, for God's sake, what about us?"

He moved restlessly around the room.

"I love you, Arik," she said.

"I love you, too, Raquela."

She leaned back on the divan and shut her eyes. He joined her and put his arms around her. He stroked her hair, his fingers traced her cheeks, her chin. "Did Dr. Yassky say how long you're to stay on Cyprus?"

"Six weeks."

He relaxed. "For heaven's sake, what's six weeks?"

She moved away from him. "You're telling me to go. Why?"

"Dearest, I'm afraid . . ."

"Afraid? Of what?"

He walked to the window. His back was to her as he spoke. "I'm afraid that I love you so much that if I married you, after a while you . . . you might grow tired of me. Because I'm too old."

Raquela went and stood beside him, looking down at the twinkling lights of Jerusalem. "Arik, why would I grow tired of you? You're the kindest, warmest, dearest man I've ever known."

He smiled. "How many men have you really known? Your feeling for Carmi was puppy love. I want you to meet more men. Young men. I want you to be sure that it is really me you love."

"Arik, you're sending me away."

"No, Raquela. The decision was yours. You knew deep down, the moment Dr. Yassky asked you, that you would say yes."

IT WAS dusk when the plane carrying Raquela to Cyprus landed in a small airport outside Nicosia. A young man approached her. "Miss Levy?"

She nodded, relieved that someone had come for her.

"I'm Yakov, from the Joint," he said. The Joint—also called the JDC—was the familiar name for the American Joint Distribution Committee. Part of the United Jewish Appeal, the JDC was the largest Jewish overseas welfare organization in the world. In the camps it ran health and welfare services, set up schools, and brought in supplies. Raquela was to be part of the JDC team.

Yakov picked up her bag. "It's too late to take you to camp. You're spending the night in a hotel in Famagusta."

YAKOV returned the next morning and they took a taxi down to the harbor. The stone seawall rising above the Mediterranean reminded Raquela of the Old City walls of Jerusalem.

"The Greeks call Cyprus 'Love's Island,'" Yakov told her. "It's Aphrodite's island."

She looked out the window at a stone turret, the remains of an old castle. "That's Othello's tower," he said, "where Othello killed Desdemona in jealousy. It's a romantic island all right. Richard the Lion-Hearted was married on it."

"Romantic? With a prison camp?"

"That's only a small part of the island. Remember, this is a British crown colony. The English love to come here for their holidays."

Soon the taxi pulled up at the entrance gate of the Karaolas camp, where a contingent of British soldiers sat at a table. While an officer scribbled a pass for Raquela, she looked through a barbed-wire fence into the compound. Thousands of people in rags moved around a giant maze of rounded iron huts.

Still outside the barbed wire, she followed Yakov to a hut on whose side the letters JDC were painted. He set down her bag, introduced her to the director, and went out.

"I'm Morris Laub," the director said in an American accent. He was in his late thirties, dark-haired, with dark glasses and a strong, sensitive face. He reminded her of Arik. "I can't tell you what your coming means to us, Miss Levy. We have a prison wing in the British Military Hospital in Nicosia. That's where we want you to set up the maternity ward."

A small, wiry man with deep, mournful eyes entered the office. "This is Josh Leibner, my associate. We are both American."

"If you're ready," Josh Leibner said, "I'll take you to the hospital in Nicosia."

"Can I see the camp before we go?" Raquela asked.

"Of course."

They entered the gate and walked through the streets of sand. Karaolas seemed to stretch to the horizon. Athlit, in comparison, seemed very small.

She saw half-naked children holding on to the wire, looking longingly at the Mediterranean. Even the cool sea is denied them, she thought bitterly.

Suddenly there was a commotion. A water truck appeared. Boys carrying tin cups flew down the streets, shouting, "Water!"

"There's no water in the camps," Josh explained. "The British have to bring it in. It comes to about a cupful for each person per day." His face was tormented. "No water is only part of the degradation. No privacy is worse. A girl came to me yesterday and asked if she could use our kitchen shack for her honeymoon. 'It's the only place in the camp where we can be alone,' she said."

They walked back to the JDC hut and Josh picked up her suitcase. A taxi with a Cypriot driver waited nearby. "He's a friend," Josh told her as they climbed inside. "A lot of the Cypriots are our friends. They want the British off their necks as much as we do."

"We?" she asked. "I thought you were American."

"I'm from Brooklyn. My wife's a New Yorker, too. But we moved to Palestine, and now we have two sabra kids."

The British Military Hospital, a vast complex of iron huts, lay on a hill on the outskirts of Nicosia. Two soldiers looked at their passes and waved them in. Josh led Raquela to a hut, introduced her to Matron White, and left.

Big-bosomed and large-bottomed, Matron White spoke in a braying voice. "Nurse Leev-eye. We work on twelve-hour shifts. One month on day shift. One on night shift. Since this is the twenty-second of November, you may start on the day shift. Beginning December one, you will work the night shift. You work the entire month. Then you get four and one-half days off."

I'll need them, Raquela thought silently.

The matron was still braying. "You work for the JDC. But at the hospital, you're under British military command. You take orders from me." She called out, "Nurse Welles, show Nurse Leev-eye to the nurses' quarters."

A kindly gray-haired English nurse led her to a long, arched metal hut. It was partitioned into small rooms, each with two cots.

After Raquela had changed into her uniform, Nurse Welles took her to the Jewish wing of the hospital. Again the dismal pattern Raquela knew all too well: the barbed-wire fence, soldiers outside the gate, and, inside, rows of desolate huts.

Are you ready for another descent into hell? Raquela heard Arik's voice.

"Here's the maternity hut," Nurse Welles was saying.

Raquela stared. "It looks like a prehistoric bird or monster." It was composed of three barracks—two elongated black wings and a short, round protrusion in front, painted white.

They entered an arched hall dominated by a coal stove—the kitchen. They walked down the right wing, which held the admitting, labor, and delivery rooms. Raquela recoiled. The delivery rooms were filthy.

Then they walked down the left wing, a long barracks with twenty-four arches and a recessed window between each arch.

Below each window a woman lay on a cot, covered with a khaki blanket. Raquela was reminded of woodcuts of medieval hospitals that she had seen in her textbooks.

In the administration hut, Raquela telephoned Josh Leibner. "We've got to clean up the filth—" Her voice faltered. "It's like an insane asylum."

"What do you need?"

"Some good strong girls and more sheets."

Cyprus, 1947. Newly arrived refugees await assignment to huts inside the barbed-wire detention camp.

"I'll try my best."

Within the hour Leibner sent six young refugee women to Raquela in the maternity ward. Each had a blue number tattooed on her left forearm—all death-camp survivors. The small battalion scrounged for basins, soap, a mop, rags. Then they set to work, dusting and scrubbing.

Raquela selected two of her aides to help sponge-bathe the patients. Gerda was Polish, short, compact. She looked like a fighter. Lili, a Hungarian, was tall and fragile and gaunt. Gently they bathed the patients, whose bodies were blotched with rashes. "It's the lack of hygiene and proper food," Raquela said. At the hospital pharmacy she found salves to alleviate their discomfort.

The maternity ward was cleaned just in time. A woman entered.

Raquela greeted her, smiling. "You're going to have your baby under the best conditions we can create for you."

The delivery was easy and fast. Later, scrubbed and clean, with the mother and baby sleeping, Raquela turned to Lili and Gerda. "I couldn't have chosen better assistants."

"Are you as excited as we are?" Lili asked.

"If you stop being excited, you'd better stop being a midwife. Let's have tea and celebrate."

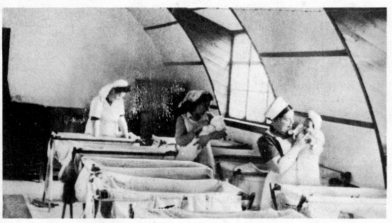

Jewish maternity ward in the British Military Hospital on Cyprus, 1947

They sat in the kitchen, around the coal stove, the experience of the birth drawing them together.

"I gave birth to my son in a cave," Gerda said. "It was winter. The Carpathian Mountains were covered with snow. My husband stood guard outside the cave. He had to watch not only for the Germans but also for the Ukrainians. They either raped the women or turned us over to the Germans for ransom."

Raquela lowered her eyes from Gerda's face.

"I was in labor—I don't know for how many hours. When my son was born, I bit the cord and tied it with a piece of cloth I tore from my skirt. He lived only a few days. I had no milk." She paused. "It was better he died so soon. He could never have survived. We lived in the woods for three years."

"Three years!" Raquela blurted out.

"We went into the cave in June 1941, and we came out in July 1944, when the Russians drove the Nazis back. But my husband was very weak—he weighed only sixty pounds. He died after we were liberated."

THE next morning Josh Leibner appeared in the maternity ward. "Can you take time off?" he asked Raquela. "I want to take you to hear Golda Meir."

"Golda Meir on Cyprus!" What could have brought the head of the political department of the Jewish Agency to the camps?

"There's an outbreak of typhus," he explained. "She's been able to convince the British to let parents with babies under one year old leave immediately."

"You mean no more seven hundred fifty a month quota?"

"Not exactly. They'll just deduct the number from a later quota. Golda Meir's here to try to convince the *refugees* to bend the first-in, first-out rule. She met yesterday with the commanding officer in charge of the camps. She learned he got a cable from the chief secretariat in Jerusalem. It said, 'Beware of Mrs. Meir. She is a formidable person.'"

Raquela laughed.

They took a cab to a second complex of camps, at Dhekelia, eighteen miles from Karaolas.

Inside, Raquela saw a straggly line of people in ragged winter coats. Obviously newcomers, they milled around, bewildered, resentful. Behind them were the black iron huts that looked like sewer pipes—their future homes.

"We've got more than thirty thousand in the camps," Josh said bitterly. Men, women, even small children were talking, arguing. They came upon a crowd of people circling a grandstand made of vegetable crates. He introduced Raquela to a small, attractive woman with curly black hair—his wife—and their two children.

Raquela shook hands. "We'd like you to visit us in Famagusta whenever you're free," Josh's wife, Pnina, said.

The air grew still as Golda Meir climbed to the top of the crates and began speaking. Her voice was strong, her words simple.

"There is typhus in the camps. We cannot allow Jewish babies to die. We owe them life. I am asking you to make a sacrifice—"

An angry voice interrupted. "Haven't we sacrificed enough?"

Golda Meir said, more softly, "We know what you have suffered. But we're asking one more sacrifice. Those of you whose turn it is to go to Palestine in December—we're asking you to give your certificates to families with babies."

A man shook his fist in the air. "Hitler did enough to me. I've been in this hell for six months. I want to get *out!*"

"Friends, listen to me!" Golda Meir's voice pealed forth. "They're talking about us right now at the United Nations. I am sure you will not have to remain on Cyprus much longer. Eventually all of you will be free to come home to us."

Derisive laughter filled the air.

"You must believe me. Whoever gives up a certificate now will be on the quota in January. If we delay getting the children out, they may be dead of typhus. We want all of you to come home."

"She's right!" a woman said. "I've waited so long, I can wait another month. Take my certificate. My babies are dead."

A few days later a "baby transport" sailed for Haifa.

RAQUELA sat with the Jewish doctors and nurses in a hut, listening to the shortwave radio. In New York, the nations of the world were about to vote on UNSCOP's recommendation that Palestine be partitioned into a Jewish state and an Arab state. Raquela's temples throbbed as the roll call began.

"Afghanistan votes no." "Argentina abstains." "Australia votes in favor of partition."

The votes continued. The Soviet bloc and most of Latin America were voting in favor of partition. The United States and France voted yes. All the Arab states voted no. Great Britain abstained.

Raquela thought, Today's the twenty-ninth of November. She had long ago decided that twenty-nine was her lucky number.

She heard the results. "Thirty-three in favor. Thirteen opposed. Ten abstentions."

Tears rolled down the cheeks of the doctors and nurses.

Golda Meir's voice came over the radio, speaking from Jerusalem. "The Jewish state will offer equal rights and opportunities to all its citizens. The Arabs have nothing to fear; we reach out to our Arab brothers the hand of friendship."

The doctors and nurses sprang up, hugging and kissing one

another. Raquela ran through the compound to the Jewish wing of the hospital. "Wake up! Wake Up! The U.N. has just voted. We are to have a state!"

Cries of joy swept through the building.

THE maternity ward had been transformed. The nursery had become a white island of bassinets lined with sailcloth and protected with white netting. The babies nestled in pieces of army blankets that had been softened by countless scrubbings and purified by the sun.

Soon Raquela's six weeks would be over. Meanwhile, she was determined to use every day to win more concessions for her mothers and babies. She had to sign for every diaper and shirt she requisitioned from the Red Cross hut. Colonel John Richardson, a pleasant, sandy-haired Englishman in charge of the hut and its supplies, told her one day, "I'm being shipped back to England soon. I want to give you extra shirts and diapers."

"You're very kind, Colonel Richardson."

The colonel went on to explain. "My replacement has just arrived. I'm afraid he's so hostile to your people he won't even give you the things you're entitled to."

The bonanza was too big a haul to handle on her own, so Raquela sped back to maternity to find Henya, one of her aides. On the way to the Red Cross hut they picked up some laundry duffel bags.

"We're here for your offer," Raquela said.

His face broke into a smile. "I'll help you."

The three of them—the tall Englishman, Raquela, and Henya—swiftly emptied the shelves and stuffed the babies' layettes into the duffel bags. Then the two women thanked him, dragged the bags to Raquela's room, and hid them in her closet.

Henya looked at Raquela's clothes hanging there. Her face changed. "I wish I could make a dress for you. I'm a seamstress. Before the war I worked for a couturier in Paris for a few months." Suddenly she drew back. "I went home to Warsaw to my husband and my two little girls just before Hitler came. See my gray hair. I know I look like an old woman. I'm thirty-eight. My hair turned gray overnight."

Henya leaned against Raquela's small table and continued talking. "One day Nazi trucks came down the street, rounding up all the children. I saw them grab my two little girls and throw them into a truck. I ran after them, screaming, 'Give me back my children.' The Nazi officer stopped the truck.

"'Which are your children?' he asked me. I pointed to them." Tears streamed down her cheeks. Raquela's eyes filled up.

Henya went on. "The Nazi officer took my two precious children to the back of the truck, where I was standing.

"'Choose one,' he said.

"I stood there screaming. How could I choose? 'Give me back my children,' I kept pleading.

"He laughed and drove away."

January 1948

Raquela had stayed the night with the Leibners after a New Year's Eve party. In the morning they all walked to Famagusta harbor. They saw British soldiers lining the dock. Out in the water, thousands of people were crowding the decks of two huge ships, the *Pan Crescent* and the *Pan York*.

Josh whispered to his wife and Raquela, "I hear there are fifteen thousand refugees on those two ships."

Raquela was appalled. "Fifteen thousand more! Where in the name of humanity are we going to squeeze them?"

"We'll have to open new compounds for them," Josh said.

"I'd better get right back to the hospital," Raquela said, "and see if I can scrounge some more supplies."

She taxied to Nicosia and hurried to maternity.

"Gerda, Lili, Henya," she called. "We've got to get to work. Fifteen thousand new refugees have arrived in Famagusta."

In the afternoon Gerda told her, "There are men outside who want to see the midwife in charge."

Raquela walked to the entrance. Two men, who looked barely out of their teens, waited. One, slight but muscular, had curly hair and light eyes. The other, taller, was also spare and muscular, with bright Mediterranean-blue eyes.

The former, who introduced himself as Ike, spoke first. "We're the captains of the *Pan Crescent* and the *Pan York*. I was the skipper of the *Exodus*."

The taller man said, "I'm Gad, captain of the *Pan York*. We have

fifteen babies who were born during the voyage. And many pregnant women in need of medical attention. We'd like to bring them
here in ambulances."

"We can arrange that," Raquela said.

The next hours were spent in feverish preparations as another
hut was set up next door to the maternity ward.

It was already dark when a convoy of ambulances moved into
the compound. Soldiers carried the women on stretchers into the
new annex. It was lighted by a few bare bulbs and there was no
flooring. Only earth. Some of the women seemed terrified. The
infants sensed their mothers' fright and began to howl.

Raquela lifted a tiny baby out of its crib. Its mother ran toward
her, pulled the baby out her arms, and screamed, "You can't have
my child. Where's my husband? They separated us when they put
me on the ambulance. It's like Auschwitz."

Raquela spoke softly. "This is a Jewish maternity ward, and
we're going to take care of you and your baby."

Women on cots stared at Raquela. One woman shouted joyfully,
"Look at her cap! The Star of David! She *is* Jewish."

Willingly now, the women surrendered their babies to the nurses,
who washed and fed them and tucked them into cribs.

All the next day doctors and nurses worked, taking time out
only for coffee. Raquela's eyes were burning with weariness. She
was suddenly consumed with longing for Mount Scopus. In a few
days her six weeks' tour of duty would be finished.

That evening Mary Gordon, the JDC's medical director, entered
the new ward. "Some of you," she said to the nurses, "are scheduled
to leave next week. We are asking you to prolong your stay. With
these fifteen thousand we need all of you. It must be your decision.
But you must make it immediately."

"How long do you think we'll have to stay?" Raquela asked.

"It could be weeks."

The nurses answered, "We'll stay."

THE lights were low in the Chanticleer nightclub in Nicosia.
Raquela and Esther Nathan, who was head nurse in surgery, were
beginning their four-and-a-half-day leave. Both Jerusalemites, they
were the same age, with the same love for nursing, the same affirmation of life, which Cyprus made more poignant each day.

418

Their escort at the club was Dr. Renzo Toaff, a gynecologist at the hospital. He was a tall, distinguished-looking man in his early thirties who had been born in Italy. Since the nurses would not go out alone at night, he had become their favorite escort.

In the muted light Raquela saw two familiar figures walking jauntily toward them—the captains of the *Pan Crescent* and the *Pan York*. "What a stroke of luck," Gad said. "Do you mind if we join you?"

Raquela introduced Dr. Toaff. "Please do join us," he said.

Gad ordered two bottles of retsina. When the waiter returned with the golden-colored wine, Gad filled the glasses. "*L'chaim.* To the two best-looking nurses in the military hospital."

Raquela looked at the captains. Ike had an impish grin and a restless manner. Gad was calm and composed.

Gad leaned toward her. "When can I see you?"

"I'm off duty tomorrow," she said. "In fact, Esther and I are off for four and a half days."

"Then why don't the two of you come visit us on our ships?"

Raquela looked at Esther. "We'd love it," Esther said.

The next morning Ike and Gad picked up the two young women in a taxi. They drove to the Famagusta harbor and walked along the dock. Ships of many countries were at anchor. An English captain in stiff whites and gold braid strutted along the waterfront.

"That's the way I thought a captain should look," Raquela said. "Not like the two of you."

"If the British knew that we're professional seamen, they'd throw us in the jug," Gad said. "They think we're refugees with a little knowledge of seamanship." He sought out a young Greek Cypriot, who took them in a motorboat to the *Pan York.*

"You'll have to climb the Jacob's ladder," Gad said.

Raquela and Esther climbed the swaying rope ladder hanging down the side of the ship. "I hope the ladder in Jacob's dream looked steadier than this one," Esther said.

Gad led Raquela around the deck. "I've never been on a ship in my life," she confessed. "The only water we see in Jerusalem is water to drink."

He laughed. "It's a long time since I've seen Jerusalem. We've been at sea for months. And now, even though we're free to move around Cyprus, we're still detainees. The British keep constant tabs on us. Ike and I had to give them our word that we and the crew won't try to get out of Cyprus."

Raquela looked down into the sun-dappled water, then at Gad. "You brought seventy-five hundred people on this ship, and Ike another seventy-five hundred. It's like those waves out there. I see waves of Jews coming into Palestine. After what happened in the Holocaust, it's something to see the strength of our people!"

Gad nodded. "That's why I can't wait to get back to Europe, so I can bring more and more people home."

Ike and Esther joined them. "How in the world did you squeeze all those people into the ships?" Esther asked.

"I'll show you," Gad said. "Just follow me." He led them down to the hold. Raquela felt she was entering a dungeon. Thousands of wooden planks were arranged like shelves in rows of twelve that reached from the floor to the ceiling.

"People actually slept here!" she gasped.

"There's not enough space for a person to sit up," Esther said.

Ike put his hand on Esther's shoulder. "This wasn't exactly billed as a luxury cruise." He explained that each refugee was allowed the same area—the size of a coffin—six feet long, two feet wide, with forty inches between the wooden planks.

"How did you feed them all?" Raquela asked.

"With American canned rations," Gad replied. "From the JDC."

Raquela shook her head. "I hear there were terrible storms."

"Some of the worst I've lived through," Gad said. "It's strange what happens to people. We had twenty-four doctors and forty nurses among the refugees. When the ship began to roll, the doctors and nurses took to their bunks—as seasick as the rest. The minute they were needed to operate, or take care of any emergency, they stopped being seasick. As soon as they finished, they got seasick all over again."

Raquela thought of Chaim Weizmann's words. *The boats in which our refugees came to Palestine are their* Mayflowers.

Gad and Ike ushered the women up to the captain's wardroom. The cook set the table with a red and white checked cloth and soon placed before them heaping platters of fried chicken, coffee, and, for dessert, a bowl of figs and grapes.

Raquela patted her stomach. "I haven't tasted food this good in years. Especially not on Cyprus."

Gad beamed. "You're always welcome aboard."

The muted light in the wardroom cast a soft glow on Gad's handsome yet rugged face. Trim and graceful, he looked younger than his twenty-seven years. Raquela felt his presence, his gentleness and inner strength. He seemed romantic, adventurous, bigger than life.

Arik, she thought. Arik, you may yet regret . . .

February 1948

The British were writing their epitaph in Palestine in violence and chaos. Each day government services disintegrated further. The railways ran only sporadically. Postal services became disorganized. Palestine was burning—the arsonists, both Arabs and Englishmen. It was a tragedy, for the British had done much that was admirable in this land.

They had changed it from a neglected Turkish outpost to a westernized land with British courts of law, British police, and British culture. Statesmen like Balfour and Lloyd George had laid the cornerstones for the Jewish national home.

But the other face of British rule now showed itself—political expediency in its most treacherous form, betrayal of promises, surrender to the Arabs for their petroleum.

Bevin decided that in these last days of British rule there would be no help in setting up the Jewish state. Immigration must be stopped, lest men of military age enter Palestine and join the Haganah forces to fight the Arabs. Despite the quota system of first into the camps, first out, the British barred all able-bodied men from leaving.

Meanwhile, the Arabs were trying to starve Jerusalem. Grocers' shelves were nearly empty. Women foraged for grass to feed their families. The cisterns were dry. Men with water wagons brought meager rations to the Jerusalemites.

The battle was for the highway dubbed the Murder Road that climbed nearly three thousand feet from Tel Aviv to Jerusalem. Hiding behind bushes, high over the winding road, the Arabs had an easy shooting gallery.

Jerusalem had to be saved. Food had to get through.

The Jews created "sandwiches"—trucks and cars covered with two sheets of steel plate with a wall of wood between. The sand-

421

wiches traveled in convoys, with armed Haganah men and women shooting back at the snipers.

Convoys broke through, but many were ambushed. The ditches along the highway were a graveyard of burned sandwiches.

The Arabs had their hands around the throat of Jerusalem.

GAD was waiting for Raquela at the Famagusta dock. Soon they were in the motorboat, speeding out to the *Pan York*.

Raquela and Esther had come aboard several times, their friendship with the two young sea captains a welcome reprieve from the hospital routine and the fears for their families in Jerusalem.

Now Gad took Raquela below to show her a newspaper photo of billboards in Jerusalem covered with obituary notices. The names of the dead were printed below the photos.

Raquela studied the faces. Two of them had been high school classmates. "What's going to happen, Gad? This is only the beginning." She continued to look at the faces. "I've read that the mufti's Arab gangs are being reinforced with German Nazis specially released from prisoner-of-war camps in Egypt. I wonder how the British officers in Palestine are reacting."

"It looks as if each British commanding officer makes his own decisions. Some are on our side, holding off the Arabs with even a few men. But others are openly siding with the Arabs; they've also withdrawn their troops from some of the borders, so Arabs from outside can join the battle. There's a so-called liberation army made up of troops from Iraq. They're battling our boys in the north; their leader is Fawzi el-Kaukji, an Iraqi Nazi. Like the mufti, he spent World War Two with Hitler in Berlin."

Gad went on. "Don't look so glum, Raquela. We're fighting back. The Haganah has just blown up six bridges leading from Palestine to the neighboring countries; the Iraqis won't have easy access. Now, let's eat."

The food was delicious; Raquela downed it with a glass of cool wine, relaxing in the salt air.

After lunch Gad put his arm around her. "I'm growing very fond of you, Raquela."

She put her hand on his. "I'm . . . I'm fond of you, too, Gad."

He cupped her face in his hands and kissed her.

She shut her eyes. She thought, Arik, am I disloyal? But it was you who told me . . . *I want you to meet more men. Young men . . . to be sure. . . .*

A knocking on the door startled them. They moved apart.

"Come in," Gad said.

Eli, the radio operator, stood in the doorway, his face white. "There's been an explosion in Jerusalem, on Ben Yehuda Street."

Raquela's hand flew to her mouth.

Ben Yehuda Street—the Fifth Avenue of Jerusalem—lined with shops, cafés, modern hotels.

She turned to Gad, her voice hoarse with fear. "Esther's family lives on Ben Yehuda Street."

They hurried down to the radio room and made contact with the radio ham in Jerusalem.

"No word yet how many were killed," the voice said.

"*Pan York:* How did it happen?"

"Arabs and British deserters—joint operation."

Arabs and deserters. Raquela felt faint. She heard the voice say, "The Vilenchik Building . . ." She had many friends living in it. "The stone wall buckled outward and collapsed. Hundreds of people are in the streets now, running out of burning buildings. Pieces of bodies are mixed in with glass and bricks."

Raquela moaned. Her eyes were blurred with tears. "Esther will go out of her mind."

Gad took his handkerchief and wiped her cheek. "When is your next leave?"

"In a week."

"Why don't the four of us go somewhere—get Esther away? Meanwhile, you alert the doctors and nurses not to mention the explosion in front of her."

Raquela dried her eyes. "Where do you want to go?"

"I'll talk to Ike. This island has some beautiful spots."

They decided to go to Mount Troodos. Esther was delighted with the plans. But Raquela found herself in a quandary. The night before they were to leave, she kept repeating Arik's idea over and over: *Younger man . . . younger man.* Was she in love with Gad?

The next morning Gad and Ike picked up Raquela and Esther in a taxi. Raquela watched the landscape change as the cab left Nicosia and drove across the wide plain—the Messaoria—that stretched across the island. They traveled southwest until, fifty miles from Nicosia, they began the ascent to Mount Troodos.

A fresh snow carpeted the mountain. Tiny villages were guarded by tall poplar trees standing like silver sentries. The cab navigated past orchards and vineyards, the foliage heavy with snow.

Finally they pulled up in front of a rustic lodge. They registered, then followed a porter up the stairs. Esther and Raquela entered a large, inviting bedroom that smelled of pine needles. Gad and Ike shared a room on the next floor.

The four changed into warm clothes and hurried out in the snow. They raced through the fields, built a snowman, and then, famished, returned to the inn for lunch. The days of their leave melted into one. They ate, drank, danced, sang, laughed, took midnight walks.

On the last evening, after dinner, they walked along a snow-covered path framed on both sides with oaks and pines. Gad drew Raquela aside. "Let them go ahead."

He held her close and kissed her. "I'm in love, Raquela."

She put her hand on his lips. "I'm in love, too, Gad."

He kissed her again. "My darling, I dream I hold you in my arms every night." He brushed his lips across her eyes, her cheeks.

"I love you, Gad. I love you." She held him tightly.

ESTHER's parents were safe. The whole family had rushed into the street wearing only their nightclothes. Their apartment, with everything they owned, was ruined.

March descended on the camps with sudden, brutal heat. Raquela was counting the days. Seventy-five days until May 15, 1948—Bevin's announced target date. On May 15 all the troops would be withdrawn. The last Englishman would be out of Palestine. The gates of Cyprus would surely fling open. She and the internees would go home.

Morale was fairly high among the adults. But among the orphaned children in the Dhekelia camp the teachers fought a desperate war against rage and frustration.

Hanoch Rinott, from Youth Aliyah, had come from Jerusalem to set up schools. Now he pleaded with the camp commander to let the children go swimming. Finally permission was granted.

Rinott invited Raquela to go along. Flanked by armed soldiers, the children were marched through the camp like prisoners. Outside, a tank led them for a mile and a half in the relentless sun. Raquela marched beside them, her own rage boiling.

The next two hours were magic as the children swam, dug castles and tunnels in the sand, and seemed to forget the camps. Then, reluctantly, they dressed for the long march back.

Raquela watched them reenter the hated gate. What could these children make of their lives? Could they be reclaimed? Could a child who had never been inside a house, whose parents had been killed in Hitler's gas chambers, ever be normal?

A few weeks later Major Maitland, a kindly British officer who spent his Sundays driving through Cyprus trying to buy shoes for the children, made an announcement. "All orphaned children who arrived on the *Pan York* and the *Pan Crescent* will be allowed to leave on the next transport to Palestine."

The camps for once were filled with smiling people. The children would go directly to Youth Aliyah children's villages and kibbutzim in Palestine. The whole country was ready to put its arms around them, adopt them, welcome them home.

A few days after the orphaned children left, Raquela received a letter from a friend:

Maybe you've heard this from somebody else. If not, I hate to be the first to write you about this tragedy. It's about Carmi. He was commander of a convoy that was trying to evacuate the people in Atarot and Neve Yaakov.

Raquela knew the places well; two communities in the hills of East Jerusalem, where Jews lived side by side with Arabs.

The Arabs had turned hostile. Carmi was in an armored truck leading the operation. He succeeded in evacuating all the Jews. Then he headed his convoy through Sheikh Jarrah to reach Mount Scopus. In Sheikh Jarrah, Arabs ambushed the convoy. Carmi jumped out and shouted, "Everyone jump into ditches." The people miraculously saved themselves. But Carmi was killed. A hero's death. I am so sad, dear Raquela, to write you this news.

Raquela wept for Carmi. She wept for all the young men and women who would die before they could have their own state.

There was a knock on the door. "Raquela, are you there?" It was Gad's voice.

She wiped her face hurriedly. "Come in," she said.

His face was distorted in agony. "There's terrible news about Mount Scopus," he said. "There's been a massacre. Seventy-seven people killed."

Raquela flung herself on him. "No! It can't be! Do you know any names?"

—"Only one so far—Dr. Yassky."

"Not Dr. Yassky!" Director of Scopus.

Gad held her in his arms. "Can you get time off?" he asked. "We can go back to the ship and get more news on the shortwave."

"I'm free this shift."

"Let's go, then. I have a cab waiting."

They hardly spoke in the taxi. She lay in his arms, her eyes shut. Maybe, she thought, if she could keep conjuring up pictures of all her friends on Mount Scopus, she could keep them alive.

Aboard the ship, Gad turned the dials of the radio. "Come in, Tel Aviv. This is the *Pan York*."

"This is Tel Aviv. Over."

"Can you give us details on the massacre at Scopus? Over."

"I've got some newspapers in front of me. I'll read from one." The radio operator began: "'Tuesday, April 13, 1948.'"

He told about how the convoy had set off from downtown Jerusalem for Scopus—one hundred and thirty doctors, nurses, patients, professors. The Haganah escort was in a "sandwich"; then came an armored ambulance with Dr. and Mrs. Yassky and eight others. Behind them came buses, trucks, another ambulance. On the road to Sheikh Jarrah a mine exploded. Arabs in ditches tossed grenades and fired guns at the stalled vehicles. A few Jews managed to turn and dash back to the city. But most were paralyzed in the narrow road.

Raquela held the arms of the deck chair tightly.

The radio operator continued the account: "'A few tried to jump from the buses. They were gunned down. The rest sat for hours in the armored buses and ambulances. As time passed, hundreds of Arabs streamed out from neighboring areas with more guns and hand grenades. British soldiers watched from their post less than a hundred yards away and did nothing.

"'From Mount Scopus, doctors could see the whole action. They telephoned downtown. The Haganah demanded it be allowed to send men to the rescue. The British refused. They told the Haganah the sight of armed Jews would only inflame the Arabs. Mobs of Arabs poured gasoline on the buses, put torches to the gasoline, and the people inside were all burned alive.'"

Dear Lord, Raquela prayed silently, don't let Arik be in one of those buses.

"'For seven hours the convoy was under fire. Half an hour later the British appeared in tanks and armored cars. The Arabs fled.'"

Armored truck-ambulance used in convoys to transport doctors, nurses, and patients to Hadassah Hospital, 1948

Gad said, "Tel Aviv. Do you have the casualty list?"

Raquela listened to the names. She knew many of the victims well. Arik's name was not among them.

May 14, 1948

Raquela sat with the doctors and nurses in their hut in the hospital compound, listening to the radio.

For days they had been debating three questions: Would Britain pull out of Palestine by Bevin's target date—May 15? Would the Jewish state be proclaimed? Would the Arabs invade?

David Ben-Gurion's advisers had told him two things were certain: the British would pull out, and the Arabs would invade. Fifty million Arabs in seven neighboring Arab states, a million Arabs in

427

Palestine—against only six hundred and fifty thousand Jews.

Ben-Gurion made his decision: the state would be born. And it would come into existence on Friday, May 14.

Now the radio came alive. Ben-Gurion spoke in a quiet voice. "I shall read the Scroll of Independence."

Independence! Tears streamed down Raquela's cheeks.

> "The land of Israel is the birthplace of the Jewish people. Here . . . they wrote and gave the Bible to the world. The State of Israel will be open for Jewish immigration and for the ingathering of the exiles."

The exiles! The fifty-two thousand men and women who had been interned on Cyprus; the two thousand babies she had helped deliver in the maternity ward. The tens of thousands in the DP camps. The thousands more fleeing persecution in Europe and the Arab lands. Now they could all be ingathered.

The dark night of the Holocaust was over. The quotas and the certificates and the illegal ships were over. The state of Israel was open to Jewish immigration.

The words washed over her.

> "We extend our hand to all neighbouring states and their peoples in an offer of peace . . . and appeal to them to establish bonds of co-operation for the advancement of the entire Middle East."

Peace . . . cooperation . . . Was it a dream? Ben-Gurion's voice rang out:

> "We hereby proclaim the State of Israel."

Raquela and Esther hugged each other. Dr. Toaff kissed them both, laughing and wiping his eyes. "Do you realize now we're a nation? For the first time in two thousand years we're in charge of our own destiny!"

The next morning Raquela taxied to Karaolas. In the camp, a mass of people paraded across the grounds. Banners waved: LONG LIVE ISRAEL. Fiddlers played. Drummers beat makeshift drums. Thousands of people were marching in different lines. Raquela joined one, marching happily. Then her group formed a circle and danced a hora, faster and faster. When the folk dance was over, they paraded toward the watchtowers.

Joyously waving their banners, the people called out to the soldiers, "Long live Israel! Now you, too, can go home."

The soldiers, smiling broadly, waved back.

Raquela caught sight of Josh and Pnina Leibner and their children. She hurried toward them.

Raquela and Pnina hugged each other. *"Israel."* Pnina said it as if she were trying out a holy word. Only yesterday they had called their land Palestine. But Palestine was derived from the name Philistine, the people who were constantly at war with the ancient Israelites. No, the name Israel was right. For thousands of years they had called it *Eretz-Israel*—"the Land of Israel."

"Josh," Raquela said, "do you know when we can all leave?"

"No. But we've heard Egyptian planes have dropped bombs on Tel Aviv. The Arab armies are massing at all the borders."

Raquela looked sadly at the people parading. In a few days, perhaps, they would be arriving in Israel, descending the gangways of Ike's and Gad's ships; they would plunge into the war.

President Truman recognized Israel immediately after Ben-Gurion's proclamation of Independence. The Soviet Union followed. But the Arabs declared war.

Egypt, Transjordan, Syria, Lebanon, and Iraq, with troops from Saudi Arabia, invaded Israel. The war of liberation began.

When would the men interned on Cyprus be allowed to join Israel's army? The refugees waited. Why the delay?

British power was ended. But Bevin had one last card—Cyprus. He gave new orders. "The Jews in the camps and aboard the impounded *Pan York* and *Pan Crescent* are guilty of having attempted illegal entry into Palestine. As such, they are still internees under our jurisdiction on the British Crown Colony of Cyprus."

No one could leave—no men, women, or children. Nor Gad and Ike. Nor would Raquela and the hospital staff leave, so long as they were needed.

The refugees reacted first with disbelief, then with outrage.

But two weeks passed and still the gates of Cyprus were sealed.

The island temperature rose to one hundred degrees, and the rage of the people mounted. For Raquela, surcease came on her evenings off with Gad. One night, as they were pacing the deck of the *Pan York*, Gad put his arm through hers. "If we don't get out of here soon, Raquela, I swear Ike and I will explode."

"Sometimes I wake up in a sweat," she said. "I dream you and Ike have somehow managed to sneak out past the British. And I'm not sure whether or not I want you to be gone."

"You would miss me, Raquela?"

"I would miss you very much. I love being with you on your ship. Out here on the water, everything seems timeless. In camp, I'm as restless as the prisoners."

He held her tightly. The dark night and the dark sea bowled around them.

She looked out at the water. Across the sea lay Jerusalem . . . and Arik.

Was it possible to love two men? Arik—the teacher, the father figure, intimately involved with her own career; Gad—romantic, exciting, young. Gad meant fun and adventure.

A line that Papa loved to quote from Goethe's *Faust* went through her mind: *Two souls dwell, alas! in my breast.*

ON MAY 28 the Old City of Jerusalem fell. Starved out of food and ammunition, seventeen hundred people in the Jewish quarter huddled into cellars and synagogues to save themselves from the bullets of Transjordan's Arab Legion. Two rabbis, defying the pleas of Haganah defenders, walked with a white flag to the Arab Legion's headquarters and surrendered.

The Legion allowed thirteen hundred women and children to pass through the gates of the crenellated wall into New Jerusalem. But the Arabs took the men to a prison in Transjordan.

On every front the newborn state was battling for its life. In the south and west the Egyptians crossed the Suez Canal, cutting the Negev off from northern Israel and driving on to Tel Aviv. In the north the Syrians, Lebanese, and Iraqis marched across the Galilee.

From the east the Arab Legion crossed the Jordan River, and now they battled for the cities on the West Bank and, most of all, for New Jerusalem.

The city was on starvation rations. Yet one hundred thousand Jerusalemites and units of the Israel Army were still holding off the soldiers of the Arab Legion.

The road to Jerusalem, the single lifeline from Tel Aviv, was immobilized by the Arab Legion. To save the city, a secret road was built through a steep wadi by hundreds of elderly men working at night. The old Murder Road was bypassed. On the new road, dubbed the Burma Road, trucks from Tel Aviv reached Jerusalem just as it was down to its last two days of bread and flour.

The siege of Jerusalem was over.

In New York, the U.N. Security Council was meeting in endless sessions. Some members sought to arrange a cease-fire, but as long as the Arabs were winning, the council failed to reach agreement.

Now, as the Arab offensive began slowing down, the Security Council agreed to a cease-fire. It would last from June 11 to July 9.

It gave both sides a breathing spell. Instructed by the U.N. to do nothing during the truce to improve their positions, both sides regrouped their forces.

Golda Meir barnstormed America, describing the war. She raised fifty million dollars. Her dollars bought arms and planes from Czechoslovakia—the only country willing to supply the new state.

Then Bevin relented a little. He announced that all refugees—*except men of military age*—could leave the Cyprus camps. Britain, he explained, must remain evenhanded. They could not allow Jewish soldiers to create an imbalance.

Imbalance! Raquela shook her head in disbelief. More than fifty million Arabs against fewer than a million Jews!

THE *Pan York* and the *Pan Crescent* were freed. They would begin ferrying the refugees to Israel.

Raquela looked up at the two ships. Some of the happiest hours of her life had been spent aboard the *Pan York*. But it now had a new name—*Komemiyut*, a Hebrew word for national pride. The *Pan Crescent* had become the *Atzamaut*, a word for independence.

Raquela climbed the gangway of the *Komemiyut* and hurried to the bridge. Gad was bending over charts, talking to his first mate. At last he looked up. "Raquela!" He pressed her into his arms.

"Will you be coming back?" she whispered.

"We'll keep making the run to Haifa until we get everyone out."

"Even the young men?"

His face grew sober. "As soon as they're released."

"Good-by, Gad."

"Good-by, my darling."

She hurried down the gangway.

Gad returned to Cyprus every few days. But he and Raquela had only minutes together. The moment the ships were in sight, the refugees queued up to board.

The day came when Gad said to Raquela, "This is my last trip. Others will finish cleaning out Cyprus. They're sending Ike and me to Europe to reoutfit our ships. From now on we'll be sailing back and forth from Naples with refugees."

Already she felt a sense of loss.

"This is not good-by, Raquela. I'll come to Jerusalem."

He walked her to the gangway and watched her descend.

She waved. "Good-by, Gad." Would she ever see him again?

A few days later her replacement on Cyprus arrived. Raquela boarded the plane bound for Israel.

PART FOUR

July 1948

At Haifa Airport, Israeli officials sped Raquela through immigration. She wanted to embrace the Israeli customs men. She was home. And the British were gone. But the war was far from over. In a few days the truce would end. Unless the Security Council could prolong the cease-fire, the war would erupt again.

Raquela took an intercity *sherut*—a seven-passenger cab—to Tel Aviv, where she was stunned to discover that there was no passenger traffic to Jerusalem. Only convoys of jeeps led by the U.N. or the Red Cross were allowed to make the journey. She sat in a café, trying to figure out how to get home to Bet Hakerem.

She was beginning to panic when an army jeep drove slowly by. Raquela caught sight of the driver, a friend. "Ze'ev," she called out. He stopped the jeep and she ran to greet him. "I've got to get to Jerusalem," she said.

"Hop in. I'm just on my way."

They joined a convoy at the outskirts of Tel Aviv and took the "Burma Road" to Jerusalem, where the signs of war were everywhere. Glass and rubble littered the streets, but the city of stone had withstood the shelling. The jeep separated from the convoy and finally stopped in front of Raquela's home. Raquela thanked Ze'ev and ran across the patio, shouting, "Mama! Papa!"

"Raquela!" They flung open the door and embraced.

"How are you?" Mama asked. "Are you feeling all right?"

Raquela laughed. "I'm fine, Mama. All I need is a shower."

"Come on inside," Mama said, businesslike. "Now I know why I saved all my water today. I must have felt you were coming home."

As they entered the house, Papa explained. Jerusalem had no running water. The Arabs controlled two of the pumping stations that brought water to Jerusalem. They had cut off the supply. But Israel held two other stations and was beginning to lay pipelines. Meanwhile, the little water they had was brought in by trucks.

After Raquela had bathed, she joined her parents in the living room, eager for news. "How are Jacob and Yair?"

"Thank God, well," Papa said. "They've been on different fronts in the war of liberation."

Mama smiled mysteriously. "You have a new brother."

"What? Have you adopted a baby?"

"We adopted him, but he's no baby. He's your age."

"I can't stand this suspense. I want to know all about him."

"I'll tell you," Mama said. "Nearly every family in Jerusalem has taken in a wounded boy or girl, to help free the beds in the hospitals. They sent us this nice young man, Itzhak Elkhanim. He's from Hungary. His family was killed in the concentration camps. He fought in the Old City and was badly wounded. Now he's convalescing." She paused. "When he wakes up, you'll meet him. Now I'm going to fix you some food."

After making Raquela a scrambled egg and a salad for lunch, Mama tiptoed to the bedroom. "Come here, Raquela," she called. "Itzhak is awake."

Raquela entered the room. A pale young man smiled at her.

"How do you feel?" she asked.

"Are you asking as a nurse—or as a sister?"

Raquela chuckled. "Both."

"In that case, I'm already feeling better."

They chatted for a little while. "You rest now, Itzhak. We'll have plenty of time to talk." She plumped up his pillow. "Good-by . . . my brother," she said.

She went to her bedroom, lay down, and was asleep instantly.

THE NEXT MORNING Raquela took the bus to Zion Square and walked to the old English Mission Hospital. Since the attack on Mount Scopus, this massive Romanesque structure had housed what was now called Hadassah A. Four other emergency hospitals had been set up by Hadassah in Jerusalem.

Raquela walked up to the department of obstetrics. In the hall she saw the back of a familiar figure. "Arik!"

He wheeled around. "Raquela!" He gathered her in his arms and kissed her.

"Arik. It's so good to see you. Are you well?"

"I'm strong as an ox. But let me look at you." He stood back. "You're more beautiful than I remembered." All around them, nurses, doctors, patients were scurrying through the corridor. "It's so hectic here," he said. "I'll be free in a couple of hours and we can get coffee."

"Fine. I'll go work in maternity. I've brought my uniform."

Raquela went to the nursery and for the next three hours changed diapers, bottle-fed babies, and took hungry infants to nursing mothers. She was tucking soft white blankets around the infants when she saw Arik in the doorway.

He was smiling. "I'm free now."

"Let's go to the Patt Bakery," she said, "for old times' sake."

In the bakery, Mrs. Patt embraced Raquela, her blue eyes wide with pleasure. "How about some of my apple strudel? With this rationing, I save it for my special friends."

"I dreamed about your apple strudel on Cyprus," Raquela said.

They sat at a table in the garden, Arik beaming. "I haven't felt this good since you left." He took her hand.

The waiter brought their coffee and a small square of strudel.

"Mrs. Patt must love you, Raquela," Arik said. "Do you know what our daily rations are this week? One tomato, half a carrot, one cucumber, two onions, one green pepper, and a few string beans."

"But that's a starvation diet!"

"Sometimes we get an egg and some milk and cheese. It's so ironic. We've got this truce commission and Count Folke Bernadotte, the U.N. mediator. They say that there mustn't be any improvement of any kind during the truce. If we had no food at the beginning of the truce, we should have none now. It's madness."

Raquela put her hands to her face. "I feel so guilty. Mama made me an egg for my lunch. I may have used up the family's ration."

"Actually, things are a little better now. But Jerusalem is still hungry." Arik sipped his coffee. "Now I want to hear about you."

For the next half hour Raquela told him about Cyprus, about the despair of the young men of military age whose wives and babies were evacuated.

"Did you meet anyone special?"

She took a long swallow of coffee. "I met the captains of the two biggest illegal ships."

"I want to hear more." He looked at his wristwatch. "But now we'd better get back to the hospital."

There was little time in the next days for Raquela and Arik to be together. On July 9, 1948, the cease-fire ended.

The Arabs had used the last days of the truce to erect strong fortifications on the walls of the Old City. From the nursery window Raquela could see the new gun positions. She hurried to Arik. "I'm uneasy. I'd like to move the babies to a safer room downstairs. Is that okay?"

He smiled. "I put you in charge."

Back in the nursery, she handed each baby to a nurse who carried it down the stairs. She brought the last infant down herself.

Minutes later, a blast pierced the air. The massive hospital trembled. Raquela heard a commotion in the corridors. Voices called out, "Is anyone hurt?"

Arik came in, shaken. He took Raquela in his arms. "A shell exploded in the nursery upstairs. It would have killed every baby—" He stopped. "It would have killed you, too."

NEW Jerusalem was encircled by the mufti's gangs, mercenaries, Kaukji's Arab Liberation Army, and by Transjordan's Arab Legion. The latter was the most formidable—twelve thousand soldiers trained and armed by the British and led by the English general Sir John Glubb.

King Abdullah of Transjordan had long hungered for Jerusalem and the West Bank of the Jordan. His desert kingdom on the East Bank had been promised to the Jews under the British Mandate. But in 1921 the British had given it to Abdullah as a reward for the assistance of his father in defeating the Turks during World War I.

Now Abdullah wanted the West Bank and Jerusalem as well.

435

THE BATTLEFRONT WAS the streets of Jerusalem. Every doctor and nurse worked to exhaustion. Basements of the five emergency Hadassah hospitals were used for operating rooms, and when the electricity gave out, the surgeons operated by flashlight.

Each day saw gruesome casualties. Many of the soldiers were new immigrants, some with little or no training. Everything was strange to them—the language, the customs, the terrain. Some could barely understand their commanders' orders. Thousands died.

Yet the tide of battle was turning. The Israelis had a secret weapon—*ein brera,* no alternative. Against all predictions the Jews were routing the Arabs.

Kaukji's troops were headquartered in Nazareth, to the north. Using diversionary tactics, the Israel Army confounded them. They took flight, and on July 16 Nazareth surrendered.

In the center of the country, Colonel Moshe Dayan led a commando unit of jeeps and half-tracks. Dayan, who believed in speed and the element of surprise, astonished the enemy by racing his commandos through the Arab lines. The vital Lydda airport was captured, as were the towns of Lydda and Ramla. The Arab Legion fled back toward the West Bank.

Later, visiting injured commandos in a hospital in the south, Dayan found two with severe eye wounds. Remembering his own feeling when he had lost an eye on a reconnaissance mission for the British during World War II, Dayan stopped at their beds to cheer them up. "Boys," he said, "for all that's worth seeing in this wretched world, one eye is enough."

IN JERUSALEM, the Israel Army sought desperately to recapture the Old City. They had already breached the New Gate. A few more hours, they felt, and they could drive out the Arab Legion. But they were forced by the U.N. to halt when a second truce went into effect at seven p.m. on July 18, 1948. With nine-tenths of Jerusalem now in Israeli hands, only the Old City and East Jerusalem flew the flag of the Arab Legion. Mount Scopus held, but the Arabs controlled Sheikh Jarrah and the road to Scopus.

Bone-weary, Raquela had little time to be with Arik. For the second truce brought as little respite as the first. The shelling continued for three months.

The U.N. mediator, Count Bernadotte, recommended that Israel, winning on nearly every front, hand over New Jerusalem and the Negev to the Arabs in exchange for peace. Outraged, three men assassinated Bernadotte on September 17. The Jewish community recoiled with horror. The provisional government, headed by Ben-Gurion, issued an ultimatum: the dissident groups must disband. The Irgun accepted the ultimatum. The leaders of the Stern group were arrested. In the aftermath of the tragedy the new state was united.

Despite the second truce, the battlefields blazed again on October 10. In the south, King Faruk of Egypt had sent his army across the Sinai Desert into the Negev to get his piece of the Israeli pie. Ben-Gurion had to choose whether to drive the Egyptians out of the Negev or the Arab Legion out of the Old City and the West Bank. Steeped in the Bible, Ben-Gurion saw the Negev as Israel's future. Here were Solomon's copper mines, gold and minerals, and, maybe, oil. He opted for the Negev.

Israel's forces attacked King Faruk's legions. At four a.m. on October 21 the Israelis entered Beersheba. At nine fifteen a.m. the ancient town was captured. It would become the capital of the Negev, Ben-Gurion's dream.

Just before the third cease-fire began, Kaukji's Arab Liberation Army was routed from the north. The entire Galilee was open.

There was no stopping now. Both sides breached the truce, and the Israelis quickly broke the Egyptian stronghold in the Negev.

On November 30 Colonel Moshe Dayan, now commander of the army in Jerusalem, and Colonel Abdullah el-Tel, the representative of all the Arab forces, met in Government House. Under the supervision of the U.N. truce commission they signed an agreement for an "absolute and sincere" cease-fire in the Jerusalem area.

On the first Shabbat of the "sincere" truce, Arik asked Raquela to go walking. The day was warm and balmy. Thousands of people thronged the streets. Young fathers wheeled their babies in carriages. Young mothers clutched their husbands' arms as if they were still telling themselves, He's alive.

But the joy was tempered. Six thousand young men and women had died to give birth to Israel. And the Old City, where Raquela and Arik had spent so many Saturday mornings, was denied them.

Instead, they walked through the quiet streets of Bet Hakerem.

Finally they rested on a wooden bench. "I've neglected you all these months, Raquela," Arik said.

"Nonsense, Arik. Many times in that operating room, when I saw your eyes red from no sleep, I was afraid you might collapse."

He caressed her hand. "We can be together again," he was saying. "Take up where we were before you went to Cyprus."

Where we were. Do you ever go back to where you were? She loved this man, his strength, his compassion.

And Gad? Memories of the *Pan York*, of the moonlit sea, kaleidoscoped in her mind.

In her bedroom that night, she asked herself, What is it you want? What's best for you?

She tossed on her bed, unable to find answers.

February 1949

At long last the gates of Cyprus opened. Britain had finally recognized the Jewish state, and soon after, the men on Cyprus were allowed to leave.

Early in February Raquela received a cable: CAN YOU MEET ME TONIGHT AT JEWISH AGENCY OFFICE ON HAIFA DOCK. GAD.

She put on her cape and walked toward the post office. She walked blindly, in a fierce rain, trying to think. She could take a few days off and go see Gad. She could see him now, tanned, blue-eyed, in his captain's uniform. She could feel his kisses.

But is it Gad I really love? Then why am I not already on my way to Haifa? *Remember,* she heard Senora Vavá's voice, *you are a ninth-generation Jerusalemite.*

Married to Gad, she would probably have to move to Haifa, waiting and watching for his ship to come in. Her life with him would be like the sea that was his life—uncertain, stormy, with days of calm and beauty, and weeks, maybe months, of loneliness.

Married to Arik, she would live in Jerusalem. She would work at his side. He would be her constant companion. But did she love Arik as a teacher? Or as a man? Or both?

The answer was suddenly clear. Raquela ran to the post office, and sent a cable: HAVE DECIDED TO STAY IN JERUSALEM. GOOD-BY DEAR GAD. RAQUELA.

She hurried to the hospital, tears mingling with rain on her cheeks. Arik, it's you I want and need . . . you and Jerusalem.

EARLY IN 1949 ON the island of Rhodes, a gifted black American, Dr. Ralph Bunche, the new U.N. mediator, had begun meeting with Arabs and Jews in armistice negotiations. By the twentieth of July, four Arab countries had signed the armistice and the War of Independence ended—twenty months after the U.N. had voted to partition Palestine and the Arabs had declared war.

Twenty months. Six thousand dead. One out of every ten Jews who had fought on the battlefield, dead.

IT WAS a warm fall day, and Raquela and Arik rode out of Jerusalem bound for Beersheba. Ben-Gurion had already begun implementing his dream of opening the Negev by asking Hadassah to establish a first-rate hospital in the ancient town.

Arik had spent most of September organizing the department of obstetrics and gynecology. Now he was returning with Raquela; she was to set up the maternity ward.

They sat in the back of the *sherut*, Raquela wondering what life would be like these next months.

"There's a sense of peace there," Arik said. "It was only after I saw it that I understood what Ben-Gurion meant when he asked us to open a hospital for the whole Negev."

"What did he say?" Raquela asked.

Arik spoke slowly. "He said, 'If the state doesn't put an end to the desert, the desert will put an end to the state.'"

Suddenly against the horizon they saw the silhouettes of camels moving in a straight line in the shimmering sunlight. A Bedouin in a flowing robe followed the camels on a donkey. Behind him walked three women, black-gowned and veiled, with baskets on their heads. The car sped past them.

Again the desert, limitless, empty to the horizon.

They entered Beersheba. Raquela saw a sleepy desert outpost with dirt streets, Arab houses in shambles, a mosque, and a police station. They got out of the cab a quarter of a mile up the road.

"This is the hospital compound," Arik said. They entered a large courtyard surrounded by a jumble of one-story stone houses. Arik was talking. "My friend Dov Volotzky and his crew have begun repairs and construction to convert these buildings into different departments. Now I'll show you your quarters."

They turned left through the courtyard to a white stone cottage.

"There are two bedrooms," Arik said as they entered. "You'll be sharing your room with another nurse."

They left Raquela's suitcase, then Arik led her to a small yellow house. "Here is the maternity building."

Excitedly Raquela walked through the building's four small rooms. Surveying. Studying. "I see the way to do it," she said. "We'll put the delivery room here, with an admission office near the door. I'll make a list of everything we'll need—from diaper pins to the delivery table."

"Okay, Sergeant. And now would you like to see where I live?"

They walked to an elegant stone villa. Several doctors had already moved in. Arik's room was large and flooded with sunlight. He embraced Raquela. "It's a new beginning," he whispered. "And you have never looked so beautiful."

She shut her eyes. Now, at last, maybe we will have time to be together, she thought.

RAQUELA was hanging green and white curtains in the maternity ward when Dov Volotzky and Arik entered with huge boxes. "We have a present for you. From Hadassah in America," Arik said.

Raquela hurried down the stepladder. "Let me see." She tore open a box and lifted out a package of white sheets. "They're beautiful. So soft. It's the best present I ever got."

"Listen," Dov said. "It's Friday. How about coming for supper?"

"I'd love it," Raquela said.

At dusk Arik and Raquela arrived at Dov's cottage, which was in back of the hospital. His eyes sparkled as he greeted them, holding his eighteen-month-old son, Chanan, in his arms. His wife, Sarah, came to the door; she seemed warm and ebullient.

Raquela felt a sharp stab of recognition. The cottage smelled of Friday night. Sabbath candles. Delicious odors of gefilte fish, chicken soup, broiled chicken, and carrots came from the kitchen.

Soon Arik was down on the floor and little Chanan was riding him like a donkey. Arik cuddled the little blond boy, tickled him, tossed him into the air.

"Arik, you're a born father." Sarah smiled. "What are you waiting for? Now, let's eat, or everything will be ruined."

They sat around the Shabbat table, talking, laughing, reminiscing. Then Sarah put Chanan to bed and the talk continued.

Finally Arik and Raquela said good night and strolled arm in arm out of the hospital courtyard.

"Let's walk to the desert," Arik said.

A full moon rode across the sky. "I saw you in a different light, Arik," Raquela said, "the way you were with Chanan."

"I love that baby as if he were my own."

"Arik—what about us?"

He bent to pick a cactus flower. "For you, my love."

Raquela slipped the flower into a buttonhole in her dress. "You haven't answered me, Arik."

He put his arms around her. "I want you, dearest."

"I want you, too, Arik."

Silently, their arms around each other, they walked back to the hospital courtyard and into the cottage.

In her room the cactus flower fell from her dress.

SWIFTLY the hospital took shape as Dov Volotzky's men fixed windows, installed plumbing, and set up medical equipment.

Most of the laborers were newcomers, Jewish refugees from Arab lands. For the war had created two great streams of refugees: Arabs fleeing Israel, and Jews fleeing Arab lands.

By the time Ralph Bunche had begun his armistice negotiations in January 1949, six hundred thousand Arabs had fled to the neighboring states, to the West Bank, and to the Gaza Strip. At the same time, six hundred thousand Jews who had been living in Arab states began their refugee trek. It was a mirror image.

The Arab refugees were housed in dismal camps, in tent cities in Arab lands. The Jewish refugees were housed in dismal camps, in tent cities in Israel. But there the mirror image ended. For the Arab refugees became the responsibility of the world. The U.N. fed and housed them. The Jewish refugees became the responsibility only of Israel—with help from Jews abroad.

The Arab refugees were kept inside the squalid camps. Israel closed down its camps and moved the people out. They built transit neighborhoods, which then gave way to new development towns. And of all these towns, Beersheba was the most important.

The Haim Yassky Hadassah Hospital for the Negev, named for the famous doctor who had been killed in the Mount Scopus ambush, was opened in December 1949.

Soon the operating theater was as busy as a big-city hospital's. Truck drivers were now hauling concrete and food down the Negev road to Eilat. That ancient harbor on the Gulf of Aqaba, where King Solomon had welcomed the queen of Sheba to his kingdom, was to be opened, to become the window to Asia and Africa. The Negev road was a hundred and forty-three miles from Jerusalem.

The truck drivers often drove twelve hours or more over this monotonous terrain. Exhausted, they sometimes fell asleep at the wheel and overturned. Other drivers, finding them, would rush them to the new hospital.

Ben-Gurion had asked Hadassah to open this hospital for the Bedouin Arabs of the Negev as well as for the Jews. But for weeks no Bedouins came.

Finally the first Bedouin sheikh arrived. Behind him came four wives, twelve children, and two camels. He carried an almost lifeless young boy. At the entrance gate he told the guard, "My son Abdullah is sick in the stomach. No food stays in him. Can your medicine make him better?"

The guard escorted the sheikh and his son into the building while the family and the animals settled themselves under a palm tree in the courtyard.

For several days the little boy hovered between life and death. The sheikh's family never moved from the courtyard.

The boy was saved.

Word about the Jewish miracle doctors spread among the Bedouins, and soon more sheikhs arrived with their families.

OVERNIGHT, it seemed to Raquela, concrete apartment houses rose from the sand. The town encroached upon the desert. New streets, new neighborhoods, new factories. The sounds of bulldozers and tractors pierced the desert air.

One night the Israel Philharmonic came to perform in Beersheba. Raquela and Arik left the hospital early to have dinner before the concert. Raquela wore a terra-cotta suit and the necklace of blue Hebron-glass beads Arik had bought her on their first walk through the Old City.

They strolled through the bustling streets. At the restaurant, Arik said, "Let's celebrate and have some wine."

"What are we celebrating?"

"Just being in love."

The waiter brought the wine. Arik lifted his glass. "To the lucky day on Scopus when we first met."

Raquela sipped her wine, looking at Arik. In these four months of intimacy in Beersheba, of nights of closeness and beauty, he had not once talked of marriage. What was holding him back?

The waiter set food before them—*humus,* chick peas and sesame seeds ground with oil. There was no meat. Israel was too poor to import beef.

"You're so quiet tonight, Raquela," Arik said.

"I'm troubled. I need advice."

"And what advice does my beautiful Raquela seek?"

"You're a very complex man, Arik. There's some barrier between us, and I can't put my finger on it."

"Our ages—"

"It's deeper that that," she interrupted. "I feel something . . . unspoken . . . between us."

"But I've never been so completely in love."

"Are you sure? Completely?" She tried to stifle her doubts.

"With every cell in my body."

She shook her head.

"You called me complex, Raquela. All right, I am. I have fears. The very things I love in you are the things I fear—your strength, your independence, your desirability."

"For God's sake, Arik, how can a man with *your* strength, *your* understanding of human nature, be scared off by me?"

"I wish things could go on just the way they are now."

"You know they never can."

Around them people began to stand up. "We'd better get to the concert," Arik said.

They crossed the street to the outdoor theater and took their seats. Raquela tried to push the conflict out of her mind. The sun was setting, and she watched the ball of flame drop abruptly out of the cobalt-blue sky.

June 1950

The army warehouse was stacked with clothing. Raquela leaned down on a table and signed for her gear—khaki shirt and jacket, khaki blouse, khaki beret, brown belt, sandals, mess kit.

She moved to the side to wait. Twenty-five Hadassah nurses milled around the warehouse in Camp Tel Nof, an army training camp twenty miles south of Tel Aviv. Was it only a week since the notice had come from Hadassah in Jerusalem? The army had requested every civilian hospital in the country to supply nurses, and they asked for twenty-five volunteers from the Hadassah staff.

Raquela leaned against the warehouse wall. Her mind flashed back. She had been in Arik's office in Beersheba.

"Arik, the army wants volunteer nurses."

"You're not thinking of—"

"The soldiers need us, Arik. I'm going to join."

His voice was strangled. "We need nurses here, too, Raquela." He came toward her and put his arms on her shoulders. "It's a fine, patriotic thing you're doing, but that's not the only reason. You're leaving me. That's part of it, isn't it?"

Her eyes filled. "Yes, Arik."

"But these months together have been so beautiful."

"They have, Arik. But I can't go on—not on your terms."

He'd returned to his desk and put his head in his hands. "I can't throw off my fears." He lifted his head to her. "I love you so, but I feel it so clearly—some morning you'll wake up and see next to you the face of an old man. I wouldn't blame you, but you might run into another man's arms. And I would die."

"It's no use, Arik. I can't deal with your fears."

In the warehouse, she already felt an emptiness. Had she made the right decision?

The next morning Raquela and the other Hadassah nurses sat in a lecture hall with a group of eighteen-year-old recruits. A scholarly-looking woman in her mid-thirties addressed them. On the wall behind her hung a huge map of Israel. With a pointer she traced the country's narrow contour. "We have five hundred and ninety-four miles of border to be defended. And here, right in the center, we're just ten miles across. It's our most heavily populated area. Within a few hours an invading army could slice us in half. Like this." She ripped her pointer across the center of the map.

"If we could have a regular standing army, we'd be in good shape. But we can't afford it. That's why every boy and girl of eighteen is drafted. That's why you're here."

"You recruits will begin your eighteen-month tour of duty with three months' basic training. Then you'll go into communications, or meteorology, or work at radar stations. You can be secretaries and clerks. Some will make officer candidate school."

She paused. "Now, we have a special group among us." She looked down at the nurses. "You nurses will do three weeks of basic training. You'll become second lieutenants and begin work in the military hospitals immediately."

She laid her pointer on a table. "We don't expect women to serve in the front lines. But every soldier must learn how to use a gun. Tomorrow you'll be issued rifles."

At five thirty the next morning the nurses dressed and marched outside. They did exercises, then breakfasted, and at seven stood at attention for bed inspection.

At eight classes began. At ten they were issued rifles.

In the next three weeks they hiked, they marched, and they learned to shoot.

Finally the course was over and Raquela reported for duty at Tel Hashomer, the military hospital outside Tel Aviv.

She entered the rehabilitation ward. Soldiers lay on beds, legs in traction, arms swathed in bandages. One soldier whistled. "Wow! Look at the new bird."

"Pinch me," another called out. "Am I dreaming?"

One young man deliberately turned his face away from her. She read his name on his chart. He was a quadriplegic.

"Can I do something for you, Aviad?" she asked.

"Nobody can."

In the next days Raquela sought ways to make Aviad comfortable, gently lifting the paralyzed arms and legs as she changed his sheets and pajamas. He neither thanked her nor protested.

His mother came and tried to talk to him. He rarely answered.

One morning he called out, "Nurse, will you come here, please?"

"Yes, Aviad?" Raquela asked.

"My girl friend is coming this afternoon for the first time. I want to be dressed."

"Of course. I'll dress you." She left the ward and returned with a new T-shirt and khaki pants. His mother helped her draw the clothes on his wasted limbs. Then they lifted him into a wheelchair. But his head—the only part of his body that moved—

collapsed on his chest. "I'll get a neck brace," Raquela said.

She returned quickly with a high leather collar and began fitting it around Aviad's neck.

Aviad looked at the soldiers watching him in the ward. "Hi, fellows. How do I look?"

Raquela heard a familiar voice say, "You look just fine."

She glanced toward the door. It was Arik.

THEY walked through the hospital grounds. "You were right, Raquela, to leave me. It made me realize that whatever years I have I want to spend with you."

"No more fears? No more doubts?"

"I want to marry you, Raquela."

She walked beside him in silence.

"You're not saying anything, Raquela. Why?"

"Arik, I've missed you terribly, but I'm committed to the army."

They found a shaded bench and sat down.

"You know, the personnel shortage at Hadassah is worse than ever," Arik said. "Especially in your department. Maybe we could convince the army to release you." He took her in his arms. "If so, will you marry me?"

She put her head on his shoulder and whispered, "Yes, Arik."

August 1950

Raquela examined herself in the long mirror, carefully buttoning the white linen suit softened with an eyelet-embroidered collar and cuffs. Then she draped the gossamer bridal veil over her head and shoulders.

She stepped away and glanced around the unfamiliar bedroom in the home of Sophia and Leon Lustig, Arik's childhood friends from Poland. Rather than a huge wedding in Jerusalem, she and Arik had agreed on a small ceremony the moment the army released her. The Lustigs had offered their cottage in the picturesque seacoast town of Nahariya, on the northernmost border of Israel.

Sophia Lustig entered the bedroom. "For the beautiful bride." She handed Raquela a corsage of pink roses.

Raquela inhaled the fragrance. "Today is so good," she said. "It's got to be good. It's the twenty-ninth. Twenty-nine is my lucky number."

"Any day would be a lucky day, marrying Arik," Sophia said. She kissed Raquela. "Now, come, they're waiting."

Raquela walked into the garden, her heart pounding. She saw four men holding wooden poles, supporting a velvet canopy—her brothers, Jacob and Yair; her adopted brother, Itzhak; and Leon Lustig. Waiting for them under the canopy was the rabbi.

The ceremony began. Arik walked down the garden path, escorted by his mother and father, to the border of the canopy. Raquela came next, walking between Mama and Papa. Arik stepped forward and led her under the canopy, facing the rabbi.

The garden smelled of pomegranates and figs and mandarins. My whole life, Raquela thought, has led to this day.

She stood at Arik's side, listening as the rabbi sanctified the wine and handed the glass to Arik, who drank a few drops. Then Arik lifted Raquela's veil and she sipped from the glass. The rabbi continued. "As you share the wine of this cup, may you share all things from this day on with love and understanding."

Raquela and Arik exchanged rings. Then Arik repeated after the rabbi, "Be thou my wife according to the Law of Moses. I faithfully promise that I will be a true husband unto thee and I will honor and cherish thee."

"And I," Raquela promised, her eyes shining, "plight my troth unto thee in affection and in sincerity."

Once more the rabbi gave them the wine. "I pronounce you husband and wife. May the Lord bless you and keep you and cause His countenance to shine upon you and bring you peace."

The rabbi now placed the empty wineglass on the grass. Arik crushed it under his heel. The traditional breaking of the glass was to remind them, even on this day of greatest joy, of the destruction of the Temple in Jerusalem in the year 70 A.D.

"Mazel tov! Mazel tov!" the wedding party shouted.

AFTER a week's honeymoon, Arik and Raquela moved into a three-room apartment at 18 Palmach Street in Jerusalem. There was little furniture in the shops, but Raquela soon found a sofa bed and a table and chairs for the living-dining room. She hung white curtains in the bedroom and covered the bed with a multicolored afghan she had knitted.

They both resumed work in Jerusalem, and each Tuesday they

drove down to the still rapidly expanding hospital in Beersheba.

One day Raquela answered the telephone in Arik's Beersheba office. A frightened voice spoke. "I'm calling from Kibbutz Revivim. One of our pregnant women is very sick. We have no doctor here."

Raquela put Arik on the phone. "What are her symptoms?"

"Her body is shaking. We think she's having convulsions."

"What kind of transportation do you have?"

"A farm truck."

Dr. Aron ("Arik") Brzezinski

"Get her in the truck and start toward the hospital. I'll meet you along the road in an ambulance."

Raquela and Arik jumped into the ambulance. Kibbutz Revivim lay twenty-five miles south of Beersheba. Midway they spotted the truck. Both vehicles pulled over to the side of the road.

Two men carried an unconscious woman into the ambulance and they all set off immediately for the hospital.

Inside the ambulance, Arik examined the woman. "It's eclampsia," he said. It was the dread toxemia of pregnancy.

At the hospital, the young woman was wheeled up the ramp. Only an operation could save her life. Arik operated.

Raquela went to the waiting room and found the young husband hunched over with anxiety. "Can I see my wife?"

"I'm sorry. Not yet. She's very ill."

"And my baby?"

Raquela put her hand out to comfort him. "The baby is dead."

Tears welled in his eyes. "Will my wife be all right?"

"If anyone can save her, it's Dr. Brzezinski. You have the best gynecologist in the country."

"Can I telephone her mother from here?"

"Of course. I'll take you to the doctor's office."

Raquela heard him tell the operator, "I'd like to call Jerusalem. The Ministry of Labor. I want to speak to Mrs. Golda Meir."

Raquela hurried out of the office—to give the man privacy, and

448

to tell Arik the woman was Golda Meir's only daughter, Sarah.

Two hours later Raquela was called to the waiting room. Golda Meir had rushed down from Jerusalem. "How is my daughter?"

Raquela's eyes fixed on the strong, commanding face she had last seen on Cyprus. Her son-in-law, Zechariah, stood beside her. "Tell me the truth."

"It's touch and go, Mrs. Meir. Dr. Brzezinski is with her."

"Can I see her?"

"No one can see her. She's too critically ill."

Golda dropped into a chair and lit a cigarette.

"I'll tell Dr. Brzezinski you're here," Raquela said.

Arik entered the waiting room. His eyes were bloodshot with fatigue. "Mrs. Meir, you have a very sick daughter. We're doing everything we can to save her."

"Please, Doctor—don't give me double-talk. What are Sarah's chances?"

His face grew solemn. "Her chances are not very good."

All night Golda sat, smoking cigarettes. At intervals Arik and Raquela came to report. No change.

In the morning Raquela took Mrs. Meir and Zechariah across the street to the staff dining room for breakfast. In the hospital courtyard, she suggested they sit on a bench in the morning sun. Golda sat down, watching a Bedouin family encamped with their goats, but her eyes kept returning to the stucco building where her daughter lay unconscious.

The second day passed. No change. The third day. The fourth. Golda hardly moved from the bench, weeping unashamedly.

Finally, on the seventh day, Sarah opened her eyes. "Where am I?" she asked.

"You're in the hospital in Beersheba," Arik said. "And you're going to be fine."

Raquela raced into the courtyard to tell Golda and Zechariah.

BACK in Jerusalem, Raquela saw the hospital filling up again with victims of Arab terrorist attacks.

David Ben-Gurion, Israel's first prime minister, had announced that he was ready to sit down at any time to talk peace with the Arabs. Only King Abdullah of Jordan—as Transjordan was now called—had agreed. And for this he paid with his life. On July 20,

1951, as he was leaving a mosque in the Old City with his young grandson, Prince Hussein, he was shot down by a relative of the former mufti of Jerusalem.

February 1951

Raquela hurried through the hospital to Arik's office. He jumped up as she entered, his eyes searching. She smiled. "I came straight from the lab. Two months pregnant. Can you believe it?"

"Believe it? I've been dreaming it. But how do you feel?"

"So excited you'd think this was the first baby ever to be born."

Through the next months Raquela watched the changes in her body as the embryo took shape. Its legs kicked her gently, a life making its presence known. Always her mind was on the date she had circled on the calendar, September 29, 1951. Our baby must be born on the twenty-ninth, she told herself.

On the morning of September 29 her pains began. She and Arik taxied to Hadassah, and Raquela went through the familiar routine, surprised at her own excitement and mounting tension.

Her husband sat at her side as the pains grew closer. She turned her head. "Arik, you look petrified. The greatest gynecologist in the country acting like any nervous father."

He bent down and kissed her tenderly.

Another pain convulsed her body. She breathed into it, telling herself, as she had told countless mothers, Breathe. Relax. Breathe. Relax.

An hour passed. Two. Three. At last she was ready. Arik helped her onto the delivery table.

"Push down," the midwife commanded. "Good. Now relax."

She was wide awake. Aware of Arik at her side. Aware of her baby, pushing its way out of her body into the world.

She heard Arik shout, "It's a boy. Oh, Raquela! We have a son."

April 1952

The El Al plane lifted off from Lydda airfield. Raquela, holding seven-month-old Amnon, put her hand in Arik's.

They were on sabbatical. Both had taken leave from their jobs so Arik could work at Beth Israel Hospital in New York with gynecologist Dr. Henry Falk.

Arik took Amnon in his lap and rumpled his curly golden hair.

How alike they are, Raquela thought. Unruffled, composed, easy to live with. She was euphoric. They would have a whole year away from pressure. Time for Arik to enjoy his baby son.

NEW YORK was a wonderland. From their Manhattan apartment Raquela explored the city, wheeling Amnon in a carriage. She stared at the shopwindows on Broadway, devouring the dresses; feasted her eyes on pyramids of fresh fruit; entered butcher shops still pinching herself that she could buy meat.

Saturdays and Sundays they picnicked in Central Park, and, after lunch, lay back while Arik—never without a volume of Sholom Aleichem—read to her.

After a few months they bought a secondhand Chevrolet. Raquela took lessons and became a passionate driver. She drove Arik to medical centers in Boston, Cleveland, and Chicago, so he could take back to Israel America's newest techniques in performing hysterectomies and cesarean sections.

They returned to Jerusalem in April 1953 and Raquela was prevailed upon to teach midwifery for Hadassah.

Each morning, leaving Amnon with her housekeeper, she drove Arik to the hospital in the Chevrolet, which they had brought from America. Then she crossed the street to the barracks where she taught student nurses. The moment her classes were over, she raced home to give Amnon lunch, and rested while he napped. Then she took him to visit Mama and Papa, played with him in Independence Park, or went marketing.

All the while the Arab states continued their threats of war. "Read this," Arik said one afternoon, handing her the newspaper.

She took the paper to the sofa. It was the king of Saudi Arabia this time. "Israel, to the Arab world, is like a cancer to the human body. The only remedy is to uproot it. Why don't we sacrifice ten million of our number to live in pride and self-respect?"

She was stunned. *"Ten million!* Willing to sacrifice ten million human beings to defeat us!"

"They won't defeat us," Arik said. "But they're preparing for it." He spoke softly. "If only there will be peace by the time Amnon grows up."

A year later Raquela became pregnant once more. But this time she contracted herpes zoster—shingles. A stripe of blisters ran along the side of her abdomen. She stopped teaching. The rashes itched and burned.

But worse than the pain was her fear. Raquela knew the herpes zoster virus might infect the fetus. It could damage the baby's brain. Its heart. Its kidneys or its liver. Raquela forced herself to keep house and take care of Arik and Amnon. She tried to hide her worry. But the months seemed interminable.

The baby was due in late January, 1955. January was a bleak month anyway. It was in January 1952 that Raquela's brother Jacob, just thirty-three, had died of Hodgkin's disease.

Raquela told Arik, "If only the baby comes on the twenty-ninth, everything will be all right."

January 29 passed. The next morning labor began.

Arik rushed her to Hadassah. This time she was to be delivered by a gynecologist, Dr. Sadowsky.

Labor was fast. Arik held her hand while Dr. Sadowsky eased the baby out of her body. "It's a boy," Arik called out.

"Is he all right?"

"He'll be all right."

"Let me see him," she said. She pushed her head up to look at the baby. "Oh, Arik. He's jaundiced. His skin is yellow."

"Raquela, honey, he'll be all right."

Her eyes filled with fear. "We must keep him alive."

"We'll keep him alive, my darling. Haven't we decided to name him Rafael—healed by God? Now you rest."

But she could not rest, not now or for days. The herpes zoster virus had circulated through the fetus and then localized in the liver, destroying some cells and causing the jaundice.

Would her baby survive long enough to allow the liver cells to regenerate?

Raquela regained enough strength to sit beside Rafi's crib in the hospital. He could hold no food. She watched the glucose drip nourishment into a tiny vein in his hand. He lay pale and listless.

Mama had taken Amnon to her house. And Arik saw Raquela withdrawing inside herself. "Raquela, you must come home from the hospital and sleep."

"Leave me alone, Arik. I can't sleep."

"You have to keep your strength. Amnon needs you, too."

"Amnon is all right. But if anything happens to Rafi—"

He put his arms around her. "I'm worried about you."

Her eyes were glazed. His words hardly penetrated her depression. She refused to leave the hospital.

Days passed. Weeks. Rafi showed little improvement.

Friends came. Judith Steiner. Her brothers, Yair and Itzhak, came with their wives. Mama and Papa and Amnon came. But not even Amnon, three and a half years old, could comfort her.

At last Rafi's liver cells began regenerating. Gradually he began to put on weight, and Arik and Raquela took him home. But two months later he was back in the hospital. His liver was inflamed again. He vomited. He screamed with pain.

The pediatricians worked around the clock to save him.

Finally, after a few weeks, the inflammation subsided. Raquela took him home, and soon the apartment, once again bright and cheerful, hummed with the sounds of her little boys and of Arik's baritone voice, singing them to sleep each night.

THE year 1955 was a year of terror. Israel's borders were penetrated by terrorist gangs called fedayeen—Arabs recruited largely from Gaza, with bases in Egypt, Jordan, and Syria. The border settlements suffered most: men and women and children indiscriminately killed by grenades and bullets. Israel retaliated, attacking the fedayeen bases.

The United Nations took note of the terrorist activities but censured Israel whenever she retaliated.

From Cairo Radio came the voice of Gamal Abdel Nasser, threatening war. "Burn, murder, and destroy," he proclaimed.

The Russians found him an eager ally. For years they had sought a foothold in the Middle East. Now they supplied Nasser with artillery and tanks, with submarines and MiGs, knowing they were to be used in the coming war against Israel.

In July 1956, turning against England and France, Nasser nationalized the Suez Canal, their lifeline to their markets in Africa and the Orient. And he barred Israel's ships from sailing through the canal. Next, he blockaded the Gulf of Aqaba and cut off Israel's southern port of Eilat.

In October Nasser concluded a military alliance with Syria and Jordan. The three armies were placed under Egyptian command. Their troops massed at Israel's borders.

On October 29 Israel dropped paratroopers inside the Sinai Peninsula. Under the command of Moshe Dayan the army pushed across the desert in tanks, jeeps, ice-cream trucks, and cars. Taking the world by surprise, they slashed into the Sinai, demolishing the fedayeen nests, knocking out Nasser's Sinai force—one-third of his total army—and capturing all the Russian hardware in Sinai and Gaza. Hordes of Egyptian soldiers were found wandering in the desert, abandoned by their officers. Five thousand were taken prisoner. Many had Arabic translations of Hitler's *Mein Kampf*.

One hundred and seventy-two Israelis were killed, eight hundred wounded. Egypt took one Israeli prisoner. He was exchanged for many of the five thousand captured Egyptians.

Britain and France were to have attacked the Suez Canal zone and invaded Egypt from the west at the same time that Israel's troops crossed the desert from the east. But they waited too long. They finally succeeded in putting troops into the canal zone.

Immediately the U.N., led by the United States and the Soviet Union, demanded that all British and French troops be withdrawn from the Sinai Peninsula and the Gaza Strip. Israel tried to point out that this was the time to negotiate a peace treaty with Nasser. But the Russians threatened rocket attacks. They sent Israel an ultimatum: if she did not withdraw, they would destroy her.

With a heavy heart Israel withdrew from the Suez Canal zone and the Sinai Peninsula, but she refused to withdraw from the Strait of Tiran and the Gaza Strip without guarantees of security.

Finally President Dwight D. Eisenhower gave Ben-Gurion his personal guarantee—the U.N. would station forces in Gaza so there would be no enemy troops grouped at Israel's borders and no fedayeen attacks. And the United States itself would guarantee Israel's free access to the waterways.

Ben-Gurion, accepting the guarantees, ordered his troops to withdraw. "This is the blackest day of my life," he said.

He knew—as Arik and Raquela knew, as all of Israel knew—this would not be the last of the wars for survival.

June 1961

It was David Ben-Gurion who selected the site for the new Hadassah–Hebrew University Medical Center, soon to open in Ein Karem, in the hills of Judaea south and west of downtown

Jerusalem. Standing on a mountain plateau overlooking the Valley of Sorek, where once Delilah had won Samson's heart, Ben-Gurion saw miles of empty land. "Magnificent!" he said. "Build here. Jerusalem will grow toward the hospital."

Now the medical center, which would replace that on Mount Scopus, was finished—a huge complex of buildings of honey-hued stone and red and white brick. The four-hundred-and-twenty-bed hospital was a semicircular fortress. In case of war, three floors were built underground, with connecting tunnels equipped to be converted instantly into emergency units. The center, unique in the Middle East, held the hospital, the medical school, the nursing school, the dental school. Later there would be the Institute of Oncology for cancer treatment and research.

As his gift to the people, Marc Chagall created twelve stained-glass windows, one for each of the twelve tribes of Israel, to be installed in the hospital synagogue.

On moving day Raquela and Arik helped transfer the maternity patients to Ein Karem. Late in the afternoon they stood in the broad courtyard in front of the hospital, watching the sun change the colors of the mountains to blue, then to pink and mauve. Arik put his arms around Raquela. "This is my dream," he said. "That you and our boys will have a long life. That we can work in this new center. We have what we need. If only—if only there will be no more war."

ARIK pushed open the apartment door. They had moved to a spacious third-floor apartment on Hameyasdim Street in Bet Hakerem. "Raquela, it came!" He handed her the letter. The U.S. National Institutes of Health was happy to inform Dr. Brzezinski that he had been awarded a grant for a five-year project to study the problems of toxemia in pregnancy. Under the controlled scientific conditions in Israel, and with his long experience, his study could provide valuable information not only for saving lives in Israel but also throughout the world.

"I knew," she said. "I knew someday you'd be famous. It's recognition you deserve."

He put his hands on her shoulders. "I want you to help me. Together we can get this project off the ground."

"I will, Arik. I want to work with you on this."

They soon broadened the scope of the study. While eclampsia was their central interest, they were also studying premature births, stillbirths, and infant mortality. Jerusalem was an ideal laboratory. Its population consisted of families from some eighty countries. Raquela and Arik were trying to find out in which ethnic groups infant morbidity was highest. Then they could plan preventive-health-care services.

"Arik," Raquela said one evening, "you look so tired. With your patients and this study, you're working too hard."

He paid no attention. He was busy making notes. Finally he looked up. "And how is our new house coming along?"

"Fine. I can't wait for us to move in."

It was to be Arik's dream house. Papa had given them the land next to his cottage in Bet Hakerem. Now the house was taking shape—long, low lines, split level, Arik's office and their bedroom on the lower level, the boys' rooms on the upper level, and a spacious sunken living room whose French doors opened out to the tropical trees and calla lilies Papa had planted.

The house was to be ready at the end of August, 1963.

ON AUGUST 15 Arik opened the door to their apartment. He was hunched over with pain. "Arik!" Raquela ran to his side.

"I'm afraid it's my gallbladder. I'll get into bed."

"Can I get you something?" Her heart pounded.

"Some Demerol."

"I'll run down to the pharmacy."

When she returned, her housekeeper said, "While you were out, Dr. Brzezinski asked me for a box from the chest in the foyer."

Raquela paled. It was where Arik kept his most precious photos. Their wedding pictures. Snapshots of Amnon and Rafi. Pictures of their stay in New York. Why did he want them now?

She hurried into the bedroom. The pictures lay on the bed, but Arik was gasping for breath, his forehead beaded with perspiration. "Arik—let me call a doctor."

"You know I've had these attacks before. They always pass. I'll be all right after a while."

Raquela called the children into the living room. Amnon, now a sturdy eleven-year-old, came toward her quietly. He seemed cut out to be a doctor like his father. Rafi, eight and a half, burst into the room. She saw herself in Rafi—her eyes, her smile, her eagerness for life.

"Children"—she controlled her voice—"Daddy is sick. I'd like you to spend the night at Grandma and Grandpa's house."

Amnon looked frightened. "Will Daddy be all right?"

"Of course," she reassured him. "It's just his gallbladder. Now, both of you—get your pajamas. And take your white shirts and khaki shorts so you'll be all set for Friday night and Shabbat."

She kissed her sons, then walked to the window and watched them disappear down the hill toward Mama's house.

That night Arik slept fitfully, waking intermittently, confessing pain. "It's in my back and right side."

By noon the next day he could no longer tolerate the pain. "All right, Raquela. Call the doctor."

He arrived within minutes. Raquela paced the floor while he examined Arik.

"It's not his gallbladder. It's his heart." The doctor telephoned for an ambulance.

At the hospital, he was rushed into the emergency room. Raquela sat in the nurses' station. The nurses—old friends— tried to divert her. But nothing worked.

Raquela and Arik's sons, Rafi and Amnon

Why did I listen to him? Why didn't I myself call a doctor sooner? she agonized. Arik . . . stay alive . . .

A team of doctors came out of the emergency room. "It's a coronary, Raquela. We don't know yet how severe it is."

All afternoon the doctors worked, barely leaving the room. Just before sundown Raquela called Mama, who spoke comfortingly. "Tell Arik how beautiful the boys look in their white Shabbat shirts. Now I'm going to light my Friday night candles and pray."

The hours dragged. At midnight a nurse appeared. "Dr. Brzezinski wants to see you. Just stay a few minutes . . . please."

Raquela sped to his bedside. "I'm here, darling."

"Ra—Raquela," he gasped. "How—how—are the boys?"

"They're fine. Mama wants you to know how beautiful they look."

"And you, my dearest, take . . . good care . . ." His voice faded.

Raquela saw the erratic movement on the heart monitor. "Save him," she cried to the nurse. "He's having another heart attack."

"Please step outside, Mrs. Brzezinski," the nurse said brusquely. Doctors and nurses hurried in and out of his room.

Raquela paced the corridor. Don't die, Arik. We need you . . . Amnon and Rafi . . . and I. You were so happy . . . the grant . . . the house. . . . I love you, Arik. Stay alive, please stay alive.

At one a.m. the doctors and nurses filed sadly out of Arik's room. Raquela screamed.

ON SUNDAY morning thousands of people filled the cemetery in the Jerusalem hills. Raquela held her children's hands as Arik's body was lowered into the earth.

"Good-by, my love," she whispered.

PART FIVE

September 1963

Dr. Moshe Prywes, associate dean of the Hebrew University–Hadassah Medical School, stood up as Raquela entered. "How are you, my dear?" He scanned her face. "Isa and I worry about you."

She took hold of his hand. "You both have been wonderful."

It had been thirty days since Arik's death, and Raquela now returned to work. She had moved into the new house and was trying to pick up the pieces of her life.

She was thirty-eight. A widow. Trying to be both mother and father. Careful not to demand too much of the boys. Wary lest Amnon try to become man of the house overnight. Forfeit his childhood. And worried that Rafi was clinging to her too much.

For the anxiety, the fears, work was the answer. This morning she had decided what she must do. Now she was discussing it with Dr. Prywes. "Moshe, I want to continue Arik's project. It's his memorial. I don't want it to—just to die."

He tilted his chair. "Raquela, you're very skilled. But America would never let a nurse head a major research project."

"Couldn't you find someone I could work with?"

Surely Moshe would find a solution, Raquela thought. Brilliant. Urbane. A world traveler. Member of the U.N. World Health Organization. French Legion of Honor. Arik, his best friend, had called him the most creative medical educator in Israel.

It was that friendship that Raquela was relying upon now. For twelve years the two families had spent vacations and weekends together at the little beach house Arik and Raquela had built at Bet Yannai. Raquela thought of the evenings on the beach when Moshe had told them stories of the war. He had always managed, with incredible ingenuity, to land on his feet.

He had been one of the very few Jewish doctors working in the university hospital in Warsaw when World War II began. The hospital was evacuated eastward. Warsaw was burning. The doctors were mobilized and Moshe became a captain. Then the Nazi-Soviet pact partitioned Poland. The Polish Army commander gave the doctors in uniform a choice: "You can go west and join the Nazis, or you can go east and become a Soviet prisoner of war." Moshe knew the Nazis would kill him. He went east.

The Russians rounded up all the officers—Poles and Jews. Ten thousand were massacred. Moshe was saved by advice from a Communist whom he had once treated as a patient. "For the Russians, better to be a simple soldier—not an officer." So before the roundup, Moshe had ripped off his captain's bars. Then he hid his medical diploma inside the heel of his boot. Finally he burned all the papers that might identify him as a member of the wealthy Prywes family of Warsaw.

As an obscure private, he was exiled to an Arctic slave-labor camp along the Pechora River near the Ural Mountains.

Moshe had been in the prison camp a year and a half when the Nazis attacked Russia in June 1941. A few days later all Russian doctors and nurses were mobilized into the Red Army. Because the twenty-eight thousand prisoners in his camp were now without a doctor, Moshe decided to reveal who he was. By now he weighed less than one hundred pounds and he was emaciated and weak from malnutrition. He felt he had nothing to lose. He was one step away from death.

He drew out his diploma from his boot and showed it to the camp commandant.

The commandant examined the document. "I'm placing you in charge of medicine for all the camps on the Pechora River," he said.

Moshe was given a house, a horse, and a white coat. For five years he traveled about the heavily forested region, operating on prisoners, delivering babies, treating illnesses.

He survived the war and returned to Warsaw. His wife, Isabella, a dentist, had also miraculously survived. She had worked as a nurse in a prison-camp hospital. They left Poland. Moshe worked for the American Joint Distribution Committee in Paris until he was invited, in 1951, to join the medical school in Jerusalem. He and Arik became friends.

Dr. Moshe Prywes

"I want to help you, Raquela," Moshe said. "I'm going to call Dr. Michael Davies. He's head of the department of medical ecology here at the school."

She listened as he spoke into the phone. "Fine, Michael. I'll write Washington and ask them to transfer the project to you." He smiled as he continued. "I'll assure them that you are the most qualified person to carry on the work. But I have one condition—that Raquela Brzezinski work with you."

Raquela leaned forward.

"Then you admire her, too. . . . Yes, she is efficient. Responsible. Agreed, then, Michael?" He hung up.

Not long after, approval arrived from Washington. Determined to succeed, Raquela threw herself into the project.

One afternoon her old friend Judith Steiner, who had become director of the nursing school, dropped in for tea.

"Will you forgive me if I give you some advice?" Judith asked.

"What kind of advice?"

"You should start going out more," Judith said. "You're a beautiful woman, Raquela. Eligible men would like to meet you."

"I'm not ready, Judith." She stood up and walked to the French doors. Papa's plants were a tropical jungle outside, framing the doorway. "I need time to mourn."

RAQUELA's best friends were Moshe and Isa Prywes. They often invited her and the boys to dinner with their two daughters.

Isa was an extraordinary woman. Warm, highly intelligent, she was quintessential wife and mother. She sought to heal Raquela's wounds. But it was Isa who needed healing. She had been fighting cancer for eleven years, and now she was dying. She was forty-nine.

Eventually Moshe had to take Isa to the Hadassah Hospital at Ein Karem. Every hour he raced up from his office, on the main floor of the medical center, to see her. She ate only when he came to feed her. Jenny, their eighteen-year-old daughter, was in the army. Her noncom gave her time off to visit her mother. Vivian, fourteen, came every day after school. Raquela visited briefly each day, hoping to bring even a few minutes of distraction. She tried not to weep, marveling how Isa, racked with unbearable pain, continued to fight.

She died in November 1965.

Jenny was transferred to Jerusalem to be closer to home, and each evening she and Vivian tried to comfort their grief-stricken father. One evening Jenny said, "Daddy, you're so alone. You're only fifty-one. You should remarry."

December 31, 1965

Moshe and Raquela were at a friend's New Year's Eve party. Raquela tried to make small talk, but the evening dragged. She wondered why she had come. Moshe, too, found the gay atmosphere intolerable.

Midnight. Husbands and wives kissed each other. Moshe approached her. "Let's get out of here, Raquela. This is no place for either you or me tonight." He drove her home.

Three days later he telephoned. "Raquela, I'm building a house in Ashkelon. You've just built a house. You know more about this sort of thing than I do. Would you come along with me and talk to the contractor?"

"Why not?"

She sat beside him in the car, drinking in the Jerusalem air as they began to descend the hills of Judaea. The once barren hills were now green, terraced with trees. Little settlements of Jews from Yemen, India, Afghanistan, and Europe peopled the Biblical hills and valleys.

Just before Latrun they turned south. How often Raquela had driven this road with Arik on their way to Beersheba. She relaxed. At last she could think of Arik without a stab of pain.

They were in the Negev. Raquela looked around and saw desert land grown fertile. Rows of lush cotton and corn marching like proud soldiers toward the horizon.

"One word made all of this possible," Moshe said.

"Water!" She said it as if it were magic.

Israel had just finished the great National Water Carrier. Giant hydraulic engines lifted the Jordan's water from the Sea of Galilee, pipelines conducted it over steep mountains, open sluiceways sped it down valleys. In the center of the country it linked with the huge Yarkon-Negev pipeline, which brought the water south from Tel Aviv's Yarkon River. The once barren desert was now a harvest of crops and flowers.

Raquela at work with
Dr. Michael Davies studying the
problems of infant mortality

Moshe drove into Ashkelon, six miles north of the Gaza Strip. Its broad avenue was lined with date palms and flower beds. Foreigners ambled along the streets. Israel had become an important tourist center, and Ashkelon, charming and rich with Biblical history, lay on the tourist route.

They turned toward the beach and drove to Moshe's cottage. The contractor was inside, plastering the walls. Moshe stood aside, smiling, while Raquela pointed out that the floor was uneven, and discussed where to put the outlets for the stove and refrigerator. The contractor began with an argument and ended with total, if reluctant, capitulation.

Raquela and Moshe lunched in a restaurant on a hill overlooking the Mediterranean. This was Samson country, and the restaurant was named Delilah. They ordered sea bass. The breeze from the Mediterranean swept the restaurant. Everything was good. Ashkelon. The sea. The fish. The beautiful day. Raquela felt vibrantly alive.

The next days were hectic. Raquela was delegated to chauffeur a group of Washington doctors to the hospitals and settlements around Jerusalem. Meanwhile, the toxemia study seemed to be growing more and more meaningful. Dr. Davies was planning a book on toxemia in pregnancy, and Moshe was to be its editor.

Raquela began to hear rumors floating around the hospital and the university linking her with Moshe. She brushed them off. Ridiculous gossip.

Early one morning, after two weeks of heavy rainstorms, Moshe telephoned. "I'm worried about what this rain is doing to your beach house, Raquela. Let's drive out there tomorrow, and we can see whether the rains have done any damage."

The next day the rain had ended, but the weather was raw. The summer colony in Bet Yannai looked cold and deserted. Raquela and Moshe walked up a sandy embankment to the house.

"First thing I'm going to do is to make us some hot coffee," Raquela said. Moshe sat in the kitchen, watching her. They munched on sandwiches and nutcake and warmed themselves with Turkish coffee.

"Now, let's look around the house," Moshe said. They examined the kitchen and the living room. "So far, so good. Now let's see the bedroom."

He followed her there. "Take off your shoes, Raquela." She kicked off her pumps. "Now stand up on the bed!"

Slowly she climbed up on the mattress. Moshe stood at the edge of the bed, reached up, and put his arms around her waist. "I think I love you, Raquela."

A smile seemed to rise from inside her body. For the first time since Arik's death.

She stepped down and looked up at his face. "I think I love you, too, Moshe."

EACH morning at six, Raquela was awakened by Moshe's telephone call telling her how he loved her. And each night, after the children in both their houses were asleep, she telephoned him.

In the next weeks he came to her late at night, parked his car a block away, and slipped into the house. Other nights, when Jenny and Vivian were away, she drove to his apartment.

It seemed her whole life had led to this joyous, mature love. The man was like a young lover. She was struck by his beauty, his masculinity; they connected on every level. They discussed her work and his. They laughed like teenagers. They took drives through the Jerusalem they loved, finding no need for words in the luminous air of the Biblical land from which they drew their strength.

One night, at her house, Raquela said, "I'm a lucky woman. Some women go through life without knowing even one great passion. I've known two."

Moshe drew her close. "We've both known love before. I think that's why we're so good together." He covered her face and throat with kisses. "I want to marry you, Raquela."

Raquela and Moshe in Beersheba

She closed her eyes. "Not yet. I need time. Why can't we go on like this? We love each other. What else matters?"

"Many things matter. For one thing, you're a young woman. You should be married. And people are talking."

"Let them talk, Moshe. We don't owe the gossips anything. I'm only concerned about our children."

"So am I. That's the very reason we ought to get married."

"Moshe, I'm afraid Amnon and Rafi would hate any man who would try to take Arik's place."

"We could overcome that. I love your boys, Raquela, and I think they love me. And they need a father. As for my daughters, if we marry, it would free them to begin living their own lives."

He looked at her. "I hate sneaking around. We have to make a decision, Raquela. Either we get married, or we stop seeing each other altogether." He paced the room, seeing her trembling, unable to make the choice. "Let's have a trial separation. We won't meet for three or four months."

Pain gripped her stomach. "If that's what you want."

"I want it. I want to see if we can live without each other. It's no good this way. Jerusalem is small, like a fish tank. Everyone knows what's going on."

The next morning there was no call from Moshe.

At seven, unable to eat breakfast, Raquela drove to her office, somehow managed to get through the morning. By noon she thought she was going mad. She tried to concentrate on the papers on her desk, but the words danced in front of her. She went home.

Suppertime. She fed Amnon and Rafi. They went to their rooms to do their homework. They kissed her good night. She sat on the sofa in the living room.

The phone was silent. Why had he decided on this separation? Why was a man as sophisticated as Moshe concerned about what people said? She stood up. Had she lost him? Would some other woman grab him? Marry him the minute he asked?

The telephone rang. "Raquela, I'm coming over to get you."

She flew to the bathroom, showered, and dressed. Moshe drove her to his apartment.

The lights were low. They sat together, drinking wine.

"Isn't this nice?" he said, as though nothing had happened.

"Very nice," she agreed.

"Let's promise," he said, "that we will never again have such a long separation—like these twenty-four hours —for the rest of our lives."

Raquela in front of her summer cottage at Bet Yannai

THEY spent their honeymoon traveling. Moshe, prominent medical educator and now vice-president of the Hebrew University, was invited to speak at conferences, describing Israel's work in aiding developing countries. They went to Teheran, New Delhi, Bangkok, Tokyo, Honolulu, San Francisco, New York. Then, after two months, back to Jerusalem.

It was January 1967.

April 1967

Dr. Kalman Jacob Mann, director general of the Hadassah Medical Organization, stood before the staff.

"Kibbutz Gadot has just been attacked by the Syrians. They're

465

using powerful Soviet cannons. Crops and homes have been destroyed. The Syrians have also shelled two kibbutzim on the Sea of Galilee. The Israel Air Force has silenced their guns and shot down six Russian MiGs."

The hall filled with whispers. "Do you think it means war?" Raquela asked Moshe.

"He's preparing us anyway."

Dr. Mann was now giving assignments to members of the staff. "As my deputy," he said to Moshe, "your duties will include maintaining contact with the front. Get information such as number of wounded, types of injuries. Pass it on to our medical teams immediately, so the moment the casualties are flown in here, they can go to the proper departments.

"And Raquela, I want you to organize five satellite hospitals that will be under army-Hadassah command. The army will help you select the best locations."

Within an hour Raquela was in her car with an army captain, driving around Jerusalem. Three of the sites she selected were hotels. A fourth was a dormitory at Hebrew University. The fifth, which she made her headquarters, was a convalescent home in Motza, the scene of the 1929 massacre.

A few weeks later, on May 15, 1967, Israel celebrated its nineteenth birthday. That evening Prime Minister Levi Eshkol was told, "Egyptian troops are moving through Cairo. Some have already reached the Sinai Peninsula."

Eshkol was caught by surprise. His advisers had assured him Egypt was not yet ready for aggression.

The next day Eshkol ordered a limited mobilization.

Nasser was moving fast. On May 18 he demanded that U Thant, Secretary-General of the U.N., remove the United Nations peace-keeping forces from the Egyptian-Israeli border—from Gaza to Eilat. U Thant capitulated. Arab forces instantly moved into the Gaza Strip. Then Nasser announced that the Gulf of Aqaba was closed to the Israelis. He imposed a total blockade of all Israeli ships and stopped all foreign vessels carrying matériel to Israel.

Abba Eban, the minister of foreign affairs, began a shuttle around the world. In Paris, President Charles de Gaulle, once Israel's great friend, told Eban the days of their cooperation were over. France, now out of Algeria, had turned to the Arabs. Even the arms which Israel had ordered and paid for were not to be delivered, de Gaulle said, "to prevent Israel from starting a war."

Eban flew to London. Prime Minister Harold Wilson recommended patience and restraint.

Eban flew to Washington. President Lyndon Johnson agreed that the blockade must be lifted. He had a brilliant idea. He would ask all the nations that guaranteed Israel's integrity to send ships to the Red Sea. An international flotilla would sail through the Strait of Tiran, escorting an Israeli vessel.

Not one country sent even a rowboat.

AMNON and Rafi, their schools closed, filled sandbags. Teenagers dug bombproof shelters in gardens and parks. They helped run the post office and deliver the mail. Women drove the milk trucks, and bakers worked around the clock. At least there would be milk and bread—if war came. The army prepared coffins, and youngsters dug graves in the parks. Tel Aviv was prepared for forty thousand deaths. Women taped and blacked out windows, stocked up with water and food, and disconnected electrical appliances whenever possible.

By the last weeks of May, Israel was totally mobilized. Every able-bodied man up to the age of forty-nine was called up. They had been practicing for years. They could be placed in the field within twenty-four hours.

Normally, married women with children were not expected to be called up, but some with essential skills were—doctors, nurses, computer operators, and intelligence officers.

Survival was the imperative—survival against the Arabs, as once it had been survival against the Germans. But this time there was a land in which to fight and an army to do the fighting.

June 5, 1967

The Arabs were marching. Saudi Arabia, Kuwait, Sudan, Egypt, Syria, Jordan, and Iraq were racing to the slaughter.

Raquela turned on the radio in the kitchen. "This is Kol Israel broadcasting from Jerusalem. The military spokesman announces the Egyptians this morning launched a land-and-air attack." She gripped the arms of her chair.

"Israel's forces went into action to repel them."

The telephone rang. It was Moshe. "You've heard the news?"

"Oh, Moshe. After all the tension, I feel something strange, almost like relief."

"Get the children to your parents' house to be closer to the shelter. The war's all in the Negev so far. We're hoping Jerusalem will be spared."

"I'll get them now. Then I'll go to the hospital in Motza."

"Promise me you'll drive carefully. I could not live if—"

"And you, Moshe . . ." She clutched the telephone. Would she ever hear his voice again?

In the car, Raquela tuned in Cairo Radio. The Egyptian commentator was exhorting, "Arise! Go forth into battle! The hour of glory is here."

A twist of the dial. Now it was Damascus Radio. "The time has come! Silence the enemy! Destroy him! Liberate Palestine!"

Back to Kol Israel. Music. Then the announcer: "Be calm."

Raquela made swift stops at the satellite hospitals. They were all fully staffed, every nurse at her station. "Keep in touch with me at Motza," she told the staffs, then raced back to her car.

Still no news on Kol Israel. The voice of General Chaim Herzog, the military commentator for Kol Israel, came on the air. He was explaining Israel's news blackout. "It is not always advisable to report on battles, for the enemy is as interested to learn the facts as we are. Under the circumstances . . . it is advisable that the Arabs continue to believe their own false stories. The fog of war hinders the enemy, and so let us leave him with it."

She heard a jolting explosion. Sirens shrieked. People raced into air-raid shelters. Raquela sped toward Motza.

Kol Israel at last was crackling with news. "Jordanians have opened fire on Jerusalem. Prime Minister Eshkol earlier sent a message to King Hussein. It said, 'We shall not initiate any action whatsoever against Jordan. However, should Jordan open hostilities, we shall react with all our might.'"

Before noon all Jerusalem was under Jordanian fire.

Syrian planes attacked Haifa. Natanya was bombed by Iraqi warplanes. At nine fifteen p.m. Tel Aviv was hit by the long-range guns of the Arab Legion.

Raquela spent the night at Motza. Every hour she turned on Kol Israel. Music. No more news. She switched to the Arab stations.

Nasser's commanders were reporting fantastic victories. The Arabs were winning on every front.

One thirty a.m. News at last. General Yitzhak Rabin, chief of staff, was holding a press conference. "The Israel Air Force has destroyed three hundred seventy-four enemy planes with a loss of only nineteen of our own. In eighty minutes Israel has destroyed Egypt's entire air force. Our armor and troops have captured Khan Yunis, in the Gaza Strip. El Arish and Rafiah, along the Mediterranean, have fallen. Gaza is encircled."

Raquela telephoned the hospital. "Moshe, Moshe! We're winning! The Arab broadcasts about their victories were lies."

The fog of battle had lifted.

By the next morning, Tuesday, June 6, Hussein's Arab Legion was being thrown back. Israeli paratroopers captured the Sheikh Jarrah quarter of Jerusalem that for nineteen years had blocked the road to Mount Scopus. Now the paratroopers began circling the hills north of the Old City. They were young soldiers who had never walked the labyrinthine streets of Old Jerusalem. Yet they knew it from their parents' stories and their Bible studies.

Advancing toward the Old City, they fought in trenches, in rooms, on roofs. There were heavy casualties everywhere.

Colonel Motta Gur led his paratroopers to the square outside the parapeted walls of the Old City. The Israel high command had given orders not to damage sites holy to any of the three religions. Colonel Gur ordered his brigade to attack. They swept the wall and not a single shot hit a holy place.

The heaviest casualties were among the commanders, who shouted to their men, "Follow me." They were racing to see who would get into the Old City first. No one could stop the momentum now. The paratroopers broke their way into narrow streets, running, crouching against the sides of deserted houses.

They reached the Wailing Wall. A soldier scrambled to the top and raised the flag of Israel. Chief Rabbi Shlomo Goren blew the shofar—the ram's horn—and the eerie notes pierced the air.

Shortly after noon on Wednesday, June 7, hundreds of soldiers came together at the wall. All day and through the night the paratroopers—dirty, tired, their uniforms bloodstained—kept coming to the wall, touching it, kissing it, weeping.

Jerusalem was reunited.

ON THE SOUTHERN front the desert was ablaze. Israeli and Soviet tanks, shelled from the ground, were blistering. Helicopters landed just long enough to pick up the wounded. Parachutes dropped out of the sky, bringing water and more ammunition. The temperature climbed to one hundred and five degrees.

Buses carrying troops trekked through the desert, followed by private cars, taxis, milk trucks, and delivery wagons.

The Israel Air Force was flying a cover over the three brigades that were now reversing the course Moses had taken to lead the children of Israel out of Egypt. Their goal was the Suez Canal.

In the northern Sinai, Brigadier General Israel Tal rushed his troops along the Mediterranean.

In the center of the peninsula, Brigadier General Avraham Yoffe sped his tanks toward the Mitla Pass, the strategic gateway through the desert to the canal.

In the southern Sinai, Brigadier General Arik Sharon's troops were fighting toward Nakhl, from which they also planned to wedge their way through the Mitla Pass to the canal.

Two o'clock Friday morning, June 9, Yoffe's forces reached the canal.

Less than five days after the Egyptian threat to fight a holy war had exploded in the Gaza Strip, the Egyptian Army was in flight across the desert. The great Soviet fleet of tanks lay burned or captured.

In New York, the Egyptian government agreed to a U.N. cease-fire. The war in the Sinai and the West Bank and in Jerusalem was over.

It was not yet over in other parts of Israel.

OF ALL the Arabs who encircled Israel, the Syrians were the most vicious. From the day the war broke out, they directed an almost ceaseless barrage of artillery fire at the northern kibbutzim and the new little development towns. For six full days these northern villages took the brunt of the war.

At seven a.m. on June 9 General Dado Elazar gave the command. From all the kibbutzim and other settlements that had endured Syrian fire for the nineteen terror-filled years since the establishment of the state of Israel, the army now moved with trucks, with infantry and tanks, and with the Israel Air Force.

They moved up the cliffs, some of which had never been scaled by men.

In Kibbutz Dan, Major Mottel, watching through binoculars, saw the first Israeli tanks burst into flames, blown apart by Syrian mines and antitank fire. He saw men leap out of turrets to pull the wounded out of the burning tractors and tanks. Under searing fire they raced to climb into other vehicles. The tanks lumbered up the Golan Heights.

The men in the kibbutzim below the cliffs saw it. Each time a tank exploded, they knew three men were trapped.

Leading a unit up a hill was Lieutenant Colonel Moshe Klein, an infantry battalion commander who had come from Hungary. The Syrians destroyed his half-track. Colonel Klein escaped from the burning vehicle and with his soldiers climbed the rest of the hill on foot—running, crouching, taking cover wherever they could. He saw two groups of his soldiers moving up the hill separately, and fearing they might mistake one another for the enemy, he stood up to coordinate the two groups. The Syrians killed him.

Behind him his deputy, Major Zohar, took over. A Syrian bullet pierced his neck. The medics carried him down the hill, past the troops racing forward. Thirty-year-old Major Alexander Krinsky, who had come with Youth Aliyah from Poland, was rushed in. He led the men up to the top of the hill, and there he was killed.

Without officers, even without orders, the soldiers continued to advance.

The hills were blocked by barbed wire protecting the Syrian trenches and by a fantastic underground network of Soviet-built concrete bunkers, from which the Syrians could blast any vehicle scaling the heights.

All Friday afternoon the Israelis fought along the Golan Heights, racing down roads, encircling camps and villages. At dawn on Saturday, with heavy air support, the Golani Brigade burst into the village of Banias, where the Syrians had sought to divert the headwaters of the Jordan River.

Another force pushed on toward Kuneitra, the largest city on the Golan plateau. The Syrian Army was collapsing, retreating as fast as it could to Damascus, forty-five miles away.

One day after General Elazar's command to advance into Syrian territory, the battle for the Golan Heights was over.

The casualties were heavy: one hundred and fifteen Israelis killed, and thirty wounded, one thousand Syrians dead, and six hundred taken prisoner. Eighty thousand Syrian soldiers and civilians had fled.

The Syrians lost the Golan Heights, the cliffs from which they had harassed and killed Israelis for nineteen years.

On Saturday afternoon silence fell on the kibbutzim. The people were told, "Turn on your lights. No more blackouts. The heights of Golan are ours."

JERUSALEM had become whole again. There had been dire predictions of bloodshed. Jews would be massacred if they entered the Old City. Arabs would be massacred if they walked down Zion Square. But the warnings were groundless. The moment the barriers came down, thousands of Jews swarmed through the Old City, welcomed again by friendly Arab merchants eager to sell their wares. On Zion Square, Arab men in long gowns and women in Bedouin dresses entered the clothing stores to study Western fashions, and pushed shopping carts through the supermarkets.

That Saturday, June 10, 1967, Raquela and Moshe were among the throngs walking through the narrow streets of the Old City. Senora Vavá had lived here, and before her, for more than three hundred years, Raquela's family had walked on these stones.

They reached the Wailing Wall. Raquela pressed her head against it. Moshe and their four children had come through the war alive.

A FEW days later Raquela entered Mama's living room. A tall woman in a black Bedouin gown stood talking animatedly to Mama. Could it be? The mysterious smell of musk and incense filled the room. "Aisha!"

The Arab woman flushed with pleasure. "Can this beautiful woman be my little Raquela?"

The two women embraced. Then Raquela stood back, a little girl again, watching Mama and Aisha, drawn to each other by some strange bond, their faces creased with nearly seventy years of living.

"I will get us coffee," Mama said in the tones she had spoken each morning on the patio before Jerusalem had been torn in half.

Raquela and Aisha sat together on the sofa and caught up with each other's lives. In 1948 Aisha and her family had gone to live with relatives in East Jerusalem. She had many grandchildren.

Mama entered, carrying a tray with cups of Turkish coffee.

"Do you remember," Aisha asked, "I always brought you eggs so fresh—the minute the chickens laid them?"

"I remember," Mama said. "You never failed me."

Raquela watched the two women. Would this euphoria last?

November 1967

In the United Nations the Security Council adopted Resolution 242. It called for "a just and lasting peace," with the withdrawal from occupied territories—though by no means withdrawal from *all* the occupied territories—and the renunciation of all forms of belligerency, blockade, or organized warfare—as well as "freedom of navigation through international waterways . . . the right to live in peace within secure and recognized boundaries . . . a just settlement of the refugee problem."

The refugee problem! Arthur Goldberg, the United States ambassador to the U.N., who drafted much of Resolution 242, explained that settling the refugee problem meant settling it for all refugees, Jewish as well as Arab.

The victory of the Six-Day War opened the borders that had been closed since 1948 and meant that a million Arabs, some in refugee camps, others living in towns and villages, came under Israeli military jurisdiction.

Yasir Arafat, head of the PLO (Palestine Liberation Organization), had set up headquarters in Nablus on the West Bank, reoccupied by Israel. The PLO had been created in 1964 as an umbrella for Arab terrorist groups. Its covenant was simple: Destroy Israel. In the months following the Six-Day War, Arafat organized saboteurs to whip up the Arabs on the West Bank and in Gaza, to terrorize not only the Jews but also the Israeli Arabs who had remained loyal to Israel throughout the war.

ONE morning in August, 1967, Moshe and Raquela visited an Arab refugee camp outside Hebron run by the United Nations.

Raquela walked through the grounds unbelieving. No tents. No iron huts. No barbed wire. Nearly a thousand one-family houses in pastel pinks and grays ran up and down the small hills. "This is like a modern town," she exclaimed.

At the clinic, they introduced themselves to the camp nurse and spent the next hour discussing the problems of the pregnant women and newborn babies.

They left the clinic and followed a line of people to a warehouse. Inside, they watched as each adult showed a ration card to a young Arab behind a counter. He added up the names listed on the card, and handed out food donated by the United States—cooking oil, bags of lentils, and fifty-pound sacks of flour.

Driving home, Raquela was trying to sort out her emotions. "Keeping any people in a camp—even one like this, which looks like a suburb—does terrible things to them." Memories of Athlit and Cyprus made her shudder. "Camps are evil," she said bitterly.

"Sure they're evil. People become demoralized in them. And they're a scandal. Take those ration cards we saw. Every person listed gets a monthly supply of food and clothes. Sometimes there are ten names on one card. People die or leave the camps, but their names are never crossed off the cards."

A few days later another scandal was revealed. The refugees had been selling their rations to buy guns and ammunition. American food—labeled "not to be sold or exchanged"—had been exchanged for guns to kill Israelis.

Then the biggest scandal of all surfaced: the United Nations camps had become proving grounds for terrorists.

Prime Minister Levi Eshkol died and Golda Meir was sworn in as interim prime minister. Terrorists blew up a supermarket, tossed grenades into a bank, and bombed the Hebrew University.

Terror on the streets, in the marketplaces. And still Yasir Arafat's fedayeen failed to disrupt daily life in Israel. His fighting arm, El Fatah, turned to a new form of terror: skyjacking.

The first plane hijacked had been an El Al jet flying from Rome to Tel Aviv on July 22, 1968. The terrorists forced the pilot to land in Algeria. Most of the world condemned the terrorists, and also Algeria, for granting them asylum, but aside from this, the world did nothing.

Still the terrorists failed to paralyze the country.

Jerusalem boomed. Mayor Teddy Kollek was now responsible for East as well as West Jerusalem. Born in Vienna in 1911, Teddy had come to Palestine as a pioneer in 1934. During World War II he was in Europe, in charge of contacts with the Jewish underground. He returned to become part of David Ben-Gurion's inner circle of idealistic men and women fighting for the birth of Israel.

Now, as mayor of Jerusalem, he drew upon his vast experience to rebuild a united city. Hadassah had taken a vow to return to Scopus. He gave them support. New apartment houses were rising on the hills all around the city. He helped choose the sites. He extended the city's services—water, electricity, garbage collection—to the Arab sectors of East Jerusalem. He met with the leaders of the three religions—Judaism, Christianity, and Islam—to help the three communities coexist in a united city.

Each day thousands of visitors flew into Israel and headed straight for Jerusalem. Christians and Jews entered the Old City to worship in churches and synagogues that had been closed to them during Jordan's occupation.

A new immigration began as Russia finally opened a crack in the Iron Curtain and allowed thousands of Jews to leave. The cities of Israel were burgeoning. The population of the country reached three million.

On the West Bank, Israel taught Arab farmers how to use twentieth-century tools. The farmers grew prosperous as Israel helped them sell their goods to Europe.

Tens of thousands of Arabs from Kuwait, Saudi Arabia, and other lands were permitted to take their sick to Hadassah and other hospitals, to travel freely about the Jewish state.

But "a just and lasting peace" was still a dream. The Arabs kept repeating what they had adopted in a summit meeting in September 1967: no recognition, no negotiation, no peace.

RAQUELA balanced her life with work and the family. The U.S. government had renewed its grant to the research team which had published its first scientific paper, "The Jerusalem Perinatal Study," in the *Israel Journal of Medical Sciences*.

In the summer of 1971 Raquela filled the house with Papa's lilies. Jenny, Moshe's firstborn, was marrying Yaakov Navot, a dark-haired young man born in Morocco. Only Papa was missing on their wedding day. Strong, loving Papa was dead.

Soon after the wedding, Raquela, Moshe, and Rafi went to Duke

University, in North Carolina, where Moshe taught medical education. Amnon stayed in Israel, where he was doing his three-year army service. Raquela, free of responsibilities for the first time in years, relaxed in the social life of academe.

In February 1972 they returned to Jerusalem. The following November, Yigal Allon, then minister of education and culture, called Moshe to his office and offered him the post of president of the University of the Negev. Moshe explained that although he was greatly honored, his interest lay not in the presidency but in the creation of a new, revolutionary type of medical school in which students would go out into the community and become involved with patients—in child-care centers and in their homes.

Allon smiled. "Your taking the presidency of the university may be helpful in promoting the building of a medical school there." While Moshe still hesitated, Allon added, "Mrs. Meir would like it very much."

Moshe agreed to take the presidency until the medical school could be created. Meanwhile, he would change the name to the Ben-Gurion University of the Negev, to honor the man whose dream it had been to open the desert frontier.

On the afternoon of December 7, 1972, Raquela sat in the front row of the university hall, Mama and the children beside her. On the podium, Moshe was being sworn in as president.

Raquela looked around the hall filled with dignitaries from Israel, Europe, and America. The dusty town of Beersheba she had come to with Arik twenty-three years ago was now a metropolis of one hundred thousand people.

She was forty-eight. More than ever, she would have to divide her life. She would spend half the week in Beersheba as Moshe's wife, and the other half in Jerusalem as a workingwoman, as mother and stepmother, and as daughter to Mama.

Feminine, aware of her beauty, Raquela always would define herself as a workingwoman. Sharing the destiny of all women of Israel. Women had to work, to stand with their men in a besieged land surrounded by hostility. Nearly half of her country's resources were spent on defense. On survival.

Yes, she could handle her life, balance it all. She looked at Moshe on the podium. She was in love. The passionate love of a mature woman. And she was happy. Fulfilled.

AGAIN RAQUELA FILLED the house with calla lilies. Vivian was marrying a handsome young army captain named Gideon Weiler. An officer in the Armored Corps, Gideon was a born leader, a career army man who adored his men and his tanks.

Gideon was Rafi's idol. Rafi, who would finish high school in August, had already told Raquela, "I'm going into the Tank Corps. I want to be with Gideon."

October 6, 1973

The synagogues of Israel were filled. It was the holiest day of the year—Yom Kippur, the Day of Atonement.

The Arabs struck.

Israelis, many with their prayer shawls still on, raced out of the synagogues to join their units.

To the survivors of Hitler's death camps this was a grim reminder. The Nazis had always chosen the Jewish holy days for an *Aktion*—systematically rounding up and murdering Jews. Yom Kippur was a favorite day for terror. It was to catch the Jews unprepared. It was to break their spirit.

Now it was not the Nazis; it was Egypt and Syria that had launched the surprise attack. And Russia had given them the tools of war.

In the south, the Egyptians flung pontoon bridges across the Suez Canal and sent Russian tanks across them. Thousands of soldiers forded the canal in rubber dinghies. The Israelis had built a line of fortresses along the canal—the Bar-Lev Line. The Egyptians surprised the soldiers in their bunkers. Some were killed before they could even reach for their guns.

In the north, one hundred Soviet MiGs streaked through the sky, bombing the Golan Heights. Beneath the MiGs, seven hundred Syrian tanks attacked. They broke through the 1967 cease-fire lines and in a wall of fire hurtled through the Golan into the kibbutzim. They were headed for the heartland of Israel.

A deep depression spread across the land. The people of Israel were stunned. How could their leaders have been taken by surprise? How could their invincible army have been caught sleeping? There had been signs, if they had only read them, that President Anwar el-Sadat was planning a new war. In March 1973 Sadat had told an American journalist, "Everything in this country is now being mobilized in earnest for the resumption of battle, which is now inevitable. . . . Everyone has fallen asleep over the Middle East crisis, but they will soon wake up."

On Friday, October 5, 1973, the Russian advisers in Syria had packed and flown home.

Then, at dawn on Yom Kippur, Egyptians began massing men and tanks along the canal. This was no military exercise. Prime Minister Golda Meir's chief of staff, General Elazar, pleaded for total mobilization and a preemptive strike. But Moshe Dayan, her minister of defense, disagreed. The United States had warned Israel against taking a preemptive strike.

It was a tragic dilemma. Whoever moves first in the Middle East has all the advantages. But weighed against the strategic advantage was the threat of losing U.S. aid.

In the end Golda Meir agreed with Dayan. No total mobilization. No preemptive strike.

Not only Israel, but the rest of the world as well, was caught by the surprise attack. And suddenly, throughout America and Europe, millions of people were galvanized into action, expressing tangibly their ties with the beleaguered country. Raquela, returning to the hospital, found a whole cadre of American, Canadian, and South African doctors who had rushed to Israel to help.

The Israel Air Force was being annihilated. Its planes were disintegrating in midair, destroyed by Russian-built surface-to-air missiles. The Israel Army, fighting on two fronts, realized its first thrust must be against the Syrians. The Sinai could wait.

Raquela's boys were in the north, on the Syrian front. Amnon was with an infantry unit. Rafi, buck private, ferried bombs to the north in a half-track. Vivian's husband, Gideon, was with the Armored Corps somewhere in the Golan Heights.

The television set was an altar; each evening, exhausted after work, Raquela sat with Mama and Vivian, who was seven months pregnant, in front of the set. Moshe was in Beersheba supervising emergency procedures. On the television screen, fire streaked through the sky. The war was in their living room. They sat anguished, watching shells lighting up the sky, watching tanks explode. Was Gideon in one of them? Where was Amnon? Was Rafi safe?

On the third night Rafi called. He was exhilarated. No news of

Gideon. But Amnon was okay. The Syrians were being pushed back!

On the fourth night the Syrians were in total retreat. Their attack in the north had failed. Now the army could turn to the war in the Sinai.

Once again the family watched the screen as the desert exploded. The battles were taking ferocious losses in lives and matériel. Russia swiftly resupplied the Arabs. On one day alone—Friday, October 12, 1973—Soviet cargo planes made sixty flights to Cairo and Damascus. Prime Minister Golda Meir appealed to President Richard Nixon to balance the aid the Russians were giving their Arab clients.

A few days passed. Then President Nixon ordered a rescue airlift of giant cargo planes. A wave of gratitude lifted the depression in the country. The United States had not forgotten its commitment. Israel was not alone. On Sunday, October 14, the planes began landing at Lydda airport, unloading tanks, ammunition, air-to-air rockets, medical supplies. Phantom jets were flown in to replace the fighters destroyed by Russian missiles.

On the day the airlift started, the army made known the terrible losses of men. Vivian, listening to the radio, rushed to the phone to call Moshe in Beersheba. "Daddy, the chief of staff has given out the figures. Six hundred and fifty-six soldiers killed so far. General Elazar said all families of the dead soldiers have been informed. It must mean Gideon's alive."

"Of course, Vivi. That's what it means," Moshe said softly.

The next day there was a knock on Vivian's door. It was Gideon's driver.

Sitting in the living room, he told her how, on the day the war broke out, Gideon had been promoted to the rank of major. He and his men had driven their tanks along the narrow ledge of the Golan. They had fought without rest, outnumbered, ten tanks to one. In a brief lull Gideon had pulled a gasoline coupon out of his pocket and written on the back:

My sweet darling, I am writing these few words in the middle of a battle in the night. Only a few seconds ago we destroyed five tanks. If, God forbid, something happens to me, know that I love you unto death and that I admire you always. I am thinking of our baby.

Three hours later a bazooka hit his tank. Gideon, standing up in the turret, was ejected thirty yards. His driver survived. It was he who found Gideon's body with the note to Vivian.

What does it mean to be a woman in Israel? Raquela thought, looking at Vivi's pale, strained face and swollen body. Widowed at twenty-three. How does one comfort a young woman who must hunger for her husband? How does one help her mourn?

Once again Israel defeated her enemies. The war ended in the most spectacular victory of all the four wars. Israel's soldiers stood twenty-five miles from Damascus, sixty miles from Cairo.

But a whole generation of young men, twenty-six hundred, had been killed. How does one comfort the wives and mothers and children of dead soldiers?

On Christmas Eve Vivian gave birth to Gideon's daughter.

THE next year, 1974, Moshe stepped down from the presidency of the university and opened the medical school of the Ben-Gurion University of the Negev. He was given full control of the three agencies concerned with health in the Negev. He was in effect the medical chief of the frontier. Raquela began to spend more time in Beersheba as Moshe led young medical students into the Bedouin settlements in the Negev, into the mother-and-child-care centers and into the old-age homes, to become involved, from the first day, in the work of saving lives.

IT WAS 1976. Amnon was in his fourth year of medical school. Rafi was ending his army stint as a lieutenant in the Armored Corps and he came home to Jerusalem. "Mother," he said, "I'm scheduled to leave the army on the fifth of August. My commanding officer has asked me to volunteer for another year."

Raquela's heart began to pound. "I thought you were all set to go to the university to study philosophy and literature."

"I know. But Mother, they've invested so much in me. They've trained me. . . . What do you think?"

Raquela put her arm on Rafi's shoulder, her fingers on his lieutenant's bars. "As a mother, Rafi, I want you to come home. I want you to go to the university. I want you to start your life." She swallowed hard. "But as an Israeli, I can't tell you to come home. Only you can make this decision."

On August 5 he telephoned. "I'm signing up for another year, Mother. I'll try to get home this weekend. . . ."

When would there be an end to terrorism and fighting? Even though the war was over, there had not been a single day of peace.

Raquela was restless. She drove to the Hadassah Hospital on Mount Scopus. It had been completely restored and reopened in October 1975. Three thousand had come to rededicate it.

Still restless, Raquela drove home and began fixing dinner. Moshe came up from Beersheba in the late afternoon.

At six thirty in the morning the doorbell rang. Moshe went to the door. Raquela heard him scream, "Rafi, Rafi, Rafi!"

She rushed out of the bedroom. "Moshe, what is it?"

Two officers stood in the doorway. One of the officers was speaking. "We regret to inform you that your son, Lieutenant Rafael Brzezinski, died last night in the line of duty."

Moshe held her close.

RAQUELA, dressed in black, stood before the iron gate leading to the soldiers' cemetery on Mount Herzl. As each mourner approached her, she extended her hand in mute recognition.

An army van pulled up. Soldiers lifted out the simple coffin draped with the flag of Israel. Rafi was carried by his closest friends through the crowded rows of graves strewn with flowers. He was being accorded a hero's funeral, laid to rest near General Dado Elazar—former chief of staff, hero of the northern command in the Six-Day War—and Yoni Nethanyahu, the brilliant commander of the Entebbe raid who was killed rescuing hostages from Uganda.

Raquela listened as Rafi's commanding officer spoke.

"We will always remember you, Rafi. Your sweet personality, how you played the guitar for us the long nights in camp, how you loved to read poetry and share it with us. You were a gifted officer and teacher in the Tank Corps. You taught your men what Israel means to you. They loved you, Rafi."

Raquela's throat was choked. Rafi. Rafi. My son. She lifted a small stone and placed it on the grave.

During the seven days of mourning—the *shivah*—Raquela composed herself to receive visitors. It was the ancient wisdom of the *shivah* that brought friends to the house, to sit with Raquela and Moshe to comfort them, to talk to them of Rafi.

Late one morning Golda Meir came. She sat on the sofa, beside Raquela. For the first few minutes all the guests withdrew into themselves in awe.

Golda Meir spoke the words on everyone's mind. "Our children," she said, "our soldiers. We mothers and fathers nurture our children like precious flowers. Then they grow up . . . and go to war."

Soon the atmosphere changed and the neighbors began chatting with Golda, as if a member of the family had entered, as if their own mother were talking to them, affectionately, informally.

Rafi

In the evening a limousine pulled up in front of the house. Soon everyone in Bet Hakerem knew that the president of Israel, Ephraim Katzir, and his wife, Nina, had come to pay their respects to Raquela and Moshe.

THE period of mourning came to an end. Raquela returned to work.

Once again she spent half the week in Jerusalem and the other half in Beersheba. She knew that work was the road to recovery, and her projects multiplied. In Beersheba she created a new study: to find the causes and a cure for the hepatitis rampant among newborn babies from Arab lands.

Her days were crowded. Friends came each evening, surrounding her with warmth. She was coping. She could control her feelings, though hardly a moment passed that she did not think of Rafi.

At night, however, the pain and grief refused to be controlled. In bed, with Moshe holding her tightly, she wept.

"How much longer, Moshe? How many more sons must die before peace comes? What can we do, Moshe?"

"We go on living," he said.

RUTH GRUBER: Author, Veteran Newspaperwoman, Expert on Israel

From the start, Ruth Gruber's special beat as an investigative reporter has been frontier societies. Her main focus: the problems of women and refugees. At the age of twenty-three she became the first foreign correspondent allowed to enter the Soviet Arctic, and her book about

Raquela Prywes with the author

the experience became a best seller. After that, assignments took her all over the world—Alaska, Puerto Rico, Europe, the Middle East, Vietnam, Korea. Always, her primary interest has been that of humanity in flight—displaced persons and parentless children who needed to be absorbed by new lands.

In 1944, when President Roosevelt wished to bring one thousand refugees to safety in the United States, she was among the official party escorting them here. They traveled on an army troopship through submarine-infested waters. Later she reported on the DP camps in Europe and the Arab refugee camps in the Middle East.

Because of her wartime assignments and her close association with Israel—which she covered for nearly two decades for the New York *Herald Tribune*—Ruth Gruber experienced firsthand many of the events that shaped Raquela's life. She was the only foreign correspondent allowed to cover the historic voyage of the *Exodus 1947*. That same year, 1947, she was the first and only foreign correspondent to enter the detention camp the British had built on Cyprus.

She began *Raquela* shortly after completing *They Came to Stay*, a Condensed Books selection which she co-authored with TV news reporter Marjorie Margolies. For nine months Ruth Gruber lived in Israel, interviewing Raquela Prywes and most of the people who appear in her story. "Writing *Raquela*," says the author, "was a journey of discovery for both of us. In the course of reliving her life, Raquela reestablished ties with many friends she hadn't seen in years."

In private life Ruth Gruber is married to Henry J. Rosner, who recently retired as New York City's assistant commissioner of social services. When not traveling, the Rosners make their home in New York City.

THE SNAKE

A CONDENSATION OF THE NOVEL BY

John Godey

ILLUSTRATED BY ALAN REINGOLD

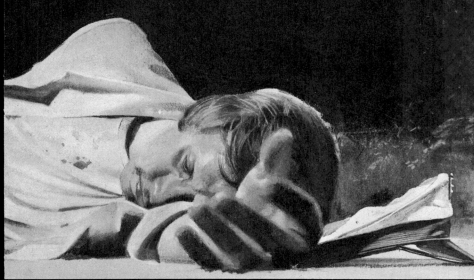

A deadly, eleven-foot snake is loose in
Central Park. By the time it has claimed two
victims New York City has the jitters.
How did it get there? What can be done?
Mark Converse, a dedicated herpetologist,
is intent on finding it before anyone else does.
He is also intent on *not* falling in love.
But he finds Holly Markham, a pretty reporter
covering the story, irresistible.
Meanwhile, trying to find one black mamba
in an eight-hundred-forty-acre park
seems an impossible task. Tension rises
unbearably as the snake strikes, again
and again, and a great city mobilizes
a massive hunt.
A creepy-crawler of a story that grips
the reader right through to its chilling end.

"The author of *The Taking of Pelham One Two
Three* has done it again....This is great."
—*Publishers Weekly*

ONE

THE box was two feet long, a foot and a half wide, and a foot and a half deep. Its outside was plywood, its inside a lining of burlap stitched onto cardboard. There were air holes drilled into the top and sides. Together with its contents, the box weighed sixteen pounds. For anyone less than Matt Olssen's size it would have been an unwieldy burden, but Matt carried it comfortably under his long arm.

Even so, a few times along the way it became a drag, and he was tempted to walk away from it. Once, he had actually forgotten it. By the time he got back to where he had left it, two characters had hefted it up onto the bar and were struggling with the knot in the blond sisal twine around its width. He had been half inclined to let them get a look at what was inside, but he had been warned that, although it would probably be lethargic, he wasn't to count on it; it might come out of the box like a shot. So he picked up the box and moved along.

He had taken it—box and animal together—from some Greek in a poker game in exchange for a handful of markers for the African money they were using. The Greek claimed it was a rare specimen that he had bought at a bargain price from a cop in Lubumbashi. The cop was said to have confiscated it from some black in the bush

country. Matt had accepted it, with the notion of turning it loose in
the downtown area of the city for laughs. But later, sobering up, he
decided instead to bring it back to the States to sell it to a zoo.
He stowed the box away under the bunk in his cabin, and aside
from sprinkling some water through the air holes a few times, paid
no attention to it on the ten-day voyage back from Africa.

His ship docked in Brooklyn in early morning. By the time he
finished supervising the off-loading it was noon, and ninety-two
degrees, and he was nearly dehydrated. He cleaned up, put the
box under his arm, and staggered to a waterfront joint a block away
from the ship's berth. It wasn't until three o'clock that he phoned
his wife. "Betty? It's me."

"Oh? You come and go, don't you?"

So it was going to be an uphill fight. Sweetening his voice, he
said, "Hey, baby, be nice. I been six months at sea."

"Six? I haven't heard from you in over a year."

"And every night I dreamed about my beautiful Betty."

She snorted. "Well, dream on. I'm hanging up."

"Wait, no, I have to tell you something."

He glanced through the phone-booth door at the box standing
on end near his barstool. Nobody was paying attention to it; he
had promised to break the nose of any man who went near it.

"I have to see you, Betty. I missed you. You know?"

"I'm busy. I have to go."

"No. Listen, baby . . . I got something for you. A present."

She hesitated. "Well, if it's a dumb statue like last time, you know
what you can do with it."

"I didn't have time to buy something"—he smiled slyly into the
transmitter—"so I'm just gonna give you cash instead. You mind?"

She came alive. "You're gonna give me money? How much?"

"Ah, don't let's spoil the surprise. But I'll give you a little hint.
It's in the four figures. Okay, sweetheart?"

"Well, okay. But don't get rolled or anything."

"See you in an hour or two, baby, soon as we're finished unloading the ship."

Ten hours later he had drunk better than a quart and a half of
whiskey and had had two or three fights. He had moved from joint
to joint on a course that led northward through Brooklyn, across
the East River into Manhattan, and on up the West Side. Now

he was the last remaining customer in a dump, and the bartender had just shut off the air conditioning to chase him.

He heaved the box up on the bar, paid his bill, and slapped down a ten-dollar tip. The bartender mumbled his thanks and then asked, "What you got in that box, sailor?"

It was a question that had been put to him often during the hours since he had left the docks. Depending on his mood, his answer had either been "A little pussycat" or "None of your business." In all cases he had made it evident, by virtue of his size and attitude, that the subject was closed.

Now he simply winked at the bartender, hiked the box up under his arm, and went out into Columbus Avenue. It was nearly two a.m., but the September heat had hardly relented since sundown.

He turned east toward Central Park, his gait rolling, part swagger, part stagger. Near the end of the block a cluster of Hispanics called out insults. He stopped and challenged them to come down off their stoop and fight. They laughed, and saluted him with their beer cans.

He moved on. The streets of New York—and of Rio and Genoa and a hundred other ports—held no terrors for him. He knew that his size was intimidating; and if it failed to intimidate, he was ready to fight, confidently.

At Central Park West he looked at the building on the corner in bafflement, checked the street sign and the building number. Dumb ox. She lived on the other side of the park. He set the box down near the curb and waved his arms wildly at an approaching cab. The cab slowed, then suddenly shot off. In the next five minutes two more cabs passed him up.

He glared into the street, knowing what the problem was; the cabbies were scared of him. He was wearing what he called his shore uniform. He had begun to put it on, item by item, at that dockside joint in Brooklyn and now, hours later, he was fully dressed. There were spots on his white nautical cap. His white linen jacket was grimy and soaked with sweat and spilled drinks. The duck pants were filthy and ripped at one knee, and he had a smear of dried blood at the corner of his mouth.

His appearance proclaimed a violent and forbidding man.

A cab stopped for a red light on the north corner of the street. Matt picked up the box and ran toward it. The driver watched him for a moment, then put his car in gear and shot past the light. Cursing loudly, Matt tucked the box securely under his arm and crossed the street toward the park.

RAMON Torres, sitting on a bench backed against the stone retaining wall that bordered the park, watched with sour lack of interest as the big sailor tried to get a cab. But when the sailor hitched up the box he was carrying, crossed to the park side of the street, and started walking north, Torres had to talk to himself to keep from jumping the guy right then and there.

When the sailor was fifty or sixty feet up the street, Torres began tailing him, walking close to the wall so he could crouch against it if the guy looked back. But the sailor didn't turn around. He kept walking, and a couple of times he paused and looked toward the park, as if he were thinking of going in.

The sailor was a giant and looked tough—he carries that box under his arm like it was a feather, Torres thought as he realized that it would be risky to tackle the guy. But Torres was desperate. The way the weather was, people were wearing hardly any clothes, had no place to carry their money, and had been leaving it home. So he wasn't going to let the man's size stop him. Besides, the way the sailor was walking, he looked pretty drunk.

The sailor stopped at Eighty-first Street, at the entrance to the transverse—the underpass road for traffic across the park.

"Go in," Torres said softly. "Go inna park, stupid. Don't be afrai', go on, walk inna park." But the big guy crossed the street past the transverse opening. He stopped again.

Torres held his breath. The sailor was turned toward the pedestrian entrance. Better than the transverse, Torres thought, no cars. Go in, man, he pleaded silently, go in.

It worked. The sailor turned into the entrance, and as he hurried after him Torres touched the short-barreled .38 he carried in his belt under his loose shirt.

Soon after he began walking through the park, Matt Olssen realized that the walkways branched and wound, and he would have to keep from wandering in circles. He knew you weren't supposed to walk in the park after dark, but it didn't bother him. Any mugger got a good look at him, he'd probably run away. And if he didn't, well, another fight was just another fight.

He tipped the box forward and shook it for balance. There was motion in it. He reached around with his free hand and tapped the cover sharply. "Lie still, pussycat," he said.

He tilted the box back and forth a few more times. The movement inside became briefly agitated and then subsided.

It was clear to Torres that the sailor didn't know what he was doing. First he went to the left, toward the kids' playground, then back around to the main path, heading east. He never once looked behind him. No hurry, Torres thought. Let him get nice and deep inside the park.

When the sailor lurched toward the path that climbed up to the Belvedere Castle, Torres whispered to himself, Hey, that's good; nice and lonesome up there. But the sailor turned away and went straight on. Ahead, on the right, was the big round Delacorte Theatre. The sailor moved on past without even looking at it.

Torres hung well back. Above him, nailed to a tree, was one of those green signs: THIS PARK CLOSES AT MIDNIGHT. He smiled to himself in the darkness. Now the sailor was stumbling past the little Belvedere Lake, with the structure on the other side looming up against the sky like something from olden times.

Torres started to quicken his pace. Just ahead was one of those arches, like a little tunnel. Go ahead in, Torres said to himself. But instead, the sailor veered off to his left.

Good enough, Torres thought. He drew his piece out of his belt, cocked it, and took off after the sailor at a light run. He had closed to within a dozen feet when the sailor heard him and turned around. Torres edged toward him a little.

"Aw ri', man," he said. "This wha' they call a mugging, okay?"

The sailor didn't look scared.

"You be smart and you don't get hurt." He waved the pistol. "I wan' you lay down on your face. Okay?"

The sailor laughed.

Being laughed at made Torres mad. He pushed the gun out at arm's length and yelled, "You hear me, man? Lay down!"

The sailor shifted the box from under his arm and threw it at Torres, shoving it out from his chest with both hands. Torres saw the box coming and, behind it, the sailor moving toward him fast. An edge of the box caught Torres on the shoulder, and then it went sailing past him and he heard something crack as it hit the pavement. The sailor was right on top of him when he pulled the trigger. He shot three times, and then the sailor's weight was bearing him backward.

They hit the ground hard, with the sailor on top. Torres braced his feet against the pavement, heaved upward, and the sailor rolled off him. He scrambled to his feet and trained the gun downward at the sailor's head. But the sailor wasn't moving. His eyes were open and staring up at the sky. His shirt was bloody. All three bullets had gone into his chest.

Torres felt a surge of pride. He had wasted him! Okay, beautiful, but think about it later. Three shots, and if there was cops cruising through the park, they maybe heard them. Hurry up and make the score and split.

The sailor was lying a couple of feet in front of the box. The wood had cracked when it landed, and the cover was broken. Torres reached toward the sailor, and his eye was caught by something in the box. He saw two points of gleaming light and a dark shape moving slowly from side to side. The shape moved upward on a long column, and Torres, staring, realized that it was the head and neck of a snake. As he watched, frozen, the snake started to slide out of the box. It poured over the rim, slow and smooth, no end to it, and Torres thought he must have been dreaming.

He looked on in fascination as the snake drew itself into a loose coil until finally a thin tail flipped out of the box. Then the snake raised its head up high and stared at Torres. Its head was small and flattened, and its eyes were shining in the darkness. It sways over the sailor's body, like, Torres thought wildly, it's guarding it.

Torres couldn't believe his eyes. He had seen some big snakes before in Puerto Rico, but never one like this. It scared him. But he wasn't gonna split without the money. He thought of trying to shoot the snake, but he knew it would have to be a very lucky hit.

The snake kept looking at him with its gleaming eyes, and its tongue kept flicking in and out. It's like we're both hypnotized, Torres thought, and staring at each other across the sailor's body. But man, Torres said to himself, you can't stay here all night. The snake had started to hiss, and it had its mouth wide open. Suddenly, remembering a movie about India, Torres had an idea. He held the gun out in front of him and moved it to the right, and the snake's head swayed to follow it. He moved the gun back to his left, and again the snake's head moved with it.

"Stupid snake," Torres said, and, to himself, Hey, you got it made. He edged forward to within three feet of the sailor's body. He extended the revolver as far to his right as his arm would reach, and when the snake's head, hissing, turned to stare at it, he crouched and with his free hand reached inside the sailor's bloody coat. His fingertips had just touched the wallet when the snake's head shot forward, so fast that it was a blur, and he felt a sharp stinging pain in his thigh. Before Torres could move, the snake struck again, in almost the same place.

Torres shouted hoarsely and jumped back. The snake was hissing again. Torres retreated half a dozen paces and looked at his thigh. His beige pants were reddened by a few tiny spots of blood. It didn't hurt there, just a feeling like pins and needles. When he looked up again the snake was in motion, curling forward over the sailor's body, moving toward him.

"Save me," Torres screamed. "Save me."

He turned and began to run at top speed.

The snake crawled off the walkway into the grass. Holding its head high, it disappeared into the darkness.

FIVE minutes after the start of his panicky flight, Torres stopped running long enough to drop his revolver into a trash basket. Then he began to run again, as fast and hard as he could.

For a while he kept turning his head to see if the snake was chasing him. From time to time he reached down to touch the place on his thigh where he had been bitten. It wasn't swollen and it didn't hurt—just the little pins-and-needles feeling. But he was becoming light-headed and having some trouble breathing. Also, he had lost his bearings and couldn't seem to find his way out of the park.

His breathing was getting worse. He knew he better get to a hospital fast. But his legs felt weak, and he was staggering more than running. He was sucking for air, and his arms and hands felt so heavy that he could hardly move them. When he tried calling out for help, he couldn't talk, only make sounds like a frog.

The pins and needles were spreading upward in his body. He couldn't feel his legs at all now. But he kept going, and after a while he saw an exit onto Fifth Avenue. He stumbled out of the park and into the middle of the street, where he collapsed. Through his closed eyelids he saw the brightness of headlights coming toward him, but he didn't try to move. He knew he was gonna die, right there, laying down in the middle of Fifth Avenue.

PATROLMAN John Nebbia, driving a Nineteenth Precinct sector car, saw the figure stagger out of the park and into the street, where it collapsed. He sped up until he reached the body. His partner, Patrolman Frank Finnerty, was out of the door and kneeling over the man before the emergency brakes were set. Nebbia turned on his revolving roof light, then got out.

As THE snake headed into heavy brush, its primal impulse was to seek a place of safety. Deep in the brush, constantly probing with its forked black tongue, it paused at the base of a tree and looked upward. Then it began to wind up the trunk of the tree, using its tail for leverage. It stopped two-thirds of the way, in an area of heavy foliage, and draped itself over the branches in an arrangement of loose loops that distributed its weight evenly.

The snake was eleven feet two inches long, and slender. Its head was coffin-sided and comparatively small for the length of its body. Its eyes, dark brown and round, were wide open. It was unable to shut its eyes because it had neither eyelids nor nictitating membrane.

The snake was asleep.

AT THREE forty-five a.m. Nurse Rosamund Johnson was at the emergency ward reception desk when the two patrolmen came into East Side Hospital with a patient. His feet were dragging, his head lolling, and he seemed to be semicomatose.

"Found this on Fifth Avenue," one of the cops said. "He's got the blue face. Probably a heart attack."

Nurse Johnson punched a key on her intercom and said, "Billy, bring a stretcher, stat," then hit another key and, after a moment, said, "Dr. Papaleo, we have a patient in a cyanosed condition who's having trouble breathing. Come immediately, please."

"Me, I diagnose it overdose," the other cop said. "I've seen hundreds of them."

An attendant came through a door rolling a stretcher. The two cops strained, helping the attendant lift their inert burden onto it.

"Put the patient in room D, Billy," Nurse Johnson said. Then she turned to the cops. "Can you fellows wait a few minutes in case the doctor wants to talk to you? There's a coffee machine around the corner."

One of the cops nodded, and the other said, "I'll call it in."

DR. CHARLES Papaleo looked down at the patient on the table in room D. He was semicomatose, unable to respond to questions. Overdose, Papaleo thought, I'll bet it's good old overdose. But he put the notion out of mind. Physicians were expected to follow form, especially first-year interns like Papaleo, who were discouraged from making snap judgments.

So, attend to the symptoms. Cyanotic. Marked hypoventilation—the patient was breathing poorly, although he didn't seem to be fighting for air, as people usually did who couldn't breathe. Oxygen. Papaleo found a nasal catheter and inserted it.

A nurse came into the room. Kelly, an old hand.

Papaleo opened the patient's mouth—thick discharge. No falling back of tongue. Didn't seem to be any obstructions, either. He sniffed the patient's breath. No alcohol smell.

"Nurse Kelly," Papaleo said, "will you get the suction apparatus, please?"

Kelly moved off briskly and came back with the apparatus: a vacuum to suction the mucus into a clear bottle so the matter could be examined. She maneuvered a tube into the patient's mouth.

Papaleo, his forehead ridged, fitted his stethoscope into his ears, opened the patient's shirt, and listened to the heartbeat. Fast but regular. He picked up the man's wrist and counted his pulse. Call it an even hundred. He wound a blood-pressure cuff around the patient's arm, pumped up the autovalve bulb, released the bulb. A hundred over forty. Combined with the pulse rate, it was slightly under normal, and it failed to suggest anything of substance.

"The oxygen doesn't seem to be helping his breathing, Doctor," Nurse Kelly said.

She was right. What now? Papaleo thought.

"Neurological check," he said, and began to test for sensation. Knee reflexes, okay. Bang the tendons, okay. Response to pain, okay. Check for head trauma—can't feel anything amiss. Shine

495

flashlight into eyes—pupils normal size and contract under stimulus of light. Heroin out.

Kelly was looking at him sidelong now and fidgeting. She opened her mouth to say something, but Papaleo intercepted her. "Lungs. Help me to get him into a sitting position."

The patient was dead weight as they pushed his shirt up over his back and tried to sit him up. Kelly held him steady and Papaleo leaned over him, placed his ear against the skin, and tapped. Sounded all right, but what could he really tell with the patient unable to breathe deeply?

They got him back down, and Papaleo studied his arms. No needle tracks. Well, the normal pupils had told him that. Pill overdose? A possibility. He realized that he was sweating profusely. He wiped the sweat from his face with his forearm. Kelly was watching, her lips pursed.

He said, "Who brought him in?"

"The police. I think they're still around."

"I'll step outside and talk to them." He started away from the table, then returned. "Maybe some kind of overdose, though the signs are absent. Still, get some Narcan, please. And set up an IV with five percent dextrose and saline."

Kelly's lips softened. Good, Papaleo thought, she approves.

"Oh yes, let's protect against an insulin overdose. Add fifty percent glucose."

Papaleo found the cops in the anteroom, drinking coffee and chatting with the security guard. They told him what they thought: overdose. And what they knew. No help.

He returned to room D, where Nurse Kelly had already hooked up the intravenous apparatus. Papaleo looked down at the patient blankly. What else was there? Take a blood sample, check for sugar? That would take at least a half hour, and the patient might not last that long.

"Doctor," Kelly said, "I think we're in trouble."

He thought so himself, but what the devil could it be? He decided to listen to the heart again—beat more rapid now and weaker. The patient's chest barely seemed to be moving. Paralysis, some kind of paralysis?

"I think we're about to lose him," Nurse Kelly said. "I think we want a Code Blue."

Code Blue was the emergency call that mobilized a surgeon, an anesthetist, the chief resident, extra nurses. It was clearly indicated.

Papaleo looked grim. "Very well. Let's do a Code Blue."

Dr. Shapiro, the chief resident, was down in less than a minute. He ran his hands over the patient's chest while Papaleo filled him in. Before Papaleo was quite finished, Shapiro interrupted.

"Nurse, get a respirator," he said. Nurse Kelly, looking righteous, moved away from the table. "He can't breathe because his muscles aren't functioning properly. We want a mechanical aid to help the chest muscles do their work."

Should have thought of it, Papaleo told himself, when I noticed that he didn't seem to be fighting for breath: a mechanical respirator to pump oxygen directly into his lungs.

When Kelly arrived with the respirator, Shapiro removed the nasal catheter and placed an endotracheal tube in the patient's windpipe. The other members of the Code Blue team had arrived, but there was nothing for them to do as yet.

Shapiro shook his head. "I don't know." Then, frowning, "What's this, on his thigh?"

The patient's light summer trousers were stained with a scuffing of grime, sweat, and a little blood. Papaleo hadn't noticed it before.

"He must have scraped it when he fell. The policemen said he collapsed in the street."

"Hand me scissors. We'll cut the pants legs off." But abruptly Shapiro bent over the patient with his stethoscope. He straightened up. "I can't raise a heartbeat. Let's get going."

The entire Code Blue team pitched in. Everyone worked with great intensity, injecting, kneading, pounding—but to no avail. The patient's heart refused to start up again.

"You can all go," Shapiro said. "We've lost this one. Death from cardiorespiratory failure due to unknown causes."

Shapiro reminded Nurse Kelly to phone the medical examiner's office and ask them to pick up the body for autopsy. In death from an undiagnosed cause, Papaleo recalled, no permission from next of kin was required.

"I should have thought of the mechanical respirator earlier," Papaleo said to Shapiro. "I'm sorry."

"Well, you'll think of it next time." Shapiro took a last look at the corpse on the table, said, "Good night," and left.

While Nurse Kelly picked up the pieces—phoned the medical examiner's office and got an orderly to wheel the body to the hospital morgue—Papaleo went to another room, where he put a dressing under the eye of a man who had been kicked in a brawl. After that his tour of duty was finished. But instead of going back to bed, he went down to the morgue.

The corpse's eyes were open, and they seemed to Papaleo to be bewildered, as if he too were trying to fathom the cause of his death. Papaleo closed them. He ran his eyes down the body from top to bottom, as if taking inventory. Then his eyes traveled upward again to the thigh, to the patch of bloodied grime on the trousers.

He took scissors from his jacket pocket, slit the trouser leg up from the cuff to the hip, and spread the material to the side. The skin was abraded, and slightly stained by blood. Bending close, he noticed four small perforations in the skin, partially obliterated by the abrasions. The perforations seemed to be in two sets: one pair about six inches above the knee, the other, two or three inches higher. The perforations in each set appeared to be about half an inch apart.

He studied the marks. They could be an injection of some sort, though with a rather large needle. But who would inject in pairs? Bites of some kind? Insect bites? No. Too large, and not with that spacing. Besides, who would stand still for *four* such bites or stings?

Fang marks, then? What had fangs? Dogs, cats, lions, tigers . . . snakes? Come on, Papaleo. A poisonous snakebite in Manhattan? Anyway, snakes didn't strike that high. And, so far as he knew, snakes secreted a hemotoxic poison, which destroyed the red blood corpuscles and resulted in discoloration and swelling of the affected area, due to local hemorrhages. Nothing like that here. Still, shouldn't he tell Shapiro about the perforations? Yeah, sure, wake up the boss. . . . Forget it, Papaleo.

He decided to read up on snakebite before he hit the sack. But by the time he got back to his room he was too exhausted to start rummaging for a textbook. He fell on his bed fully clothed and went to sleep.

A half hour later Torres' corpse was taken to the city morgue for storage until the medical examiner's office could schedule it for postmortem examination.

Tʜᴇ snake woke shortly before dawn. At once its long tongue began to flick in and out through a rostral opening in the margin of its upper jaw that allowed it to emerge even when its mouth was shut.

The two tips of the forked tongue fitted into ducts communicating with the snake's Jacobson's organ, which lay in a depression in the roof of the mouth. The sensory epithelium of the Jacobson's organ responded to odor substances conveyed to it by the tongue, and interpreted them as a chemical computer might do, in terms of quality of the atmosphere, of presence of animals, of prey.

The findings of the Jacobson's organ disquieted the snake. And so, when it slipped down the tree trunk, it chose not to wander off in search of water. Moving in slow ripples, it drank the dew from the grass. Then, despite its hunger, it wound back up the tree to the place where it had been before. It slept again.

Aᴛ ᴍᴜᴄʜ the same moment Arthur Bennett stumbled on a huge body. His first thought when he saw it lying on the walk was that it was a wino, like himself, sleeping it off. Then the saw the bloodstains on the T-shirt and the linen jacket.

Bennett recoiled, then stepped forward again and looked at the body. The eyes were open and glassy. One arm was bent back underneath. A white sailor hat lay nearby, and there was a good-looking box, its cover broken, a little distance away.

Bennett found the wallet sticking up from the breast pocket of the jacket. He leafed through it quickly and cackled with delight: bills half an inch thick—twenties and fifties and even a few hundreds. He stuffed the money (nine hundred and eighty-four dollars) into his pants pocket and looked around. Nothing in sight. He grabbed the sailor cap and put it on his matted white hair. Then he picked up the box and tucked it under his arm.

He decided to get out of the park real fast.

Tʜᴇ snake basked on the surface of a large black rock a short distance from the tree it had sheltered in, its eleven-foot length spread out to the sun. It was seven thirty in the morning on the third day of the heat wave, and the sun already burned relentlessly.

The snake was poikilothermic—a cold-blooded animal. Its temperature was not constant, like that of most animals, but modulated with the temperature of its environment. Because cold exerts a narcotic, potentially killing effect, snakes predominate in the tropics and subtropics and thin out in number and species in the temperate regions. Yet a common viper is known to inhabit an area above the Arctic Circle and parts of Siberia.

Scarcely stirring, the snake warmed up its blood until some thermostatic reflex warned it that it had reached the optimum temperature. Then it slid away from its exposed position on the rock and into the shaded underbrush.

THE sailor's body was discovered a little after eight thirty by a parks department grass cutter. The police were notified, and a car was dispatched to the scene. The medical examiner's office collected the remains, which were brought to the morgue on First Avenue, near Bellevue Hospital, and placed not far from the remains of Ramon Torres.

Examination of Matt Olssen's effects offered no clues to his identification. But later in the day the corpse was identified by its fingerprints, which were on record as the result of a number of arrests over the past five years, all for aggravated assault. An address on the East Side was given for one Betty Parker Olssen, listed as the victim's wife.

Two policemen arrived at Betty Olssen's small apartment to perform the uncomfortable duty of informing her that her husband had been shot in the course of a robbery. The widow took the news calmly. She nodded her head. "I knew he was crazy enough to get himself killed sooner or later."

ARTHUR Bennett bought a pint of muscatel, then wandered down to the Bowery, picking up eighty cents in handouts along the way.

He couldn't dispose of the sailor's box, for which he was asking a dollar. When he became too persistent in pushing the sale of the box, someone became annoyed, grabbed it from him, smashed it by jumping on it, then threw the remnants into the street, where, in time, passing cars splintered it further.

Two men cornered him in a doorway and emptied his pockets of his coins, some peanuts, and the dead sailor's wallet.

THE OLIVE-SLATE COLOR of the snake's back blended with the shadowed leaves of the tree, and the starling, lighting on a bough, did not see it.

The snake's vision was highly developed, with particular acuity for perception of movement, and because of the placement of the eyes at the side of the head, it commanded a large field. This vision had picked up the bird in flight and watched it flutter to its perch, which was four feet from the snake's head.

Now the snake's darting tongue picked up the odor of prey. Frozen in that extraordinary immobility peculiar to reptiles, the snake stared at the bird. Then, anchoring itself by its tail, it shot forward in a blur of speed and sank its fangs. The bird squawked and flew off. But before it had gone twenty feet its wings began to flutter erratically and it dropped to the ground, into a patch of undergrowth.

For five minutes the snake waited patiently before it circled down the tree. On the ground, it trailed the bird unerringly by means of the special scent left by an injected prey.

The snake's poison was a digestive juice in the form of a highly specialized proteinaceous saliva. Thus the venom, in addition to killing the prey, had begun the process of digesting it.

The snake maneuvered its length until the bird lay directly in front of its mouth. The bones supporting the snake's lower jaws moved in the skull, the elastic ligaments between the halves of the jaw stretched, and the mouth opened to an astounding width, which would accommodate a prey far bigger than the starling and even larger than the diameter of the snake itself.

The snake hooked the teeth of one side of its mouth into the bird's body. Using this purchase as a fulcrum, it pushed the other side of the mouth forward, engaged its recurved teeth (useless for chewing), then repeated the ratcheting process, side after opposite side. In this way the snake gradually ingested the starling.

THIS evening's performance at the Delacorte Theatre was to be Richard Sheridan's *The School for Scandal.* By seven o'clock all twenty-two hundred-odd free tickets had been distributed.

Before the play at least half the ticket holders picnicked in the park, mainly in the areas adjacent to the Delacorte: up by the Belvedere Castle, on the banks of the Belvedere Lake, by the Shakespeare Garden. On the Great Lawn the grass was barely visible for the blankets that covered it.

At eight o'clock, in dusk, the performance began. The house-lights dimmed, and the audience, sitting on wooden seats in the circular theater, prepared for its pleasure.

THE snake crept swiftly through the darkness, its slender length curved into a continuous flowing S movement. Its locomotion was by a series of gentle curves, with the body forced against the sub-strate at each curve. This horizontal undulation was made possible by the hundreds of vertebrae that constituted its backbone. The scales of its lower surface were enlarged overlapping plates whose free edges were directed backward, and to each of which was attached a pair of movable ribs. When the ribs moved forward they carried the plate, or scute, with them. Since the scute was smooth and its leading edge was protected by the one over it, it slipped comfortably over any irregularity in the surface. There was one disadvantage: when the scute was moved backward, its free rear edge snagged. Thus, for all practical purposes, the snake could move in only one direction: forward.

Although it had no awareness of it, the snake was, in part, re-tracing its movements of the night before, after it had escaped from the box. It passed the place on the pavement where Matt Olssen had died, where it had bitten Torres. Its path then took it over a segment of the Great Lawn and across a walkway, toward the Belvedere Lake. It veered to the left, away from the fling of light from the Delacorte Theatre, and crawled down to the water's edge. As it drank, a great shout of laughter rose from the theater. The snake didn't hear it. It lacked an external ear, an eardrum, a tympanic cavity, and eustachian tubes. It was deaf.

RODDY Bamberger leaned toward the girl and whispered, "Let's duck out of here and go to my place and turn on the air conditioner and . . ." He brushed her cheek with his lips.

The girl didn't answer. She was sitting forward in her chair, seemingly transported by the play. But Roddy had seen college dramatic society versions of *The School for Scandal* that were bet-ter than this. And in London he had been present at a National Theatre performance. After that, this was sacrilege!

He should have had more sense than to have allowed himself to be conned into coming here. Free theater—like free anything else—was bound to be inept. It was all a mess: the play, the ridiculous heat, the girl herself, gazing at the stage with idiot rapture.

"Arline . . ." He breathed softly on her cheek. "Arline, let's go back to my place."

She made an abrupt gesture, stilling him so that she could catch the next line of the play. Somebody in the row above was shushing him.

Okay. Chalk up the evening as a disaster. "I'm sorry, Arline," he said, "I'm feeling dreadfully sick."

He was on his feet. She glanced at him in distress, started to say something, but he was already moving toward the aisle. At the end of the row he looked back. She was looking at him, uncertain, but it was too late. Even if she were to chase after him, he would have none of it.

It occurred to him as he left the theater that he would be walking through the park alone. But he wasn't overly nervous about it. There was a reassuringly sizable police detail on hand. He headed eastward between the Belvedere Lake and the Great Lawn.

He saw it an instant before he stepped on it. He saw it but didn't quite believe it, which was perhaps why, with his right foot on the way down to the pavement, his reflexes didn't react to compel the foot to step clear over it instead of coming down flatly on its tail. Then, in his effort to step free, he lost his balance and fell on it.

Immediately the snake whipped back on itself, twisting to free itself of the man's weight. Its head curved back, and it struck. It bit again. It launched a third strike, but the man was rolling away from it, so that, although one of its fangs penetrated, the other only grazed the target. Quickly, with powerful surging curves, the snake pushed itself off the walkway and into the grass.

For Roddy Bamberger the sense of unreality persisted. He lay still on the pavement, as one did in the aftermath of a nightmare. It was real, it had happened. A snake had actually bitten him. The incredibly long, swift strike, the impact of the fangs, had not really been all that painful, however. He had been bitten on the back of the thigh, below the buttocks. He eased his hand down to his thigh. Some blood, not much. Suddenly he felt awful. He was having trouble breathing. He rolled over and with a good deal of

effort got to his feet. He felt weak, dizzy. He wanted to lie down again, but resisted the impulse.

He began to run back toward the halo of light that marked the Delacorte Theatre. He ran poorly, stumblingly; his legs were trembling, he couldn't breathe, his mouth was choked with saliva. But he kept on, driven by terror.

He collapsed a hundred feet from the theater, where a cop, strolling down the walk for a smoke, found him. He tried to tell the cop about the snake, but he was unable to talk. He was only barely conscious.

THERE was not even time to call a Code Blue; the patient died thirty seconds after being wheeled into the emergency ward at East Side Hospital.

Dr. Pranay Mukerjee folded his stethoscope away in the pocket of his white jacket and looked at the man on the table as a person. In his mid-thirties, well nourished, well dressed. Dr. Mukerjee, an experienced physician, lifted the corpse's hand, noted the fingernails. Cyanotic. What was the cause of death? Drug overdose? Not likely. The heartbeat had been fast and thready, but not abnormally so. The pupils were not dilated.

Dr. Mukerjee's eye was caught by a small smear of blood on the table. But no wound was visible. Beneath him, perhaps? He turned the corpse over and saw it at once: a slight bloodiness on the trousers, high up on the left thigh. Doesn't look much, Dr. Mukerjee thought, yet—shall we see?

He cut the left leg of the man's trousers away and bent low over the thigh. After a moment he straightened up. Shaking his head, he said aloud, "Ah, no, it is not possible, is it?"

He swabbed the thigh clean of blood and studied the affected area intently. There were two pairs of perforations, and a third perforation by itself. No, not quite by itself—in company with a light surface scratch. Below each perforation he could make out a series of tiny indentations, dropping down in a straight vertical.

He addressed the nurse. "Ask the chief resident to come here. Stat, please."

When Dr. Mukerjee described the symptoms of the dead man, Dr. Shapiro looked startled. "We had one like that last night." He frowned down at the body.

"It is thoroughly outlandish, of course," Dr. Mukerjee said, "but the clinical symptoms are remarkably consistent."

"Consistent with what?"

"I direct your attention to these perforations," Mukerjee said. "This pair here, and this second pair"—his long brown finger touched the white skin—"and this single one, a seeming anomaly which I will presently explain. You will also notice, please, the tiny indentations below each—"

"Do you know what those punctures are, Dr. Mukerjee?" Shapiro spoke sharply. He was very direct himself, and he suspected Mukerjee of milking the suspense.

"I believe they are fang marks."

"Of what sort of animal?"

"Of a poisonous snake, Doctor," Mukerjee said.

Shapiro said, "I've never seen snakebite. I presume you have?"

"Yes."

"What about the single perforation?"

"I believe the snake struck twice successfully, and a third time inaccurately, so that only one of its fangs penetrated. The small indentations are the impression of its back teeth."

"Okay," Shapiro said with a strained smile. "Somewhere in Manhattan there is a rattlesnake at large."

"Oh, no," Mukerjee said. "Rattlesnakes secrete a hemotoxic venom. In that case the flesh in the area around the punctures would be heavily swollen, discolored. From the patient's symptoms, this would be a neurotoxic venom. If I am to venture a guess as to the identity of the animal, I would say cobra, Doctor. I have seen a number of victims of its bites at home in India."

"Cobra? We're a long way from India, aren't we, Doctor? Are you certain of your diagnosis?"

"If we were in India, I would say yes, flat out. Here I will simply say that the indications strongly suggest the bite of a snake distilling a powerful neurotoxic poison." Mukerjee paused. "Did you not mention a similar case last night?"

"Paralysis of the chest muscles. Semicomatose, so he couldn't tell us anything. He died on us."

"Ah," Mukerjee said. "Fang marks, too?"

"No, but . . ." Shapiro's voice faltered as he remembered the bloodstains on the patient's trousers. Damn that Papaleo! Mukerjee was looking at him politely, waiting. Well, he wasn't about to bad-mouth one of his interns to another physician. What he would say to Papaleo was something else again. "Not to my knowledge. We're waiting for the ME's report. Meanwhile, professional caution to one side, you're really convinced, aren't you?"

"I wouldn't stake my entire reputation on it, but—"

"The question is," Shapiro said impatiently, "shall I tell the police about it?"

"I should do so," Mukerjee said.

Dr. Shapiro returned to his room and phoned the police, who said they would send someone to see him. He tried to get Dr. Papaleo, but it was his night off duty. He called the medical examiner's office and requested rush reports on Ramon Torres and a second cadaver, Roderick Bamberger, soon to arrive at the morgue; suspected injection of neurotoxic venom by snakebite.

He picked a textbook from his bookshelves and began to read up on snakebites and their treatment. Before he had gotten very far he was summoned to the hospital reception room, where a stocky, hard-faced man introduced himself as Detective Robert Dark. "About this snake?"

"We haven't established as an absolute fact that it *is* a snake, we just *suspect* snakebites," Shapiro explained.

"You're a doctor," the detective said. "You oughta *know*."

Dark's tone was peevish, even challenging. Shapiro felt annoyed. He said, "Detective Dark, the diagnosis of snakebite was made by an Indian doctor who is familiar with cobra bites."

"A cobra?" Dark almost smiled. "I can see why you're not standing on that diagnosis, Doc."

"We're standing on it, Officer, unless we're contradicted by autopsy reports. I asked the ME to expedite them. The soonest they can get around to them is early tomorrow morning."

Dark said, "So what do you want me to do?"

"Well," Shapiro said, "check out the zoos, pet shops—"

"This time of the night? When we don't even know for sure that there's a snake? Tell you what, Doc. I think we ought to wait for the autopsy reports. There ain't a thing we can *do* right now."

"Detective Dark, two men have been bitten in the park—*al-legedly* bitten—and who is to say that by morning there won't be a third?"

"I tell you, Doc, anybody who goes into that park at night is likely to get killed one way or another. Fact, we had a guy shot dead in the park just last night around three in the morning."

Shapiro sighed. "Well, I'm just trying to do what I think is best."

"Me, too," Dark said.

DURING the night the snake had lost its fangs, but by morning new fangs had already moved into position.

The snake's upper jaw contained only two teeth, the poison fangs, ankylosed to the inside of the jawbone. Connected to the poison gland, the fangs conducted venom from it through a canal. The fangs were subjected to much wear, and had to be replaced from time to time. Sometimes they broke off prematurely, but substitute fangs, always growing just behind the functioning ones, would move up to take their place. This cycle of loss and replacement continued throughout the snake's life.

Because of the heat wave—now in its fourth day—the snake had lost little body heat during the night. It basked on the black rock for only a brief time before it glided down into its adopted territory and then climbed up into its tree. The snake spread out amid dense foliage, which provided concealment and shelter from the rays of the sun.

THREE

WHEN Dr. Shapiro finished his morning rounds he went down to the hospital cafeteria for a second breakfast. Papaleo appeared beside his table. He seemed pale and nervous.

"Did you hear it?"

Shapiro sopped up runny egg with a piece of toast. Then he looked up and said, "Hear what, Dr. Papaleo?"

"On the radio. A news flash. Less than five minutes ago. They said two people had been bitten by a snake in the park and died at East Side Hospital."

Shapiro stared at Papaleo. "Did they say where the information came from?"

"I don't think so."

Shapiro nodded and turned back to his eggs, but Papaleo lingered, fidgeting.

"On the one I tried to treat," Papaleo said, "there were perforations on the thigh. After you left, I cut the patient's pants off and saw them. I thought of snakebite, but it didn't make sense."

"It was your duty to wake me and tell me."

"But you had gone back to sleep, and . . . I'm sorry, Doctor."

My fault, Shapiro thought. He didn't tell me because he was afraid I'd either ream him out or laugh at him. He said, "It's my fault for not insisting on removing the patient's pants."

"Oh. Well, anyway." Papaleo tried to smile, then hurried away.

After Shapiro finished his breakfast he phoned the medical examiner's office. He asked for the pathologist who had performed the autopsy on Torres, and was connected with Dr. Borkowski.

"How do you like that?" Borkowski seemed tickled. "Fatal snakebite in the middle of Manhattan—isn't that terrific?"

"Your enthusiasm is infectious," Shapiro said, "but I've been waiting for your call, Doctor. I don't mind your making hay with the media, but you might have phoned me first."

Borkowski was silent for a moment, then said stiffly, "The reports are on their way over. Meanwhile, to sum up my findings—"

"Never mind. I'll get them from the radio like the rest of the public." Shapiro jiggled the phone, cutting Borkowski off. He had been hearing a page, and asked the operator what she wanted.

"There are some gentlemen here to see you," the operator said. "From the press. And also from the television."

"Oh, damn," Shapiro said.

THE police commissioner and "Hizzonner" the mayor were in a meeting at city hall when they were informed about the snake.

At eleven thirty a.m. one of the mayor's aides, mindful of his boss's unpredictability in an election year, entered the room with the early edition of the New York *Post* and placed it on the desk beneath Hizzonner's eyes.

KILLER SNAKE SLAYS
TWO IN PARK

The mayor goggled. The news story on page three, to which the aide obligingly turned, was brief, with photographs and quotations from Dr. Shapiro, Dr. Mukerjee, Dr. Papaleo, and Dr. Borkowski. An inset box contained a few facts about Central Park. Acclaimed masterpiece of its architects, Frederick Law Olmsted and Calvert Vaux. Its eight hundred and forty acres larger than London's Hyde Park, Paris' Tuileries, Berlin's Tiergarten, Copenhagen's Tivoli Gardens. Not as large as Rome's Villa Borghese or Vienna's Prater. Purchased for five and a half million dollars in 1856; real estate market value today—untold billions.

The lead editorial consisted of three sentences.

> There is a snake in Central Park. It is killing people. What is the mayor doing about it?

"Dirty pool," the aide said indignantly. "It's one thing for them to endorse your opponent, but—"

"I'll show 'em," Hizzonner said. "I'm leaving no stone unturned, that's what I'm doing about it!"

Later, at a news conference, he amplified on this declaration by telling his audience that the Central Park Precinct was out in full force, combing every nook and cranny for the interloper.

"Give 'em the details, Francis," the mayor said to the police commissioner.

The PC, who had just learned the details himself by phone, declared that the men and women of the Central Park Precinct were finecombing the park in cars, on horseback, and on foot, ably assisted by parks department gardeners and groundsmen.

"How many is that, all told?" a reporter asked.

The police commissioner, frowning, ignored the question. He knew that the total strength of the Central Park Precinct was in the neighborhood of one hundred and twenty, which broke down to forty per shift. Subtract clerical personnel, special duty officers, anticrime detective units on stakeout detail, officers on vacation and sick call, and the precinct probably had no more than fifteen men available for finecombing the park.

"Cars equipped with loudspeakers," the commissioner said, "are instructing people to stay on the walkways and out of heavily brushed areas, to make no attempt to deal with the snake if they spot it but to inform a police officer immediately."

"Mr. Mayor," a reporter said, "are you considering closing the park for the citizens' safety until the snake is found?"

"You may rest assured, the matter is under intense study."

After the news conference broke up, the mayor, alone with the police commissioner, said, "How'd you like that reporter asking if I was going to close the park? In the middle of a heat wave, when people are gasping for air?"

"You'd need a thousand cops to keep people out," the commissioner said, "and even then you couldn't do it. You know people in this city. They'd find a hundred ways to get in. Believe me, they'd try to get in."

"Believe me," the mayor said, "I believe you."

AFTER a brief opening citation of the weather—"near record-breaking heat for September with no relief in sight"—the early evening news program on the mayor's favorite television network devoted eight full minutes to the snake.

The sequence opened with a panoramic sweep of the park—"the most valuable parcel of real estate in the civilized world"—from a circling helicopter. Then the anchorman said, "Somewhere in this famed park lurks an unwelcome visitor to the city—a venomous snake whose deadly bite has claimed the lives of two victims."

The mayor watched the screen from an armchair in his bedroom at Gracie Mansion. From time to time he groaned.

The helicopter's camera focused fleetingly on a policeman on horseback, then on one riding a scooter. The anchorman went on, "From noontime on, police from the Central Park Precinct have been scouring the park, thus far without result. But the search continues. It's hot work, and dangerous. . . . Earlier today, reporter Bill Stevens was at East Side Hospital."

Dr. Papaleo, described by Stevens as "the earnest young intern who treated the first victim of the snake, Ramon Torres," told how he had watched helplessly as Torres had died of causes unknown at that time.

Dr. Mukerjee, soft-eyed and soft-spoken, reminded the reporter that his "brilliant snap diagnosis" was as yet not proved. "It was the bite of a snake *similar* to that of a cobra, shall we say."

Dr. Shapiro, chief resident of the hospital, answered questions brusquely. When asked what he would do if another snakebite victim were brought in, he opened a refrigerator and took out a small cardboard box.

"All hospitals in the area received this polyvalent, wide-spectrum antivenin from the curator of herpetology at the Bronx Zoo. If another victim is brought in, he'll be injected with this serum."

"May I ask which snakes this serum is effective against?"

Dr. Shapiro said, "*Bitis, Naja, Dendroaspis. Bitis* covers various vipers and adders, *Naja* the cobras; *Dendroaspis* are arboreal snakes, such as the mambas of Africa. If our snake is one of these, the antivenin *may* be effective. The most effective antivenins are specific: cobra serum for cobra bite, Gaboon viper serum for Gaboon viper bite, and so forth. Identifying the snake in the park is of paramount importance. Now, if you'll excuse me, I must attend to a patient."

The anchorman said, "Where did the snake come from, and how did it get into the park? Thus far, we do not know. And perhaps we shall never find out." He explained that zoos, pet shops, laboratories, exotic animal farms—all had been queried; none had reported a missing snake. Nor had any individuals who owned pet snakes come forward. Perhaps an individual existed who didn't wish to make a self-incriminating admission?

The deputy commissioner of the New York Police Department made a plea: "If you are such an individual, and your snake has escaped, call the NYPD anonymously. It is vital that we know exactly what *kind* of snake the killer snake is, so that the proper antidote can be stocked." A special police number was flashed onto the screen.

The news report continued, with an interview at the American Museum of Natural History, where a herpetologist declared that a drastic turn in the weather, a rapidly falling thermometer, was highly desirable. This would cause the snake to become lethargic, disoriented, thus sharply decreasing the danger of anyone else's being bitten. Meanwhile, some general advice: "Stay out of the underbrush, watch where you walk." Although many snakes could strike with incredible speed, they could not locomote swiftly; the average human could easily outrun just about any snake in the world. "Don't worry"—smiling—"about the snake chasing you." Except in very rare instances, such as during the breeding season, or in protection of their eggs, snakes would not pursue a man.

The herpetologist offered advice on what to do in case of snakebite. "Avoid strenuous activity, alcohol, panic—all of these speed up the heartbeat and circulate the venom more quickly through the body. Lie down, apply a tourniquet above the wound in the direction of the heart, inject antivenin as quickly as possible. As to incising and sucking out the venom, it goes in and out of fashion. If you do suck the venom, make sure there are no lesions in your mouth or on your lips."

The mayor paid little attention to the herpetologist. He was waiting for the inevitable man-in-the-street interviews, which, idiotic as they might seem, must be attended to seriously by the politician, for, however cracked and inarticulate, they were truly the voice of the people.

The first interview took place in the playground at Central Park West and Eighty-first Street, near the Hunters' Gate. A young woman in halter and shorts, filmed against a background of swings and seesaws, speaks aggrievedly above the penetrating screams of toddlers. "Where do I go if I don't come here with my child—the French Riviera? Besides, can a snake be any worse than the winos that hang around this park?"

A middle-aged couple, coming up out of a subway station. The woman: "Maybe the snake will eat up some muggers. If that's the case, they should have one on every street." Her husband: "Sylvia, it's nothing to laugh at!" Woman: "Do you see me laughing?" Husband: "Sylvia!"

On Central Park West and Seventy-third Street, the spokeswoman for an angry group of mothers, surrounded by milling children: "They must close the park, and keep it closed until they find the snake. That mayor, he's trifling with human lives."

On Cathedral Parkway, several dozen resentful black and Hispanic women. The spokeswoman, large and forceful: "He close that park over our dead body. We stifling in our apartments. Where else we got to go to beat the heat? He close that park and he hear from us come election time."

The final clip was light in tone. Three teenage girls, giggling. One of them says, "It's kicky." Reporter: "Kicky? What do you mean by kicky?" The girl: "Kicky? Well, like a groove." The reporter, shaking his head and smiling: "I'm kicking it back to you, Jerry."

Jerry, the anchorman, smiling: "You're in the groove, fella." He pauses, adjusts his face to appropriate sobriety, and says, "To re-

513

capitulate, a deadly venomous snake, origin unknown, suspected to be a cobra, is at large in Central Park. Two men have already succumbed to its fatal poison. The city has the jitters."

The mayor shut off the television set and telephoned the police commissioner.

"When are you going to catch that snake?" the mayor said.

"I wish I knew," the commissioner said. "It'll be dark in a half hour, and we'll call off the search until tomorrow."

"And what are you going to do tomorrow?"

"More of the same. A diligent, quiet search."

"Forget quiet, Francis. Do it noisy."

"What do you mean, sir?"

"It's war," the mayor said. "Two people have been slain, and everybody is blaming the snake on me. It's the TV's fault, getting the public all worked up. Are you listening, Francis?"

"I am, sir."

"Follow me explicitly. The snake has become Topic A. Everybody is saying we're not doing enough. Your handful of cops was invisible in that big park. We have to make them visible, so the people can see the mayor is working for them. That means a very big police presence, Francis. I want five hundred cops in that park tomorrow morning."

"Five hundred? Where am I going to get them?"

"Just get them. I don't care if you have to bring off-duty cops back on emergency duty."

"I don't dare. The police association would crucify us."

"Then take them out of Harlem and Bedford-Stuyvesant and the South Bronx. I want the people to see that their mayor is leaving no stone unturned."

"Sir, pulling police out of high-crime areas is an invitation to riot."

"No excuses. I order you to put five hundred cops in the park tomorrow morning. Good night, Francis."

The mayor hung up.

THE special police number provided on the news broadcast began to ring within minutes of the announcement. Several callers denounced by name the culprit who had turned the snake loose in the park; in these cases the person they named was a neighbor who, as subsequent questioning brought out, happened to have children who broke windows and cursed, or owned a dog that barked all night. Several individuals who preferred to remain anonymous, and a number of activist organizations which did not, claimed "credit" for introducing the snake into the park.

It was a familiar story to the police, who had learned to practice patience in these circumstances. Except for the most outlandish calls, they methodically logged all that came in. There were people who had spotted the snake in their apartment house elevator, crawling through a subway tunnel, in a branch library. About seventy percent of the sightings were within Central Park. The snake was observed drinking at the Pulitzer Fountain at Fifth Avenue and Fifty-ninth Street; slithering through the grass of the Sheep Meadow; riding the Friedsam Memorial Carousel; sunning itself on Cherry Hill; climbing the steps of the Metropolitan Museum of Art; at the top of the Obelisk.

The police checked out as many of the plausible reports as they could, given their manpower limitations. They knew that, as in all branches of police work, there were a thousand false leads to a single authentic one; but the thousand-and-first might crack the case.

SPECIAL Operations Division, with headquarters in Flushing Meadow, Queens, consists of the following units: emergency service, tactical patrol, street crime, auto crime, aviation, harbor, and mounted (known as horse soldiers). The most widely publicized is the emergency service unit (ESU), specialists in the oddball assignment. If there's a cat at the top of a pole, a sniper to be dislodged, a riot to be quelled, a finger stuck in a soda machine, the ESU comes to the rescue.

The man who was placed in charge of the field operation to find the snake in the park was Captain Thomas Eastman of ESU. He was presented with his assignment by his boss, Deputy Inspector Vincent Scott.

Eastman, who had left his office at six o'clock for his home, was recalled by telephone. He arrived back at headquarters at eight forty-five.

"About the killer snake in the park," DI Scott said sourly. "You know anything about snakes?"

Eastman pondered for a moment. "You're supposed to catch

them behind the head with a long stick with a clamp at the end that closes up when you press a handle. Like the thing grocers use to bring packages down from a high shelf?"

"You don't have to catch it," the DI said. "Just get rid of it. Just get in the park and find it and kill it."

"That's what they were trying to do today, and didn't do it. The problem is the size of the park. You know how big it is, Chief? It's eight hundred and forty acres. Fifth Avenue to Central Park West, Fifty-ninth to Hundred-and-tenth. I don't have any idea how to cover all that area."

The DI shook his head. "You don't need an idea, you need manpower. You're getting manpower."

"How much?" Eastman asked cautiously.

"Five hundred." The DI paused to savor Eastman's astonishment. "They want that snake real bad. It's political, a red-hot item. You hear the news this evening?"

Eastman nodded. "John Q. Public has the jitters."

"Right. *That's* why you got a whole army of cops to play with. Planning and Operations is putting the package together."

"I wouldn't mind some technical help, Chief," Eastman said.

"We already got one of these characters, herpa-something, from the Natural History Museum, he's supposed to be helping us."

"I saw him on the tube," Eastman said. "Maybe he's okay, but there's this young fellow at the Bronx Zoo. He doesn't fool around. About seven or eight months ago there was this rattlesnake some nut kept in an apartment in Washington Heights. It escaped, and I went in with a detachment. We had a couple of those snake-catching sticks. Anyway, we evacuated all the tenants and tossed that house, really *tossed* it, cellar to roof. We must have been four or five hours at it. Then this young fellow from the zoo came down, and inside of five minutes he found the snake curled up near the boiler in the cellar. He lifted it up on a stick, popped it into a bag, and took it off to the zoo."

"An apartment house," the DI said. "That can't compare to Central Park."

"What impressed me, Chief," Eastman continued, "was not only that he knew right away where to look for it, but he *saw* it. Right away. It was there all the time, only we didn't see it."

"Yeah. Get hold of this kid, if you want to."

MOLTING WAS ONE OF THE imperatives that governed the snake's existence. Unlike most animals, the snake never stopped growing, from birth to the moment of death. It literally outgrew its horny outer skin and was obliged to shed three or four times a year.

For several days now the snake's skin had been darkening and dulling, and its eyes, sheltered behind transparent protective lenses, had begun to dim. It was time to molt.

Because it was defenseless during molting, the snake sought the shelter of the topmost branches of its tree. It stretched out almost to its full extent and began to rub its face against a branch. The skin around its lips broke away. Squirming vigorously, over the next few hours the snake advanced laboriously, like a finger being pulled out of a tight glove, until it had worked itself completely out of the old skin, which ended up at the tail, inside out.

The new skin was bright, the colors fresh and attractive. The snake was at its handsomest. Its eyesight was keen behind its new transparent lenses. The old, discarded skin, feathery and translucent, dropped a few feet and was caught in a net of twigs, undetectable from ground level.

As always after molting, the snake was hungry. In the darkness, it coiled down the tree and sped away in search of food.

FOUR

WHEN Mark Converse opened his eyes, the python was in the direct line of his vision. It was sprawled on the bottom of its glass cage and appeared to be staring at him, though he was sure it was asleep.

The python was under four feet long, just a baby, but lately it had taken to having notions about the cat. A few days ago it had curled down the lamp standard and begun to constrict the cat. The cat had raked a claw across the python's ventral area before bounding away.

Converse knew that when he went to Australia he would have to dispose of both the python and the cat. Better start thinking about it. He could probably farm out the cat, but who would take a python? So it would doubtless go to the zoo. Meanwhile, it had made a nice pet, and even seemed to show some affection, or at least tolerance, for him.

It was quarter of seven in the morning, and the telephone was ringing. Converse reached across the bed and picked up the phone as it rang for a third time.

"This is Captain Eastman of the New York Police Department. Excuse me for calling you at this hour."

Converse's heart began to thump. "Who?"

"Captain Eastman, NYPD. Emergency service unit. Remember me? That rattlesnake up in Washington Heights last year?"

Converse didn't remember any Captain Eastman, only a faceless lot of jittery, blundering cops. "Got another snake?"

There was a very long pause, during which Converse thought he heard Eastman muttering to himself. But when he spoke it was in an apologetic tone. "I got your home number from the night man at the zoo. He said you're not with the zoo anymore."

"Yeah, I quit a few weeks ago. I'm going off to Australia with an expedition, to bring back specimens. . . ." Autobiography at seven a.m.? Forget it. Converse said, "Where's this one?"

There was another silence, and now Eastman spoke with exaggerated clarity. "I must have woken you from a pretty deep sleep, Mr. Converse. I'm talking about the snake in Central Park."

"There's a snake in Central Park? On the loose?"

Eastman's voice became edgy. "Are you putting me on?"

Converse reacted to Eastman's tone. He said peevishly, "I don't know what you're talking about."

"Where on earth have you been since twelve noon yesterday?" Eastman asked with wonder in his voice. "Haven't you turned on the TV or the radio or seen a newspaper?"

"Well, no. Honestly, I didn't know. Is there a law against it?"

"Look," Eastman said, "I haven't got time to fill you in on everything, except to tell you that this particular snake has bitten two citizens and they're both dead."

"You're kidding. *Killed* two people? In Central Park? What kind of a snake is it?"

"We don't know. The reason I'm calling—I remember how quickly you found that rattler. I'd like you to help us again."

"In Central Park?" Converse said. "Incredible. Absolutely unbelievable."

"Look, the point is—can you help us?" Eastman sounded tired and exasperated.

"Of course."

Eastman let his breath out in relief. "There isn't much time. We've got a big search operation set up at nine o'clock this morning. I'd like to talk to you before we begin."

"Where are you, where can I meet you?"

"I'm phoning from police headquarters, but I'm leaving directly for the park. Do you know where all those statues of Latin American liberators are, at the Sixth Avenue entrance?"

"I know. I'll be there in half an hour."

Converse got out of bed and dressed quickly in jeans and a T-shirt imprinted with the legend DUCHY OF LIECHTENSTEIN ALL STARS. He ran down the steps into Charles Street and went around to Seventh Avenue and bought a couple of papers. The *Daily News* headline read: SNAKE, SLAYER OF TWO, STILL AT LARGE. The *Times* was predictably more circumspect: POLICE SEARCH OF PARK FAILS IN EFFORT TO FIND SNAKE; TWO ARE DEAD OF BITES.

Converse found a cab cruising on Seventh. The driver picked him up and went along Charles Street to Hudson, where he turned north. Then he spoke to Converse, who was trying to read his newspapers. "The snake in Central Park? What'll they think of next? But, tell the truth, it actually don't surprise me."

"Well, it surprises *me*," Converse said.

The driver gave him a pitying look. "Come on, man. This city?"

FIFTEEN or twenty police vehicles, massed along Central Park South, clogged the Artists' Gate where the Avenue of the Americas ran into the park. Close by, just inside the park, were three huge television trucks and a few cars with PRESS placards on their windshields. The area was swarming with cops. Some were armed with shotguns, others with cans of Mace. A few carried crowbars.

Barriers had been put up on the downtown side of Central Park South, and a dozen policemen wearing the distinctive white helmets of the tactical patrol unit (TPU) were trying to keep spectators from overflowing the curb. The Avenue of the Americas had been closed off at Fifty-seventh Street, with traffic diverted to the east and west. Inside and outside the park, loudspeakers were urging the crowd to remain behind the barriers.

Converse started into the park, but his way was barred by a TPU cop who eyed him with suspicion. "Captain Eastman is waiting for me," Converse said. The cop guided him through a small mob to what he said was the command post. Its center was a large folding campaign table with a map of Central Park pinned to it. Half a dozen policemen were bent over the table.

The TPU cop spoke to a tall officer wearing silver oak leaves on his collar. "This fella says Captain Eastman wants to see him, sir."

"My name is Converse. I'm the herpetologist."

The officer stared at Converse's T-shirt with distaste, then called out, "Eastman, the ologist-something is here."

A face turned up out of the heads bent over the map. It was broad, pink, sweating. "Yeah," Eastman said, "tell him to wait a minute."

"Stay put right here," the tall officer said, and moved off.

Someone tapped Converse on the shoulder. It was a young woman. She was holding a shorthand pad and a ballpoint pen. "Aren't you that herpetologist from the Bronx Zoo?" she said. "I'm sorry, I forget your name."

"Mark Converse."

"I did a piece for my paper when you caught that rattlesnake last year. Holly Markham. I don't suppose you remember?"

"Why, yes. How you doing?"

She was pretty, but in a cool, self-contained way. He preferred outwardness, even a suggestion of mischief in a woman's face. But when she put out her hand and smiled, her face opened up. If it didn't exactly suggest abandonment, it had become immediately charming. He smiled back and shook her hand. Her grip was firm and without coquetry.

"Are you helping the police again, Mr. Converse?"

He glanced toward the campaign table. "If I can."

She wrote his name down and asked him his title at the zoo.

"Formerly assistant curator of herpetology. I've joined an expedition to Australia to bring back specimens. Australia has some terrific species of poisonous snakes."

She smiled and tilted her head and said, "How does someone get into anything as funny as snakes? You don't mind my asking?"

"Funny is in the eye of the beholder. I've been into snakes ever since I was a kid. I'm twenty-nine now, in case you're wondering. How old are you?"

"Twenty-five, and snakes make me crawl."

"Yeah." Converse sighed. "That's how people feel about them. Not me. I like them."

"Because they're cute and cuddly?"

He looked at her sharply. Maybe there was some mischief there, after all. "Because I understand them. And maybe because I'm for the underdog."

"What makes them underdogs?"

"They're seriously disadvantaged animals. No limbs. No hearing. No true voice. No teeth for chewing, so that they're obliged to swallow their food whole. No lids or nictitating membrane—can't shut their eyes. Cold-blooded, meaning that they're at the mercy of the environment for survival. No charm. Underdogs, right?"

She looked up from her notebook. "That underdog in the park has killed two people."

"Accidents happen. Snakes don't bite people; people get bitten."

"And there are no muggers, just people who get mugged?"

He sighed again. "Look, I'll tell you something about snakes. They have three defensive attitudes when they're threatened. One, they try to hide. Two, they try to run away. Three, if it's impossible to hide or run away, they defend themselves by biting. It's a last resort. Snakes are shy of people. They don't hunt them, don't hate them, don't eat them. It's the other way around."

"I read somewhere that those huge constrictors do eat people."

"That's nonsense. The very largest reticulate constrictors, which can engorge animals of quite surprising size, can't swallow a man."

"That's a comforting thought." Her face was solemn, but there was a twitch at the corners of her lips. Then, "I spoke to the Museum of Natural History herpetologist yesterday. He doesn't think the snake is a cobra."

"It probably isn't. According to the news stories, the perforations are clean, injection-type bites, in and out quickly. Cobras have a tendency to hang on, so the perforations aren't that neat."

"Do you have any idea of what kind of snake it might be?"

He shook his head. "I just know what it *isn't*. American snakes like rattlers or copperheads or moccasins distill a hemotoxic venom. The eastern coral snake, the only other poisonous snake in the States, does secrete a neurotoxic venom like the venom that killed those two people, but the coral is a chewer like the cobra, and not all that deadly."

She nodded. They both listened to a loudspeaker. "Attention, all police personnel, take up your positions."

"They're going to form a single line abreast," Holly Markham said, "all the way from Central Park West to Fifth Avenue, and sweep the park from end to end, south to north."

Converse shook his head. "They'll never find it that way."

"Why not?"

"Because they've got five hundred cops out here. That's four hundred and ninety-nine too many." Eastman was sitting on an edge of the campaign table, watching him. Their eyes met, and Eastman beckoned to him. "I have to go now. Nice talking to you, Holly."

"Too bad. It was just beginning to get interesting. In case this thing fizzles, how do I get in touch with you?"

He told her his phone number and she wrote it down. He walked over to Eastman, who said, "Sorry to keep you waiting, Mr. Converse. Do you have any suggestions?"

Sure, Converse thought, call off your cops. He said, "I might, if I knew what kind of snake it was."

"We find it, we'll know what kind it is."

The mass of policemen was now attenuating, spreading toward the east and west ends of the park. Converse said, "I've never seen this many cops in one place."

"Neither have I. It tells you something about how bad we want that snake." Eastman's blue eyes were bleak. "I would appreciate any help you could give us in finding and killing it."

"What do you want to kill it for? It's no harder to capture it than it is to kill it."

"It's a murderer, and I believe in capital punishment."

Converse shook his head. "It has to be caught before somebody else is hurt, but it's a fact that a snake doesn't attack out of malice. It bit those people because it felt threatened."

"Whose side are you on—ours or the snake's?"

As it happens, Converse thought, I want to prevent anybody else from being bitten and I want to save the snake. But it would be best to leave Eastman's question unanswered. He waved toward the line of cops. "That's not the way to find it. You can beat an area and drive a tiger out into the open, but not a snake. Snakes are among the most accomplished hiders in the animal kingdom."

The loudspeakers were blaring, urging speed on the flanks.

"Poor bastards," Eastman said. "Imagine what it's like out there in the sun? They're going to be dropping like flies."

"Once, in my office at the zoo," Converse said, "just a little cubbyhole, mind you, I misplaced a two-foot-long snake, and it was missing for three weeks. I turned the place upside down and couldn't find it. It turned up in a desk drawer."

"We're going to toss the whole park," Eastman said. "Every last inch of it, except water—" He stopped abruptly. "Do snakes swim?"

"They sure can. But this one obviously isn't a water snake, so you can skip the water."

"Thank God. There's a hundred and fifty acres of water, and we would have had to bring in divers."

"How many trees are there?"

Eastman groaned. "They hide in trees?"

"Some snakes live in trees and never come down to the ground. Others are strictly terrestrial. Still others are *both* arboreal and terrestrial. And some of those also live underground in burrows."

"Trees and burrows. Anything else I ought to know?"

"Snakes live by stealth, and they have to be caught by stealth. Snakes are deaf, but they're sensitive to vibrations of the substrate. Five hundred heavy-footed cops are going to sound like an earthquake to that snake out there. It'll hide, and that's that. You don't need five hundred men, just one man who knows what he's doing."

Eastman barked a short unamused laugh. "I get your point."

A series of loudspeakers burst into sound. "Attention, all sergeants. We're moving out. Remember, walk as straight a line as you can, eyes down to the ground, concentrate on heavily brushed areas. But everything is included—playgrounds, walks, buildings. Move on out. Move out."

"Eyes down," Converse said. "They won't look up in the trees."

The loudspeakers were addressing the people in the park: "Please keep back and do not impede the officers. If you do not have business in the park, please leave."

Eastman stood up. "I'd better put that dope about the trees into the loudspeakers. Come along?"

Converse shook his head. "No sense to it. After this is over and the dust settles, I'll come back."

Eastman turned abruptly and hurried away.

Converse walked out of the park. There was a group of reporters at the exit, and he wondered if Holly Markham was among them. She wasn't.

IF I WANTED to die of thirst, Police Officer Fleming told himself, I would've joined the French Foreign Legion. The only thing keeping him going was the promise of a lunch break once they had finished sweeping the area between the Seventy-ninth and Eighty-fifth Street transverses.

He was positive the search was hopeless. But still he trudged on, pouring sweat, keeping his eyes on the ground. As for looking up into trees, he had quit doing that when he had heard a parks department gardener say that there were over a hundred thousand trees in the park. Even with five hundred cops that figured out to better than two hundred trees per man!

Suddenly a loudspeaker blared, "Okay, boys, we're finishing up this part of the park, then it's lunch and all the beer you can drink." Fleming took a deep breath, plowing into an area full of trees and thick brush. A low-hanging branch snapped across his face, and he wiped at his mouth as if the snake itself had brushed him. If this isn't over soon, he thought, I'm gonna start screaming.

THE snake was near the top of its tree when it first saw the approaching figure. As the figure came closer, the snake moved downward, silent, swift, its skin blending with the background leaves and branches. Its flicking tongue picked up odor substances.

When the figure was directly below the tree it disturbed a low-hanging branch. The snake anchored itself by its tail as the figure paused. It retracted the anterior portion of its body, tensed to strike downward.

The figure moved on.

The snake held its threatening posture, hissing softly, until the figure disappeared from sight. Then it climbed back up to the top-most branches.

The Reverend Sanctus Milanese, leader of the well-known religious sect called Puries, or members of the Church of the Purification, stood motionless before his carved, gleaming doorway. Despite the heat, the reverend wore his long black cloak with its

scarlet lining, and a small skullcap (scarlet with black lining).
He was encircled by his security guards.

If the reverend had called a press conference for any ordinary
reason, he might have been ignored. But the announcement that
he would issue a statement defining the position of his church with
respect to the snake in the park had intrigued the media. A blend
of the snake and the unpredictable Puries represented a mix of
volatile elements certain to produce an interesting explosion.

The Reverend Sanctus Milanese was a tall man with black eyes
under strongly arched black eyebrows, iron-gray hair, thin lips,
and a long, unsmiling face. He did not move. His eyes, tilted upward, did not blink. He was waiting for the TV crews to set up
their equipment.

Holly Markham was one of a number of reporters massed on the
sidewalk in front of Purity House, the Fifth Avenue mansion of
the Reverend Sanctus Milanese. The building, in the style of a
French château, had been built some eighty years before by a
highly respected robber baron. It had been purchased three years
ago, for cold cash raised by popular subscription of the reverend's
followers, and presented to him as a fiftieth-birthday gift. It thus
became the third notable real estate holding of the Church of the
Purification. The others were the Tabernacle, located in the east
Thirties in a former Greek Orthodox church; and a Dutchess
County estate consisting of over a hundred acres and seven buildings, including a forty-room main house. This complex, called Eden
Paradise, was a training center for novitiate members.

With the cameras in place and their crews at the ready, the Reverend Sanctus Milanese began to speak. His voice was booming
evangelical, Holly thought, a hard-sell voice.

"It has not been given to the police to uproot the serpent," the
reverend said sonorously, "for only God knows where the serpent
lurks. Shall He impart His knowledge to those who follow tem-
poral sway?"

A television reporter shouted, "To whom will God impart His
knowledge, Reverend?"

"I shall speak the truth. He has instructed me as follows: Let
your flock go into the park and their purity shall overcome the evil
serpent, and they shall find this messenger of Satan where it hides
and then they shall destroy it."

That's it, Holly thought, the kernel of news in the shell of bombast. He's giving the police notice that he will defy them.

A reporter said, "City officials have warned against vigilante action. They have asked the public not to search for the snake. Will you disregard this warning?"

"Reverend turns piercing eyes on speaker," Holly wrote in her notebook. "Bodyguards turn eyes too, not piercing but cold, bleak, inaccessible."

"Suppose one of your people gets bitten?" a reporter asked.

"Guards give newsman death-ray looks," Holly wrote.

"Then it is the Lord's will."

The Reverend Sanctus Milanese turned abruptly, with a theatrical swirl of his cape that displayed its scarlet lining, and strode toward the massive, ornately carved door of his house. At the last moment the door opened from the inside, and he passed through.

"He makes a classy exit," Holly wrote, and shut her notebook.

MARK Converse passed the afternoon in fitful catnaps and short dreams, all involving Holly Markham.

It was his nature to be insanely susceptible to falling in love with the women he met. It was partially in an effort to cure himself of his affliction that he had quit his job at the zoo, which he liked very much, and signed on to hunt snakes in Australia. The Outback would offer few temptations. But the expedition had been delayed, and he had been left with almost two months with nothing to do. He had recognized his idleness as fallow ground for the forming of a liaison. Now Holly seemed to be tempting him.

Holly Markham, the girl with the calm, unassertively confident face? Not his type. Then why had he looked for her in the crowd of reporters before he left the park? Just a reflex; he turned toward good-looking women like a flower turning toward the sun. Pretty? Only when her face opened up in its transforming smile.

Converse got out of bed and switched on the television set in time for the evening news. Almost immediately Eastman appeared. He was admitting to a reporter that the police sweep had failed and that he didn't know "at this time" what the next move would be. His face was eroded by fatigue and frustration.

Converse got up from his chair and made himself a drink. The phone rang. It was Captain Eastman.

THE MAYOR, HIS STAFF, several high city officials, and the police commissioner were gathered in the conference room at city hall. The police operation had ended officially at five forty-five, although its failure had been conceded long before the last few exhausted cops straggled out of the park. Now the mayor called upon the commissioner for a report.

"In a nutshell," the PC said, "we didn't find the snake. And that's the good news, Mr. Mayor. The bad news is that there's been an upsurge of crime in those areas of the city where we pulled out personnel to try to find this damned snake. That there have been twenty-odd fires of suspicious origin. That there are traffic snarls that won't be unsnarled until nine o'clock. That more than seventy-five cops ended up in the hospital with heat prostration, though all but half a dozen were treated and released. That eight cops were hurt in scuffles in the park with Puries who refused to move out of the way of the police line. And that the police association has threatened a job action because of what they call cruel and inhumane treatment of their membership."

"You don't have to say it with such relish, Francis. Sit down." The mayor turned to the meeting at large. "Gentlemen, we gave it everything we have today, and now we're confronted with a very large problem—what to do for an encore?" He surveyed the room. "I'm open for suggestions."

Nobody met his eyes. Everybody was frowning. "Francis?"

The PC said, "I'll tell you what we can't do—we can't mount another operation like today. I'll have a mutiny on my hands."

The mayor glared around the room. A young bearded aide was muttering.

"Speak up if you've got something to say," the mayor said.

"Okay. First things first. How do you deal with the press?"

"Well, what *do* I say to the press?"

"You praise the devotion and courage of the police. After that, Your Honor, something about no further sweeps on the scale of today's operation under consideration at this time. Instead, twenty-four-hour patrol of the park—"

He was interrupted by another aide. "Okay. But you know the big question—are we planning to close the park?"

"Tell them it is still under intensive study."

"How many times can you keep saying that?"

"As many as I have to," the mayor said emphatically. "I'm never going to answer that question."

A voice said, "They're sure to quiz you about the Puries."

The mayor nodded grimly. "Why on earth are they mixing in this thing anyway?"

The bearded aide replied, "Publicity. Their enrollment has been down lately, they're falling behind in their mortgage payments. This is an opportunity to get exposure on the tube and in the papers, and attract recruits and money."

"Well, I don't like it," the mayor said.

"From the political point of view, it isn't all negative," the bearded aide said. "Anything the Puries are for, the recognized churches are automatically against, so we'll pick up a large sympathy vote."

The remainder of the meeting was desultory. There were, Hizzonner said, other matters to occupy them besides a lousy snake. Would anybody advance the claim, for instance, that dealing with those creeps in Washington and Albany wasn't of more moment than a lousy snake? Nobody advanced such a claim. The mayor adjourned the meeting.

FIVE

THE Central Park Precinct is located midway through the Eighty-fifth Street transverse, on the south side of the road. Its appearance is far and away the most distinctive of any police precinct in the city. Constructed in 1871 as a stable, it consists of a series of quaint, two-storied, handsomely weathered red brick buildings in a horseshoe shape around a central courtyard. It is an official landmark, jealously protected against demolition; jealously protected also, its officers suggest, against air conditioning.

A taxi pulled off the transverse road and dropped Converse at the precinct courtyard. Inside the main entrance, a heavily sweating policeman directed him down a narrow corridor lined with offices to the last room on the park side of the building. Converse knocked on the door and went in. Captain Eastman sat behind a desk in a round-shouldered slump.

"I thought your headquarters were in Flushing," Converse said.

"They are, but I'm on detached duty at this precinct for the duration. This is the precinct commander's office. He's on vacation, the lucky dog. Sit down."

"I was a little fresh this morning," Converse said. "I'm sorry. But I knew you wouldn't find the snake, and that search struck me as a pure waste of manpower."

Eastman's lids fluttered tiredly. "How old are you?"

Converse was surprised. "Twenty-nine. Why?"

"I'm forty-eight. If I learned any one thing since I was your age, it was never to be sure about anything. Anyway, we *had* to sweep the park today, whether we found the snake or not. We're dealing with people and their anxieties, not cold abstractions."

"You're not planning on doing the same thing tomorrow, I hope."

"I don't know. Maybe you'll find the snake for us tonight, so we don't have to worry about tomorrow."

Converse shook his head. "In one night? It isn't likely."

"Mr. Converse"—Eastman's voice became urgent—"I'd like to find that snake before it bites anybody else."

So would I, Converse thought, but I have a problem: nobody else realizes that the snake is just as much a victim of circumstances as the people it bites. It had to be *brought* to the park, by somebody acting out of malice or ignorance. Okay, but I mustn't let my feelings about snakes get out of hand. We can't have anybody else bitten, no matter *what* happens to the snake. Still, it's perfectly possible to save human lives without killing the snake. But Eastman would hit the ceiling if I said so. Not that I have to say it. Eastman is smart, he reads me very well.

What he did say was, "You know, Captain, it won't bite anybody who doesn't bother it."

Eastman laughed bitterly. "We keep getting reports that the park is lousy with citizens hunting for the snake. In the dark, mind you. Armed with forked sticks and crowbars and axes. We're pulling some of them in to discourage them."

"Can you hold them legally?"

"No," Eastman said flatly. "We escort them out of the park and warn them. But some come right back in again and take up where they left off, poking their sticks into bushes."

"Well," Converse said, "they're going to make it harder for us to find the animal. It's going to be scared to come out."

Eastman sighed. "What are you going to do?"

"Try to find the snake. I wish I knew what it was."

"Yeah, well, as I said, you'll know when you find it." He added without much conviction, "Somebody said something about a mongoose for killing snakes. Anything to it?"

"A mongoose can kill a snake, most times, and so can a hedge-hog. Both are resistant to snake venom. But they're not natural enemies of snakes, and their tendency is to avoid each other. The fights you see are always staged. Actually, the most efficient snake-killing animal is an African bird called the secretary bird. It's about four feet high, with long, taloned legs that it uses to stomp and gash a snake to death." He glanced at Eastman. "No, it isn't prac-tical to put a secretary bird in Central Park."

"I guess not." Eastman's fleeting expression of hope disappeared.

"There are two things we can try tonight," Converse said. "We can shine a powerful flashlight beam around, and if the animal is nearby, the light bounces off its retina and you pick up the eye shine. Trouble is, it's a local effect. You can't shine a light in the snake's eye if it's a block away."

Eastman grunted. "What's the other thing?"

"Stake out a watering place. Snakes are mostly nocturnal. If it wants a drink, it'll probably come out for it at night."

"You know how much water there is in the park?"

"You told me—about a hundred and fifty acres. It's a long shot. The odds might be a little better tomorrow morning. Snakes are cold-blooded, and have to lie in the sun to warm themselves up for an hour or so. Maybe less than that in this weather, because they don't lose much heat during the night. They bask early in the morning, and they like lying on a rock if there's one around."

"You know how many rocks there are in the park?"

"It's a problem. But if you give me a week or so, I'll turn it up. We need time."

"We haven't got any," Eastman said.

CONVERSE decided to stake out the Belvedere Lake because it was near there that Roddy Bamberger had been bitten.

Eastman said, "We know the snake was around the lake a cou-ple of nights ago. Is it their custom to hang around in one place?"

"It depends on the species. As a rule, only when they're breed-ing. But at least the lake's a starting place."

"Why don't we stake out *all* of the possible watering holes?" Eastman suggested.

"Because there's only one of me," Converse said, "and your cops would probably miss it or else step on it in the dark and get bitten."

They left the precinct and the park around nine in a squad car driven by a patrolman. From Central Park West they reentered at the Hunters' Gate and drove on the pedestrian walks past the Shakespeare Garden and the darkened Delacorte Theatre. Except for a group of young people whom they took to be Puries, there was no evidence that citizens were still searching for the snake.

The police car pulled over to one side of a walkway. Converse and Eastman got out and walked to the lake.

"This is as good as anyplace else," Converse said. "We might as well sit down. Of course, if it comes for a drink on the other side of the lake, we won't see it. But that fellow was bitten near here."

"You're *sure* it's okay to sit down?"

"Sure. That way there's no chance of our stepping on it."

"If you say so." Eastman touched the Pillstrom tongs that Converse had brought. "I know what this stick is for. And your pillow-case—I remember you putting that rattlesnake into some kind of a yellow bag."

"It was a yellow pillowcase. Listen, Captain, it would be better if we didn't talk. Okay?"

"I thought snakes were deaf."

"They are. I'm not. I want to be able to hear it if it comes."

Eastman fell silent. Behind them, the driver had turned off the car's motor and lights. Above them, the sky was the color of lead, except where it was tinged with red from the uplifting of neons in the center of the city. The oppressiveness of the heat seemed worse than ever. The park was quiet, except for an occasional auto horn or a noisy transmission as a car accelerated.

Eastman was sitting motionless on the grass with his head bowed. If the snake came along, Converse thought, Eastman wouldn't give them away. Not that there was much chance of it. Even if the snake was still in the area, it would be next to impossible to detect unless it practically ran into them.

Converse kept his head raised, peering through the gloom for something that, if it did come, might go unseen and unheard. He felt something on the back of his hand. A raindrop.

THE SNAKE PROPELLED ITS great length forward swiftly toward the water it had drunk from on the previous nights. When it felt raindrops it stopped, raised its head high, and tested the air with its darting tongue. When the rain came down in a sudden torrent, the snake slid into a coil, lowered its head to within an inch or two of the ground, and moved from side to side in an almost dancelike rhythm. The downpour pelted its body, colder than it liked. The snake uncoiled, curving forward again toward the lake. Then it stopped, dipped its head, and drank from a puddle. Afterward it returned to its tree.

AFTER the first warning drop or two the rain fell in sheets. In a few seconds Converse and Eastman were soaked to the skin.

They ran to the squad car and jammed in beside the driver.

"We can go," Converse said. "It won't come tonight, not now."

INCREDIBLE as it might seem, he had actually offered to go to the Central Park Zoo with her. Now, at three thirty in the morning, while they drank coffee, Jane Redpath was praising him for his courage in offering to accompany her to the park. She told him that he was the gutsiest man she had ever met. It was probably true, she thought, and he was incontestably the stupidest.

They prepared to leave. She gathered up her tripod and slung her Hasselblad over her shoulder. Jeff stuck a hefty tire iron in his belt and picked up a forked wooden stick and a burlap bag. She thought the tire iron was a pretty good idea, in case of muggers, but she wasn't so sure about the stick and bag. They reminded her that there *was* a snake in the park. The knowledge made her squirm, but she rationalized her fear in terms of the enormous size of the park. Still, she might have postponed the expedition if her paper hadn't already been badly overdue.

In the taxi that took them downtown through deserted streets, she went on about her photographic project, which was to constitute the thesis for her master's degree in physiology. "Whenever people think of sleep problems," she said, in what she hoped was a calm, serious voice, "they tend to think in terms of human beings. But we can learn much from animals—"

"Jane, I love you," he said fervently. He was nuzzling her neck with his handsomely broken athlete's nose.

"Jeff," she whispered, "I'm scared. If we meet that snake . . . I mean, it's not too likely, but—"

"Relax, baby. If we run across it, we'll just catch it. It's simple. You spear the snake behind the head with a forked stick, then you grab it with your hand—behind the head, so it can't nip you—and just pop it in a bag. Nothing to it."

She shivered.

"Keep in mind," Jeff continued, "that snakes have a very low IQ. When they're threatened and can't run away, they attack. All they can think of is that they have to bite something. So you give them the stick, and they bite *that*. Then you shake them off the stick and pin them down. It's easy."

"Easy." She tried to put an enormous amount of admiration in her voice.

"Anything's easy, if you really know what you're doing."

THE snake glided onto the pavement, dry again since the cloudburst. It moved slowly, cautiously, as its tongue brought in the mingled odor substances of many animals. Once or twice it lifted its head high and peered into a cage. In one cage two lions were asleep; their powerful smell was familiar to the snake and disturbing. It moved on.

THE cab dropped them at Fifth Avenue and Sixty-fifth Street. They entered the park through the Children's Gate, and walking softly on their sneakered feet, they skirted the ivy-covered Arsenal, where the park's administrative offices are housed.

They circled to their right and came into the zoo. It was dark and shadowy except for the thin light from the lampposts.

Jane felt very nervous. Not Jeff. He was fully tooled up for the venture. "Okay," he said. "Where do we start?"

In the nighttime hush his voice echoed like a gunshot.

"*Shsh. Quiet.* You'll wake everything up."

He lowered his voice to a creditable whisper. "You're gonna wake them all up anyway with your flash."

"I'm not using a flash. I'm doing a time exposure with a very fast film. ASA four hundred. It should work with the light from the streetlamps."

Something moved to her right. She turned quickly and saw two

533

points of light. She gasped and clung to Jeff, then realized that an animal was watching through the bars of its cage. It was a shadowy gray bulk, and she couldn't make out what it was.

Trembling, she rested her head on his chest. "It scared me."

"Relax, you're with Jeff, okay?" His voice was soft.

She took a deep breath. "Okay, let's go to work."

She moved on to the next cage. Inside were two Barbary sheep, tan animals with strangely curved horns. Both were asleep.

She opened the metal legs of the tripod and fitted the Hasselblad to it. She adjusted the settings and sighted through the finder. Behind her, Jeff gave a tiny cluck of impatience.

She said, "You're making me nervous. Go check out the other cages, see what I can shoot next. Okay?"

He strode off to the south end of the line of cages. She sighted on the sheep, but before she could press the shutter release, they bounded to their feet, bleating. He's done it, she thought, the clumsy oaf somehow startled them. She whirled, catching up the camera and tripod, and started toward him angrily. Then she stopped dead. He was crouched, his back to her, facing a snake. Its head was high off the ground, its mouth agape.

She let out a cry of terror. The urge to turn and run was overwhelming, but she knew she couldn't desert Jeff. He was moving the forked stick toward the snake and whispering softly, laughing a little at himself. *"Toro.* Ho, *toro,* make your move."

The snake was tensed, hissing hollowly. Its body seemed incredibly long and slender, the neck swelling on a vertical axis. Barely aware of what she was doing, she planted the tripod and put her eye to the finder. Peering through, holding her breath, she saw Jeff extend the stick at full length. She pressed the shutter release almost by reflex, and it seemed to trigger off movement. The picture in the finder became unfrozen. The snake and the stick seemed to meet, and then Jeff dropped the stick with a clatter.

She shut her eyes, shaking with fear. When she opened them, Jeff's left hand was clasped over his right forearm. He seemed flushed but calm.

"It's okay," he said. "It's gone. It ran away."

He lifted his left hand from his arm and she saw two small spots of oozing blood an inch below the crook of his elbow. He slipped his belt out of his trousers, looped it around his arm just

below the biceps, and pulled it very tight. "The thing is to keep calm," he said quietly. "If you get excited, the heart pumps quicker and the poison circulates that much faster. So everybody concerned has to relax, okay?"

Behind her, a voice called out roughly, and she turned, her heart thumping. A figure was moving toward them out of the shadows. A brilliant light came on and blinded her.

JANE Redpath was alone in the waiting room. The cops who had brought them into the emergency ward had been called by the zoo's night watchman, the man who had flashed his light at them after Jeff was bitten.

The police car had responded quickly, and Jeff was rushed to East Side Hospital. He had walked in under his own power, smiling at her and telling her not to worry, to go home and catch some sleep. He'd give her a call later on.

She sat on the edge of a chair, remembering how in the park he had calmed her down and then calmed the watchman. While the watchman went for help he had stretched out on the pavement, slowing up the action of the venom. He said it didn't hurt, he felt just a kind of pins and needles. . . .

The emergency ward door opened and a man in a white jacket came over to her. "I'm Dr. Moran."

"Yes." She couldn't say any more. The doctor looked grave.

"We've administered a polyvalent serum; he seems to be responding moderately well. He's remarkably calm, and that helps."

"Then he's going to be all right?"

The doctor made an ambiguous movement of his head that was neither affirmation nor denial. "He wasn't able to describe the snake with any certainty. Did you get a good look at—"

"My camera! I left it in the police car! I took a picture of it!"

Dr. Moran was sprinting toward the emergency ward entrance.

FUMBLING for the phone in the darkness, Converse knew with certainty that it would be Eastman, and it was.

"Sorry again." Eastman was grim. "Another snake victim. I'm at East Side Hospital. We have a picture of the snake. It's being developed. Can you come over?"

"Right away."

WHEN THE SNAKE left the Central Park Zoo it ranged far afield, questing, as it had been ever since the rain had stopped, driven once again by an age-old imperative of its species.

It went northward, to the more uncultivated section of the park. Its movements were swift, urgent. It did not move in a straight line, but quartered an area, delving into wild patches, probing with its small head.

It was already light when it came upon a burrow concealed under a fallen tree in a tangle of heavy growth. The faintness of the odors analyzed by the Jacobson's organ indicated that the burrow had been vacant for some time. The snake broached the entrance, careful not to disturb the covering brush. It slid cautiously downward to make certain that the burrow was large enough for its length and that it had at least one additional exit.

The burrow fulfilled the snake's requirements in every way, and it slid all the way inside. It tried the second exit hole, again careful not to dislodge the brush that hid the opening but would not obstruct quick escape. The snake coiled its long body comfortably inside the burrow and went to sleep.

THE picture taken by Jane had been enlarged to five by nine inches, and had been placed, still wet, on a table in an empty emergency room. Captain Eastman was studying it with a mingled expression of revulsion and fascination. The snake was curled upward on the stick, and its mouth was gaped wide open over Jeff's arm. The snake's posterior section trailed off at the bottom of the stick, strongly curved, as if to brace itself against the pavement.

The receptionist told Converse to go right in to Eastman.

When he came through the doorway Converse said, "How is the patient?"

"Not too bad. He's young and strong, so—"

Converse had spotted the picture and brushed by him. He bent over the table and let out a low whistle. "It's a black mamba." He leaned over the picture for another look, then said, almost reverently, "It's beautiful."

Converse told Eastman that, although the black mamba was covered by the polyvalent antivenin, the Bronx Zoo had a specific black mamba serum in its reptile house.

Eastman said, "I'll call the precinct up in that area and have them shoot the stuff down here to the hospital in a squad car. After that, I'd like you to go to the Central Park Zoo with me."

"Okay. But don't bet that the snake's there. Black mambas are very wide ranging. They move like something shot out of a gun. It could be a couple of miles away from the zoo by now."

Eastman went out to call the Bronx precinct. He paused by the open door of room D, where the Code Blue team was working on Jeff. The doctors and nurses had left. There were only two figures beside the table. One was Dr. Shapiro. The other was a nurse, attaching a tag to the patient's big toe.

Eastman went into the room. "What happened?"

"We lost him," Shapiro said. "We thought he was going to make it, and then he just went out, he simply blinked out on us."

"Damn," Eastman said.

"When he began to go, it took us by surprise," Shapiro said. "Then somebody got the bright idea of turning him over, and we saw the hives on his back. If they had appeared on his front, as they usually do, we'd have shot some Adrenalin into him."

"What did the hives mean?"

"Anaphylactic shock. Antivenin is extracted from the blood serums of horses that have been injected with snake poison. Some people are allergic to horse serum and go into shock if they're given it. It can be fatal if it's not treated."

Eastman nodded. "I've heard of that. But I thought there was a way of testing for it beforehand."

"There is." Shapiro's voice was weighted with fatigue, and Eastman thought, Everybody is bone-tired, only the snake is full of energy. "But you don't stop to test for allergic reaction when somebody is dying of snakebite. In other circumstances we'd have recognized the symptoms of anaphylactic shock. The trouble is, they're very similar to the symptoms of neurotoxic poisoning from snakebite, so we couldn't tell. The hives were on his back, and we didn't see them until it was too late."

"Yeah," Eastman said. "Has anybody told that girl out there?"

Shapiro said, "I'm going right out to tell her."

Eastman started toward the door. "I'm sorry, Doc."

As Eastman left the room he saw Converse. "That serum from the Bronx could make a big difference," Converse said.

"Not really," Eastman replied.

SIX

Converse said, "The name of the snake is black mamba. It is the largest poisonous snake in Africa and the deadliest."

It was eight thirty in the morning, and Jeff had been dead for almost two hours. Converse was sitting behind a scarred oak desk in the shooting range of the Central Park Precinct. The press was facing him, and he was flanked by Captain Eastman and Deputy Inspector Scott. The desk was cluttered with radio and television microphones. TV cameramen roamed the long room.

The DI had opened the press conference with a flat announcement that the perpetrator had been identified, and that Converse would provide background information and answer questions.

Holly Markham was sitting halfway back in the press section. She was wearing a yellow silk blouse that went beautifully with her black hair. She looked up from her notebook and smiled.

Converse said, "The black mamba is not actually black at all, but dark olive on top and whitish underneath. But in bright sunlight it has the appearance of being black, hence the name."

Someone asked, "What part of Africa does it come from?"

"It's distributed throughout most of Africa, except for the northernmost parts. Incidentally, there are three different kinds of mambas: the black; green, which is found in savanna country and riverine forests and is exclusively arboreal; and Jameson's, a rain-forest snake. All are slender, with a small, coffin-sided head."

"From the picture, how big do you judge our snake to be?"

"At least ten feet, maybe eleven. It's a superb specimen."

The DI muttered impatiently. Converse looked at him questioningly, then went on.

"In Africa the black mamba is held in awe, much as a tiger or lion might be. Some of the stories you hear about it are exaggerations, especially its speed. For example, there's a persistent claim that it can overtake a galloping horse."

"Can it?"

"It's unlikely. But it's undoubtedly the swiftest snake in the world. Estimates of its speed vary between seven and twenty miles per hour. My guess would be about ten miles an hour. I saw a few black mambas in Africa when I was a student. I can tell you that it's a genuinely intimidating sight to see an irritated black mamba racing across the ground with its head a foot and a half in the air and its mouth wide open. Being chased by an extremely venomous and aggressive snake doing ten miles an hour is the stuff nightmares are made of."

A reporter in the front row spoke up. "Isn't it pure myth that snakes chase people?"

"For the most part, yes," Converse said equably. "But certain snakes—the king cobra, the black mamba, others—will sometimes take out after somebody, usually on their breeding grounds during the mating season, or when they're highly irritated. And if a black mamba was chasing *you*, sir, I'd bet on the snake."

"You'd probably cheer the slimy thing on." The man scowled.

"As most people know by now," Converse said mildly, "snakes aren't slimy; they're dry and rather pleasant to the touch."

Holly Markham stood up. "Will it help you to find the snake now that you've identified it?"

Converse said, "It defines the problem without simplifying it. So far as its habits go, the black mamba is an all-purpose snake. It's arboreal part of the time—it lies in the low branches of trees or in bushes to take birds. It may bask on a treetop too, though, like most snakes, it likes a rock better. Most of the time it's terrestrial. It hides in thickets, under rocks, and very often in a well-concealed burrow."

Someone asked if the black mamba was as dangerous as a cobra.

"In my opinion, more so. It's a lot more aggressive, and it doesn't have to go into a set posture before it bites. In fact, it can strike with extreme effectiveness in any direction while it's running at top speed. The cobra strikes inaccurately in daylight. The black mamba is deadly by day or night. Taking everything into account, I'm inclined to think it's the most dangerous snake in the world."

"You mean the most poisonous?"

"It's not the most poisonous, although two tiny drops are sufficient to kill a man in as little as twenty minutes." He paused. The audience seemed impressed. "There are three elements that make a snake dangerous: potency of venom, position of fangs, and aggressiveness or disposition to bite. The black mamba rates high on all counts."

Someone called out, "What do you mean by position of fangs?"

"Some species have fangs situated at the rear of the mouth, so it's harder for them to bite accurately and efficiently. The venom of the boomslang of Africa, for example, is terrifically potent, but because it's rear-fanged it doesn't deliver its venom as effectively as the black mamba, whose fangs are in the front."

A small white-haired man asked what the most poisonous snake known was.

"The king cobra, largest of all poisonous snakes, can kill in fifteen minutes. But in highly venomous snakes the exact degree of potency doesn't make much difference. They all kill very quickly if antivenin isn't administered shortly after the bite."

Holly spoke up, asking him to define aggressiveness more fully.

"In simplest terms, willingness to bite when threatened or irritated. Some deadly snakes won't bite at all, except for food. Sea snakes, for example, are among the most poisonous known to man, but when fishermen bring them in in their nets, they just pick them up and throw them back into the water, and rarely seem to get bitten."

The DI was stirring restlessly. Converse, warming to his subject, ignored him.

"There's a very poisonous snake called the blue-banded krait. It's absolutely deadly at night, but simply can't be made to bite during daylight. Children play with them in African villages. People have been known to beat them with a stick, subject them to torture, without being bitten."

Someone called out, asking what the black mamba ate.

"Small mammals," Converse said. "Mainly rodents. As to frequency, snakes are erratic. They can go for long periods, months, without eating. It's largely a matter of opportunity; if food is around, they'll eat fairly often."

A television reporter said, "What about the old wives' tale about snakes not dying until sundown?"

"There's a fair amount of truth to it. Chop a snake's head off, and the body will continue to writhe for several hours. And a poisonous snake can inflict a fatal bite up to forty minutes after its head has been severed."

There were exclamations all around the room, and a good deal of note taking. It's the sensational details they want, Converse thought. They don't give a damn about what makes snakes tick.

A hand rose in the rear of the room. "Young man? How many

more people is this snake of yours going to bite before you kill it?"

"Why kill it? Why not capture it and put it into a zoo? If you're looking for a villain, blame the person who turned that black mamba loose in the park. He's the one to hate, not the snake."

The DI was on his feet. Unmindful of the microphones, he shouted, "Zoo, my foot. We're going to kill that damned snake."

He motioned imperiously to Converse, who changed seats with him. Eastman hitched his chair closer to the DI's. Together they began to grapple with questions about whether another sweep of the park in force was contemplated ("Not at this time"), what additional steps would be taken to protect the public ("The commissioner's office is working on the problem"), whether or not these steps might include closing the park ("We're just cops, we don't make that kind of decision").

Converse caught Holly's eye and she gave him a quick smile before she turned her attention back to the DI and Eastman. He continued to stare at her, compelling her to look at him. She did. Their eyes locked and held. He felt light-headed, giddy. The rest of the room was blurring, voices fading. Knowing his weakness, he knew himself to be in serious trouble.

Eastman's voice, coming as from a great distance, tugged at his attention. . . . "Unless Mr. Converse has anything to add?"

He shook his head. Eastman adjourned the press conference.

Converse threaded his way between the rows of chairs and made for the door. From the corner of his eye he saw Holly getting to her feet. He stopped abruptly. Awkwardly, they avoided looking at each other.

"Well," Holly said. She gave him a quick glance, then turned her eyes down and said, "Better get back to work."

"Well," Converse said. "See you around."

"See you."

Maybe they both wanted to linger, Converse thought, and maybe that was why neither of them did. No declaration of any kind, no exchange of phone numbers. Just "See you." All for the best.

HOLLY left the precinct to go back to her office. Converse decided to have a chat with the precinct's anticrime detectives.

The policeman at the main desk directed him to a small office opposite the desk, where four bearded men were polluting the air with cigarette smoke. They were dressed in dirty jeans, shirts that exposed their chests, leather belts. They were a part of the Central Park anticrime unit.

"You guys know the park," Converse said. "Where's the best place to hide? The least people, the most wild areas?"

One of the detectives said, "Uptown. North of Ninety-sixth Street. You could get lost in some parts up there."

Another detective said, "I thought the snake was biting people around Eightieth."

"Was," Converse said. "But its instinct would be to find a wilder and less frequented territory." He thanked the anticrime squad, and they wished him luck.

Converse left the park. At Amsterdam Avenue a New York *Post* truck hurled a pile of papers in the direction of a stationery store. He read the headline: SNAKE THREE, PEOPLE ZERO.

THE handout from the office of Hizzonner the mayor read: "I profoundly regret the tragic death of this fine young man to whose athletic prowess we thrilled so many times in the past." Jeff had been a second-string guard on the Columbia football team. "Yet, even in this moment of tragedy I cannot pass up the observation that he was foolhardy. If he had not tried to catch the snake, but had merely retreated, no harm would have befallen him.

"I take this opportunity once again to urge the public to exercise the utmost caution. Do not attempt to take matters into your own hands. The police, with the help of experts, are redoubling their efforts. Do not hamper them in their work. Do not endanger your own life. Please cooperate."

In response to the handout the Reverend Sanctus Milanese, whose views were now being sought by the media, told a reporter, "The members of the Church of the Purification are conscripted in the army of God to destroy the personification of evil. Can soldiers sit on the sidelines while this messenger of Satan crushes the city? The police are powerless. Only the godly are sanctioned for this work. They shall prevail who are pure."

"You're going to continue to search for the snake in defiance of the orders of the police and the mayor's instructions?"

"We will continue as before, and there may be new initiatives as God proposes them."

The police commissioner, told about the reverend's statement, said that the police would not tolerate vigilantism. Whoever disobeyed the police directives would be dealt with sternly.

CONVERSE went home, played with the python, played with the cat, and went to bed to catch up on his sleep.

Near ten o'clock that night he arrived back at Central Park headquarters with his stick and pillowcase, looking so refreshed and rested that Eastman, nervous and exhausted, almost hated him for it. Youth. But the prospect of getting out of the precinct house and doing something other than sitting at his desk palliated Eastman's sourness.

A police driver took Converse and Eastman to the Engineers' Gate, at Ninetieth and Fifth Avenue, and then followed the East Drive around the Receiving Reservoir. The park seemed to be twinkling with lights, and they could make out shadowy figures, some of whom must have been police personnel, others Puries. Driving, they were almost blinded by the sweeping floodlight of an emergency service unit truck.

"Where do you want to stop?" Eastman said.

"No place," Converse said. "What black mamba in its right mind would turn up with all this going on? Those lights? People clumping around everywhere? Forget it. It's going to hole up and stay hidden until everybody goes away."

Eastman's definition of "doing something" did not include riding around in a police car. "How the hell can you find it, if you don't get out and look for it?" he said.

"No way," Converse said. "If I knew all this was going on, I would have stayed home. And there's no sense getting sore, Captain. You want to get out, I'll keep you company, but it's a waste of time."

Eastman sat hunched against the window of the car, glowering.

Converse said, "Anyway, our best chance is to catch it basking. I'll be out here tomorrow morning just before first light."

Eastman sighed. "I guess you're right. Tomorrow morning—you going to pick me up?"

"I could," Converse said. "But . . ." His voice trailed off.

"But you'd rather not?"

Converse nodded. "It's really a one-man job."

Some seven hours later Converse stood in the center of the North Meadow. The invisible presence of the sun, hidden beneath the rooftops of Fifth Avenue, backlit the buildings and turned them into cutout silhouettes. Above, the sky was a mottled gray; to the west, it was still dark. But the approach of daylight was reassuring, and it evaporated the uneasiness Converse had felt when he had entered the park from Central Park West and begun to walk along the eerily deserted walkways.

The size of the area he had to cover was intimidating. Already, in his short walk, he had seen half a dozen heavily overgrown sites that might suit a black mamba as a hiding place. The question was where to start. At the moment he simply didn't know. It all seemed hopeless.

No. He shook his head, as if to reprove himself. He was a good herpetologist, he knew snakes, and he would turn up the black mamba no matter how much territory he had to scour. The real problem was that everyone was in such a hurry.

The sun was a whitish watery semicircle above the rooftops, and already he was beginning to feel its heat. So would the black mamba. At this very moment it might be moving, in its swift elegant glide, toward the rock it would bask on. Maybe. In this alien terrain it might feel safer basking in the top branches of a tall tree, then swinging down to shade in the thick foliage below.

He hoped its inclination would be otherwise; it would be very difficult to spot in a tree. As a rule, black mambas weren't all that shy. They were secure in the knowledge of their speed and the potency of their bite, and since this one was obviously highly aggressive, it was reasonable to expect that it would choose to bask on a luxurious rock.

Okay, Converse told himself, let's get organized. No point trying to check out any rocks today, too random, not likely to produce results. The sun was already climbing fast; the snake wouldn't require much exposure in this heat. Best idea would be to explore the whole northern sector, east to west, from the Ninety-seventh Street transverse to the end of the park, marking out likely places for closer examination.

There were lots of likely places—wild, untended areas with tangled brush, fallen trees, piles of leaves and dead branches. He moved slowly and methodically. The watchword was patience.

WITHIN THIRTY-SIX HOURS after Jeff's well-publicized death, the mood of the public had turned hysterical, to something approaching mass neurosis. This mood was nourished by what the newspapers took to calling "snake-associated" events.

The first of these incidents took place in a crowded movie house. A voice (whether female, or male screaming in falsetto, was never established) called out, "Snake! The snake is here!" In the panicky rush toward the exits, people were injured badly enough to be hospitalized. After the theater was emptied, the police searched the house but found no snake.

In the incident at Macy's department store, more than a hundred and fifty people were injured when a live snake appeared suddenly in the aisles of the main floor. Several women saw it at the same time and uttered piercing screams. The snake, in a panic of its own, scudded behind a counter, then disappeared. When it was found, after the entire floor had been cleared and the casualties had been taken away in ambulances, it was identified as a black racer, a thoroughly harmless snake but one which superficially resembled a black mamba. The perpetrator was never found, although the police checked the stories of several witnesses who claimed to have seen a shifty-eyed man carrying a wicker basket.

BY THE end of the third day, Converse had covered about sixty percent of the area between Ninety-seventh Street and the north end of the park. Each day he would arrive at the park before dawn and position himself where he could watch a likely rock. When he had convinced himself that the snake was not going to appear, he would try a second rock. By that time the sun would have been up for a couple of hours and the snake, wherever it was, would have finished basking. He would then start checking out trees, although the snake's olive-slate coloration would make it difficult to spot in the shadow-dappled foliage. He would finish up by wading through heavily overgrown patches where the black mamba might have found a burrow.

At ten a.m., exhausted, he would call it quits and check in at the precinct house. By then, anyway, there were too many people around—amateur herpetologists (averaging about fourteen years of age), uniformed officers and detectives, and, of course, the omnipresent Puries.

This morning, when Converse walked into the office of the commander of the Central Park Precinct, Eastman looked alert, as though he had caught up on some sleep. But his face sagged when he saw the empty pillowcase.

"I didn't find the black mamba," Converse said primly, "but I've eliminated another area, and that's progress."

"Yeah, I guess so, I guess you could call it progress."

"Count your blessings, Captain. Since that fellow in the zoo, nobody else has been bitten. Maybe it's dead."

"You believe that?"

Converse shook his head. "No."

"It hasn't bitten anybody else, but it's still a threat. Anyway, even if it is dead, that won't be the end of it unless we can prove it. You been reading the papers?"

Converse nodded. "They're all crazy in this city. That's not the snake's fault." He got to his feet. "Maybe I'll find it tomorrow," he said as he left the office. He felt depressed.

At eleven thirty that night he phoned Holly Markham. He had looked her up in the Manhattan phone book.

"Yes?" Her voice was tentative, wary.

He said, "I'm sorry. This is Mark Converse."

"Why are you calling at this hour?"

He couldn't tell if she was glad to hear from him. He said, "I'm calling because I have a very strong feeling for you."

He heard her make a little sound of surprise. Then she said, "Well, I have a very strong feeling for you too. But that's no reason to call up in the middle of the night."

"You have a strong feeling for me? You're joking?"

"I'm not joking, Mark."

"You're not joking?"

"No, I'm not." There was apprehension in her voice; it quavered.

"Look, I've got to see you. I need you very badly. Can I come to your place? Will you come down here?"

After a long silence she said, "What you mean is that you *want* me. That's honorable, but it's different from needing me. If you ever really need me, call me and I'll come right over. Okay?"

He hung up the phone without answering. He went to bed and ran the conversation over and over in his mind. In the end, he vowed never to call her again, and to stop loving her at once.

THE SNAKE NO LONGER came out of its burrow during daylight hours, except briefly each morning to bask on a nearby rock.

On this night, as it had on several previous nights, it drank from the Loch, midway between the East and West drives. On the way back to its burrow it surprised a squirrel. The squirrel leaped for the base of a tree and began to scramble up, but the snake launched an upward strike and sank its fangs just above the bushy tail. The squirrel slipped back momentarily, but recovered and scampered upward.

The snake waited below, staring up into the shadowed branches. Its sharp eyes picked up the squirrel when it began to fall, and followed its descent to the ground. After eating the squirrel, the snake returned to its burrow; digestion, already begun by the injection of venom, would take approximately six hours.

SEVEN

Holly showed her press card, and a tall, muscular, expressionless Purie, wearing the armband of the reverend's security squad, led her down an aisle of the Tabernacle to a seat in the front row. The man sitting next to her was a city news reporter from the Associated Press.

The reverend's recruitment meeting had drawn a full house. The crowd was young—mostly in its early twenties—and was hushed and expectant. Holly looked at the flier she had been given at the door. It was an application form for membership in the Church of the Purification. No selling copy, no hype, just a few dotted lines for name, address, age, present religious affiliation.

"They're getting members," the AP man said. "According to our church-news man, they've been signing up in droves, the usual white kids from good families."

The Purie membership was overwhelmingly middle class, with access to money from parents, no matter how much the parents opposed the reverend. Whatever else you said about him, Holly thought, he was shrewd. His latching on to the issue of the snake looked certain to result in enlarged membership and increased revenue, which would help support his real estate holdings, the cost of his limousines, his personal French chef . . .

The organ played a sudden monitory chord in A minor and held it in a trembling vibrato. A dazzling spotlight settled on a white door at the side of the stage. The door opened and the Reverend Sanctus Milanese strode to the podium, the spotlight accompanying him.

It wasn't a very good show, Holly thought. Not that it was bad, either. Her notes read: "Usual burning eyes, evangelical tones. Star in fine fettle, but material old hat. Snake is Satan's messenger. Can be captured only by the pure in heart—guess who? The location of the lair in which the evil serpent lurks will soon be vouchsafed to us by Him. All in good time, however, for He moves in mysterious ways His miracles, etc. Drama trite, leading man terrific."

Nevertheless, the audience was eating it up.

The AP man was obviously disappointed. He whispered, "I was half hoping he would come up with something wild—like the Chinese thing." A year earlier, for some fancied slight, the reverend had had his adherents try to set fire to the Chinese consulate.

The reverend was expounding on the villainous role the snake had played throughout history. Symbol of evil from time immemorial, servant of Satan, eager to do his heinous bidding.

Holly let the sound of the reverend's voice wash over her. She had really been glad that Mark Converse had phoned her. She had really wanted to go to him, and only the intervention of her guardian angel, who checked in whenever she became too susceptible to her emotions, had prevented it. Right, guardian angel. Chaps lose respect for a girl who's that available. Right? Wrong. Better to follow where the heart led.

The reverend was making his pitch for recruits. Come to us, enlist in the legions of the pure, who shall inherit the earth more surely than the meek, step forward and offer a sign that you long to be purified.

With an operatic swirl of his cape, red and black mingling richly, the reverend walked off, attended by the faithful spotlight.

Holly started up the aisle. At the door, a wooden box was overflowing with membership applications. The reverend was on the beam, Holly thought; he was riding the snake's tail to glory.

IF THREE years as a reporter of city news had taught Holly Markham anything at all, it was to take nothing on faith. And so, late that afternoon, she went around to the public library and, sitting in the north reading room with a stack of books, compiled notes on the relationship of snake and man from "time immemorial." Her findings not only refuted much of the reverend's sweeping claim but overturned a few conceptions of her own.

"Rev's assertion"—she wrote in her racing shorthand—"that snake 'symbol of evil from time immemorial' is nonsense. Actually such is case only two thousand years, and even then only in *Western* theologies. Fact is, from 'time immemorial' man's reaction to snake highly contradictory: worshipped, feared, hated, admired. Many civilizations, both primitive and advanced, held snake to be deity or semideity; Hopi Indians used snakes as go-betweens to plead with rain gods to make rain.

"More snake worship: pythons in Africa; king cobra in Burma. Cobra also venerated in India; in old days, Dravidians believed headmen reincarnated as cobras. Mexico: famous Quetzalcoatl, feathered serpent, god of civilization, inventor of agriculture, metallurgy, patron of all the arts!

"Babylon: snake symbol for Ishtar, goddess of sexual love. Snake obvious phallic symbol, ancients knew it before Freud. Greeks and Romans both used to regard snakes as sacred creatures. Household pets in old Rome. Egyptians supposed to have kept snakes in home too—tamed asps. Check with M. Converse, can poisonous snakes be tamed? *Don't* check with M. Converse, ulterior motive involved—right?

"Ancient Greece: snake regarded as healer. *Vide* Aesculapius, god of medicine. Caduceus, staff wreathed with two snakes, carried by Hermes, still familiar emblem of physicians and medicine. Go fight the American Medical Association, Reverend!

"But with coming of Christianity, snake firmly established as symbol of evil. Christians opposed idea of snake worship (one God, right?) so fingered it as epitome of evil. Snake tricked Adam and Eve into original sin and expulsion from Eden. Medieval artists put shoulder to wheel, selling idea of snake as symbol of evil.

"Fact: although people die of snakebite—most in Asia, Australia, Africa, fewest in Europe, U.S.A.—number comparatively small. Many more humans poison snakes than other way around. Most common—sprays used to kill insects, insects swallowed by snakes, accumulate in liver, liver swells until snake dies painful death. No snakes eat humans, but humans eat snakes. In Hong Kong, discerning diners eat poison kraits and cobras. U.S.A.—rattlers on menus, used to be known as prairie eel.

"Theories on why people hate snakes: they prefer upright animals, reflecting own image; they like expressive animals such as dogs; snakes are stony-eyed because have no way of closing eyes. Probably not poisonousness of snakes that fills humans with revulsion so much as slitheriness. But children two and three years old like snakes. Around four, begin to develop aversion. (Proves no *innate* fear of snakes, but assigned fear by parents?)

"Medicine: snakeskins used to cure everything from lumbago to hot flashes. U.S.A.—in more innocent times, hustlers sold 'snake oil' as panacea. Pliny prescribed snake fat to cure baldness. Central American Indians drank rattlesnake venom as aphrodisiac.

"Talk to editor about using some of this stuff as shirttail piece to reverend story? Remember bits and pieces to show M. Converse how terrifically knowledgeable I am?"

THE snake cornered a rat near the retaining wall along Central Park West, but the surprise was not complete. The rat heard the slight sound of the snake's movement and, before the snake could strike, ran away along the base of the wall. At an opening to the street, the rat rounded the wall into the four-a.m. stillness of Central Park West. It paused briefly at the curb. When the snake slid around the wall onto the pavement, the rat fled across the street. Halfway up the street the rat tired, and the snake gained on it. The rat darted to its left, scampered behind a brownstone stoop, and hopped through the bars of an open window leading into a basement apartment.

The snake crawled past the stoop to the window. It inserted its head and neck through the bars, swaying, then slid forward onto a table beneath the window. Without stopping, without waiting for its posterior to clear the bars, it began to wind down the table leg to the floor. It paused, then glided through an open doorway into another room. It paused again, and now its flicking tongue brought in odors other than those of the rat.

WEBSTER McPeek would never truly know whether he heard the snake or was simply awakened by instinct. He sat upright in bed, and saw the snake almost at once and very clearly, in a fling of light from the streetlamp outside. McPeek shouted, loud and hoarse, his voice clogged by fear. His wife awoke in panic and, when she saw the snake, screamed. The snake started to curl its long, slender body forward, and when McPeek realized that it was heading toward the children's bedroom, he leaped out of bed and ran after it toward the open door.

But the children, roused by the shouting, appeared wide-eyed and frightened in the doorway. The snake was between McPeek and the children. He tried to wave them back into their room, but they ran toward him, arms outstretched. He ran to them blindly, his wife just behind him.

IN THE darkness the snake struck out in a panic at the threshing legs, the stamping feet that threatened it. It struck several times, until the feet and legs retreated. Then it turned in a tight arc and glided swiftly back the way it had come, its head high. It wound up the table leg in a continuous motion and slid through the window bars.

The snake pushed itself down the street toward the park. Pressing down hard with its scutes, throwing its body into powerful curves, it ran along the base of the retaining wall until it found the opening it had come through in pursuit of the rat. In the park, it slid into the concealment of grass and brush.

WEST Side Hospital, although it was accustomed to the presence of the police, had never known such a convocation of high brass as it now had in its waiting room. It was five thirty in the morning, and such was the haste with which the group had gathered that most were unshaved. Captain Eastman had made the call that set the meeting in motion. As soon as the report came in, he had phoned DI Scott, who had in his turn called the deputy chief of the Special Operations Division, parent organization of the emergency service unit. The deputy chief had phoned the borough commander, and so it had gone, upward through the ranks, to the commissioner himself.

In the emergency ward, an augmented Emercrit group (West Side's equivalent of East Side's Code Blue team) was working to save the lives of Webster McPeek, his wife, Emily, and the two McPeek children—Webster junior, nine years old, and Charlene, six. All had been administered black mamba antivenin immediately upon arrival at the hospital. The two males seemed to be responding well, but Mrs. McPeek and Charlene were touch and go.

The police brass were deep in conference. Presently the division deputy chief separated himself from the group and beckoned DI Vincent Scott to one side.

"The heat's on," the chief said. "When it starts biting people outside of the park, it's going too far. Those people that got bitten. They're a fine, wonderful family. You get the point?"

"Yes, sir. There's going to be a public outcry."

The chief nodded. "Your job is on the line, Vincent. You've got forty-eight hours to get the snake. After that, you'll be reassigned to someplace dirty. Nobody's fooling around now. This comes straight from the top."

As THE chief finished speaking to DI Scott, Converse's alarm clock went off. He sipped a cup of instant coffee while he shaved and dressed, and turned off the air conditioner before he left. A cab took him to One Hundredth Street and Central Park West. He got out near the Boys' Gate, shifted the Pillstrom tongs to his shoulder, and headed into the park.

The sky was lightening, but the sun was not yet up. It was the eleventh or twelfth day of the heat wave—he had lost count—and this was going to be another ninety-plus day.

He ambled eastward along the walkways, dreaming about Holly Markham. By the time he reached his first target area of the day, not far from the short road (CLOSED TO THE PUBLIC—POLICE ONLY) that connected the East and West drives, the sun was starting to clear the buildings on Fifth Avenue.

The site was a hollow in a heavily wooded area, dense with undergrowth, bushes, ground creeper, weeds, a couple of fallen trees, and, above it, a large flat plateau of rock. It was a beautifully convenient rock, Converse thought, within the perfect neighborhood for a black mamba's home. But that had been the case, to be sure, in a dozen previous sites he had checked out.

He inched forward toward the rock, careful to avoid setting up vibrations that a snake might "hear." He took cover behind a thick bush, where, if he didn't move about unduly, he wouldn't be likely to be spotted by a snake's sharp eyes.

A long bar of sunlight appeared on a margin of the rock. Converse shut his eyes against the brightness, and when he next opened them the entire rock was bathed in sunshine, providing an irresistible basking place for a black mamba.

When he first heard the sound—or *thought* he heard it; it might have been wishful thinking—he pushed his head forward, straining. Nothing. Silence. Then he heard it again, a mere whisper of sound, but continuous now, and his heartbeat accelerated with an almost painful abruptness. Not daring to move, he listened with terrific intensity, and presently he was sure of it.

It wasn't much of a sound, and an untrained person might not have heard it at all, or, hearing it, have dismissed it as of no consequence. But to a herpetologist it was unique and unmistakable—an innocent enough rustle, much like the sound of a jump rope being drawn through grass. His heart was thumping so hard that for a moment he entertained the ludicrous notion that it was straining the thin material of his T-shirt.

As the sound came perceptibly closer beneath the rock, he thought joyously, Converse, you're a lucky man. No—it wasn't luck at all, but a reward. He had been doing all the right things, he had been patient and painstaking, and sooner or later it was inevitable that he would find it.

Tingling with excitement, Converse looked out over the flat sunbathed surface and knew that in just another moment a small head would appear over the rim of the rock. The rope-dragging sound intensified, and he braced himself for his first sight of the snake.

Then the sound stopped.

THE snake felt the vibrations first at a distance. It paused below the rock and raised its head warily. It could see nothing threatening. But the disturbing vibrations continued. Then all at once the ground began to shake, leaves and small stones flew, and there was a great wind. The snake whipped around and turned into the brush. It pushed past the debris around the entrance to the burrow and slid inside to safety.

LATER, Converse was to realize that he should have heard it long before he did—but he was intensely concentrated on the top of the rock and the sound of dragging rope.

When the leaves and small stones stung his legs, and the trees and bushes began swaying, the sound crashed in on him with a roar. He looked up just as the blue-and-white police helicopter passed over him, so low that it barely seemed to clear the treetops. No longer cautious, he leaped up onto the flat shelf of the rock. He shook his fist up at the helicopter and screamed, "You idiots! You dumb, stupid saboteurs!"

THE Central Park Precinct was seething with activity when Converse arrived. Nobody paid any attention to him as he went down the corridor to the commander's office. Eastman barely glanced at him. He was on the phone, speaking about the deployment of police from other precincts to duty in the park. He was unshaved, his clothes were rumpled, his blue eyes puffy.

By the time Eastman finished his phone call, Converse's anger had simmered down. Nevertheless, the first words he said were, "Well, you ruined it, Captain."

Eastman looked startled, but he didn't say anything.

"A helicopter," Converse said. "It would have been cheaper to call the snake up on the telephone and warn it to take cover. Why didn't somebody ask me about it? I could have told you it wouldn't work. You promised to give me time."

"Time ran out a few hours ago," Eastman said. He took note of Converse's puzzlement. "You didn't hear about it?"

Converse shook his head, and Eastman told him about the McPeek family. "The little girl died a few hours ago. The wife is still on the critical list."

"Oh, God." Converse knew it to be the kind of accident that occurred from time to time in Africa, when a black mamba would pursue a rodent into a house. His eyes welled with tears.

"We have no more time for the scientific approach," Eastman said. "We're putting every man we can spare into the park, and we're going through the houses on the street where the family was bitten. And that's why we put the helicopter in the air."

"It's awful," Converse said. He brushed at his eyes. "But you won't help anybody by using a helicopter." Remembering how the ground had trembled, Converse's indignation returned. "That stupid machine, just when the snake . . . might have been coming out to bask."

555

He had almost given himself away. Had Eastman detected the slight hesitation?

"What happened this morning?" Eastman's voice was heavy with suspicion. "Were you on its trail?"

"If I was on its trail, I'd have picked it up after the helicopter was gone, wouldn't I?"

And so he should have done. He should have waded into that hollow and turned it over until he found the snake. But he had been carried away by anger.

"Because," Eastman said, "if I find out that you located it and aren't telling, so help me, I'll beat the daylights out of you."

Converse said calmly, "Relax, Captain, you sound like an old-fashioned tough-guy cop. I know you're not, but—"

The hand that closed on the back of his neck was like a steel clamp. Converse wrenched himself free and whirled around to see whose hand it was.

"Get the hell out," DI Scott said, "and don't come back."

Converse walked slowly along Central Park West, touching his neck tenderly from time to time. Nobody had manhandled him that way since he was a kid, but his indignation was tempered by the thought that he had lied to Eastman. He liked Eastman. But, like everybody else, Eastman wanted to kill the snake.

There was no hurry. He would return to the park later, after the police had cleared out. He would go down into that hollow and stay there until he found the black mamba. He would catch it, bag it, and . . . then what? Sneak it up to the Bronx Zoo and give it to his old boss for safekeeping? What he would really like to do was shove it down DI Scott's shirt collar.

He passed a group of Puries being herded by some cops into patrol cars. More work for the reverend's lawyer, who had been kept busy for the last few days bailing out the flock.

Converse crossed the street and caught a bus. The man beside him had a newspaper. The headline announced the death of Mrs. Emily McPeek. Converse wept. The man moved to another seat.

The attack on the McPeek family affected the city as no previous event had done. The fact that the snake had invaded a victim's living quarters created a new level of terror.

556

That evening the mayor phoned the police commissioner. "The snake," he said. "It's making national and even international news. The hotels and restaurants and theaters and airlines are driving me crazy. Hundreds of cancellations. We need those tourists, Francis. Destroy that snake before it destroys *us*."

EIGHT

GRAHAM Black, humble soldier in the army of the Church of the Purification, stood on the flat rock and stared down into the hollow. It was deeply shadowed with the dark of evening and the over-hanging miasma of evil. Down there, he was sure, lurked the beast, the messenger of Satan, upon whom the beloved Reverend Sanctus Milanese had declared holy war.

If Graham Black had been capable of detachment, he might have recognized the familiarity of the revelation that he was experiencing. He'd known it each time he explored another possible hiding place in his assigned sector of the park. But Graham Black did not question himself. He knew only certainty.

As he started off the rock and down into the shadows, he felt himself trembling in expectation. He ducked his head and swept aside the low-hanging branches of a tree.

Now, responding to another of the imperatives that directed its behavior, the snake had defined the perimeters of its territory and would defend them jealously. It would be more than usually alert to threat, more irritable and willing to bite. So that, when it felt the impact of footsteps on the substrate, it did not withdraw into its burrow, but instead began to hiss harshly, its head inclined forward, its mouth gaped wide, its body tensed to strike.

GRAHAM Black was gazing at Evil, its mouth open to an astonishing width, swaying, hissing. He wondered if he might not advance upon the beast, seize its terrible head in his hands, and throttle it. But the Reverend Sanctus had forbidden such an action. "Do not attempt to deal with the serpent yourself. Only note where it hides, and then justice will be done. Anything else is vanity."

Perhaps it was as well. The serpent was truly horrifying, and, looking into its terrible staring eyes, he felt fear.

557

His mission was accomplished; he had found out the serpent. But the snake's wide stare was compelling, hypnotic, and he lingered. Then, just as he turned to leave, the snake began to move toward him, gliding over the leaves. But he remembered being told that a snake only rarely pursued a man and that, in the event that it did, a man could easily outdistance it.

He put his back to the advancing snake and, lifting his feet high to clear the underbrush, started running. When he began to climb upward from the hollow toward the rock, he turned to look over his shoulder. The serpent was still pursuing, and it had closed the gap between them, its head high on a forward slant.

Graham Black did not look behind him again. Straining, he pushed upward toward the rock, and he had almost reached it when he felt a blow against the calf of his right leg.

WHEN Captain Eastman arrived at East Side Hospital, the reception room was crowded with reporters. His ID got him past the security man guarding the entrance to the emergency ward, but no farther. At the door of the room where the Code Blue team was working on Graham Black, the guard wouldn't budge.

Eventually the door opened and Dr. Shapiro came out.

"How is he, Doc?" Eastman asked.

Shapiro said, "He's responding to the antivenin. We think he's going to make it."

"Thank God," Eastman said. "He can tell us where the snake is. Can I go in and see him?"

Shapiro shook his head. "No. Anyway, he won't talk to you. He won't even talk to *us*. He flatly refuses to say a word to anybody but the Reverend Sanctus Milanese."

THE Reverend Milanese's gleaming Rolls-Royce turned into the emergency ward driveway, and was surrounded by reporters before it had come to a stop. Cameras focused through the windows to the back of the car, where the reverend's saturnine face, shrouded in the stiff collar of his cloak, could barely be discerned.

The limousine door opened, and the Reverend Milanese emerged with a flash of scarlet cape lining. Surrounded by his bodyguards, he swept through the crowd to the entrance and on into the emergency ward, ignoring the protesting hospital security guard.

Presently those in the reception room heard shouts and the sound of scuffling. Later, the guard posted in front of Graham Black's room told reporters that the Puries had forced their way into the room and roughed him up in the process. He exhibited a welt on his right cheekbone, and said that he would bring suit against the Church of the Purification for aggravated assault.

In the hospital cafeteria, Captain Eastman drank his coffee, looking at the phone at the cashier's elbow. Dr. Shapiro had promised to call him as soon as the reverend arrived, the arrogant, phony Reverend Sanctus Milanese.

Eastman had no patience for the fanatical Puries. It was inevitable, the way they had been roaming through the park, that one of them would get bitten. And now, what new idiocy would the reverend dream up to harass an already overworked police force?

When the telephone rang he reached across the counter and took it out from under the cashier's hand. The Reverend Milanese had just left the emergency room, he was told.

Eastman yelled, *"Left?"* and slammed the phone down. He ran up the stairs to the reception room.

The reverend, surrounded by his bodyguards, faced newsmen who were shouting questions: "Did you speak to him?" "What did he tell you?" "Do you know where the snake is?"

The reverend held his hand out, palm up, for silence. "I have seen Graham Black and I have prayed with him."

"Is that all? Didn't he say anything about the snake?"

The reverend faced the speaker. "Graham Black beseeched me to carry on the task imposed upon us, namely, to exterminate the messenger of Satan and so purify the tainted city. I pledged new initiatives to destroy the wicked serpent."

There was another volley of questions: "What new initiatives?" "Will you tell the police what Graham Black told you?" "Are you going to defy the warning about vigilante actions?"

"We shall do God's bidding in the way that He prescribes. We obey His laws, not the police commissioner's."

The reverend nodded to his guards, who began to push against the crowd toward the exit. The reporters followed, still shouting. A TV newsman reached over with his microphone. "Reverend, how soon can we expect these new initiatives to start?"

The reverend, after a moment's hesitation, said, "Armageddon is tomorrow. The emissary of Satan will be extirpated."

The reverend's guard swept out into the courtyard and the reporters piled out after them. Eastman crossed the almost empty reception room and went into the emergency ward. Shapiro was in the corridor, sitting on a stretcher, his legs dangling.

"You promised to call me when he got here," Eastman said.

Shapiro looked up with a bitter smile. "They manhandled us. Those Purie goons just charged in and shoved us all to one corner, so they could talk without being overheard. I had no way of calling you, I was under *restraint*."

"Did it look as if he was interrogating the patient?"

Shapiro nodded. "He showed Graham a sheet of paper, a map maybe, and he looked at it and pointed at it."

"You couldn't make out *anything* they were saying?"

"Not a word. They were whispering, and we were off in the corner with those goons glowering at us. I swear, you could *smell* the violence in them. In a hospital. In a *hospital*."

"Will you let me talk to him now?"

Shapiro shrugged. "Why not? But you won't get anything out of it. He won't talk to you."

For all of the time Eastman was in the room bending over him, Graham Black looked up at the ceiling. He gave no indication that he knew Eastman was speaking to him, or even that he was there.

After two minutes Shapiro escorted Eastman from the room. "I'm sorry," Shapiro said, "but I told you."

WHEN Holly still hadn't shown up by seven forty-five for a seven-o'clock date, Converse knew that the day—which had begun with the helicopter and gone on with his being fired by the DI and having his neck squeezed—was going to be a red-starred calamity.

For a while he had been sure he was going to turn the day around. He had phoned Holly at her newspaper. When he heard her voice he said, "This is Mark Converse. Can I see you tonight?"

"Yes, of course."

"I don't think you could classify it as a case of actual need. I just want to see you."

"I want to see you too."

She had named the time and the place. The place was a five-minute walk from his apartment on Charles Street, and was called, for no reason he could fathom, the Blue Griffin. Before he realized that she was so late, he had sat at the bar and amused himself by trying to think of more appropriate names.

At seven thirty he decided to leave. Half an hour late was already too much leeway; it bespoke indifference, at the very least. But he ordered another drink, to delay broaching the heat outside.

He became aware that someone was calling out his name. There was a phone call for him. He took his drink and found the phone booth in the deeper recesses of the room. It was Holly.

". . . trying to get you, but the phone there was busy. I looked for you at the hospital. . . . What did you say?"

He had groaned.

She said, "You don't know? Didn't Captain Eastman call you?"

"Dead?"

"He's going to recover. He's a Purie. Why didn't they tell you?"

"I got fired this morning. Was he able to talk?"

"Fired? What do you mean you were fired? How did it happen?"

"Come down here," he said, "and I'll tell you."

"Tell me now." She spoke hurriedly. "I'm at the office, finishing up my story. It belongs in the story."

"No." It's unimportant, he thought, and the only thing that matters is your getting here as soon as possible.

"If you won't tell me yourself, I'll have to phone Captain Eastman and ask him."

"What do you mean *have* to?"

"And then it'll take me longer to get downtown to meet you. But if you tell me now—"

"It's a question of priorities, right?" He was deliberately sloshing his drink around. She was silent. "Right?" he asked.

"Don't be unreasonable."

"Unreasonable. Unreasonable is what it's all about, isn't it?" He waited. "Well, isn't it?" The line hummed. He hung up.

CONVERSE stood at the bedroom window of his apartment. With masochistic zeal he totted up the disasters: helicopter, getting fired, DI squeezing neck, Holly's clay feet, and—why had he put it out of mind?—the biting of the Purie. If he had gone down into the hollow after the helicopter incident, instead of screaming at Eastman like a piqued adolescent, he would have deprived the Purie of the opportunity of getting bitten. It had never occurred to him that someone else would find the snake's hiding place.

"Converse," he said aloud, "you're a murderer and a punk."

The self-accusation was exaggerated. The Purie was alive, thank God. Nevertheless, he himself had behaved very badly. Tomorrow morning—a new, unsullied day—he would go to the park, descend into that hollow, and catch that damn snake once and for all.

It was, he thought, quite a snake. How many had it killed—four, five? He had heard of a black mamba in Africa that had killed some eleven people before it was taken. The herpetologist who had told him about it had characterized it as a rogue.

Well, he was inclined to give the snake in the park the benefit of the doubt. Irritable, yes, but with good reason, what with being in an alien terrain and under the constant strain of being threatened. But whether it was a rogue or simply a snake instinctively defending itself, it was sure as hell an aggressive individual of an aggressive species.

He decided to take a leaf from his boyhood when, on disaster-filled days, his mother would pop him into bed early. He would now declare this day finished by going to sleep at eight thirty. Moodily he fell into bed.

He woke with the ringing of the doorbell. He got up and felt his way through the darkness to the living room. Without bothering to ask who was there, he opened the door. Holly. She was wearing tailored yellow slacks and some kind of a slipover blouse. He was wearing ragged denim shorts.

She said, "I went to the Blue Griffin first, thinking you might still be there. Can I come in?"

He said, "Sorry, I'm not talking to the press today."

"Please?"

He stepped aside to let her in. She walked halfway across the dim room. He stood near the door and watched. She turned to face him and said, "You could use some light in this room. Can I have a drink?"

"I don't give drinks to reporters." He heard his own voice with a feeling of surprise. It was choked.

She said, "I do believe you care," and walked back across the room toward him, smiling.

CAPTAIN EASTMAN LAY on a cot in the office of the Central Park Precinct's commander and slept intermittently and poorly. Earlier he had attended a meeting at the borough commander's office on East Twenty-first Street. The borough commander had said that there was no doubt that the Puries knew the whereabouts of the snake, and that they would go after it tomorrow, as their reverend had promised. Their headquarters were under surveillance. Dozens of Puries had been coming and going ever since the reverend's return from the hospital. Therefore, the park would be saturated with police beginning an hour before dawn. There were augmented patrols out tonight, with orders to pick up anybody on foot and run them out of the park.

Eastman dozed briefly and woke, remembering his telephone conversation with Holly Markham, who wanted to know why Converse had been fired. She kept pressing him, and finally, in exasperation, he went beyond the scope of her questions and blurted out that Converse knew where the snake was hiding. But when she asked what evidence he had to back up his statement, he said that there wasn't any evidence, it was just a hunch.

But Eastman knew that he was right, that Converse *did* know. The longer he thought of it, tossing on the lumpy mattress, the angrier he became. What I should do, he said, half aloud, is go down there and beat on him until he tells me where the snake is.

CONVERSE said, "I want to pay you a compliment."

Holly smiled. She had an infinite variety of smiles, all bewitching; this one was a half smile, mysterious and tender.

"The compliment is, you're the brightest girl I ever met."

She laughed, then she drew his head down and kissed him. Her hand trailed lightly down his chest.

They exchanged playful kisses, until suddenly Converse was speaking to her seriously, even anxiously. "I know exactly where that black mamba is," he said. "I could have caught it this morning, even after the helicopter, but I didn't. So that Purie found it and got bitten. I'm responsible for that. And the Puries are going after it tomorrow, and someone else might get bitten, maybe even tonight."

He started to slip on his shoes.

"What are you doing?"

"I'm going to catch the black mamba," Converse said. "Before it bites anybody else."

"Mark, I don't want you to leave me, I really don't. Besides, it's dangerous at night, isn't it?"

A buzzer sounded. Converse went to the window and looked out. He said, "It's Eastman," and called out, "I'll be right down."

Holly said, "I'm going along."

"No way."

"Listen, if you're going to act like a herpetologist, you can't stop me from acting like a reporter, can you?"

SHE was a lovely girl, Eastman thought. She was in love with Converse, and he felt the bite of envy.

Converse, who was carrying his snake-catching stick and a large flashlight, looked at the waiting taxi in surprise. "How did you know I would come? After all, your boss gave me the boot this morning."

"I'm a pretty good judge of character." They got in the cab, and Eastman said to Holly, "Where can we drop you?"

She shook her head. "I'm going with you."

Eastman started to protest. Converse said, "Save your breath, Captain. I tried."

"She might get hurt."

"Don't worry, I'll see to it."

The driver was looking back at them. Eastman said, "Where do we go?"

"The Boys' Gate, One Hundredth Street and Central Park West," Converse said. The snake's territory was closer to the east side, but he was more familiar with the approach from the west.

The taxi made good time until it reached Eighty-sixth Street, and then it began to crawl and, finally, stopped at the end of a long line of stalled traffic.

"What's all this?" Eastman said to the driver. "Can you see anything?"

"Fya rengines," the driver said. "Fya rengines and cop cars."

Eastman rolled down his window and heard a clangorous blend of emergency sounds: sirens, wailers, hooters. He pushed the door open and ducked his head out beneath the cab's roof.

"The whole damn park is on fire!" he said.

NINE

Operation Pillar of Fire had begun at the tick of midnight; thus, the night had technically become "tomorrow," and none would be able to accuse the Reverend Sanctus Milanese of having borne false witness.

Approximately sixty Puries took part in the operation. Eight "diversionary" squads were designated by consecutive letters of the alphabet, A through H. The larger, ninth squad went by the letter S for serpent. All, men and women alike, were dressed in black slacks, black polo shirts, black socks and shoes. Squads A to H carried three five-gallon drums of gasoline. Squad S carried five drums, and its members were armed with shovels, axes, hoes, rakes, baseball bats, and roughly hewn forked sticks.

The members of Operation Pillar of Fire assembled at widely dispersed points. They entered the park in cars through nine different gates. Several cars passed patrolling police, but there were no incidents; they were indistinguishable from any other cars driving through the park. The squads were dropped off as near as possible to their assigned destinations; then the cars drove away.

The diversionary sites were spread throughout the park and away from the prime target area. The two southernmost locations were near the zoo and along the Bridle Path near the Dalehead Arch. The northernmost sites were located in the Conservatory Garden and across the park on the Great Hill. One group penetrated a wild area of the Ramble, another, the opposite side of the Lake, at Cherry Hill. The seventh group was at the King Jagiello monument, a slight way from the Seventy-ninth Street transverse, and the eighth in the center of the East Meadow.

Later, many people were to express astonishment that a plan of such complexity could have been mounted in the four hours since the reverend had returned from East Side Hospital. But that was not the case. The operation, in a different form, had been drilled meticulously for the past three days. At its inception, Operation Pillar of Fire had been a scattershot affair, in which more than twenty-five wild areas of the park were to be set on fire in the hope that the snake would be driven from cover. But when Graham Black had pinpointed on a parks department map the precise location of the snake, everything changed.

Operation Pillar of Fire was under the command of its architect, Buckley Pell, a former Marine Corps sergeant. After his expulsion from the corps with a less than honorable discharge for "undue savagery," Buck Pell had repented of his massively godless past and joined the Church of the Purification. He became an organizer and leader of the reverend's bodyguards.

Buck Pell had trained his squads to concert pitch, and their performance was exemplary. Each diversionary squad arrived at its target area no later than five minutes past midnight. They proceeded to saturate the ground, the bushes, and the lower branches of trees with gasoline. The squad leader, meanwhile, had laid a trailer—a ten-foot length of fast-burning fuse—leading outward from the target area. With the exception of the leader, the squad then withdrew fifty feet from the critical territory.

At exactly twelve fifteen each leader of squads A to H lit the end of his trailer fuse.

AFTER they piled out of the cab, the driver yelled, "Hey, who's gonna pay?" and Eastman knew that he was elected. Mostly because he was the only one left. Converse had taken off like a shot, with Holly right behind him. Eastman tossed some bills into the cabby's lap and started running, but he knew that he would never catch up with Converse.

The street intersections were a mess. There were cops at every corner, frantically trying to shunt passenger cars off Central Park West and into the side streets. It looked hopeless. From nowhere, with their infallible talent for smelling out trouble, people were pouring onto the scene of the disaster.

All over the park, orange flames were shooting up, enveloped in thick black smoke boiling upward to the soiled sky.

THE two cars holding the ten men comprising squad S pulled off the East Drive at the point where it intersected with the police department's connecting road to the West Drive. The squad members piled out and the cars drove off at once.

Buck Pell gave a hand signal and began to run. The squad followed him, awkward with their burden of gasoline drums, shovels, axes. Hidden from the road, they went through heavy brush to the landmark rock that overlooked the hollow where Graham Black had been bitten. Buck Pell pointed down into the hollow and in a whisper warned his men to be on the alert, to check out exactly where each foot was going to land, to make sure they didn't spill gasoline on their clothing.

He led the way into the hollow, carrying one of the gasoline drums himself.

As HE ran, Converse recognized the sound of Holly's footsteps, smooth and regular, and although she didn't seem able to catch up with him, she was holding her own.

He felt a surge of pride—beautiful girl, beguiling smiles, and a good runner too! But he didn't slow up for her. He pounded on, awkward but tireless, almost unaware of the clamor of police cars and fire engines roaring by, and of the flame and smoke heaving upward all over the park.

When he turned his head for a glance at Holly, he was surprised to see Eastman behind her, head down, running doggedly. He felt sorry for Eastman, who was too heavy for the pace. But he couldn't wait for him. The Boys' Gate was just a few hundred yards away now. When he looked behind again, Eastman was still well back, but Holly was no longer in sight. He felt a pang of regret, then a sense of relief. He wouldn't have to worry about her, he could concentrate on trying to catch the black mamba before it could be destroyed by a pack of maniacs.

AFTER he had emptied his own gasoline drum, Buck Pell supervised the activities of squad S. He was grinning.

When he had first broached Operation Pillar of Fire, a few people had protested that green vegetation wouldn't burn. It was a common fallacy; he knew that gasoline made the hottest of all fires, and the heat parched out foliage around it, and green stuff wasn't green anymore and would burn like tinder. Look at the way the diversionary fires were blazing all over the park—that was green stuff, and it was burning real good.

When the gasoline drums had been emptied, Buck Pell chased his squad all the way back to the big rock. Once they were on their way he laid his trailer fuse.

"Okay, now, you Puries," he sang out. "I'm gonna touch it off. And when the fuse burns down to the gasoline, she's gonna blow.

I want every eye peeled on the fire. She's gonna burn real bright, so if the snake is in there, you'll see it. Look sharp, Puries. And if you see it, I want you to sing out."

Still grinning, Buck Pell crouched over the fuse and cupped his hand around his lighter.

DEEP in its burrow, the snake felt the vibrations of footsteps. They moved around for a long time, very close to the burrow. The smell was heavy and alien, and the snake was alarmed. It was the disturbing smell, after the footsteps had receded, that made the snake glide upward toward the second hole of the burrow and stick its head out.

It saw the shadowy figures standing on the rock. Another figure was running toward the rock. Nearby, on the ground, a bright, sputtering flame was approaching. The snake slid out of the burrow and watched the brightness crawling toward it.

As SOON as the fuse was lit, Buck Pell ran for the rock. Someone on the rock put a hand out and hauled him up. Seconds later, with a *pffft,* there was a blinding burst of flame.

The squad members were leaning forward, peering intently. Suddenly one of them screamed, "There it goes."

Buck Pell caught a glimpse of the snake, behind the flames, and it was moving so fast that he knew it was not burned or injured. "Okay," he shouted, "let's go get him! Move it!"

He headed off around the burning hollow in a wide arc to his left, his troops streaming after him.

ONCE, before he pulled so far ahead that Eastman had trouble seeing him, Converse turned and looked back. He wants to make sure he's losing me, Eastman thought, so he can play Good Samaritan to that stinking snake. Panting, he tried to turn on an extra burst of speed.

SQUADS A to H had left the area of their fires once they were burning satisfactorily. The Puries walked through the park in formation, singing. They offered no resistance to being gathered in by the police.

All of the detainees were taken to the Central Park Precinct,

where they were booked, charged, and fingerprinted. Because the Central Park Precinct had no lodging facilities, the suspects were dispersed for the rest of the night to other precincts.

As HE rounded into the park, Converse saw flames and black smoke boiling upward almost directly to the east, and he knew that the Puries had ignited the snake's territory. Still he ran on. If the snake had not died in the flames, but had been driven out into the open, it might fool them. In Africa, during the seasonal burning of dried grass, black mambas frequently survived by remaining in a burrow under a dead tree or a disused ant heap. It was reasonable to suppose that the snake in the park had found such a burrow.

A few hundred yards short of the snake's territory, Converse heard excited voices. He stopped. Then they came into view, black-clad Puries running, waving their improvised weapons. He watched as they streamed past him. From their purposiveness, it seemed that they had flushed the snake and might actually be on its trail.

Converse hesitated, then, on instinct, ran after the Puries.

THE snake crawled into a thicket and rested, its eyes fixed on pursuing lights. Suddenly a light shone directly into its eyes, and behind the light the snake could make out a figure.

BILL Hextall, at the extreme right flank of squad S, saw the snake when his flashlight beam reflected in its eyes. The snake, except for its head and neck, was hidden in brush. As its head withdrew, Hextall let out a hoarse shout.

The other members of squad S started to run back toward him. He pointed toward the thicket where he had seen the snake, and half a dozen of them began to beat the area with their weapons. Then someone spotted it gliding across an open area, speeding westward. Shouting, squad S took up the pursuit.

The snake fled before them and ran through an opening out of the park and onto the pavement of Central Park West.

A well-dressed man wearing a pinstriped seersucker suit and a cocoa straw hat was the first to see the snake crawl onto the street. This man, who shouted in a strangulated voice described by those who heard it as sounding like "a man having his throat cut," saw the snake reverse itself and curve back toward the shelter of the park's retaining wall.

From north and south along Central Park West, crowds of people, hearing screams and shouts, converged on the scene. Squad S poured out of the park behind Buck Pell.

The snake panicked, swerved outward from the wall, and, with the crowd retreating before it, crawled toward the curb. It turned toward the entrance to the park, but there were many figures blocking its path. It changed direction to its left and the figures moved with it; to the right, and the figures moved with it. It stopped, piled its length into a coil, lifted its head high, hissed dryly, opened its mouth wide, and swayed menacingly.

By the time Converse burst out of the park, hurdling the stone wall, the snake was in the center of a ring of black-clad Puries, which in its turn was surrounded by a mass of onlookers. Holding the Pillstrom tongs over his head, pushing, pleading, using his shoulders and elbows, Converse strained to break through the crowd. Once, when he raised his head to take a deep breath, he caught a glimpse of Holly, her face pale, her body cramped by the press of other bodies.

"Close in," Buck Pell shouted, "but slow, careful."

With their weapons extended, the Puries of squad S shuffled forward, contracting their circle. The snake turned its head to follow their movements, hissing, its anterior rigid and swaying. Suddenly a Purie leaped forward and, running to keep pace with the snake's movement, smashed his shovel down on it.

"Death to the Devil," he screamed.

The snake rolled over completely, writhing. A ragged cry rose from the crowd, half horror, half exultation. The snake moved forward again, dragging.

Buck Pell signaled, and the Puries closed in, flailing downward with their weapons. The snake's head rose, and it launched a strike at a Purie that fell short. A swinging blow from a rake knocked the snake to the ground, bleeding. It flopped over, and its light underside was turned up before it succeeded in righting itself. As it started to crawl forward again, Buck Pell went to meet it, an axe raised high over his head.

Converse was still struggling against the density of the crowd when he saw the axehead flash upward and then down in a gleaming arc. He heard the thud and ring of the axe, and from the crowd a concerted gasp like a sudden gust of wind. At the same time, in awe or revulsion or both, the crowd eddied back, flowed around him, and he stood at the forefront.

The black mamba lay on the blood-smeared pavement, its head severed.

EASTMAN watched a squad of helmeted cops form a wedge and start to bull their way through the crowd. If they were going to try to collar the Puries, they were in for serious trouble. Never mind that the Puries had burned up the park—they had killed the killer, hadn't they? They were the heroes, weren't they?

He saw someone burst out of the crowd like a cork popped from a bottle, elbows flailing, face dark and scowling. It was Converse, still carrying his snake-catching stick. For a moment they came face to face.

Eastman started to speak, but Converse muttered, "So long," and moved on.

Sore loser, Eastman thought.

MARVIN Thurman, a television reporter shooting "man in the street" reactions, spotted the police commissioner's limousine two blocks south of where the snake had been killed. The PC and the mayor were in the car, which was barely able to move because of the hordes of people who had poured out into the street.

Pushing his microphone through the limousine window, Thurman said, "Mr. Mayor, did you know the snake has been killed?"

The mayor's pale, unshaved face lit up. "Wonderful. I didn't doubt for an instant that New York's finest would once again display their ability to cope with a difficult and unique problem." He turned to the PC. "Congratulations, Commissioner, to the dedicated and tireless men of the NYPD."

Thurman refrained from telling the mayor who had killed the snake. Instead he said, "What about the Puries? What will be done with them?"

"They will be prosecuted to the fullest extent of the law." The mayor pounded on the side of the limousine for emphasis. "There is no room for lawlessness and vigilantism in this great city, and it will be punished accordingly."

"I see," Thurman said. "Does that include the Puries who killed the snake?"

The falling open of the mayor's mouth was recorded for posterity in full color.

It MIGHT have been high noon, Converse thought, as he walked aimlessly southward on Central Park West. At two o'clock in the morning, the streets were alive with people, some streaming to the center of the action, others returning from it.

The streets were still clogged by police cars, fire engines, several ambulances. The fires all seemed to be under control, but smoke still climbed upward from half a dozen different areas. It would be a long night for the six fire companies in the park. For hours after the flames had died, firemen would be overhauling the areas, raking and chopping the vegetation until no spark remained.

"Hey, Mark, wait up."

Her voice sounded winded. She looked terribly pale, and he guessed that she had witnessed the slaughter of the black mamba.

She said, "I got a stitch in my side before, that's why I couldn't follow you."

"Yes, well . . ." He really didn't feel like talking to anybody, even Holly.

They walked slowly, ambling. He was looking straight ahead, but he was aware that her face was turned up to him, in some sort of silent pleading, or at least questioning. From time to time her shoulder brushed against him. Then she reached for his hand. He withdrew it from her.

"Okay," she said. "You want me to go away?"

He shrugged.

"I guess I can take that any way I choose," she said. "I choose to take it as meaning that you don't want me to go but are too proud to say so. Well, all right, but I can be proud too, and if I don't get any response soon—"

He reached down and took her hand.

"Better," she said. "But talk to me. Or at least look at me."

He said, choking with anger, "I could have bagged it. There wasn't any need to kill it."

She shook her head. "There *was* a need. The situation cried out for an execution, for catharsis."

573

"They savaged it." He swore under his breath. "Damn it. Damn everything. Things will be better in Australia."

"Australia? It's too far."

"By plane?" He glanced at her face.

"I mean too far from *me*. Didn't you for heaven's sake know that's what I meant?"

"I'll only be gone a couple of months. Wouldn't you wait that long?"

"I could try, but we're living in a very impatient century. Nobody ever waits for anybody anymore."

He said, "You're not being reasonable."

"Not being reasonable—that's what it's all about, Buster."

She looked angry, and there were tears in her eyes. Damn it, Converse thought, I can't make up my mind this fast. I need time—say until we reach the next streetlamp.

THE flames had swept over the burrow and scorched the earth black. It had set the fallen tree afire and seared the two entrances, but it had not reached inside, and if the snake had remained in the burrow she might have survived unharmed.

She had mated in the spring at the breeding grounds near Lubumbashi, and laid her eggs in the burrow in New York three days ago. If they survived hunting animals and winter cold, they would hatch next spring. Each egg would produce a twelve-inch-long black mamba, resembling the full-grown snake in every particular except color. Each would be light green on top, pure white on the underside. Each would be highly aggressive, in the way of young snakes, and its venom, from the instant of birth, would kill a large rat.

The snakes would grow very rapidly toward their mature size of ten or eleven feet. But long before then their venom would be potent enough to kill a man or a horse.

The eggs were approximately the size of a hen's eggs, oval in shape and white in color. There were thirteen of them.

JOHN GODEY
The Man Who Loves New York

An authentic New Yorker, John Godey was born in Brooklyn, brought up in the Bronx, then moved to Manhattan. When it comes to writing, his favorite setting is his city—with its crowds, its excitement, its madness and its fads. He points up the city's soft spots as only a native can. He did this in his story of a daring subway hijacking in *The Taking of Pelham One Two Three*, a Condensed Books selection and a major motion picture. Currently, he says, he enjoys the idea of "shaking up the town with a poisonous snake."

"When I started this thriller, I knew nothing about snakes. I didn't even know if they could survive in Central Park. So I read every book I could find on the subject and I had a lot of help."

John Godey's real name is Morton Freedgood. He started using his pen name in the 1940s, because, he explains, "I was writing serious books, and I wanted to write thrillers, but under a pseudonym." He and his wife now live on the Palisades, across the Hudson from Manhattan. "We are on the thirty-third floor, with a fabulous view that takes in the skyline from the Statue of Liberty to the George Washington Bridge. It's a perfect setting for a writer who spends long hours at a desk. The panorama set out before me is as interesting as Venice."

All Godey will give away about his next thriller is that it's set in New York!

ACKNOWLEDGMENTS

Page 3: Tlingit Indian headdress of leather and carved
wood (Alaska, nineteenth century), courtesy of the
Museum of the American Indian, Heye Foundation, New York.

Pages 108, 359: maps by George Buctel.

Pages 371, 374, 375, 427: Hadassah Picture/Slide Archives.

Page 378: Marc Riboud/Magnum.

Page 460: Werner Braun, Jerusalem.

Page 462: David Harris, Jerusalem.